CONTENTS

PART THREE

A
T. A. BARRON
COLLECTION

The Lost Years of Merlin

The Seven Songs of Merlin

The Fires of Merlin

PHILOMEL BOOKS • NEW YORK

PATRICIA LEE GAUCH, EDITOR

The Lost Years of Merlin
Text copyright © 1996 by Thomas A. Barron
Frontispiece illustration © 1996 by Mike Wimmer
Map illustration © 1996 by Ian Schoenherr

The Seven Songs of Merlin
Text copyright © 1997 by Thomas A. Barron
Frontispiece illustration © 1997 by Mike Wimmer
Map illustration © 1996 by Ian Schoenherr

The Fires of Merlin
Text copyright © 1998 by Thomas A. Barron
Frontispiece illustration © 1998 by Mike Wimmer
Map illustration © 1996 by Ian Schoenherr

Library of Congress Cataloging-in-Publication Data
Barron, T. A. [Novels. Selections]
A T. A. Barron collection / written by T. A. Barron. p. cm
Contents: The lost years of Merlin—The seven songs of Merlin—
The fires of Merlin.
ISBN 0-399-23734-8
1. Children's stories, American. 2. Merlin (Legendary character)—Juvenile fic-
tion. [1. Merlin (Legendary character)—Fiction. 2. Wizards—Fiction. 3.
Fantasy.] I. Title. PZ7.B27567 Tab 2001 [Fic]—dc21 2001016385

3 5 7 9 10 8 6 4 2

T. A. BARRON

THE LOST YEARS OF MERLIN

PHILOMEL BOOKS · NEW YORK

This book is dedicated to
PATRICIA LEE GAUCH
loyal friend, passionate writer, demanding editor

with special appreciation to
BEN
age four, who sees and soars like a hawk

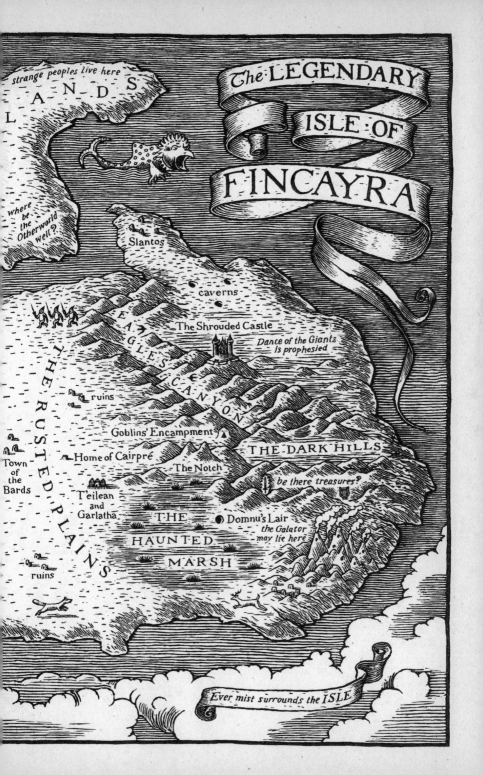

AUTHOR'S NOTE

I don't know much about wizards, but I have learned this much: They are full of surprises.

As I finished writing *The Merlin Effect*, a novel that follows a single strand of Arthurian legend from ancient Druid times almost to the dawn of the twenty-first century, I realized that the strand had bound me up so tightly that I could not escape. As I tugged on it, the strand tugged back. As I unraveled it, the strand entangled me more completely.

The strand was Merlin himself. He is a mysterious and captivating fellow, this wizard who can live backward in time, who dares to defy even the Threefold Death, and who can seek the Holy Grail while still speaking with the spirits of rivers and trees. I realized that I wanted to get to know him better.

Modern scholars have argued that the myth of Merlin may have sprung from an actual historical figure, a Druid prophet who lived somewhere in Wales in the sixth century A.D. But that is a matter for historians to debate. For whether or not Merlin was ever real in the realm of history, he is certainly real in the realm of imagination. There he has long lived, and there he continues to thrive. He even accepts visitors on occasion. And since I wanted to write a work of imagination, not history, Merlin's door was wide open.

So before I could even begin to protest, Merlin made his own plans for me. My other books and projects had to wait. It was time to explore another aspect of his legend, one deeply personal to the wizard himself. I suspected that, like most things in life, the more I learned about Merlin, the less I would really know. And, to be sure, I was well aware from the outset that making even a small contribution to such a marvelous body of myth would pose a daunting challenge. But curiosity can be a powerful motivator. And Merlin was insistent.

Then came the wizard's first surprise. As I immersed myself in the traditional tales about Merlin, I found an unexplained gap in the lore. Merlin's youth—the crucial, formative time when he most likely discovered his own shadowy origins, his own identity, and his own powers—was only fleetingly mentioned, if it was mentioned at all. Where he first tasted sorrow, where he first knew joy, where he first gained a particle or two of wisdom, remained unexplored.

Most of the traditional tales follow the same approach as Thomas Malory and ignore Merlin's early life entirely. A few stories speak of his birth, his tormented mother, his unknown father, and his precocious infancy. (In one account, he speaks fluently in his mother's defense when only one year old.) Then we hear nothing more of him—until, when considerably older, he is found explaining the secret of the fighting dragons to the treacherous King Vortigern. In between lies a gap of several years. Perhaps, as some have supposed, he wandered alone in the woods during those years lost from legend. Or perhaps, just perhaps . . . he traveled somewhere else.

This gap in Merlin's early life contrasts starkly with the volumes and volumes of material about his later years. As an adult, he assumes many (sometimes contradictory) forms, being variously described as prophet, magician, Madman of the Forest, trickster, priest, seer, and bard. He appears in some of the earliest myths of Celtic Britain, some of them so ancient that their sources were already obscure when the great Welsh epics of the *Mabinogion* were first set down a thousand years ago. In Spenser's *Faerie Queene* and in Ariosto's *Orlando Furioso*, Merlin the wizard is present. He counsels the young king in Malory's *Morte d'Arthur*, assembles Stonehenge in Robert de Boron's twelfth century poem *Merlin*, delivers many prophecies in Geoffrey of Monmouth's *Historia Regnum Brittaniae*.

More recently, writers as diverse as Shakespeare, Tennyson, Thomas Hardy, T. H. White, Mary Stewart, C. S. Lewis, Nikolai Tolstoy, and John Steinbeck have spent time with this fascinating figure, as have many others in many lands. Yet, with rare exceptions such as Mary Stewart, few have dealt at all with Merlin's youth.

And so the early years of Merlin remain strangely mysterious. We are left wondering about his early struggles, fears, and aspirations. What were his deepest dreams? His passions? How did he discover his own unusual talents? How did he deal with tragedy and loss? How did he come to know, perhaps even to accept, his own dark side? How did he first encounter the spiritual works of the Druids— and, for that matter, the ancient Greeks? How did he reconcile his own yearning for power and his horror at its abuses? In sum, how did he become the wizard and mentor to King Arthur whom we celebrate still today?

Questions such as these are not answered by the traditional lore. Nor do the words attributed to Merlin himself shed much light. Indeed, one gets the impression that he was determined to avoid talking about his own past. A reader of the traditional lore could fairly easily picture Merlin as an old man, seated beside the boy Arthur, musing distractedly about the "lost years" of his youth. Yet one can only speculate whether he might have been remarking on the brevity of life, or perhaps referring to a missing chapter from his own past.

My own view is that, during Merlin's lost years, he not only disappeared from the world of story and song. Rather, I believe that Merlin *himself* disappeared—from the world as we know it.

This tale, spanning a few volumes, will attempt to bridge the gap. The story begins when a young boy, without any name and without any memory of his past, washes ashore on the coast of Wales. It concludes when that same boy, having gained and lost a great deal, is ready to step into a central role in Arthurian legend.

In between, much happens. He discovers his second sight, but pays dearly for the privilege. He begins to speak with animals, trees, and rivers. He finds the original Stonehenge, far older than the circle of stones that tradition credits him with constructing on England's Salisbury Plain. First, however, he must learn the meaning of Stonehenge's Druid name, *Dance of the Giants*. He explores his first crystal cave. He voyages to the lost Island of Fincayra (spelled *Fianchuivé* in the Gaelic), known in Celtic myth as an island beneath the waves, a bridge between the Earth of human beings and the Otherworld of spiritual beings. He encounters some figures whose names are familiar in ancient lore, including the great Dagda, the evil Rhita Gawr, the tragic Elen, the mysterious Domnu, the wise Cairpré, and the vital Rhia. He also encounters others not so familiar, such as Shim, Stangmar, T'eilean and Garlatha, and the Grand Elusa. He learns that true sight requires more than eyes; that true wisdom unites qualities often separated, like faith and doubt, female and male, light and dark; that true love mingles joy with grief. And, most important of all, he gains the name Merlin.

Some words of thanks are necessary: to Currie, my wife and best friend, for guarding so well my solitude; to our pandemonious children Denali, Brooks, Ben, Ross, and Larkin, for their abundant sense of humor and sense of wonder; to Patricia Lee Gauch, for her unwavering faith in the power of a story to be true; to Victoria Acord and Patricia Waneka, for their invaluable assistance; to Cynthia Kreuz-Uhr, for her understanding of the interwoven sources of myth; to those who have encouraged me along the way, especially Madeleine L'Engle, Dorothy Markinko, and M. Jerry Weiss; to all the bards and poets and storytellers and scholars who have contributed over many centuries to the tales of Merlin; and, of course, to the elusive wizard himself.

Come with me, then, as Merlin reveals to us the story of his lost years. In this journey, you are the witness, I am the scribe, and Merlin himself is our guide. But let us beware, for a wizard, as we know, is full of surprises.

T. A. B.

He that made with his hond
Wynd and water, wode and lond;
Geve heom alle good endyng
That wolon listne this talkyng,
And y schal telle, yow byfore,
How Merlyn was geten and bore
And of his wisdoms also
And othre happes mony mo
Sum whyle byfeol in Engelonde.

—From the thirteenth-century ballad
OF ARTHOUR AND
OF MERLIN

PROLOGUE

If I close my eyes, and breathe to the rolling rhythm of the sea, I can still remember that long ago day. Harsh, cold, and lifeless it was, as empty of promise as my lungs were empty of air.

Since that day, I have seen many others, more than I have the strength left to count. Yet that day glows as bright as the Galator itself, as bright as the day I found my own name, or the day I first cradled a baby who bore the name Arthur. Perhaps I remember it so clearly because the pain, like a scar on my soul, will not disappear. Or because it marked the ending of so much. Or, perhaps, because it marked a beginning as well as an ending: the beginning of my lost years.

A dark wave rose on the rolling sea, and from it lifted a hand.

As the wave surged higher, reaching toward sky as smoky gray as itself, the hand reached higher as well. A bracelet of foam swirled around the wrist, while desperate fingers groped for something they could not find. It was the hand of someone small. It was the hand of someone weak, too weak to fight any longer.

It was the hand of a boy.

With a deep sucking sound, the wave began to crest, tilting steadily toward the shore. For an instant it paused, hovering between ocean and land, between the brooding Atlantic and the perilous, rock-bound coast of Wales, known in those days as Gwynedd. Then the sucking swelled into a crashing roar as the wave toppled over, hurling the boy's limp body onto the black rocks.

His head smacked against a stone, so violently that his skull would surely have split open were it not for the thick mat of hair that covered it. He lay completely still, except when the whoosh of air from the next wave tousled his locks, black beneath the stains of blood.

A shabby seagull, seeing his motionless form, hopped over the jumble of rocks for a closer look. Bending its beak toward the boy's face, it tried to pull a strand of sea kelp that was wrapped around his ear. The bird tugged and twisted, squawking angrily.

At last the kelp broke free. Triumphantly, the bird jumped down to one of the boy's bare arms. Beneath the shreds of a brown tunic still clinging to him, he seemed small, even for a boy of seven years. Yet something about his face—the shape of his brow, perhaps, or the lines around his eyes—seemed far older.

At that instant, he coughed, vomited seawater, and coughed again. With a screech, the gull dropped the kelp and fluttered off to a stony perch.

The boy remained motionless for a moment. All he could taste was sand, slime, and vomit. All he could feel was the painful throbbing of his head, and the rocks jabbing into his shoulders. Then came another cough, another gush of seawater. A halting, labored breath. Then a second breath, and a third. Slowly, his slender hand clenched into a fist.

Waves surged and subsided, surged and subsided. For a long while, the small candle flame of life in him wavered at the edge of darkness. Beneath the throbbing, his mind seemed strangely empty. Almost as if he had lost a piece of his very self. Or as if a kind of wall had been erected, cutting him off from a portion of himself, leaving nothing but a lingering sense of fear.

His breathing slowed. His fist relaxed. He gasped, as if to cough again, but instead fell still.

Cautiously, the seagull edged closer.

Then, from whatever quarter, a thin thread of energy began to move through his body. Something inside him was not yet ready to die. He stirred again, breathed again.

The gull froze.

He opened his eyes. Shivering with cold, he rolled to his side. Feeling the rough sand in his mouth, he tried to spit, but succeeded only in making himself gag from the rancid taste of kelp and brine.

With effort, he raised an arm and wiped his mouth with the tatters of his tunic. Then he winced, feeling the raw lump on the back of his head. Willing himself to sit up, he braced his elbow against a rock and pushed himself upright.

He sat there, listening to the grinding and splashing sea. Beyond the ceaseless pulsing of the waves, beyond the pounding inside his head, he thought for an instant that he could hear something else—a voice, perhaps. A voice from some other time, some other place, though he could not remember where.

With a sudden jolt, he realized that he could not remember *anything*. Where he had come from. His mother. His father. His name. *His own name.* Hard as he tried, he could not remember. *His own name.*

"Who am I?"

Hearing his cry, the gull squawked and took flight.

Catching sight of his reflection in a pool of water, he paused to look. A strange face, belonging to a boy he did not know, peered back at him. His eyes, like his hair, were as black as coal, with scattered flecks of gold. His ears, which were almost triangular and pointed at the top, seemed oddly large for the rest of his face. Likewise, his brow rose high above his eyes. Yet his nose looked narrow and slight, more a beak than a nose. Altogether, his face did not seem to belong to itself.

He mustered his strength and rose to his feet. Head swirling, he braced himself against a pinnacle of rock until the dizziness calmed.

His eyes roamed over the desolate coastline. Rocks upon rocks lay scattered everywhere, making a harsh black barrier to the sea. The rocks parted in only one place—and then only grudgingly—around the roots of an ancient oak tree. Its gray bark peeling, the old oak faced the ocean with the stance of centuries. There was a deep hollow in its trunk, gouged out by fire ages ago. Age warped its every branch, twisting some into knots. Yet it continued to stand, roots anchored, immutable against storm and sea. Behind the oak stood a dark grove of younger trees, and behind them, high cliffs loomed even darker.

Desperately, the boy searched the landscape for anything he might recognize, anything that might coax his memory to return. He recognized nothing.

He turned, despite the stinging salt spray, to the open sea. Waves rolled and toppled, one after another after another. Nothing but endless gray billows as far as he could see. He listened again for the mysterious voice, but heard only the distant call of a kittiwake perched on the cliffs.

Had he come from somewhere out there, beyond the sea?

Vigorously, he rubbed his bare arms to stop the shivers. Spying a loose clump of sea kelp on a rock, he picked it up. Once, he knew, this formless mass of green had danced with its own graceful rhythm, before being uprooted and cast adrift. Now it hung limp in his hand. He wondered why he himself had been uprooted, and from where.

A low, moaning sound caught his ear. That voice again! It came from the rocks beyond the old oak tree.

He lurched forward in the direction of the voice. For the first time he noticed a dull ache between his shoulder blades. He could only assume that his back, like his head, had slammed against the rocks. Yet the ache felt somehow deeper, as if something beneath his shoulders had been torn away long ago.

After several halting steps he made it to the ancient tree. He leaned against its massive trunk, his heart pounding. Again he heard the mysterious moaning. Again he set off.

Often his bare feet would slip on the wet rocks, pitching him sideways. Stumbling along, his torn brown tunic flapping about his legs, he resembled an ungainly water bird, picking his way across the shoreline. Yet all the time he knew what he really was: a lone boy, with no name and no home.

Then he saw her. Crumpled among the stones lay the body of a woman, her face beside a surging tidal pool. Her long, unbraided hair, the color of a yellow summer moon, spread about her head like rays of light. She had strong cheekbones and a complexion that would be described as creamy were it not tinged with blue. Her long blue robe, torn in places, was splotched with sand and sea kelp. Yet the quality of the wool, as well as the jeweled pendant on a leather cord around her neck, revealed her to have been once a woman of wealth and stature.

He rushed forward. The woman moaned again, a moan of inextinguishable pain. He could almost feel her agony, even as he could feel his own hopes rising. *Do I know her?* he asked himself as he bent over her twisted body. Then, from a place of deeper longing, *Does she know me?*

With a single finger he touched her cheek, as cold as the cold sea. He watched her take several short, labored breaths. He listened to her wretched moaning. And, with a sigh, he admitted to himself that she was, for him, a complete stranger.

Still, as he studied her, he could not suppress the hope that she might have arrived on this shore together with him. If she had not come on the same wave, then at least she might have come from the same place. Perhaps, if she lived, she might be able to fill the empty cup of his memory. Perhaps she knew his very name! Or the names of his mother and father. Or perhaps . . . she might actually *be* his mother.

A frigid wave slapped against his legs. His shivers returned, even as his hopes faded. She might not live, and even if she did, she probably would not know him. And she certainly could not be his mother. That was too much to hope for. Besides, she could not have looked less like him. She looked truly beautiful, even at the edge of death, as beautiful as an angel. And he had seen his own reflection. He knew what he looked like. Less like an angel than a bedraggled, half-grown demon.

A snarl erupted from behind his back.

The boy whirled around. His stomach clenched. There, in the shadows of the dark grove, stood an enormous wild boar.

A low, vicious growl vibrating in its throat, the boar stepped out of the trees. Bristling brown fur covered its entire body except for the eyes and a gray scar snaking down its left foreleg. Its tusks, sharp as daggers, were blackened with the blood of a previous kill. More frightening, though, were its red eyes, which glowed like hot coals.

The boar moved smoothly, almost lightly, despite its hulking form. The boy stepped backward. This beast outweighed him several times over. One kick of its leg would send him sprawling. One stab of its tusk would rip his flesh to shreds. Abruptly the boar stopped and hunched its muscular shoulders, preparing to charge.

Glancing behind, the boy could see only the onrushing waves of the ocean. No escape that way. He grabbed a crooked shard of driftwood to use as a weapon, though he knew it would not even begin to pierce the boar's hide. Even so, he tried to plant his feet on the slippery rocks, bracing for the attack.

Then he remembered. The hollow in the old oak! Although the tree stood about halfway between him and the boar, he might be able to get there first.

He started to dash for the tree, then suddenly caught himself. The woman. He could not just leave her there. Yet his own chance for safety depended on speed. Grimacing, he tossed aside the driftwood and grabbed her limp arms.

Straining his trembling legs, he tried to pull her free from the rocks. Whether from all the water she had swallowed or from the weight of death upon her, she felt as heavy as the rocks themselves. Finally, under the glaring eyes of the boar, she budged.

The boy began dragging her toward the tree. Sharp stones cut into his feet. Heart racing, head throbbing, he pulled with all his power.

The boar snarled again, this time more like a raspy laugh. The whole body of the beast tensed, nostrils flaring and tusks gleaming. Then it charged.

Though the boy was only a few feet from the tree, something kept him from running. He snatched a squarish stone from the ground and hurled it at the boar's head. Only an instant before reaching them, the boar changed direction. The stone whizzed past and clattered on the ground.

Amazed that he could have possibly daunted the beast, the boy quickly bent to retrieve another stone. Then, sensing some movement over his shoulder, he spun around.

Out of the bushes behind the ancient oak bounded an immense stag. Bronze in hue, except for the white boots on each leg that shone like purest quartz, the stag lowered its great rack of antlers. With the seven points on each side aimed like so many spears, the stag leaped at the boar. But the beast swerved aside just in time to dodge the thrust.

As the boar careened and snarled ferociously, the stag leaped once again. Seizing the moment, the boy dragged the limp woman into the hollow of the tree. By folding her legs tight against her chest, he pushed her entirely into the opening. The wood, still charred from some ancient fire, curled around her like a great black shell. He wedged himself into the small space beside her, as the boar and the stag circled each other, pawing the ground and snorting wrathfully.

Eyes aflame, the boar feigned a charge at the stag, then bolted straight at the tree. Hunched in the hollow, the boy drew back as far as he could. Yet his face remained so close to the gnarled bark of the opening that he still could feel the boar's hot breath as its tusks slashed wildly at the trunk. One of the tusks grazed the boy's face, gashing him just below the eye.

At that moment the stag plowed into the flank of the boar. The bulky beast flew into the air and landed on its side near the bushes. Blood oozing from a punctured thigh, the boar scrambled to its feet.

The stag lowered its head, poised to leap again. Hesitating for a split second, the boar snarled one final time before retreating into the trees.

With majestic slowness, the stag turned toward the boy. For a brief moment, their eyes met. Somehow the boy knew that he would remember nothing from that day so clearly as the bottomless brown pools of the stag's unblinking eyes, eyes as deep and mysterious as the ocean itself.

Then, as swiftly as it had appeared, the stag leaped over the twisted roots of the oak and vanished from sight.

◼ PART ONE ◼

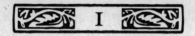

A LIVING EYE

I stand alone, beneath the stars.

The entire sky ignites into flame, as if a new sun is being born. People shriek and scatter. But I stand there, unable to move, unable to breathe. Then I see the tree, darker than a shadow against the flaming sky. Its burning branches writhe like deadly serpents. They reach for me. The fiery branches come closer. I try to escape, but my legs are made of stone. My face is burning! I hide my eyes. I scream.

My face! My face is burning!

I awoke. Perspiration stung my eyes. Straw from my pallet scratched against my face.

Blinking, I drew a deep breath and wiped my face with my hands. They felt cool against my cheeks.

Stretching my arms, I felt again that pain between my shoulder blades. Still there! I wished it would go away. Why should it still bother me now, more than five years since the day I had washed ashore? The wounds to my head had long since healed, though I still remembered nothing of my life before being thrown on the rocks. So why should this wound last so much longer? I shrugged. Like so much else, I would never know.

I started to stuff some loose straw back into the pallet when my fingers uncovered an ant, dragging the body of a worm several times its size. I watched, almost laughing, as the ant tried to climb straight up the miniature mountain of straw. It could have easily gone around one side or another. But no. Some mysterious motive drove it to try, spill over backward, try again, and spill again. For several minutes I watched this repeating performance.

At last I took pity on the little fellow. I reached for one of its legs, then realized that it might twist off, especially if the ant struggled. So I picked up the worm instead. Just as I expected, the ant clung to it, kicking frantically.

I carried the ant and its prize up and over the straw, dropping them gently on the other side. To my surprise, when I released my hold on the worm, so did the ant. It turned toward me, waving its tiny antennae wildly. I caught the distinct feeling that I was being scolded.

"My apologies," I whispered through my grin.

The ant scolded me for a few more seconds. Then it bit into the worm and started to drag the heavy load away. To its home.

My grin faded. Where could I find my own home? I would drag behind me this whole pallet, this whole hut if necessary, if only I knew where to go.

Turning to the open window above my head, I saw the full moon, glowing as bright as a pot of molten silver. Moonlight poured through the window, and through the gaps in the thatched roof, painting the interior of the hut with its gleaming brush. For a moment, the moonlight nearly disguised the poverty of the room, covering the earthen floor with a sheath of silver, the rough clay walls with sparkles of light, the still-sleeping form in the corner with the glow of an angel.

Yet I knew that it was all an illusion, no more real than my dream.

The floor was just dirt, the bed just straw, the dwelling just a hovel made of twigs bound with clay. The covered pen for the geese next door had been constructed with more care! I knew, for I sometimes hid myself in there, when the honking and hissing of geese sounded more to my liking than the howling and chattering of people. The pen stayed warmer than this hut in February, and drier in May. Even if I did not deserve any better than the geese, no one could doubt that Branwen did.

I watched her sleeping form. Her breathing, so subtle that it hardly lifted her woolen blanket, seemed calm and peaceful. Alas, I knew better. While peace might visit her in sleep, it escaped her in waking life.

She shifted in her slumber, rolling her face toward mine. In the lunar light she looked even more beautiful than usual, her creamy cheeks and brow thoroughly relaxed, as they were only on such nights when she slept soundly. Or in her moments of silent prayer, which happened more and more often.

I frowned at her. If only she would speak. Tell me what she knew. For if she did know anything about our past, she had refused to discuss it. Whether that was because she truly did not know, or because she simply did not want me to know, I could never tell.

And, in the five years we had shared this hut, she had revealed little more about herself. But for the kind touch of her hand and the ever present sorrow at the back of her eyes, I hardly knew her at all. I only knew that she was not my mother, as she claimed.

How could I be so sure that she was not my mother? Somehow, in my heart, I knew. She was too distant, too secretive. Surely a mother, a real mother, wouldn't hide so much from her own son. And if I needed any more assurance, I had only to look at her face.

So lovely—and so very different from my own. There was no hint of black in those eyes, nor of points on those ears! No, I was no more her son than the geese were my siblings.

Nor could I believe that her real name was Branwen, and that mine was Emrys, as she had tried to convince me. Whatever names we had possessed before the sea had spat us out on the rocks, I felt sure somehow that they were not those. As many times as she had called me Emrys, I could not shake the feeling that my true name was . . . something else. Yet I had no idea where to look for the truth, except perhaps in the wavering shadows of my dreams.

The only times that Branwen, if that was really her name, would show even a hint of her true self were when she told me stories. Especially the stories of the ancient Greeks. Those tales were clearly her favorites. And mine, too. Whether she knew it or not, some part of her seemed to come alive when she spoke of the giants and gods, the monsters and quests, in the Greek myths.

True, she also enjoyed telling tales of the Druid healers, or the miracle worker from Galilee. But her stories about the Greek gods and goddesses brought a special light into her sapphire eyes. At times, I almost felt that telling these stories was her way of talking about a place that she believed really existed—a place where strange creatures roamed the land and great spirits mingled with humans. The whole notion seemed foolish to me, but apparently not to her.

A sudden flash of light at her throat curtailed my thoughts. I knew that it was only the light of the moon reflected in her jeweled pendant, still hanging from the leather cord about her neck, although the green color seemed richer tonight than ever before. I realized that I had never seen her take the pendant off, not even for an instant.

Something tapped on the dirt behind me. I turned to see a bundle of dried leaves, slender and silvery in the moonlight, bound with a knot of grass. It must have fallen from the ridge beam above, which supported not only the thatch but also dozens of clusters of herbs, leaves, flowers, roots, nuts, bark shavings, and seeds. These were only a portion of Branwen's collection, for many more bundles hung from the window frame, the back of the door, and the tilting table beside her pallet.

Because of the bundles, the whole hut smelled of thyme, beech root, mustard seed, and more. I loved the aromas. Except for dill, which made me sneeze. Cedar bark, my favorite, lifted me as tall as a giant, petals of lavender tingled my toes, and sea kelp reminded me of something I could not quite remember.

All these ingredients and tools she used to make her healing powders, pastes, and poultices. Her table held a large assortment of bowls, knives, mortars, pestles, strainers, and other utensils. Often I watched her crushing leaves, mixing powders, straining plants, or applying a mixture of remedies to someone's wound or wart. Yet I knew as little about her healing work as I did about her. While she allowed me to watch, she would not converse or tell stories. She merely worked away, usually singing some chant or other.

Where had she learned so much about the art of healing? Where had she discovered the tales of so many distant lands and times? Where had she first encountered the teachings of the man from Galilee that increasingly occupied her thoughts? She would not say.

I was not alone in being vexed by her silence. Oftentimes the villagers would whisper behind her back, wondering about her healing powers, her unnatural beauty, her strange chants. I had even heard the words *sorcery* and *black magic* used once or twice, although it did not seem to discourage people from coming to her when they needed a boil healed, a cough cured, or a nightmare dispelled.

Branwen herself did not seem worried by the whisperings. As long as most people paid her for her help, so that we could continue to make our way, she did not seem to care what they might think or say. Recently she had tended to an elderly monk who had slipped on the wet stones of the mill bridge and gashed his arm. While binding his wound, Branwen uttered a Christian blessing, which seemed to please him. When she followed it with a Druid chant, however, he scolded her and warned her against blasphemy. She replied calmly that Jesus himself was so devoted to healing others that he might well have drawn upon the wisdom of the Druids, as well as others now called pagan. At that point the monk angrily shook off her bandage and left, though not before telling half the village that she was doing the work of demons.

I turned back to the pendant. It seemed to shine with its own light, not just the moon's. For the first time I noticed that the crystal in its center was not merely flat green, as it appeared from a distance. Leaning closer, I discovered violets and blues flowing like rivulets beneath its surface, while glints of red pulsed with a thousand tiny hearts. It looked almost like a living eye.

Galator. The word sprung suddenly into my mind. *It is called Galator.*

I shook my head, puzzled. Where did that word come from? I could not recall ever having heard it. I must have picked it up from the village square, where numerous dialects—Celt, Saxon, Roman, Gaelic, and others even more strange—collided and merged every day. Or perhaps from one of Branwen's own stories, which were sprinkled with words from the Greeks, the Jews, the Druids, and others more ancient still.

"Emrys!"

Her shrill whisper startled me so much that I jumped. I faced the bluer-than-blue eyes of the woman who shared with me her hut and her meals, but nothing more.

"You are awake."

"I am. And you were staring at me strangely."

"Not at you," I replied. "At your pendant." On an impulse, I added, "At your *Galator.*"

She gasped. With a sweep of her hand she stuffed the pendant under her robe. Then, trying to keep her voice calm, she said, "That is not a word I remember telling you."

My eyes widened. "You mean it is the real word? The right word?"

She observed me thoughtfully, almost started to speak, then caught herself. "You should be sleeping, my son."

As always, I bristled when she called me that. "I can't sleep."

"Would a story help? I could finish the one about Apollo."

"No. Not now."

"I could make you a potion, then."

"No thanks." I shook my head. "When you did that for the thatcher's son, he slept for three and a half days."

A smile touched her lips. "He drank a week's dose at once, poor fool."

"It's almost dawn, anyway."

She gathered her rough wool blanket. "Well, if you don't want to sleep, I do."

"Before you do, can't you tell me more about that word? Gal—Oh, what was it?"

Seeming not to hear me, she wrapped herself in her customary cloak of silence, even as she wrapped herself in the wool blanket and closed her eyes once more. In seconds, she seemed to be asleep again. Yet the peace I had seen in her face before had flown.

"Can't you tell me?"

She did not stir.

"Why don't you ever help me?" I wailed. "I need your help!"

Still she did not stir.

Ruefully, I watched her for a while. Then I rolled off the pallet, stood, and splashed my face with water from the large wooden bowl by the door. Glancing again at Branwen, I felt a renewed surge of anger. Why wouldn't she answer me? Why wouldn't she help me? Yet even as I looked upon her, I felt a small prick of guilt that I had never been able to bring myself to call her Mother, although I knew how much it would please her. And yet . . . what kind of mother would refuse to help her son?

I tugged against the rope handle of the door. With a scrape against the dirt, it opened, and I left the hut.

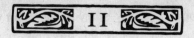

AN OWL IS COMING

The western sky had darkened, as the moon had nearly set. Streaks of silver, shading into gray, lined the thick clouds above the village of Caer Vedwyd. In the dim light, its humped roofs of thatch looked like a group of shadowed boulders. Somewhere nearby I heard lambs crying. And my friends, the geese, began to wake up. A cuckoo in the bracken called twice. Under the dripping oak and ash trees, the fresh scent of bluebells mingled with the smell of wet thatch.

It was May, and in May even a dreary village before dawn could seem lovely. I pulled a burr from the sleeve of my tunic, listening to the quiet stirrings. This month excited me like no other. Flowers opened their faces to the sky, lambs birthed, leaves sprouted. And as the flowers blossomed, so did my dreams. Sometimes, in May, I swallowed my doubts and believed that one day I would find the truth. Who I really was, where I really came from. If not from Branwen, then from someone else.

In May, anything seemed possible. If only I could learn to harness time itself. To make every month like May! Or, perhaps, to live *backward* in time, so that whenever the end of the month arrived, I could turn May right around and live it all over again.

I chewed my lip. Whatever the month, this village would never be my favorite place. Nor my home. I knew this early hour would be the finest of the day, before the sun's rays revealed its tattered huts and fearful faces. Like most villages in this rolling, thickly wooded country, Caer Vedwyd existed only because of an old Roman road. Ours ran along the north bank of the River Tywy, which flowed south all the way to the sea. Although the road had once carried streams of Roman soldiers, it now carried mainly vagabonds and wandering traders. It was a towpath for horses bringing barges of grain down the river, a route for those seeking the Church of Saint Peter in the city of Caer Myrddin to the south, and also, as I remembered well, a passage to the sea.

A metal tool clanged in the smith's shop under the great oak. I could hear a horse tramping somewhere up the towpath, its bridle jingling. In another hour, people would be gathering in the square under the tree, where the village's three main paths converged. Soon the sounds of bartering, arguing, cajoling, and of course thieving, would fill the air.

Five years in this place, and it still did not feel like home. Why? Perhaps because everything, from the local gods to the local names, was changing. Fast. The newly arrived Saxons had already started to call Y Wyddfa, whose icy ridges towered over everything, Snow Hill or Snowdon. Likewise, people were now calling this region, long known as Gwynedd, the country of Wales. But to call it a country at all was to imply a kind of unity that did not really exist. Given the number of travelers and dialects that passed through just our little village every day, Wales seemed to me less a country than a way station.

Following the path down to the mill house, I saw the last traces of moonlight touching the slopes of Y Wyddfa. The sounds of the waking village melted into the splashy clatter of the river flowing under the stone bridge by the mill. A frog bellowed, somewhere by the mill house, the only building in the village made of real brick.

Without warning, a quiet voice within me whispered, *An owl is coming*.

I whirled about just in time to see the square head and massive brown wings sail past me as fast as the wind and as silent as death. Two seconds later it dropped into the grass behind the mill house, its talons squeezing the life out of its prey.

Stoat for supper. I grinned to myself, pleased that I had somehow known that the owl was approaching, and that its invisible quarry was a stoat. How did I know? I had no idea. I simply knew, that's all. And I supposed that any reasonably observant person would have known as well.

More and more, though, I wondered. I did sometimes seem a step ahead of other people in sensing what was about to happen. This talent, if you could call it a talent, had only just appeared in the last few weeks, so I didn't even begin to understand it. And I hadn't shared it with Branwen, or with anyone else. It could be nothing more than a string of lucky guesses. But if, in fact, it was something more, it might at least provide some entertainment. Or even prove useful in a pinch.

Only the day before, I had seen some village boys chasing one another with imaginary swords. For a brief moment, I longed to be one of them. Then the group's leader, Dinatius, spied me and pounced on me before I could get away. I had never liked Dinatius, who had spent the years since his mother's death as the smith's servant. He struck me as mean, stupid, and quick-tempered. But I had tried never to offend him, less out of kindness than the fact that he was much older and much larger than I—or any other boy in the village. More than once, I had seen him struck by the smith's

powerful hand for shirking his duties, and just as often I had seen
Dinatius do the same to someone smaller. Once he badly burned the
arm of another boy who had dared to question his Roman ancestry.

All this ran through my mind the day before as I struggled to get
away from him. Then I chanced to see a low-flying gull overhead.
I pointed to the bird and cried, "Look! Treasure from the sky!"
Dinatius turned his face skyward at just the moment that the bird
released an especially pungent sort of treasure—which splatted him
right in the eye. While Dinatius cursed and tried to wipe his face,
the other boys laughed, and I escaped.

Smiling, I thought of yesterday's close call. For the first time, I
wondered whether I might possess a talent—a power—even more
precious than predicting events. Suppose, just suppose . . . I could
actually *control* events. Make something happen. Not with my
hands, my feet, or my voice. With nothing but my thoughts.

How exciting! It was probably just another May dream. But what
if it was more? I would give it a try.

As I approached the stone bridge over the river, I knelt beside a
low, tightly cupped flower. Concentrating all my thoughts on the
flower, I grew oblivious to everything else. The chilled air, the crying
lambs, the smith's noises, all faded away.

I studied the flower's lavender hue, touched on the east by the
golden light of the emerging sun. Minuscule hairs, wearing droplets
of dew, embroidered the edges of each petal, while a tiny brown
aphid scurried across the collar of fringed leaves at the top of the
stalk. Its aroma seemed fresh, but not sweet. Somehow I knew that
its hidden center must be the color of aged yellow cheese.

Ready at last, I began willing the flower to open. *Show yourself,*
I commanded. *Open your petals.*

I waited for a long moment. Nothing happened.

Again I focused on the flower. *Open. Open your petals.*

Still nothing happened.

I started to stand. Then, very slowly, the collar of leaves began to flutter as if touched by the barest of breezes. A moment later one of the lavender petals stirred, unfurling an edge ever so slightly, before gradually beginning to open. Another petal followed, and another, and another, until the whole flower greeted the oncoming dawn with petals outstretched. And from its center sprouted six soft sprigs, more like feathers than petals. Their color? Like aged yellow cheese.

A brutal kick struck me in the back. Coarse laughter filled the air, crushing the moment as swiftly as a heavy foot crushed the flower.

III

RIDING
THE STORM

With a groan, I pushed myself to my feet. "Dinatius, you pig."

The older boy, square-shouldered with bushy brown hair, smirked at me. "You're the one with pointed ears like a pig. Or like a demon! Anyway, better a pig than a bastard."

My cheeks grew hot, but I held my temper. I looked into his eyes—gray as a goose's back. This required me to tilt my head back, since he was so much taller. Indeed, Dinatius' shoulders could already lift loads that made many grown men wobble. In addition to stoking the smith's fire—hot, heavy work on its own—he cut and carried the firewood, worked the bellows, and hauled iron ore by the hundredweight. For this the smith gave him a meal or two a day, a sack of straw to sleep on, and many a blow about the head.

"I am no bastard."

Dinatius slowly rubbed the stubble on his chin. "Where then is your father hiding? Maybe he's a pig! Or maybe he's one of those rats who lives with you and your mother."

"We don't have any rats in our home."

"Home! You call that a home? It's just a filthy hole where your mother can hide and do her sorcery."

My fists clenched. The taunts about me cut deep enough, but it was his crass mention of *her* that made my blood boil. Still, I knew that Dinatius wanted me to fight him. I also knew what the outcome would be. Better to hold my temper, if I could. It would be very hard to keep my arms still. But my tongue? Even harder.

"He who is made of air should not accuse the wind."

"What do you mean by that, bastard whelp?"

I had no idea where the words came from that I spoke next. "I mean that you should not call somebody else bastard, since your father was just a Saxon mercenary who rode through this village one night and left nothing but you and an empty flask in his wake."

Dinatius' mouth opened and then closed without a word. I realized that I had spoken words he had always feared, but never admitted, were true. Words that struck more violently than clubs.

His face reddened. "Not so! My father was a Roman, and a soldier! Everyone knows that." He glared at me, "I'll show you who's the bastard."

I stepped backward.

Dinatius advanced on me. "You are nothing, bastard. Nothing! You have no father. No home. No name! Where did you steal the name Emrys, bastard? You are nothing! And you'll never be more!"

I winced at his words, even as I saw the rage swell in his eyes. I glanced about for some way to escape. I couldn't possibly outrun him. Not without a head start. But there were no birds flying overhead today. A thought hit me. *No birds flying overhead.*

Just as I had done yesterday, I pointed to the sky and cried out, "Look! Treasure from the sky!"

Dinatius, who had just leaned forward to lunge at me, did not look skyward this time. Instead, he hunched as if to protect his head from a blow. That was all that I could hope for. I turned and ran as fast as a frightened rabbit across the rain-soaked yard of the mill house.

Roaring with rage, he flew after me. "Come back, coward!"

I cut across the grass, leaped over a broken grinding stone and some scraps of wood, and dashed over the bridge, my leather boots slapping on the stones. Even before I reached the opposite side, I could hear Dinatius' footsteps above my own panting. Veering sharply, I turned up the old Roman road on the riverbank. To my right, the Tywy's waters churned. To my left, dense forest stretched unbroken, except by the pathways of deer and wolves, all the way to the slopes of Y Wyddfa.

I sped up the stony path for sixty or seventy paces, all the while hearing him draw closer. As I topped a small rise, I left the path, hurling myself into the thicket of bracken bordering the forest. Despite the thorns tearing into my calves and thighs, I plunged frantically ahead. Then, breaking free of the bracken, I jumped a fallen branch, leaped a rivulet, and scrambled up the mossy outcropping of rock on the other side. Finding a slender deer trail, winding like an endless snake along the forest floor, I raced along until I found myself in a grove of towering trees.

I stopped just long enough to hear Dinatius crashing through the branches behind me. Without pausing to think, I crouched on the cushion of needles underfoot and sprung up to the lowest branch of a great pine tree. Like a squirrel, I worked my way upward, one branch after another, until I had climbed to the height of three men above the ground.

At that very instant, Dinatius entered the grove. Directly above him, I clung to the branch, heart racing, lungs aching, legs bleeding. I tried to remain motionless, to breathe quietly, though my lungs screamed for more air.

Dinatius stared to his left and to his right, straining to see in the dimly lit grove. At one point, he looked up, but caught a flake of bark in his eye and thundered, "Curse this forest!" Hearing some slight rustling beyond the grove, he threw himself in that direction.

For most of the morning, I waited on that branch, observing the slow sweep of light over the needled boughs, and the still slower movement of wind walking among the trees. At length, convinced that I had eluded Dinatius, I dared to move. But I did not climb down.

I climbed up.

Ascending the stairway of branches, I realized that my heart was still racing, though not with fear, nor with exertion. It pounded with anticipation. Something about this tree, this minute, thrilled me in a way I could not explain. Each time I tugged my body to a higher branch, I found my own spirits lifted as well. It was almost as if I could see farther, hear clearer, and smell deeper the higher I climbed. I imagined myself soaring beside the small hawk that I could see circling above the trees.

The vista below me enlarged. I followed the course of the river as it wound its way down from the hills to the north. The river reminded me of a huge serpent, something out of Branwen's stories. And the hills sat in rumpled rows, like the folds of an ancient, exposed brain. What thoughts, I wondered, had that brain produced over the great stretch of time? Was this forest one of them? Was this day one of them?

Out of the mists curling among the steepest hills rose the great mass of Y Wyddfa, its summit gleaming, cloaked in white. Cloud shadows, dark and round, moved across its ridges like the footprints of giants. If only I could see the giants themselves! If only I could witness their dance!

In the western sky the clouds themselves gathered, though I could still see the occasional glint and sparkle of light on the sunlit sea. The sight of the endless ocean filled me with a vague, indefinable longing. Somehow I knew. My true home, my true name, lay out there . . . somewhere. Currents as bottomless as the sea itself churned within me.

Reaching for the next limb, I struggled to pull myself higher. I clasped my hands around the base of the branch, then threw one leg over. Several twigs broke off and spiraled gracefully to the ground. With a grunt, I pulled as hard as I could and finally mounted it.

Ready to rest, I wedged myself into the notch of the branch and leaned back against the trunk. Feeling my hands, so sticky from pine sap, I brought them to my face. I filled my lungs with the sweet, resiny smell.

Suddenly something brushed my right ear. I spun my head around. A bristling brown tail disappeared around the trunk. As I stretched to peer behind the trunk, I heard a loud whistle. The next instant, I felt tiny feet scamper lightly across my chest and down my leg.

I sat up again, just in time to see a squirrel leap from my own foot to a lower branch. Grinning, I watched the bustling animal chatter and squeak. The squirrel dashed up the trunk and then down and then up again, waving its tail like a furry flag, all the while chewing on a pinecone almost as large as its head. Then, as if it had just noticed me, it stopped short. It considered me for a few seconds, squealed once, and jumped to the outstretched bough of a neighboring tree. From there it scurried down the trunk and out of sight. I wondered whether I had looked as amusing to the squirrel as the squirrel had looked to me.

The thrill rose in me again, driving me to climb. As the wind lifted, so did the elixir of scents from the trees. Resins from chafing branches on every side poured over me, immersing me in a river of aromas.

Again I saw the hawk, still circling overhead. I could not be sure, but I felt somehow that it was watching me. Observing me, for reasons of its own.

The first rumble of thunder came as I hauled myself up to the highest branch that could support my weight. With it came a rumble more powerful still, the collective calling of thousands of trees bending with the same wind. I gazed across the sea of trees, their branches rippling like waves on water. I found that beneath the rumble I could hear their varying voices: the deep sighing of oak and the shrill snapping of hawthorn, the whooshing of pine and the cracking of ash. Needles clicked and leaves tapped. Trunks groaned and hollows whistled. All these voices and more joined to form one grand, undulating chorus, singing in a language not so distant from my own.

As the wind swelled, my tree started to sway. Almost like a human body it swung back and around, gently at first, then more and more wildly. While the swaying intensified, so did my fears that the trunk might snap and hurl me to the ground. But in time my confidence returned. Amazed at how the tree could be at once so flexible and so sturdy, I held on tight as it bent and waved, twisted and swirled, slicing curves and arcs through the air. With each graceful swing, I felt less a creature of the land and more a part of the wind itself.

The rain began falling, its sound merging with the splashing river and the singing trees. Branches streamed like waterfalls of green. Tiny rivers cascaded down every trunk, twisting through moss meadows and bark canyons. All the while, I rode out the gale. I could not have felt wetter. I could not have felt freer.

When, at last, the storm subsided, the entire world seemed newly born. Sunbeams danced on rain-washed leaves. Curling columns of mist rose from every glade. The forest's colors shone more vivid, its smells struck more fresh. And I understood, for the first time in my life, that the Earth was always being remade, that life was always being renewed. That it may have been the afternoon of this particular day, but it was still the very morning of Creation.

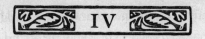

IV

THE RAG PILE

Late afternoon light heightened the hues and deepened the shadows before I felt a subtle pang in my abdomen. Quickly the pang grew. I was hungry. Hungry as a wolf.

Taking a last look at the vista, I could see a golden web of light creeping across the hills. Then I began to climb down from my perch. When at last I reached the bottommost branch, still wet from rain, I wrapped my hands around the bark and let myself drop over the side. For a moment I hung there, swaying like the tree in the gale. For some reason, I realized, the usual ache between my shoulder blades had not bothered me since I had first ascended the branches. I let go, falling into the bed of needles.

Gently, I placed my hand upon the ridged trunk of the old tree. I could almost feel the resins moving through the tall, columnar body, even as the blood moved through my own. With a simple pat of my hand, I gave thanks.

My gaze fell to a bouquet of tan mushrooms wearing shaggy manes, nestled among the needles at the base of the pine. From my forages with Branwen, I knew them to be good eating. I pounced. In short order, I had consumed every one—as well as the roots of a purple-leafed plant growing nearby.

I found the deer trail and followed it back to the rivulet. Cupping my hands, I drank some of the cold water. It chilled my teeth and awakened my tongue. A new lightness in my step, I returned to the towpath leading to the village.

I crossed the bridge. Beyond the mill, the thatched roofs of Caer Vedwyd clustered like so many bundles of dry grass. In one of them, the woman who called herself my mother was probably mixing her potions or tending to someone's wound, ever secretive and silent. To my own surprise, I found myself hoping that, one day, this place might yet feel like home.

Entering the village, I heard the playful shouts of other boys. My first impulse was to seek out one of my usual hideaways. Yet . . . I felt a new surge of confidence. This was a day to join in their games!

I hesitated. What if Dinatius was about? I would need to keep a wary eye on the smith's shop. Still, perhaps even Dinatius might soften in time.

Slowly, I approached. Beneath the great oak tree, where the three main pathways converged, I saw farmers and merchants gathered, peddling their goods. Horses and donkeys stood tethered to posts, their tails swishing at flies. Nearby, a bard with a somber face was entertaining a few listeners with a ballad—until one of the swishing tails slapped him right in the mouth. By the time he quit gagging and composed himself again, he had lost his audience.

Four boys stood at the far side of the square, practicing their aim by throwing rocks and sticks at a target—a pile of torn rags stuffed against the base of the oak. When I saw that Dinatius was not among them, I breathed easier. Soon I drew near enough to call out to one of the boys.

"How is your throw today, Lud?"

A squat, sandy-haired boy turned to me. His round face and small eyes gave him the look of being perpetually puzzled. Although he had not been unfriendly to me in the past, today he seemed cautious. I could not tell whether he was worried about Dinatius—or about me.

I stepped nearer. "Don't worry. No birds are going to empty themselves on your head."

Lud watched me for an instant, then started to laugh. "A good shot, that was!"

I grinned back. "A very good shot."

He tossed me a small stone. "Why not try your aim?"

"Are you sure?" one of the other boys asked. "Dinatius won't like it."

Lud gave a shrug. "Go ahead, Emrys. Let's see you throw."

The boys traded glances as I hefted the stone in my palm. With a snap of my arm, I threw at the rag pile. The stone flew high and wide, hitting the goose pen and causing a great commotion of honking and flapping.

I muttered sheepishly, "Not too good."

"Maybe you should get closer," ridiculed one of the boys. "Like right under the tree."

The others laughed.

Lud waved them quiet and tossed me another stone. "Try again. Some practice is what you need."

Something about his tone restored my confidence. As they all watched, I took aim again. This time, as I positioned myself, I took a moment to gauge the distance to the target and the weight of the stone in my hand. Keeping an eye on the pile of rags, I wound back my arm and released.

The stone made a direct hit. Lud clucked in satisfaction. I could not keep from smiling proudly.

Then something odd caught my attention. Instead of sailing

through the rags and hitting the trunk of the tree behind, my stone had bounced away, as if the rags themselves were made of something solid. As I looked more closely, my heart missed a beat. For as I watched, the rag pile shifted. From it came a piteous groan.

"It's a person!" I cried in disbelief.

Lud shook his head. "That's no person." He waved carelessly at the rag pile. "That's a Jew."

"A filthy Jew," echoed one of the other boys. He hurled his own stone at the rags. Another hit. Another groan.

"But—but you can't." I started to say more, then caught myself. That would risk losing any chance I might have to be accepted by the group.

"Why not?" Lud reared back to throw a weighty stick. "The Jew should never have come through here. They are Hell born, like demons, with horns and tails. They carry diseases. Bring bad luck."

The rag pile whimpered.

I swallowed hard. "I don't believe it. Why don't we let the beggar go and aim at something else instead?"

Lud eyed me strangely. "You'd best not defend the Jew. People might wonder whether . . ." He paused, picking his words. "Whether you come from the same stock."

Before I could reply, Lud let fly the heavy stick.

With a sweep of my arm, I cried out. "No! Don't hit him!"

The stick abruptly stopped its flight in midair and fell to the ground.

It was as if the stick had slammed into an invisible wall of air. The boys stood astonished. My jaw dropped. I was no less amazed than they were.

"A spell," whispered one boy.

"Sorcery," said another.

Lud's round face whitened. Slowly, he backed away from me. "Get away, you— you—"

"Demon's child," finished another voice.

I turned to find myself face-to-face with Dinatius, his tunic ripped and splattered with mud from his long trek through the forest. Despite his grimace, he looked satisfied at having cornered his prey at last.

I straightened my back, which only made me more aware of his considerable size advantage. "Let's not be enemies."

He spat on my cheek. "You think I would be the friend of a demon's whelp like you?"

My dark eyes narrowed as I wiped my face clean. It was all I could do to contain my anger enough to try again. My voice shaking, I declared, "I am no demon. I am a boy just like you."

"I know what you are." Dinatius' voice rolled down on me like a rock slide. "Your father was a demon. And your mother does the wicked work of demons. Either way, you are a child of the devil!"

With a shout, I lunged at him.

Deftly, Dinatius stepped to one side, swung me into the air, and threw me hard to the ground. He kicked me in the side for good measure, sending me rolling in the dirt.

I could barely sit up for the pain in my ribs. Above me towered Dinatius, his bushy head thrown back in laughter. The other boys laughed, too, even as they urged him on.

"What's your trouble, demon's child?" taunted Dinatius.

Though my pain was great, my rage was greater. Clutching my side, I struggled to roll onto my knees, then rise to my feet. I growled like a wounded beast, then charged again, arms flailing.

An instant later, I found myself facedown in the grass, barely able to breathe. I could taste blood in my mouth. The thought of playing dead crossed my mind, in the hope that my tormentor would lose interest. But I knew better.

Dinatius' laughter ceased as I forced myself to stand, blood trickling down my chin. I planted my unsteady feet and looked into his eyes. What I found there caught me off guard.

Beneath his belligerence, he was clearly surprised. "God's sweet death, but you're stubborn."

"Stubborn enough to stand up to you," I replied hoarsely. My hands clenched into fists.

At that moment, another figure swept out of nowhere to stand between us. The boys, except for Dinatius, fell back. And I gasped in surprise.

It was Branwen.

Though a shadow of fear crossed his face, Dinatius spat at her feet. "Move aside, she-demon."

Eyes alight, she glared at him. "Leave us."

"Go to the devil," he retorted. "That's where you both belong."

"Is that so? Then it is you who had better flee." She raised her arms menacingly. "Or I will bring the fires of Hell down on you."

Dinatius shook his head. "You will be the one to burn. Not me."

"But I am not afraid of fire! I cannot be burned!"

Lud, watching Branwen nervously, pulled on Dinatius' shoulder. "What if she speaks the truth? Let's go."

"Not until I finish with her whelp."

Branwen's blue eyes flashed. "Leave now. Or you shall burn."

He stepped backward.

She leaned toward him, then spoke a single word of command. "Now."

The other boys turned and ran. Dinatius, seeing their flight, looked uncertain. With both hands, he made the sign to protect himself from the evil eye.

"Now!" repeated Branwen.

Dinatius glowered at her for a moment, then retreated.

I took Branwen's arm. Together, we walked in slow procession back to our hut.

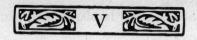

SACRED TIME

Stretched out on my pallet, I winced as Branwen massaged my bruised ribs. Odd patches of light, streaming through the holes in the thatched roof, fell on her left shoulder and hand. Her brow wrinkled in concern. Those blue eyes studied me so intensely that I could almost feel them boring into my skin.

"Thank you for helping me."

"You're welcome."

"You were wonderful. Really wonderful! And you appeared just in time, out of empty air. Like one of your Greek gods—Athena or somebody."

Branwen's wrinkles deepened. "More like Zeus, I'm afraid."

I laughed, which I regretted because it made my side hurt. "You mean you showered them with thunder and lightning."

"Instead of wisdom." She gave a sullen sigh. "I only did what any mother would do. Even if you never . . ."

"What?"

She shook her head. "It doesn't matter."

She rose to prepare a poultice that smelled of smoke and cedar. I heard her chopping and grinding for several minutes before returning to my side. Then, placing the poultice against my ribs, she laid her hands on top, pressing gently. Gradually I felt a steady warmth flowing into my bones, as if the marrow itself had turned into fire coals.

In time she closed her eyes and began to sing a low, slow chant that I had heard her use before in her healing work. In the past, I had never been sure whether she sang it to heal the person in her care or, in some way I could not understand, to heal herself. This time, studying her face, I had no doubt: The chant was for her, not for me.

> *Hy gododin catann hue*
> *Hud a lledrith mal wyddan*
> *Gaunce ae bellawn wen cabri*
> *Varigal don Fincayra*
> *Dravia, dravia Fincayra.*

The words, I felt, came from another world, an ocean away. I waited until she opened her eyes, then asked what I had wondered so often before, not expecting to receive any answer.

"What does it mean?"

Again she examined me with eyes that seemed to pierce my very soul. Then, choosing her words with care, she replied, "It is about a place, a magical place. A land of allurement. And also illusion. A land called Fincayra."

"What do those words at the end say? *Dravia, dravia Fincayra.*"

Her voice dropped to a whisper. "Live long, live long Fincayra." She lowered her eyes. "Fincayra. A place of many wonders, celebrated by bards of many tongues. They say it lies halfway between our world and the world of the spirit—neither wholly of Earth nor wholly of Heaven, but a bridge connecting both. Oh, the stories I could tell you! Its colors are more bright than the brightest sunrise; its air more fragrant than the richest garden. Many mysterious creatures are found there—including, legend has it, the very first giants."

Shifting my hips on the straw, I rolled so that my face was closer to hers. "You make it sound like a real place."

Her hands tightened against my ribs. "No more than any other place I've told you stories about. Stories may not be real in the same way as this poultice, my son, but they are real nonetheless! Real enough to help me live. And work. And find the meaning hidden in every dream, every leaf, every drop of dew."

"You don't mean that stories—like the ones about the Greek gods—are true?"

"Oh, yes." She thought for a moment. "Stories require faith, not facts. Don't you see? They dwell in sacred time, which flows in a circle. Not historical time, which runs in a line. Yet they are true, my son. Truer in many ways than the daily life of this pitiful little village."

Puzzled, I frowned. "But surely the Greeks' mountain Olympus is not the same as our mountain Y Wyddfa."

Her fingers relaxed slightly. "They're not so different as you think. Mount Olympus exists on land, and in story. In historical time, and in sacred time. Either way, Zeus and Athena and the others can be found there. It is an *in between place*—not quite our world and not quite the Otherworld, but something in between. In the same way that mist is not really air and not really water, but something of both. Another place like that is the Isle of Delos, the Greek island where Apollo was born and makes his home."

"In story, sure. But not in reality."

She eyed me strangely. "Are you sure?"

"Well . . . no, I guess not. I've never been to Greece. But I've seen Y Wyddfa a hundred times, right out that window. There are no Apollos walking around here! Not on that mountain, and not in this village."

Again she eyed me strangely. "Are you sure?"

"Of course I'm sure." I grasped a handful of straw from my pallet and threw it in the air. "This is the stuff of this village! Dirty straw, broken walls, angry people. Ignorant, too. Why, half of them think you really are a sorceress!"

Lifting the poultice, she examined the bruise running down my ribs. "Yet they still come here to be healed." She reached for a wooden bowl containing a greenish brown paste that smelled pungent, like overripe berries. Tenderly, using two fingers of her left hand, she began to apply the paste to my bruise.

"Tell me this," she said without taking her eyes off my wound. "Have you ever been out walking, away from the clatter of the village, when you felt the presence of a spirit, of something you couldn't quite see? Down by the river, perhaps, or somewhere in the forest?"

My thoughts drifted back to the great pine tree swaying in the storm. I could almost hear the swishing of branches, the wafting of resins, the feeling of bark on my hands. "Well, sometimes, in the forest . . ."

"Yes?"

"I've felt as if the trees, the oldest trees especially, were alive. Not just like a plant, but like a person. With a face. With a spirit."

Branwen nodded. "Like the dryads and hamadryads." She gazed at me wistfully. "I wish I could read to you some of the stories about them, in the Greeks' own words. They tell them so much better than I can! And those books . . . Emrys, I have seen a room full of books so thick and musty and inviting that I would sit down with one on my lap and do nothing but read all day long. I would keep on reading late into the night until I fell asleep. And then, as I slept, I might be visited by the dryads, or by Apollo himself."

She stopped short. "Have I never told you any stories about Dagda?"

I shook my head. "What does that have to do with Apollo?"

"Patience." Taking another scoop of the paste, she continued working. "The Celts, who have lived in Gwynedd long enough to know about sacred time, have many Apollos of their own. I heard about them as a child, long before I learned to read."

I jolted. "You are Celtic? I thought you came from . . . wherever I came from, over the sea."

Her hands tensed. "I did. But before I went there, I lived here, in Gwynedd. Not in this village but in Caer Myrddin, which was not so crowded as it is today. Now let me continue."

I nodded obediently, feeling buoyed by what she had said. It wasn't much, but it was the first time she had ever told me anything about her childhood.

She resumed both her work and her story. "Dagda is one of those Apollos. He is one of the most powerful Celtic spirits, the god of complete knowledge."

"What does Dagda look like? In the stories, I mean."

Branwen took the last of the paste from the bowl. "Ah, that's a good question. A very good question. For some reason known only to him, Dagda's true face is never seen. He assumes various forms at various times."

"Like what?"

"Once, in a famous battle with his supreme enemy, an evil spirit named Rhita Gawr, both of them took the forms of powerful beasts. Rhita Gawr became a huge boar, with terrible tusks and eyes the color of blood." She paused, trying to remember. "Oh, yes. And a scar that ran all the way down one of its forelegs."

I stiffened. The scar under my eye, where the boar's tusk had ripped me five years ago, started to sting. On many a dark night since that day, the same boar had appeared again, and attacked again, in my dreams.

"And in that battle, Dagda became—"

"A great stag," I completed. "Bronze in color, except for the white boots. Seven points on each side of its rack. And eyes as deep as the spaces between the stars."

Surprised, she nodded. "So you have heard the story?"

"No," I confessed.

"Then how could you know?"

I exhaled long and slow. "I have seen those eyes."

She froze. "You have?"

"I have seen the stag. And the boar as well."

"When?"

"On the day we washed ashore."

She studied me closely. "Did they fight?"

"Yes! The boar wanted to kill us. Especially you, I would guess, if it really was some kind of evil spirit."

"Whatever makes you say that?"

"Well, because you were . . . you! And I was just a scrawny little boy then." I cast an eye over myself and grinned. "As opposed to the scrawny big boy I am now. Anyway, that boar would surely have killed us. But then the stag appeared, and drove it off." I touched the spot under my eye. "That's how I got this."

"You never told me."

I glanced at her sharply. "There is much you have never told me."

"You're right," she said ruefully. "We may have shared a few stories about others, but very few about ourselves. It's my fault, really."

I said nothing.

"But I will share this much with you now. If that boar—Rhita Gawr—could have killed just one of us, it would not have been me. It would have been *you*."

"What? That's absurd! It's you who has such knowledge, such powers to heal."

"And you have powers more vast by far!" Her gaze locked into mine. "Have you begun to feel them yet? Your grandfather told me once that his came in his twelfth year." She caught her breath. "I did not mean to mention him."

"But you did! Now can you tell me more?"

Grimly, she shook her head. "Let's not talk about it."

"Please, oh please! Tell me something, at least. What was he like?"

"I can't."

My cheeks grew hot. "You must! Why did you mention him at all unless there was something about him I should know?"

She ran a hand through her yellow locks. "He was a wizard, a formidable one. But I will tell you only what he said about you. Before you were born. He told me that powers such as he possessed often skipped a generation. And that I would have a son who . . ."

"Who what?"

"Who would have powers even greater than his own. Whose

magic would spring from the very deepest sources. So deep that, if you learned to master them, you could change the course of the world forever."

My jaw fell open. "That's not true. And you know it. Just look at me!"

"I am," she said quietly. "And while you are not now what your grandfather described, perhaps you will be someday."

"No," I protested. "I don't want that. I only want my memory back! I want to know who I really am."

"What if who you are involves such powers?"

"How could it?" I scoffed. "I'm no wizard."

She cocked her head. "One day you might be surprised."

Suddenly I remembered what had happened to Lud's stick. "Well . . . I *was* surprised. Out there, before you came. Something strange happened. I'm not even sure I did it. But I'm not sure I didn't, either."

Without saying a word, she retrieved a torn piece of cloth and started wrapping it around my ribs. She seemed to be observing me with new respect, perhaps even a touch of fear. Her hands moved more gingerly, as if I were almost too hot to touch. Whatever she was feeling, whatever I was sensing, it made me very uncomfortable. In the same moment that I had started to feel closer to her, it made her seem more distant than ever.

At length, she spoke. "Whatever you did, you did from your powers. They are yours to use, a gift from above. From the greatest of the gods, the one I pray to more than any other, the one who gave each of us whatever gifts we have. I have no idea what your powers might be, my son. I only know that God didn't give them to you without expecting you to use them. All God asks is that you use them *well*. But first you must, as your grandfather put it, come to master them. And that means learning how to use them with wisdom and love."

"But I didn't ask for powers!"

"Nor did I. Just as I did not ask to be called a sorceress. But with every gift comes the risk that others may not understand it."

"Aren't you afraid, though? Last year in Llen they burned someone they said was a sorceress."

She raised her eyes to the shafts of light coming through the holes above our heads. "Almighty God knows I am no sorceress. I only try to use whatever gifts I may have as best I can."

"You try to blend the old wisdom with the new. And that frightens people."

Her sapphire eyes softened. "You see more than I realize. Yes, it frightens people. So does almost everything these days."

She gently tied off the bandage. "The whole world is changing, Emrys. I have never known a time like this, even in . . . the other place. Invasions from across the sea. Mercenaries whose loyalties shift overnight. Christians at war with the old beliefs. Old beliefs at war with the Christians. People are afraid. Deathly afraid. Anything unknown becomes the work of demons."

Stiffly, I sat up. "Don't you sometimes wish . . ." My voice disappeared, and I swallowed. "That you didn't have your gifts? That you weren't so different? That nobody thought you were a demon?"

"Of course." She bit her lip thoughtfully. "But that's where my faith comes in. You see, the new wisdom is powerful. Very powerful. Just see what it did for Saint Brigid and Saint Colombe! Yet I know enough about the old wisdom to know it has great power, too. Is it too much to hope that they can live together, old and new? That they can strengthen each other? For even as the words of Jesus touch my soul, I cannot forget the words of others. The Jews. The Greeks. The Druids. The others, even older."

I watched her somberly. "You know so much. Not like me."

"There you are wrong. I know so little. So very little." A sudden look of pain crossed her face. "Like . . . why you never call me *Mother*."

An arrow jabbed my heart. "That is because . . ."

"Yes?"

"Because I really don't believe you are."

She sucked in her breath. "And do you believe that your true name is Emrys?"

"No."

"Or that my true name is Branwen?"

"No."

She tilted her head upward. For a long moment, she stared into the thatch over our heads, blackened with the soot of countless cooking fires. At length, she looked at me again.

"About my own name, you are right. After we landed here, I took it from an old legend."

"The one you told me? About Branwen, daughter of Llyr?"

She nodded. "You remember it? Then you remember how Branwen came from another land to marry someone in Ireland. Her life began with boundless hope and beauty."

"And ended," I continued, "with so much tragedy. Her last words were, *Alas that I was ever born.*"

She took my hand in her own. "But that is about my name, not yours. My life, not yours. Please believe what I am telling you! Emrys is your name. And I am your mother."

A sob rose inside my throat. "If you are really my mother, can't you tell me where my home is? My true home, the place I really belong?"

"No, I can't! Those memories are too painful for me. And too dangerous for you."

"Then how do you expect me to believe you?"

"Hear me, please. I don't tell you only because I care for you! You lost your memory for a reason. It is a blessing."

I scowled. "It is a curse!"

She watched me, her eyes grown misty. It seemed to me that she was about to speak, to tell me at last what I most wanted to know. Then her hand squeezed mine—not in sympathy, but in fright.

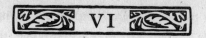

VI

FLAMES

A shape filled the doorway, blocking the light.

I jumped up from the pallet, knocking over Branwen's wooden bowl. "Dinatius!"

A hefty arm pointed at us. "Come out, both of you."

"We will not." Branwen rose to her feet and stood beside me.

Dinatius' gray eyes flashed angrily. He shouted over his shoulder, "Take her first."

He entered the hut, followed by two of the boys from the village square. Lud was not with them.

I grabbed Dinatius by the arm. He shook me off as if I were a fly, throwing me backward into the table bearing Branwen's utensils and ingredients. Spoons, knives, strainers, and bowls sprayed across the dirt floor of the hut as the table collapsed under my weight. Liquids and pastes splattered the clay walls, while seeds and leaves flew into the air.

Seeing him wrestling with Branwen, I sprung to my feet and leaped at him. He wheeled around and smacked me with such force that I flew backward into the wall. I lay there, momentarily dazed.

When my head cleared, I realized that I was alone in the hut. At first, I wasn't certain what had happened. Then, hearing shouts outside, I stumbled over to the doorway.

Branwen lay twenty or thirty paces away, in the middle of the path. Her hands and legs were bound with a length of spliced rope. A wad of cloth, torn from her dress, had been stuffed into her mouth so she could not cry out. Apparently the merchants and villagers in the square, busy with their work, had not yet noticed her—or not wanted to intervene.

"Look at her," laughed a slim, grimy-faced boy, pointing at the crumpled figure on the path. "She's not so scary now."

His companion, still holding some rope, joined the laughter. "Serves the she-demon right!"

I started to run to her aid. Suddenly I caught sight of Dinatius, bending over a pile of loose brush that had been stacked under the wide boughs of the oak. As he slid a shovel full of flaming coals from the smith's shop under the brush, fear sliced through me. *A fire. He's starting a fire.*

Flames began crackling in the brush. A column of smoke swiftly lifted into the branches of the tree. At this point Dinatius stood upright, hands on his hips, surveying his work. Silhouetted before the fire, he looked to me like a demon himself.

"She says she is not afraid of fire!" declared Dinatius, to the nods of the other boys. "She says she cannot be burned!"

"Let's find out," called the boy with the rope.

"Fire!" shouted one of the merchants, suddenly aware of the flames.

"Put it out!" cried a woman emerging from her hut.

But before anyone could move, the two boys had already grabbed Branwen by the legs. They began dragging her toward the blazing tree, where Dinatius stood waiting.

I ran out of the hut, my eyes fixed on Dinatius. Rage swelled within me, such rage as I had never known before. Uncontrollable and unstoppable, it coursed through my body like an enormous wave, knocking aside every other sense and feeling.

Seeing my approach, Dinatius grinned. "Just in time, whelp. We'll cook you both together."

A single wish overwhelmed me: *He should burn. Burn in Hell.*

At that instant, the tree shuddered and cracked, as if it had been ripped by a bolt of lightning. Dinatius whirled around just as one of the biggest branches, perhaps weakened by his fire, broke loose. Before he could escape, the branch fell directly on top of him, pinning his chest and crushing his arms. Like the breath of a dozen dragons, the blaze leaped higher. Villagers and merchants scattered. Branches exploded into flames, the sound of their snapping and splitting nearly drowning out the cries of the trapped boy.

I rushed to Branwen. She had been dropped only a few paces from the burning tree. Fire was licking at the edges of her robe. Quickly I pulled her away from the searing flames and untied her bonds. She pulled the wad from her mouth, staring at me with both gratitude and fear.

"Did you do that?"

"I—I think so. Some kind of magic."

Her sapphire eyes fixed on me. "Your magic. Your power."

Before I could reply, a spine-shivering scream erupted from inside the inferno. It went on and on, a cry of absolute agony. Hearing that voice—that helpless, human voice—my blood froze within my veins. I knew at once what I had done. I also knew what I must do.

"No!" protested Branwen, clutching at my tunic.

But it was too late. I had already plunged into the roaring flames.

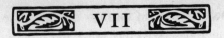

VII

HIDDEN

Voices. Angelic voices.

I sat bolt upright. Could they really be angels? Was I really dead? Darkness surrounded me. Blacker than any night I had ever known.

Then: the pain. The pain on my face and my right hand told me I must indeed be alive. It was searing pain. Clawing pain. As if my very skin were being ripped away.

Beneath the pain, I grew aware of a strange weight on my brow. Cautiously, I reached my hands to my face. The fingers of my right hand, I realized, were bandaged. So were my brow, my cheeks, my eyes—swathed in cold, wet clothes that smelled of pungent herbs. Even the barest touch cut me with daggers of pain.

A heavy door creaked open. Across an expanse of stone floor, footsteps approached, echoing from a high ceiling above my head. Footsteps whose cadence I thought I recognized.

"Branwen?"

"Yes, my son," answered the voice in the darkness. "You have awakened. I am glad." Yet she sounded more dismal than glad, I thought, as she lightly caressed the back of my neck. "I must change your bandages. I am afraid it will hurt."

"No. Don't touch me."

"But I must, if you are to heal."

"No."

"Emrys, I must."

"All right, but be careful! It hurts so much already."

"I know, I know."

I tried my best to remain still as she carefully unwrapped the bandages, touching me as delicately as a butterfly. While she worked, she dripped something over my face which smelled as fresh as the forest after a rain and seemed to numb the pain a little. Feeling somewhat better, I spouted questions like a fountain. "How long have I slept? Where is this place? Who are those voices?"

"You and I—forgive me if this stings—are at the Church of Saint Peter. We are the guests of the nuns who live here. It is they you hear singing."

"Saint Peter! That's in Caer Myrddin."

"So it is."

Feeling a cold draft from a window or door somewhere, I drew my rough wool blanket about my shoulders. "But that is several days' travel, even with a horse."

"So it is."

"But—"

"Be still, Emrys, while I untie this."

"But—"

"Still, now . . . that's right. Just a moment. Ah, there."

As the bandage fell away, so did my questions about how we had come to be here. A new question crowded out all the rest. For although my eyes were no longer covered, I still could not see.

"Why is it so dark?"

Branwen did not answer.

"Didn't you bring a candle?"

Again she did not answer.

"Is it nighttime?"

Still she did not answer. Yet she did not need to, for the answer came from a cuckoo, alive with song, somewhere nearby.

The fingers of my unbandaged hand quivered as I touched the tender area around my eyes. I winced, feeling the blotches of scabs, the still-burning skin underneath. No hair on my eyebrows. No eyelashes, either. Blinking back the pain, I traced the edges of my eyelids, crusted and scarred.

I knew my eyes were wide open. I knew I could see nothing. And, with a shiver, I knew one thing more.

I was blind.

In anguish, I bellowed. Suddenly, hearing again the sound of the cuckoo, I flung off my blanket. Despite the weakness of my legs, I forced myself to rise from the pallet, pushing away Branwen's hand as she tried to stop me. I staggered across the stones, following the sound.

I tripped on something and crashed to the floor, landing on my shoulder. Stretching out my arms, I could feel nothing but the surface of the stones beneath me. They felt hard and cold, like a tomb.

My head spun. I could feel Branwen helping me to my feet, even as I could hear her muffled sobs. Again I pushed her away. Staggering forward, my hands hit a wall of solid rock. The sound of the cuckoo drew me to the left. The groping fingers of my unbandaged hand caught the edge of a window.

Grasping the sill, I pulled myself closer. Cool air stung my face. The cuckoo sang, so close to me that I might have reached out and touched its wing. For the first time, it seemed, in weeks, I felt the splash of sunshine on my face. Yet as hard as I tried to find the sun, I could not see it.

Hidden. The whole world is hidden.

My legs buckled beneath me. I fell to the floor, my head upon the stones. And I wept.

VIII

THE GIFT

During the weeks stretching into months that followed, my torment filled the halls of the Church of Saint Peter. The nuns residing there, moved both by the strength of Branwen's piety and the severity of my burns, had opened the gates of their sanctuary. They must have found it difficult to feel anything but sympathy for this woman who did little else but pray all day and tend to her wounded boy. As to the boy himself, they mostly avoided me, which suited me just fine.

For me, every day was dark—in mood as well as sight. I felt like an infant, barely able to crawl around the cold stone chamber that I shared with Branwen. My fingers came to know well its four rigid corners, its uneven lines of mortar between the stones, its lone window where I sometimes stood for hours, straining to see. Instead of lighting me, though, the window only tortured me with the jovial call of the cuckoo and the distant bustle of Caer Myrddin's marketplace. Occasionally the smell of someone's cooking pot or a flowering tree might waft to me, mingling with the scents of thyme and beech root that rose from Branwen's low table by her pallet. But I could not go out to find such things. I was a prisoner, confined in the dungeon of my blindness.

Two or three times, I summoned the courage to walk, feeling

with my hands past the heavy wooden door and into the maze of corridors and chambers beyond. By listening carefully to the echoes of my footsteps, I discovered that I could judge the length and height of passageways and the size of rooms.

One day I found a stairway whose stone steps had been worn into shallow bowls over the years. Feeling the wall carefully as I descended, I pushed open a door at the bottom and found myself in a fragrant courtyard. Wet grass touched my feet; warm wind breathed on my face. I remembered, all at once, how good it felt to be outdoors, on the grass, in the sun. Then I heard the nuns singing in the cloisters nearby. I started walking faster, eager to find them. Without warning, I strode right into a stone column, so hard that I fell over backward into a shallow pool of water. As I struggled to get up, I stepped on a loose rock and pitched sideways. The left side of my face bashed against the base of the column. Bruised and bloody, my bandages torn, I lay there sobbing until Branwen found me.

After that I didn't stir from the pallet in my chamber, convinced I would spend the rest of my days as a helpless burden to Branwen. Even when I tried to think of other things, my mind always returned to the day that had been my undoing. The sight of her, bound and gagged by the tree. The rage that boiled over so violently. The laughter, melting into shrieks, of Dinatius. The searing flames all around. The crushed arms and broken body beneath the branches. The sound of my own screams when I realized that my face was burning.

I could not remember our trek to the walls of Caer Myrddin, though from Branwen's spare description I could imagine it well enough. I could almost see Lud's round face watching us ride over the hill in the cart of the passing trader who had taken pity on the woman with sapphire eyes and her badly burned son. I could almost feel the swaying of the horse-drawn cart, almost hear the squealing of the wheels and the pounding of the hooves on the towing path. I could almost taste my own charred skin, almost hear my own delirious wailing as we rode through those long days and nights.

Now, very little broke the regularity of my days. The singing of the nuns. The shuffling of their footsteps to cloisters, to meals, to meditations. Branwen's quiet prayers and chants as she did her best to heal my skin. The continuing calls of the cuckoo, perched in a rustling tree that I could not name.

And darkness. Always darkness.

Sometimes, as I sat on my pallet, I ran my fingers gingerly over the scabs on my cheeks and under my eyes. The ridges on my skin felt terribly deep, like the bark of a pine tree. I knew that, despite Branwen's skills, my face would be scarred forever. Even if, by some miracle, my sight were ever restored, those scars would announce my folly to the world. I knew, of course, that such thoughts were foolishly vain. Yet they came to me anyway.

Once I found myself longing to grow a beard. I imagined a great, flowing beard—the kind an ancient sage, hundreds of years old, might wear. What a beard that was! All curly and white, it covered my face like a mass of clouds. I even suspected that a bird or two might try to nest there.

But such wistful moments never lasted long. Increasingly, I felt gripped by despair. Never again would I climb a tree. Never again would I run freely through a field. Never again would I see Branwen's face, except in memory.

I began to leave my meals untouched. Despite Branwen's insistence that I eat more, I had no desire. One morning, she knelt beside me on the stones of our chamber, wordlessly dressing my wounds. As she tried to replace my bandage, I leaned away from her, shaking my head.

"I wish you had left me to die."

"It was not your time to die."

"How do you know?" I snapped. "I feel like I've died already! This is not a life! This is endless torture. I prefer to live in Hell than to live here."

She seized me by the shoulders. "Don't talk that way! It is blasphemy."

"It is the truth! See what your powers, the ones you called a gift from God, have done for me? Curse these powers! I'd be better off dead."

"Stop it!"

I shook free, my heart pounding. "I have no life! I have no name! I have nothing!"

Branwen, swallowing her sobs, began to pray. "Dear Lord, Savior of my soul, Author of all that is written in the Great Book of Heaven and Earth, please help this boy! Please! Forgive him. He knows not what he says. If only you would restore his sight, even a little, even for a while, I pledge to you he will earn your forgiveness. He will never use his powers again, if that is what it takes! Only help him. Please help him."

"Never use my powers again?" I scoffed. "I would gladly give them up in exchange for sight! I never wanted them anyway."

Bitterly, I tugged the bandage on my brow. "And what kind of life do you have now? Not much better than mine! It's true. You may talk bravely. You may fool those nuns out there. But not me. I know you are miserable."

"I am at peace."

"That's a lie."

"I am at peace," she repeated.

"At peace!" I shouted. "At peace! Then why are your hands so chafed from all your wringing? Why are your cheeks so stained with your—"

I never finished the sentence.

"Good God," she whispered.

"I . . . don't understand." Hesitantly, I extended a hand toward her face, lightly brushing her cheek.

In that instant, we both realized that I could, somehow, *sense* her tear stains. Though I could not see them with my eyes, I nonetheless knew they were there.

"It is another gift." Branwen's voice was full of awe. She clasped my hand tightly. "You have the *second sight*."

I didn't know what to think. Was this the same ability that I once used to open a flower's petals? No. It felt different. Less willful somehow. What about seeing the colors inside the flower before it opened? Perhaps. Yet this felt different from that, too. More like . . . an answer to Branwen's prayer. A gift from God.

"Can it be?" I asked meekly. "Can it really be?"

"Thanks to God, it can."

"Test me," I demanded. "Hold up some fingers."

She obliged.

I bit my lower lip, trying to perceive her fingers.

"Two?"

"No. Try again."

"Three?"

"Try again."

Focusing my thoughts, I instinctively closed my eyes, though of course that made no difference. After a long pause, I said, "Two hands, not one. Am I right?"

"Right! Now . . . how many fingers?"

Minutes passed. Perspiration formed on my scarred brow, stinging the sensitive skin. But I didn't waver. At length, I asked a hesitant question.

"Could it be seven?"

Branwen sighed with relief. "Seven it is."

We embraced. I knew, in that moment, that my life had changed completely. And I suspected that, for the rest of my days, I would continue to ascribe special importance to the number seven.

Most important of all, though, I knew that a promise had been made. It didn't matter whether it had been made by me, by Branwen, or by us both. I would never again move objects with my mind. Not even a flower petal. Nor would I read the future, or try to master whatever other powers might once have been mine. But I could see again. I could live again.

Right away, I started eating. And hardly stopped—especially if I could get bread-in-milk, my favorite. Or blackberry jam on bread crusts. Or mustard mixed with raw goose eggs, which gave me the added fun of making any nearby nuns ill. One afternoon, Branwen went out to the market and found a single, succulent date—which was, for us, as splendid as a royal feast.

And my spirit revived along with my appetite. I began to explore the hallways, the cloisters, the courtyards of Saint Peter. The whole church was my domain. My castle! Once, when no nuns were about, I stole into the courtyard and took a bath in the shallow pool. The most difficult part was to resist singing at the top of my lungs.

Meanwhile, Branwen and I worked together every day for long hours, trying to sharpen my second sight. For my first practice sessions, we used spoons, pottery bowls, and other ordinary utensils that she found somewhere in the church. In time, I moved on to a small altar with subtle contours and grains in its wood. Eventually, I graduated to a two-handled chalice with intricate carvings on its surface. Although it took the better part of a week, I finally came to read the words inscribed on its rim: *Ask, and ye shall receive.*

As I practiced, I realized that I could see objects best if they were stationary and not far away. If they moved too quickly or remained too distant, I often lost them. A flying bird simply melted into the sky.

Furthermore, as the light around me grew dimmer, so did my second sight. At dusk I could see only the blurred outlines of things. I could not see anything at night, unless a torch or the moon pushed back the darkness. Why my second sight should need light at all, I could only wonder. It was, after all, not like normal sight. So why should darkness smother it? Then again, second sight seemed to be partly inward, and partly outward. Perhaps it relied on what was left of my eyes, in some way I could not comprehend. Or perhaps it required something else, something inside me, which failed to pass the test.

Thus, while second sight was certainly better than no sight at all, it was not nearly as good as the eyesight I had lost. Even in daylight, I could discern only the barest wisps of colors, leaving most of the world painted in variants of gray. So while I could tell that Branwen now wore a cloth veil around her head and neck, and that it was lighter in color than her loose robe, I could not tell whether the veil was gray or brown. I began to forget much of what I had learned about the colors of things since arriving in Gwynedd.

Yet I could accept such limitations. Oh, yes—and gladly. With my emerging ability, I walked to the cloisters or to meals with Branwen. I sat beside a nun and conversed for some time, seeming to look at her with my eyes, without her suspecting that those eyes remained useless. And one morning I actually ran around the courtyard, weaving in and out of the columns, leaping right over the pool.

That time I didn't hold back my singing.

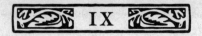

THE YOUNG BIRD

As my second sight improved, Branwen helped me to read the Latin inscriptions in the religious manuscripts at the church. Strong smells of leather and parchment washed over me every time I cracked open one of those volumes. And the images, stronger still, carried me away—to the flaming chariot of Elijah, the last supper of Jesus, the stone tablets of Moses.

Sometimes, as I pored over those texts, my troubles melted away. I became one with the words, seeing deeds and colors and faces with richness and clarity that I could never see with my eyes. And I came to understand, in a way I never had before, that books are truly the stuff of miracles. I even dared to dream that someday, somehow, I might surround myself with books from many times and many tongues, just as Branwen had once done.

With each passing day, my vision grew a little stronger. One morning I discovered that I could read Branwen's expression by the curl of her lips and the glint in her eyes. Another morning, as I stood by my window watching the wind toss the branches, I realized that the rustling tree where the cuckoo lived was a hawthorn, broad and dark. And one night I glimpsed, for the first time since before the fire, a star shining overhead.

On the next night, I positioned myself in the center of the

courtyard, far from any torches. Low on the northern horizon, a second star glittered. The next night, three more. Then five more. Eight more. Twelve more.

Branwen joined me in the courtyard the following evening. Together we lay on our backs on the stones. With a sweep of her hand, she pointed out the constellation Pegasus. Then, slowly and rhythmically, she told me the tale of the great winged horse. As she spoke, I felt I was soaring through the sky on Pegasus' broad back. We leaped from one star to another, sailed past the moon, galloped across the horizon.

Every night after that, unless clouds completely covered the sky, Branwen and I lay there under the dome of darkness. As much as I loved reading the church's manuscripts, reading the manuscript of the heavens thrilled me even more. With Branwen as my guide, I spent my evenings in the company of Cygnus, Aquarius, and Ursa—whose claws raked my back several times. I tied the sails of Vela, swam far with Pisces, marched beside Hercules.

Sometimes, while exploring the stars, I imagined the entire sky shrinking down into a single, glorious cape. In a flash, I would put it on. Deep blue, studded with stars, the cape fell over my back, sparkling as I moved. The stars riding my shoulders. The planets ringing my waist. How I would love to own a cape like that one day!

Yet even as I celebrated, I could not forget how much lay hidden from me. The clouded sky obscured some of the stars; my clouded vision obscured more. Still, the thrill of all I could see far outweighed the frustration with what I could not. Despite the clouds, the stars had somehow never seemed so bright.

And yet . . . there remained a dark place inside of me that even the light from stars could not reach. The ghosts of my past continued to haunt me. Especially what I had done to Dinatius. I still heard his screams, still saw the terror in his eyes, still felt the twisted and useless remains of his arms. When I asked Branwen whether he had survived, she couldn't say. She only knew that he was still hovering at the edge of death when we had left the village. Still, this much was clear. While he had done plenty to provoke my rage, his brutality could not obscure my own.

On top of that, something else continued to plague me, something deeper than guilt. Fear. About myself, and my dreadful powers. The merest thought of them threw up a wall of flames in my mind, flames that seared my very soul. If I lacked the strength to keep my promise, would I use those powers or would they use me? If, in the grip of uncontrollable rage, I could destroy both a person and a tree with such ease, what else might I one day destroy? Could I annihilate myself completely, as I did my own eyes?

What kind of creature am I, really? Perhaps Dinatius had been right after all. Perhaps the blood of a demon really did flow through my veins, so that terrible magic could rise out of me at any moment, like a monstrous serpent rising out of the darkest depths of the sea.

And so it was, even in the new brightness of my days, that I remained troubled by the darkness of my own fears. As the weeks passed, my vitality, as well as my vision, continued to grow. Yet my unease continued to grow as well. I knew, down inside, that I could never put my fears to rest—until I somehow learned my true identity.

There came an afternoon when I heard a new sound outside the window of my chamber. Eagerly, I moved closer. By stretching my second sight, I found the source of the sound, nestled among the boughs of the hawthorn tree. I watched and listened for a while. Then I turned back to Branwen, who sat in her customary place on the floor next to my pallet, grinding some herbs.

"The cuckoo has nested in the hawthorn tree." I spoke with a mixture of certainty and sadness that made Branwen put down her mortar and pestle. "I have watched her—seen her—sitting in the nest every day. She laid her only egg there. She guarded it from enemies. And now, at last, the egg has hatched. The young bird has emerged from the darkness."

Branwen studied my face carefully before responding. "And," she asked in a trembling voice, "has the young bird flown?"

Slowly, I shook my head. "Not yet. But very soon he must."

"Can he not . . ." She had to swallow before trying again. "Can he not stay with his mother for a while longer, sharing their nest for a little more time?"

I frowned. "All things must fly when they are able."

"But where? Where will he go?"

"In this case, he must find his own self." After a pause, I added, "To do that, he must find his own past."

Branwen clutched at her heart. "No. You don't mean that. Your life will be worth nothing if you go back . . . there."

"My life will be worth nothing if I stay here." I took a step toward her. Though my eyes were useless, I probed her with my newfound gaze. "If you cannot, or will not, tell me where I came from, then I must find out myself. Please understand! I must find my true name. I must find my true mother and father. I must find my true home."

"Stay," she begged in desperation. "You are only a boy of twelve! And half blind, as well! You have no idea of the risks. Listen to me, Emrys. If you stay with me for just a few more years, you will reach manhood. Then you can choose whatever you want to be. A bard. A monk. Whatever you like."

Seeing my blank look, she tried a different approach. "Whatever you do, don't decide right now. I could tell you a story, something to help you think through this madness. What about one of your favorites? The one about the wandering Druid who saved Saint Brigid from slavery?" Without waiting for me to answer, she began. "There came a day in the life of young Brigid when she—"

"Stop." I shook my head. "I must learn my own story."

Weakly, Branwen clambered to her feet. "I left behind more than you will ever know. Do you know why? So we could be safe, you and I. Is that not enough for you?"

I said nothing.

"Must you really do this?"

"You could come with me."

She leaned against the wall for support. "No! I could not."

"Then tell me how to get back there."

"No."

"Or at least where to begin."

"No."

I felt a sudden urge to probe the inside of her mind, as if it were the inside of a flower. Then the flames ignited, overwhelming my thoughts. I remembered my promise—and also my fears.

"Tell me just one thing," I pleaded. "You told me once that you knew my grandfather. Did you also know my father?"

She winced. "Yes. I knew him."

"Was he, well, not human? Was he . . . a demon?"

Her whole body stiffened. After a long silence she spoke, in a voice that seemed a lifetime away. "I will say only this. If ever you should meet him, remember: He is not what he may seem."

"I will remember. But can't you tell me anything more?"

She shook her head.

"My own father! I just want to know him."

"It is better you do not."

"Why?"

Instead of answering, she just shook her head sadly. She went to the low table bearing her collection of healing herbs. Deftly, she picked a few, then ground them into a coarse powder which she poured into a leather satchel on a cord. Handing me the satchel, she said resignedly, "This might help you live a little longer."

I started to respond, but she spoke again.

"And take this, from the woman who would have you call her Mother." Slowly, she reached into her robe and pulled out her precious pendant.

Despite my limited vision, I could see the flash of glowing green.

"But it's yours!"

"You will need it more than I."

She removed the pendant and squeezed its jeweled center one last time before placing the leather cord around my neck. "It is called . . . the *Galator*."

I caught my breath at the word.

"Guard it well," she continued. "Its power is great. If it cannot keep you safe, that is only because nothing outside of Heaven can."

"You kept me safe. You built a good nest."

"For a while, perhaps. But now . . ." Tears brimmed in her eyes. "Now you must fly."

"Yes. Now I must fly."

Gently, she touched my cheek.

I turned and left the room, my footsteps echoing down the corridor of stone.

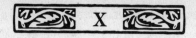

X

THE OLD OAK

As I stepped through the carved wooden gates of the Church of Saint Peter, I entered the bustle and confusion of Caer Myrddin. It took some time for my dim vision to adjust to all the commotion. Carts and horses clattered along the stony streets, as did donkeys, pigs, sheep, and a few hairy dogs. Merchants bellowed about their wares, beggars clutched at the robes of passersby, spectators gathered around a man juggling balls, and people of all descriptions strode past, carrying baskets, bundles, fresh greens, and stacks of cloth.

I glanced over my shoulder at the hawthorn tree, whose branches I could barely make out above the church wall. For all the pain I had experienced in that place, I would miss the quiet calm of my room, the slow singing of the nuns, the bird in the boughs of that tree. And, more than I ever expected, I would miss Branwen.

Watching the blur of people, animals, and goods, I noticed some sort of shrine on the opposite side of the street. Curious, I decided to get closer, although that would require swimming across the fast-flowing river of traffic. Biting my lip, I started across.

Instantly, I was pushed and kicked, turned and buffeted. Since I could not see well enough to stay out of the way, I crashed into a man carrying a load of firewood. Sticks flew in all directions. So did curses. Then I walked straight into the flank of a horse. Seconds later, I nearly lost my toes under a cart wheel. Somehow, though, I made it to the other side. I approached the shrine.

It was not much of a monument, just a carved image of a hawk above a bowl of muddy water. If any people took care of it, they had not done so in years. The hawk's wings had broken off. The stones around the base were crumbling. Probably only a handful of the people who strode by here every day even noticed it.

Yet something about this old, forgotten shrine intrigued me. I drew closer, touched the hawk's worn beak. I knew enough from Branwen's descriptions to guess that the shrine was probably made to honor Myrddin, one of the ancient Celts' most revered gods, who sometimes took the form of a hawk. One of their Apollos, as she would say. Although I still could not quite accept her notion that such spirits still walked the land, I wondered again about the stag and the boar who had fought over us so long ago. If they were, in fact, Dagda and Rhita Gawr, was it just possible that the spirit of Myrddin still lived as well?

A donkey, loaded down with heavy sacks, knocked into me. I fell into the shrine, plunging my hand into the murky water. As I stood and shook my hand dry, I tried to imagine what Caer Myrddin might have looked like centuries ago. Branwen had told me that, instead of a bustling city, it was just a peaceful hill with a spring where wandering shepherds might pause to rest. Then, over time, it grew into a trade center, taking goods from the farms of Gwynedd, and regions as distant as Gwent, Brycheiniog, and Powys Fadog. When the Romans came, they built a fortress on the River Tywy's high banks. And now the old military roads, such as the one to Caer Vedwyd, linked the city to the lush valleys and deer-filled forests of the north, and also down the river to the sea. Whether or not anyone today took the time to remember such things, this crumbling shrine—and the name of the city itself—still connected Caer Myrddin to its distant past.

That, I realized, was the purpose of my own journey. To connect myself with my past. To find my name. My home. My parents. And though I had no idea where this journey might take me, nor where it might end, I suddenly knew where it should begin.

The sea. I must return to the sea. To the very spot where I had tumbled onto the rocky shore more than five years ago.

Perhaps, when I arrived at that forbidding shore, I would find nothing but jagged rocks and screeching gulls and pulsing waves. Or perhaps I would find the clue that I sought. Or at least a clue to the clue. It was not much of a hope, but it was the only hope I had.

For what seemed like hours, I wandered through the city, trying to keep to the smaller side streets to avoid being trampled in the traffic. As if I were not already aware of the limits of my vision, I tripped and stumbled enough times to make my toes horribly tender within my leather boots. Even so, I made my way. While I am sure many people concluded—correctly—that I was a clumsy oaf, I am just as sure none of them guessed that my eyes were totally useless. The occasional words of sympathy I received were for my scars, not for my blindness.

At last, I found my way to the road that ran beside the River Tywy. I knew that if I followed it far enough to the north, I would return to my old village. From there I would make my way to the sea.

At last I came to the walls of the city, ten paces thick and twice as tall. I crossed the wide bridge, taking care not to trip on the uneven stones. Then I continued into the wooded valley beyond.

As I plodded along beside the river, I concentrated on each step. If my attention wavered, even briefly, I was likely to end up on the ground. Too often, I did. Once I tripped in the middle of a village square, where a donkey almost stepped on my back.

Still, I managed well enough. For three days I walked, eating raspberries and bramble berries along with the round of cheese given to me by one of the nuns. During that time I spoke to no one, and no one spoke to me. One day at dusk I helped a shepherd pull his lamb out of a pit, receiving a crust of bread in thanks, but that was my only contact with others.

In time the road turned into the old towpath through Caer Vedwyd. Barges floated down the river, sliding past the families of ducks and swans. As I drew near the village, I kept to the cover of the woods, staying parallel to the path without actually walking on it. That way no one saw me. Occasionally, I feasted on roots and berries and edible leaves. I drank once again from the rivulet below the great pine tree where I rode out the gale, but I wished that I had never climbed down. In a strange way I felt more at home here, in the wild woods, than anywhere else in Gwynedd.

Late that afternoon, I paused near the bridge at Caer Vedwyd. I caught a glimpse of a tall but twisted figure standing at the other end of the bridge. I strained to make it out more clearly, as the wind swelled around me. It could have been a decrepit tree, except that I had never noticed a tree in that spot before. I could not shake the feeling that it was, instead, the bent body of a person—a person with nothing but stumps for arms.

I did not linger. Despite the obstacles, I tromped through the woods for some distance, avoiding the next several villages as well. As the shadows grew longer, my vision worsened and my progress slowed. Finally, having left any signs of people behind, I broke into a wide meadow. Scraped from my falls and exhausted from my trek, I found a hollow in the soft grass and curled up to sleep.

Sunlight on my face woke me. Crossing the meadow, I rejoined the road near the point where it left the river. But for one elderly man, whose scraggly white beard bounced on his chest as he walked, I met no one else on this stretch. I observed the old man, wishing again that I too could grow a beard, to hide those miserable scars. One day, perhaps. If I lived so long.

Despite the lack of settlements, I did not feel disoriented. My memories of the way to the sea remained surprisingly clear. For though I had traveled this route only once in my life, I had walked it many times in my dreams. My slow shuffle started to gain speed. I could almost hear the distant sound of slapping waves.

Every so often, I reached into my tunic and touched the Galator. As little as I knew about it, I felt oddly comforted to know it was there. The same was true for Branwen's leather satchel, slung over my shoulder.

The old road gradually deteriorated until it became no more than a grassy trail. At last it passed through a cleft in a wall of crumbling cliffs. I smelled the barest whiff of salt on the air. I knew this place, knew it in my bones.

Black rock rose vertically to twenty times my own height. Kittiwakes called and swooped among the crags. The trail bent sharply to the right, ending where I knew it would.

At the ocean.

Before me stretched the gray-blue waters, without any end and without any bottom. The smell of kelp tickled my nostrils. Waves rushed forward and withdrew, grinding sand against rock. Gulls, circling above the shore, shrieked noisily.

I crossed the black barrier of rocks, stepping over tidal pools and shards of driftwood. Nothing has changed, I told myself. As waves washed over my feet, I gazed westward. The fog of my vision merged with the fog on the water. I strained to see more clearly, but it was impossible.

Nothing has changed. The black rocks, the briny breeze, the endless rhythm of the waves. Just like before. Did they hide a clue somewhere? If so, how could I ever hope to find it? The sea was so enormous, and I was so . . . tiny. My head dropped lower on my chest. Aimlessly, I started to walk, my leather boots splashing in the chill water.

Then I saw one shape that had changed. The ancient oak, though still mammoth, had been shorn of most of its bark, which sat in tattered strips among the roots. Several branches, broken and splintered, lay strewn across the rocky beach. Even the hollow in the trunk, where I had endured the attack of the boar, had been punctured, its walls split and buckled. The old tree had finally died.

As I approached its remains, I tripped, stabbing my shin on a pointed rock. But I cut short my own howl of pain, not wanting to alert any wild boars that might be near. Whether or not the boar I had met here was really Rhita Gawr, it had certainly wanted blood on its tusks. If a boar appeared now, I would have no place to hide. And, almost certainly, no Dagda to rescue me.

My shoulders ached, as did my legs. I sat down on the lifeless roots. As I ran my hand along the edge of the hollow, I could still feel the marks of the boar's slashing tusks. That experience felt so close. So recent. And yet this ancient tree, whose strength had then seemed eternal, was now nothing more than a skeleton.

I kicked at a shred of bark by my foot, knowing that I myself had fared little better. I had returned to this spot, if not yet dead, then perilously close. I was nearly blind. I was utterly lost.

I sat there, my head in my hands. Absently, I stared at the shoreline. The tide, I could tell, was beginning to retreat. Gradually, the border widened between the harsh rocks and the sea, leaving a strip of sand whose contours contained their own tiny mountains and oceans.

A hermit crab skittered across this landscape of sand. I watched as the crab wrestled with a half-buried shell at the edge of a tidal pool. After much clawing and scraping, the crab finally retrieved its prize, a conch streaked with a color that reminded me vaguely of orange. I imagined the crab celebrating that it had, at last, found a new home. But before it could savor its success, a sudden sea breeze blew the shell out of its grasp. The shell slid into the shallow pool, floating like a tiny raft, bouncing on the ripples.

Seeing the stranded crab watch its hard-earned treasure float away, I allowed myself a sardonic grin. That is how it works. You think you have found your dream, then you lose it forever. You think you have found your home, then you see it float away.

Float away. Despite my better judgment, I felt suddenly possessed by an idea. A wild, hopeless, mad idea.

I would build a raft! Perhaps this very tree, which had helped me once before, could help me again. Perhaps this very tide, which had borne me once to shore, could bear me out to the sea. I would trust. Simply trust. In the tree. In the tide.

I had nothing to lose except my life.

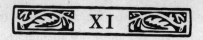

XI

SAILING

Using the broken limbs of the ancient oak, lashed together with ropelike shreds of bark, I built my raft. Relying only on my second sight, I often misjudged the fit of limbs and the strength of knots. Yet plank by plank my raft came together. In its center, I placed a large slab from the hollow of the tree, which provided a slightly cupped seat where I could ride. Finally, I bound the edges with several long strands of kelp that I found among the rocks.

By the time I finished, the sun was starting to set. I dragged the meager craft to the edge of the waves. On a whim, before pushing off, I ran back to the tidal pool where the conch shell still drifted. Scooping it up, I dropped it on the sand so that the crab might find its home again.

Gulls screeched, in laughter it seemed, as I waded into the cold waves. Before climbing on my feeble vessel, I hesitated. Opposing worlds tugged at me. I stood exactly on the edge—of land and sea, of past and future. For a moment I lost my resolve. Water lapped about my thighs, the same water that had nearly drowned me before. Perhaps I was acting too hastily. Perhaps I should return to shore to think of a better plan.

Just then I noticed a hint of gold shining on the remains of the old tree. The sunset had struck the trunk, etching it in fire. It reminded me of another tree on fire, a tree whose flames still burned me deeply. And I knew I must try to find the answers to my questions.

I pulled myself aboard the raft. Settling into the cupped center, I folded my legs in front of me. I looked one more time at the black cliffs, then turned away from shore. Dipping my hands in the chilly water, I paddled for some distance, until my arms grew too tired. The fading sun, still strong enough to warm my wet skin, made the water sparkle with many more colors than I could detect. Yet even though I could not truly see, I could sense the web of pink and golden light dancing just beneath the waves.

As the tide carried me farther from shore, a breeze leaned against my back. Where the sea might take me, I did not know. All I could do was trust.

I thought about ancient seafarers like Bran the Blessed, Odysseus, and Jonah, whose tales I had heard from Branwen. And I wondered whether anyone but Branwen would ever care about my own ocean voyage. I wished that someday I might be able to describe it to her. But in my heart I knew that I would never see her again.

A black-headed gull swooped past, skimming the surface of the waves in search of supper. With a loud squawk, it careened toward the raft and settled on one of the strands of kelp dangling from the side. Clamping its beak on a green frond, it pulled and twisted madly.

"Away!" I waved my hands in its face. The last thing I needed at this moment was to have my little craft pulled apart by a hungry bird.

The gull dropped the kelp, lifted off with a screech, then circled the raft. A few seconds later it landed again—this time on my knee. The bird's eye, which seemed as yellow as the sun, examined me.

Apparently concluding that I looked too large (or too tough) for a ready meal, the gull cocked its black head and took flight, heading back to shore.

As I watched the gull depart, I yawned. The continuous rocking of the waves was making me drowsy, more so because I was spent from my days of trekking from Caer Myrddin. Yet how could I sleep? I could fall off the raft, or worse, miss something important.

I tried to rest without sleeping. Curling my back, I leaned my head against my knees. To keep myself awake, I concentrated on the slowly setting sun. By now the great burning globe was resting just above the water, sending a shimmering band of light across the waves, right to my raft. It might have been an avenue of gold, a pathway across the water.

I wondered where that path might lead. Just as I wondered where my own might lead.

Checking over my shoulder, I could tell that I had already drifted some distance from shore. Although the breeze had subsided, I realized that the raft might have caught a current. I bounced over the waves, which splashed me constantly. Despite the jostling, my lashings looked still taut, the wood still sturdy. Licking my lips, I tasted the salty spray. As I laid my head again on my knees, I could not help but yawn again.

The sun, swollen and scarlet, ignited the clouds with colors, colors that I could see only subtly. The shape of the sun I could sense more clearly, as it grew flatter on the horizon. An instant later, as if it were a bubble that had finally burst, it disappeared below the waves.

But I did not notice the onset of darkness, for I had fallen asleep.

A sudden splash of cold water woke me. Night had arrived. A host of stars clustered around the thinnest crescent moon I had ever known. I listened to the ceaseless heaving and sucking of the waves, to the bashing of water against wood. I slept no more during that night. Shivering, I drew my legs tightly to my chest. I could only wait for whatever the sea wished to show me.

As the sun rose behind me, I discovered that the coast of Gwynedd had disappeared. Not even the imposing cliffs were visible anymore. Only a faint wisp of a cloud stretched like a pennant from what I guessed might be the summit of Y Wyddfa, though I could not be sure.

I spied a timber that had slipped out of its lashing, and quickly bound it up again. As the day dragged on, my back and legs grew painfully stiff, but I couldn't stand to stretch them without flipping over. Waves slapped relentlessly against the raft and against me. The hot sun burned the back of my neck. Meanwhile, my mouth and throat felt an even stronger burning, which increased as the day wore on. Never before had I felt so thirsty.

Just at sunset, I perceived a group of large, streamlined bodies leaping above the ocean surface. Although seven or eight individuals comprised the group, they swam in perfect unity. They moved like a single wave, surging and subsiding. Then, as they passed near my raft, they changed direction and swam a complete circle around me. Once, twice, three times, they ringed me, leaping in and out of the bubbles of their own wakes.

Were they dolphins? Or sea people, perhaps? The ones Branwen called *people of the mer,* who were said to be part human and part fish? I could not see well enough to tell. Yet the glimpse of them filled me with wonder. As they swam away, their bodies gleaming in the golden light, I promised myself that if I should ever live long enough, I would do whatever I could to explore the mysterious depths under the sea.

Another night passed, as cold as before. The crescent moon vanished completely, swallowed by the stars. Suddenly I remembered the constellations, and Branwen's stories about their origins. After much searching, I managed to find a few, including my favorite, the winged Pegasus. I imagined that the constant rocking of my raft was the galloping, galloping of the steed across the sky.

I fell asleep, dreaming that I was carried aloft on the back of some great winged creature, although whether or not it was Pegasus I could not be sure. Suddenly we were swooping into battle. A darkened castle, manned by ghostly sentinels, rose up before us. And yes! The castle was spinning, turning on its foundation. It drew us down, down, toward its spinning edifice. I tried with all my might to change course, yet I could not. In seconds we would slam straight into the castle walls.

At that point, I woke up. I shivered, from more than cold. The dream filled my thoughts deep into the following day, though its meaning continued to elude me.

Late that afternoon, the western horizon grew dark. Waves rose to new heights, throwing my vessel this way and that, as winds hurled sheets of spray. The raft groaned and creaked. Several strands of kelp burst apart, and a crack appeared in the large slab of wood from the hollow of the old oak. Still, for the most part, the storm passed me by. With twilight, calmer waters returned. I was soaked, to be sure, and terribly thirsty, but both my craft and I remained intact.

That night, I did my best to repair the broken lashing. Then, as I sat cross-legged, a biting wind smacked my face. Another shadow, darker than before, swept across the stars. Swiftly it covered the southern sky, then the dome above me, until finally the entire sky went black.

As darkness swallowed me, my second sight flickered out, useless in such utter blackness. I couldn't see! I was no less blind than I had been on the day I first arrived at the church.

Mighty waves began lifting and swirling, tossing my raft around like a mere twig. Water drenched my face, my back, my arms and legs. And this time the storm did not dissipate. Rather, it swelled, gathering strength with each passing minute. Bending low in my seat, I curled up as tight as I could, like a hedgehog fearing for its life. I wrapped my hands around the outermost edges of the raft, clinging to the scraps of wood that were keeping me afloat.

My powers! For an instant I considered calling on them. Perhaps I could bind the raft together, or even calm the waves! But no. I had promised. Besides, those powers frightened me deeply, even more than this terrible gale. The truth was I knew nothing about magic except its terrible consequences—the smell of scorched flesh, the screams of another person, the agony of my own burning eyes. However my powers might have helped me, I knew that I would never use them again.

All through the black night the storm howled and raged. Curtains of water fell on me. Enormous waves pounded me. At one point I recalled the story of Bran the Blessed surviving a fierce storm at sea, and it gave me a brief burst of hope that I, too, might survive. Yet this hope was soon drowned in the ocean's onslaught.

Both of my hands went numb with the cold, yet I dared not release their grip to try to warm them. More of my lashing popped. One timber split down the middle. My back ached, though not as much as my heart. For something inside me knew that this storm would spell the end of my voyage.

The rising sun brightened the sky only a little, but it was enough that I could begin to sense shapes again. My second sight had only barely returned when a powerful wave crashed down so hard that it knocked the breath right out of me. The raft buckled and finally broke apart.

In that terrifying instant I was cast down into the seething sea, battered by the currents. By luck I touched a floating timber and grasped it. Another wave toppled over me, and another, and another.

My strength ebbing, I started to lose my grip. The wild storm continued thrashing and pounding. As the new day dawned, I felt sure that it would be my last. I barely noticed the odd-shaped cloud hovering low over the water, though it looked almost like an island made of mist.

With a plaintive cry, I let go. Water poured into my lungs.

PART TWO

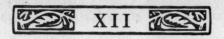

XII

FALLEN WARRIOR

Not swaying anymore.

Not drowning anymore.

Once again, I awoke to find myself on an unknown shore. The same sound of surf filled my ears. The same brackish taste soured my mouth. The same feeling of dread twisted my stomach.

Were the torments of my years in Gwynedd just a dream? A terrible, twisted dream?

I knew the answer, even before my sand-crusted fingers touched my scarred cheeks, my useless eyes. And the Galator dangling from my neck. Gwynedd had been real. As real as the strange, potent smell that spiced the air of this place, wherever this place might be.

I rolled onto my side, crunching a shell under my hip. Sitting up, I drank in the air. Sweet as a summer meadow it tasted, but with an edge to it. Sharper. Truer.

While I could hear the waves sloshing and slapping, not far away, I could not view them with my second sight. That was not because of my poor vision, however. The waves lay hidden behind a rolling wall of mist, mist so thick that it obscured everything beyond.

Within the wall of mist, curious shapes seemed to coalesce, hold together for a few seconds, then vanish. I saw something like a great archway, with a door swinging closed. As it melted away, it was replaced by a spiked tail, big enough for a dragon. Then, as I watched, the tail transformed into an enormous head with a bulbous nose. Like a giant made of mist, it turned slowly toward me, moving its mouth as if to speak, before dissolving into the shifting clouds.

Turning my stiff back, I looked around. This beach, unlike the north coast of Gwynedd, formed a gentle meeting of land and sea. No piles of jagged rocks littered the coast, only shells of pink and white and purple, strewn over the fine-grained sand. Next to my foot, a leafy vine crawled across the beach like a shiny green snake.

Pink. Purple. Green. My heart leaped. I could sense colors! Not so well as my memories before the fire, perhaps, but much better than before the sea tore my raft to shreds.

But wait. That could not be true. As I examined my own skin, and then the folds of my tunic, I knew that they were no more brightly colored than before.

With a glance back at the beach, I understood. It was not that I could see any better. It was that this landscape simply radiated color. The shells, the shining leaves, even the sand of this place felt brighter and deeper somehow. If they seemed this vivid with only my second sight, how vivid they would be if I had eyes that could truly see!

I picked up one of the spiral-shaped shells. Purple lines wound around its body of gleaming white. It felt comfortable in my hand, like one friend meeting another.

I put the shell to my ear, expecting to hear the watery sound within its chambers. Instead, I heard a strange, breathy sound, like the voice of someone far away. Whispering to me in a language I could not understand. Trying to tell me something.

I caught my breath. Lowering the shell, I peered into its chamber. It seemed ordinary enough. I must have just imagined it. Again I brought it to my ear. The voice again! This time clearer than before.

In spite of myself, I thought I heard it say *bewaaare . . . bewaaare.*

Quickly, I put down the shell. My palms felt sweaty, my stomach knotted. I stood up. My legs, arms, and back ached with stiffness. I glanced down at the shell, then shook my head. Seawater in my ears. Maybe that was it.

Water. I must find fresh water. If only I could find some to drink, I would feel more alive.

I climbed to the ridge of a dune arching above the beach. What I saw took my breath away.

A dense forest, where colorful birds flitted among the spires of towering trees, stretched far to the west. Near the horizon rose waves of misty hills, where the green of the forest deepened into blue. Between here and there, a lush valley unfurled as soft as a carpet. Sunlit streams cascaded out of the woods and over the meadows, merging into a great river that rushed toward the sea. In the distance, more trees grew, though in orderly rows that seemed less wild than the forest, more like an orchard that someone had planted long ago.

I was about to descend into the valley and quench my thirst when something else caught my attention. Although I could see only a little of the eastern bank of the river, it seemed far less green than the other side. Rather, it looked brownish red, the color of dried leaves. Or rust. At first it gave me an unsettled feeling, but then I realized that it was probably just some strange sort of vegetation. Or perhaps a trick of the light, caused by the mass of dark clouds hovering over the eastern horizon.

Feeling my parched throat, I turned back to the verdant valley and forest before me. Time for that drink! Then I would investigate this mist-shrouded island, if indeed it was an island. Although I could not quite put my finger on it, something about this place made me want to stay and explore—despite the strange experience with the shell. It might have been the vibrant colors. Or it might have been the simple fact that I had trusted in the waves and they had brought me here. Whatever the reason, I would remain for a while—but only for a while. If I did not discover any clues to my past, I would promptly leave. I would build myself another boat, sturdier than the last, and continue my quest.

I started down the dune. The sand soon gave way to grasses, their slender stalks bowing in the fragrant breeze. Though still stiff from my voyage, I gathered speed as I descended. Soon I was running across the open field. Feeling the wind in my face, I realized that this was the first time I had run since leaving Caer Myrddin.

Approaching a stream of bright water, I knelt by the mossy stones along its border. Immediately I immersed my whole head in it. The cold, clear water slapped my skin, shocking me no less than the colors and smells of this land had first shocked me. I swallowed enough to feel bloated, belched, then swallowed some more.

Satisfied at last, I leaned on my elbow, now drinking not the water but the crisp, spicy air. Grasses tickled my chin. With so much tall grass surrounding me, anyone passing near might have thought me just a brown log by the streambed. I listened to the subtle rustling of stems rubbing together, the rising and falling of wind in the forest, the steady dancing of the stream. A long-legged beetle, red in hue, crawled lazily across the folds of my tunic.

A sudden whoosh of air, just above my head, jolted me out of my reverie. Whatever it was had flashed past with the speed of an arrow, so fast that I had no idea what it could have been. Cautiously, I lifted myself higher. My second sight detected some movement in the grass downstream. I rose to my feet.

A piercing whistle erupted from the grass, followed by hissing and snarling. The angry sounds swelled as I approached. A few steps later, I halted, amazed.

The largest rat I had ever seen, as thick as my own thigh, with powerful legs and teeth as sharp as dagger points, wrestled before me. Its adversary was a small hawk with a banded brown tail and gray back. A merlin. Despite the fact that the rat was at least three times the bird's size, they appeared evenly matched.

Furiously, they battled. The merlin's strong talons clung tight to the back of the rat's neck. The rat writhed, trying to bite and claw its enemy's head, bashing the bird against the ground. But the bird's courage outweighed its compact body, for it only screeched and dug its talons deeper, drawing blood from the rat's tough hide. Feathers flew, as blood splattered the grass. Clawing, biting, and snarling, they tumbled over each other in a wild frenzy.

This fight might have continued for some time with no victor, except that another rat emerged from a thicket by the stream. Whether out of loyalty to its kind, or more likely, desire for some easy prey, it joined in the fray. Clamping its jaws on one of the merlin's wings, it tore at the bird viciously.

The merlin shrieked in pain, but somehow held on. The second rat, its face ripped by the bird's beak, released its grip and circled around to the other side. Meanwhile, the merlin's torn wing hung at its side, flapping uselessly, while one of its talons came loose. Sensing victory at hand, the second rat brushed away some feathers caught in its teeth. Its legs tensed as it readied to pounce on the weakened bird.

At that instant I ran forward and kicked the second rat in the chest, so hard that it rolled into the thicket. Seeing this, the first rat stopped its thrashing, glaring at me with blood red eyes. With a violent shake, it threw the merlin to the grass. The bird lay on its back, too weak to move.

The rat hissed shrilly. I took a step closer. Then I raised my hand as if to strike. The rat, apparently tired of battling for the moment, turned and slipped away through the blades of grass.

I stooped to examine the merlin. Although its eyes, two dots of black encircled in yellow, remained barely half open, they watched me intensely. As I reached for the bird, it whistled and lashed out with one of its talons, slashing the skin of my wrist.

"What are you doing, fool bird?" I yelped, sucking the bloody wrist. "I'm trying to help you, not hurt you."

Again I reached toward the fallen warrior. Again the bird whistled and struck with its talon.

"Enough of this!" Shaking my head in dismay, I rose to leave.

As I left the spot, I glanced one more time at the merlin. Its eyes had finally closed. It lay there on the grass, shivering.

I took a deep breath, and returned. Cautiously, I picked up the bird, avoiding the talons in case it suddenly came alive again. I held the warm, feathered body in my hand, wondering that any creature so fierce could also feel so soft. Stroking the injured wing, I could tell that, while skin and muscles had been shredded, no bones had been broken. I reached into the satchel that Branwen had given me, removed a pinch of the dried herbs, and added to this a few drops of water from the stream. Using the edge of my tunic, I cleaned the gashes made by the teeth of the rat. There were several deep ones, especially along the wing's upper edge. Carefully I applied the herbs as a poultice.

The merlin stiffened and opened an eye. This time, however, it did not slash at me. Apparently too weak even to whistle, it could only watch me warily.

When I had finished, I held the small bird and pondered what to do next. Leave it here by the stream? No, the rats would surely return and finish their work. Take it with me? No, I had no need for a passenger, certainly not one so dangerous.

Spotting an oak with wide branches at the edge of the woods, an idea came to me. I put down the bird long enough to pull up some grasses and twist them together into a rough-hewn nest. Gathering both the nest and the bird under my arm, I climbed to a low branch that wore a rich coat of moss. I wedged the nest into place where the branch joined the trunk, then placed the helpless bird within.

I looked into the defiant, yellow-rimmed eyes for a moment. Then I climbed down and strode into the forest.

XIII

A BUNDLE OF
LEAVES

As I walked among the spires and the intertwined branches of this ancient forest, an odd sensation crept up on me.

It had nothing to do with my second sight, although the light proved dim indeed in these dark groves where only occasional rays reached all the way to the forest floor. It had nothing to do with the resins filling the air, stronger than I had ever smelled, although they brought back the memory of the day I outlasted the storm in the arms of the great pine beneath Y Wyddfa. It had nothing to do with the sounds all around me—winds rushing through leaves, branches clacking and creaking, needles crunching underfoot.

The odd sensation stemmed from none of these things. Or perhaps it came from all these things combined. A sound. A smell. A dimly lit grove. Above all, a feeling. That something in this forest knew I was there. That something was watching me. That a strange whispering, much like what I had heard in the shell, was now happening all around me. I spotted a knobby stick, nearly as tall as myself, leaning against the trunk of an old cedar. A good staff might help me work my way through the dimly lit groves of this forest. I reached for it. Just as my hand was about to squeeze its middle, where a cluster of twigs protruded, I gasped and pulled back.

The stick moved! The twigs, joined by others above and below, began churning like little legs. The knobby shaft bent as it clambered down the cedar's flaky bark, over the roots, and into a patch of ferns. In a few seconds, the stick creature had vanished. So too had my desire to find a staff.

Then I felt a familiar urge. Climb one of these trees! Not all the way to the top, perhaps, but high enough to gain a view of the upper canopies of branches. Choosing a lanky linden tree, whose heart-shaped leaves trembled like the surface of a running river, I started up. My feet and hands found plenty of holds, and I moved swiftly higher.

From the distance of five times my own height above the ground, the view changed dramatically. Much more light pierced the mesh of limbs, improving my vision. Through the quivering linden leaves I noticed a round, green clump of moss near my head—although given my experience with the stick I decided not to touch it. Then I glimpsed a pair of orange and blue butterflies floating among the branches. A spider, its web pearled with dew, swung freely from a nearby limb. Squirrels with large eyes chattered noisily. A golden-plumed bird moved from branch to branch. Yet one quality from the forest floor did not change: The strange whispering continued.

Turning toward the edge of the forest, I could make out the grassy field where I had encountered the merlin. Just beyond, flowing toward the wall of mist that I knew marked the sea, I spied the sparkling water of the great river. To my surprise, a strange wave lifted from its rapids, a wave that seemed almost like a huge hand. I knew that it could not be so. Yet as the hand of water emerged from the river, dripping water through its broad fingers before plunging back down with a splash, I felt a surge of wonder and fear.

Then, from far above me, a huge bundle of leaves broke loose. Rather than falling straight downward, though, it flew outward and across to another tree. Miraculously, the second tree's branches caught the bundle, cradling it in sturdy boughs, before flinging it outward again. Another branch caught it, bent with the weight, then flung it back. The bundle spun through the air, sailing over branches and between trunks, spinning like a dancer. It seemed almost as if the trees of this grove were playing catch with one another, throwing this bundle as children might throw a ball of string.

In time, the bundle of leaves dropped lower and lower among the limbs. Finally, it rolled onto the forest floor, coming to rest at last in a bed of brown needles.

I gasped. From the bundle, a long, leafy branch suddenly protruded. No, not a branch. An arm, wearing a sleeve of woven vines. Then another arm. One leg, then another. A head, its hair bedecked with shining leaves. Two eyes, as gray as beech bark with a touch of blue.

The leaf-draped figure rose and laughed out loud. The laughter, full and clear, rang through the trees with all the beauty of a bell.

I leaned forward on my limb, trying to discern more detail. For I could tell already that this bundle of leaves was, in truth, a girl.

XIV

RHIA

Without warning, the limb gave way. I tumbled to the ground, my fall broken by several boughs along the way. My chest smacked hard into one limb, as did my lower back, my shoulder, and both thighs. With a thud, I landed in a cushion of needles.

Groaning, I rolled to the side. In addition to the stiffness from my voyage, and the usual pain between my shoulder blades, my entire body ached. Slowly, I sat up—and found myself face-to-face with the girl.

Her laughter ceased.

For a long moment, neither of us moved. Although the light was spare, I could tell that she was about my own age. She watched me, standing as still as one of the trees. But for the touch of blue in her eyes, her garb of woven vines consisted of so much green and brown that she could almost have passed for a tree. Yet the eyes could not be missed. They flashed angrily.

She uttered a command in a strange, rustling language, waving her hand as if to brush away a fly. Immediately, the heavy branches of a hemlock wrapped themselves around my middle, as well as my arms and legs. The branches held me tightly, and the more I struggled the harder they squeezed. Swiftly they lifted me into the air. I hung there, suspended, unable to move.

"Let me down!"

"Now you will not fall again." The girl spoke in my own tongue, the Celtic language I had spoken in Gwynedd, but with a curious, lilting accent. Her expression shifted from wrath to mirth. "You remind me of a big brown berry, though not a tasty one."

She picked a plump purple berry growing in the moss by her feet and put it in her mouth. Puckering, she spat it out again. "Ecchh. No sweetness left."

"Let me down!" I roared. I twisted to break free, but the branch around my chest tightened so much that I could hardly breathe. "Please," I croaked. "I meant . . . no harm."

The girl eyed me severely. "You broke the law of Druma Wood. No outsiders are allowed here."

"But . . . I didn't . . . know," I wheezed.

"Now you do." She plucked another berry. Evidently it tasted better than the first, because she bent and picked another one.

"Please . . . let me . . . down."

Ignoring me completely, the girl went about her berry picking, swallowing them almost as fast as she plucked them. At length she started to leave the glade, not bothering even to glance in my direction.

"Wait!"

She stopped. Looking annoyed, she faced me. "You remind me of a squirrel who has stolen someone else's nuts and gets caught. Now you want to give them back, but it's too late. I'll come back for you in a day or two. If I remember."

She turned to go, stepping quickly away.

"Wait!" I gasped.

She disappeared behind a curtain of branches.

I tried again to wriggle free. The hemlock squeezed tighter, pressing the Galator, still under my tunic, deep into my ribs. "Wait! In the name of . . . the Galator."

The girl's face reappeared. Tentatively, she returned to the grove. She stood beneath the mighty hemlock, looking up at me for some time. Then she flicked her wrist and spoke more rustling words that I could not understand.

Instantly, the branches unfurled. I dropped facedown onto the ground. Pulling a handful of needles out of my mouth, I struggled to stand.

She held her hand up to me. Not wishing to be imprisoned by branches again, I obeyed and did not move.

"What do you know about the Galator?"

I hesitated, realizing that the Galator must be famous indeed to be known even in this remote land. Cautiously, I revealed as much as I dared. "I know what it looks like."

"So do I, at least by legend. What else do you know?"

"Only a little."

"Pity," she said, more to herself than to me. Drawing closer, she peered at me curiously. "Why do your eyes look so far away? They remind me of two stars that are hidden by clouds."

I stiffened. Defensively, I snapped, "My eyes are my eyes."

Again she studied me. Then, without a word, she pressed the last of her purple berries into my hand.

Unsure, I sniffed them. Their aroma brought back just how hungry I was, so against my better judgment I popped one into my mouth. A sudden burst of sweetness struck my tongue. I ate the rest in another swallow.

The girl studied me thoughtfully. "I see that you have suffered."

I frowned. She had noticed the scars. As would anyone who looked at my face. And yet . . . it seemed as though she had seen something beneath the surface, as well. I felt an inexplicable urge to unburden myself to this strange girl of the woods. Yet I resisted. I didn't know her, after all. Only a moment ago she would have abandoned me to the trees. No, I would not be so foolish as to trust her.

She rotated her head slightly, listening to some distant whispering of the branches. I noticed the intricate dressing of leaves in her curly brown hair. Although I could not be sure in the dim light of the grove, it appeared that her ears were somewhat triangular in shape, pointed at the top much like my own.

Did that mean that she, like myself, had endured teasing from others for having ears like a demon? Or . . . might everyone in this strange land have pointed ears? Was it possible that this girl and I actually belonged to the same race?

I shook myself back to reality. It was just as likely that angels themselves would have pointed ears. Or that demons would have lovely white wings!

I continued to watch her as she listened. "Do you hear something?"

Her gray-blue eyes swiveled back to me. "Only the words of my friends. They tell me that an outsider is in the forest, but that I already know." She paused. "They also tell me *beware*. Should I?"

I tensed, recalling the voice of the shell. "A person should always beware. But you need not be frightened of me."

She seemed amused. "Do I look frightened?"

"No." I felt myself grinning, as well. "I'm not very scary, I suppose."

"Not very."

"Your friends you spoke of. Are they . . . the trees?"

"They are."

"And you speak with them?"

Once again the bell-like laughter echoed in the grove. "Of course! Just as I speak with the birds and beasts and rivers."

"And also the shells?"

"Naturally. Everything has its language, you know. You only need to learn how to hear it." She raised an eyebrow. "Why do you understand so little?"

"I come from . . . far away."

"So that is why you know nothing of Druma Wood, or its ways." Her brow furrowed. "Yet you know of the Galator."

"Only a little, as I said before." I added wryly, "Although I would have said anything to get those horrible branches off me."

The hemlock boughs overhead wavered slightly. The sight made me cringe.

"You know more than a little about the Galator," declared the girl confidently. "One day you will tell me." She began to walk, somehow certain that I would follow. "But first, tell me your name."

I stepped carefully over a fallen branch. "Where are we going?"

"To get something to eat, of course." She bore to the left, following a trail that only she could detect through a patch of hip-deep fern. "Now will you tell me your name?"

"Emrys."

She glanced at me in a way that told me she did not quite believe me. But she said nothing.

"And what is yours?"

She stopped beneath a beech tree, which, though old and twisted, had bark as smooth as a young sapling. Raising a hand toward the graceful boughs, she said, "My friend will answer."

The leaves of the old beech stirred in gentle rustling. At first the sound meant nothing at all to me. I looked at the girl quizzically. Then, slowly, I began to hear a particular cadence. *Rrrrhhhhiiiaaaa. Rrrrhhhhiiiaaaa. Rrrrhhhhiiiaaaa.*

"Your name is Rhia?"

Again she started walking, passing through a stand of long-needled pines, sturdy and straight. "Rhiannon is my full name, though I don't know why. The trees call me Rhia."

Curious, I questioned her. "You don't know why? Didn't your parents tell you?"

She hopped across a slow-moving stream, where a plump mallard drifted among the reeds. "I lost my family when I was young, very young. The whole thing reminds me of a fledgling who falls out of the nest before she can fly." Without turning toward me, she added, "It also reminds me of you."

I stopped short, grabbed her by the arm. Seeing some branches bend menacingly lower, I released my grip. "What makes you say such a thing?"

She looked straight at me. "You seem lost, that's all."

We strode farther into the forest without speaking, past a red-tailed fox who did not stir from a meal of fresh grouse. The terrain began to slope upward, rising into a steep hill. Yet even as the walking grew more arduous, Rhia's pace did not slacken. In fact, it seemed to me that her pace only increased. Puffing hard, I struggled to keep up with her.

"You're like . . . Atalanta."

Rhia slowed a bit, her expression quizzical. "Who is that?"

"Atalanta," I panted. "A heroine . . . in a Greek legend . . . who could run . . . so fast . . . nobody could . . . catch her . . . until somebody . . . finally tricked her . . . with some . . . golden apples."

"I like that. Where did you ever learn such a story?"

"From . . . someone." I mopped my brow. "But I . . . wish I had . . . some of . . . those apples . . . right now."

Rhia smiled, but did not slow down.

As we ascended, enormous boulders, cracked and covered with pink and purple lichens, sprouted like giant mushrooms from the forest floor. The spaces between the trees grew wider, allowing more sunlight through the canopy of branches. More ferns, as well as sprinklings of flowers, crowded around massive roots and tumbled trunks.

At one point, Rhia paused to wait for me beneath a white-barked tree by a ledge. As I labored to catch up with her, she cupped her hands to her mouth and made a curious hooting sound. An instant later, three small owl faces, flat and feathery with enormous orange eyes, poked out of a hole about halfway up the trunk. The owls watched us intently. Then they hooted twice in unison and disappeared back inside the hole.

Rhia turned to me and smiled. Then she continued to climb the hill. At long last she reached the crest and halted, hands on her hips, taking in the view. Even before I caught up, I sniffed a new, juicy fragrance in the air. When at last I stood beside her, panting, the sight before me took away what little breath I still had.

In the rounded clearing before us, trees of all sizes and shapes and colors twined together, covering the entire top of the hill. Their branches, heavy with fruit, draped almost to the grass. And what fruit! Bright orange spheres, slender green crescents, tightly packed bunches of yellow and blue gleamed amidst the flashing wings of butterflies and bees. Round ones. Square ones. Hefty ones. Wispy ones. Most of the varieties of fruit I had never seen, nor even dreamed of, before. But that did not stop my mouth from watering.

"My garden," announced Rhia.

Seconds later, we were devouring whatever fruits we chose. Juices ran down my chin, my neck, my hands, my arms. Seeds stuck to my hair, while half-chewed rinds clung to my tunic. From a distance, I might have passed for a fruit tree myself.

The orange spheres exploded with tangy flavor, so I peeled and ate my fill of them before I started trying other kinds. One variety, shaped like an urn, contained so many seeds that I spat it out in disgust. Rhia laughed, as did I. Then I tried another, circular with an open hole in the middle. To my relief, it tasted like sweet milk and bore no seeds at all. Next I swallowed half of a gray, egg-shaped fruit. Although it had almost no taste, it somehow made me feel sad, aching with longing for all the things my life lacked.

When she saw that I had tried that particular kind, Rhia pointed me toward a spiral-shaped fruit, pale purple in color. I took a bite. A flavor like purple sunshine burst in my mouth. Somehow, it swept all the aching feelings away.

For her part, Rhia swallowed a huge quantity of tiny red berries growing in bundles of five or six on a stem. I tried one, but it was packed with such overpowering sweetness that it made me nauseous. I had no desire to eat more.

I watched in astonishment as Rhia downed them ten at a time. "How can you eat so many of those?"

She ignored me and continued eating.

At last, I started to feel full. More than full. I sat down, leaning against one of the thickest trunks in the garden. Afternoon light sifted through the leaves and fruit, as a gentle breeze flowed over the hill. I watched as Rhia eventually reached her limit of the sweet red berries. She joined me by the trunk, her shoulder nudging my own.

She opened her arms to the wondrous array of trees around us. "All this," she said gratefully, "from a single seed."

My eyes widened. "A single seed? You can't mean that."

"Oh yes! The seed of the shomorra tree yields not just one tree, but many, not just one fruit, but hundreds. And though the shomorra yields so much, it is so difficult to find that its scarceness is legendary. *As rare as a shomorra,* the old saying goes. In all the Druma, there is but this one."

I drank deeply of the scented air of this clearing. "This is not my home, yet I feel I could stay here long and gladly."

"Where then is your home?"

I sighed. "I don't know."

"So you are searching for that?"

"That and more."

Rhia twirled a vine from her sleeve. "Isn't your home wherever you are?"

"You aren't serious," I scoffed. "Home is the place you come from. The place where your parents live, where your past is hidden."

"Hidden? What in the world do you mean by that?"

"I have no memory of my past."

Although she seemed intrigued, Rhia asked no more questions. Instead, she reached for another cluster of red berries and popped them in her mouth. Through this mouthful, she said, "Perhaps what you are seeking is nearer than you know."

"I doubt it." I stretched my arms and shoulders. "I will explore some more of this place, but if I can't learn anything about my past, I will build a new boat and sail as far as I must. To the very horizon, if that's what it takes."

"Then you won't be long here, I suppose."

"Probably not. Where is here, anyway? Does this place have a name?"

"It has."

"What is it?"

Her expression darkened. "This place, this island, is called Fincayra."

XV

TROUBLE

I jumped as if I had been struck by a whip. "Fincayra?"

Rhia eyed me with interest. "You have heard of it?"

"Yes. Someone told me a little. But I never imagined it could be real."

She sighed somberly. "Fincayra is real enough."

So it is, I thought to myself. As real as Y Wyddfa. As real as Olympus. If only I could tell Branwen! I tried to call back what she had said about Fincayra. *A place of many wonders,* she had called it. *Neither wholly of Earth nor wholly of Heaven, but a bridge connecting both.* She had mentioned bright colors, too. That part I knew was true! And something else. Something about giants.

As we sat together in silence, immersed in private thoughts, the blanket of evening began to envelop the garden of the shomorra. With each passing minute, colors became shadows and shapes became silhouettes.

Finally, Rhia stirred. She rubbed her back against the trunk. "Night already! We have no time to travel to my house."

Feeling drowsy after our feast, I slid lower on the bed of soft grass beneath the tree. "I have slept in worse places."

"Look." Rhia pointed to the sky, where the first stars glimmered through the branches laden with fruit. "Wouldn't you love to be able to fly? To sail among those stars, to be one with the wind? I wish I had wings. Real wings!"

"So do I," I replied, searching for some sign of Pegasus.

She turned to me. "What else do you wish for?"

"Well . . . books."

"Really?"

"Yes! I would love, really love, to bury myself in a whole room full of books. With stories from all peoples, all times. I heard about such a room once."

She watched me for a moment. "From your mother?"

I drew a long breath. "No. From a woman who wanted me to believe that she was."

Rhia seemed puzzled, but said nothing.

"The room," I continued, "would have every kind of book imaginable. Surrounding me, everywhere I turned. Being in a room like that would be a lot like flying, you know. I could fly through those pages, anywhere I like."

Rhia laughed. "I'd rather have real wings! Especially on a night like this. See?" She looked up through the branches. "You can already see Gwri of the Golden Hair."

"That's a new constellation for me. Where is it?"

"Right there."

Though I strained with my second sight, I could see nothing in that part of the sky but a single star that I knew would eventually become part of Pegasus' wing. "I don't see it."

"Can't you see a maiden?"

"No."

She took my arm and aimed it upward. "Now?"

"No. All I see is a star that will be part of Pegasus. And there. I can see another star for Pegasus."

Rhia shot me a puzzled look. "Stars? Constellations of stars?"

Puzzled myself, I demanded, "What else?"

"My constellations are not made from the stars, but from the spaces *between* the stars. The dark places. The open places, where your mind can travel forever and ever."

From that instant onward, I could not view the heavens in the same way. Just as I could not view the girl beside me in the same way. "Tell me more. About what you see up there."

Rhia tossed back her brown curls. In a lilting voice, she began to explain some of the strange wonders of the Fincayran sky. How the broad band of stars across the middle of the night sky was truly a seam sewn in the two halves of time, one half always beginning, the other half always ending. How the longest patches of darkness were really the rivers of the gods, connecting this world and others. How the spinning circle of the stars was actually a great wheel, whose endless revolutions turned life into death, death into life.

Late into the night we drew pictures in the sky and traded tales. When at last we slept, it was soundly. And when warm rays awoke us, we realized that we did not want to leave this place. Not yet.

So for another day and another night we lingered at the bountiful hilltop, feasting on fruit and conversation. Though I remained guarded about discussing my deepest feelings, I discovered more than once that Rhia had an unnerving way of reading my thoughts as if they had been her own.

We sat beneath the fruity canopy, eating a hearty breakfast of tangy orange spheres (for me) and sweet red berries (for her). As we finished the meal by sharing one of the spiral-shaped fruits, Rhia turned to me with a question.

"That woman, the one who said she was your mother. What was she like?"

I looked at her with surprise. "She was tall, with very blue—"

"No, no, no. I don't care what she looked like. What was she *like?*"

For a moment I considered Branwen. "Well, she was kind to me. More kind than I deserved. Most of the time, anyway. Full of faith—in her God, and in me. And quiet. Too quiet. Except when she told me stories. She knew a lot of stories, more than I can begin to remember."

Rhia examined a berry for a moment before dropping it into her mouth. "I'm sure she learned some of them in that room full of books."

"That's right."

"And even though she wasn't your real mother, did you feel different because she was there, beside you? A little less lonely? A little . . . safer?"

I swallowed. "I guess so. Why are you so curious about her?"

Her face, which usually seemed at the very edge of laughter, turned serious. "I was just wondering what a mother, a real mother, would be like."

I lowered my eyes. "I wish I knew."

Rhia nodded. She ran her hand along a drooping bough of fruit, though she seemed to be looking past it, to some place or time far away.

"So you don't remember your mother?"

"I was so very young when I lost her. I only remember feelings. Being safe. And warm. And . . . held. I'm not even sure I really remember those things. It might just be my longing for them."

"What about your father? Any brothers or sisters?"

"I lost them. All of them." She spread her arms to the branches above us. "But I found the Druma. This is my family now. And while I don't have a true mother, I do have someone who protects me. And holds me. She is almost my mother."

"Who is that?"

Rhia smiled. "A tree. A tree named Arbassa."

I imagined her seated in the boughs of a great, sturdy tree. And I, too, smiled.

Then I thought about Branwen, my own almost-mother, as a strange warmth filled my chest. She was so distant from me and yet, at times, so close. I thought about her stories, her healing work, her sorrowful eyes. I wished that she had been willing to share more, about her own struggles as well as my mysterious past. I hoped that I might see her once again someday, although I knew it could not be so. Haltingly, I said a silent prayer to the God to whom she prayed so often, a prayer that wished her the peace she so longed to find.

Suddenly a sharp whistle pierced the air above my head. I looked up to find a familiar form perched on one of the branches.

"I don't believe it."

"A merlin," observed Rhia. "A young male. And look. His wing is hurt. See how it's missing some feathers." She twitched her neck, in the way a hawk often does, and released a sharp whistle of her own.

The bird, cocking his head, whistled back. This time the whistle warbled a bit, incorporating some more throaty tones.

Rhia's thick eyebrows lifted. She turned to me. "He said to me—not very politely, I might add—that you saved his life a while ago."

"He told you that?"

"Is it not true?"

"Yes, yes, it's true. I patched him up after he got into a fight. But how did you learn to talk with birds?"

Rhia shrugged as if the answer were obvious. "It's no more difficult than talking with trees." She added a bit sadly, "Those that are still awake, that is. Anyway, who was the merlin fighting?"

"I couldn't believe his pluck. Or foolishness. He picked a fight with two giant rats, each of them at least three times his size."

"Giant rats?" Rhia's whole body stiffened. "Where? In the Druma?"

I shook my head. "No, but right on the edge. Near a little stream that flows out of the trees."

Gravely, Rhia glanced at the merlin, who was pecking ravenously at a spiral-shaped fruit. "Killer rats, on our side of the river," she muttered, shaking her head. "They are forbidden to enter Druma Wood. That's the first time I've heard of them so close. Your friend the merlin may not have any manners, but he was right to attack them."

"That bird just likes fighting, if you ask me. It could just as easily have been you or me that he attacked. He is no friend of mine."

As if to contradict me, the merlin fluttered down from the fruit and landed on my left shoulder.

Rhia laughed. "Looks like he disagrees with you." She observed the hawk thoughtfully. "It's possible, you know, that he came to you for a reason."

I grimaced. "The only reason is the same bad luck that follows me everywhere."

"I don't know. He doesn't seem like such bad luck to me." Whistling in a light, friendly cadence, she extended her hand toward the merlin.

With a screech, the bird lashed out with one of his talons. Rhia quickly withdrew, though not before the talon sliced across the back of her hand.

"Oh!" Scowling, she licked the blood from her wound, then whistled a sharp reprimand.

The merlin reprimanded her in return.

"Stop that," I barked. I tried to brush the merlin off my shoulder, but the talons held tight, piercing my tunic and digging into my skin.

"You keep him away from me," declared Rhia. "That bird is trouble."

"I told you so."

"Don't act so smug!" She got up to leave. "Just rid us of him."

I rose also, with the unwanted passenger still on my shoulder. "Can't you help me somehow?"

"He's your friend." She stalked off, heading down the hill.

Again I tried to remove the merlin. But he refused to budge. Fixing an eye on me, he whistled angrily, as if he were threatening to tear off my ear if I did not cooperate.

Growling with frustration, I ran after Rhia as she disappeared into the forest. The bird clung tight to my shoulder, wings flapping. When I finally caught up with her, she was sitting on a low, rectangular rock, licking her gash.

"I don't suppose you could fix my hand the way you fixed your friend's wing."

"He's not my friend!" I shook my left shoulder, but the merlin hung on, eyeing me coldly. "Can't you see? It's more like he's my master and I'm his slave." I glared at the bird. "I can't make him leave."

Rhia's expression turned sympathetic. "I'm sorry. It's just that my hand hurts so."

"Let me see it." I took her hand, studying the deep cut. Blood continued to flow. Swiftly, I reached into my satchel and sprinkled some of the powdered herbs into the open wound. Pulling a broad leaf off a nearby bush, I laid it over the gash, taking care to draw the skin together as I had seen Branwen do dozens of times. Then, using a vine from Rhia's own sleeve, I wrapped her hand securely.

She lifted her hand gratefully. "Where did you learn to do this?"

"From Branwen. The woman who told me stories. She knew a lot about healing." I closed the satchel. "But she could only heal wounds to the skin."

Rhia nodded. "Wounds to the heart are much more difficult."

"Where are you going next?"

"To my house. I hope you will come." She waved at the hawk, who raised a vicious talon in response. "Even with your, ah, companion there."

"Generous of you," I replied grimly. Despite the bothersome bird, my curiosity to learn more about this place, and about Rhia herself, remained strong. "I would like to come. But I won't stay for long."

"That's fine. As long as you take that bird with you when you go."

"Do I have any choice?"

With that, we strode into the forest. For the rest of that morning and well into the afternoon we followed a trail only visible to Rhia. We rounded hills, leaped streams, and slogged through marshes where the air hummed with all kinds of insects.

Halfway across one such marsh, Rhia pointed to a dead tree that seemed to be painted bright red. She clapped her hands once. A split second later, a scarlet cloud billowed out of its branches. Butter-flies—hundreds of them, thousands of them—rose into the air, leaving the tree as bare as a skeleton.

I watched the scarlet cloud rise. So bright were the wings of the butterflies, flashing in the sun, that I wondered whether slices of the sun itself had been set like jewels within them. And I began to hope that my second sight was continuing to improve. If I could see such a stunning burst of color as this without my eyes, then one day, perhaps, I might be able to see all the world's colors as vividly as I had seen them before the fire.

On we went, stepping through glades of hip-high fern, crossing over tumbled trees whose trunks and limbs were melting steadily into soil, passing beneath roaring waterfalls. When we paused to gather some berries or take a drink of water, it was only briefly. Yet those moments were always long enough to glimpse the tail of a scurrying beast, catch the spicy scent of a flower, or hear the several voices of a stream.

I did my best to keep up, although Rhia's pace and my poor vision in shadowy places kept my chest heaving and my shins bruised. All the while, the bird continued to pinch my shoulder. I started to doubt that those talons would ever let me go.

As the late afternoon light wove luminous threads through the loom of branches, Rhia came to a sudden halt. I approached, huffing, to find her looking up at the trunk of a linden tree. There, wrapped around the middle of the trunk, hung a spiky wreath of glittering gold.

"What is it?" I asked in wonderment.

Rhia smiled at me. "Mistletoe. The golden bough. See how it holds the light of the sun? It is said that one who wears a mantle of mistletoe may find the secret path to the Otherworld of the spirits."

"It's beautiful."

She nodded. "Second only to the long-tailed alleah bird, it's the most beautiful sight in the forest."

I studied the shining wreath. "It seems so different from other plants."

"And so it is! It's neither a plant nor a tree, but a little of both. It's something in between."

Something in between, I repeated to myself, remembering the words. Once Branwen had used them to describe those special places, like the Greeks' Mount Olympus, where mortals and immortals could live side by side. And those special substances, like mist, where elements as distinct as air and water could merge to form something both alike and unlike themselves. Something in between.

Rhia beckoned. "We should go. We will need to move quickly to reach my house before dark."

Through the towering trees we marched. As the light grew dim, my ability to see grew worse. As did my bruises and scrapes. Despite Rhia's repeated urgings, I lost speed in the darkening forest. I stumbled more and more often, tripping on roots and rocks. Every time I fell, the merlin dug in his talons and screeched at me angrily, so loud that my ear stung as much as my shoulder. The trek became a torture.

At one point, I misjudged a branch and walked straight into it. The branch jabbed one of my sightless eyes. I howled in pain, but Rhia was too far ahead to hear. Then, trying to regain my balance, I did not see an animal's den and stepped in it, twisting my ankle.

I crumpled on a fallen trunk, my eye stinging and my ankle throbbing. I lowered my head toward my knees, prepared to wait out the night if necessary.

To my surprise, the merlin finally lifted off. An instant later, he pounced on a mouse, bit the creature's neck in two, then carried it aloft. He landed next to me on the trunk and began attacking his meal. While sorry for the mouse, I rubbed my sore shoulder thankfully. But my relief was muted. I felt sure that the bird, who continued to eye me even as he ate, would soon return to his favorite perch. Why, of all the places in this entire forest, did he have to choose my poor shoulder?

"Emrys!"

"Over here," I answered dismally. Even the sound of Rhia's voice failed to lift my spirits, for I did not look forward to telling her that I could not see well enough to go any farther that night.

I heard a crackling of twigs, and she appeared out of the darkness. Suddenly I realized that she had not come alone. Beside her stood a slight figure, thin as a sapling, whose long face remained hidden in shadow. And although I could not be sure, the figure seemed to exude a potent fragrance, as sweet as apple blossoms in the spring.

I rose to meet them. My ankle felt somewhat stronger, but I still wobbled unsteadily. With the onset of night, I could see less well by the minute.

Rhia indicated her thin companion. "This is Cwen, my oldest friend. She took care of me when I was young."

"Sssso young you could not sssspeak, nor even feed yoursssself," whispered Cwen in a voice like the wind rustling a field of dry grasses. Sounding wistful, she added, "You were assss young then assss I am old now." She pointed a narrow, knobby arm at me. "And who issss thissss?"

At that instant a deafening whistle and a flapping of wings filled the air, followed by a shriek from Cwen. Rhia swatted at something, then pulled her friend away. I myself cried out as sharp talons closed once more on my left shoulder.

"Akkkhh!" hissed Cwen, glaring at the merlin. "That thing attackssss me!"

Furious, Rhia whistled at the bird. Yet he merely cocked his head at her, not even bothering to respond.

Rhia glared at me. "That bird is trouble! Nothing but trouble!"

With a glance at my shoulder, I nodded glumly. "I wish I knew how to lose him."

"Sssskewer him," urged Cwen, keeping her distance. "Pluck out hissss featherssss!"

The merlin ruffled his pointed wings and she fell silent.

Rhia scratched her chin thoughtfully. "This bird reminds me of a shadow, the way he sticks to you."

"He reminds me more of a curse," I grumbled.

"Hear me out," Rhia went on. "Is there any possibility, no matter how small, that you might be able to tame him?"

"Are you insane?"

"I am serious!"

"But why should I want to tame him?"

"Because if you can come to know him, even a little, you might find out what he really wants. And then you might find some way to free yourself from him."

Cwen scoffed. "Nonsssssense."

As the darkness closed in, I didn't feel at all hopeful. "It will never work."

"Do you have a better idea?"

I shook my head. "I suppose, if I am going to try to tame him—and I would have better luck taming a dragon, I think—then I should first give him a name."

"Right," agreed Rhia. "But the name will be tricky. It must be something fitting."

I groaned. "That part is easy. You just said it yourself. The name for him is Trouble. Nothing but Trouble."

"Good. Now you can start his training."

Dejectedly, I turned to the dark form on my shoulder.

"Come then," said Rhia as she took Cwen's thin arm. "We are only a few hundred paces from my house."

I brightened a bit. "Really?"

"Yes. You are welcome there, so long as that bird is not too much—"

"Trouble," finished Cwen.

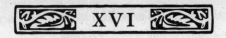

XVI

ARBASSA'S DOOR

As Rhia led us out of the deep forest into a nearby clearing, I noticed the sudden brightness of the night sky. Then, as the web of branches fell away, I wondered whether a star might be exploding above us, filling the sky with light. At once I realized that the light came not from a star, nor even from the sky.

It came from Rhia's house. From the center of the clearing rose a great oak, mightier than any tree I had ever seen. Its burly branches reached outward and upward from the trunk, so thick that it seemed to be made of several trunks fused together. Set in the midst of those branches, glowing like a giant torch, was an aerial cottage whose beams and walls and windows curled with the twisting limbs. Layers of leaves overlaid the tree house, so that the light radiating from its windows shone through multiple curtains of green.

"Arbassa." Rhia lifted her arms high as she spoke the name.

In response, the branches above her head shimmered just enough to drop a light rain of dew on her upturned face.

I watched, my chest feeling warm again, as Rhia approached the base of the tree. Peeling off her snug shoes, which appeared to be made of a leathery type of bark, she stepped into a cup-shaped portion of the massive roots. As she spoke a quiet, swishing phrase, the root gradually closed around her feet, so that she and the tree stood planted together as one single being. Rhia stretched her arms wide and embraced the great trunk, even though she could only reach a tiny portion of the way around. At the same time, one of the tree's enormous branches unfurled like the frond of a fern, wrapping itself over her back to return the embrace.

A few moments later, the branch lifted and the root parted. With a creaking sound, the trunk creased, cracked, and opened into a small doorway. Rhia ducked her head and entered. Cwen, walking stiffly, slipped in beside her.

"Come." Rhia motioned to me to join her.

As I stepped toward the cavern, however, the tree shuddered. The bark-edged doorway began to close. Rhia shouted a sharp command, but the tree ignored her and continued to seal itself. I called out to her, while Trouble fluttered his wings nervously. Despite Rhia's protests, the doorway shut tight.

Helpless, I stood before the tree. I knew as little about what this meant as I knew what to do about it. But one thing was clear. I had been rejected—no doubt thanks to the troublesome bird on my shoulder.

Just then the trunk creased again. The door reopened. Rhia, her face red from shouting, beckoned to me to come. Glancing uncertainly at the fidgeting bird, I entered the dark cavern.

Rhia said nothing. She merely turned and started to climb the spiraling stairway within the trunk. I followed, hoping that Trouble would not cause any.

The gnarled platforms of the stairs grew right out of the inner walls of the trunk, so that the whole stairway smelled as rich and moist as a glade after a rain. As we climbed higher, the stairs grew lighter, revealing intricately carved script that flowed over the inner walls. Thousands of lines of this tightly written script covered the stairwell, as beautiful as it was indecipherable. I wished I could read what it said.

At last we reached an open platform. Rhia pushed against a drapery of leaves, and entered her house. I came right behind, although Trouble clawed angrily at the leaves when they brushed against his feathers.

I found myself standing on a floor of tightly meshed boughs, sturdy yet uneven. A fire burned in the hearth in the middle of the room, so bright that I wondered what fuel could be burning within it. The branches of the great tree curled around us, though they were not as closely woven as the floor, so that window slats opened in all directions.

Every piece of furniture in this one-room house rose out of the branches, as naturally as the branches themselves sprang from the trunk. A low table by the hearth, a pair of simple chairs, a cabinet containing utensils made of carved wood and beeswax, all were produced by living branches twisted into shape. Next to the cabinet, Cwen was stirring something.

I stepped closer to Rhia. "What happened down there?"

Cautiously, she looked from me to the sharp-taloned bird on my shoulder. "My friend Arbassa did not want to let you in."

"That much I could tell."

"It would only have done that for one reason. To keep out of my home someone who could do me great harm."

I felt a new surge of resentment against Trouble. If his presence had almost prevented me from entering Rhia's house, might it also prevent me from finding my past, my identity? "I wish I'd never met this cursed bird!"

Rhia frowned. "Yes. I know." She waved toward Cwen, still bending over the cabinet. "Come. Let's have some supper."

The slim figure poured something that looked like honey over her concoction, a platter of rolled leaves crammed with reddish-brown nuts. The whole thing gave off a hearty, roasted smell. As she carried the platter over to the low table by the hearth, she glanced sharply at Trouble. "I have no ssssupper for that viciousss beasssst."

For the first time, I realized that Cwen was truly more tree than human. Her skin, gnarled and ridged, looked very much like bark, while her tangled brown hair resembled a mass of vines. Her root-like feet remained unshod, and she wore no adornment but the silver rings on the smallest of her twelve knobby fingers. Beneath her robe of white cloth, her body moved like a tree bending with the wind. Yet her age must have been considerable, for her back bent like a trunk leaning under a winter's weight of snow, and her neck, arms, and legs seemed twisted and frail. Even so, the fragrance of apple blossoms wafted around her. And her recessed brown eyes, shaped like slender teardrops, shone as bright as the fire.

Staying clear of me, and especially my passenger, she set down the platter. Her aim was off, however, and she knocked over an oaken flask of water on the table.

"Cursssse thessse old handsssss!" Cwen grabbed the flask and brought it over to the cabinet. As she refilled it, I heard her muttering, "The cursssse of time, the cursssse of time." She continued to grumble as she returned it to the table.

Rhia sat in one of the chairs, indicating with a nod for me to take the other. I watched as she took one of the rolled leaves in her hand. This she plunged into the jar of honey on the platter.

She flashed me a slightly guilty smile. "A person can never get enough honey."

I grinned. Tilting my head toward Cwen, I whispered, "She is not a person, like you or me, is she?"

Rhia looked at me curiously. "A person, she certainly is. But like us, she is not. She is the last survivor of the treelings—a race of part trees, part people. They used to be common in Fincayra, back in the days when giants were the masters of this land. But they are gone now, except for Cwen."

She stuffed the food, dripping with honey, into her mouth, then reached for the flask of water. After several swallows, she offered it to me. Since by then I had tried some myself and found the rolled leaves so sticky that they were very difficult to chew, I accepted the water gladly.

As I replaced the flask on the table, I noticed that the fire, intensely bright though it was, produced no smoke and no heat. In a flash I understood that this fire was really not a fire at all. Thousands of tiny beetles, pulsing with light of their own making, crawled across a pile of rounded river stones in the center of the hearth. The stones appeared to be their home, for the beetles crawled over and under them continuously, like bees in a hive. While each one of the beetles comprised only a subtle spot of light, collectively they produced a powerful glow which illuminated the entire tree house.

As I finally swallowed the sticky food, Trouble shifted on my shoulder, digging his talons deep into my skin. I cried out, then turned angrily toward him. "Why do you punish me like this? Get off my shoulder, I say! Get off!"

Trouble merely stared at me, unblinking.

I turned to Rhia. "How am I supposed to tame him? Not even the Galator could tame him!"

Cwen, standing near one of the window slats, stiffened.

Caught off guard, I instinctively touched the tunic over my chest, feeling the pendant hanging beneath. Then, realizing what I had done, I did my best to disguise the motion, reaching higher to rub my free shoulder. In a casual voice, I said to Rhia, "Wouldn't it be wonderful to find something magical, like the Galator? But if I ever did, I wouldn't waste it on the bird. I'd use it to mend my sore body."

Rhia nodded sympathetically. "Where are you sore?"

"My legs mostly. But I also have this ache between my shoulder blades. It's been with me for as long as I can remember."

Her eyebrows lifted, but she remained silent. I somehow had the feeling that she, too, knew more than she was saying.

She reached beneath the table and pulled out two small, silvery blankets, made from the most delicate linen I had ever seen. She spread one over her thighs, then handed the other to me. "A good night's sleep will help."

I held the shimmering blanket up to the light. "What is this cloth?"

"It is silk, made by moths."

"Moths? You're joking."

She smiled. "Their silk is just as warm as it is light. Try it yourself."

Keeping a safe distance from the hawk, Cwen approached. "Would a ssssong be ssssoothing to you?"

"Please," Rhia answered. "It reminds me of all the times you sang to me when I was small."

Cwen nodded, her teardrop eyes expressionless. "I will ssssing you a ssssong that ussssed to help you ssssleep."

As she passed a thin hand over the glowing beetles, their light dimmed. Then, like an old tree weaving in the wind, Cwen began to project a rolling, vibrating sound. It swelled and faded, repeating a comforting pattern over and over again. Almost a voice, yet not quite a voice, the sound wound wordlessly around us. Coaxing us to relax, to let go. I pulled the blanket over my chest and leaned back in the chair, my eyes feeling heavy. Rhia, I could tell, was already asleep, and even Trouble's head had drooped low on his chest. I watched Cwen's flowing motions for a while, but it was not long before I too drifted into slumber.

I dreamed that I lay alone, fast asleep, in a deep forest. Tall trees surrounded me, weaving in the wind. Honey, from somewhere, dripped into my mouth. Then, all at once, enemies appeared. I couldn't see them. But I could feel them. They were hiding in the trees. Or perhaps they were the trees themselves! Worse yet, as hard as I tried, I couldn't wake up, not even to protect myself. Slowly, one of the thin, twisted trees nearby bent down over my sleeping form, slipping a fingerlike branch into my tunic. *The Galator. It wants the Galator.* With a supreme effort, I managed to rouse myself.

I was still sitting in the chair by the dimly glowing hearth. The silk blanket had fallen to the floor beside me. I reached for the Galator, and to my relief, felt it was still there under my tunic. Listening, I heard the sporadic chattering of birds outside, telling me that sunrise was an hour or so away. Rhia slept curled as tight as a ball in her chair, while Cwen lay snoring on the floor by the cabinet. Trouble sat on my shoulder, his yellow-rimmed eyes wide open.

I wondered whether Arbassa itself ever slept. Even now, as it held us in its arms, was it still watching the hawk with concern? I wished I could ask the great tree whether Fincayra held the answers to my questions. Had the time come to leave Druma Wood and explore other parts of this island? Or should I be building a boat to search for another place entirely?

I sighed. For I knew once again, in that hour before dawn, how little I really did know.

XVII

THE ALLEAH
BIRD

Rhia shrieked suddenly. She sat rigid in her chair, not moving, not breathing. Even the golden light of sunrise, pouring through the window slats and over her suit of leafy vines, could not hide the look of terror on her face.

I bounced out of my chair. "What's wrong?"

Her wide eyes peered into mine. "Everything."

"What do you mean?"

She shook the forest of curls on her head. "A dream. So real, like it was truly happening." She took a deep breath. "It frightened me."

I watched her, remembering my own dream.

Cwen's slender form approached. "What dream wassss thissss?"

Rhia faced her. "Every night I dream about the Druma. Without fail."

"Sssso? I do assss well."

"It's always safe. Always comforting. Always . . . home. Even when I go to sleep worried about the troubles in other parts of Fincayra—which happens more and more—I know I can always find peace in my dreams of the Druma."

Cwen wrung her knobby hands. "You don't sssseem sssso peaceful now."

"I'm not!" Rhia's eyes filled with terror again. "Last night I dreamed that the whole Druma—all the trees, the ferns, the animals, the stones—started bleeding! Bleeding to death! I tried and tried, but I couldn't do anything to stop it. The forest was dying! The sky darkened. Everything turned the color of dried blood. The color of—"

"Rust," I finished. "Same as the other side of the river."

She nodded grimly, then lifted herself from her chair and strode to the eastern wall, where rays of lavender and pink now mixed with gold. Propping her hands on both sides of a slat, she gazed at the dawn. "For months, I've tried to convince myself that the sickness across the River Unceasing would never reach the Druma. That only the Blighted Lands would fall, not the whole of Fincayra."

"Sssso wrong," put in Cwen. "In all my yearssss, which are now sssso very many, I have never felt the Druma in sssssuch danger. Never! If we are to ssssurvive, we need new ssssstrength—from whatever sssssource." The last phrase rang rather ominously, though I was not sure why.

Rhia's brow creased. "That too was part of my dream." She paused, thinking. "A stranger came into the forest. A stranger who knew no one at all. He had some sort of power . . ." She swung around to face me. "And he—and only he—could save the Druma."

I blanched. "Me?"

"I'm not sure. I woke up before I could see his face."

"Well, I'm not your savior. That's certain."

She watched me closely, though she didn't say anything.

Trouble's talons squeezed tighter on my shoulder.

I turned from Rhia to Cwen and back to Rhia. "You're mistaken! Badly mistaken. Once I had . . . But I can't . . . I can't do anything like that! And even if I could, I have my own quest to follow." I shook my left arm. "Despite this bird on me."

"Your own quesssssst?" demanded Cwen. "Sssso you care nothing for otherssss?"

"I didn't say that."

"But you did." Rhia looked at me sharply. "You care about your own quest more than you care about the Druma."

"If you put it that way, yes." My cheeks burned. "Don't you understand? I have to find my own past! My own name! The last thing I need is to get caught up in whatever is happening here. You can't ask me to give up my quest just because you had one bad dream!"

She glared at me. "And how far would your quest have gone if the Druma had not been kind to you?"

"Far enough. I got here on my own, didn't I?"

"You remind me of a baby who says he fed himself on his own."

"I am no baby!"

Rhia sucked in her breath. "Listen. I'm the only creature of my kind who lives in this forest. No other woman or man or child can be found here, except for the rare outsider who slips through, as you did. But do I think, even for an instant, that I live here alone? That I could have survived without the others—like Arbassa, or Cwen, or the alleah bird, whose beauty I treasure even if I should never be lucky enough to see it again? If the Druma is in trouble, then all of them are in trouble. And I'm in trouble, too."

Imploringly, she opened her hands to me. "Please. Will you help?"

I looked away.

"He will not help ussss," spat Cwen.

Rhia strode to the stairway entrance. "Come. I want you to see what else will die if the Druma dies."

As she started down the stairs within Arbassa's trunk, I followed her, but only reluctantly. For the feeling was growing inside me that my own quest must take me elsewhere—to other parts of Fincayra, and perhaps beyond. In any case, to places far from the Druma. And even if I stayed here for a while, how could I try to help Rhia without being tempted to call on my forbidden powers? I shook my head, certain that our new friendship was already lost.

I glanced over my shoulder at Cwen. She showed no emotion at my departure—with one exception. Her teardrop eyes glared at Trouble, making clear that she was glad to see the irascible bird go. As if in response, he lifted one leg and raked his talons savagely in her direction.

Winding down the stairway, I smelled the familiar moist fragrance, all the while doubting I would ever stand here, in this great tree, again. I paused to examine the curious script that covered Arbassa's walls.

Rhia, already at the bottom, called up to me. "Let's go."

"I am just taking a last look at this writing."

Even in the spare light of the stairwell, her puzzlement was clear. "Writing? What writing?"

"On the wall here. Don't you see it?"

She climbed back up to me. After staring at the spot where I pointed, she seemed baffled, as if she saw nothing there. "Can you read it?"

"No."

"But you can see it?"

"Yes."

For a moment she scrutinized me. "There is something different about the way you see, isn't there?"

I nodded.

"You see without your eyes."

Again I nodded.

"And you can see something I can't see *with* eyes." Rhia bit her lip. "You are even more of a stranger to me now than when I first met you."

"Maybe it's better for you I stay a stranger."

Trouble fluttered his wings nervously.

"He doesn't like it in here," she observed, heading down the stairs.

I followed. "He probably knows what Arbassa thinks of him." After a pause, I added, "Not to mention what I think of him."

The doorway creaked, then opened. We stepped through it into the morning light scattered by the leafy boughs overhead, even as the passage snapped shut behind us.

Rhia glanced upward into the broad boughs of Arbassa, then quickly moved into the forest. As I followed, my walking jarred Trouble, and his talons squeezed me tighter than ever.

Before long, she came to a large beech tree, its gray bark folded with age. "Come here," she called. "I have something to show you."

I approached. She took her hand and laid it flat against the trunk.

"No tree is as ready to speak as a beech. Especially an elder. Listen."

Gazing up into the branches, she started making a slow, swishing sound with her voice. Immediately, the branches began to wave in response, whispering gently. As she varied her pace, pitch, and volume, the tree seemed to reply in kind. Soon the girl and the tree were engaged in full and lively conversation.

After a time, Rhia turned to me and spoke again in our own language. "Now you try it."

"Me?"

"You. First put your hand on the trunk."

Still doubtful, I obeyed.

"Now before you speak, listen."

"I already heard the branches."

"Don't listen with your ears. Listen with your *hand*."

My palm pressed into the folds of the trunk; my fingers joined with the cold, smooth bark. Presently I could feel a vague pulsing at the edges of my fingertips. The pulsing moved gradually into my whole hand and then up my arm. I could almost feel the subtle rhythm of air and earth flowing through the body of the tree, a rhythm that combined the power of an ocean wave surging with the tenderness of a small child breathing.

Without thinking, I started making a swishing sound like Rhia. To my surprise, the branches responded, waving gracefully above me. A whisper stirred the air. I nearly smiled, knowing that while I did not understand its words, the tree was indeed speaking to me.

Both to Rhia and the old beech, I said, "One day I would like to learn this language."

"It would do you no good if the Druma dies. Only here are the trees of Fincayra still awake enough to talk."

I hunched my shoulders. "What can I possibly do for you? I already told you I'm not the person in your dream."

"Forget my dream! There is something remarkable about you. Something . . . special."

Her words warmed me. Even if I didn't really believe them, it meant something that she did. For the first time in what seemed like ages, I thought of myself, seated on the grass, concentrating on a flower, making it open its petals one by one. Then I remembered where that path had taken me, and I shuddered. "Once there was something special. But that part of me is gone."

Her gray-blue eyes burrowed deeper. "Whatever it is you have, it is with you right now."

"I have only myself and my quest—which will probably take me far from here."

Adamantly, she shook her head. "That is not all you have."

All at once I understood what she must be talking about. The Galator! She didn't want me, after all. She wanted the pendant I wore, whose power I did not begin to understand. It didn't matter how she had concluded that I carried it. What mattered was that, somehow, she knew. How foolish of me to have believed, even for an instant, that she had seen something special about me. About my person, rather than my pendant.

"You don't really want me," I growled.

Her face turned quizzical. "You think not?"

Before I could answer, Trouble's talons dug into my shoulder with sudden force. I winced with pain. It was all I could do to keep myself from swiping at the bird, but I knew that he might attack me as ferociously as he had attacked the killer rat by the stream. All I could do was try to tolerate the pain, while despairing that he had chosen me to be his perch. But why had he chosen me? What did he really want? I had absolutely no idea.

"Look!" Rhia pointed at a brilliant flash of iridescent red and purple disappearing into the trees. "The alleah bird!"

She started after it, then paused, glancing back at me. "Come!

Let's get closer. The alleah bird is a sign of good fortune! I have not seen one for years."

With that, she dashed after the bird. I noticed that the wind seemed to sweep through the trees at that very moment, causing the branches to chatter vigorously. Yet if they were truly saying something, Rhia was not paying any attention. I rushed after her.

Over fallen branches and through needled bracken we chased the bird. Each time we drew close enough to get a better look, it flew off in a burst of brilliant color, showing only enough of its plumed tail to make us want to see more.

Finally, the alleah bird settled on a low branch in a stand of dead trees. Most likely it had chosen this place to perch because the supple, living branches all around were swaying so wildly in the wind. For the first time, no leaves hid its bright feathers. Rhia and I, panting from the chase, held ourselves as still as possible, studying the flaming purple crest on the bird's head and the explosions of scarlet along its tail.

Rhia could hardly contain her excitement. "Let's see how near we can get." She started to creep closer, pushing past a dead limb.

Suddenly Trouble whistled sharply. As I cringed from the blast in my ear, the hawk took flight. My heart missed a beat when I realized that he meant to attack the beautiful bird.

"No!" I cried.

Rhia waved her arms wildly. "Stop! Stop!"

The merlin paid no attention. Releasing another wrathful whistle, he shot like an arrow straight into his prey. The alleah bird, taken unaware, shrieked in pain as Trouble sunk his talons deep into its soft neck and pecked at its eyes. Still, it fought back with surprising savagery. The branch snapped beneath them. Feathers flying, the two birds tumbled to the ground.

Rhia ran forward, with me right behind. Reaching the spot, we both froze.

Before us on the brown leaves, Trouble, his talons smeared with blood, stood atop the body of his motionless prey. I noticed that the alleah bird seemed to have only one leg. Probably the other one had been torn off in the attack. I felt sick at the sight of those crumpled feathers, those luminous wings that would never fly again.

Then, as we watched in amazement, the alleah bird began to metamorphose. As it changed, it pulled away from its former skin, much like a snake that is shedding. This left behind a brittle, almost transparent skin, marked with ridges where the feathers had been. Meanwhile the bird's wings evaporated, as the feathered tail transformed into a long, serpentine body covered by dull red scales. The head grew longer and sprouted massive jaws, filled with jagged teeth that could easily bite off a hand. Only the eyes, as red as the scales, remained unchanged. The serpentlike creature lay dead, the thin skin of its former body clinging to its side.

I took Rhia's arm. "What does this mean?"

Her face drained of color, she turned slowly toward me. "It means that your hawk has saved our lives."

"What is that . . . thing?"

"That is—or was—a shifting wraith. It can change into whatever shape it wants, so it is especially dangerous."

"Those jaws look dangerous enough."

Grimly, Rhia poked at the shed skin with a stick. "As I said, a shifting wraith can change into anything. But there is always a flaw, something that gives it away, if you look closely enough."

"The bird had only one leg."

Rhia motioned toward the still-whispering branches beyond the dead stand. "The trees tried to warn me, but I wasn't listening. A shifting wraith in the Druma! That has never happened before. Oh, Emrys . . . my dream is coming true before my eyes!"

I bent low and extended my hand toward the merlin, now preening his wings. Trouble cocked his head to one side, then the other, then hopped onto my waiting wrist. With quick, sideways steps, he climbed up my arm and sat once more on my shoulder. Yet this time his weight didn't feel so troublesome.

I faced Rhia, whose brow was wrinkled with foreboding. "All of us were wrong about this little fighter. Even Arbassa was wrong."

She shook her head. "Arbassa was not wrong."

"But—"

"When Arbassa closed the door, it was not to keep out the merlin." She drew a long breath. "It was to keep out *you.*"

I stepped backward. "The tree thinks I could be dangerous to you?"

"That's right."

"Do you believe that?"

"Yes. But I decided to let you in anyway."

"Why? That was before your dream."

She studied me curiously. "One day, perhaps, I will tell you."

XVIII

THE NAME OF
THE KING

My second sight moved from the skin of the shifting wraith, as brittle as a dried leaf, to the living, whispering boughs of the Druma. "Tell me what is happening to Fincayra."

Rhia frowned—such an unnatural expression for her. "I only know a little, what I've learned from the trees."

"Tell me what you know."

She reached toward me, wrapping one of her forefingers around one of mine. "It reminds me of a basket of sweet berries that turns sour. Too sour to eat." She gave a sigh. "Some years ago, strange things—evil things—started happening. The lands east of the river, once nearly as green and full of life as this forest, fell to the Blight. As the land darkened, so did the sky. But until today, the Druma has always been safe. Its power was so strong, no enemies dared to enter. Until now."

"How many wraiths are there?"

Trouble fluttered his wings, then grew quiet again.

"I don't know." Her frown deepened. "But the shifting wraiths are not even our worst enemies. There are warrior goblins. They used to stay underground, in their caves. But now they run free, and they kill just for pleasure. There are ghouliants—the deathless warriors who guard the Shrouded Castle. And there is Stangmar, the king who commands them all."

At the mention of that name, the living branches surrounding the stand of dead trees started shaking and clacking. When at last they grew still, I asked, "Who is this king?"

Rhia chewed her lip. "Stangmar is terrible—too terrible for words. It's hard to believe, but I've heard the trees say that when he first came to power, he wasn't so wicked. In those days, he sometimes rode through the Druma on his great black horse, even pausing to listen to the voices of the forest. Then something happened to him—no one knows what—that made him change. He destroyed his own castle, a place of music and friendship. And where it stood, he built the Shrouded Castle, a place of cruelty and terror."

She sat solemnly for a moment. "It lies far to the east, in the darkest of the Dark Hills, where the night never ends. I've heard of no one, other than the king's own servants, who has gone there and returned alive. No one! So the truth is difficult to know. Yet . . . it is said that the castle is always dark, and always spinning, so fast that no one could ever attack it."

I stiffened, remembering my dream at sea. Even now, that terrible castle felt all too real.

"Meanwhile, Stangmar has poisoned much of Fincayra. All the lands east of the Druma, and some to the south, have been *cleansed,* as those loyal to him would say. What that really means is that fear—cold, lifeless fear—has covered everything. It reminds me of snow, except snow is pretty. Villages are burned. Trees and rivers are silent. Animals and birds are dead. And the giants are gone."

"Giants?"

Her eyes burned angrily. "Our first and oldest people. Giants from every land call Fincayra their ancestral home. Even before the rivers began rolling down from the mountains, the footsteps of giants marked Fincayra. Long before Arbassa first sprouted as a seedling, their rumbling chants echoed over ridges and forests. Even now, the Lledra, their oldest chant, is the first song many babies ever hear."

The Lledra. Had I heard that name before? It seemed familiar somehow. But how could it be? Unless, perhaps, it was one of Branwen's chants.

"They can grow taller than a tree, our giants. Or even a hillside. Yet throughout the ages, they've stayed peaceful. Except for the Wars of Terror long ago—when goblins tried to overrun the giants' ancient city of Varigal. Usually, unless someone makes them angry, they are as gentle as butterflies."

She stamped her foot on the ground. "But some years ago, Stangmar issued a command—for some reason known only to him—to kill the giants wherever they were found. Since then, his soldiers have hunted them ruthlessly. Although it takes twenty or more soldiers to kill just one, they nearly always succeed. The city of Varigal, I've heard, is now just a ruin. It's possible that a few giants still survive, disguised as cliffs or crags, but they must always stay in hiding, afraid for their lives. In all my travels through the Druma, I've never seen a single one."

I gazed at the corpse of the shifting wraith. "Isn't there any way to stop this king?"

"If there is, no one has found it! His powers are vast. Besides his army, he has assembled almost all of the Treasures of Fincayra."

"What are they?"

"Magical. Powerful. The Treasures were always used to benefit the land and all its creatures, not just one person. But no more. Now they are his—the Orb of Fire, the Caller of Dreams, the Seven Wise Tools. The sword called Deepercut—a sword with two edges, one that can cut right into the soul, and one that can heal any wound. The most beautiful one, the Flowering Harp, whose music can bring springtime to any meadow or hillside. And the most hateful one, the Cauldron of Death."

Her voice fell to a whisper. "Only one of the legendary Treasures hasn't yet fallen into his hands. The one whose power is said to be greater than all the rest combined. The one called the Galator."

Beneath my tunic, my heart pulsed against the pendant.

Her finger wrapped tighter around mine. "I've heard the trees saying that Stangmar has given up searching for the Galator, that it disappeared from Fincayra some years ago. Yet I've also heard that he is still searching for something that will make his power complete—something he calls *the last Treasure*. That could only mean one thing."

"The Galator?"

Rhia nodded slowly. "Anyone who knows where it's hidden is in the gravest danger."

I could not miss the warning. "You know I have it."

"Yes," she replied calmly. "I know."

"And you think it could help save the Druma."

She pursed her lips in thought. "It might, or it might not. Only the Galator itself can say. But I still think *you* could help."

I stepped back, jabbing my neck on a broken limb. Trouble screeched at me reproachfully.

Yet the pain in my neck, like the pain in my ear, didn't distress me. For I had heard in her voice that certain something I had not allowed myself to hear before. She really did see something of value in me! I felt sure that she was mistaken. But her faith was a kind of treasure itself, as precious in its way as the one around my neck.

The words jumped out at me. *As precious as the one around my neck.* Suddenly I realized that I had my clue! The clue I'd been seeking!

Until now I had assumed that the Galator was simply known in Fincayra—not that it truly *belonged* in Fincayra. Now I knew better. It was the most powerful of this land's ancient Treasures. And it may have disappeared around the time Branwen and I washed ashore on Gwynedd. If only I could find out how the Galator had come into Branwen's hands, or at least learn some more of its secrets, then I might find some of my own secrets as well.

"The Galator," I said. "What else do you know about it?"

Rhia released my hand. "Nothing. And now I must go. With or without you."

"Where?"

She started to speak, then froze, listening. Trouble, clinging firmly to my left shoulder, also froze.

Rhia's loose brown hair stirred like the branches as yet another wind moved through the forest. As her features hardened with concentration, I wondered whether her laughter like bells would ever ring again among these trees. The sound swelled steadily, a chorus of swishing and creaking, drumming and moaning.

As the wind subsided, she leaned toward me. "Goblins have been seen in the forest! I have no time to lose." She caught a fold of my tunic. "Will you come? Will you help me find some way to save the Druma?"

I hesitated. "Rhia . . . I'm sorry. The Galator. I need to find out more about it! Can't you understand?"

Her eyes narrowed. Without saying good-bye, she turned to go.

I strode up to her and caught a vine from her sleeve. "I wish you well."

"And I wish you well," she said coldly.

A sudden crashing came from the underbrush behind us. We whirled around to see a young stag, with the beginning of a rack above its bronze-colored head. The stag leaped over some fallen timber, eager to get away from something. For a split second I caught a glimpse of one of its brown eyes, dark and deep, filled with fear.

I tensed, recalling the one time before when I had seen a stag. Yet that time the fear was in my own eyes. And that time the stag did everything in its power to help me.

Rhia pulled free, then started to go.

"Wait! I will come with you."

Her whole face brightened. "You will?"

"Yes . . . but only until our two paths diverge."

She nodded. "For a while, then."

"And where are we going?"

"To find the one creature in all the Druma who might know what to do. The one who is called the Grand Elusa."

For some reason, I wasn't sure I liked the sound of that name.

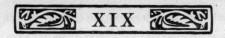
HONEY

As swiftly as the stag, Rhia bounded off. Although my legs still felt stiff, I tried my best to keep up with her through dense thickets and over moss-banked streams. Even so, she often needed to stop and wait for me.

Because the sun rode high above us, sending shafts of light to the forest floor, I could see obstacles much more easily than the night before. Even so, I stumbled often enough that Trouble finally took off from my shoulder. He stayed close by, flying from branch to branch. And while my shoulder felt grateful for the rest, I did not resent his watchful eye as I had only a while ago.

Animals of all kinds were on the move. Birds with small gray bodies or bright green wings or huge yellow bills, traveling sometimes in flocks and other times alone, flew overhead. Large-eyed squirrels, beavers, a doe with its fawn, and a golden snake also passed me. In the distance, wolves howled. At one point an enormous shape, black as night, ambled out of the trees. I froze, fearful, until two smaller shapes appeared just behind—and I knew that I had encountered a family of bears. All these creatures shared the same look of fear I had seen in the stag. And all of them, it seemed, were heading in the opposite direction from Rhia and myself.

Late in the morning, perspiration dripping from my brow, I stepped into a shadowed glade. Cedars, very old from the looks of them, stood arranged in a perfect circle. So shaggy was their bark that at first glance they might have been mistaken for an assembly of ancient men whose long manes and beards flowed down over their stooped bodies. Even the sound of their gently stirring branches seemed different from the whispers of other trees. More like people at a funeral, humming a solemn, mournful lament.

Then I noticed, in the center of the glade, a narrow earthen mound. No wider than my body, it stretched at least twice my own height in length. It was surrounded by round, polished stones, which glistened like blue ice. Cautiously, I moved closer.

Trouble flew back to my shoulder. But instead of perching himself as usual, he paced back and forth with sharp, agitated steps.

I caught my breath. *I have been here before.* The notion—the conviction—came to me in a fleeting instant. Like a scent of some flower that appears and then vanishes before you have time to find its source, some dim memory touched me briefly and then fled. Perhaps it was only a dream, or the memory of a dream. Yet I could not shake the feeling that, in some way I could not quite identify, this mound within the circle of cedars was familiar.

"Emrys! Come on!"

Rhia's call jarred me back to the present. With a final glance at the mound, and at the mournful cedars, I left the glade. Soon I could hear the strange humming no more. But it continued to haunt the darkest corners of my mind.

The terrain grew steadily wetter. Frogs piped and bellowed so loudly that sometimes I could not even hear my own breathing. Herons, cranes, and other water birds called to one another in eerie, echoing voices. The air began to reek of things rotting. At last I saw Rhia, standing by the tall grasses at the edge of a dark swath of land. A swamp.

Impatiently, she beckoned. "Let's go."

I viewed the swamp skeptically. "We have to cross that?"

"It's the quickest way."

"Are you sure?"

"No. But we are running out of time—did you see all the animals fleeing?—and if it works it could save us an hour or more. Just on the other side of the swamp are the hills of the Grand Elusa."

She turned to cross the swamp, but I caught her arm. "Just what *is* the Grand Elusa?"

She shook loose. "I don't really know! Her true identity is a secret, even to Arbassa. All I know is that the legends say she lives among the living stones of the Misted Hills. That she knows things no one else knows, including some things that haven't happened yet. And that she is old, very old. I've even heard that she was present when Dagda carved the very first giant from the side of a mountain."

"Did you say . . . living stones?"

"That's what they're called. I'm not sure why."

I glanced toward the murk, studded with dead trees and stagnant pools. A crane cried out in the distance. "Are you sure this creature will help us?"

"No . . . but she might. That is, if she doesn't eat us first."

I rocked back on my heels. "Eat us?"

"The legends say she is always hungry. And fiercer than a cornered giant."

Trouble cocked his head toward Rhia. He piped a long, low whistle.

She lifted her eyebrows.

"What's wrong?"

"Trouble promises to keep us safe. But this is the first time I've heard that note of worry in his voice."

I sniffed. "I feel sorry for the Grand Elusa if she should try to eat Trouble. This bird doesn't know the meaning of fear."

"That's why I'm not happy to hear him sounding worried."

With that, she turned again to the swamp. She stepped on a slab of caked mud, from which she leaped to a rock. As I followed, I noticed we had left our footprints in the mud, but dismissed any concern about leaving tracks. We were already so deep into the forest, it could not matter.

We hopped from rock to log to rock again, making our way slowly across the swamp. Snags reached out to us with long, withered arms. Strange voices, somehow different from birds or frogs, echoed across the murky water, joining the occasional whistle from Trouble. Often, as we struggled to keep to the shallower places, something would slap the surface of the water or seem to stir within its darkened depths. I could never quite tell what might be causing such disturbances. Nor did I really want to know.

At length, the swamp faded, even as gray mist began to thicken the air. We came to a wet field of tall grasses, which gradually lifted into solid ground. Ahead of us stood a steep, rock-strewn hill, where vaporous arms unfurled toward us.

Rhia halted. "The Misted Hills. If only I could find a cluster of sweet berries! We could use an extra dose of strength for the climb." She glanced at me uncertainly. "And for whatever else lies ahead."

As we started to ascend, Trouble lifted off from my shoulder. He flew in silence, making slow, stately circles in the air above our heads. Although I guessed that he was scanning the forest for any sign of danger, he also seemed to be enjoying himself, savoring the freedom of soaring on high.

Boulders, some as big as Rhia's whole house, appeared here and there among the trees. The trees themselves grew farther and farther apart, their gnarled roots grasping the hillside. Yet despite the greater distance between the trunks, the forest didn't seem any lighter. Maybe it was the shadows of the immense boulders. Or the curling mist surrounding them. Or something else. But the forest felt increasingly dark.

As we labored to climb the steep slope, doubts flowed over me like the mist. Whatever kind of being this Grand Elusa was, she certainly didn't pick such a place to live because she enjoyed having visitors. And what if the goblins in the forest found us first? I clutched the Galator beneath my tunic, but I did not feel any better.

Suddenly, a great gray stone loomed directly before me. I froze. Perhaps it was only a trick of the mist, confusing my second sight. But it looked less like a boulder than like a face, craggy and mysterious. A face staring straight at me. Then I heard, or thought I heard, a grinding sound, almost like someone clearing his throat. The boulder seemed to shift its weight ever so slightly.

I didn't wait to learn what happened next. Up the hill I raced, tripping over roots, rocks, and my own feet.

At last I topped the rise. Above my panting, I heard an angry, buzzing sound. Bees. Thousands of bees, swarming around the broken trunk of a dead tree. Although it was hard to be certain in the mist, it looked as if the tree had broken off, probably in a storm, not long ago. What was not hard to tell was that the bees were not pleased about it.

Rhia, hands on her hips, watched the furious buzzing with interest.

Reading her thoughts, I shook my head. "You're not thinking," I panted, "about going after their honey . . . are you?"

She grinned slyly. "A person can never get enough honey! It would take just a minute to fetch some. It wouldn't slow us down."

"You can't! Look at all those bees."

Just then Trouble dropped down, enjoying a final flying swoop before landing on my shoulder. This bird clearly loved to fly. As he settled in, he gave a satisfied chirp. I felt surprised at just how familiar, almost natural, it felt to have him there. So different from yesterday! He folded his banded wings upon his back, cocking his head toward me.

On a whim, I winked at him.

Trouble winked back.

Rhia continued to examine the broken trunk. "If only I could find some way to distract the bees, just for a few seconds. That would be enough."

With a sudden screech, Trouble took off again. He flew straight into the swarm. He swooped and dived among the bees, batting them with his wings, then raced away into the mist. The swarm sped after him.

"Madness! That bird likes a fight as much as you like . . ."

I didn't bother to finish, since Rhia was already scaling the severed trunk in search of the bees' stores of honey. I listened for any buzzing, but heard none. I ran to join her. As I pulled myself up on a low branch, the trunk cracked and wobbled unsteadily on its base.

"Careful, Rhia!" I called. "This whole thing could topple over anytime."

But she could not hear. Fully occupied, she was already leaning over the jagged top of the trunk.

Standing on the branch, I leaned over beside her. A golden pool of honey, surrounded by walls of honeycomb as thick as my chest, lay beneath us. Bits of broken branches, bark, and honeycomb floated in the heavy syrup. I plunged in my hand, scooped out a heaping handful, then drank the sweet, gooey liquid. I had never in my life tasted such satisfying honey. Rhia apparently agreed, since she was busy feasting with both hands at once, her cheeks and chin dripping.

"We should go," she declared at last. "Have your last swallow."

Seeing a large chunk of honeycomb floating just below me, I grabbed it. As I tugged, however, the honeycomb refused to budge. Bracing myself, I pinched it as hard as I could and yanked with all my might.

At that instant, the object rose out of the pool with a deafening howl. I suddenly realized that I had been holding not a honeycomb but the tip of a huge, bulbous nose. Rhia shrieked as I jerked sideways to get away from the head, covered with honey, that was lifting toward us. Just then the base of the thick trunk cracked, tilted, and split apart. It toppled over the side of the hill, taking both of us with it.

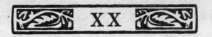

XX

SHIM

Rhia and I cascaded down the slope. Ahead of us the weighty log, loaded with honey and whatever had boiled up from its depths, rolled and bounced down the ridge, gathering speed as it descended. Finally it smashed into a gigantic boulder, splintering into bits.

When at last I stopped, the world around me kept spinning for some time. Half dazed, I made myself sit up. "Rhia."

"Over here." She lifted her head from the grass just below me, her brown wisps of hair matted with honey and twigs.

Simultaneously we turned to the moaning sound coming from the wreckage of the trunk. Rhia reached for me, wrapping her forefinger around mine. We stood and carefully crept closer.

What we saw was a little mound, completely covered with honey, sticks, and leaves, lying beneath the boulder. Then the mound rolled over, shook itself vigorously, and sat up.

"It's a man." My words were filled with awe. "A tiny little man."

"A dwarf," corrected Rhia. "I didn't know there were any dwarves left in Fincayra."

Two pink eyes popped open in the mask of honey. "You both is wrong. Totally, horribly, disgustingly wrong! I is no dwarf."

Rhia looked quite skeptical. "No? Then what are you?"

The little man blew a blast of honey out of his bulbous nose. As more honey dripped off his chin, he licked his fingers, palms, and wrists. Having cleaned his hands, he looked nervously from one side to the other. "You isn't a friend of the king's, is you?"

Rhia scowled. "Of course not."

"And what about your black-haired friend there, who pullses on other people's noses?"

"He's not either."

"Certainly, definitely, absolutely not?"

Rhia could not keep herself from grinning. "Certainly, definitely, absolutely not."

"All right then." The little man struggled to unstick himself from the ground so that he could stand. He strode up to Rhia. Although he came to only just above her knee, he threw his head back with pride.

"I is no dwarf. I is a giant."

"A what?" I exclaimed, starting to laugh.

The little man glared at me, pink eyes shining. "I is a giant." Then his pride seemed to melt away. His face fell, and his shoulders drooped. "I is just a very, very, very *small* giant. I wishes, I truly wishes, that I could be big. Like a giant should be."

"I don't believe it." I stooped lower to get a better view. "You don't look like a giant to me. Not even a small one."

"But I is!"

"Then I'm a fungus."

"And why is a fungus going around pullsing other people's noses?"

Rhia burst out laughing, shaking every leaf on her suit of vines. "Leave him alone, Emrys. If he says he's a giant, well then, I believe him."

Seeming vindicated, the tiny fellow patted his bulging belly. "I is having a nicely meal, too, bothering nobodies, until I is interrupted."

"My name is Rhia. What's yours?"

Glancing nervously over his shoulder, he muttered, "Can't be too careful these dayses." He took a tiny step closer. "My name is Shim."

I observed him suspiciously. "And tell us, Shim, do you always go swimming in your honey when you drink it?"

"Certainly, definitely, absolutely! If you would like not to get stingded by the bees, that is the best way to do it."

Amused, Rhia smiled. "You have a point. But getting out again must be difficult."

The little giant sputtered, "You is, you is, makings fun of me!"

"Not at all," I teased. "You're not funny in the least." I tried my best to hold back my laughter, but it spewed out of me all at once. I roared, clutching my side.

The tiny fellow darted up to me and kicked me as hard as he could in the foot. My mirth vanished. With a growl, I started after him.

"No, stops! Please, stops!" cried Shim, hiding behind Rhia's legs. "I doesn't mean to hurts you. Really, truly, honestly."

"You certainly did!" I tried to grab hold of the sticky mass behind Rhia. "When I catch you I'll pinch more than your nose."

"Wait," commanded Rhia. She held me by the shoulder. "We don't have time for this. We've dawdled long enough!"

Reluctantly, I backed away. "I suppose you're right. Anyway, those bees will be coming back any second, with their stingers ready for battle." I shot a glance at Shim. "If I were you, I'd take a good bath before they descend on you."

The pink eyes swelled in fright. "On me?"

"Certainly, definitely, absolutely."

The little giant gasped. "I truly hates to get stingded!"

With that, he tore off into the swirling mist behind the boulder. He had only just disappeared, however, when he screamed with terror. Rhia and I both ran to see what had happened.

A few seconds later, we too screamed. We fell, spinning head over heels, into a deep pit plunging straight into the ground. Eventually, we rolled to a stop. The world had gone totally dark.

"Ohhhh, my head," I grumbled.

Something wriggled beneath me. "Gets you off me, you fool!"

An arm or a leg, sticky and caked with dirt and leaves, struck me square in the face. "Ow! Watch out, you blundering ball of honey!"

"Stop it," cried Rhia. "We must find our way out of here."

"Where is here, anyway?" I asked. "We must have fallen into a hole. A deep one. So deep I can't even see any light up there. And feel the floor! It's all poky, not like normal rock."

"I caaan aaanswer yooour queeestion," boomed a thunderous voice from deeper in the darkness. "Youuu haaave fouuund my laaair."

"Whose lair?" we all asked at once.

A long pause ensued.

"The laaair of the Graaand Eluuusa."

XXI

THE GRAND
ELUSA

The chamber's walls seemed to shake with the force of the voice.

Rhia pressed against my side. I tried my hardest to see, but my second sight was useless in such total darkness. For an instant I considered breaking the promise made at Caer Myrddin and tapping whatever powers I might still possess. To protect us however I could. But the very thought rekindled all my old fears, and I sat frozen.

"Is you," whispered Shim into the darkness, "the creature who, who, who eatses everything?"

"I eeeat whaaatever I choose." The deep voice echoed, its vibrations continuing to pummel us. "Nooow teeell meee whooo youuu aaare, befooore I eeeat youuu."

Bravely, I cleared my throat. "I am called . . . Emrys."

"Emryyys of wheeere?"

This time my voice was weaker. "I don't know."

"And I am Rhia, of Druma Wood."

After a silence, the Grand Elusa boomed, "Whooo eeelse is heeere?"

No answer.

"Whooo eeelse is heeere?" So loud came the voice that flakes of dirt shook loose and fell on our heads.

No answer. Only a gasping sound that I assumed was the rapid panting of the frightened little giant.

"He is Shim," answered Rhia. "Also of the Druma." She drew in a deep breath. "Please don't eat us. We need your help."

"Fooor whaaat?"

"To save the Druma! My home!"

I added, "Your home as well."

For a moment, no one spoke.

Then, all of a sudden, light filled the chamber. We looked at one another, truly amazed. For we found ourselves in an enormous cavern cut from the rock. Although the walls around us fairly glowed, there was no clear source of the light. More mysterious yet, there was no sign at all of the Grand Elusa. But for ourselves, the radiant cavern looked empty.

"Where is she?" I scanned the glowing cavern walls.

Rhia's brow furrowed. "I have no idea."

Shim, meanwhile, sat with his face in his hands, shivering.

"And this light . . ." I reached a hand to the wall. "Look! It comes from the rocks themselves!"

"Crystals," said Rhia in wonderment. "A cave of glowing crystals."

Indeed, the walls, ceiling, and floor of this cave radiated a clear, dancing light. Crystals sparkled and flashed all around us, as if the sunlight shining on a rippling river had been poured into the very Earth. And I am quite sure that my own face glowed as well, for even in the days when I could see with my own eyes, when colors ran deeper and light shone brighter, I had never seen anything as beautiful as this crystal cave.

Then I felt a sudden surge of warmth against my chest. Peering into the neck of my tunic, I jumped. The Galator was glowing as bright as the walls! Vibrant green light flowed from the pendant's jeweled heart. I looked up to find Rhia watching me, smiling.

"You like my cave?" A new voice, airy and small, floated to us from one of the walls.

While Shim continued to shiver with fear, Rhia and I leaned closer to the source. There, amidst a massive curl of crystals, hung a delicate web. Its strands radiated out from the center like the light from a star. Upon this web dangled a single spider, the size of a thumbnail. Its tiny head and back were covered with minuscule hairs which glowed as white as the crystals themselves.

"I like it very much," I replied.

"It reminds me of all the stars I have ever seen," said Rhia.

I watched the spider, the round hump of her back jiggling as she climbed to a higher strand. "Are you—"

"I am," declared the spider, "the Grand Elusa."

"But your voice was so much . . . *larger* before."

Ignoring me, the white spider hooked a silken thread to the strand. Throwing a line over a torn section of the web, she leaped down to a lower level. With a quick motion, two of her eight arms tied off the line. Having completed her repair, she scurried back to the center.

"How could you have sounded so large?" I asked again.

"Oh, I can be large when I please." The spider waved at Shim. "Large enough to eat that shivering morsel over there with one bite."

The little giant, his face still in his hands, gave out a groan.

"If I am not in the mood to eat my guests," she continued in her airy little voice, "I make myself smaller for a while. My stomach shrinks, even if my appetite doesn't. Anyway, image and reality are rarely the same. As you surely know by now, Emrys, that is the first rule of magic."

I caught my breath. "I know nothing about magic! Except that it's dangerous, very dangerous."

"Then you do know something about magic."

"That is all I will ever know."

"Too bad. You might have found it useful in the future."

"Not me. There is no magic in my future. At least not of my own making."

The spider seemed to observe me for a moment. "If you say so."

Spying a beetle twice her size who had flown into the web, she rushed over, bit its neck, then waited for it to cease struggling. In a flash, she secured it tightly with a strand of silk. She plucked off one of its legs and started munching. "I do enjoy eating, though. That much of the image is reality."

"Can you help us?" pleaded Rhia. "The Druma . . . it's in trouble."

The Grand Elusa pulled off another leg from the beetle. "Of course it is in trouble! Like all the rest of Fincayra! As much trouble as this poor beetle, being consumed bit by bit. Have you only just realized that?"

Rhia hung her head. "I . . . didn't want to believe it."

"Until now, when the Blight is practically at your door! You have waited too long."

"I know! But maybe there's still time. Will you help?"

The spider took another bite, chewed avidly. "Just what do you expect me to do?"

"You could explain why it's happening."

"Why?" More chewing. "It would take too long to tell you everything. I will run out of food and then I will have to eat all of you."

"Just tell me if it can be stopped. By anything." Then Rhia added, with a glance in my direction, "Or anyone."

The spider reached a leg up and scratched the hump of her hairy back. "I will tell you this. Fincayra—and that includes the Druma—is doomed, unless the king you call Stangmar can be toppled."

"Toppled! Is that possible?"

"It all depends," declared the spider, "on what Stangmar calls *the last Treasure*. Something he once had, then lost long ago."

I looked down at my tunic, under which the Galator glowed. "Can you tell us its powers?"

The spider considered the question for a while before answering. "The last Treasure carries great powers, greater than you know." She grabbed another leg and bit off the bottom half. "Stangmar is convinced that when he finds it, his power will be complete."

Rhia sighed. "He is right."

"No! He is wrong. It is not his power that will be complete, but his servitude."

"Servitude?"

"To the most terrible spirit of all, the one known as Rhita Gawr." I stiffened.

"To Rhita Gawr, your king is nothing but a tool for his greater goal." She nibbled on the beetle's knee, then gave a satisfied smack of her lips. "To dominate all of this world, the Earth, and the Otherworld. That is his true desire."

She smacked her lips again, before crunching into the joint. "His supreme adversary, Dagda, is battling him on many fronts, too many to name. Yet Rhita Gawr has already won over Stangmar, and he has used the king to gain control of much of Fincayra. Few things now stand in his way, and the most important of them is . . ."

Another smack, another crunch. "The last Treasure. If that too falls into his hands, he will certainly win Fincayra. Then Rhita Gawr will control the bridge between the Earth and the Otherworld. He will be within reach of winning the Earth itself. Tough, but tasty— this leg, I mean. And if that ever happens, all is lost."

Frowning, I tried to understand. "Doesn't the king know he's being used in this way?"

"He knows. But he was corrupted by Rhita Gawr long ago." She swallowed the last section of the last leg. Then she carefully wiped her mouth, using the two arms nearest to her head. "Stangmar has lost the ability to choose for himself."

"Yet if he could be toppled somehow, Rhita Gawr might still be stopped."

"Perhaps."

Rhia, looking discouraged, leaned against a wall of glowing crystals. "But how?"

The Grand Elusa bit into the beetle's belly. "Mmmm, tender as could be."

"How?" repeated Rhia.

The spider swallowed. "There is only one possibility left. No, no. It is not really a possibility at all."

"What is it?"

"The king's castle must be destroyed."

Rhia blinked. "The Shrouded Castle?"

"Yes. It is the creation of Rhita Gawr, and through its walls the evil spirit's power flows into Stangmar and his army. The ghouliants themselves are part of the castle they guard, you know." She took another bite of the belly. "*Mmmm.* Very good. What was I saying? Oh yes, the ghouliants. That is why they never venture outside the castle walls. If you can destroy the castle, you can also destroy them."

"It can't be done!" exclaimed Rhia. "The Shrouded Castle is always spinning, always dark. It would be impossible to attack, let alone destroy."

"There is a way." The spider, still chewing, turned toward me. "Just as there is a way for a man who is blind to see again."

I started. "How do you know that?"

"In the same way you can see things with your second sight that others cannot see with their eyes."

At that I faced Rhia. "The writing on the walls inside Arbassa! That's why it was invisible to you."

"And if you should survive," continued the Grand Elusa, "your second sight could improve further. One day you might not only see, but understand."

"You mean it could help me read the writing?"

"If you survive."

"Really?"

"Do not underestimate your second sight! One day, you might come to rely on it. To love it. Maybe even more than you once loved your own eyes." She paused long enough to nibble on the beetle's forehead. "Though I happen to love eyes myself."

Rhia addressed the spider. "You said there is a way."

Using three of her arms, the white creature grasped the remainder of the beetle and ate some more of the belly. She chewed slowly, savoring its flavor. "I may not have time to explain it to you. In fact, you ought to leave while you can. I will finish this morsel quite soon, and then, with my appetite, I am afraid it will be your turn next."

Again Shim groaned from behind his hands.

"What is the way?"

"Do you know about the Cauldron of Death?" asked the spider, cleaning one of her arms.

Grimly, Rhia nodded. "Just that anyone who is thrown into it is killed instantly."

"True enough. But it is also true that it bears a fatal flaw. If someone were to crawl into it willingly, not by force, then the cauldron itself would be destroyed."

"Crawl into it willingly? Who would ever do such a thing?"

"No one who wants to live to see another day." The spider munched some more, lips smacking. "Yet, in the same manner, the castle itself has a flaw. A tiny one, perhaps, but a flaw nonetheless."

"What is it?"

"There is an ancient prophecy, as ancient as the giants themselves."

At this, Shim spread his fingers just wide enough to peek through.

The spider swung to another strand, pulled free an old antenna that some victim had left behind, and gobbled it in one bite. Returning to the nearly eaten beetle, she chanted:

> *Where in the darkness a castle doth spin,*
> *Small will be large, ends will begin.*
> *Only when giants make dance in the hall*
> *Shall every barrier crumble and fall.*

"What does it mean?" demanded Rhia. "*Only when giants make dance in the hall . . .*"

"*Shall every barrier crumble and fall.*" I pushed some black hairs back from my face. "So the castle walls would crumble if giants ever danced there?"

Having finished off the beetle's belly, the spider tore off one of the wings. "So goes the prophecy."

Rhia's expression darkened. "So that's why Stangmar has been hunting down all the giants! He must have heard this prophecy, too. He's doing everything he can to make sure it never comes true."

The spider crunched on the remainder of the wing. "Including destroying Varigal, the most ancient city of all."

"Ohhh," moaned Shim. "I doesn't means it when I says I wishes to be big. I doesn't means it. Really, truly, honestly."

The Grand Elusa eyed the shivering mass of dirt, twigs, and honey. "I pity you, shrunken one. For though your parents came from the giants' race, you have not learned that bigness means more than the size of your bones."

"But I is happy being small! Just a foolish whim to gets big. Big and dead! I is happier small but alive."

"So be it," said the spider. "Now, I ought to warn all of you. This little morsel has only one wing left, and also part of the head." She pulled off the wing, crammed it into her mouth, and chewed for a few seconds. "*Hmmm.* Now just the head. I am still very hungry. And also tired of being this size. If you do not leave my crystal cave quite soon, I will be forced to sample a few of your arms and legs."

Rhia clutched my arm. "She's right. Let's get out of here."

"But how?"

"I am not certain," the spider answered, "but I think you might be able to climb out on the crystals."

"Of course!" exclaimed Rhia. "Let's go."

She began to scamper up the radiant wall, using the larger crystals as holds for her hands and feet. Shim pushed past her, scaling the steep wall as rapidly as his stubby arms and legs could manage. He left behind a trail of gooey syrup on the crystals.

Seeing me standing beneath her, Rhia called down. "Quick! Or you'll follow that beetle."

I hesitated, driven to ask the Grand Elusa one thing more.

"Come on!"

"Go ahead," I called back. "I'll be there right away."

"You had better do just that." The spider reached for the beetle's head, leaving nothing but an empty noose of silk. "On the other hand, you do look scrawny but edible."

"Please tell me one last thing," I begged. "About my home. My true home. Can you tell me where it is? The Galator—glowing right here—is my only clue."

"Ah, the Galator! Come closer and show it to me."

"I don't dare. You might . . ."

"My, but you *do* look more meaty than I thought."

"Please!" I cried. "Then can you tell me how to find my mother? My father? My true name?"

Swallowing the very last of the beetle, the spider answered, "I cannot say. That is for . . . I daresay, you do smell unusually interesting. Come closer, boy. Come closer. Yes! Leeet meee taaake a cloooser loook!"

As the spider's voice swelled in size, so did the spider. But I did not stay to watch the change. I scurried out of the cave with all the speed I could muster.

ENCOUNTER
IN THE MIST

I emerged from the cave into the swirling mist. I could barely make out Rhia, even though she was only a few paces away. Beside her stood Shim, so covered with sticks and dirt and leaves that he looked more like a miniature mountain than a miniature person. Glancing down at the Galator, I noticed that it no longer glowed.

Rhia sat in a small grove of elms, where five young saplings had sprouted around an elder. She watched me exit the cave, clearly relieved. Then she leaned close to the old elm tree in the center of the grove. She began talking with it, whispering in low, swishing tones. In response, the tree rocked slowly on its roots, creaking with a voice that seemed terribly sad.

In time, Rhia turned to me, her eyes clouded. "This tree has seen more than two hundred springs in Druma Wood. Yet now it's sure it has seen its very last. It weeps every day for the future of its children. I told it not to lose hope, but it said it has only one hope left. To live long enough to do at least some small thing to keep the Druma safe from warrior goblins. But it expects just to die of grief instead."

Shim, standing beside her, rubbed his dirt-caked nose and looked down.

I could only nod sadly and watch the streaming mist. All at once I picked up the sweet scent of apple blossoms.

"You ssssseem sssso very glum," said a familiar voice.

"Cwen!" Rhia leaped to her feet. "What ever brings you here? You almost never go out walking anymore."

Passing a branched hand before her face, Cwen emerged from the mist. "I sssshouldn't have followed you." She hesitated, a touch of fear in her teardrop eyes. "Issss it possible you can sssstill forgive me?"

Rhia's eyes narrowed. "You have done something terrible."

At that instant, six huge warrior goblins stepped out of the mist. Swiftly they surrounded us. Their thin eyes glinted beneath pointed helmets, their muscular arms protruded from shoulder plates, their three-fingered hands grasped the hilts of broad swords. Beads of perspiration gathered on their gray-green skin.

One of them, wearing red armbands above his elbows, brandished his sword at Cwen. In a wheezing, rasping voice, he demanded, "Which one has it?"

Cwen glanced furtively at Rhia, who was glaring at her in astonishment. "They promissssed me I could usssse the Galator to make mysssself young again." She waved her shriveled fingers. "Don't you ssssee? My handssss will wither no more!"

Rhia winced with pain. "I can't believe you would do this, after all the years—"

"Which one?" rasped the goblin.

Cwen pointed a knobby finger at me.

The warrior goblin stepped into the grove of elms and aimed his sword at my chest. "Give it to me now. Or shall I make it very painful for you first?"

"Remember what you ssssaid," urged Cwen. "You promisssssed not to harm them."

The goblin wheeled around to face the aging treeling. A thin smile curled his crooked mouth. "I forgot. But did I make any promise about you?"

Cwen's eyes widened in fright. She started to back away.

"No!" cried Rhia.

It was too late. The goblin's sword whizzed through the air, slicing off one of Cwen's arms.

She shrieked, grasping the open wound as brown blood gushed from it.

"There." The goblin's wheezing laughter filled the air. "Now you won't have to worry about that old hand any more!" He advanced at Cwen. "Now let's do the other one."

Screaming in terror, blood pouring from her stunted arm, Cwen stumbled off into the mist.

"Let her go," rasped the goblin. "We have more important work to do." He jabbed his sword, dripping with brown blood, at my throat. "Now, where were we?"

I swallowed. "If you kill me, you'll never know how it works."

A sinister look filled the goblin's face. "Now that you remind me, my master did tell me to keep alive the person who wears it. But he said nothing about keeping your friends alive."

I sucked in my breath.

"Perhaps if I agree to spare your friends, though, you will tell me how it works." He winked at another goblin. "Then my dear master and I will have some bargaining to do."

He pivoted to Shim, who was shaking in fear, and kicked him so hard he flew across the grove. "Shall I start our fun with this dirty little dwarf? No, I think not." He turned to Rhia, his thin eyes gleaming. "A girl of the forest! What an unexpected pleasure."

Rhia stepped backward.

The goblin nodded, and two members of his band lunged at her. Each of them seized one of her leaf-draped arms.

"Give it to me," ordered the goblin.

I glanced at Rhia, then back at him. How could I possibly give up the Galator?

"Right now!"

I did not move.

"All right then. We'll amuse ourselves while you make up your mind." He flicked his wrist at Rhia. "To start with, break both of her arms."

Instantly the goblins wrenched Rhia's arms behind her back. At the same time, she cried out, "Don't do it, Emrys! Don't—"

She shrieked with pain.

"No!" I pleaded. I pulled the Galator out of my tunic. The jewels glinted darkly in the mist. "Spare her."

The goblin smiled savagely. "Give it to me first."

Rhia's captors twisted her arms harder, almost lifting her off the ground. She shrieked again.

I removed the cord from my neck. The grove was silent, except for the sad creaking of the old elm. I hefted the precious pendant, then handed it over.

The goblin snatched it from me. As he gazed into the jeweled object, he wheezed excitedly. Meanwhile, his greenish tongue danced around his lips. Then he smirked at me. "I have changed my mind. First I will kill your friends, and then I will ask you how it works."

"No!"

All the goblins wheezed in laughter. Their immense chests shook at their leader's joke, while Rhia winced painfully.

"All right," rasped the goblin. "Maybe I will be merciful. Show me how it works. Now!"

I hesitated, not knowing what to do. If there was ever a moment to break my vow and call upon my powers, this was it. Did I dare? Yet even as I asked myself the question, my mind filled with surging, searing flames. The screams of Dinatius. The smell of my own burning flesh.

Try, you coward! a voice within me cried. *You must try!* Yet, just as urgently, another voice answered: *Never again! Last time you destroyed your eyes. This time you will destroy your very soul. Never again!*

"Show me!" commanded the goblin. Even through the thickening mist, I saw his muscles tighten. Raising his sword, he aimed the blade at Rhia's neck.

Still I hesitated.

Just then a strange wind, wilder by the second, shook the branches of the old elm in the center of the grove. Its creaking rose to a scream. As the goblin looked up, the tree snapped free of its roots and toppled over. He had only enough time to howl in agony as the tree crashed down on top of him.

I reached for the Galator, which had dropped to the ground. I slung the leather cord over my neck. With my other hand, I grabbed the fallen goblin's sword and started slashing at another member of the band. The goblin, far stronger than I, quickly backed me against the trunk of the downed tree.

The goblin reared back to strike me down. Suddenly, he froze.

A look of sheer horror came over his face—horror that I had seen only once before, in Dinatius when the flames swallowed him.

I whirled around. Then I, too, froze. The sword fell from my hand. For out of the swirling mist came a gargantuan white spider, her jaws slavering.

"Huuungry," bellowed the great spider in a blood-curdling voice. "I aaam huuungry."

Before I knew what was happening, Rhia grabbed me by the wrist and pulled me out of the path of the Grand Elusa. To the shrieks of the cornered goblin, we ran down the hill, closely pursued by Shim. The little giant sprinted almost as fast as we did ourselves, his feet kicking up a cloud of dirt and leaves.

Two of the warrior goblins dodged the monster, leaving their companions to fend for themselves, and chased after us. Wheezing and cursing, waving their swords in the air, they pursued us through the mist-shrouded boulders. Though we charged with all our speed down the hillside, they gained on us steadily. Soon they were almost on top of Shim.

Suddenly a river appeared out of the mist. Rhia cried out, "The water! Jump in the water!"

With no time to ask questions, Shim and I obeyed. We hurled ourselves into the fast-flowing water. The goblins plunged in after us, thrashing their swords in the current.

"Help us!" Rhia shouted, although I had no idea to whom. Then she slapped her hands wildly against the water's surface.

At once, a wave began to crest in the middle of the river. A great, glistening arm of water rose up, bearing Rhia, Shim, and myself in the palm of its hand. The liquid fingers curled over us like a waterfall, as the hand lifted us high above the river's cascading surface. Spray, sparkling with rainbows, surrounded us. The arm of water whisked us downstream, leaving our pursuers far behind.

Minutes later, the arm melted back into the river itself, dumping us on a sandbar. We climbed out of the water, bedraggled but safe. And, in the case of Shim, considerably cleaner as well.

XXIII

GREAT LOSSES

Rhia collapsed on the bank, her garb of leaves wet and glistening in the sun. As the surface of the river returned to normal, a thin finger of water splashed across her hand. It clung there for an instant before dissolving into the sand.

But she did not seem to notice. Morosely, she kicked at the emerald reeds by the river's edge.

I sat down beside her. "Thank you for saving us."

"Thank the river, not me. The River Unceasing is one of my oldest friends in the forest. He bathed me as an infant, watered me as a child. Now he has saved us all."

I glanced at the waterway, then at Shim, who had flopped down on his back in the sun. For the first time, no dirt and honey covered his clothing, and I noticed that his baggy shirt was woven of some sort of yellowish bark.

Suddenly, I remembered the yellow-rimmed eye of Trouble. Had the brave hawk eluded that swarm of bees? If he had not, had he survived their wrath? And if he had, would he ever be able to find me again? My shoulder felt strangely bereft without him sitting there.

I turned back to Rhia, who looked more glum than I. "You don't seem very glad."

"How can I be glad? I lost two friends today—one old, one new." Her eyes wandered across my face. "Cwen I've known ever since she found me abandoned so long ago. The old elm I met only a few minutes before she felled herself to spare us harm. They couldn't be more different—one crooked and bent, the other straight and tall. One stole my loyalty, the other gave me life. But I grieve for both."

I heaved a sigh. "That elm won't see its saplings ever again."

She lifted her chin a bit. "Arbassa wouldn't agree. Arbassa would say that they'll meet again in the Otherworld. That we all will, someday."

"Do you really believe that?"

She drew a deep breath. "I'm . . . not sure. I know I *want* to believe it. But whether we really will meet after the Long Journey, I don't know."

"What Long Journey?"

"It's the voyage to the Otherworld, after a Fincayran dies. Arbassa says the more a person needs to learn when she dies, then the longer her Long Journey must be."

"In that case, even if the Otherworld is real, it would take me *forever* to get there."

"Maybe not." She glanced at the rushing river, then back at me. "Arbassa also told me that, sometimes, the bravest and truest souls are spared the Long Journey completely. Their sacrifice is so great that they are brought right to the Otherworld, at the very instant of death."

I scoffed at this. "So instead of dying, they just . . . disappear? One second they're here, writhing in pain, and the next second they're in the Otherworld, dancing merrily? I don't think so."

Rhia lowered her head. "It does sound hard to believe."

"It's impossible! Especially if they're not capable of such a sacrifice anyway."

"What do you mean by that?"

"If they're too cowardly!" I bit my lip. "Rhia, I . . . could have done more, much more, to help you."

She looked at me sympathetically. "What more could you have done?"

"I have some, well, powers. Nothing to do with the Galator. I don't begin to understand them. Except that they are strong—too strong."

"Powers like your second sight?"

"Yes, but stronger. Fiercer. Wilder." For a moment I listened to the churning water of the River Unceasing. "I never asked for such powers! They just came to me. Once, in a rage, I used them badly, and they cost me my eyes. They cost another boy much more. They weren't meant for mortals, these powers! I promised never to use them again."

"Who did you promise?"

"God. The Great Healer of Branwen's prayers. I promised that, if only I might somehow see again, I would give up my powers forever. And God heard my plea! But still . . . I should have used them back there. To save you! Promise or no promise."

She peered at me through her tangle of curls. "Something tells me that this promise isn't the only reason you didn't want to use your powers."

My mouth went dry. "The truth is, I fear them. With all my heart I fear them." I pulled a reed out of the shallow water and twisted it roughly with my fingers. "Branwen once told me that God gave me those powers to use, if I could only learn to master them. To use them *well*, she said, with wisdom and love. But how can you use wisely something that you fear to touch? How can you use lovingly something that could destroy your eyes, your life, your very soul? It's impossible!"

She waited quite a while before responding. Then she waved toward the white-capped waters. "The River Unceasing appears to be just a line of water, flowing from here to there. Yet he is more. Much more. He is all that he is—including whatever hides beneath the surface."

"What does that have to do with me?"

"Everything. I think Branwen was right. If someone—God, Dagda, or whoever—gave you special powers, they are for you to use. Just as the River Unceasing has his own powers to use. You are all that you are."

I shook my head. "So I should ignore my promise?"

"Don't ignore it, but ask yourself if that is really what this God wanted you to do."

"He gave me back my sight."

"He gave you back your *powers*."

"That's insane!" I exclaimed. "You have no idea—"

A loud snort from somewhere nearby cut me off. I jumped, thinking it came from a wild boar. Then came the snort again, and I realized that it was not a boar after all. It was Shim. He had fallen asleep on the sandbar.

Rhia watched the tiny figure. "He snores loud enough to be a true giant."

"At least, with him, you can see what he really is with just one look. With me, it's not so simple."

She turned back to me. "You worry about who you are too much. Just be yourself, and you'll find out eventually."

"Eventually!" I stood angrily. "Don't try to tell me about my life. Stick to your own life, if you please."

She stood to face me. "It might help you to think about some-body's life besides your own! I've never met anybody more wrapped up in himself. You're the most selfish person I've ever met! Even if you are—" She stopped herself. "Forget it. Just go away and worry about yourself some more."

"I think I'll do just that."

I stomped off into the thick forest by the River Unceasing. Too angry to watch where I was going, I crashed through the under-brush, bruising my shins and scraping my thighs. This made me all the angrier, and I cursed loudly. Finally, I sat down on a rotting trunk that was already mostly a mound of soil.

Suddenly I heard a gruff voice shout, "Get him!"

Two warrior goblins, the same ones we had eluded upstream, jumped from the underbrush and threw me to the ground. One of them pointed a sword at my chest. The other produced a large sack made of roughly stitched brown cloth.

"None of your tricks this time," growled the goblin with the sword. He beckoned to the other with a burly, gray-green hand. "Get him in the sack."

At that instant, a piercing whistle shot from the sky. The goblin with the sword cried out and fell back, his arm bleeding from the gouges of talons.

"Trouble!" I rolled out of the fray and jumped to my feet.

The merlin, talons slashing and wings flapping in the face of the goblin, drove him back several paces. Every time the goblin slashed with his sword, Trouble dived into his face, ripping at the eyes beneath the pointed helmet. Despite the huge size advantage of the goblin, the small hawk's ferocity was proving too much.

But Trouble did not count on the other goblin joining the battle. Before I could shout any warning, the second warrior whipped his powerful hand through the air. He caught the hawk in mid-dive. Trouble slammed into the trunk of a tree and fell stunned to the ground. He lay there, utterly still, his wings spread wide.

The last thing I saw was the first goblin raising his sword to chop the merlin into pieces. Then something smashed me on the head and day turned into night.

XXIV

THE SWITCH

Conscious again, I sat bolt upright. Though my head still swam, I could make out the massive boughs of trees all around me. I inhaled the rich, moist air. I listened to the quiet whispering of the branches, which sounded strangely somber. And I knew that I must still be in Druma Wood.

No sign anywhere of the goblins. Or of Trouble. Was it all a bad dream? Then why did my head hurt so much?

"You is awake, I sees."

Startled, I turned. "Shim! What happened?"

The little giant examined me warily. "You is never very nicely to me. Is you going to hurts me if I tells you?"

"No, no. You can be sure of that. I won't hurt you. Just tell me what happened."

Still reticent, Shim rubbed his pear-shaped nose thoughtfully.

"I won't hurt you. Certainly, definitely, absolutely."

"All rights." Keeping his distance, he paced back and forth on the mossy soil. "The girl, the nicely one, she hears you fightsing. She is upset the goblinses capture you. She wants to finds you, but I tells her this is madness. I do try, I do try!"

At this point he sniffed. His eyes, more pink than usual, squinted at me. A tear rolled down his cheek, making a wide curve around his nose.

"But she does not listen to Shim. I comes with her, but I is scared. Very, very, very scared. We comes through the woods and finds the place where you fights the goblinses."

I grabbed him by the arm. Small though it was, it felt as muscled as a sailor's. "Did you see a hawk? A little one?"

The little giant pulled away. "She finds some feathers, all bloody, by a tree. But no hawk. She is sad, Shim can tell. This hawk, he is your friend?"

Friend. The word surprised me as much as it saddened me. Yes, the bird I would have given anything to lose just a day ago had, indeed, become my friend. Just in time to leave me. Once again I knew the pain of losing what I had only just found.

"You is sad, too."

"Yes," I said quietly.

"Then you is not going to like the rest. It isn't nicely, not at all."

"Tell me."

Shim stepped over to a hefty hemlock root and sat down dejectedly. "She follows your trail. Shim comes, too, but I is more and more scared. We finds the place where goblinses camp. They is fightsing. Pushing and shouting. Then . . . she makes the switch."

I gasped. "The switch?"

Another tear rolled down his cheek, rounding the edge of his nose. "I tells her not to do it! I tells her! But she shushes me quietly and sneaks up to the sack holding you. She unties it, pulls you out, over to these bushes. She tries, we both tries, to wakens you. But you is like dead. So she climbs into the sack herself! I tries to stop her, but she says . . ."

"What? Tell me!"

"She says that she must do it, for you is the Druma's only hope."

My heart turned into lead.

"Then the goblinses stop fightsing. Without looksing into the sack, they carries her off."

"No! No! She shouldn't have done that!"

Shim cringed. "I knows you is not going to like it."

"As soon as they find her, they'll . . . oh, it's too horrible!"

"It is horrible, it is."

Images of Rhia crowded my mind. Feasting beneath the fruity boughs of the shomorra. Showing me constellations in the darkest parts of the night sky. Greeting Arbassa with a shower of dew on her face. Wrapping her finger around my own. Watching me, and the glowing Galator, within the crystal cave.

"My only two friends, gone in the same day." I slammed my fist against the moss-covered turf. "It's always the same for me! Whatever I find, I lose."

Shim's tiny shoulders drooped. "And there's nothing we can do to stops it."

I swung my face toward his. "Oh, yes there is." Wobbly though I was, I forced myself to stand. "I'm going after her."

Shim recoiled, and nearly fell backward off the root. "You is full of madness!"

"Maybe so, but I'm not going to lose the one friend I have left without a fight. I'm going after them, wherever they took her. Even if it means going all the way to the Shrouded Castle itself."

"Madness," repeated Shim. "You is full of madness."

"Which way did they go?"

"Down the river. They is marching fast."

"Then I will, too. Good-bye."

"Wait." Shim grabbed hold of my knee. "I is full of madness myself."

Though touched by the little giant's intention, I shook my head. "No. I can't take you, Shim. You'll just get in the way."

"I is not any fighter. That is truly. I is scared of almost everything. But I is full of madness."

I sighed, knowing I was not much of a fighter myself. "No."

"I asks you, please."

"No."

"That girl. She is sweet to me, sweet like honey! I only wants to help her."

For several seconds, I studied the upturned face by my knee.

"All right," I said at last. "You may come."

▣ PART THREE ▣

XXV

A STAFF AND
A SHOVEL

For hours, we followed the River Unceasing, clambering over smooth stones and low branches. Finally the river curled to the south, and we reached the eastern edge of Druma Wood. Through the thinning trees, I viewed the bright line of the river and, beyond that, the shadowed plains of the Blighted Lands. From this vantage point, there could be no doubt that the River Unceasing had been the sparkling waterway that I had glimpsed from the dune on my first day on Fincayra.

Downriver some distance, I could make out a group of egg-shaped boulders. They straddled both sides, and at least one sat in the middle of the waterway. The channel looked wider and shallower in that area. If so, it would make a good place to cross. On the opposite bank, a stand of trees had been planted in parallel rows, like an orchard. Yet if indeed it was an orchard, it was the most scraggly one I had ever come across.

Twigs snapped behind me. I whirled around to see Shim, struggling to get through some ferns. Several green arms wrapped around his stubby legs. As he twisted and jumped in the ferns, his floppy yellow shirt, hairy feet, and prominent nose combined to make him look more like a poorly dressed puppet than a person. But his coarse brown hair (still wadded with honey, dirt, and sticks), not to mention his fiery pink eyes, made it clear that he was alive. And angry.

"Madness," he muttered as he finally broke free of the ferns. "This is madness!"

"Turn back if you like," I suggested.

Shim scrunched his bulbous nose. "I knows your thinking! You wants me not to goes!" He drew himself up, which still made him only a bit taller than my knee. "Well, I goes. I goes to rescue her."

"It won't be easy, you know."

The little giant folded his arms and frowned at me.

I turned my second sight once more toward the lands across the river. It struck me that everything, including the trees in the orchard, wore blander colors than I had seen in the Druma. Whatever vividness the rest of Fincayra had added to my vision would vanish as soon as we crossed the river. I had grown accustomed to seeing brighter colors in the forest, and even dared to hope that my second sight had improved. But now I knew the truth. My second sight was just as faded as before, as faded as the landscape in front of me.

And, as before, the strange reddish brown color painted the plains beyond. All the eastern lands, but for the black ridges in the distance, showed the color Rhia had described as *dried blood*.

I drew a deep breath of fragrant forest air. I listened, perhaps for the last time, to the continuous whispering of the boughs. I had only barely begun to sense the variety and complexity of this language of the trees, sometimes subtle, sometimes overwhelming. I wondered what they might be saying to me even now, if only I could understand their voices. Silently, I promised myself that if I should ever return to this forest, I would learn its ways, and cherish its secrets.

Just above my head, a hemlock branch quivered, filling the air with spicy scent. Reaching up, I rubbed some of its flat needles between my thumb and forefinger, half hoping that this would make my hand smell forever of the forest. On an impulse, I wrapped my fingers around the middle of the limb. I squeezed tight as if I were clasping another person's hand. I pulled, just enough to feel the branch sway.

Suddenly the branch broke off. Still clasping it, I tumbled into the ferns—and onto Shim.

"You stupidly fool!" The miniature fellow regained his feet, took a swipe at my arm, missed, and fell back into the ferns. "What is you doings?" he cried from the tangle of green fronds. "You almost crushes me."

"Sorry," I replied, trying hard to keep a serious face. "The branch broke."

From behind the mountainous nose, two pink eyes glared at me. "Shim almost broke!"

"I said I'm sorry."

He stood again, growling furiously. "I makes you sorrier." Clenching his fist, he prepared for another swipe.

Just then, I noticed the branch in my hand. To my astonishment, its bark started to peel away. At the same time, the smaller branches attached to the main stem began snapping off, one by one, dropping their needles on my lap. The peeling bark rolled into large curls, then fell away, as if shaved by an invisible knife.

Catching sight of this, Shim lowered his fist. A look of wonder filled his face.

By now the branch in my lap was no longer a branch. It was a sturdy, straight stick, thick and gnarled at the top, tapered at the bottom. Lifting it higher, I could see it stretched a full head taller than myself. I twirled it in my hands, feeling the smooth wooden skin. In a flash, I understood.

Using the stick as support, I lifted myself from the ferns. Standing before the fragrant hemlock tree, I recalled my clumsy attempt to find a staff when I had first entered this forest. I bowed my head to the tree in thanks. Now I held my staff. And more precious by far, I held a small piece of the Druma that would travel with me beyond its borders.

"You isn't going to hit me with that stick, I hopes," said Shim rather meekly.

I looked at him sternly. "If you won't hit me, I won't hit you."

The little figure stiffened. "I didn't want to hurts you."

I raised an eyebrow, but said nothing. Hefting my new staff in my hand, I started striding toward the egg-shaped boulders downriver. Shim followed behind, fighting through the brush, grumbling as much as before but not quite so loudly.

A few moments later we reached the spot. Here the river widened considerably, flowing over a bed of white stones. As I had hoped, the water, while still fast flowing, looked quite shallow. Beneath the boulders, the mud on both banks showed tracks of large, heavy boots.

"Goblinses," said Shim, observing the tracks.

"I'm sure the River Unceasing did not make it easy for them to cross."

Shim glanced up at me. "Myself, I hates to cross rivers. Really, truly, honestly."

I leaned against my staff, grasping the gnarled top. "You don't have to do it. It's your choice."

"How far will you goes?"

"To wherever Rhia is! Since those goblins think they have the Galator in their sack, they are probably heading to Stangmar's castle. I don't know if we can catch them before they get there, but we must try. It's our only hope, and Rhia's."

My second sight scanned the shadowed hills in the distance. A wall of clouds, blacker than any storm clouds that I had ever seen, rose above them, plunging the easternmost hills in total darkness. Rhia's own description of the location of the Shrouded Castle came back to me. *In the darkest of the Dark Hills, where the night never ends.* I must find her before she reached those hills! *Where the night never ends.* For in such darkness I would have no vision. And almost no hope.

Shim swallowed. "All right. I goes. Maybe not alls the way to the castle, but I goes."

"Are you sure? We won't find much honey over there."

He answered by starting to wade into the river. He made his way for a few paces, struggling against the water. As he neared the partly submerged boulder, though, he stumbled. Suddenly he found himself in much deeper water. He shouted, thrashing his little arms. I leaped to his aid just before he went under. Hauling him onto my shoulders, I began to cross.

"Thanks you," panted Shim. He shook himself, spraying water all over my face. "This water is muchly wet."

Carefully, I stepped through the surging water, using my staff for support. "I'd be grateful if you'd keep your hands away from my nose."

"But I needs a handle to holds on to."

"Then hold on to your own nose!" I exclaimed, certain now that I had made a mistake to let him come along.

"All right," he replied with such a nasal voice that I knew he was holding tight to his own nose.

With every step through the rapidly flowing river, I felt something pulling backward against my leather boots, tugging me back toward the forest. It was not the current itself. Rather, it seemed that hundreds of invisible hands were trying to restrain me from leaving the Druma. Whether these hands were in the water, or in myself, I could not tell. But my feet grew increasingly heavy as I neared the opposite bank.

A feeling of foreboding swelled in me. At the same time, I felt an image forming in my mind, an image from some source other than my second sight. I saw strange lights, dozens of them, moving toward me. Suddenly I realized that my hidden powers were at work. This was going to be an image of the future!

"No!" I cried, shaking my head so violently that Shim had to grab my hair to avoid falling off.

The image disappeared. The powers receded. Yet the feeling of foreboding remained, deeper than before.

As I crossed onto the eastern bank, Shim wriggled down from my shoulder. Not without punching me in the ear, however.

"Ow! What was that for?"

"For makings me holds my nose all that way."

The thought of throwing him back into the river crossed my mind, but somehow I resisted. And my anger was swiftly crowded out by the closer view of the orchard. The trees, thin and tormented, looked considerably more frail than even the oldest trees in the Druma. Indeed, those farthest away from the river seemed positively sickly, mere ghosts of living things. We had arrived in the Blighted Lands.

I approached one of the sturdier trees, whose branches draped over the river. Reaching up, I plucked a small, withered fruit. Turning it in my hand, I puzzled at the leathery toughness, the rusty brown color, the wrinkled skin. Sniffing it, I confirmed my suspicion. It was an apple. The scrawniest apple I had ever encountered.

I tossed it to Shim. "Your supper."

The little giant caught it. He looked unsure as he brought the fruit to his lips. Finally, he took a bite. The bitter expression on his face said it all.

"Bleh! You wishes to poison me!"

I smirked. "No. I didn't think you'd take a bite."

"Then you wishes to trick me."

"That I cannot deny."

Shim placed his hands on his hips. "I wishes the girl is here!"

Grimly, I nodded. "I do, too."

At that instant I saw in the distance, beyond the last row of trees, a band of six figures marching out of the eastern plains. They seemed to be heading straight for the orchard. Warrior goblins! Their swords, breastplates and pointed helmets gleamed in the late afternoon sun. I watched them disappear behind a rise. Although the slope hid them, their gruff voices grew steadily louder.

Shim, who had seen them too, stood petrified. "What is we goings to do?"

"Hide someplace."

But where? From where we stood, I could not find even a single rock to crouch behind. The withered vegetation offered no protection. The slope along the bank ran low and smooth, with not so much as a gully.

The goblins neared the top of the rise. Their voices grew louder, as did the heavy stamping of their boots. My heart raced. I scanned the terrain to find any possible hiding place.

"You!" whispered a voice. "Over here!"

I turned to see a head poking out from among the roots of the trees at the far end of the orchard. Shim and I dashed to the spot. We found a deep, newly dug ditch that had not yet been connected with the river. In the ditch stood a broad-shouldered, sunburned man with a strong chin and brown hair, the more so because it was flecked with dirt. Below his bare chest, he wore loose leggings of brown cloth. He gripped his shovel as effortlessly and securely as a practiced soldier grips his sword.

He waved at us with his shovel. "Get in here, lads. Quick."

We did not hesitate to follow the command. I tossed aside my staff and dived into the ditch. Even as Shim dived in behind me, the goblins marched over the rise and entered the orchard. Quickly, the man covered us with dirt and leaves. He left only a small hole where each of us could breathe.

"You there!" called a goblin's voice. From beneath the blanket of dirt, it sounded a bit higher, though no less grating, than the voice of the goblin who had led the band in the Druma.

"Yes?" answered the ditch digger. He sounded perturbed at being interrupted in his work.

"We're searching for a dangerous prisoner. Escaped this morning."

"From who?" asked the man.

"From guards, you buffoon! Former guards, that is. Lost their prisoner, then their heads." He gave a high, wheezing laugh. "Have you seen anybody cross this river? Speak up, man!"

The laborer paused for some time before speaking. I started to wonder whether he might yet give us away.

"Well," he said at last, "I did see somebody."

Beneath the dirt, my stomach clenched.

"Who?"

"It was . . . a young man."

Sweat, mixed with dirt, stung my lips. My heart pounded.

"Where and when?" barked the goblin.

Again the man paused. I debated whether I should try to bolt, hoping to outrun the warriors.

"A few hours ago," answered the laborer. "Heading downstream. Toward the ocean."

"You'd better be right," rasped the goblin.

"I'm right, but I'm also late. Got to finish this irrigation ditch before nightfall."

"Ha! This old orchard needs a lot more than a ditch to save it."

Another goblin voice, slower and deeper than the other, joined in. "Why don't we chop down a few of these trees to lighten this poor fellow's load?"

The whole band wheezed in laughter.

"No," declared the first goblin. "If we're going to catch the prisoner by nightfall, we have no time to lose."

"What did they do with that fool girl?" rasped another goblin as the band marched off, boots pounding on the soil.

I pushed my head out of the dirt too late to hear the full reply. All I caught were the words *of the king* and, a bit later, *better off dead*.

I shook the dirt off my tunic. As the gruff goblin voices faded away, finally swallowed by the sound of the churning river, I crawled out of the ditch and faced the man. "I am grateful. Most grateful."

He planted his shovel in the loose dirt, then extended a burly hand. "Honn is my name, lad. I may be just a common ditch digger, but I know who I like and who I don't. Anyone who is an enemy of those overgrown toads is surely a friend of mine."

I took the hand, which nearly swallowed my own. "I am called Emrys." I nudged the pile of dirt beside my foot. "And my brave companion here is Shim."

Shim popped out, spat some dirt from his mouth, and glared at me.

"We must go now," I said. "We have a long journey ahead of us."

"And where are you bound for?"

I drew a deep breath. "For the castle of the king."

"Not the Shrouded Castle, lad?"

"Yes."

Honn shook his head in disbelief. The gesture revealed his ears, somewhat triangular in shape and pointed at the top, beneath the mat of brown hair. "The Shrouded Castle," he muttered. "Where the Seven Wise Tools, hewn ages and ages ago, are kept. I remember when they belonged to the people. Now they belong just to the king! The plow that tills its own field . . . the hoe that nurtures its seeds . . . the saw that cuts only as much wood as is needed . . ."

He caught himself. "Why do you want to go there?"

"To find someone. A friend."

He stared at me as if I had lost my mind.

"Can you tell me where the castle sits?"

Raising his shovel, he jabbed it at the air in the direction of the Dark Hills. "That way. I can tell you no more, lad, except that you would be wise to change your plans."

"That I can't do."

He grimaced, studying me with care. "You are a stranger to me, Emrys. But I wish you whatever luck there is left in Fincayra."

Honn reached for his shirt beside the ditch. He pulled out a worn dagger with a narrow blade. He twirled it once in his hand, then handed it to me. "Here. You will need this more than I."

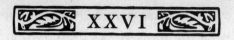 **XXVI**

THE TOWN OF
THE BARDS

I strode across the tundra, trekking toward the rising waves of the Dark Hills. My satchel of herbs felt heavier, now that it also carried Honn's dagger. As my boots crunched on the dry, crusty soil, my staff clicked against the ground. Every so often my shoulder rubbed against the staff's knotty top and I caught a faint scent of hemlock.

Shim, grumbling to himself about madness, struggled to keep pace with me. But I would not slow down for him. We had no time to lose. Over and over the goblin's words *better off dead* echoed in my mind.

Despite the blades of grass, clumps of bracken, and groves of scraggly trees that managed to survive on this tundra, the dominant colors of this plain, stretching to the dark horizon, were dull grays and browns, tinged with rust. Several times I looked over my shoulder at the fading green hills of Druma Wood, trying to recall the lushness of that land. As the sun sank lower against our backs, our shadows grew longer and darker.

I noticed in the distance a stand of dark, leafless trees. Then, drawing nearer, I realized the truth. What had looked like trunks and limbs were really the skeletons of houses and stables—all that remained of a village about the size of Caer Vedwyd. No people or animals were left. The buildings had been burned to the ground. The stone walls had been torn apart. By the side of the ash-strewn road through the village, a wooden cradle, once the bed of a child, lay in splinters. Why this village had been destroyed, no one remained to tell.

We pushed on toward the Dark Hills. Although I stretched both my ears and my second sight for any sign of goblins, I found none. But that was no cause to relax. The first hint of sunset already streaked the sky. In another hour, night would fall. I could only imagine what creatures might prowl this terrain after dark.

Meanwhile, Shim fell farther behind. He kept stopping to rest, I kept urging him to move. His strength was ebbing, just like my vision. Reluctantly, I concluded that we would need to find some sort of shelter before the day ended. Where, though? This desolate plain didn't offer many choices.

We continued to trek over the long, gradual rises and depressions of the land. As our shadows grew, so did my fears. Strange howling sounds, half wolf and half wind, reached our ears. Despite my pleas, Shim lagged ever more.

At last, as I topped a rise, I glimpsed a village below. Warm yellow torches blazed in the streets, while fires burned in the hearths of low houses made of mud brick. My mouth watered when I realized that the smell of burning wood mingled with roasting grain.

Shim approached and traded glances with me. With a joyful cry, he started running down to the village gates. Clumsily, but full of hope, I ran after him.

A man, sitting on the ground by the gates, suddenly leaped to his feet as we came near. He was tall and gaunt, and he held a spear. He wore a simple tunic. A thick black beard covered most of his face. But his unusually large, dark eyes were his most striking feature. Even in the dwindling light, his eyes shone eerily. Yet I could not shake the feeling that their light came less from intelligence than from fear. Indeed, his eyes seemed nearly crazed, like the eyes of an animal frightened to the very edge of death.

Bracing himself, the man pointed his spear at my chest. Though he said nothing, his expression was grim.

"We come in peace," I declared. "We are strangers in this land and seek only some shelter for the night."

The man's large eyes opened still wider, but he said nothing. Instead, he thrust his spear closer, nicking the wood of my staff and barely missing my hand.

"We is hungry," moaned Shim. "Hungry and sleepily."

Again the silent man thrust his spear at us. Only then did I notice the sign behind him, hanging at an angle from one of the gate posts. Carved into a weathered slab of wood, it read, *Welcome to Caer Neithan, Town of the Bards.* Below that were inscribed the words *Here song is ever,* but the phrases that followed had been damaged somehow. I could not be sure, but they seemed to have been scraped away.

Through the gates, I watched a woman, tall and dark like the man, scurry across the town square. Before she slipped into one of the houses, she paused to beckon to two children, perhaps four or five years old, their black hair falling over their shoulders. They darted up to her and the door closed with a slam. It struck me as odd that we heard the padding of their bare feet, but not their voices. The woman, as well as the children, were as silent as the man with the spear.

Then I realized that, in this entire village, not a single voice could be heard. No babies crying. No friends laughing. No neighbors arguing over the price of wheat, the cause of lice, or the likelihood of rain. No sounds of rage, or joy, or sorrow.

No voices at all.

The man jabbed again with his spear, nearly brushing the folds of my tunic. I backed slowly away, still pondering the eerie glow of his eyes. Through my frown, I said to him, "Whatever happened to you and your village, I am sorry."

The spear slashed the air again near my chest.

"Come, Shim. We are not welcome here."

The little giant whimpered, but turned to follow me. We trudged across the tundra, as wordless as the Town of the Bards. In time we left its flickering torches far behind, though its sorrowful silence continued to cling to us.

Behind us, sunset draped a curtain of rich purple over Druma Wood. Before us, the dark night swiftly deepened. I reluctantly gave up hope of finding any shelter on this featureless plain. Yet I knew that I must keep searching, right up to the moment I could no longer see my own staff. Otherwise, like whatever creatures howled hungrily in the distance, Shim and I would have to spend the night in the open.

At that moment I spotted a shape of some sort ahead. It appeared to be a rock—and on the rock, a person.

As we approached, I saw to my surprise that it was a girl. She looked a few years younger than Rhia. Swinging her bare feet, she sat on the rock, watching the purples and blues streak the darkening sky. She did not seem at all afraid to see approaching travelers.

"Hello." She tossed her brown curls that reached almost to her waist. A playful smile illuminated her face.

Cautiously, I drew closer. "Hello."

"Would you like to watch the sunset with me?"

"Thank you, but no." I studied her bright, exuberant eyes, so different from the eyes of the man we had just left. "Shouldn't you be getting back to your home? It's rather late."

"Oh no," she chirped. "I love watching the sunset from here."

I stepped nearer. "Where is your home?"

The girl giggled shyly. "I'll tell you if you'll tell me where you're going."

Perhaps because of her friendly manner, or because she reminded me a little of Rhia, I felt drawn toward this spirited girl. I wanted to speak with her, if only for a moment. I could pretend, in some remote corner of my heart, that I was once more speaking with Rhia herself. And if her village was somewhere nearby, we might yet find shelter for the night.

"Where are you going?" she repeated.

I smiled. "Oh, wherever my shadow may lead me."

Once more she giggled. "Your shadow will disappear fairly soon."

"As will yours. You should go home before it gets any darker."

"Don't worry. My village lies just over that rise there."

While we spoke, Shim edged nearer to the rock on which she sat. Perhaps he too felt drawn to her, for the same reasons as I. For her part, she did not seem to notice his approach. Then, for whatever reason, he halted and started slowly backing away.

Thinking nothing of Shim's movements, I asked the girl, "Do you think it might be possible for us to stay in your village tonight?"

She threw back her head with a hearty laugh. "Of course."

My spirits lifted. We had found shelter after all.

Just then Shim tugged on the bottom of my tunic. As I bent down, the little giant whispered, "I isn't sure, but I think something is strangely about her hands."

"What?"

"Her hands."

Not expecting to find anything, I glanced quickly at the girl's hands. At first, I saw nothing strange. And yet . . . they did seem somehow different. In a way I couldn't quite define. Suddenly, I knew.

Her fingers. Her fingers are webbed.

The alleah bird! Rhia's warning that shifting wraiths always show a flaw of some kind! I reached for the dagger Honn had given to me.

Too late. The girl had already begun to metamorphose into the shape of a serpent. Her brown eyes transformed to red, her skin to scales, her mouth to ruthless jaws. Even as the wraith leaped at my face, a thin veil of discarded skin crackled as it floated to the ground.

I drew the knife barely in time to lash out as the serpent bowled me over backward. Shim shrieked. We rolled on the tundra, a knot of teeth and tail, arms and legs. I could feel the wraith's claws digging into the flesh of my right arm.

Then, almost as swiftly as it had started, the battle stopped. Our two entwined bodies lay utterly still on the ground.

"Emrys?" asked Shim meekly. "Is you dead?"

Slowly, I stirred. I extracted myself from the grasp of the serpent, whose throat had been slashed open by the dagger. Rancid-smelling blood poured out of the gash and down the scaled belly. Weakly, I staggered over to the rock and propped myself against it, clutching my wounded arm.

Shim looked at me admiringly. "You has saved us."

I shook my head. "Plain luck saved us. That . . . and one observant little giant."

XXVII

CAIRPRÉ

The little light remaining fled swiftly. We settled for the night by a barely trickling stream a few hundred paces from the remains of the shifting wraith. Each consumed by his own thoughts, neither of us spoke. While Shim stared hard at the eroded banks to make sure that no deadly creatures hid there, I mixed a poultice from my satchel of herbs.

The herbs smelled vaguely of thyme. And beech root. And Branwen. Gingerly, I patted the poultice on the claw marks on my arm, knowing full well that she would have done much better. I tried to hum to myself one of her soothing chants, but couldn't remember more than a few notes.

I knew, as the darkness submerged us, that my second sight would soon be no help at all. I laid down my staff and leaned back against a rotting tree stump, the dagger clutched in my hand. I hefted the narrow blade that had slain the wraith. Had Honn used it in his labors? Or had he carried it just for protection? Either way, I was now twice indebted to him.

A few faint stars began to appear overhead. I tried to search for some of Rhia's constellations, made not from the stars but from the spaces between them. I thought about the shomorra tree, heavy with fruit. The writing on Arbassa's walls. The crystal cave, all aglow. Yet all that seemed so long ago, so far away.

To my disappointment, the stars were so few and so scattered that I found no patterns at all. Then I realized that even those stars were not growing brighter as the sky darkened. They seemed shrouded somehow. And not by clouds, at least not by ordinary clouds. Something held them back, kept them from lighting this land.

At that moment, I sensed a faint smoky smell in the air, as if a fire burned nearby. I sat up straight, straining my second sight. But I found no flame anywhere.

Stranger still, I noticed that a vague circle of light brightened the area where we lay upon the ground. It came not from the dimly lit stars, but from somewhere else. What else could be shining down on us? Puzzled, I looked closer.

Suddenly I understood. The gentle illumination came not from above, but from below. It came, in fact, from the rotting tree stump!

I rolled away. Cautiously, I took a closer look. I noticed a glowing circle in the top of the stump, as though a door had been cut in the wood, allowing the ring of light to shine through.

"Look here, Shim."

My companion strode over. Seeing the glowing stump, he sucked in his breath. "Now I is sure we camps in the wrong place."

"I know. But this light feels good somehow."

Shim frowned. "The snakely girl feels good at first, too."

Then, without warning, the door popped open. From it emerged a shaggy head with a tall brow and dark, observant eyes. The head of a man.

The eyes, deeper than pools, gazed at me, then at Shim, for a long moment.

"All right," said the stranger in a low, resonant voice. "You can come in. But I don't have any time for stories."

The head disappeared down into the trunk. Shim and I exchanged looks of bewilderment. Stories? What could he mean?

At length, I announced, "I'm going down there. Come with me or stay here, as you choose."

"I stays!" answered Shim decisively. "And you should forgets this foolery and stays, too."

"It's worth the risk if it means we won't have to camp out in the open."

As if to emphasize my point, the distant howling resumed.

"Supposing this man becomes another snakely snake? Supposing you is trapped down in his hole?"

I did not answer. I peered through the door and into a narrow tunnel. Although it was well lighted, which restored my second sight, all I could see from this position was a rough-hewn ladder leading downward. I hesitated, pondering Shim's warning.

The howling swelled in volume.

Clutching my dagger in one hand, I put my feet into the entrance and began to climb down. I noticed as I descended that the wooden rungs were heavily worn, as if many hundreds of hands and feet had entered by them. And, I hoped, left by them.

Down I climbed, one rung after another. Soon a leathery, musty smell drifted up the tunnel. It was a smell that excited me, for I had encountered it only one place before, in the Church of Saint Peter at Caer Myrddin. The farther I descended, the stronger it became.

It was the smell of books.

When at last I reached the bottom, I stared in astonishment. For hundreds and hundreds of volumes surrounded me. They covered the walls and floor of this underground room from end to end and top to bottom.

Books everywhere! Books of all thicknesses, colors, heights, and also languages—judging from the varied scripts and symbols on the covers. Some bound in leather. Some so tattered that they wore no covers at all. Some formed of papyrus scrolls from the Nile. Some, made of pergamentium from the land the Greeks called Anatolia and the Romans called Lesser Asia, with the feel of sheepskin.

Books sat in rows on the sagging shelves that lined the walls. They lay stacked in piles on the floor, so many that only a narrow path remained from one side of the room to the other. They huddled in a mound beneath the heavy wooden table, itself cluttered with papers and writing supplies. They even covered most of the bed of sheepskins in the corner.

Across from the bed, a small but adequate pantry held shelves of fruits and grains, breads and cheeses. Two low stools sat to one side, and a hearth to the other. The hearth crackled with a flame bright enough to light the living space as well as the tunnel leading to the stump above. Next to the fire sat a cauldron made of iron. Bowls, grimy with leftover food, lay stacked beside the cauldron, perhaps in the hope that given enough time they might eventually wash themselves.

Sitting in a high-backed chair by the far wall, the long-haired man sat reading. His tangled brows, streaked with gray, sprouted like brambles above his eyes. He wore a flowing white tunic, with a high collar that nearly touched his chin. For a moment or two, he did not seem to notice that I had joined him.

I put the dagger back into my satchel. The man did not move. Feeling uncomfortable, I cleared my throat.

Still the man did not look up from his book.

"Thank you for inviting me."

At this the man stirred. "You are most welcome. Now would you mind shutting the hatch to my front door? Drafts, you know. Not to mention the unmentionable beasts who like to prowl at night. You'll see the lock."

He paused, noticing something. "And tell your diminutive friend that he is under no obligation at all to join us. He need not feel awkward in the least. Of course, it is too bad that he will miss out on my fresh clover honey."

Suddenly, I heard a slam up the tunnel. Seconds later, Shim stood beside me.

"I changes my mind," he said sheepishly.

The man closed the book, replaced it on the shelf behind his chair. "Nothing like a good read to finish a day of good reads."

Despite myself, I grinned. "I have never seen so many books."

The man nodded. "Stories help me. To live. To work. To find the meaning hidden in every dream, every leaf, every drop of dew."

I blanched. Had not Branwen said almost the same thing to me once?

"I only wish," continued the man, "that I had more time to enjoy them. These days, as you surely know, we have other distractions."

"You mean goblins and the like."

"Yes. But it is *the like* that I most dislike." He shook his head gravely, pulling down another book. "That is why I have so little time for my favorite stories right now. I am trying to find some sort of answer in the books, so that Fincayra's own story does not have to end before its time."

I nodded. "The Blight is spreading."

Without looking up from his book, he replied, "So it is! Sophocles—do you know the Greek playwrights?—had a stunning phrase. In *Oedipus,* as I recall. *A rust consumes the buds.* And that is indeed what has been happening to our land. Rust. Consuming the buds. Consuming everything."

He pulled down another book and placed it on top of the first one, still on his lap. "Yet we mustn't lose hope. The answer just might lie hidden in some forgotten volume. *It's worth a look in every book.*" He raised his head, looking slightly embarrassed. "Forgive the rhyme. They just slip out, it seems. Even if I try to stop making them, I can't. As I was saying, *There are sages in these pages.*"

He cleared his throat. "But enough of that now." He waved toward the pantry. "Are you hungry? Do help yourselves. Honey is on the left, by the plums. Breads of many kinds are there, twice-baked in the manner of the Slantos to the north."

"I've not heard of them," I confessed.

"Not surprising." The man went back to flipping through pages. "Most of those northerly reaches are unexplored and uncharted. And consider the Lost Lands! There may be people there, most unusual people, who have never been visited by anyone."

He bent closer to the book, pondering a particular page. "And may I ask your names?"

"I am called Emrys."

The man lifted his head, eyeing me in an odd sort of way. "Called? You say it as if you were not sure it is your true name."

I bit my lip.

"What about your companion?"

I glanced at the small figure who was already at the pantry, devouring some bread slathered with fresh clover honey. "That is Shim."

"And I am Cairpré, a humble poet. Forgive me for being too preoccupied to be a good host. But I am always glad to welcome a visitor."

He closed the book, still observing me. "Especially a visitor who reminds me so much of a dear friend."

I felt a strange surge of fear as I asked, "What friend might that be?"

"I was a close friend . . . of your mother."

The words fell on me with the weight of anvils. "My—my mother?"

Cairpré dropped the books on his lap onto the chair. He stepped over to me and placed a hand on my shoulder. "Come. We have much to discuss."

A SIMPLE
QUESTION

Cairpré led me to the twin stools by the pantry. After removing some leather-bound books from the seats, we sat down. Shim, for his part, had already climbed onto the pantry's bottom shelf and seemed very comfortable, surrounded by ample supplies for his supper.

The poet observed me silently for several seconds. "You have changed since I last saw you. Quite a lot! So much I didn't even recognize you at first. Though you could, I suppose, say the same about me. It has been five or six years, after all."

I could not contain my excitement. "You have met me before? And my mother as well?"

His eyes darkened. "You don't remember?"

"I don't remember any of my childhood! Up to the day I washed ashore, it's all a mystery." I grasped the sleeve of his white tunic. "But you can help me! You can answer my questions! Tell me everything you can. First—about my mother. Who is she? Where is she? Why did you say she *was* a friend?"

Cairpré leaned back on his stool, clasping his knee with both hands. "It seems as though I will be telling you a story, after all."

After a pause, he began. "There came a day when a woman, a

human woman, arrived on the shores of this island. She came from the land of the Celts, from a place called Gwynedd."

A sudden pang of doubt struck me. Had I been wrong all along about Branwen? Hesitantly, I asked, "What was her name?"

"Elen."

I breathed a sigh of relief.

"Now, Elen looked very different from us Fincayrans. Her skin was lighter than most, more creamy than ruddy. Her ears were shaped differently, too—more round than triangular. Truly, she was beautiful. But her most striking feature was her eyes. They glowed with a color unlike any ever seen on this island. Pure blue, untinted with gray or brown. Blue as a sapphire. So she was called Elen of the Sapphire Eyes."

I shuddered.

"She came here," he continued, "because of her love for a man of Fincayran blood. A man from this world, not her own. And soon after she arrived, she discovered yet another love." He glanced around the room. "Books! She loved books, from all lands and all languages. In fact, we met over a book, when she came here to collect one I had borrowed that was slightly overdue—a decade or so. After that, she came here often to read and talk. She sat in the very chair where you sit now! Especially, she was interested in the art of healing, as it has been practiced through the ages. She herself had a gift for healing others."

Again I shuddered.

Remembering something, Cairpré smiled to himself. "But her favorite books of all, I think, were the stories of the Greeks."

"Is this true?" I demanded. "Do you swear this is true?"

"It is."

"She told me so little. Not even her name! She only called herself Branwen."

Cairpré turned toward a high shelf of books. "How like her to choose a name from legend. Yet it grieves me to hear that she chose such a tragic one."

"Alas that I was ever born," I quoted.

The poet gazed at me. "So you know the legend?"

"I know it." My lower lip trembled. "But I didn't know *her*. Not at all. She said so little about herself that I refused . . ."

A knot filled my throat, and I started to sob quietly. The poet watched me with the compassion of someone feeling the same stab of pain. Yet he did not try to comfort me. He merely let me shed the tears that I needed to shed.

Finally, in a hoarse whisper, I finished the sentence. "I refused . . . to call her Mother."

Cairpré said nothing for some time. When at last he spoke, he asked a simple question.

"Did she love you?"

Raising my head, I nodded slowly. "Yes."

"Did she care for you when you needed help?"

"Yes."

"Then you did know her. You knew her down to her soul."

I wiped my cheeks with my tunic. "Perhaps. But it doesn't feel that way. Can you tell me some . . . about my father?"

A strange, faraway look came into Cairpré's eyes. "Your father was an impressive youth. Strong, willful, passionate. *Full of zest, the ardent quest.* No, the rhythm's all wrong. Let me try again. *Awake! Alive! A startling drive.* There, that's better. In our most ancient tongue, his name means Tree Climber, because as a boy he so enjoyed climbing trees. Sometimes he would even climb to the top of a tall tree and stay there just for the experience of riding out a fierce storm."

I laughed out loud, understanding more fully than the poet knew.

"Yet Tree Climber's childhood, I believe, was far from joyous. His mother, Olwen, was a daughter of the sea, one of those beings the Earth folk call *mer people,* though Fincayrans prefer *people of the mer.* So he—like you—was born with the strange depths of the sea in his bones. Yet Olwen's Long Journey came too soon."

"I've heard about this Long Journey."

Cairpré sighed. "And long it is. Arduous, too, according to *The Glories of Dagda.* Unless, of course, you happen to be one of the few who are taken to the Otherworld right in the moment of death. But that is rare, extremely rare."

"You were talking about my father."

"Oh, yes. Your father. Since Olwen died when he was but an infant, your father was reared by his own father, a Fincayran known as Tuatha, son of Finvarra. Now Tuatha was a masterful wizard and a powerful man. It is said that even the great spirit Dagda would sometimes come to his home to confer on high matters. But alas, this wizard had very little time for his own son's needs. And Tuatha had even less time when he discovered—when your father was about the age you are now—that the boy lacked the gift of making magic. *The powers,* as Tuatha called them."

I swallowed hard, knowing that such powers were not a gift, but a curse. I recalled the prophecy of my grandfather, as told to me by Branwen—Elen—my mother. That she would one day have a son who would possess powers even greater than his own. *Whose magic would spring from the very deepest sources.* Such folly! He might have been a great wizard, but he could not have been more wrong.

"Your father's life changed, however, when he first met Elen during one of his travels to Earth. They fell deeply in love. Although it is rarely done, and still more rarely done with success, this man and woman of different worlds were married. Elen came to live in Fincayra. And because of her love, a new strength came into his heart, a new calm into his eye. *The loving bond may reach beyond.* Their happiness was great, for a time, though I am afraid that time was all too brief."

Grasping the edge of the stool where my own mother had sat long ago, I leaned forward. "What happened?"

Cairpré's face, so serious already, grew still more serious. "Your father," he began, then paused to clear his throat. "Your father was part of the royal circle of Stangmar. When the evil spirit Rhita Gawr, who has long had designs on Fincayra, began courting the king, your father was present. And your father—like the rest of the circle—slipped gradually into trouble. The same trouble that eventually corrupted the king, as well as the whole of Fincayra."

"Didn't my father try to resist Rhita Gawr? Didn't he try to keep the king from listening to him?"

"If he tried, he failed." The poet sighed. "You must understand. Many good people have been fooled by Rhita Gawr's treachery. Your father was only one of them."

I felt heavier than a boulder. "So my father helped to bring the Blight to Fincayra."

"That is true. But all of us bear some of the blame."

"What do you mean?"

Cairpré winced, so painful was the memory. "It all happened gradually, you see. So gradually that no one quite understood what was happening—until it was too late. No one but Stangmar himself understands just how it started. All anyone else knows is that, somehow, Rhita Gawr offered to protect the king in a time of need. To have refused this help would have placed the king, and therefore Fincayra, in some sort of danger. Rhita Gawr must have planned it out very carefully, because he made it almost impossible for the king not to accept his help. And Stangmar did just that."

He paused to lift a small brown moth off his white collar and place it gently on top of a pile of books by his stool. "That one little decision has led to a cascade of tragedies, one after another. When Rhita Gawr convinced Stangmar that his enemies were plotting to overthrow him, the king forged a questionable alliance with the warrior goblins and the shifting wraiths. Out of their dark crevasses they crawled! Then came the rumors that the giants, Fincayra's most ancient people, had suddenly become dangerous. Not only to the king, but to the rest of us, as well. So not many objected when Stangmar ordered the giants hunted down. Giants always seemed so . . . *different* to most people. Those of us who did object were either ridiculed or battered into silence. Next Stangmar heeded Rhita Gawr's warnings and began a campaign to cleanse the land of all the king's enemies—and to confiscate the Treasures of Fincayra because they might somehow fall into enemy hands."

"Didn't anyone try to stop this?"

"Some brave souls tried, but they were too few and too late. Stangmar stamped out any opposition, burning whole villages to the ground on the slightest suspicion of treason. Yet even that was preferable to what he did to the village of Caer Neithan."

I jumped. "You mean . . . the Town of the Bards?"

"You know of it? Oh, what a loss, to our world and all the others! For ages beyond memory, that town has been a fountain of music and song, home of our most inspired storytellers, nurturer of generations of bards. Laon the Lame was born there! Pwyll wrote her first poem there! *The Vessel of Illusion* was composed there! I could go on and on. *Here song is ever in the air, while story climbs the spiral stair.*"

With a nod, I observed, "The words on the sign."

"Quite so. They were written in truth, though now they are but a mockery. I should know, since I wrote them myself." He sighed. "Caer Neithan was my birthplace, as well."

"What happened there?"

Cairpré studied me sadly for a while. "Of all the fabled Treasures stolen by Stangmar—the sword Deepercut that can slice to the soul, the Flowering Harp that can call forth the spring, the Cauldron of Death that can end any life—the one most celebrated by bards throughout time was the Caller of Dreams. It was a horn with the power to bring wondrous dreams to life, and for centuries it was used only sparingly and wisely. But with the help of Rhita Gawr, Stangmar used it to punish Caer Neithan for harboring some who dared to oppose his policies. He called to life the most horrible dream ever beheld by any bard—and inflicted it upon the entire town."

Remembering the half-crazed eyes of the man with the spear, I was almost afraid to ask, "What dream was that?"

The poet's eyes grew cloudy. "That every man, woman, and child in that village would never speak, nor sing, nor write again. That the instruments of their souls—their very voices—would be silenced forever."

His voice a mere whisper, he continued. "By this time, no one was left to protest when Rhita Gawr urged Stangmar to destroy his own castle, the grandest yet most welcoming home any king or queen could ever ask for, including its library of books, a library more vast than my own by a thousandfold. And why? On the grounds that it was not safe enough from attack! So Rhita Gawr, calling it a gesture of friendship no doubt, built a new castle for Stangmar, a castle infused with his own evil power. Thus arose the Shrouded Castle, ever spinning on its foundation, from which spreads the impenetrable cloud that now darkens our sky and the terrible Blight that now strangles our soil."

He rubbed his chin. "The castle is guarded by Rhita Gawr's own deathless warriors, the ghouliants. Their lives, if you can call them lives—for they are actually men whose bodies were raised from the dead by Rhita Gawr—will never end, at least not by mortal blows. For their lives are sustained by the very turning of the Shrouded Castle! So as long as the castle keeps turning, they will remain there, performing deeds even darker than the Shroud itself."

I ached for Rhia. If she was still alive, she was probably in the bowels of that very castle! She would be at the mercy of the ghouliants, and of Stangmar himself. What would become of her when he concluded that she neither could nor would help him obtain the Galator, the last Treasure? I shuddered at the thought. And I despaired at the Grand Elusa's belief that the only way to topple Stangmar was to destroy the Shrouded Castle. I might as well wish to sprout wings!

"Now you can see," Cairpré added, "That Stangmar is truly the prisoner of Rhita Gawr. And as Stangmar is imprisoned, so are we all."

"Why hasn't Dagda intervened to stop all this? He is battling Rhita Gawr on other fronts, isn't he?"

"That he is. In the Otherworld as well as in this world. But Dagda believes, as Rhita Gawr does not, that to win ultimately he must respect people's free will. Dagda allows us to make our own choices, for good or ill. So if Fincayra is to be saved, it must be saved by the Fincayrans."

XXIX

LOST WINGS

Cairpré reached around Shim, who had managed to spread himself (as well as clover honey) across the pantry shelf. The long-haired man tore off a slab of dark, grainy bread and ripped it in half. Keeping one piece, he handed me the other.

"Here. Before your little friend eats it all."

Shim did not seem to notice and continued stuffing himself.

I half grinned and took a bite of the crusty bread. It felt hard, almost like wood, until some vigorous chewing softened it up a bit. Then, to my surprise, it swiftly dissolved into liquid, filling my mouth with a tangy, minty flavor. Almost as soon as I swallowed, a wave of nourishment flowed through me. I straightened my back. Even the usual pain between my shoulder blades eased a little. I took another bite.

"You like ambrosia bread, I can see," said Cairpré through a mouthful. "One of the Slantos' finest achievements, without doubt. Still, it is said that no one from other parts of Fincayra has ever tasted any of the Slantos' most special breads, and that they guard those precious recipes with their lives."

I scanned the walls and floor of the room, so densely jammed with volumes. Being here felt like being in the hold of a ship whose cargo consisted of nothing but books. I remembered Branwen's wistful look when she had spoken about being in a room full of books—this very one, no doubt. Even with the spreading Blight, it must have been difficult for her to leave this room, this land, forever.

I turned back to Cairpré. "Bran—I mean, my mother—must have loved being here, with all your books."

"Indeed she did. She wanted to read the teachings of the Fincayrans, the Druids, the Celts, the Jews, the Christians, the Greeks. She called herself my student, but it was really more the other way around. I learned so much from her."

He glanced at a mound of books at the base of the ladder. On the leather cover of the book on top, a gold-leaf portrait, showing a figure driving a blazing chariot, gleamed in the light of the hearth fire.

"I remember once," he said in a distant voice, "when we talked the whole night through about those remarkable places where beings of mortal flesh and beings of immortal spirit live side by side. Where time flows both in a line and in a circle. Where sacred time and historical time exist together. *In between places,* she called them."

"Like Mount Olympus."

The poet nodded. "Or like Fincayra."

"Was it all the mounting troubles that made her want to leave Fincayra? Or was there something more?"

He eyed me strangely. "Your suspicion is correct. There was something more."

"What?"

"You, my boy."

My brow furrowed. "I don't understand."

"Let me explain. Do you know about the Greek Isle of Delos?"

"Apollo's birthplace. But what does that have to do with me?"

"It was another *in between place*, both sacred and historical at once. That is why the Greeks never allowed anyone to give birth on Delos. They didn't want any mere mortal to be able to claim a birthright to soil that belonged first to the gods. And they killed or banished anyone foolish enough to disobey."

"I still don't see what this has to do with me."

At this moment, Shim released an immense belch, far bigger than one would expect from a person so small. Yet the little giant did not seem aware of it, just as he seemed to have forgotten about Cairpré and myself. He merely patted his belly and returned to the serious matter of fresh clover honey.

Cairpré's shaggy eyebrows lifted in amusement, then his expression darkened. "In the same manner as Delos, it is strictly forbidden that anyone with human blood should ever be born on the island of Fincayra. This is a land not of the Earth, nor of the Otherworld, though it is a bridge between them both. Visitors come here from either world, and they sometimes stay for years. Yet they cannot call this place home."

I leaned closer. "I have been searching for my own home. So help me understand this. If my mother had to leave Fincayra to give birth to me, where did she go? Do you know where I was born?"

"I know," replied the poet, his tone grave. "It was not where you should have been born."

I caught my breath. "Are you saying that I was born on Fincayra, even though I have human blood?"

His face told me everything.

"Does that mean I am in danger?"

"More danger than you know."

"How did that happen? You said it is forbidden."

"I can explain what, but not why." Cairpré scratched the top of his head. "It happened this way. Your parents, aware of Fincayra's ancient law, knew that Elen must sail to another land to give birth. But they also knew that no one can be sure, when setting sail from Fincayra, whether or not he or she will ever return. The passage here is a strange one, as you are well aware. Sometimes the door is open; sometimes it is not. Many who have left this island, hoping desperately to return, have found only a shred of mist upon the waters. Others have met their deaths in the stormy seas. *Nothing is known but we sail alone.*"

He shook his head. "Your mother and father loved each other deeply, and did not want to part. If Tuatha had not commanded your father to stay, I believe he would have sailed with her. Moreover, I suspect that Elen could sense trouble brewing, and did not want to leave him. So they lingered long before parting. Too long. Your mother was already in her ninth month when at last she set sail."

Feeling something warm against my chest, I looked down at my tunic. Beneath the folds, the Galator was glowing faintly, making a circle of green light over my heart. Swiftly, I covered the place with my hand, hoping that Cairpré would not notice and interrupt his tale.

"Soon after the ship had launched, a terrible storm arose on the waves. It was the kind of storm that few sailors since Odysseus have survived. The ship was battered, nearly drowned, and forced back to shore. That very night, huddled in the wreckage of the ship, your mother gave birth." He paused, thinking. "And she named the boy Emrys, a Celtic name from her homeland."

"So that is my true name?"

"Not necessarily! Your true name may not be your given name."

I gave a nod of understanding. "Emrys has never felt right to me. But how do I find my true name?"

The deep-set eyes pondered me. "Life will find it for you."

"I don't know what you mean."

"With luck, you will in time."

"Well, my true name is a mystery, but at least now I know I belong in Fincayra."

Cairpré shook his gray head. "You do, and you do not."

"But you said I was born here!"

"Your place of birth may not be where you belong."

Feeling a surge of frustration, I pulled the Galator out of my tunic. Its jeweled center, still glowing faintly, flared in the light of the fire. "She gave me this! Does this not prove I belong here?"

A new depth of sadness filled the pools beneath Cairpré's brows. "The Galator belongs here, yes. Whether or not you belong here, I do not know."

Exasperated, I demanded, "Must I destroy the castle and the king and all his army, before you will tell me I belong here?"

"I may tell you that one day," answered the poet calmly. "If you tell me the same."

His demeanor, if not his words, soothed me somewhat. I replaced the pendant under my tunic. Feeling again the pain between my shoulder blades, I stretched my arms out wide.

Cairpré observed me knowingly. "So you too feel the pain. In that way you are certainly a son of Fincayra."

"This pain in my shoulders? How should that make any difference?"

"It has made all the difference in the world." Seeing the confusion in my face, he once again leaned back on his stool, clasped his knee, and began to tell a story.

"In the far, far reaches of time, the people of Fincayra walked upon the land, as they do now. Yet they also could do something else. They also could fly."

My eyes widened.

"The gift of flight was theirs. They had lovely white wings, the old legends say, sprouting from between their shoulder blades. So they could soar with the eagles and sail with the clouds. *Wings of white to endless height*. They could venture high above the lands of Fincayra, or even to lands beyond."

For an instant, I could almost feel the flutter of the feisty hawk who would swoop through the air before landing on my shoulder. Trouble had so enjoyed the gift of flight! I missed him, almost as much as I missed Rhia.

I smiled sadly at Cairpré. "So the Fincayrans had both the ears of demons and the wings of angels."

He looked amused. "That's a poetic way to put it."

"What happened to their wings?"

"They lost them, though it's not clear how. That is one story that has not survived, though I would gladly give away half of my books just to hear it. Whatever happened, it took place so long ago that many Fincayrans have never even heard that their ancestors could fly. Or if they have, they simply dismiss it as untrue."

I watched the poet. "But you believe it's true."

"I do."

"I know someone else who would believe it. My friend Rhia. She would love to be able to fly." I bit my lip. "First, though, I must save her! If she still lives."

"What happened to her?"

"Carried off by goblins! She tricked them into taking her instead of me, though what they really wanted was the Galator. She is probably at the Shrouded Castle by now."

Cairpré tilted his head, frowning. From that angle his face looked like a stern statue, made of stone rather than flesh. At last he spoke, his resonant voice filling the room so crowded with books.

"Do you know the prophecy of the giants' dance?"

I tried to recall it. *"Only when giants make dance in the hall, Shall every . . ."*

"Barrier."

"Shall every barrier crumble and fall. But I don't have any hope of destroying the castle! All I can hope to do is save my friend."

"And what if that requires destroying the Shrouded Castle?"

"Then all is lost."

"No doubt you are correct. Destroying the castle would destroy Rhita Gawr's presence in Fincayra. And neither he nor Stangmar is about to let that happen! A warrior as great as Hercules would find it impossible. Even if he carried some weapon of enormous power."

Suddenly an idea struck me. "Perhaps the Galator is the key! It is, after all, the last Treasure, the one that Stangmar has been searching for."

Cairpré's shaggy mane wagged from side to side. "We know very little about the Galator."

"Can you at least tell me what its powers are?"

"No. Except that they are described in the ancient texts as *vast beyond knowing.*"

"You're no help at all."

"Too true." Cairpré's sad face brightened only a little. "I can, however, give you my own theory about the Galator."

"Tell me!"

"I believe that its powers, whatever they are, respond to love."

"Love?"

"Yes." The poet's gaze rambled over his shelves of books. "You shouldn't be so surprised! Stories about the power of love abound." He stroked his chin. "As a start, I believe the Galator glows in the presence of love. Do you recall what we were talking about when it started shining under your tunic?"

I hesitated. "Was it . . . my mother?"

"Yes. Elen of the Sapphire Eyes. The woman who loved you enough to give up everything in her life in order to save yours! That, if you really want to know the truth, is why she left Fincayra."

For a long while, I could find no words to speak. Finally, I said regretfully, "What an ass I was! Never calling her my mother, never putting her pain ahead of my own. I wish I could tell her how sorry I am."

Cairpré lowered his eyes. "As long as you stay in Fincayra, you will never have that chance. When she left, she swore she would never come back."

"She should never have given me the Galator. I know absolutely nothing about how it works or what it can do."

"I just told you my theory."

"Your theory is mad! You say it glows in the presence of love. Well, you should know that I've seen it glow once before since I came back to Fincayra. In the presence of a bloodthirsty spider!"

Cairpré froze. "Not . . . the Grand Elusa?"

"Yes."

He almost smiled. "That strengthens my theory all the more! Do not be fooled by the Grand Elusa's alarming appearance. The truth is, her love is as great as her appetite."

I shrugged. "Even if your theory is correct, what good does it do? It doesn't help me save Rhia."

"Are you determined to go after her?"

"I am."

He scowled. "Do you know what the odds are against you?"

"I have some idea."

"But you don't!"

Cairpré stood up and started pacing down the narrow path between the stacks of books. His thigh brushed against one large, illuminated volume, and it fell to the floor in an explosion of dust. As he bent to retrieve it, stuffing loose pages back between the covers, he looked my way. "You remind me of Prometheus, so certain he could steal the fire of the gods."

"I'm not that certain. I just know I must try. Besides, Prometheus finally succeeded, didn't he?"

"Yes!" exclaimed the poet. "At the price of eternal torture, being chained to a rock where an eagle would gnaw forever upon his liver."

"Until Hercules rescued him."

Cairpré's face reddened. "I can see that I taught your mother too well! You are right that Prometheus found freedom in the end. But you are wrong if you think for a minute that you will be so fortunate. Out there, in the lands controlled by Stangmar, people are at risk just by showing themselves! You must understand me. All your mother's sacrifices will have been wasted if you go to the Shrouded Castle."

I folded my arms. While I certainly did not feel courageous, I did feel resolved. "I must try to save Rhia."

He stopped pacing. "You are no less stubborn than your mother!"

"That sounds to me like a compliment."

He shook his head in defeat. "All right, then. You ignore my warnings. *Thou withered breath, approaching Death.* I suppose then I should at least give you some advice that might conceivably help."

I slid off my stool. "What is it?"

"More likely, though, it will only hasten your death."

"Please tell me."

"There is one person in all of Fincayra who might have the power to help you enter the castle, though I doubt that even she can help you beyond that point. Her powers are old, very old, springing from the same ancient sources that brought the very first giants into being. That is why Stangmar fears to crush her. Even Rhita Gawr himself prefers to leave her alone."

Cairpré stepped closer, wading through the sea of books. "Whether or not she will choose to help you, I cannot say. No one can! For her ways are mysterious and unpredictable. She is neither good nor evil, friend nor foe. She simply *is*. In legend, she is called Domnu, which means Dark Fate. Her true name, if it ever was known, has been lost to time."

He glanced at Shim, now sleeping soundly on the pantry shelf, his hand inside the empty jar of honey. "You and your little friend may not have the pleasure of meeting her, however. Getting into her lair will be very dangerous." He added under his breath, "Though not as dangerous as getting out again."

I shivered slightly.

"To find her you must start before sunrise. Although the light of dawn is now only a pale glow through the spreading darkness, it will be your best guide. For just to the north of the sunrise, you will see a notch, cut deep into the ridge of the highest row of hills."

"I should head for the notch?"

Cairpré nodded in assent. "And you will miss it at your peril. If you cross the ridge to the north of the notch, you will find yourself in the middle of Stangmar's largest encampment of goblins."

I sucked in my breath. "No risk of that."

"And if you cross the ridge to the south of the notch, you will be even worse off, for you will enter the Haunted Marsh."

"No risk of that, either."

At that moment, Shim released a loud, prolonged snort. The books lining the shelves seemed to jump in surprise, as did Cairpré and I.

The poet frowned, but continued. "Passing through the notch itself will not be easy. It is guarded by warrior goblins. How many, I don't know. But even one can mean trouble enough. Your best hope is that these days they are unused to travelers, for reasons you can well understand. It is just possible they will not be paying much attention. There is at least a chance you could slip past them."

"Then what?"

"You must proceed straight down the ridge, being careful not to veer to one side or the other, until you reach a steep canyon. Eagles once soared among its cliffs, but no more, since now the canyon is always darker than night. Turn south, following the canyon to the very edge of the Haunted Marsh. If you make it that far, you will encounter the lair of Domnu. But not before you have met some other creatures almost as strange as she is."

Feeling weak, I leaned against my stool. "What does her lair look like?"

"I have no idea. You see, no one who has ventured there has ever returned to describe it. All I can tell you is that, according to legend, Domnu has a passion for games of chance and wagers—and dearly hates to lose."

Cairpré bent down to the floor and pushed a pile of books aside. He threw a sheepskin on the spot. With deep sadness, he said, "If you mean to pursue this idea of yours, you had better try to rest now. Sunrise will come before long."

He pondered my face. "I can see by the scars on your cheeks and the strange distance in your eyes that this is not the first time you have shown bravery. Perhaps I have underestimated you. Perhaps you possess all the hidden strengths of your forebears and more."

I waved away the comment. "If you knew me better, you would know that I am no credit to my forebears! I have no special powers, at least none that I can use. All I have is a stubborn head, and the Galator around my neck."

He rubbed his chin thoughtfully. "Time will tell. But I will say this. When first you entered my home, I was looking for an answer in some forgotten volume. Now I am wondering whether I should be looking for that answer in some forgotten person."

Wearily, I stretched myself out on the sheepskin. For some time I lay awake, watching the firelight dance on the walls of books, the scrolls of papyrus, the piles of manuscripts. Cairpré had returned to his high-backed chair, absorbed in his reading.

So this is where my mother learned her stories. I felt a swell of desire to stay many days in this room filled with books, to travel wherever their pages might carry me. Perhaps one day I would do just that. But I knew that I must travel somewhere else first. And that I must depart before dawn.

XXX

T'EILEAN AND GARLATHA

Shim scrunched his pear-shaped nose in puzzlement. "Why is she called Dumb Now? That is muchly strange."

"Domnu," I replied, pushing myself up from the sheepskin. "I've told you everything I know, which isn't much." I glanced at Cairpré, fast asleep in his chair with three open books in his lap. His long gray hair fell over his face like a waterfall. "Now it is time to go."

Shim's gaze moved to the pantry, whose bottom shelf glistened from spilled honey. "I is not gladly to leave this place."

"You don't have to come, you know. I will understand if you want to stay."

The pink eyes kindled. "Really, truly, honestly?"

"Yes. I am sure Cairpré will make you welcome, although he probably doesn't have much food left."

The little giant smacked his lips. Then, glancing toward the wooden ladder up the tunnel, his expression clouded. "But you is going?"

"I am going. Now." For a few seconds, I studied the little face at my knee. Shim had turned out to be not such a bad companion after all. I took one of his tiny hands in my own. "Wherever you go, may you find plenty of honey there."

Shim scowled. "I is not happy about going."

"I know. Farewell."

I moved to the ladder and grasped a worn rung.

Shim ran over and pulled on my tunic. "But I is not happy about staying, either."

"You should stay."

"Is you not wantsing me?"

"This will be too dangerous for you."

Shim growled with resentment. "You is not saying that if I is a real giant, big and strong. Then you begs me to come."

Sadly, I smiled. "Maybe so, but I still like you the way you are."

The little fellow grimaced. "I don't! I still wishes I am big. Big as the highlyest tree."

"You know, when Rhia was irked at me once, she told me *Just be yourself.* I've thought about it now and then. It's much easier to say than to do, but she had a point."

"Bah! Not if you don't likes the self you are being."

"Listen, Shim. I understand. Believe me, I do. Just try being at home with who you are." I paused, a little surprised to hear myself say such a thing. Then, with a final look around Cairpré's crowded walls of books, I began climbing up the tunnel.

As I squeezed through the door in the stump, I scanned the eastern horizon. Dry, reddish soil stretched as far as I could see, broken only by the occasional scrawny tree or cluster of thorned bracken. Although no birds were around to announce the dawn, a faint line of light was already appearing above the Dark Hills, which stood blacker than coal. To the north of the glow, I made out two sharp knobs, divided by a narrow gap. The notch.

Standing beside the stump, I concentrated on the formation, trying to memorize its position. I did not want to miss the notch, even by a small margin. And I couldn't be certain it would remain visible as the day progressed.

Seeing my staff on the ground, I stooped to pick it up. Dew frosted its twisted top, making the wood slippery and cold to the touch. Suddenly I noticed several deep gashes along the shaft. Teeth marks. I had no way to tell what kind of beast had made them. I only knew that they had not been there when I climbed down into Cairpré's tunnel last night.

I reached to close the door, when Shim's bulbous nose emerged. The little body followed, clambering through the opening.

"I is coming."

"Are you sure?" I showed him the staff. "Whatever chewed on this last night could still be near."

Shim swallowed, but said nothing.

I waved toward the dimly glowing horizon. "And to find Domnu, we have to make it through that notch in the Dark Hills. No room for error, either. To one side lies an army of goblins, to the other lies the Haunted Marsh."

The little giant planted his feet firmly. "You is not leaving me."

"All right then. Come."

Hopping over the trickling stream by the stump, I strode off in the direction of the notch. Shim, hustling to keep up, followed.

For the rest of that morning—if such grim, lightless hours could be called morning—we trekked across the open tundra. The soil crackled under the weight of our feet. Heading toward the notched ridge, we followed no roads or trails, though we crossed several. Yet the roads were as empty as the village that had been burned to the ground.

Conversation was just as sparse as the surrounding vegetation, and almost as brittle, for both of us knew how easily we could be spotted by anyone loyal to Stangmar. Even when Shim reached into the pocket of his shirt and offered to share a hunk of ambrosia bread from Cairpré's pantry, he did so without speaking. I merely nodded in thanks, and we pressed on.

As the land gradually lifted toward the Dark Hills, I did my best to guide us. Although the notch no longer stood out against the sky, as it did during the brief glow that had passed for sunrise, it remained barely visible. Yet it seemed to me less a sign of the route than a sign of foreboding. Suppose we somehow passed through the notch, and even made it to Stangmar's castle, only to find that Rhia was not there? Or worse, that she was there but no longer alive?

Every so often, we encountered sparse signs of habitation. An old house here, a dilapidated pen there. Yet these structures seemed as lifeless as the landscape. They sat there, rotting, like bones on a beach. If anyone still lived there, they lived in hiding. And they existed somehow without trees or gardens or greenery of any kind.

Then, to my surprise, I sensed a subtle splash of green ahead. Thinking it might be just a mistake of my weak vision, I concentrated on the spot. Yet the color seemed real enough, contrasting with the rusty browns and grays on all sides. As I drew nearer, the green deepened. At the same time, I detected the outlines of trees, arranged in regular rows, with some sort of fruit clinging to their boughs.

"An orchard! Can you believe it?"

Shim rubbed his nose. "Looks dangerously to me."

"And see?" I pointed at a boxy shape behind the trees. "There's some sort of hut in the cleft of the hill."

"I thinks we better stays away. Really, truly, absolutely."

Whether because the green trees reminded me of the Druma, or because the hut reminded me of my days with the woman I now knew to be my mother, I felt curious to learn more. I looked down. "You can wait here for me if you want. I'm going closer."

Shim watched me depart, swearing under his breath. A few seconds later, he trotted to catch up to me.

As he approached, I stopped and turned to him. "Smelled some honey, did you?"

He growled. "Goblinses, more likely." Nervously, he glanced over his shoulder. "But even if no goblinses are there, they is not far away."

"You can be sure of that. We won't stop long, I promise. Just long enough to see who lives there."

As we neared the orchard, I discerned a rough stone wall bordering the trees. It was made of the same gray rock, splotched with rust-colored lichen, as the hut. Judging from the gaps and toppled portions of both, neither hut nor wall had been repaired in quite some time. Just as the crumbling wall embraced the trees, the trees themselves embraced the hut, flowing over its roof and sides with leafy branches. Beneath the boughs, several beds of green, speckled with brighter colors, thatched the ground.

I crouched, as did Shim. Cautiously, we crept closer. A fresh aroma wafted over us, the scent of wet leaves and newborn blossoms. It struck me how long it had been since I smelled the fragrance of living, growing plants. And then it struck me that this was not just an orchard. This was a garden.

Just then a pair of shapes, as gray as the stones in the wall, emerged from the hut. Taking wobbly steps, the pair slowly advanced toward the nearest bed of plants. They moved with an odd, disjointed rhythm, one back straightening as the other curved, one head lifting as the other drooped. As different as their motions were, however, they seemed unalterably connected.

As they came nearer, I could tell that these two people were old. Very old. White hair, streaked with gray, fell about both of their shoulders, while their sleeveless brown robes hung worn and faded. Had their backs not been so bent, they would have stood quite tall. Only their arms, muscular and brown, seemed younger than their years.

The pair reached the first bed of plants, then separated. One of them, a woman whose strong cheekbones reminded me of my mother, stooped to retrieve a sack of seeds and started working them into the soil on one side of the hut. At the same time the other, a man with a long banner of whiskers waving from his chin, picked up a basket and hobbled toward a tree laden with the same spiral fruit that I had tasted at the shomorra tree. Abruptly, the old man halted. He turned slowly toward the spot where we crouched behind the wall.

Without taking his eyes off us, he spoke in a low, crusty voice. "Garlatha, we have visitors."

The old woman looked up. Though her face creased with concern, she answered calmly, in a voice that creaked with age. "Then let them show themselves, for they have nothing to fear."

"I am T'eilean," declared the man. "If you come in peace, you are welcome here."

Slowly, we lifted our heads. I stood up and planted my staff on the ground. As my hand brushed over the place that had been raked by teeth only hours before, a chill passed through me. Meanwhile, Shim rose beside me and squared his shoulders, although only his eyes and frantic hair poked above the top of the wall.

"We come in peace."

"And what are your names?"

Feeling cautious, I hesitated.

"Our names is secret," declared Shim. "Nobody knows them." For good measure, he added, "Not even us."

One corner of T'eilean's mouth curled upward. "You are right to be cautious, little traveler. But as my wife has said, you have nothing to fear from us. We are simple gardeners, that is all."

I stepped across the wall, trying not to crush the slender yellow vegetables growing from a vine on the other side. I offered a hand to Shim, who pushed it aside and climbed over the jumble of rocks unaided.

T'eilean's expression became serious again. "These are dangerous times to travel in Fincayra. You must be either very brave or very foolish."

I nodded. "Time will tell which we are. But may I ask about you? If it's dangerous to travel here, it must be more so to live here."

"Too true." T'eilean beckoned to Garlatha to join him. "But where could we go? My wife and I have lived here together for sixty-eight years. Our roots are deep, as deep as these trees." With a wave at their unadorned home, he added, "Besides, we have no treasure."

"Not that could be stolen, that is." Garlatha took his arm, smiling at him. "Our treasure is too big for any chest, and more precious than any jewels."

T'eilean nodded. "You are right, my lady." Leaning toward me, he grinned mischievously. "She is always right. Even when she is wrong."

Garlatha kicked him hard in the shin.

"*Owww,*" he howled, rubbing the spot. "After sixty-eight years, you should have learned some manners!"

"After sixty-eight years, I have learned to see right through you."

Garlatha looked at him full in the face. Slowly, she grinned. "Yet, somehow, I still like what I see."

The old man's dark eyes glittered. "Come now, what of our guests? Can we offer you a place to sit? Anything to eat?"

I shook my head. "We have no time for sitting, I'm afraid." I pointed toward the spiral-shaped fruits dangling from the branch. "I would take one of those, though. I had that kind once before and it was wonderful."

T'eilean reached up and, with surprising dexterity, plucked one of the fruits with his large, wrinkled hand. As he gave it to me, he said, "You may certainly have this, but you have not had its kind, the larkon, before."

Puzzled, I shook my head.

"These grow nowhere else in Fincayra," explained the gardener, his voice solemn. "Years ago, long before you were born, trees bearing them dotted the hills east of the River Unceasing. But they have succumbed to the Blight that has afflicted the rest of our land. All but this one."

I took a bite of the fruit. The flavor like purple sunshine burst inside my mouth. "There is one other place this fruit still grows, and there I have eaten it before."

In unison, T'eilean and Garlatha asked, "Where?"

"In Druma Wood, at the shomorra tree."

"The shomorra?" sputtered Garlatha. "You have truly been there, to the rarest of trees?"

"A friend who knows it well took me there."

T'eilean stroked his wispy beard. "If that is true, you have a remarkable friend."

My face tightened. "I do."

A slight breeze stirred the branch above me, rustling the living leaves. I listened for a moment. I felt like a man, deprived of water for days, who finally heard the sound of a burbling stream. Suddenly, Shim reached up and yanked the spiral fruit from my hand. Before I could protest, he took two large bites.

I glared at him. "Don't you know how to ask?"

"*Mmmpppff,*" said the little giant through a mouthful of fruit.

Garlatha's eyes shone with amusement. Turning to her husband, she said, "It appears that I am not the only one without manners."

"You are right," he answered. Hobbling a few steps away, he added with equal amusement, "As always."

Garlatha grinned. Her strong arm reached up to the branch, picked another spiral fruit, and handed it to me. "Here. You can start again."

"You are most generous, especially if this is the last tree of this kind east of the Druma." I sniffed the larkon's zesty fragrance, then took a bite. Once again, my tongue exploded with sunny flavor. Savoring the taste, I asked, "How has your garden survived so well in the midst of this Blight? It's a miracle."

The couple traded glances.

T'eilean's face hardened. "It is no more of a miracle than all of these lands once were. But our wicked king has changed all that."

"It has broken our hearts to watch," said Garlatha, her voice cracking.

"Stangmar's Shroud blocks out the sun," continued the old man. "More with each passing month. For as the Shrouded Castle grows in power, the sky grows ever darker. Meanwhile, his armies have sown death across the land. Whole villages have been destroyed. People have fled to the mountains far to the west, or left Fincayra altogether. A vast forest, as remarkable as Druma Wood, once grew on those hills to the east. No more! What trees have not been slaughtered or burned have retreated into slumber, never to speak again. Here on the plains, what soil has not been soaked with blood has taken on its very color. And the Flowering Harp, that could perhaps coax the land back to life, has been stolen from us."

He looked down at his weathered hands. "I carried the Harp only once, when I was just a boy. But after all these years, I still cannot forget the feel of its strings. Nor the thrill of its melody."

He grimaced. "All that and more is lost." He motioned toward the cleft in the hill behind the hut. "See our once joyous spring! Hardly a trickle. As the land has withered, so has the water that nourished it. Half of my day I now spend hauling water from afar."

Garlatha took his hand. "As I spend half of mine searching the dry prairie for seeds that still may be revived."

Awkwardly, Shim offered to her the remains of his fruit. "I is sorry for you."

Garlatha patted his unruly head. "Keep the fruit now. And do not feel sorry for us. We are far more fortunate than most."

"That we are," agreed her husband. "We have been granted a long life together, and a chance to grow a few trees. That is all anyone could ask for." He glanced at her. "That and our one remaining wish, that one day we might die together."

"Like Baucis and Philemon," I observed.

"Who?"

"Baucis and Philemon. They are characters in a story from the Greeks, a story I learned from . . . my mother, long ago. They had but one wish, to die together. And in the end the gods turned them into a pair of trees whose leafy branches would wrap around each other for all time."

"How beautiful," Garlatha sighed, looking at her husband.

T'eilean said nothing, though he studied me closely.

"But you have not told me," I continued, "how your garden has survived in this terrible time."

T'eilean released Garlatha's hand and opened his sinewy arms to the greenery, the roots, the blossoms surrounding them. "We have loved our garden, that is all."

I nodded, thinking how wondrous this region must have been before the Blight. If the garden where Shim and I now stood was only a small sampling of its riches, the landscape would have been as beautiful—though not as wild and mysterious—as the Druma itself. The kind of place where I would have felt alive. And free. And possibly even at home.

Garlatha observed us worriedly. "Are you certain you cannot rest here for a while?"

"No. We cannot."

"Then you must be extremely careful," warned T'eilean. "Goblins are everywhere these days. Only yesterday, at sunset, when I was coming back with water, I saw a pair of them. They were dragging away a helpless girl."

My heart stopped. "A girl? What did she look like?"

The white-bearded man looked pained. "I could not get very close, or they would have seen me. Yet, while I watched, part of me wanted to attack them with all my strength."

"I am glad you did not," declared his wife.

T'eilean pointed at me. "The girl was about your age. Long, curly brown hair. And she wore a suit that seemed to be made of woven vines."

Shim and I gasped.

"Rhia," I whispered hoarsely. "Where were they going?"

"There can be no doubt," the old man answered dismally. "They were traveling east. And since the girl was alive at all, she must be someone Stangmar wants to deal with personally."

Garlatha moaned. "I cannot bear the thought of a young girl at that terrible castle."

I felt for the dagger in my satchel. "We must go now."

T'eilean extended his hand to me, clasping my own with unexpected firmness. "I do not know who you are, young man, nor where you are going. But I suspect that, like one of our seeds, you hold much more within than you show without."

Garlatha touched Shim's head again. "The same, I think, could be said for this little fellow."

I did not reply, although I wondered whether they would have spoken so kindly to us if they had known us better. Even so, as I crossed over the crumbling wall, I found myself hoping that I might one day see them again. I turned to wave to the elderly couple. They waved back, then resumed their work.

I noticed that the Galator felt warm against my chest. Peeking under my tunic, I saw that its jeweled center was glowing ever so slightly. And I knew that Cairpré's theory about the Galator was true.

XXXI

THEN CAME
A SCREAM

For several hours, we trekked toward the notch in the ridge, my staff rhythmically punching the dry soil and dead grass. A cold wind out of the Dark Hills blew down on us. Its bitter gusts slapped our faces. Despite the wind, Shim did his best to stay by my side. Even so, I had to stop several times to help him through some thorny bracken or up a steep pitch.

As the land sloped increasingly upward, the wind blew ever more fiercely. Soon it smacked with such piercing cold that my hand holding my staff no longer pulsed with pain, but started to go numb. It felt as wooden as the staff itself. Flying bits of ice began to whip against us. I lifted my free arm to protect my cheeks and sightless eyes.

The bits of ice turned into needles, then shards, then daggers. As the icy blades rained down on us, Shim, who had resisted complaining since leaving the garden, whined piteously. But I could only hear him in the lulls between gusts, for the howling of the wind grew fiercer.

Although it remained light enough for my second sight to help, the swirling ice and blowing dirt confused my sense of direction. Suddenly I stumbled against a low, flat outcropping of some sort. With a cry, I crumpled to the ground, dropping my staff.

Shivering, I crawled over to the outcropping, hoping to use it as a slight shelter against the storm. Shim tucked himself into the folds of my tunic. We sat there, our teeth chattering from the cold, for minutes that seemed like weeks.

In time, the ice storm abated. The howling wind hurled itself at us a few last times, then finally retreated. Although the air seemed no warmer, our bodies slowly revived. I opened and closed my hands, which made my palms and fingertips sting. Hesitantly, Shim poked his head out of my tunic, his wild hair embedded with icicles.

All at once, I realized that the outcropping that had partially shielded us was nothing more than an immense tree stump. All around us, thousands of such stumps littered the hills, separated by a vast web of eroded gullies. Though frosted with a glaze of ice, the stumps did not sparkle or gleam. They merely sat there, as lifeless as burial mounds.

In a flash, I understood. This was all that remained of the vast forest that T'eilean had described. *Stangmar's armies have sown death across the land.* The old man's words lifted like ghosts out of the rotting stumps, the blood red soil, the broken hills.

Shim and I looked at each other. Without a word, we stood up on the frosted ground. I picked up my staff, knocking a chunk of ice off the top. Then I located the notch again, stepped over the brittle remains of a branch, and started up the slippery terrain. Shim scrambled to stay with me, muttering under his breath.

As the day wore on, we continued to climb, over hills scarred with countless stumps and dry streambeds. All the while, the sky grew darker. Soon the notch disappeared, swallowed in the deepening darkness. I could only trust my memory of where I had last glimpsed its two sharp knobs, though that memory itself was fading with the light.

Slowly, we gained elevation. Despite the dim light, I detected a few thin trees rising amidst the stumps and dead branches. Their twisted forms resembled people writhing in pain. Seeing one tree wearing the bark of a beech, I approached it. Laying my hand on the trunk, I made the swishing, rustling sound that Rhia had taught me in Druma Wood.

The tree did not respond.

I tried again. This time, as I made the swishes, I imagined the living, breathing presence of a healthy tree before me. The powerful roots thrusting into the soil. The arching branches lifting toward the sky. The deep-throated song rising through the trunk, thrilling each and every leaf.

Perhaps it was just my imagination, but I thought I could sense the barest beginnings of a quiver in the uppermost branches. Yet if they had actually moved, they quickly fell still again.

Giving up, I trudged on. Shim huffed at my heels. As we climbed the rising slope, the ground grew more rocky. With each passing minute, the light dimmed further. The sky blackened, while the stumps and rocks around us melted into shadows.

Although my second sight was swiftly fading, I fought to see whatever I still could. And with all my concentration, I listened. I knew that any movement, no matter how slight, could provide our only warning of attack. As I tried to avoid tripping on rocks and snapping dead branches, my steps grew less certain.

Ahead, I discerned a barely visible gap, where twin knobs of dark rock lifted into the still darker sky. Might it be the notch? I edged closer, as quietly as I could.

Abruptly, I stopped. I stood as still as one of the twisted trees, listening.

Shim crept to my side. "You hears something?"

"Not sure," I whispered. "I thought I did, somewhere ahead of us."

Minutes passed. I heard no sound apart from our breathing and the thumping of my own heart.

Eventually, I touched the little giant's arm. "Let's go," I whispered. "But keep quiet. Goblins are near."

"Oooh," moaned Shim. "I is scared. Certainly, definitely, abs—"

"Quiet!"

Out of the shadows ahead of us came a raspy cry and a sudden pounding of feet. Torches flared, searing the darkness.

"Goblins!"

Across the rocky ridge we fled. Dead branches snapped under our feet. Thorns ripped at our shins. I could hear, just behind, the heaving of the goblins' chests, the clanking of their armor, the sputtering of their torches.

Shim and I tore across the rocks, trying not to stumble. Darkness pressed closer. We did not know where we were going, nor did we care. We only knew that the goblins were gaining on us.

In a desperate effort to lose them, I veered sharply to one side. Shim followed closely, and we crossed over the ridge. The vista before us could not have been more chilling. Against the darkened sky, more hills loomed even darker. Worse yet, the valley below us looked utterly black, but for the glint of hundreds of tiny lights. Despite the goblins at our backs, we hesitated for an instant.

A spear whizzed past, passing between my head and the top of my staff. Even as the spear clattered against the ground, to a chorus of raspy curses, we plunged down the slope. My foot struck a rock and I fell, sprawling. Shim waited long enough for me to roll back to my feet, grab my staff, and resume running. We charged downward into the black valley.

Total darkness swept over us like a wave. The ground became wet and mushy under our feet. The air turned rancid. Before long we splashed through something like an enormous puddle, covering a bed of oozing murk.

All at once I halted, causing Shim to run straight into my back.

"What is you stopping for?" he demanded angrily.

"Listen."

"I hears nothing, except the throbbings of my tenderly nose."

"That's just it. The goblins stopped. Somewhere back there."

"You is right." The little giant shifted nervously in the murk. "Do you think they is scared to goes here?"

I felt something cold oozing into my leather boots. "We may be in . . . the Haunted Marsh."

As if in answer, a faint, wavering light appeared some distance away. It hovered in the darkness, seeming to examine us. Then another appeared, followed by another. Soon more than twenty of the eerie lights swam around us, moving slowly closer.

Shim squeezed my hand.

A reeking smell, like festering flesh, drifted over us. I gagged, my lungs rebelling. As the lights drew nearer, the smell grew stronger.

Then came a thin, unsteady wailing. An ancient dirge pulsing with anguish, with undying pain. The wailing made me cringe, as it welled out of the ground, the lights, the rotting air. It came from one side. It came from the other. It came from every direction at once.

Shim released a terrified shriek. Letting go of my hand, he dashed away from the cluster of floating lights.

"Wait!"

I hurled myself after him. I had only gone a few steps, however, when something caught my foot. I tumbled headlong into a puddle of slimy liquid. Pulling myself and my staff free, I shook the murk from my arms. They stunk of mold and decay.

The ominous lights circled, gathering again. The wailing swelled. The stench of death flooded over me.

"Shim!"

No answer.

"Shim!"

Then came a scream.

The lights pressed closer, staring down on me like so many eyes. So this was how my quest would end! I would have rather drowned in the sea off the coast of Gwynedd than die like this, wretched and alone.

Yet the loss of my own quest pained me less than the loss of Rhia. She, like the brave merlin, had given her life for me. I did not deserve such friendship. Yet she did not deserve to die. She was so full of life, so full of wisdom that I did not begin to comprehend. The pain of losing her made my heart sting, as if it were on fire.

Suddenly I realized that the Galator was blazing with heat against my chest. I tore it out of my tunic and held it high. The jeweled center sparkled with its own green light, pushing back the darkness just enough that I could see my own hand and arm.

The eerie lights faltered, stopped their advance. The wailing ceased. A touch of freshness wafted on the air. At the same time, the Galator's glow started to expand. In a few seconds, the circle of green illuminated my entire body as well as my staff.

"Shim! Where are you?"

"Here!" Soaked in murk, he staggered to my side. His chest, legs, arms, and one side of his face dripped with black ooze.

As the glowing circle expanded, the floating lights wavered, then slowly drew back into the darkness. The wailing resumed, but transformed into an angry murmur.

Heartened by the retreat of the lights, I pressed ahead. I would find some way out of this swamp, whatever it took.

Holding the Galator above my head with one hand, grasping my staff with the other, I made sure Shim held tight to my tunic. Then I started to trudge through the marshy pools. The mud was soft and sticky, sucking at my boots. Suddenly I stepped into a shallow pit. I fell forward with a splash, almost dropping the pendant. Instantly the eyes of light crowded closer and the murmur swelled louder.

As I regained my balance, the menacing lights pulled back a little. It took me a moment to extract my staff from the grasping mud of the pit, though it finally came free with a loud slurp. We slogged onward. I could tell, however, that Shim could not travel very far in this terrain. Although he was struggling to stay with me, the water was up to his waist, and the work of pushing through it was tiring him fast.

My own legs, as well as the arm holding the Galator, began to feel increasingly heavy. Nevertheless, I helped Shim climb up to the shoulder of my arm holding the staff. It was the same shoulder that Trouble had once claimed as his perch. But this load felt much heavier than the hawk ever did.

Each step grew more difficult, each breath more labored. I felt weaker and weaker, as if the marsh itself was sapping my strength. My shoulder ached. The murk from Shim's legs dripped onto my face, while the rancid taste burned my tongue.

As my stamina faded, the lights pressed ever closer. The murmur swelled, like a pack of wolves howling in my ears. The marsh seemed endless, stretching far beyond the limits of my flagging endurance.

My powers! Should I try to use them? I needed them so much. Yet I feared them so much. The flames rose again in my mind, snapping at my face, searing my flesh, scorching my eyes.

Suddenly I stumbled. I fell to my knees, barely hanging on to both my staff and the Galator. Shim gave a shout and clung to my neck, sobbing. Again the lights crowded around, waiting to see if I would rise again.

With all my remaining strength, I pushed myself out of the slime. I tried to lift the Galator, but could not bring it higher than my chest. I took another exhausted step—and stumbled again.

I heard the Galator smack against something hard, like stone. I heard Shim scream as the murmur grew almost deafening.

Then I heard no more.

DARK FATE

Is you alive?"

"Not sure," was my only answer. I sat up and shook the fog from my second sight. Shim sat on one side while my staff, caked with rancid-smelling mud, lay on the other.

Shim, his small face lined with worry, pulled on my tunic. "Where is we?"

Surveying our surroundings, I took in the strangest room I had ever seen. Polished stone walls, floor, and ceiling enclosed us, without even a slit for a window. Yet a quivering blue light filled the room, like the light from a candle just before it burns out. But no candle could be seen.

I shivered, though not from cold. I could not be certain why, but a feeling of foreboding hung in the air. As if Shim and I were about to be sliced up for someone's supper.

Shim slid closer. "This place is frighteningly. Like a dungeon."

"I agree."

Suddenly he pointed. "Bones!"

With a start, I viewed the shadowy pile next to us. It was indeed a mass of bones, picked perfectly clean. In the quivering light I could make out ribs, leg bones, and more than a few skulls. People's skulls.

I swallowed, wondering whether our own remains would soon rest there.

Then I noticed that several other piles, though not of bones, surrounded us. One held thin slabs of gray stone, stacked almost as tall as my staff. Another contained polished balls of wood, carved in varied sizes and etched with strange signs. Some smaller than fingernails and others larger than heads, the balls seemed to have been carefully arranged for some purpose. Still another pile contained bundles of sticks, sorted by size as well as number. In the far corner of the room, I noticed strange white cubes marked with black dots on their sides. Spools of black and white yarn were piled here, bizarre shells from the sea there. Iron bowls overflowed with pebbles and seeds of many shapes.

In the middle of the floor sat a thick, square rug that was divided into smaller red and black squares. On many of these squares stood carved wooden pieces, each of them about as high as my waist. Attacking dragons, galloping horses, howling wolves, warring goblins, kings and queens, plus others I could not begin to recognize. Back in Caer Vedwyd, I had heard of the game called *esches*, sometimes shortened to *chess,* but that game was played on a board, not a rug. And in any event, chess pieces did not include dragons. Or goblins.

On the stone wall opposite us, a dense jumble of blue markings wavered in the light. Columns of slashes, dots, and squiggles, running in several directions, covered much of the surface. There were thousands of squares, triangles, and meshes of crossed lines, as well as circles divided into sections, much as a round loaf of bread is sliced. There were runes, letters, numbers, and symbols squeezed over and under, inside and outside, the rest of the markings.

262 · THE LOST YEARS OF MERLIN

"Too bad," growled a deep voice behind us.

We spun around to see a pale, hairless head poking through the crack of a door. Slowly, the door swung open, revealing a body as round as the head, wearing a robe resembling a cloth sack with several pockets, a necklace of rough stones, and bare feet. I froze, fearful that this was another shifting wraith. Or perhaps something worse.

The hairless head, with rows of wrinkles gathering about two triangular ears, leaned toward us. One large, shriveled wart sprouted like a horn from the middle of the forehead. Eyes even blacker than my own watched us, unblinking, for several seconds. Then the mouth full of misshapen teeth opened again. "Definitely too bad."

Reaching for my staff, I scrambled to my feet, which was made more difficult by Shim's clinging to my leg. "Who are you?"

"Almost no chance they'll live out the day," muttered the strange figure, entering the room. "Definitely too bad."

Though my voice quaked, I repeated my question. "Who are you?"

The black eyes, seeming terribly old, observed me for a moment. "That's a difficult question, my pet."

Something about the words *my pet* made me cringe.

"Who am I?" continued the creature, pacing slowly around us like a vulture examining its carrion. "Hard to tell. Even for me. Today I'm someone, tomorrow someone else." The wrinkled face bent toward me, showing more crooked teeth. "And who are you?"

I gave a sigh. "The truth is, I'm not really sure."

"At least, my pet, you are honest." The circling continued, the bare feet slapping on the stone floor. "Perhaps I can tell you a bit about who you are. Though I should warn you, it's rather disappointing. For starters, you are too skinny to provide more than a mouthful or two, even with your little friend thrown in."

Shim squeezed my leg harder.

"Worse still, my pet, you look far too weak to be of any help to my wager. And I do *so* detest losing."

An icy finger ran down my spine. "I know who you are. You are Domnu."

"Very clever, my pet." The hairless hag stopped circling. She ran a hand across the top of her head, ruminating. "But cleverness won't be enough to win my wager."

"What wager are you talking about?"

"Oh, nothing of any importance. I merely made a little wager with someone who expects you not to survive until tomorrow." She shrugged. "Die today. Die tomorrow. What difference does it make? I should not have bet on you, but I could not resist the odds."

I shuddered, remembering what Cairpré had said about this being whose name means Dark Fate. *Neither good nor evil, friend nor foe. She simply is.* "Who did you wager against?"

Domnu's bare feet slapped across the stone floor as she moved to the wall covered with strange markings, still trembling in the unsteady light. She spat on the index finger of her left hand, which immediately turned blue. Then, using the finger as a paintbrush, she stretched to reach as high as she could and drew a squiggly line through one of the circles.

"Time to start using a new wall," she grumbled. With a glance in our direction, she added, "Must keep score, my pets. I do dislike losing a wager, but I must keep score. And it certainly does look like I will lose this one."

"You mean," piped Shim, "that we is going to die?"

Domnu shrugged again. "It certainly looks that way."

I demanded, "Who did you wager against?"

"No one you know. Although he does seem to have developed a genuine dislike for you."

"Who?"

She scratched the back of her bald head. "That fool Rhita Gawr, of course."

"Rhita Gawr? The spirit battling Dagda?"

Domnu grunted carelessly. "I suppose so. At least it was so a few thousand years ago when last I checked. But as to who is winning and who is losing, my pet, I have no idea. They must keep their own tallies."

"But it's not a game! It's serious."

Domnu stiffened. "Games *are* serious, my pet. As serious as life itself, for that too is just a game."

"You don't understand." I stepped closer, with Shim still holding tight to my leg. "Their battle is for all of Fincayra. As well as the Earth. And more beyond that."

"Yes, yes," said the hag, yawning. "They have an ongoing wager."

"No! It's more than that."

She stared at me, dumbfounded. "More than that? How can anything be more than that? A wager is the purest chance of all! Make your choice, place your bet. Then whatever happens, happens. Up or down. Life or death. It doesn't matter, as long as you collect your winnings in the end."

I shook my head. "It *does* matter. Whether Dagda or Rhita Gawr wins will determine—"

"What the odds will be on their next wager. Yes, I know."

Domnu's feet slapped over to the rug of red and white squares. She bent low to face one of the pieces, the figure of a red dragon. Nonchalantly, she tickled under its scaly chin. In the quivering light, I could not be sure, but it almost seemed that the dragon's head jerked slightly, and that two thin trails of smoke drifted out of its nostrils.

"Their little game is of no interest to me," she concluded, even as she gave the dragon's ear a tweak. "I have enough trouble keeping track of my own."

Shim clutched tighter. "I is scared. Very, very, very scared."

"I don't know why you should be," replied Domnu with a crooked grin. "Dying isn't so bad after the first time."

She placed her foot on the back of the dragon piece, reached for the figure of the black king, and grabbed it roughly by the neck. I could have been mistaken, but as she lifted the king off the rug, I thought I heard a faint, anguished squeal. Still grasping the neck, she began polishing the king's crown on her sacklike robe. "I suppose we should play a game of some kind before I send you on your way, my pets. It will take our minds off your impending deaths and my impending loss. Do you prefer dice or sticks?"

"We need your help," I pleaded.

She replaced the black king, dropping the piece with a thud. Then, feet slapping on the floor, she ambled over to the pile of sticks. She plucked a small bundle from the pile and contemplated it. "I think threes would be better than thirteens today, don't you? I have the feeling in my bones that this is a low number day. Bones! Perhaps you would rather play bones?"

"Please! We need to get to the Shrouded Castle."

"The Shrouded Castle?" She pulled a stick from the bundle and spat on it. "Why ever would you want to go there?"

"A goodly question," muttered Shim, hugging my shin.

"Besides," Domnu continued, all the while examining the stick, "if I send you there, then you will *certainly* die and I will lose my wager."

"Won't you please help us?"

"I am afraid not, my pet." She twirled the stick in the palm of her hand.

I scowled. "If you're not going to help us, then why don't you just put us back in the Haunted Marsh and get it over with?"

Shim looked up at me with amazement.

"I may well, my pet. After all, I did promise Rhita Gawr that I would not keep you safe here all day. Rules of the wager, you understand. And I never break the rules." She lowered her voice. "Besides, he would notice if I did."

She inserted the stick back into the bundle, then tossed it carelessly onto the pile. "But why the hurry? We still have time for a game or two."

"We do not have time!" I exclaimed. "Isn't there any way we can convince you?"

"The only question," she went on, scanning the room, "is which game to choose. Of course! Chess! Though I don't suppose you know anything about the rules, young as you are. No matter. Just come over here and I will teach you a bit. And bring that brave warrior there. The one clinging to your leg."

She walked back over to the rug and glanced around at the chess pieces. "Too tall, I think."

With an expression of concentration, she placed the palm of her hand on the crown of the red queen. She muttered a phrase softly, then began to press slowly downward. To my astonishment, the red queen—as well as all the other chess pieces—grew steadily smaller, until they were only half of their original size. Now the tallest pieces were about the same height as Shim.

Proudly, Domnu waved at the chess pieces. "It really is one of my better inventions, this game. A great success wherever it goes. Even the humans, with their limited powers of concentration, have adopted it. Though it grieves me to see how they try to oversimplify the rules of the game. The only drawback is that it is best played with two people. And finding the right partner can be very difficult indeed."

Raising her thin eyebrows, she sent waves of wrinkles across the top of her scalp. "Especially if you have as few visitors as I do. By the way, most of my visitors come by the front door. What ever possessed you to use the back door? I might never have found you, if you hadn't knocked on the doorstep."

"I didn't knock."

"Of course you did! Though I almost didn't hear you with that awful din outside."

"But I didn't knock."

"My pet, you are forgetful! You knocked with something hard. It must have been your head. Or perhaps that unattractive little pendant of yours."

Suddenly remembering the Galator, I clutched it tightly. It was no longer glowing. Swiftly I replaced it under my tunic.

"I might have left you there, but I haven't had any company for games in so long. Two centuries at least! Then, after I brought you in, I realized you must be the ones Rhita Gawr had wagered would not survive the day, if you should ever turn up here." Her ancient eyes narrowed. "I only wish I had seen you before I agreed to the wager."

Domnu started pacing around the rug, inspecting each of the

chess pieces carefully. Although the wavering light made the whole room seem to vibrate, it struck me that each of the chess pieces trembled slightly as she approached. Then, when she passed in back of a gallant looking black stallion, the horse seemed to shift its hind leg ever so slightly. Instantly, Domnu whirled around.

"You wouldn't be wanting to kick me, now, would you?" The black eyes flashed, as she ran her finger slowly down the horse's mane. "No, your manners are better than that. Much better. You must be wanting a bit more weight on your back. Yes, I am certain that's it."

The barest whinny seemed to come from the stallion. Its carved muscles almost tensed.

Domnu bent over it and blew a long, gentle breath. Out of nowhere, a rough black stone, half the size of the horse itself, appeared on the middle of its back. While the stallion seemed to sag under the weight, it continued to hold its head high.

"There now," declared Domnu. "That's much better."

She spun to face me. "Time for a little game of chess," she said in a voice more threatening than inviting. "Before I return you to your, shall we say, friends waiting outside. You make the first move."

THE WAGER

My heart pounded. I could not bring myself to step onto the rug with Domnu.

"Come, my pet. I don't have all day." She smirked, baring her uneven teeth. "Neither do you."

"Don't goes near her," whispered Shim frantically.

"I am waiting," growled Domnu.

Perspiration beaded on my brow. What was I to do? Maybe, if I humored her, I could still find some way to win her help. Yet no sooner had I formed this thought than I knew it was impossible. Domnu would never send us to the castle, for she believed that to do so would guarantee that we would lose our lives—and she her wager. And, I admitted grimly to myself, she was probably right.

Even so, dragging a whimpering Shim with me, I moved toward the edge of the rug. I had no idea what to do next, either about Domnu's game or my own quest to help Rhia. I only knew that we had traveled too far, survived too much, to give up before trying every possibility.

When I reached the edge of the rug, Domnu pointed to the black horse weighed down by the stone. "Make your move," she commanded.

"But—but," I stammered, "I don't know the rules."

"That has not stopped you before, I'll wager."

Unsure of her meaning, I tried again. "Can you tell me the rules?"

"The way I play, you can make up your own rules. Until you break one of mine, that is."

I faltered. "I don't know how to begin."

"In the game of chess, unlike the game of life, you get to choose how you begin."

"But what if I choose poorly?"

"Ah," she said, wrinkling her scalp. "In that way the two games are quite alike. One way or another, your choice will make all the difference."

Drawing a deep breath, I stepped onto the rug of red and black squares. Hesitantly, I laid down my staff. Then, with effort, I lifted the black stallion and carried it all the way over to the other side of the rug. I placed it on a square directly in front of the red king.

"Hmmm," observed Domnu. "You chose a very risky move, my pet." She eyed me curiously. "Though no more risky than storming the Shrouded Castle without an army."

She shoved the red king to a square where he could hide behind a pair of goblins. "You must have some sort of reason."

"I do. It is—"

"A terrible shame you are so eager to die. Especially when you are just learning how to play the game. Normally, I would be quite happy to help you die sooner. But a wager is a wager."

"What if I made you a wager myself?"

Domnu scratched her hairless head. "What kind of wager?"

"Well," I replied, my mind racing, "If you can get me to the castle—"

"Us," corrected Shim. Although his whole body was quaking, he let go of my leg and stood on his own beside me. "We goes together. I is still feeling the same old madness."

I nodded at him, then turned back to Domnu. "If you can get us to the castle, then I will wager you that . . . that we will *still* survive this day. Even with Stangmar and all his goblins and ghouliants there to greet us. You could wager the opposite, that we won't succeed."

Domnu pulled thoughtfully on one of her ears. "Ah, so you are raising the stakes, are you?"

"That's right."

"And what happens if you don't survive the day?"

"Well, then you would have lost one wager, against Rhita Gawr, but you will have won another, against me. So at the end of the day, you will be no worse off. Whereas if you *don't* wager me, you will finish the day merely having lost."

She frowned. "Not a chance! What sort of a novice wagerer do you take me for, boy? I am giving you something of value by sending you to the castle. Whether or not you win, you get that much. And what do I get? Nothing."

My face fell. "But I have nothing to give you."

"Too bad." Her head wrinkled. "Time for your next move."

"Wait." I pulled out the dagger from Honn. "You could take this."

Domnu frowned again, waving it away. "A weapon? Why would I ever need that?"

"Then what about this?" I removed the satchel that Branwen had given to me. "These herbs are good for healing."

Domnu hissed. "What use would I have for such a thing?"

As I picked up my staff, she declared, "I have no need of that, either."

I knew well that my one truly valuable possession was the Galator. I suspected that Domnu knew it also. Yet . . . if I parted with that, my quest would be ruined.

"Here," said Shim, starting to peel off his baggy shirt of woven bark. "You can keeps this. Made by my own mother, when I is a babesy." He sighed. "A shame I never outgrows it."

Domnu scowled. "Keep it yourself." The black eyes probed me. "If you have nothing more to offer, then we have nothing more to discuss. Except, of course, the game of chess."

My head was whirling. While I knew almost nothing about the Galator's powers, they were clearly extraordinary. *Vast beyond knowing*, Cairpré had said. I could not possibly part with this, the last Treasure! It had already saved our lives once. It might well do so again. Besides, if Stangmar wanted it so badly, I might somehow be able to use it to bargain for Rhia's life. Though I had no way of knowing if she was still alive, I could be sure that, without the Galator, I could never save her. Moreover, this jeweled pendant had been worn by my own mother. She had given it to me to keep, to protect. To give it away would also be to give away some of her love for me.

And yet . . . if I did not offer it to Domnu, she would never help me. And I could not possibly reach the castle without her help! So I, in turn, could not help Rhia. Then again, what good was it to reach the castle without the Galator?

"Your move." She nudged me impatiently. "Make your move."

"All right, I will." Slowly, I removed the Galator from my neck. "You know this pendant, don't you?"

Domnu yawned, showing all her unruly teeth. "I have seen it a few times over the ages, yes. What about it?"

"Then you also know its value."

The hag remained dispassionate. "I have heard rumors."

Shim tugged hard on my tunic. "Don't do this! This is foolishly!"

Ignoring him, I declared, "I will wager you . . . with the Galator. If you can get us to the castle of Stangmar, I will . . ." I choked on the words. "I will give it to you."

The black eyes swelled.

"No!" cried Shim. "We needs it!"

I took a step toward her. "But if either Shim or I should ever return to you alive, no matter how much time has passed, then you must give the Galator back." Grasping the leather cord, I held up the pendant. Its jewels gleamed darkly in the shifting light. "Those are the terms of my wager."

Domnu clucked, as if she were about to swallow something tasty. "And if you should ever return—which I doubt, my pet—you would trust me to give it back to you?"

"No!" protested Shim.

I regarded her sternly. "You said you never break the rules."

"That is true." Then she added in passing, "With minor exceptions here and there, of course." All of a sudden her hand shot out and snatched the pendant. "You have a wager."

My heart sank. The Galator was gone.

Domnu gazed briefly into the Galator, her eyes reflecting its green hue. She plunged it into one of the sagging pockets in her robe. Then she smiled the smile of someone who has just won a grand wager.

For my part, I felt sure that I had just given away my last, best hope. "You wanted that all the time," I said bitterly.

"I suppose that is true, my pet."

"Why didn't you just take it from me, then? Why did you drag it out like this?"

Domnu looked offended. "Me? Take something that does not belong to me? Never!" She patted the pocket with the Galator. "Besides, the Galator must be given freely. Not stolen. Or else its powers are useless. Did no one ever tell you that?"

I shook my head.

"Too bad." She released an extended yawn. "Definitely too bad."

"Let's get on with your part," I said grimly. "How are you going to get us to the castle?"

"You wouldn't mind a slight delay, would you?" she asked. "I am feeling quite tired at the moment."

"Delay!"

"Yes." She yawned again. "Just until tomorrow sometime."

"No! You promised!"

"That's dishonestly!"

She scrutinized us for a moment. "Well, all right. I suppose I can get you there today. But you should be ashamed for denying a poor old woman her much needed rest." Her bald head wrinkled in thought. "The only question is how to do it."

She patted the top of her head, her dark eyes roaming around the room. "Ah, that's it. Wings. You will need wings. Perhaps even a pair you are accustomed to."

My heart leaped, as I wondered whether she might be referring to the legendary wings that Cairpré had told me about. Was Domnu about to restore to me what all Fincayrans had lost long ago? I flexed my shoulders in anticipation.

Her feet slapped across the floor to the doorway. She opened the heavy door, reached into the darkness, and pulled out a compact iron cage. It contained a small, tattered hawk. A merlin.

"Trouble!"

I rushed at the cage. The bird flapped and whistled enthusiastically, ripping at the iron bars with his talons.

"Let him out," I pleaded, my fingers stroking the warm feathers through the bars.

"Careful," warned Domnu. "He is feisty, this one. A real fighter. Small in body, large in spirit. He could rip you to shreds if he chose."

"Not me he won't."

She shrugged. "If you insist."

She tapped the cage lightly and it instantly disappeared. Trouble found himself falling, but caught himself just before he hit the floor. With two flaps and a whistle, he landed on the top of my staff, before hopping down to my left shoulder. With his feathered neck, he nuzzled my ear. Then he turned to Domnu and raked the air angrily with his talons.

"How did you find him?" I asked.

She scratched the wart on her forehead. "He found me, though I have no idea how. He looked, well, rather feeble when he arrived. Like someone had tried to make him into mincemeat. How the little wretch could fly at all is a miracle. I fixed him up a bit, hoping I might be able to teach him to play dice. But the ungrateful savage refused to cooperate."

At this, Trouble whistled sharply and clawed the air again.

"Yes, yes, I threw him in the cage against his will. But it was for his own good."

Trouble whistled another reprimand.

"And for my own protection! When I told him I had no interest in finding his friend, he flew at me. Tried to attack me! I could have turned him into a worm right then and there, but I decided to keep him around in case his manners improved. At any rate, he should prove useful to us now."

Puzzled, Trouble and I cocked our heads in unison.

"I should warn you," Domnu continued, "that while I can get you to the castle, I cannot get you *into* the castle. That much you will have to do on your own. Not to mention getting out again."

She peeked inside the pocket holding the Galator. "Since I will not be seeing you again, allow me to thank you for giving me this."

I sighed, but the familiar weight on my shoulder tempered my sadness. I indicated the bird. "And thank you for giving me this."

Domnu slid toward us. As Trouble eyed her warily, she placed her hands on both my head and Shim's. With the same look of concentration she had shown when shrinking the chess pieces, she started muttering.

All at once, I felt myself growing smaller. Beyond Shim's shriek, I heard Domnu calling some sort of instructions to Trouble. In a flash, the hawk was no longer riding on my shoulder. Instead, it was I who was riding on Trouble's feathery shoulder, flying high above the Dark Hills.

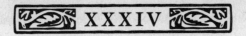

FLIGHT

Flying through the darkness, I wrapped my arms tightly around Trouble's neck. By the angle of the bird's back, I could tell that we were steadily gaining altitude. In one hand I held my staff, now almost as small as myself. I wondered where Shim might be at this moment, hoping that he was at least safe.

Chilled air flowed over us, so strongly that my sightless eyes began to water, sending thin streams of tears across my cheeks and over my ears. Neck feathers quivered with every gust, brushing against my face and hands. Being no larger than Trouble's own head, I realized that the hawk's feathers were much more than the soft, fluffy plumage they had once seemed. Each quill combined the flexibility of a branch with the sturdiness of a bone.

Gradually, the motions of the body bearing me became my own. With every upstroke of the powerful wings, I inhaled. With every downstroke, I exhaled. I could feel Trouble's shoulder and back muscles tense before each beat, then spring into action with startling strength.

As we flew, I listened with all my concentration to hear whatever I could in the blackness. I felt surprised to realize how little sound the beating wings themselves made. Only a quiet *whoosh* of air accompanied every downstroke, the barest creak of shoulder bones every upstroke.

For the first time in my life, I tasted the freedom of flight. The surrounding darkness only enhanced my sensation of soaring without limits, without boundaries. Wind in my face, I caught at least a hint of the sublime experience that the people of Fincayra had once known, then lost—an experience that I recalled not in my mind, but in my bones.

The wind shifted, and I heard a faint whimpering coming from below the talons. I realized that Trouble was also carrying another passenger, just as on a different day the hawk might carry a field mouse. And I knew that Shim, now littler than little, must be just as distraught as a mouse about to be eaten.

I tried to stretch my second sight to the limit and beyond. To push back the darkness that seemed to thicken as we progressed. Yet I felt the limits of my vision more than its gifts. The castle's Shroud poured over the Dark Hills. It enveloped them just as it did the three of us. For we were flying into the land, as Rhia had once put it, *where the night never ends.*

With effort, I sensed some of the contours of the hills rising below. No trees dotted this terrain, no rivers creased its slopes. At one point I felt the land fall away into a steep but narrow canyon, and I heard the faint cry of what might have been an eagle. To the north, a dense group of flaming torches mingled with the raspy shouts of goblins. And to the south, eerie lights flickered that chilled me deeper than the wind.

On the slopes above the canyon, I detected a few clusters of buildings, which once had been villages. A strange, uncertain yearning arose in me. Might I, as a young child, have lived in one of those villages? If I could somehow view this land in the light, would it bring back at least a little of my lost memory? But the villages below were as dark and silent as my own childhood. No fires burned in any hearths; no voices lifted in any squares.

I doubted that any laborers like Honn still toiled away in this terrain, as their ancestors had for centuries before the rise of Stangmar and the onset of never-ending darkness. It was even less likely that any gardeners could have survived in such a place. For the land of T'eilean and Garlatha at least still clung to twilight, while the lands below existed in permanent eclipse.

The darkness deepened, pressing against us like a heavy blanket. I felt Trouble's rapid heartbeat, pulsing through the veins of the bird's neck. At the same time, the beating of the wings slowed down just a notch, as if the darkness inhibited flight in the same way that it inhibited vision.

The merlin leveled off. More and more, his wings faltered, sometimes not completing a stroke, other times missing a stroke entirely. As the cold winds gusted, he weaved unsteadily. His head cocked to one side and then the other. He seemed confused, trying to see what could not be seen. He struggled to stay on course.

I clutched my feathered steed. If Trouble was having such difficulty seeing, how could he possibly guide us safely into the ever-spinning castle? Perhaps that was the point of Domnu's final warning, that getting near the castle would be less difficult than getting inside it.

With a slap of fear, I realized that our only hope now lay in my own second sight. I, whose own eyes were blind, must somehow see for the hawk! Although my second sight had always grown weaker as the light around me faded, I could not let that happen this time.

Perhaps second sight did not require light after all. Perhaps I could see despite the dark. I summoned all of my energy. I must try to pierce the darkness.

Minutes passed. I could sense nothing different. And why should I? I had never before been able to see at night, even when my eyes functioned. What made me think I could change that now?

Yet I continued to try. To probe with my mind's eye. To see beyond the grays, beyond the shadows. To fill in the swaths of darkness, just as Rhia showed me how to fill in the empty places between the stars.

Meanwhile, Trouble's flight grew more erratic and uneven. His wings labored as the fierce winds buffeted us. The bird hesitated, changed direction, hesitated again.

So very gradually that I myself did not at first notice the shift, I began to sense wispy images through the thickening darkness. A curve in a ridge. A depression that might once have been a lake. A twisting road. An uneven line that could only be a wall of stone.

Then, in the deep distance, I detected something odd. A vague, throbbing glimmer on a far ridge. It seemed both moving and stationary, both light and dark. I was not even certain that it really existed. Firmly, sinking my arms deep into his feathery neck, I turned Trouble's head toward the spot. The bird resisted at first, then started to shift the angle of his wings. Slowly, he changed direction.

In time I detected a structure of some kind, mammoth in size. It rose from a high hill like a black ghost of the night. I thought I could see strange rings of light on its sides, and some sort of pinnacles at its top. As foreboding as Domnu's lair had felt, this structure felt a hundred times worse. Still, pushing firmly on Trouble's neck, I guided us closer. By now Trouble not only accepted my steering, but also seemed heartened by it. The wings beat with renewed strength.

I reached farther and farther with my second sight. Now I could see the flat hilltop, scattered with stones, where the strange structure sat. Yet even as the land surrounding it became clearer, the structure itself remained blurred. A low, rumbling sound swelled as we approached, a sound like stone grinding against stone.

At once I understood: The structure was slowly turning on its foundation. We had found the Shrouded Castle.

Biting my lip in concentration, I steered the hawk to fly in a circle around the revolving castle. The blurred outlines immediately sharpened. The pinnacles revealed themselves as towers, the rings of light as torches seen through the spinning windows and archways. Every so often, within the torch-lit rooms, I glimpsed soldiers wearing the same pointed helmets as the warrior goblins.

I focused my vision on one lower window where no soldiers seemed to be present. Then I guided Trouble into a dive. We aimed straight at the window. The battlements, the towers, the archways drew near. Suddenly, I realized that we were flying too slow, dropping too far. We were going to hit the wall! Across my mind flashed the terrifying dream I had experienced at sea.

I pulled with all my might, forcing the hawk to veer sharply upward. Shim, clasped in the talons, screamed. We whizzed past the battlements, barely above the stones. In another split second, we would have crashed.

Refocusing, I brought Trouble around again. This time, as we circled the castle, I tried to gauge our relative speeds more closely. Yet I faltered. The truth was, I had no eyes, no real vision. Did I dare try again, guided only by my second sight?

I sucked in my breath, then urged the hawk into another dive. We shot down toward the same open window as before. Wind tore at me, screaming in my ears.

As the window neared, my stomach tightened like a fist. Even the slightest error would send us smashing into the wall. Our speed accelerated. We could not turn back now.

We tore through the window. In the same instant, I saw a stone column straight ahead. Leaning hard, I caused Trouble to swing left. We brushed past the column, slid across the floor, and slammed into a wall somewhere in the bowels of the Shrouded Castle.

THE SHROUDED CASTLE

When I regained consciousness, the first thing I noticed was how small Trouble had become. The valiant bird sat on top of my chest, poking at me with one wing and then the other. At once I realized the truth. It was I, not the bird, who had changed size. I had grown large again.

Seeing me wake up, the merlin hopped down to the stone floor. He released a low, quiet whistle, much like a sigh of relief.

A similar sound came from the far corner of the bare, shadowy room, beneath a sputtering torch fixed to the wall with a black iron stand. Shim sat up, looked at Trouble, patted himself from hairy head to hairy toes, blinked, and patted himself again.

The little giant turned to me, his nose cradled by a bright smile. "I is gladly to be big and tall again."

I raised an eyebrow, but kept myself from smirking. "Yes, we are both big again. Domnu must have worked her magic so that it would wear off if we entered the castle."

Shim scowled. "How kindly of her."

"I am grateful to her for that much." I reached to stroke the hawk's banded wings. "And more."

Trouble gave a resolute chirp. The yellow rims of his eyes shone in the torchlight. He scratched his talons on the stone floor, telling me that once again he was ready for battle.

Yet the hawk's feistiness buoyed my spirits for only an instant. I scanned the rough, imposing stones surrounding us. The walls, floor, and ceiling of this room showed no adornment, no craftsmanship whatsoever. The Shrouded Castle had been built not out of love but out of fear. If there had been any love at all during its construction, it was merely the love of cold stone and sturdy defenses. As a result, unless this room was an exception, the castle would hold no beauty, no wonder. But it would in all likelihood outlast the Dark Hills themselves. I felt sure it would outlast me.

Only then did I notice the continuous rumbling around us. The rumbling swelled, faded, and repeated, as incessantly as ocean waves. The sound of the castle turning on its foundation! As I clambered to my feet, I felt thrown off balance, both by the continuous shaking of the floor and the steady pull toward the outside wall of the room. I stooped to pick up my staff. Even with its support, I needed a moment to stand firmly.

I turned to Shim. "I would feel a lot better if I still had the Galator."

"Look," he replied, standing on his tiptoes by the open window. "It's all so darkly out there! And feels the floor moving and shaking all the time. I doesn't like this place."

"Neither do I."

"I is scared. Very, very, very scared."

"I am, too." I nodded in his direction. "But it gives me courage to be with friends."

A new gleam appeared in Shim's tiny eyes. "Courage," he said softly to himself. "I gives him courage."

"Come." Carefully, I crept to the doorway. It led to a dark corridor, lit only by a hissing torch at the far end. "We must try to find Rhia! If she is alive, she is probably below in the dungeon."

Shim's small chest inflated. "Such a terribly place! I will fights anybody who is hurtsing her."

"No you won't," I countered. "The castle is guarded by warrior goblins and ghouliants."

"Oooh." He swiftly deflated. "We should not fights them."

"Right. We must outfox them, if we can. Not fight them."

Trouble fluttered up to my shoulder, and we set off. Down the dimly lit corridor we stole, keeping as quiet as possible. Fortunately, the steady rumbling of the revolving castle covered most of our sounds, but for the slightest clacking of my staff against the stones. I reasoned that as long as we could keep ourselves from being discovered, the castle guards were probably not alert for intruders. On the other hand, I vividly recalled expecting the same thing of the goblins patrolling the notch near the Haunted Marsh.

When we reached the hissing torch, crudely jammed into a niche in the stones, the corridor turned sharply to the right. Arched doorways lined both sides of the next section, while only one narrow window slit opened to the outside. As we approached the window, I tensed as I saw shafts of darkness streaming through it, as shafts of light would pour through a window in any land not choked by the Shroud.

Gingerly, I placed my hand in the path of one of the shafts. Its coldness nipped at my fingers. My skin felt withered, half alive.

With a shiver, I withdrew my hand and moved on. Shim's bare feet padded softly by my side, as Trouble's talons hugged my shoulder securely. One corridor led to another, one sputtering torch to the next. All the rooms that we encountered were empty except for the writhing shadows of torchlight. I could only imagine how many such empty floors lay within this vast castle. Yet, for all our wandering, we did not discover any stairs.

Cautiously, we prowled the maze of corridors, turning left then right, right then left. I began to wonder whether we were traveling in circles, whether we would ever find any stairs to the lower levels. Then, as we approached one doorway, Trouble fluttered against my neck. Suddenly I heard several raspy voices trading rough remarks.

Goblins. Several of them, from the sound of it.

We waited outside the arched door, unsure how to get past without being seen. Trouble paced agitatedly on my shoulder. Then an idea struck me. I tapped the merlin on the beak, while pointing inside the doorway.

The hawk seemed to understand instantly. Soundlessly, he floated down to the floor. Keeping to the shadows by the wall, he slipped into the room. Just outside the doorway, Shim and I traded nervous glances.

A few seconds later, one of the goblins yelped in pain. "You stabbed me, you fool!"

"I did not," another retorted, over the crash of something metallic.

"Liar!"

Something heavy thudded against the stone floor. A sword slashed through the air.

"I'll show you who's a liar."

A brawl began. Swords clanged, fists struck, curses flew. In the commotion, Shim and I sneaked past the doorway. Pausing only long enough for Trouble to swoop back to his perch on my shoulder, we scuttled down the corridor. As we turned a corner, we found ourselves facing a stairwell.

Faintly lit by a flickering torch on the landing, the stone stairs wound downward in near darkness. I led the way, with Trouble riding close to my cheek, both of us trying to sense whatever might lurk in the shadows. Shim, whispering nervously to himself, stayed close behind.

The stairs spiraled down to another landing, sinister in the torch-light. Swaying shadows crawled across the walls. As we descended, the rumbling and groaning of the turning foundation increased, as did the stale odor in the air. We followed the stairs down to another level, gloomier than the last. And to another level, still gloomier. Here the stairs ended, opening into a high stone archway. Beyond that lay a dark cellar that reeked of putrid air.

"The dungeon," I whispered above the constant rumbling.

Shim made no reply except to open his eyes to their widest.

From the darkened entrance to the dungeon came a long, painful moan. A moan of sheer agony. The voice sounded almost human, though not quite. As the moan came again, louder than before, Shim froze as stiff as stone. Cautiously, I moved forward without him, poking at the blackest shadows with my staff.

Passing under the archway, I peered into the dungeon. To the left, beneath one of the few torches in the cavernous room, I viewed a man. He lay on his back on a bench of stone. From his slow, regular breathing, he appeared to be asleep. Although a sword and a dagger hung from his belt, he wore no armor except for a narrow red breastplate over his leather shirt, and a pointed helmet on his head.

Yet the strangest thing about this man was his face. It looked like paper, it was so pale. Or like a mask without any expression. What-ever the reason, the face seemed alive—and yet not alive.

The man suddenly started moaning and wailing. As the sound echoed in the dungeon, I realized that he must be dreaming, recall-ing in his sleep some moment of pain. Though I felt tempted to wake him, to spare him such torment, I dared not take the risk. As I spun around to tell Shim, I gasped. The little giant was gone.

Quickly, I darted back to the stairwell. I called his name, loud enough to be heard over the rumbling of the castle, but not so loud as to wake the sleeping soldier. Looking frantically, I could see no sign of him. I called again. No answer.

How could Shim have vanished? Where could he have gone? Maybe he had, at last, lost his nerve completely. He might be hiding somewhere, quaking. In any case, I had no time to look for him now.

With Trouble riding tensely on my shoulder, I turned around and crept past the sleeping soldier under the sizzling torch. Deeper into the dungeon I pushed. Where chains hung from the walls, the stones beneath were darkened with dried blood. I passed cell after cell, some with their heavy doors wide open, some still locked tight. Scanning through the slit in each of the locked doors, I found bones and rotting flesh still on the floor. I could not imagine Rhia, with all her zest for life, imprisoned in such a gruesome place. Yet, given the alternative, I desperately hoped that she was.

Since the day the sea returned me to Fincayra, I had discovered a little, but only a little, about my past. And I had learned even less about my true name. Yet those unfinished quests now pulled on me far less strongly than my desire to find Rhia. I was willing to put aside my own unanswered questions, perhaps forever, if only I could somehow reach her in time.

I found a cell with a skull crushed beneath a heavy rock. Then one in which two skeletons, one the size of an adult and the other no bigger than a baby, embraced each other for eternity. Then one that was completely empty but for the pile of leaves in one corner.

More despairing with every step, I trudged on. Had I come all this way to find nothing more than scattered bones and a pile of leaves?

I halted. *A pile of leaves.*

I sprinted back to the cell. My heart pounding, I peered again into the narrow slit. Just loud enough to be heard above the rumbling, I made the sound that Rhia had shown me to make a beech tree come to life.

The pile of leaves stirred.

"Rhia," I whispered excitedly.

"Emrys?"

She leaped to her feet and bounded to the door. Her garb of vines was tattered and filthy, but she was alive. "Oh, Emrys," she said in disbelief. "Is it you or your ghost?"

In answer, I slipped my forefinger through the slit. Tentatively, she wrapped her own around it, as she had so many times before.

"It is you."

"It is."

"Let me out."

"First I must find the key."

Rhia's face fell. "The guard. By the entrance. He has the key." She squeezed my finger fearfully. "But he is—"

"A soundly sleeper," finished another voice.

I whirled around to see Shim gazing up at me, an unmistakable look of pride on his small face. The little giant held out his hand. In it sat a large key wrought of iron.

I stared at him in amazement. "You stole this from the guard?"

Shim blushed, his bulbous nose turning almost as pink as his eyes. "He is a soundly sleeper, so it isn't hard."

Trouble, seated on my shoulder, whistled in admiration.

I grinned. It struck me that Shim might not be so small as he seemed after all.

With a rattle of the key, I unlocked the door. Rhia emerged, her face haggard but relieved. She embraced me, Trouble, and finally Shim, whose nose blushed more vividly than before.

Turning to me, she asked, "How do we get out of here?"

"I haven't figured out that part yet."

"Well, then, let's begin."

"I only wish I still had the Galator."

Rhia's jaw dropped. "You lost it?"

"I . . . gave it up. To get here."

Even in the dungeon, her eyes glowed. She hooked her finger around my own again. "You still have us."

Together, we started walking toward the entrance. Trouble fluttered against my neck. Even without the Galator against my chest, my heart felt a bit warmer.

But only a bit. As we passed the cell with the crushed skull, I told Rhia, "Getting in here was difficult, but getting out will be even more difficult. That is . . . getting out alive."

"I know." She stood as straight as a young beech. "In that case, all we can do is hope that Arbassa was right."

Trouble, who had started to pace across my shoulder, stopped. He cocked his head as if he were listening.

"About meeting again in the Otherworld?"

Rhia gave an uncertain nod. "After the Long Journey."

I could only frown. I was sure that, if we died today, there would be no more journeys for us—long or short.

Shim tugged on my tunic. "Let's get goings! Before that snoringly guard wakes—"

Suddenly the soldier stepped out of the shadows. His face, deathly pale under his helmet, showed no expression at all. Slowly, he slid his sword out of its scabbard. Then he lunged at me.

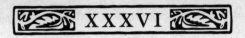
THE LAST
TREASURE

Look out!'' cried Rhia.

I threw up my staff, deflecting the blow with its gnarled top. As chips of wood flew, I pulled out my dagger. At the same time, the soldier drew back his sword. He prepared to make another thrust.

Screeching, talons gouging, Trouble flew straight into his face. One talon slashed his cheek. Without even a cry of pain, he swatted at the attacking bird. I seized the moment to bury my dagger deep in the soldier's chest, just below the breastplate.

I stepped back, expecting to see him fall. Trouble flitted back to his customary perch on my shoulder.

Astonishingly, the soldier merely stood there, his emotionless gaze fixed on the hilt of the dagger. Dropping his sword, which clattered on the stone floor, he grasped the dagger with both hands. With a sharp tug, he pulled it from his body and cast it aside. Not so much as a single drop of blood trickled from the wound.

Before he could retrieve his sword, Rhia grabbed me by the arm. "Flee!" she cried. "He is a ghouliant! He cannot die!"

We dashed through the dungeon's entrance and ran up the stairs. Not far behind, the deathless soldier bounded after us. Rhia led the way, trailing torn vines from her leggings, followed closely by me and Shim.

Up the spiraling stairs we raced, nearly tripping over the stone steps in our frenzy. Past the next landing, with its sputtering torch. And the next. And the next. The stairwell grew narrower as we climbed higher. Rhia, her legs as strong as ever, pulled farther ahead of me, while Shim fell farther behind. Panting, I glanced over my shoulder. The ghouliant had drawn within a few steps of him.

Seeing Shim's danger, Trouble took off, his wing slapping the side of my neck. His angry screech echoed in the stairwell as he flew again into the face of our pursuer.

The ghouliant fell back a few steps, trying to fight off the bird. As they battled, so did their shadows on the dimly lit stone walls. I hesitated. Should I follow Rhia, or go back to assist Trouble?

I heard a scream from up the stairwell.

"Rhia!"

I practically flew up the stairs, taking them two at a time. The stairwell curled tighter and tighter, narrowing almost to a point. Breathing hard, I rounded a bend and arrived at a landing much larger and better lit than the lower ones. At once, I stopped.

Before me spread an enormous hall, its walls lined with flaming torches and glittering objects, its ceiling vaulting high overhead. But my attention was fixed on the center of the hall. Rhia had been captured by a warrior goblin! His tongue flitting around his gray-green lips, the goblin had pinned her arms behind her back. His burly hand covered her mouth so that she could not cry out again.

"Welcome to our castle," thundered a powerful voice.

I swung around to see a large man, his face as stern as chiseled stone, seated upon a red throne that shimmered eerily. His mouth seemed etched in a permanent frown. Grim though he was, he looked darkly handsome as well. Beneath the gold circlet he wore on his brow, his black eyes glared intensely. Over his face and body wavered some strange shadows, although I could not tell what caused them.

Gathered around Stangmar's throne stood five or six ghouliants, their faces as hollow as corpses'. Two Fincayran men stood among them, their coal black hair brushing against the shoulders of their red robes. One of the men stood tall and thin, like a great insect, while the other was built like the stump of a thick tree.

Recalling what Cairpré had told me, I scanned closely the faces of the two men, wondering if one of them might actually be my own father. Yet as much as I had once longed to find my father, I now dreaded the prospect. For I could only despise a man who would serve a king as wicked as Stangmar.

I just want to know him, I had said to Branwen at our last conversation. *It is better you do not,* she had replied. Alas, if he had fallen to the state of the group before me, I now understood why.

Rhia, seeing me, struggled ferociously to free herself. The warrior goblin merely wheezed in laughter and held her more tightly.

"We suspected you would come here eventually," declared Stangmar with his fixed frown. "Especially with your friend here to bait the trap."

I started, wondering why he should care where I was. Then I realized that Stangmar still believed that I wore the Galator, the last Treasure he had long been seeking. How I could take advantage of that mistake, I was not certain, but I resolved to try.

Rhia struggled again to break loose, to no avail. As she twisted in her leafy clothing, I caught the barest whiff of the freshness of the forest we had left behind.

I stepped closer, planting my staff on the stones to help keep my balance on the slowly spinning floor. "Let her go. She has done nothing to harm you."

The king's eyes burned, as the shadows danced over his features. "She would if she could. As would you."

At this, both of the Fincayran men nodded in agreement, while the ghouliants in unison laid their hands on the hilts of their swords. The taller man glanced at me, his face tight with worry. He leaned toward the king and started to say something, but Stangmar waved him silent.

Just then the ghouliant from the dungeon marched up the stairs behind me. Although his face had been savagely scratched, he showed no sign of bleeding. In one of his hands he held Trouble by the talons, so that the upside-down bird could only flap his wings and whistle angrily.

"Another friend, is it?" Stangmar's shadowy face turned to a pair of ghouliants. "Go see if there are any more."

Instantly, the two soldiers rushed past me and descended the stairwell. I then remembered that I had lost track of Shim. I could only hope that my small companion had found a secure place to hide.

Frantically, I turned from Rhia, smothered in the arms of the warrior goblin, to Trouble, dangling helplessly in the grip of the ghouliant. "Set them free!" I shouted to the king. "Set them free or you will regret it."

Stangmar's frown deepened. "We are not accustomed to taking orders from a mere boy! Especially when that boy also threatens our royal person."

Despite the continuous wobbling of the revolving castle, I stood as tall and steady as I could.

Then Stangmar leaned forward in his throne. For an instant the shadows departed from his face. With his square jaw and intense eyes, he looked even more handsome, while no less rigid, than before. "Nevertheless, your valor impresses us. For that reason, we shall be merciful."

Suddenly the shadows reappeared, moving frantically across his face, his chest, and the gold circlet on his brow.

"We know what we are doing!" he growled, though it was not clear to whom. Regally, he waved to the goblin holding Rhia. "Set her free, we command you. But watch her closely."

The warrior goblin grimaced, but obeyed. Roughly, he shoved Rhia onto the stone floor in front of the throne. Trouble, still hanging upside down, screeched wrathfully at the goblin. But he could do no more.

"What about the hawk?" I demanded.

Stangmar leaned back in his throne. "The hawk remains where he is. We trust him as little as we trust you! Moreover, keeping him as he is will encourage you to cooperate."

My spine stiffened. "I will never cooperate with you."

"Nor will I," declared Rhia, shaking her brown curls.

Trouble screeched again, making his own position clear.

For the first time, Stangmar's frown eased slightly. "Oh, you shall cooperate. In fact, you already have! You have brought us some-thing we have long desired. You have brought us *the last Treasure.*"

I winced, but said nothing.

Shadows flickering over his face, Stangmar spread his arms to indicate the objects displayed on the walls. "Here in this hall we have collected many articles of legendary power. Hanging on the wall above our royal throne is Deepercut, the sword with two edges: the black one, that can slice into the soul, and the white one, that can heal any wound. Over there is the famous Flowering Harp. That silver horn is the Caller of Dreams. Beside it, you can see the plow that tills its own field. No more will these Treasures or the others pose any risk to our sovereignty."

His face hardened as he pointed to an iron cauldron set by the opposite wall. "We even have the Cauldron of Death."

At the mention of this object, the two men in red robes traded knowing glances. The taller one shook his head somberly.

"Yet the one Treasure we have most wanted is the one not hanging from our walls." Stangmar's voice boomed inside the hall, drowning out even the steady rumble of the spinning castle. "It is the one you have brought us."

I knew that he would soon discover that I did not have the Galator. Emboldened by the certainty of death, I squared my shoulders. "I would never bring anything that could help you."

The grim king observed me for a moment. "You think not?"

"I know not! I once carried the Galator, but it is no longer with me. It lies beyond your grasp."

Stangmar, his face shadowed, eyed me coldly. "It is not the Galator that we seek."

I blinked. "You said you were seeking the last Treasure."

"We are indeed. But the last Treasure is no mere item of jewelry." The king clasped the arms of his throne. "The last Treasure is my son."

A wave of horror flowed through me. "Your . . . son?"

Stangmar nodded, though his face showed no joy. "It is you I have been seeking. For you are my son."

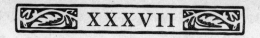

XXXVII

DEEPERCUT

Dark shadows played across the king's features, while his large hands squeezed the throne. "And now we must complete the promise we made before you fled with your mother."

"Promise?" I asked, still reeling from Stangmar's revelation. "What promise?"

"Do you not remember?"

I looked morosely at the man who was my father. "I remember nothing."

"That is fortunate." Stangmar frowned more deeply than before. The shadows wavered on his face, even as they spread slowly down both of his arms. The king clenched his fists, then pointed to me and issued his command. "Throw him into the Cauldron."

In unison, the ghouliants turned toward me.

Trouble, still in the grasp of one of the ghouliants, beat his wings and struggled to free himself. His enraged screeches echoed in the cavernous hall, rising above the rumbling of the spinning castle.

"No!" cried Rhia, jumping to her feet. Quick as a viper, she leaped at Stangmar, closing her hands around his neck. Before his guards could come to his aid, the king wrestled himself free and threw her back to the stone floor. She landed in a leafy heap at the boots of the warrior goblin.

Rubbing the scratches on his neck, the wrathful king stood up. His entire body writhed in shadows. He barked at the goblin, "Kill her first! Then we shall deal with the boy."

"Gladly," rasped the goblin, his narrow eyes alight. He reached for the hilt of his sword.

My heart pounded. My cheeks burned. Rage surged through me, the same violent rage I had felt against Dinatius. I must stop this from happening! I must use my powers!

Then searing flames engulfed my mind. The stench of charred flesh. My own flesh. My own screams. I feared those powers, no less than I feared the Cauldron of Death.

The warrior goblin, grinning savagely, slowly lifted his sword. Its blade glinted in the torchlight. In the same instant, Rhia turned toward me, looking at me with sorrowful eyes.

A new feeling, more powerful even than my rage and fear, filled my heart. I loved Rhia. Loved her spirit, her vitality. *You are all that you are,* she had said to me once. Then the words of the Grand Elusa, spoken within her glowing crystal cave, came back to me. *The last Treasure carries great powers, greater than you know.* My powers were my own. To fear, perhaps, but also to use.

The goblin's powerful shoulders tensed for the blow. Trouble screeched again, fighting to free himself from the ghouliant's grip.

But what about my promise? Again I heard Rhia's voice: *If someone gave you special powers, they are for you to use.* My mother, her sapphire eyes piercing into my soul, joined in. *All God asks is that you use your powers well, with wisdom and love.*

Love. Not rage. That was the key. The same love that caused the Galator to glow. The same love for Rhia that filled me now.

Make your move! commanded the voice of Domnu. *In chess, as in life, your choice will make all the difference.*

Just as the warrior goblin started to bring down his sword on Rhia's head, I focused all of my concentration on the great sword Deepercut, suspended from the wall just behind the throne. The flames rose again in my mind, but I persisted, pushing them back. Beyond the gleeful snort of the goblin, I heard nothing. Beyond the sword and the iron hook that held it, I saw nothing.

Fly, Deepercut. Fly!

The iron hook burst apart. The sword ripped free of the wall and flew toward the goblin. Hearing it slice through the air, he turned. Half a second later, his severed head rolled onto the stone floor.

Rhia screamed as the heavy body fell on top of her. Stangmar roared in anger, his face a mass of shadows. The two red-robed men cried out and stepped back in fright. Only the ghouliants, their faces utterly blank, stood watching in silence.

In the commotion, I let go of my staff and raised my hands high. Deepercut spun through the air toward me. With both hands, I seized the silver hilt.

The ghouliants, seeing this, drew their own swords. Moving as a single body, they rushed at me. Suddenly the voice of the king rang out.

"Stop!" His downturned lips released a long, low snarl. "This duel is ours. No one else's." The shadows roiled across his body. For an instant, he hesitated. Then, with a violent shake, he declared to someone only he could see, "We said this duel is ours! We need no help."

Bounding down from the throne, he swiftly retrieved the sword of the fallen warrior goblin. Glowering at me, he slashed his blade through the air. Only then did I notice that the shadows had again departed from his face. Stranger yet, when I glanced at the red throne, the dark shadows were still there, hovering just above the seat. I felt gripped by the feeling that, somehow, those shadows were watching me closely.

"So," he taunted, "you have *the powers*, do you? Just like your grandfather before you." He took a pace toward me. "But even with all his powers, your grandfather could not escape a mortal death. Nor will you."

I barely had time to lift Deepercut to block Stangmar's first swipe. The swords clanged, echoing among the stone arches of the hall. The force of his blow made my sword vibrate down to the hilt. My hands strained to hold on. I realized that Stangmar had the triple advantages of greater strength, more skill, and—even with my improved vision—better eyesight.

Despite all this, I fought back as well as I could. Although the spinning floor and its constant vibration threw off my balance, I pressed the attack. Slashing wildly, I parried and dodged. Sparks flew when our blades clashed.

Perhaps my sheer ferocity made Stangmar cautious. Perhaps Deepercut itself somehow strengthened me. Or perhaps Stangmar was merely toying with his prey. Whatever the reason, it seemed as we worked our way up and down the hall studded with precious objects, that I was actually holding my own.

All of a sudden Stangmar drove down on me. With a powerful blow that rang through the hall, he smashed into Deepercut. The sword ripped from my hands and clattered to the stone floor.

The king brought his sword to my throat. "Now we shall keep our promise." He indicated the terrible Cauldron by the wall. "Go."

Still panting, I stood my ground. "Who made you promise to kill me?"

"Go."

"And why should that promise mean so much to you, when you have broken all of your promises to your own people?"

"Go!"

I folded my arms. "You promised Rhita Gawr, didn't you?"

Stangmar's frown hardened, even as the shadows danced over the throne. "Yes. And you would be wise to speak of our good friend with respect. Now go!"

I looked imploringly at the man whose eyes and hair mirrored my own. "Can't you see what Rhita Gawr has done to you? To your realm? He wants you to poison your lands. Blacken your sky. Terrify your people. And even . . . kill your own son!"

As I spoke, the mysterious shadows thrashed wildly on the throne.

Stangmar's face reddened. "You have no understanding of these things. No understanding at all!" He pushed the tip of the sword against my neck.

With difficulty, I swallowed. "Rhita Gawr is not your friend. He is your master, and you are his slave."

Eyes aflame, he prodded me toward the Cauldron.

"Would Elen—your wife, my mother—want this?"

Stangmar's rage boiled over. "We will spare the Cauldron and strike you down with this very sword!"

With that he lifted his weapon to whack off my head. Seeing my opening, I concentrated on Deepercut, lying on the floor just behind him.

To me, Deepercut. To me!

But I was too late. The sword had only just begun to move, tilting up on one edge, when the grim king planted his feet firmly to deliver the blow.

As his rear foot came down, however, it grazed the upturned

blade of Deepercut. The black edge, with the power to slice deep into the soul, pierced his leather boot and pricked the base of his heel.

Stangmar cried in agony and crumpled to the ground. The shadows flailed, seeming to shake the very throne. The ghouliants, swords drawn, started to come to the king's aid. But he raised his hand. Abruptly, the soldiers halted.

Slowly, Stangmar lifted his head. He gazed up at me, his face growing softer by the second. His jaw loosened. His eyes widened. Only the frown did not change.

"You spoke the truth," he declared, speaking with difficulty. "We—that is, I—confound this royal speech! I . . . am no more than a slave."

The throne rocked violently from side to side.

Stangmar turned to the thrashing shadows. "You know it is true!" he cried. "I am nothing more than your lowly puppet! My head is now so filled with your threats and delusions that it spins as incessantly as this cursed castle!"

At that a chilling, hissing sound arose from the shadows. They ceased their wild movements and started shrinking, congealing into something still darker.

The king struggled to stand, but the wound had made his whole lower body immobile and he fell back. Somberly, he faced me again. "You must understand. It was never our—that is, my—intention that Fincayra should come to this! When I made that first promise, I had no idea what grief it would bring."

"Why?" I demanded. "Why did you ever make a promise to Rhita Gawr?"

Stangmar's brow furrowed. "I did it . . . to save Elen."

"Elen? My mother?" All at once, I remembered her final words about my father. *If ever you should meet him, remember: He is not what he may seem.*

"Yes. Elen of the Sapphire Eyes." He took a deep breath and exhaled very slowly, his elbows propped against the stone floor. "When she gave birth to you on the shores of Fincayra, it broke one of our oldest laws, one handed down by the spirits themselves, that no one with human blood should ever be born here. Otherwise, humans would have a birthright to a world that is not their own! The punishment for this high crime has always been harsh but clear. The half-human child must be exiled forever from Fincayra. And, what is worse, the human parent must be thrown into the Cauldron of Death."

He tried again to stand, with no success. The ghouliants, who appeared increasingly agitated, started toward him again. The ghouliant holding Trouble joined with the others, his sword in one hand and the struggling hawk in the other.

"Stop!" ordered Stangmar. "I do not need your miserable help."

The ghouliants obeyed, though they continued to watch warily, fidgeting with their swords. Meanwhile, the shadows on the throne continued to shrink. As they condensed, they grew thicker and darker, like the center of a gathering storm.

Stangmar shook his head. "I did not know what to do. How could I condemn to death my own fair Elen? She lifted me higher than the trees I once climbed as a child! Yet I was the king, the one responsible for enforcing the laws! Then Rhita Gawr first came to me. He offered me his help, in exchange for my help in solving a problem of his own."

"What problem was that?"

Stangmar looked away. "Rhita Gawr told me that he had learned in a dream that his gravest danger would come from a child who was half human and half Fincayran. So, knowing of you, he believed that as long as you lived, you would pose some sort of threat to him."

My whole body trembled, even apart from the quaking of the floor. "So you agreed to kill me instead of her?"

"I had no choice, don't you see? Rhita Gawr promised to protect Elen and all of Fincayra from any punishment by the spirits for this violation of the law."

"And you promised to throw me in the Cauldron!"

"I did. Sometime before the end of your seventh year. For that entire time, I kept my promise a secret from Elen. I only told her that the spirits had agreed that she need not die, and you need not be exiled. She was so relieved, I could not bear to tell her the truth. She trusted me completely."

His voice took on a faraway tone. "As it happened, during that seven years, the alliance with Rhita Gawr grew more and more strong. And necessary. He alerted me to the giants' plot to overrun Fincayra. He helped me to cleanse our land of dangerous enemies. He gave me a castle where I could be truly safe. He . . ."

The words trailed off as the king slumped lower. "He made me his slave."

Touched by his anguish, I completed the story for him. "And when Elen—my mother—found out that she had been spared only so that I could die, she fled Fincayra, taking me with her."

Stangmar gazed at me in despair. "So in the end, I lost you both."

"And so much more," added Rhia, standing next to the corpse of the beheaded warrior goblin.

I nodded, then turned to the ghouliants. For some reason, they had drawn closer about the throne, surrounding it with their bodies. Yet despite the nearness of the other soldiers, Trouble continued to wriggle and flap his wings fiercely. The ghouliant who held him did not seem to notice that one of the hawk's talons had almost pulled free.

"Too true," admitted Stangmar. "Rhita Gawr has assured me that if I can find my half-human son and put him to death, my power will then be complete. But what he really means is that I will have done his bidding—ridding him of whatever threat you might represent. So who, I ask, is ruler now?"

At that instant, the ghouliants stepped in unison away from the red throne. Parting like two curtains, they revealed an impenetrable knot of blackness writhing on the seat. Darker than the Shroud itself, the shifting knot released a shrill, shrieking hiss. With the sound came an icy gust that chilled me to the marrow of my bones.

"Rhita Gawr!" shouted Stangmar, desperately trying to raise himself off the floor.

The knot of darkness leaped off the throne, flew past Rhia, and landed on the floor next to Deepercut. Before I could even take a breath, it wrapped itself completely around the silver hilt. Like a dark hand of evil, it raised the sword and slashed at Stangmar, slicing one side of his face from ear to chin. Blood streaming down his jaw, the king howled in pain and rolled to the side.

Suddenly Stangmar froze. His expression began to change from terror to wrath. His eyes narrowed, his frown tightened, his fists clenched so hard they went white. Then, to my shock, he grabbed the other sword and jumped to his feet. He stood beside me, proud and strong despite his bloody face.

"Help us!" I cried.

But instead of aiming his sword at the black knot holding Deepercut, he pointed it straight at me. "You are a fool, boy! We are not so easily defeated as that."

I backed away. "But you said—"

"We said nothing of importance," he declared, with a wave toward the undulating mass of darkness that was Rhita Gawr. "Our friend here has healed us! By striking us with the edge that can heal any wound, he has cured our whimpering soul. And in doing so he has brought us back to our senses. We know who our enemies are, and now we will strike you down!"

Rhia started to charge at the king, but two of the ghouliants stepped in front of her. She tried her best to dodge them, but they blocked her path.

As Stangmar drew back his sword, preparing to run me through, Rhita Gawr gave another shrieking hiss. Stangmar faltered. Slowly, he lowered his weapon.

Looking somewhat ashamed, the king shook his head. "We would not fail you again," he protested. "We were deceived! Deluded! Allow us to fulfill our promise to you now."

An angry, ear-splitting hiss was Rhita Gawr's only answer. As Stangmar looked on obediently, the pulsing knot of darkness lifted its own sword once again. Swinging the blade around, Rhita Gawr prepared to end my life.

Just then, another shrill cry filled the hall. Trouble had finally broken free from the ghouliant's grip. As the soldier tried in vain to pierce the hawk with his sword, Trouble soared toward the ceiling of the great hall.

Swooping up to the highest possible point, the merlin released a screech that echoed from every wall. He careened sharply in the air, pausing for a split second above our heads. Then this small but spirited creature, whose life ever since our first meeting had consisted of one brave deed after another, did the bravest deed of all.

At the very instant that the sword started slicing toward me,

Trouble beat his wings mightily and plunged faster than an arrow into the very center of the black mass. Taken by surprise, Rhita Gawr let go of the sword, which flew across the hall, skittering over the stones. As the cold arms of blackness wrapped around Trouble, he slashed and pecked and whipped his wings furiously. Hissing and screeching, the dark knot and the merlin rolled over each other on the floor.

Desperately, I searched for some way to help Trouble. But how? I could try wielding Deepercut, but he and Rhita Gawr had embraced each other so tightly that I couldn't possibly hit one without hitting the other. I could try using my powers to strike a different kind of blow, but that would surely fail for the same reason. My heart burst to watch—yet that was all I could do.

Trouble fought on valiantly. Still, Rhita Gawr's chilling embrace and superior strength proved too much. Slowly, inexorably, the mass of darkness was swallowing the bird. Consuming him, bit by bit. First his talon. Then his wing. Then half of his tail. And, in a few more seconds, his head.

"Oh, Trouble!" wailed Rhia, still flanked by the ghouliants.

With a final, piercing whistle, the merlin lifted his head as high as he could, then plunged his beak right into the uttermost heart of the blackness. Suddenly, a thin edge of bright light surrounded the grappling pair. A strange, sucking sound rent the air, as if the wall separating two worlds had been ruptured. Both the dark mass and the hawk it had consumed grew swiftly smaller, until only a tiny black speck remained, hovering in the air. An instant later, that too disappeared.

Trouble was gone. Though he had somehow taken Rhita Gawr with him, I was as sure that the wicked spirit would one day return as I was sure that my friend would not. My sightless eyes brimming with tears, I bent to pick up a lone feather that had come to rest on the floor by my feet.

I slowly twirled the banded brown feather between my fingers. It was from one of Trouble's wings, the same wings that had borne me aloft not so long ago. Those wings, like myself, would never fly again. Gently I slipped the feather into my satchel.

Suddenly the point of a sword pushed at my chest. I looked up to see Stangmar, half his face and neck smeared with blood, scowling at me.

"Now we will fulfill our promise," he declared. "And in the way it was meant to be done. So that when our friend returns, he will know beyond doubt where our loyalty lies."

"No," pleaded Rhia. "Don't do it! This is your chance to be a true king, don't you understand?"

Stangmar snorted. "Waste not your breath on such lies." He turned to the ghouliants. "Guards! Throw him into the Cauldron."

ANCIENT WORDS

Instantly, the ghouliants not guarding Rhia tramped across the hall, converging on me. Swords drawn, faces emotionless, they began marching me toward the Cauldron of Death.

I did not even try to resist them. Whether from the loss of Trouble or from the continuous shaking of the floor, my legs felt wobbly and weak. Moreover, even if my powers could have helped me now, I had no heart to try anymore. My only thoughts were of the empty place on my shoulder.

Rhia tried to run after me, but the soldiers restrained her.

Grimly, Stangmar watched. He stood as rigid as a statue, his eyes smoldering, his hand squeezing the hilt of his sword. The dried blood on his face had turned the same color as the Blighted Lands of his realm.

Pace by pace, the procession drew nearer to the Cauldron. It seemed to glower at me as I approached, dark and silent as death itself. For a moment I considered throwing myself into it willingly, in the hope that I might be able to destroy the Cauldron as well as myself. But even that small satisfaction would not be mine, for the ghouliants were flanking me so closely that they would surely have killed me before I broke free.

Crestfallen, I turned to Rhia. Reaching through a gap between two of the soldiers, I extended a bent forefinger toward her. Although her eyes were clouded, she returned the gesture, symbolically wrapping her finger around mine for the last time.

The ghouliants stopped just short of the Cauldron. Although it reached only up to my waist, its iron mouth yawned so wide that a fully grown man or woman could easily have fit inside. And within that mouth lay only blackness—even thicker and deeper than the Shroud. The ghouliants shoved me almost to the Cauldron's rim, then turned to Stangmar, awaiting his orders.

Rhia pleaded with the king. "Don't, please!"

Stangmar paid no attention. His voice rising above the rumble of the ever-spinning castle, he gave his command.

"Into the Cauldron!"

At that instant, a tiny figure dashed out of the shadows near the stairwell. With only a fleeting glance at Rhia and myself, Shim sped across the floor, his small feet slapping on the stones. Before the ghouliants realized what was happening, he clambered up to the rim of the Cauldron. He hesitated for a fraction of a second, then threw himself into its mouth.

A thunderous explosion shook in the hall, rocking the revolving castle to its very foundation. Although the spinning never ceased, the power of the blast caused the rotations to wobble erratically. I tumbled to the floor, as did Rhia and several of the ghouliants. Torches fell from their mountings, sizzling on the stones. The Flowering Harp swayed precariously from the wall, held by a single string.

As the sound of the explosion reverberated among the walls, as well as the Dark Hills beyond, I regained my feet. What I saw was the Cauldron of Death, split into two great halves. And there, in the center of the destroyed Cauldron, lay the body of the little giant.

"Shim!" I bent over my companion, tears again filling my eyes. My voice a mere whisper, I spoke to the corpse. "You always wanted to be big. To be a true giant. Well, a giant you are, my friend. A giant you are."

"What treachery is this?" Stangmar slashed his sword through the air as he raged at the ghouliants. "We told you to find any other intruders!"

Angrily, he grabbed one of the ghouliants' swords and thrust it straight into the soldier's belly. The ghouliant shuddered, but did not utter any sound. Then he slowly pulled the sword out again, facing Stangmar as if nothing had happened.

Stangmar strode up to me, still kneeling at the edge of the shattered Cauldron. His face taut, he raised his sword high above me. As I turned toward him, my head tangled with black hair so like his own, he hesitated for an instant.

"Curse you, boy! The sight of you—and the cut of that cursed blade—has awakened feelings in us. Feelings we thought we had forgotten, and wish only to forget again! And now our task is twice as wretched. For though we must do what we must do, the pain will be all the greater."

Suddenly, Stangmar's mouth dropped open in astonishment. He faltered, stepping backward in fright.

For within the remains of the Cauldron, a strange thing was happening. As if a gentle breeze had started to blow through the hall, the hairs on Shim's head were stirring, quivering. Slowly at first, then with increasing speed, his nose started to grow larger. Then his ears. Then the rest of his head, neck, and shoulders. His arms too began swelling, followed by his chest, hips, legs, and feet. His clothes expanded with him, growing larger by the second.

Then came the greater miracle. Shim opened his eyes. More

amazed, perhaps, than anyone else, he groped at his expanding body with his swelling hands.

"I is getting bigger! I is getting bigger!"

By the time Shim's head was pushing against the ceiling, Stangmar recovered his senses. "It's a giant!" he cried to the ghouliants. "Attack him before he ruins us all!"

The nearest ghouliant dashed forward and ran his sword into the part of Shim's body that was closest. That happened to be his left knee.

"Oww!" howled Shim, clutching his knee. "Stingded by a bee!"

Instinctively, the once-little giant curled himself up into a ball. This only made him an easier target, however. The ghouliants gathered around, poking and stabbing him with the fury of an angry swarm. Meanwhile, Shim's body continued to expand, with no sign of slowing. Before long, the pressure of his shoulders and back against the ceiling made it start to buckle. Chunks of stone rained down on us. A hole opened in the ceiling.

One of the towers on the battlements fell, crashing into Shim's still-growing nose. But instead of making him curl up tighter to escape harm, the blow made something else happen. It provoked his wrath.

"I is angry!" he thundered, swinging his fist, now nearly as large as the king's throne, through a section of wall.

Stangmar, visibly frightened, started backing away. Following his lead, the ghouliants also retreated. The two Fincayran men, who had been cowering by the throne, dashed madly for the stairs, tripping over each other in their haste.

I ran to join Rhia, pausing only to retrieve Deepercut, which lay near the stairwell. Together we huddled in a far corner that seemed safe—for the moment, at least—from falling stones.

Then, for the first time in his life, Shim had a very giantlike experience. He saw his attackers running *away* from him. And the gleam in his enormous pink eyes made it clear that the experience was one he just might enjoy.

"I is bigger than you," he bellowed. "Muchly bigger!"

Shim, whose hairy feet alone had swelled bigger than boulders, stood up. He stretched his body to its fullest height, bringing down another piece of the ceiling. With a vengeful grin spreading over his gargantuan face, he began stomping on the ghouliants. Each of his stomps shook the entire castle, and sections of the floor itself began to give way.

But the deathless soldiers survived even these crushing blows. After each attack, they merely stood, shook themselves, and resumed slashing at Shim's feet with their swords. Shim's eyes flamed with rage. He stomped harder than ever. The more the ghouliants scurried beneath him, the more weight he threw into every step.

As I sat with Rhia in the corner, fervently hoping that Shim would not move to our end of the hall, I watched crumbling pieces of the ceiling crash around him. He was clearly angry—and clearly enjoying himself.

Then, beyond the sound of splintering stones and stomping feet, I began to hear a strange, rhythmic sound coming from somewhere beyond the castle. Distant at first, then closer, the sound swelled steadily. I suddenly realized that it was the sound of voices, the deepest voices I had ever heard. They were singing a simple chant, consisting of three profoundly low notes. And there was something else about the chant, something familiar, that stirred in me a feeling I could not quite identify.

Then an enormous face, craggy as a cliff and wearing a shaggy red beard, appeared in the gap in the ceiling. It was followed by another, with curly gray hair and full lips. And another, with skin as dark as a shadow, a long braid, and earrings made from chariot wheels. Each of them nodded in greeting to Shim, but remained outside the castle walls.

"Giants," said Rhia in wonderment. "They have come."

Indeed, rising from their secret hiding places all across Fincayra, the giants had come. Responding to some long-awaited call, perhaps the explosion from the Cauldron of Death, they had lumbered out of the darkened canyons, remote forests, and unknown ridges of this land. Bearing huge, flaming torches, they arrived from many directions. Some wore heavy nets of stones, which would have allowed them to rest unnoticed in fields of boulders. Others still carried branches, even whole trees, on their flowing manes. And others, perhaps because they were too foolish or too proud to disguise themselves at all, wore vests and hats and capes as colorful as the fruited trees of Druma Wood.

Swiftly, the giants arranged themselves in a circle around the castle. Following Shim's example, they began stomping the ground together, with the combined force of an earthquake. All the while, they lifted their voices in the rhythmic chant, singing in their most ancient language, the language of Fincayra's first people:

> *Hy gododin catann hue*
> *Hud a lledrith mal wyddan*
> *Gaunce ae bellawn wen cabri*
> *Varigal don Fincayra*
> *Dravia, dravia Fincayra.*

In a flash, I recalled hearing my mother sing the very same chant. But was that memory from our time in Gwynedd, or from sometime before? Had I, perhaps, even heard it as a baby? I could not quite tell.

Somehow I caught the feeling, perhaps from that vague, uncertain memory, that the meaning of this chant had something to do with the timeless bond between the giants and Fincayra. With the notion that as long as one lasted, so would the other. *Dravia, dravia Fincayra. Live long, live long Fincayra.*

The more the giants danced by the light of their great torches, the more the castle crumbled. While the stones behind Rhia and me continued to hold, other sections of the wall were buckling. And as the castle's walls weakened, so did its enchantment. The spinning started to slow, the rumbling to fade. Then, with a grinding scrape of stone against stone, the castle came to a wrenching halt. Pillars and arches collapsed, filling the air with dust and debris.

At that moment, the ghouliants, whose power had sprung from the turning castle itself, released a unified shout—more of surprise than of anguish—and dropped wherever they stood. I could not help but think, as I viewed their bodies sprawled among the stones, that their faces at last showed a touch of emotion. And that the emotion was something akin to gratitude.

With the death of the ghouliants, Shim climbed through a missing section of wall and joined the rest of the giants outside. As I listened to the pounding of their heavy feet all around the castle, I remembered more ancient words. Words that had foretold this Dance of the Giants:

> *Where in the darkness a castle doth spin,*
> *Small will be large, ends will begin.*
> *Only when giants make dance in the hall*
> *Shall every barrier crumble and fall.*

Shim, I realized, had been saved by an older form of magic. Older than the Shrouded Castle, older than the Cauldron of Death, older perhaps than the giants themselves. For even as his act of courage had destroyed the Cauldron, his very footsteps in running across the stone floor of the hall had begun the dance that would destroy the castle in its entirety. *Small will be large, ends will begin.* The Grand Elusa had told Shim that bigness meant more than the size of his bones. And now, through the bigness of his own actions, he towered above the battlements of this crumbling castle.

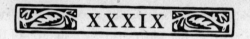

HOME

The wall behind us started to groan. I turned to Rhia, whose tattered suit of vines still smelled of the forest. "We must go! Before the whole castle collapses."

She shook some chips of stone from her hair. "The stairs are blocked. Should we try to climb down somehow?"

"That would take too long," I replied, leaping to my feet. "I know a better way." Cupping my hands around my mouth, I shouted above the din. "Shim!"

Even as a crack split the wall, a face appeared through a hole in the ceiling. The face would have been familiar if only it had been many, many times smaller.

"I is big now," boomed Shim with pride.

"You got your wish! *To be as big as the highlyest tree.*" I waved to him to bend closer. "Now put your hand through that hole, will you? We need a ride out of here."

Shim grunted, then thrust his immense hand through the hole in the ceiling. The hand came to rest on the floor beside us, though so near to a chasm that only one of us at a time could squeeze past to climb into Shim's palm. Rhia chose to go first.

While she carefully worked her way around the chasm, I hefted Deepercut in my hand. Although its silver hilt still felt cold from the clutch of Rhita Gawr, the twin edges gleamed with a luster that reminded me of moonlight on the rolling surface of the sea.

Suddenly I remembered the Treasures of Fincayra. They too must be saved! Whatever time remained before the final collapse of the castle, I must use it to find the Treasures that had not already been destroyed by falling debris.

"Come on!" called Rhia, holding onto Shim's thumb.

"You go first," I answered. "Send Shim back for me." As she watched me worriedly, I cupped my hands and shouted toward the ceiling. "All right, Shim. Lift!"

As Rhia rose through the ceiling, I placed Deepercut on the safest looking slab of stone I could find. Immediately, I began prowling around the remains of the once-cavernous hall. Crawling over tumbled columns and the corpses of ghouliants, dodging falling chunks of stone, stepping over fissures snaking across the floor, I moved as swiftly and carefully as possible. All the while, beyond the groans and crashes of the castle, I could hear the ongoing pounding of the Dance of the Giants.

In short order, I found the Flowering Harp, with all but a few strings intact, and a glittering orange sphere that I guessed must be the Orb of Fire. Quickly, I carried them over to Deepercut and returned for more. Near the toppled red throne, I discovered my own staff, a treasure at least to myself. At the far end of the hall, I uncovered the half-buried Caller of Dreams, as well as the hoe that Honn had said could nurture its own seeds.

All in all, I found only six of the Seven Wise Tools. After the hoe, I located the plow that tills its own field, although it proved almost too heavy for me to lift. Then I discovered a hammer, a shovel, and a bucket, whose powers I could only guess. Last of all I turned up the saw that I knew from Honn's description would cut only as much wood as needed. Although part of the handle had been crushed by a huge chunk of stone, the tool remained usable.

I had just deposited the saw with the other Treasures when Shim's face reappeared through the hole in the ceiling.

"You must comes!" he thundered. "This castle is readily to fall in."

I nodded, though I still wished that I had been able to locate the missing one of the Seven Wise Tools. Not knowing what it might look like had only made my task of finding it more difficult. Even so, as Shim lowered his great hand and I began loading it with the Treasures, I occasionally paused to scan the hall for any sign of the seventh Wise Tool.

"Is you done yet?" Shim bellowed impatiently.

"Almost." I hurled the last of the objects, my staff, onto his palm. "Just one more minute while I climb on."

"Quickerly!" called Shim. "You might not haves another minute."

Indeed, as he spoke, I felt the stones of the floor under my feet shift drastically. I started to climb onto his hand, giving a final glance to the hall.

Just then I spotted, in the shadows behind a smashed pillar, something that made my whole body tense. It was not the missing Wise Tool. It was a hand, groping helplessly. The hand of Stangmar.

"Comes on!" Shim implored. "I can sees the ceiling about to fall."

For an instant I hesitated. Then, even as a section of the ceiling came crashing down beside me, I turned and raced across the floor of the foundering castle. The crumbling of the walls, floor, and ceiling seemed to accelerate, as did the chanting and stomping of the giants outside.

When I reached Stangmar, I bent over him. He lay chest down on the floor, the gold circlet still on his brow. A large slab of stone had fallen across his lower back and one of his arms. His hand, now clenched into a fist, had ceased groping. Only his half-open eyes revealed that he was still alive.

"You?" he moaned hoarsely. "Have you come to watch us die? Or do you plan to kill us yourself?"

I gave my answer by reaching over and gripping the slab. With all my strength, I tried to lift it. Legs trembling, lungs bursting, I felt not even the slightest movement in the stone.

As the king realized what I was doing, he eyed me with scorn. "So you would save us now to kill us later?"

"I would save you now so you might live," I declared, though the floor beneath us started to sway.

"Bah! Do you expect us to believe that?"

Concentrating hard, I heaved, calling on all the powers within me. Perspiration slid down my brow, stinging my sightless eyes. At last, the slab budged just a little, though not enough to free Stangmar.

Before I could try again, the floor burst open. The two of us tumbled into the darkness below, amidst the rising roar of the castle's final collapse.

All at once something broke our fall. Stangmar and I rolled together in a heap. At first I had no idea what had caught us, except that it was far softer than stone. Then, as the light from the giants' torches returned, I viewed the ruins of the castle below us, as well as a familiar face above us. And I understood.

"I catches you!" crowed Shim. "It's a goodly thing I has two hands!"

"Yes," I replied, sitting in the center of his palm. "A goodly thing."

The giant's enormous mouth frowned. "The wickedly king is with you." He roared with rage, "I will eats him!"

A look of terror filled Stangmar's face.

"Wait," I cried. "Let us imprison him, not kill him."

Stangmar gazed at me with astonishment.

Shim growled again, scrunching his mountainous nose with displeasure. "But he is bad! Completely, totally, horribly bad."

"That may be true," I replied. "But he is also my father." I turned and looked into the dark eyes of the man beside me. "And there was a time, long ago, when he liked to climb trees. Sometimes just to ride out a storm."

Stangmar's eyes seemed to soften ever so slightly, as if my words had cut almost as deep as the blade of Deepercut. Then he turned away.

Shim set us down on a knoll of dry grass at the edge of the hill where the Shrouded Castle once stood so formidably. Then he stepped away, the ground shaking under his weight. I watched him sit down, propping his back against the hillside. He stretched his immense arms and gave a loud yawn, though not so loud as the snore that I knew would soon come.

Seeing Rhia nearby, I left the crumpled form of Stangmar to join her. She stood looking westward, beyond the castle ruins, toward a faint line of green on the distant horizon.

Hearing the crunch of my footsteps, she spun around. Her eyes, wide as ever, seemed to dance. "You are safe."

I nodded. "As are most of the Treasures."

She smiled, something I had not seen her do for some time.

"Rhia! Am I mistaken, or is it growing lighter?"

"You are not mistaken! The Shroud is going the same way as the castle and the ghouliants."

I pointed toward the giants, who had ceased their chanting and stomping. Singly and in clusters of two or three, they were beginning to drift away from the ruins. "Where are they going?"

"To their homes."

"To their homes," I repeated.

Peering across the hillside, we observed what was left of the Shrouded Castle. While much of it had been crushed in the Dance of the Giants, a ring of mammoth stones remained standing in a stately circle. Some of the stones stood upright, others leaned to the side, and still others supported hefty crosspieces. Whether the giants had placed the stones in this fashion, or had simply left them standing, I knew not.

In silence, as the first rays of sunlight started piercing the sky above the Dark Hills, I contemplated this imposing circle. It rose like a great stone hedge upon the land. It struck me that this ring of stones would make a lasting monument to the fact that no walls, however sturdy, can forever withstand the power of what is true. Vision that is true. Friendship that is true. Faith that is true.

All of a sudden, I realized that I could remember my own childhood in this very place! On this very hill! *Only when giants make dance in the hall, Shall every barrier crumble and fall.* The prophecy, I now understood, had not applied only to walls of stone. My own inner walls, that had cut me off from my past since the day I washed ashore on Gwynedd, had begun to crumble along with those of the castle.

First in gentle wisps, then in surging waves, memory after memory came floating back to me. My mother, wrapped in her shawl before a crackling fire, telling me the story of Hercules. My father, so confident and strong, leaping astride a black stallion named Ionn. The first time I ever tasted larkon, the spiral fruit. The first swim in the River Unceasing. The final, sorrowful minutes before we fled for our lives, my mother and I, praying that the sea might somehow deliver us to safety.

And then, from my distant childhood, came the words of a chant called the Lledra. It was a chant that had been sung by my mother long ago, just as it had been sung by the giants themselves today:

> *Talking trees and walking stones,*
> *Giants are the island's bones.*
> *While this land our dance still knows,*
> *Varigal crowns Fincayra.*
> *Live long, live long Fincayra.*

"Rhia," I said quietly. "I've not yet found my true home. Nor am I sure that I ever will. But, for the very first time, I think I know where to look."

She raised an eyebrow. "And where is that?"

I waved toward the circle of stones, luminous in the swelling rays. "All this time I've sought my home as though it could be found somewhere on a map. And now I remember a home that I once knew. Here, on this very spot! Yet, at the same time, I have the feeling that if my true home exists anywhere, it isn't on a map at all. More likely, it's somewhere inside of myself."

Her voice wistful, she added, "In the same place that our memories of Trouble are found."

I reached my hand into my satchel and pulled out the feather. Softly, I stroked its edge with my finger. "I have an idea of what happened to him when he vanished. I can't quite believe it—but I can't quite dismiss it, either."

Rhia studied the feather. "I have the same idea. And I think Arbassa would agree."

"If it's true, and his bravery opened the door to the Other-world—then he and Rhita Gawr must have fallen through that door together."

She smiled. "It wasn't a journey Rhita Gawr had planned! But it gave us the chance we needed. So if it's true, Trouble is somewhere out there right now, still soaring."

"And Rhita Gawr is out there too, still fuming."

She nodded, then her face turned serious. "Still, I'm going to miss that hawk."

I dropped the feather, watching it spin slowly downward into my other hand. "So will I."

Rhia kicked at the brittle grass under our feet. "And see what else we have lost! This soil is so parched, I wonder whether it will ever come back to life."

With a slight grin, I announced, "I already have a plan for that."

"You do?"

"I think the Flowering Harp, with its power to coax the spring into being, might be able to help."

"Of course! I should have remembered."

"I plan to carry it to every hillside and meadow and stream that has withered. As well as to one particular garden, down on the plains, where two friends of mine live."

Rhia's gray-blue eyes brightened.

"I was even hoping . . ."

"What?"

"That you might want to come along. You could help revive the trees."

Her bell-like laughter rang out. "Whether I come or not, this much is clear. You may not have found your true home. But I think you have found a few friends."

"I'd say you're right."

She watched me for a moment. "And one thing more. You have found your true name."

"I have?"

"Yes. You remind me of that hawk who once sat on your shoulder. You can be fierce as well as gentle. You grab hold with all your strength and never let go. You see clearly, though not with your eyes. You know when to use your powers. And . . . you can fly."

She glanced toward the circle of stones, gleaming like a great necklace in the light, then turned back to me. "Your true name ought to be Merlin."

"You can't be serious."

"I am."

Merlin. I rather liked the name. Not enough to keep it, of course, though I knew that names sometimes had a strange way of sticking. *Merlin.* An unusual name, to say the least. And all the more meaningful because of the sorrow and joy it brought to my mind.

"All right. I shall try it. But only for a while."

THE SEVEN SONGS OF
MERLIN

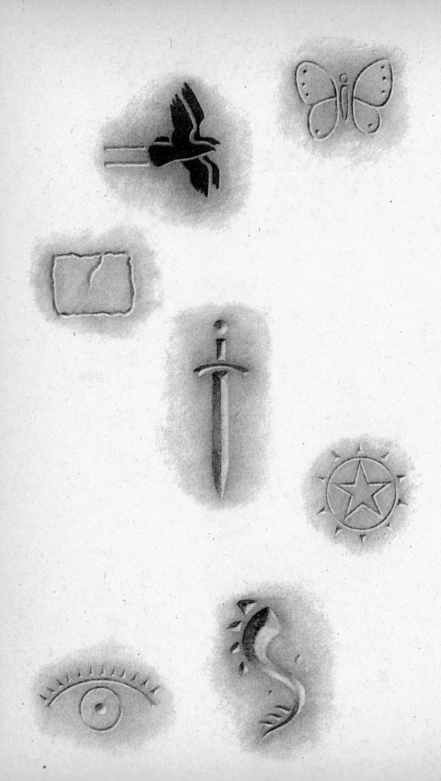

T. A. BARRON

THE SEVEN SONGS OF
MERLIN

BOOK TWO OF
THE LOST YEARS OF MERLIN

PHILOMEL BOOKS • NEW YORK

This book is dedicated to
Currie
who sings her life as if it were a verse
of the seventh Song

with special appreciation to
Ross
age two, who sees so well with his heart

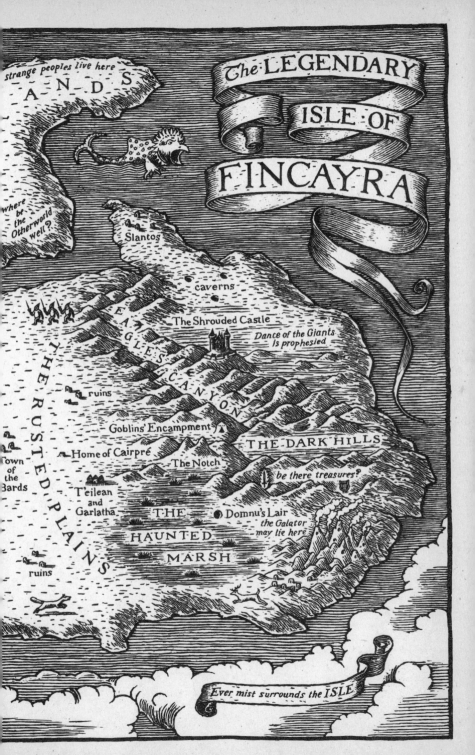

The LEGENDARY ISLE·OF FINCAYRA

strange peoples live here

...ANDS

where be the Otherworld well?

Slantos

caverns

The Shrouded Castle

Dance of the Giants is prophesied

EAGLES' CANYON

ruins

THE·RUSTED·PLAINS

Goblins' Encampment

THE·DARK·HILLS

Home of Cairpré

The Notch

be there treasures?

Town of the Bards

Teilean and Garlatha

THE HAUNTED MARSH

Domnu's Lair
the Galator may lie here

ruins

Ever mist surrounds the ISLE

CONTENTS

AUTHOR'S NOTE

Sometimes, in the long hours before dawn, I lie awake, listening. To the boughs of cottonwood, stirring in the wind. To the great horned owl, hooting quietly. And, on rare occasions, to the voice of Merlin, whispering. Before I could even begin to hear Merlin's voice—let alone hear it clearly enough to tell the tale of his lost youth—I needed to learn a little. And to unlearn a lot. Most of all, I needed to listen with care, using more than just my ears. For this wizard is full of surprises.

The Lost Years of Merlin, volume one of this sequence, revealed the strange events that began his years lost from time. Why should those years have disappeared from the traditional lore, only to come to light now, centuries later? The answer may have something to do with the profound changes—and terrible pain—that Merlin himself experienced in that period. Yet those years proved to be exceptionally important ones for the person who would one day serve as the mentor to King Arthur.

The story of Merlin's lost years began when, as a boy at the very edge of death, he washed ashore on the rugged coast of Wales. The sea had robbed him of everything he had once known. Completely unaware that he would, one day, become the greatest wizard of all

2 · THE SEVEN SONGS OF MERLIN

time, he lay tormented by the shadows of things he could not recall.
For he had no memory. No home. And no name.

From Merlin's own words, we can feel the lasting trauma, and hidden hope, of that day:

> *If I close my eyes, and breathe to the rolling rhythm of the sea, I can still remember that long ago day. Harsh, cold, and lifeless it was, as empty of promise as my lungs were empty of air.*
>
> *Since that day, I have seen many others, more than I have the strength left to count. Yet that day glows as bright as the Galator itself, as bright as the day I found my own name, or the day I first cradled a baby who bore the name Arthur.*
>
> *Perhaps I remember it so clearly because the pain, like a scar on my soul, will not disappear. Or because it marked the ending of so much. Or, perhaps, because it marked a beginning as well as an ending: the beginning of my lost years.*

Now the young Merlin's story continues. He may have solved the riddle of the Dance of the Giants, but a dark knot of riddles lies just ahead. Whether he can successfully pull them apart, in time to complete his quest, remains to be seen. The challenge is enormous. While Merlin has stumbled upon his hidden powers, he has not nearly mastered them. While he has heard some of the wisdom of the Druids, the Greeks, and the Celts, he has only begun to understand it. And while he has discovered his own name, and a hint of his true destiny, he has yet to find the secret of his innermost self.

In short, he does not yet know what it means to be a wizard.

If he is to find the wizard in himself, the young Merlin, who has already lost so much, must lose something more. Along the way, he may gain a few things, as well. He may finally learn the truth about his friend Rhia. He may grasp the difference between sight and insight. He may even find, to his sorrow, that he holds both the dark and the light within himself—even as he finds, to his joy, that he also holds other qualities often called opposites: youth and age, male and female, mortal and immortal.

Legendary heroes sometimes ascend through the three levels of self, world, and Otherworld. First he or she must discover the hidden pathways within. Next the hero must triumph over the enemies of mortal life on Earth. Finally, he or she must confront the perils and possibilities of the spirit. In a sense, Merlin alters this traditional pattern by attempting to voyage to the Otherworld in this book, only the second volume of the sequence. But Merlin, as we have seen, is not very good at following the rules. The truth is that in this book, as in the others, Merlin finds himself exploring all three levels at once.

Yet it is the Otherworld, the realm of the spirit, that holds the key to this quest. It is a mysterious place, rarely visited by mortals, full of danger as well as inspiration. If Merlin can somehow master the Seven Songs of Wizardry, defeat the same forces that destroyed his own grandfather, and discover the secret of the Otherworld Well, he could indeed find his way to the spiritual realm. If he does, he may meet both the mysterious Dagda and the treacherous Rhita Gawr . . . and whatever might be left of his loyal friend Trouble.

And, in the process, he may find something more. As W. B. Yeats once wrote, humanity has always yearned to find some connection with the cosmic order, "to reunite the perception of the spirit, of the divine, with natural beauty." That is why the young Merlin, who first sensed his own powers of renewal by riding out a storm in the branches of a tree, struggles to make such a connection as he follows the winding path to wizardry.

This portion of Merlin's journey begins where the last one ended, on the legendary isle of Fincayra. The Celts believed it to be an island beneath the waves, a halfway point between this world and the Otherworld. An *omphalos*, the Greeks might say. But Fincayra's best description came from Elen, Merlin's mother, who called it simply an *in between place*. Like the mist, which is neither quite water nor quite air, Fincayra is neither quite mortal nor quite immortal. It is something in between.

Merlin, too, is something in between. He is not truly a man, yet not truly a god. He is not really old, yet not really young. Carl Jung would have found him a compelling character, for Merlin's mythic powers sprang from both the unconscious and the conscious, just as his wisdom flowed from both nature and culture.

It is no accident that the most ancient tales of Merlin give him a saintly mother and a demonic father, metaphors for the light and the dark sides within us all. And Merlin's greatest wisdom came not from expelling or eliminating his dark side, but rather from embracing it, owning it as part of himself. Ultimately, it is this sense of human frailty, along with human possibility, that makes Merlin the fitting mentor for King Arthur.

I remain deeply grateful to all those people named in the Author's Note of the first volume, most especially my wife and best friend, Currie, and my immensely wise editor, Patricia Lee Gauch. In addition, I would like to thank Lloyd Alexander, whose works continue to inspire us all; Susan Cullinan, who understands the wisdom of humor; and Sasha, our gentle Labrador, who often warms my feet as I write.

Once again, Merlin whispers. Let us listen, but with care. For this wizard, as we know, is full of surprises.

T. A. B.

I was taken out of my true self.
I was a spirit and knew...
the secrets of nature,
bird flight,
star wanderings,
and the way fish glide.

—Merlin,
    quoted in Geoffrey of Monmouth's
    twelfth-century book *VITA MERLINI*

PROLOGUE

How the centuries have flown . . . Faster, by far, than the brave hawk who once bore me on his back. Faster, indeed, than the arrow of pain that lodged in my heart on the day I lost my mother.

Still I can see the Great Council of Fincayra, gathering in the circle of standing stones, all that remained of the mighty castle after the Dance of the Giants. Not for many ages had a Great Council been called on that spot; not for many ages would one be called again. Several difficult questions awaited resolution by the delegates, including how to punish the fallen monarch, and whether or not to choose a successor. But the gravest question of all was what to do with the enchanted Treasures of Fincayra, especially the Flowering Harp.

I cannot forget how the meeting began. Nor, hard as I try, can I forget how it ended.

A cluster of shadows more dark than the night, the circle of stones stood erect on the ridge.

No stirring, no sound, disturbed the night air. A lone bat swooped toward the ruins, then veered away, perhaps out of fear that the Shrouded Castle might somehow rise again. But all that remained of its towers and battlements was the ring of standing stones, as silent as abandoned graves.

Slowly, a strange light began rippling over the stones. It was not the light of the sun, still hours from rising, but of the stars overhead. Bit by bit the stars grew steadily brighter. It seemed as if they were somehow drawing nearer, pressing closer to the circle, watching with a thousand thousand eyes aflame.

A broad-winged moth, as yellow as butter, alighted on one of the stones. Soon it was joined by a pale blue bird, and an ancient horned owl missing many feathers. Something slithered across a fallen pillar, keeping to the shadows. A pair of fauns, with the legs and hoofs of goats and the chests and faces of boys, gamboled into the clearing inside the circle. Next came the walking trees, ashes and oaks and hawthorns and pines, sweeping across the ridge like a dark green tide.

Seven Fincayran men and women, their eyes full of wonder, stepped into the circle alongside a band of red-bearded dwarves, a black stallion, several ravens, a pair of water nymphs raucously splashing each other in a pool beneath one of the stones, a speckled lizard, popinjays, peacocks, a unicorn whose coat shone as white as her horn, a family of green beetles who had brought their own leaf to sit on, a doe with her fawn, a huge snail, and a phoenix who stared at the crowd continuously without ever blinking.

As more delegates arrived, one of the Fincayrans, a shaggy-headed poet with a tall brow and dark, observant eyes, stood watching the scene unfold. In time, he stepped over to a tumbled pillar and sat down next to a robust girl dressed in a suit of woven vines. On her other side sat a boy, holding a twisted staff, who looked older than his thirteen years. His eyes, blacker than charcoal, seemed strangely distant. He had recently taken to calling himself Merlin.

Screeching and fluttering, buzzing and growling, hissing and bellowing filled the air. As the sun rose higher, painting the circle of stones with golden hues, the din rose higher as well. The cacophonous noise subsided only once, when an enormous white spider, more than twice as big as the stallion, entered the ring. As the other creatures hushed, they moved quickly aside, for while they might have felt honored to be joined by the legendary Grand Elusa, they also suspected that she might well have worked up an appetite on her journey from her crystal cave in the Misted Hills. She had no difficulty finding a seat.

As the Grand Elusa positioned herself on a heap of crushed rock, she scratched the hump on her back with one of her eight legs. Using another leg, she pulled a large, brown sack off her back and placed it by her side. Then she glanced around the circle, pausing for an instant to gaze at Merlin.

Still more came. A centaur, wearing a beard that fell almost down to his hooves, strode solemnly into the ring. A pair of foxes, tails held high, pranced in his wake, followed by a young wood elf with arms and legs nearly as wispy as her nut brown hair. A living stone, splotched with moss, rolled into the center, barely missing a slow-moving hedgehog. A swarm of energetic bees hovered close to the ground. Near the edge, a family of ogres viciously scratched and bit each other to pass the time.

And still more came, many Merlin could not identify. Some looked like bristling bushes with fiery eyes, others resembled twisted sticks or clumps of mud, and still others seemed invisible but for a vague shimmer of light they cast on the stones. He saw creatures with bizarre faces, dangerous faces, curious faces, or no faces at all. In less than an hour, the silent ring of stones had transformed into something more like a carnival.

The poet, Cairpré, did his best to answer Merlin's questions about the strange and wondrous creatures surrounding them. That, he explained, was a snow hen, who remained as elusive as a moonbeam. And that, a glyn-mater, who ate food only once every six hundred years—and then only the leaves of the tendradil flower. Some creatures he could not recognize were known by the leaf-draped girl, Rhia, from her years in Druma Wood. Yet there remained several that neither Cairpré nor Rhia could identify.

That came as no surprise. No one alive, except possibly the Grand Elusa, had ever seen all of the diverse residents of Fincayra. Soon after the Dance of the Giants had occurred, toppling the wicked king Stangmar and destroying his Shrouded Castle, the call had risen from many quarters to convene a Great Council. For the first time in living memory, all the mortal citizens of Fincayra, whether bird or beast or insect or something else entirely, were invited to send representatives to an assembly.

Almost every race had responded. The few missing ones included the warrior goblins and shifting wraiths, who had been driven back into the caves of the Dark Hills after the defeat of Stangmar; the treelings, who had disappeared from the land long ago; and the mer people, who inhabited the waters surrounding Fincayra but could not be found in time to be invited.

After studying the crowd, Cairpré observed sadly that the great canyon eagles, one of the oldest races on Fincayra, were also not present. In ancient times the stirring cry of a canyon eagle always marked the beginning of a Great Council. Not this time, however, since the forces of Stangmar had hunted the proud birds to extinction. That cry, Cairpré concluded, would never again echo among the hills of this land.

Merlin then glimpsed a pale, bulbous hag with no hair on her head and no mercy in her eyes. He shivered with recognition. Although she had taken many names across the ages, she was most often called Domnu, meaning Dark Fate. No sooner had he caught sight of her than she vanished into the throng. He knew she was avoiding him. He also knew why.

Suddenly a great rumbling, even louder than the noise of the assembly, shook the ridge. One of the standing stones wobbled precariously. The rumbling grew still louder, causing the stone to crash to the ground, almost crushing the doe and fawn. Merlin and Rhia looked at each other—not with fright, but with understanding. For they had heard the footsteps of giants before.

Two gargantuan figures, each as tall as the castle that had once stood on this spot, strode up to the circle. From far away in the mountains they had come, leaving the rebuilding of their ancestral city of Varigal long enough to join the Great Council. Merlin turned, hoping to find his friend Shim. But Shim was not among the new arrivals. The boy sighed, telling himself that Shim would probably have slept through the meeting anyway.

The first giant, a wild-haired female with bright green eyes and a crooked mouth, grunted and bent down to pick up the fallen stone. Although twenty horses would have strained to move it, she placed it back in position without any difficulty. Meanwhile, her companion, a ruddy-skinned fellow with arms as thick as oak trunks, placed his hands on his hips and surveyed the scene. After a long moment, he gave her a nod.

She nodded in return. Then, with another grunt, she lifted both of her hands into the air, seeming to grasp at the streaming clouds. Seeing this, Cairpré raised his bushy eyebrows in puzzlement.

High in the sky, a tiny black dot appeared. Out of the clouds it spiraled, as if caught in an invisible whirlpool. Lower and lower it came, until every eye of every creature in the circle was trained on it. A new hush blanketed the assembly. Even the irrepressible water nymphs fell silent.

The dot grew larger as it descended. Soon massive wings could be seen, then a broad tail, then sunlight glinting on a hooked beak. A sudden screech ripped the air, echoing from one ridge to another, until the land itself seemed to be answering the call. The call of a canyon eagle.

The powerful wings spread wide, stretching out like a sail. Then the wings angled backward, as enormous talons thrust toward the ground. Rabbits and foxes squealed at the sight, and many more beasts cringed. With a single majestic flap, the great canyon eagle settled on the shoulder of the wild-haired giant.

The Great Council of Fincayra had begun.

As the first order of business, the delegates agreed that no one should leave the meeting until all the questions had been decided. Also, at the request of the mice, each of the delegates promised not to eat anyone else during the course of the proceedings. Only the foxes objected to this idea, arguing that the question of what to do with the Flowering Harp alone could take several days to resolve. Even so, the rule was adopted. To ensure compliance, the Grand

Elusa herself kindly offered to enforce it. Though she never said just how she planned to do that, no one seemed inclined to ask her.

As its next act, the assembly declared the circle of stones itself a sacred monument. Clearing her throat with the subtlety of a rock slide, the wild-haired giant proposed that the ruins of the Shrouded Castle receive a new name: Dance of the Giants, or *Estonahenj* in the giants' own ancient tongue. The assembled delegates adopted the name unanimously, though a heavy silence fell over the circle. For while the Dance of the Giants signified Fincayra's hope for a brighter future, it was the kind of hope that springs only from the most profound sorrow.

In time, the discussion turned to the fate of Stangmar. While the wicked king had been overthrown, his life had been saved—by none other than Merlin, his only son. Although Merlin himself, being only part Fincayran, was not allowed to voice his own views at the assembly, the poet Cairpré offered to speak on his behalf. After hearing the boy's plea that his father's life, no matter how wretched, should be spared, the Great Council argued for hours. Finally, over the strong objections of the giants and the canyon eagle, the assembly decided that Stangmar should be imprisoned for the rest of his days in one of the inescapable caverns north of the Dark Hills.

Next came the question of who should rule Fincayra. The bees suggested that their own queen could rule everyone, but that notion found no support. So fresh was the agony of Stangmar's kingship that many delegates spoke passionately against having any leader at all. Not even a parliament of citizens would do, they argued, for in time power always corrupts. Cairpré, for his part, denounced such thinking as folly. He cited examples of anarchy that had brought ruin to other peoples, and warned that without any leadership at all Fincayra would again fall prey to that nefarious warlord of the Otherworld, Rhita Gawr. Yet most of the delegates dismissed his concerns. The Great Council voted overwhelmingly to do without any leadership whatsoever.

Then came the gravest question of all. What should be done with the Treasures of Fincayra?

As everyone watched in awe, the Grand Elusa opened the sack by her side and removed the Flowering Harp. Its oaken sound box, inlaid with ash and carved with floral designs, gleamed eerily. A green butterfly wafted over and alighted on its smallest string. With the swipe of one enormous leg, the Grand Elusa shooed the butterfly away, causing the string to tinkle gently. After pausing to listen, she then removed the rest of the Treasures: the sword Deepercut, the Caller of Dreams, the Orb of Fire, and six of the Seven Wise Tools (the seventh one, alas, had been lost in the collapse of the castle).

All eyes examined the Treasures. For a long interval, no one stirred. The stones themselves seemed to lean forward to get a closer look. The delegates knew that, long before the rise of Stangmar, these fabled Treasures had belonged to all Fincayrans, and were shared freely throughout the land. Yet that had left the Treasures vulnerable to thievery, as Stangmar had demonstrated. A spotted hare suggested that each Treasure ought to have a guardian, someone responsible for guarding it and seeing that it was used wisely. That way the Treasures could be shared, but still protected. Most of the representatives agreed. They urged the Grand Elusa to choose the guardians.

The great spider, however, declined. She declared that only someone much wiser could make such important selections. It would take a true wizard—someone like Tuatha, whose knowledge had been so vast, it was said, that he had even found a secret pathway to the Otherworld to consult with Dagda, greatest of all the spirits. But Tuatha had died years ago. In the end, after much urging, the Grand Elusa agreed to watch over the Treasures in her crystal cave, but only until the right guardians could be found.

While that solved the problem of the Treasures for the time being, it did not answer the question of the Flowering Harp. The surrounding countryside, afflicted by the Blight of Rhita Gawr, showed no sign of life, not even a sprig of green grass. The Dark Hills, especially, needed help, for the damage there had been the most severe. Only the magic of the Harp could revive the land.

Yet who should be the one to carry it? The Harp had not been played for many years, since Tuatha himself had used it to heal the forest destroyed by the dragon of the Lost Lands. While that forest had eventually returned to life, Tuatha had admitted that playing the Harp had required even more of his skill than lulling the enraged dragon into enchanted sleep. The Harp, he had warned, would only respond to the touch of someone with the heart of a wizard.

The oldest of the peacocks was the first to try. Spreading his radiant tail feathers to the widest, he strutted over to the Harp and lowered his head. With a swift stroke of his beak, he plucked one of the strings. A pure, resonant tone poured forth, lingering in the air. But nothing else happened. The Harp's magic lay dormant. Again the peacock tried, again with no result beyond a single note.

One by one, several other delegates came forward. The unicorn, her white coat glistening, slid her horn across the strings. A stirring chord resulted, but nothing more. Then came an immense brown bear, a dwarf whose beard fell below his knees, a sturdy-looking woman, and one of the water nymphs, all without success.

At last, a tan-colored toad hopped out of the shadows by Merlin's feet and over to the Grand Elusa. Stopping just beyond the great spider's reach, the toad rasped, "You may not be a wizarrrrd yourrrrself, but I rrrreally believe you have the hearrrrt of one. Would you carrrry the Harrrrp?"

The Grand Elusa merely shook her head. Lifting three of her legs, she pointed in the direction of Cairpré.

"Me?" sputtered the poet. "You can't be serious! I have no more the heart of a wizard than the head of a pig. *My knowledge so spare, my wisdom too rare.* I could never make the Harp respond." Stroking his chin, he turned to the boy by his side. "But I can think of someone else who might."

"The boy?" growled the brown bear skeptically, even as the boy himself shifted with unease.

"I don't know whether he has the heart of a wizard," Cairpré acknowledged, with a sidelong glance at Merlin. "I doubt even he knows."

The bear slammed his paw against the ground. "Then why do you propose him?"

The poet almost smiled. "Because I think there is more to him than meets the eye. He did, after all, destroy the Shrouded Castle. Let him try his hand with the Harp."

"I agree," declared a slender owl with a snap of her jaws. "He is the grandson of Tuatha."

"And the son of Stangmar," roared the bear. "Even if he can awaken its magic, he cannot be trusted."

Into the center of the circle stepped the wood elf, her nut brown hair rippling like a stream. She bowed slightly to Rhia, who returned the gesture. Then, in a lilting voice, she addressed the group. "The boy's father I know not, though I am told that, in his youth, he often played in Druma Wood. And, like the twisted tree that might have grown straight and tall, I cannot say whether the fault lay with him or with the elders who did not give him their support. Yet I did know the boy's mother. We called her Elen of the Sapphire Eyes. She healed me once, when I was aflame with fever. There was magic in her touch, more magic than even she understood. Perhaps her son has the same gift. I say we should let him try the Harp."

A wave of agreement flowed through the assembly. The bear paced back and forth, grumbling to himself, but finally did not object.

As Merlin rose from the pillar, Rhia wrapped her leaf-draped arm around his own. He glanced at her gratefully, then stepped slowly over to the Harp. As he carefully retrieved it, cradling the sound box in his arms, the assembled delegates fell silent once again. The boy drew a deep breath, raised his hand, and plucked one of the strings. A deep note hung in the air, vibrating, for a long moment.

Sensing nothing remarkable had happened, Merlin turned a disappointed face toward Rhia and Cairpré. The brown bear growled in satisfaction. All at once, the canyon eagle, still perched on the giant's shoulder, screeched. Others joined the cry, roaring and howling and thumping with enthusiasm. For there, curling over the toe of Merlin's own boot, was a single blade of grass, as green as a rain-washed sapling. He smiled and plucked the string again, causing several more blades of grass to spring forth.

When, at last, the commotion subsided, Cairpré strode over to Merlin and clasped his hand. "Well done, my boy, well done." Then he paused. "It is a grave responsibility, you know, healing the lands."

Merlin swallowed. "I know."

"Once you begin this task, you must not rest until it is finished. Even now, the forces of Rhita Gawr are making plans for a renewed assault. You may be certain of that! The Dark Hills, where many of the forces lie hidden in caves and crevasses, are the lands most scarred from Blight—and also most vulnerable to attack. Our best protection is to restore the hills quickly so that peaceful creatures may return there to live. That will discourage the invaders, and also ensure that the rest of Fincayra will have warning of any attack."

He tapped the oaken instrument gently. "So you must begin in the Dark Hills—and remain there until the job is done. Save the Rusted Plains, and the other lands yearning to live again, until later. The Dark Hills must be healed before Rhita Gawr returns, or we will have lost our only chance."

He chewed his lip thoughtfully. "And one thing more, my boy. Rhita Gawr, when he does return, will be looking for you. To show his gratitude for how much trouble you have caused him. So avoid doing anything that might attract his attention. Just stick to your work, healing the Dark Hills."

"But what if, after I've left here, I can't make the Harp work?"

"If the Harp simply does not respond to your touch, we will understand. But remember: If you can make it work but shirk your task, you will never be forgiven."

Merlin nodded slowly. As the delegates looked on, he started to slip the Harp's leather sling over his shoulder.

"Wait!"

It was the voice of the hag, Domnu. Advancing toward the boy, she opened wide her eyes, sending waves of wrinkles across the top of her scalp. Then she lifted her arm and pointed a knobby finger at him. "The half-human boy cannot carry the Harp. He must leave this island! For if he stays, Fincayra is doomed."

Nearly everyone cringed at her words, none more than Merlin himself. They carried strange power, cutting deeper than any sword.

Domnu shook her finger. "If he does not leave, and soon, all of us will perish." A chill wind passed through the circle, making even the giants shiver. "Have you all forgotten the prohibition, laid down by Dagda himself, against anyone with human blood remaining long on this island? Have you all forgotten that this boy was also born here, despite an even more ancient prohibition? If you let him carry the Harp, he will surely claim Fincayra as his rightful home. He probably has no intention of returning to the world beyond the mist. Heed my warning. This boy could upset the very balance between the worlds! He could bring the wrath of Dagda down upon us all. Even worse," she added with a leer, "he could be a tool of Rhita Gawr, like his father before him."

"I am not!" Merlin objected. "You just want me banished so you don't have to give me back the Galator."

Domnu's eyes flamed. "There, you see? He is speaking to the Great Council, even though he is not truly one of us. He has no respect for Fincayra's laws, just as he has no respect for the truth. The sooner he is exiled, the better."

Many heads nodded in the crowd, caught by the spell of her words. Merlin started to speak again, but someone else spoke first.

It was Rhia. Her gray-blue eyes alight, she faced the hairless hag. "I don't believe you. I just don't." Drawing a deep breath, she added, "And aren't you the one who has forgotten something? That prophecy, that very old prophecy, that only a child of human blood can defeat Rhita Gawr and those who serve him! What if that means Merlin? Would you still want us to send him away?"

Domnu opened her mouth, baring her blackened teeth, then shut it tight.

"The giiirl speeeaks the truuuth," thundered the deep voice of the Grand Elusa. Lifting her vast bulk with her eight legs, she peered straight at Domnu. "The boooy shooould staaay."

As if the spell had been broken, delegates of all descriptions thumped, growled, or flapped their agreement. Seeing this, Domnu grimaced. "I warned you," the hag grumbled. "That boy will be the ruin of us all."

Cairpré shook his head. "Time will tell."

Domnu glared at him. Then she turned and disappeared into the crowd—but not before shooting a glance at Merlin that made his stomach clench.

Rhia turned to Cairpré. "Aren't you going to help him put it on?"

The poet laughed, tossing his shaggy mane. "Of course." He lifted the Harp's leather sling over Merlin's head, resting it on the boy's shoulder. "You know this is a responsibility, my boy. All of us depend on you. Even so, may it also be a joy! With every strum of those strings, may you bring another field to flower."

He paused, gazing thoughtfully at Merlin. Lowering his voice, he added, "And may you heal yourself, even as you heal the land."

A roar of approval echoed around the sacred ring. With that, the Great Council of Fincayra disbanded.

PART ONE

I

RESCUER

Reaching the top of the rise, I hoisted the Flowering Harp a little higher on my shoulder. The first rays of dawn streaked across the sky, painting the clouds scarlet and crimson. Ruby light licked the farthest hills, igniting the few spindly trees that stood like forgotten hairs on the horizon. Yet despite the flaming trees, the hills themselves remained darkened, the same color as the brittle blades of grass under my leather boots—the color of dried blood.

Even so, as my feet crunched against the parched hillside, I began to smile. I barely noticed the chill wind that pierced my brown tunic and bit my cheeks. For I felt already warmed by my task. The task I had pursued now for more than three weeks. The task of reviving the land.

Just as the great wizard Tuatha, my father's father, had done long ago, I had borne the Harp across the remains of fields and forests. And, like Tuatha himself, I had coaxed those lands back to life—with surprising ease, I might add. The Harp responded more easily with each passing day. It seemed almost eager to do as I wished. As if it had been waiting for me since the days of Tuatha.

To be sure, even in the midst of my success I realized that I was no wizard. I knew only the barest rudiments of magic. I couldn't have lasted a day as an apprentice to someone like Tuatha. And yet . . . I was *something*. I had saved my friend Rhia from sure death at the hand of Stangmar. I had brought down his whole castle. On top of destroying the plans of his master, Rhita Gawr. It seemed only fitting that the Great Council had entrusted the Harp to me. And that the Harp should do my bidding.

As I approached a shadowy outcropping of rock, I noticed a dry gully that ran beneath it. Clearly, this gully had not seen a drop of water in years. Whatever soil had not already blown away looked as cracked and withered as a sunbaked carcass. But for a lone, scraggly tree wearing only a thin strip of bark on its trunk and bearing not even a single leaf, nothing lived here. No plants. No insects. No animals of any kind.

Smiling confidently, I rubbed the knotted top of my staff, feeling the deep grooves in the wood and smelling the spicy scent of hemlock. I laid it on the ground. Then I pulled the Harp's leather sling off my shoulder, careful not to tangle it with the cord of the satchel of herbs that my mother had given me in our last moments together. Holding the Harp in my left arm, I observed its intricately carved floral patterns, its inlaid strips of ash, its carefully spaced sound holes. The strings, made of goat gut, gleamed darkly in the early morning light. And the neck, joining the sound box to the pillar, curved as gracefully as the wing of a swan. Someday, I promised myself, I would learn how to make a harp such as this.

As another cold gust blew against me, I drew my fingers across the strings. A sudden burst of music poured forth, a lilting, magical music that lightened my heart like nothing I had heard since the singing of my mother so long ago. Although I had now carried the

Harp over dozens of these hills, I had not grown the least bit tired of its resonant song. I knew I never would.

A small sprig of fern lifted out of the ground and started to unfurl. Again I plucked the strings.

All at once, the hillside sprang to life. Brittle stems turned into flexible, green blades of grass. A rivulet of water started splashing down the gully, soaking the thirsty soil. Small blue flowers, sprinkled with droplets of dew, popped up along the banks. A new fragrance filled the air, something like lavender and thyme and cedar combined.

I drank in this melody of aromas, even as I listened to the Harp's own melody still pulsing in the air. Then my smile faded, as I recalled the fragrances of my mother's collection of herbs. How long it had been since I had smelled them! Since before I was born, Elen of the Sapphire Eyes had surrounded herself with dried petals, seeds, leaves, roots, shavings of bark, and whatever else she might use to heal the wounds of others. Sometimes, though, I suspected that she filled her life with such things just because she enjoyed the aromas. So did I— except for dill, which always made me sneeze.

Yet, far more than the aromas that she nurtured, I enjoyed my mother's company. She always tried to make me feel warm and safe. Even when the world did not let her succeed—which was all too often. She provided for me during all those brutal years in Gwynedd, called Wales by some, without ever asking for thanks. Even when she made herself aloof and distant in the hope of shielding me from my past, even when I nearly choked with rage at her refusal to answer my questions about my father, even when I struck back in my fear and confusion by refusing to call her by the one word she most wanted to hear—even then I loved her.

And now that I understood at last what she had done for me, I could not thank her. She was far, far away, beyond the mist, beyond the ocean, beyond the rugged coast of Gwynedd. I could not touch her. I could not call her that word: Mother.

A curlew chirped from the branch of the tree, pulling my thoughts back to the present. Such a glad, full-throated song! I plucked the harp strings once more.

Before my eyes, the tree itself burst to life. Buds formed, leaves sprouted, and bright-winged butterflies flew to the branches. Smooth, gray bark coated the entire trunk and limbs. The roots swelled, grasping the bank of the stream, now swiftly tumbling down the hillside.

A beech. I grinned, seeing its burly branches reaching skyward. The breeze rippled its silvery leaves. Something about the sight of a beech tree always filled me with feelings of peace, of quiet strength. And I had saved it. I had brought it back to life. As I had this entire hillside, like so many before. I felt the thrill of my own power. The Great Council had chosen well. Perhaps I did, indeed, have the heart of a wizard.

Then I noticed my own reflection in a puddle that had formed between the tree's roots near the bank. Caught short by my scarred cheeks and my black, sightless eyes, I stopped smiling. How had Rhia described my eyes, on the first day we met? *Like a pair of stars hidden by clouds.* I wished I could see with my eyes, my own eyes, again.

Seeing with my second sight was, of course, better than blindness. I could never forget that miraculous moment when I had discovered that I could actually see without my eyes. Yet second sight was no substitute for real eyesight. Colors faded, details blurred, darkness pressed all the closer. What I would give to heal my eyes! Burned and useless though they were, I always knew they were there. They reminded me constantly of everything I had lost.

And I had lost so very much! I was only thirteen, and already I had lost my mother, my father, and whatever homes I had known, as well as my own eyes. I could almost hear my mother, in her encouraging way, asking whether I had also gained anything. But what? The courage to live alone, perhaps. And the ability to save all the blighted lands of Fincayra.

I turned back to the beech tree. Already I had rescued a good portion of the Dark Hills, stretching from the ruins of the Shrouded Castle, now a sacred circle of stones, almost to the northern reaches of the Haunted Marsh. Over the next few weeks, I would bring life back to the rest. Then I could do the same for the Rusted Plains. Although it held more than its share of mysteries, Fincayra was not, after all, a very big place.

Setting down the Harp, I stepped nearer to the beech. Laying my hands on the smooth, silver bark, I spread my fingers wide, feeling the flow of life through the imposing trunk. Then, pursing my lips, I made a low, swishing sound. The tree shuddered, as if it were breaking free from invisible chains. Its branches quivered, making a swishing sound much like my own.

I nodded, pleased with my skills. Again I swished. Again the tree responded. This time, however, it did more than quiver. For I had given a command.

Bend. Bend down to the ground. I wanted to seat myself in its highest branches. Then I would command it to straighten again, lifting me skyward. For as long as I could remember, I had loved to perch in the tops of trees. Regardless of the weather. But I had always needed to climb there myself—until today.

Hesitantly, with considerable popping and creaking, the great beech began to bend lower. A section of bark ripped away from the trunk. I craned my neck, watching the highest branches descend. As the tree bent before me, I selected my seat, a notch not far from the top.

Suddenly I heard another swishing sound. The tree stopped bending. Slowly, it began to straighten itself again. Angrily, I repeated my command. The tree halted, then started bending toward me once more.

Again a swishing sound filled the air. The tree ceased bending and began to straighten.

My cheeks grew hot. How could this be? I dug my fingers into the trunk, ready to try again, when a clear, bell-like laughter reached my ears. I spun around to see a leaf-draped girl with gray-blue eyes and a mass of curly brown hair. Glistening vines wrapped around her entire body as if she were a tree herself. She watched me, still laughing, her hands on her belt of woven grass.

"Rhia! I should have guessed."

She tilted her head to one side. "Tired of speaking beech so soon? You're sounding like a Celt again."

"I'd still be speaking to the beech if you hadn't interrupted us."

Rhia shook her brown curls, enmeshed with leaves. "I didn't interrupt your speaking. Only your commanding."

Exasperated, I glanced up at the tree, which by now stood perfectly straight again, its silvery leaves tossing in the wind. "Leave me, will you?"

The curls shook again. "You need a guide. Otherwise, you might get lost." She looked with concern at the beech tree. "Or try something foolish."

I grimaced. "You're not my guide! I invited you to join me, re-member? And when I did, I didn't think you'd try to interfere."

"And when I started teaching you the language of trees, I didn't think you'd use it to hurt them."

"Hurt them? Can't you see what I'm doing?"

"Yes. And I don't like it." She stamped her foot on the ground, flattening the grass. "It's dangerous—and disrespectful—to make a tree bend like that. It might injure itself. Or even die. If you want to sit in a tree, then climb up there yourself."

"I know what I'm doing."

"Then you haven't learned anything in the last three weeks! Don't you remember the first rule of tree speech? *Listen before you speak.*"

"Just watch. I'll show you how much I've learned."

She strode up to me and squeezed my elbow with her strong hand. "You remind me of a little boy sometimes. So sure of yourself, with so little reason."

"Go away," I barked. "I saved this tree! Brought it back to life! I can make it bend if I want to."

Rhia frowned. "No, Merlin. You didn't save the tree." Releasing her grip, she pointed at the instrument lying on the grass. "The Flowering Harp saved the tree. You are just the one who gets to play it."

II

A Fitting Welcome

Where has all the sweetness gone?"

I leaned back on the soft, fragrant grass of the gently sloping meadow, careful not to bump my head against the Harp. Even without the use of my eyes, my second sight could easily pick out the plump, pink berries in Rhia's hand. I knew that her question referred to the berries, which were not nearly sweet enough for her taste. But in the days since our confrontation at the beech tree, I had often asked the same question myself—about our friendship.

Though she appeared and disappeared at unpredictable times, Rhia never left me for long. She continued to accompany me over the ridges and valleys, sometimes in silence, sometimes in song. She continued to camp nearby, and share most of her meals with me. She even continued to call herself my guide, although it was perfectly obvious that I needed no guide.

Yet despite her continuing presence, an invisible wall divided us now. While in some ways we traveled together, we really traveled separately. She just didn't understand. And that continued to rankle me. The thrill of bringing the land back to life, of turning it green with buds and promise, I couldn't even begin to explain to her. Whenever I tried, she gave me one of her lectures on the Flowering Harp.

Or, worse, one of her looks that seemed to pierce right through me. As if she knew everything I was thinking and feeling, without even needing to ask. After all I had done for her! Were all girls as maddeningly difficult as she was?

I waved at the bush, its tangled branches heavy with pink berries. "If you don't like them, why do you keep eating them?"

She answered, still pulling berries off the branches. "There must be some sweeter ones here someplace. I *know* it."

"How do you know?"

She shrugged carelessly, even as she popped a handful into her mouth. "Mmmff. I just do."

"Did someone tell you?"

"A little voice inside me. A voice that understands berries."

"Be sensible, Rhia! This bush just isn't ripe yet. You'd be better off waiting to find another."

She ignored me, continuing to chew.

I tore a clump of grass and threw it down the slope. "What if you eat so many tart berries that you haven't any room left for sweet ones?"

She turned to me, her cheeks as packed with berries as a squirrel's would be with acorns. "Mmmff," she said with a swallow. "In that case, I guess it would have to be a day for tart berries, not sweet ones. But that little voice tells me there are some sweeter ones here. It's a matter of having trust in the berries."

"Trust in the berries! What in the world are you saying?"

"Just what I said. Sometimes it's best to treat life as if you're floating down a great river. To listen to the water and let it guide you, instead of trying to change the river's course."

"What do berries have to do with rivers?"

Her brown curls flopped as she shook her head. "I wonder . . . are all boys as difficult as you are?"

"Enough of this!" I pushed myself to my feet and slung the Flowering Harp over my back, wincing from the old pain between my shoulders. I started across the meadow, the base of my staff leaving a trail of tiny pits in the grass. Noticing a revived but still drooping hawthorn tree to my left, I reached over my shoulder and plucked a single string. The hawthorn instantly straightened and exploded with pink and white blossoms.

I glanced back at Rhia, hoping she might at least offer a word of praise, even something halfhearted. But she seemed completely occupied with fingering the branches of her berry bush. Turning to the rust-colored hill that rose from the edge of the meadow, I stepped briskly toward it. The crest of the hill was covered with shadowed rock outcroppings, the kind that could have concealed the caves of warrior goblins. Although I had seen many such places during my travels in the Dark Hills, I had yet to find any sign of goblins themselves. Perhaps Cairpré's worries had not been justified after all.

Suddenly I halted. Recognizing the pair of sharp knobs that rose from the crest, I toyed with my staff, twirling it in my hand, even as I toyed with a new idea. I veered westward, down the slope.

Rhia called out.

Planting my staff, I looked her way. "Yes?"

She waved a berry-stained hand toward the hill. "Aren't you going the wrong direction?"

"No. I have some friends to see."

Her brow furrowed. "What about your task? You are not supposed to rest until you've finished the Dark Hills."

"I'm not going to rest!" I kicked at the rich grass beneath my boots. "But no one said I had to avoid my friends along the way. Especially friends who might actually appreciate what I'm doing."

Even with my limited vision, I could not miss her reddening cheeks. "My friends have a garden. I am going to make it grow as never before."

Rhia's eyes narrowed. "If they are genuine friends, they'll be truthful with you. They'll tell you to go back and finish your task."

I stalked off. A stiff gust of wind blew in my face, making my sightless eyes water. But I pushed on down the slope, tunic flapping at my legs. *If they are genuine friends, they'll be truthful.* Rhia's words echoed in my mind. What, indeed, was a friend? I had thought Rhia was one, not long ago. And now she seemed more like a burr in my side. Do without friends! Maybe that was the answer. Friends were just too undependable, too demanding.

I bit my lip. The right kind of friend would be different, of course. Someone like my mother—totally loyal, always supportive. Yet she was one of a kind. There was no one like her on Fincayra. And yet . . . perhaps, with enough time, I might come to feel that way about others. Like the two people I was about to visit, T'eilean and Garlatha. With a single stroke of my harp strings, I would enrich both their garden and our friendship.

The wind relented for a moment. As I wiped my eyes with my sleeve, I heard Rhia's soft footsteps on the grass behind me. Despite my frustration with her, I felt somehow relieved. Not because I needed her company, of course. I simply wanted her to see all the thanks and admiration that I would soon be receiving from real friends.

I turned to face her. "So you decided to come along."

Somberly, she shook her head. "You still need a guide."

"I'm not going to get lost, if that's what you mean."

She merely frowned.

Without another word, I started down the slope, my heels digging into the turf. Rhia stayed close, as silent as a shadow. When we reached the plains, the remaining wind died away. Mist hovered in the muggy air, while the sun baked us. Now when I wiped my eyes it was because of the sting of perspiration.

Through a long afternoon we trekked in silence. Every so often, when the fields turned dry and brittle, I strummed a little, leaving behind us a wake of verdant grasses, splashing streams, and all manner of life renewed. Yet while the sun continued to warm our backs, it could not do the same for our moods.

Finally, I spied a familiar hillside, split by a deep cleft. Within it, seeming to sprout from the rocks and soil of the hill itself, sat a gray stone hut. It was bordered by a dilapidated wall and surrounded by a few trailing vines and thin fruit trees. Not much of a garden, really. Yet in the days before the fall of the Shrouded Castle, it had seemed like a genuine oasis in the middle of the Rusted Plains.

How surprised my old friends T'eilean and Garlatha would be when I brought endless bounty to their meager garden! They would be grateful beyond words. Maybe even Rhia would finally be impressed. On the other side of the wall, in the shade of some leafy boughs, I could make out two white heads. T'eilean and Garlatha. Side by side over a bed of bright yellow flowers, their heads bobbed slowly up and down, keeping time to some music only they could hear.

I smiled, thinking of the wondrous gift I had for them. When I had last seen them, on my way to the Shrouded Castle, I was nothing more than a ragged boy with only the faintest hope of living out the day. They had expected never to see me again. Nor had I expected to return. My pace quickened, as did Rhia's.

Before we were twenty paces from the crumbling wall, the two heads lifted as one, like hares in a morning meadow. T'eilean was the first to his feet. He offered a large, wrinkled hand to Garlatha, but she waved it away and rose without any help. They watched us approach, T'eilean stroking his unruly whiskers, Garlatha shading her eyes. I stepped over the wall, followed by Rhia. Despite the weight of the Harp on my shoulder, I stood as tall as I possibly could.

The wrinkles of Garlatha's face creased into a gentle smile. "You have returned."

"Yes," I replied, turning so they could see the Harp. "And I have brought you something."

T'eilean's brow creased. "You mean you have brought someone."

Rhia stepped forward. Her gray-blue eyes shone at the sight of the two aging gardeners standing before their simple hut. Without waiting to be introduced, she nodded in greeting.

"I am Rhia."

"And I am T'eilean. This is my wife of sixty-seven years, Garlatha."

The white-haired woman frowned and kicked at his shin, barely missing the mark. "Sixty-eight, you old fool."

"Sorry, my duck. Sixty-eight." He backed away a step before adding, "She is always right, you see."

Garlatha snorted. "Be glad you have guests, or I'd come after you with my trowel."

Her husband glanced at the trowel half buried in the flower bed, waving his arm in the air with the playfulness of a bear cub. "Right again. Without occasional guests to protect me, I doubt I would have survived this long."

Rhia suppressed a laugh.

Garlatha, her face softening, reached for T'eilean's hand. They stood together for a quiet moment, as gray as the stones of their hut. Leaves quivered gently all around them, as if in tribute to the devoted hands that had nurtured this garden for so many years.

"You remind me of two trees," observed Rhia. "Trees that have shared the same soil for so long they have grown together. Roots and all."

Garlatha, her eyes sparkling, glanced at her mate.

I decided to try again. "Speaking of things growing, I have brought you—"

"Yes!" exclaimed the old man, cutting me off. "You have brought your friend, Rhia." He turned toward her. "We welcome you, no less than we welcome the sunshine."

Garlatha tugged on the sleeve of my tunic. "What of your friend who came with you before, the one with the nose as big as a potato?"

"Shim is fine," I answered brusquely. "And now—"

"Though his nose," interrupted Rhia, "is even bigger than before."

Garlatha raised an eyebrow. "He did look full of surprises, that one."

With a dramatic tone, I cleared my throat. "And now I have a magnificent surprise for both of you."

Yet before I had even finished my sentence, the old woman was again speaking to Rhia. "Are you from Druma Wood? Your garb is woven in the way of the wood elves."

"The Druma is my home, and has been all my life."

Garlatha leaned closer. "Is it true what I have heard? That the rarest of all the trees, whose every branch yields a different kind of fruit, can still be found there?"

Rhia beamed. "What you have heard is true. The shomorra tree is indeed there. You might even say it's my garden."

"Such a garden you have, then, my child. Such a garden you have!"

My frustration growing, I pounded my staff on the soil. "I have a gift to bestow upon this very garden."

Neither of the elders seemed to hear me, as they continued to ask Rhia questions about Druma Wood. They seemed more interested in her than in me. Me, who had brought them something so precious!

Finally, T'eilean's muscular arm reached for a spiral-shaped fruit dangling from a branch overhead. With a graceful sweep of his hand, he plucked it. The pale purple color of the fruit glowed in his palm. "A larkon," he intoned. "The loveliest gift of the land to our humble home." He observed me quietly. "I remember that you enjoy the flavor."

At last, I thought. Even as I extended my hand to grasp the fruit, however, T'eilean swiveled and handed it to Rhia. "So I am sure that your friend will enjoy it just as much."

As I watched her take the fruit, my cheeks burned. Before I could say anything, though, he plucked another spiral fruit and offered it to me. "We are honored that you have returned."

"Honored?" I asked, my voice tinged with disbelief. I felt tempted to say more, but restrained myself.

T'eilean traded glances with Garlatha, then brought his gaze back to me. "My boy, to welcome you as a guest in our home is the greatest honor we can bestow. It is what we did for you last time, and it is what we do for you now."

"But now, T'eilean, I carry the Flowering Harp."

"Yes, yes, I have seen as much." The corners of his mouth drooped, and for the first time he seemed to show the weight of his many years. "My dear boy, the Flowering Harp is the most wondrous of all the Treasures, blessed with the magic of the seed itself. Yet in our home, we do not welcome guests for what they carry on their backs. We welcome them for what they carry elsewhere."

Riddles! From someone I had thought a friend. Scowling, I pushed some straggly hairs off my face.

T'eilean drew a long breath before continuing. "As your hosts, we owe you our hospitality. As well as our candor. If the weight of the Harp lies upon your back, then so does the far greater weight of healing our lands before it is too late. Much depends on you, my boy. Surely, you have precious little time for visits with simple folk like us."

My jaw clenched.

"Forgive me, but I am only trying to be truthful."

"Wait, Merlin," protested Rhia.

I did not hear the rest of her words, for I had already stepped over the stone wall. Alone, I strode off across the plains, the strings of the Harp jangling against my back.

ing longer. Much longer. Bigger and bigger they grew, curling around like the tusks of a wild boar. Those daggerlike points were aiming straight for my eyes! As my teeth continued to lengthen, I flew into a panic. I screamed. My mother came running, but too late to help. I clawed at my face, trying to pull my teeth out bare-handed. I couldn't remove them. I couldn't stop them.

Slowly, inexorably, the teeth curled around until the tips reached my eyes. My own eyes! In just a few seconds they would be punctured. With a shriek of pain, I felt them rupture. I was blind again, utterly blind.

I awoke.

There was the stream, splashing beside me. There was Pegasus, sailing overhead. I lifted my head from the rushes. It was only a dream. Why then was my heart still pounding? Gingerly, I touched my cheeks, scarred from the fire that had blinded me in real life. They ached terribly from the new scratches I had just given them. Yet my heart ached even more. All this from a fire of my own making! To have lost my eyes was bad enough. To have done it to myself was still worse. For the first time in months, I wondered whether Dinatius, the other boy trapped in the fire that I had started, had survived. I could still hear his screams of agony, his whimpers of fear.

I put my face into the rushes and wept. As the stream flowed, so did my tears. In time, my sobbing subsided. Yet it seemed that the sound of sobbing continued, somewhere beyond the splashing of the stream. I lifted my head, listening closely.

More sobbing, punctuated by long, heaving moans. Patting my wet and sore cheeks with the sleeve of my tunic, I crept closer to the water's edge. Despite the darkness, my second sight traced the

III

WARM WIND

With nothing but the stars for my blanket, I spent that night curled up in the hollow of a stream bank. Rushes, moist with dew, lay under my head. With one hand, I could touch the splashing water that cascaded over the steps of stones carpeted with green moss. With the other, I could feel the Flowering Harp and my staff resting among the reeds.

I should have felt glad to be alone. Free of what the world called friends. Yet stroking the magical strings at this spot, bringing this stream to life, had given me no joy. Nor had watching the rushes and mosses spring from the dry soil. Nor had even spotting Pegasus in the midnight sky, though it had long been my favorite constellation, ever since the night my mother had first shown it to me.

This night, sleeping fitfully, I did not ride upon Pegasus' winged back as I had so many times before in my dreams. Instead, I found myself in a different dream. I sat upon a scarlet stone, watching my mother approach. Somehow, my eyes had healed. I could see again. Really see! Sunlight glinted on her golden hair, and a different kind of light played in her vibrant blue eyes. I could even see the tiny sprig of hemlock that she held in her hand.

Then, to my shock, I discovered that my front teeth were grow-

stream's path for some distance. Yet I couldn't find the source of the dismal sound. Maybe it was just my own echoing memory.

Leaning over the coursing water, I groped among the rushes with my hands. My knee kept sliding off the edge of the muddy bank, almost landing in the water. I continued to search, though I found nothing. Nothing at all. Yet the sobbing and moaning seemed to come from somewhere very near, almost in the stream itself.

In the stream itself. That was it! But how could that be?

I started to plunge my left hand into the water, then caught myself. The old pain throbbed between my shoulder blades. Could this be some sort of trick? One of Fincayra's hidden perils, like the shifting wraiths who take the form of something pleasant just long enough to lure you to your death? Rhia would know. But Rhia, I reminded myself bitterly, was no longer with me.

The moaning welled up again. Starlight sparkled on the dark surface of the stream, making it look like a river of crystals. Biting my lip, I thrust in my hand. A frigid wave washed over my wrist and forearm. My skin reeled from the shock of cold. Then my fingers touched something. Smooth. Round. Softer than stone. Fumbling to get a grip on the slippery object, I seized it and pulled it free from the water. It was a flask, not much bigger than my fist, made from a heavy bladder. Its leather cap had been sealed tight with a thick coating of wax. Bloated with air, the dripping flask glinted darkly.

I squeezed it. A loud wailing struck my ears. Then came sobs, heavy with heartache. Using the base of my wooden staff, I cut away the ring of wax. It came off only gradually, as if reluctant to loosen its grip. Finally it fell away. I tore open the cap. A rush of air blew across my cheeks. It felt warm and soothing, and smelled vaguely of cinnamon. As the flask collapsed, the gust of air flowed over my face and hair like a living breath.

"Thank you, person, thank you," came a wispy little voice from behind my head.

I dropped the flask and whirled around. But I saw nothing between me and the distant stars.

"Or should I say," whispered the voice again, "thank you, Emrys Merlin?"

I caught my breath. "How do you know my names?"

"Oh yes," the voice went on breezily, "I like the Merlin part so much better than dusty old Emrys."

Reaching up, I groped at the night air. "How do you know so much? Who are you? And where are you?"

A soft, breathy laughter rose out of the air before me. "I am Aylah, a wishlahaylagon." The laughter came again. "But most people simply call me a wind sister."

"Aylah," I repeated. "Wind sister." Again I reached skyward, and this time my fingertips passed through a warm current of air. "Now tell me how you know so much."

The smell of cinnamon grew stronger. Warm air swept slowly around me, fluttering my tunic. I felt embraced by a whirling circle of wind.

"I know as much as the air itself, Emrys Merlin. For I travel fast and far, never sleeping, never stopping."

Aylah's invisible cloak continued to spin slowly around me. "That is what a wind sister does, Emrys Merlin." A slight sob made her pause. "Unless she is captured, as I was."

"Who would do such a thing?"

"Someone evil, Emrys Merlin." The warm air spun away, leaving me with a sudden chill.

"Tell me."

"Someone evil, ahhh yes," breathed Aylah from near the bank where I had slept. "Her names are many, but most know her as Domnu."

I shivered, though not from the night air. "I know Domnu. I know her treachery. Yet I wouldn't exactly call her evil."

"She is surely not good, Emrys Merlin."

"She is neither good nor evil. She simply *is*. A little like fate."

"Dark Fate, you mean." Aylah's breeze blew across the strings of the Harp, tingling them lightly. "She is one of the few who are old and powerful enough to catch the wind. I don't know why, Emrys Merlin, I only know that she locked me away in that flask and cast me aside."

"I'm sorry for you."

A warm breath of air caressed my cheek. "If you hadn't helped me this night, Emrys Merlin, I believe I would have died."

My voice too a whisper, I asked, "Can the wind really die?"

"Oh yes, Emrys Merlin, it can." Once again she brushed my cheek. "The wind, like a person, can die from loneliness."

"You are not alone now."

"Nor are you, Emrys Merlin. Nor are you."

IV

TREASURES

The thrill of playing the Harp, which I had not felt since leaving the Dark Hills, filled me once again. Indeed, as I walked across the rolling plateaus of the Rusted Plains, the land seemed to erupt with new life even before I paused to pluck the oaken instrument. The driest grasses bent before me, as the most lifeless leaves arose from the ground, twirled, and danced in spirals at my feet. For Aylah moved beside me. Her gentle breeze often brushed against my arms, and her wispy laughter lifted every time I played the magical strings.

Even so, my steps sometimes grew heavy. Whenever I came across a stone hut, or a grove of fruit trees, I leaned against my staff, frowning at the memory of my encounter with T'eilean and Garlatha. I wished that I had never thought of visiting them and their garden. In addition, every time I glanced at the shadowed ridges to the east, I felt the gnawing sense that I was making a mistake by not returning to the hills to finish my work there. Yet . . . I just didn't feel ready to go back. Not yet. Let Rhia and the others fret a while longer.

Flushed with anger, I strummed the Harp. To my surprise, this time the brittle grass beneath my boots did not transform into lush, green blades. Instead, the entire meadow seemed to darken slightly, as if a cloud had covered the sun. Puzzled, I looked skyward. But I found no clouds.

Impatiently, I strummed again. But the grass only stiffened, darkened. I frowned at the instrument. What was wrong with it?

A warm wind billowed my tunic. "You are angry, Emrys Merlin."

I stiffened. "How do you know that?"

"I don't know things," breathed Aylah. "I feel them. And I feel your anger even now."

I strode faster, eager to leave this meadow behind. The darkened blades of grass jabbed at my boots like thousands of thorns.

"Why are you so angry, Emrys Merlin?"

Having moved beyond the darkened patch of grass, I stopped. I drew a deep breath and exhaled slowly. "I don't really know."

Aylah's airy form encircled me, filling my nostrils with the scent of cinnamon. "Could it be you are missing someone?"

I squeezed the shaft of my staff. "I am missing no one."

"Not even your mother?"

My knees nearly buckled, but I said nothing.

The wind sister swirled about me. "I never met her, Emrys Merlin, though I know many who did. She must have been a good friend."

I blinked the dew from my sightless eyes. "Yes. She was my good friend. Maybe my only friend."

Aylah's warm breath touched my cheek. "Tell me about her, would you please? I would like to hear."

Twisting my staff in the dry, rust-colored grass, I started walking again. "She loved the night sky, with all its stars and dreams and mysteries. She loved stories about ancient places like Olympus and

Apollo's Isle of Delos. She loved green, growing things, and all the creatures who soar or shamble or swim. And she loved me."

Although her spinning slowed, Aylah seemed closer to me than ever. Her winds embraced me.

"You're right," I admitted. "I do miss her. More than I ever believed possible." Haltingly, I took a breath. "If only I could be with her again, Aylah! Even for just an hour."

"I understand. Ahhh yes, I do."

It occurred to me that Aylah, despite her airy form, shared some qualities with my mother. She was warm, she was caring. And she did not try to give me advice.

Just then I noticed, not far ahead, a patch of low bushes with bluish bark and broad leaves. I knew from watching Rhia that they made good eating. Setting down the Flowering Harp and my staff, I went to the bushes and pulled up one by the roots, revealing a thick, blue tuber. After cleaning its skin with my tunic, I bit into the tangy flesh.

"Can I share this meal with you, somehow? I don't know what you eat, but whatever it is, I could try to find some for you."

The broad leaves of the bush fluttered as Aylah passed over them. "I eat only the faraway fragrances of lands I have not yet explored. I am made to wander, you see." Gently, she tousled my hair. "And now, I am afraid, it is time for us to part."

I stopped chewing. "Part? Why?"

The airy voice spoke into my ear. "Because I am the wind, Emrys Merlin, and I must fly. Always soaring, always circling, that is my way. I have many places to see, on Fincayra and the other worlds as well." For a moment, she seemed to hover near the Harp. "And you must fly, as well. For you still have work to do in the Dark Hills."

I frowned. "You too, Aylah? I thought at least you wouldn't try to tell me what to do."

"I am not telling you what to do, Emrys Merlin. I am only telling you that the winds bring tidings of disturbing things, evil things, in the Dark Hills. Rhita Gawr's allies are beginning to stir again. They grow bolder by the day. Before long the goblins will emerge from their caves, and with them the shifting wraiths. Then it will be too late for you to heal the lands."

My stomach knotted at her words. I recalled Cairpré's warning as he gave me the Harp. *The Dark Hills must be healed before Rhita Gawr returns, or we will have lost our only chance. Remember: If you shirk your task, you will never be forgiven.*

I surveyed the ridges on the horizon. Shadows of clouds stalked them. "If what you say is true, I must go back now. Won't you come with me? So we can travel together a while longer?"

"I have already stayed with you, Emrys Merlin, longer than I have ever been with a person who did not have wings of his own." She breathed against my neck. "And now I must fly."

Somberly, I tossed aside the tuber. "I've heard that Fincayrans once had wings of their own. Maybe it's just an old fable, but I wish it were true. I wish they had never lost them. Then I might have some myself, so I could fly with you."

I felt an eddy of wind across my shoulders. "Ahhh, Emrys Merlin, you know about that, do you? To have wings and then lose them. Such a tragedy that was! Even if many Fincayrans have forgotten how it happened, they cannot forget the lingering pain between their shoulders."

I stretched my arms stiffly, feeling the old pain. "Aylah, do you know how it happened? Even Cairpré, with all the many stories he has heard, doesn't know how the Fincayrans lost their wings. He told me once that he'd give away half of his library just to find out."

The warm wind encircled me now, spinning slowly. "I know the story, Emrys Merlin. Perhaps one day I might tell you. But not now."

"You're really leaving? It's always like this with me. It seems whatever I find, I lose."

"I hope you will find me again, Emrys Merlin."

A sudden gust of wind flapped the sleeves of my brown tunic. Then, just as swiftly, it was gone.

I stood there for a long while. Eventually, my stomach growled with hunger. I ignored it. Then, hearing it again, I bent down to retrieve the tuber I had discarded. I took another bite, thinking about Aylah, sister of the wind. At last, when I had finished it, I started walking—east, toward the Dark Hills.

All around me, the Rusted Plains rose and fell in great rolling waves. I shuffled along, dry grasses snapping beneath my feet. A soft wind blew against my back, cooling the heat of the sun, but it was not the wind that I wished for. And even more than Aylah's company, I missed the feeling of joy in my task that I had only just regained—and lost once again. The Harp felt heavy on my shoulder.

Sometimes, as I walked, I touched the pouch of healing herbs that my mother had given to me just before we said farewell, in that dank room of stone in Caer Myrddin. I missed her more than ever. And I also knew that she missed me. If she were here, she would not desert me as the others had done. Yet she was as far away as the farthest wind.

As the golden sun dropped lower in the sky, I neared a scraggly group of trees planted in six or seven rows. Although I could see no fruit among the branches of the orchard, a few white flowers gleamed, wafting a familiar scent in my direction. Apple blossoms. I took a deep, flavorful breath. Yet it did little to lift my spirits. Perhaps playing the Harp, feeling again the joy of bringing new life to the land, would help.

I cradled the instrument in my arms. Then I hesitated, remembering my strange experience in the darkened meadow. Merely a fluke, I assured myself. Slowly, I drew my fingers across the strings. All at once, a luminous paintbrush swept across the trees and the grassy fields surrounding them. Apples burst from the branches, swelling to hefty size. Trunks thickened, roots multiplied. The trees lifted skyward, waving their fruited branches proudly. My chest swelled. Whatever had happened at the darkened meadow was certainly not a problem now.

Suddenly a voice cried out. A bare-chested boy, about my own age, fell out of one of the trees. He landed in an irrigation ditch that ran beneath the branches. Another shout rang out. I ran to the spot.

Out of the ditch clambered the boy, with hair and skin as brown as the soil. Then, to my surprise, another figure emerged, looking like an older, broader version of the boy. He was a man of the soil. He was a man I recognized.

Neither he nor the boy noticed me as I stood in the shadow of the apple tree. The shirtless man straightened his broad back and then clasped the boy by the shoulders. "Are you hurt, son?"

The boy rubbed his bruised ribs. "No." He smiled shyly. "You made a good pillow."

The man eyed him with amusement. "You don't often fall out of branches."

"The branches don't often stand up and shake me out! And look, Papa! They're loaded down with apples."

The man gasped. Like the boy, he stared, jaw dangling, at the transformed trees. I too began to smile. This was the reaction that I had hoped to get from Rhia and the others—the reaction that I would have surely gotten from my mother. She had always delighted in the beauty and flavor of fresh apples.

"'Tis a miracle, son. 'Tis a gift from the great god Dagda himself."

I stepped out of the shadows. "No, Honn. It is a gift from me."

The man gave a start. He looked from me to the tree spreading above us, then back to me. At last he turned to his son. "It's him! The lad I told you about."

The boy's eyes widened. "The one who crushed the evil king? Who calls himself after a hawk?"

"Merlin," I declared, cuffing the boy on the shoulder. "Your father helped me once, when I badly needed it."

Honn ran a hand through his hair, flecked with dirt. "Good gracious, lad. Until I heard the tales of your success, I had given you up for dead thrice over."

Leaning on my twisted staff, I grinned. "With good reason. If it hadn't been for that handy blade you gave me, I surely would have been dead thrice over."

Rubbing his strong chin, Honn examined me for a moment. Below his bare chest he wore nothing but loose brown leggings. His hands, cracked and calloused though they were, looked as powerful as tree roots.

"I am glad the old dagger proved useful, my lad. Where is it now?"

"Somewhere in the ruins of the Shrouded Castle. It failed to slay a ghouliant, one of Stangmar's deathless soldiers. But it did buy me a few precious seconds."

"Of that I am glad." His gaze moved to the magical instrument. "I see that you found the Flowering Harp." He nudged the boy. "You see, my son, it was indeed a miracle! No mere mortal, not even one so talented as the young hawk here, could have done such a thing. It was the Harp, not the lad, that revived our orchard."

I cringed, then started to speak. Before I could say anything, however, Honn continued.

"To my mind, son, all the Treasures of Fincayra are the stuff of miracles, wrought by Dagda himself." In a quiet, almost reverent voice, he added, "There is even a plow, one of the Seven Wise Tools, that knows how to till its own field. Truly! It is said that any field it touches will yield the perfect harvest, neither too much nor too little."

The boy shook his head in amazement. Waving toward the rickety wooden plow that lay beside the ditch, he laughed. "No chance of mistaking it for that one, Father! My back hurts just to watch whenever you pull it."

Honn beamed. "Not so much as my own back hurts after you jump on me from a tree."

The pair laughed together. Honn wrapped a burly arm around his son's shoulder and turned to me, his face full of pride. "The truth is, I have a treasure of my own. My young friend here. And he's more precious to me than an ocean full of miracles."

I swallowed, running a finger over my mother's leather satchel. I could smell its sweet herbs even over the aroma of ripe apples. "What would you do, Honn, if you ever lost that treasure? That friend?"

His face became as hard as stone. "Why, I'd do everything in my mortal power to get it back."

"Even if it meant leaving your work unfinished?"

"No work could be more important than that."

I nodded grimly. *No work could be more important than that.*

Stepping over the ditch, I started walking. When I reached the edge of the orchard, I paused to face the Dark Hills, glowing like coals in the setting sun. The long, thin shadow of my staff seemed to point straight at the notched hill where I had turned aside from my task.

Slowly, I swung around to the north. I would return to those hills, and to my task, before long. And then I would revive every last blade of grass I could find. First, however, I needed to do something else. I needed to find my own mother again. And, like Honn, I would do everything in my mortal power to succeed.

V

THE JESTER

Late the following day, as strands of golden light wove gleaming threads through the grasses of the Rusted Plains, I stood on the crest of a rise. Below me sat a cluster of mud brick houses, arranged in a rough circle. Their thatched roofs glowed as bright as the surrounding plains. Long wooden planks stretched between their walls, connecting the houses like the arms of young children standing in a ring. The aroma of grain roasting on a wood fire tickled my nose.

I felt rising anticipation—and an undercurrent of dread. For this was Caer Neithan, the Town of the Bards. I knew that the poet Cairpré had promised to come here following the Great Council, to help repair the damage inflicted by Stangmar. And I also knew that if there was one person in all of Fincayra who could help me find my mother, it was Cairpré himself.

He would not be pleased to see me again, with so much of my work still unfinished. Yet he, too, had known Elen of the Sapphire Eyes, having tutored her years ago. I believed that he, too, longed for her return. Hadn't he once told me that he had learned more about the art of healing from her than she had ever learned from him? Maybe, just maybe, he might know some way to bring her through the curtain of mist surrounding this island. Then, reunited with her at last, I could finish my work in the Dark Hills with a glad heart.

I descended the slope, my staff striking the crusty soil in time to the Harp thumping against my back. Listening to the swelling sounds of the village, I could not forget the eerie silence that had shrouded it during my last visit. A silence that had been, in its way, louder than a thundering tempest.

Indeed, the Town of the Bards had only rarely known silence. No settlement in Fincayra possessed a richer history of story and song. For over the ages it had been home to many of this land's most inspired storytellers, and had witnessed many of their first performances. Even Cairpré himself, whose fame as a poet I had learned about only from others, had been born in one of those mud brick houses.

As I drew nearer to the village gates, which gleamed with golden light, more people started to emerge from their doors. Clad in long tunics of white cloth, they stood out sharply against the dry, caked mud of their homes, the dark planks of wood connecting the buildings, and the empty flower boxes clinging to most windowsills. I reached for the Harp, tempted to fill those flower boxes with something more than shadows. But I caught myself, deciding to wait before announcing my arrival.

More and more people emerged. They looked strikingly different from one another in skin color, age, hair, shape, and size. Yet they shared one common characteristic, in addition to their white tunics. All of them seemed hesitant, uncertain about something. Instead of congregating in the open circle in the middle of the houses, they kept to the outer edge. A few stood by their doorways, pacing anxiously, but most sat down on the wooden planks that ringed the open area. They seemed to be gathering for some purpose, but I couldn't shake the feeling that there was something grudging about their actions.

At that moment, a tall, gaunt fellow, wearing a brown cloak over his tunic, stepped into the center of the ring. Upon his head rested an odd, three-cornered hat that tilted precariously to one side like someone who had drunk too much wine. Dozens of gleaming metal spheres dangled from the hat's rim. The man began waving his long, spidery arms, flapping his loose sleeves, while bellowing some words I could not quite make out.

At once I understood the circular arrangement of the houses. The whole town was a theater! And I had arrived in time for some sort of performance.

As I reached the village gates, I halted. Unlike the last time I was here, no guard met me with a spear aimed at my chest. Instead, my greeting came from a newly carved sign attached to one of the gateposts. Shining in the late afternoon light, it read, *Caer Neithan, Town of the Bards, welcomes all who come in peace.* Below those words, I recognized one of Cairpré's own couplets: *Here song is ever in the air, while story climbs the spiral stair.*

No sooner had I stepped inside the gates when a slender, shaggy-haired man jumped up from one of the planks and strode over. His tangled brows, as unruly as brambles, hung over his dark eyes. I waited for him, leaning against my staff.

"Hello, Cairpré."

"Merlin," he whispered, spreading his arms as if he were about to clap his hands with joy. Then, glancing over his shoulder at the gaunt man who was reciting some passage, he apparently changed his mind about clapping. "Good to see you, my boy."

I nodded, realizing that he must have assumed that my work in the Dark Hills was done. It would not be easy to tell him the truth.

Again he glanced at the man reciting, and at the somber, almost tearful faces of the people in the audience. "I am only sorry you didn't arrive for a happier performance."

"Oh, that's all right," I whispered. "From all those sullen faces, it appears that fellow has a gift for making people feel sad. What is he reciting? Some sort of tragic poem?"

Cairpré's eyebrows climbed high on his forehead. "Unfortunately not." He shook his shaggy mane. "Believe it or not, the poor fellow is *trying* to be funny."

"Funny?"

"That's right."

Just then a clamorous clinking and rattling reached my ears. I turned back to the performer to see him shaking his head wildly, tossing his pointed hat from side to side. The sound came from the metal spheres. They were bells! Of course, I thought. Just right for making people laugh. Too bad they sounded so jarring, more like banging swords than ringing bells.

I observed the man for a moment. His hands drooped, his shoulders sagged, and his back stooped. In addition, his entire face—including his brow, his eyes, and his mouth—seemed to frown. The effect was compounded because, despite his thin frame, he had a flabby neck with row upon row of extra chins. So when his mouth turned down once, it turned down five or six times.

Suddenly he drew his heavy cloak around himself as if he were about to deliver a speech. Then, in sad, slow tones, he started to sing—or, more accurately, to wail. His voice seemed to cry, his breathing came like sobs. Like Cairpré, and most of the villagers, I winced. The man may have been trying to be funny, but his singing conveyed all the joy of a funeral dirge.

> *When bells reach your ears,*
> *Abandon all fears!*
> *Your lingering sadness*
> *Will turn into gladness.*
>
> *Be joyful, have cheer:*
> *The jester is here!*
>
> *I frolic and skip*
> *With laughs on my lip!*
> *My bells jingle sweetly,*
> *I thrill you completely.*
>
> *Be joyful, have cheer:*
> *The jester is here!*

As the wailing continued, I turned to Cairpré. "Doesn't he know how he sounds? He is the least funny person I have ever heard."

The poet heaved a sigh. "I think he does know. But he keeps on trying anyway. His name is Bumbelwy. Ever since he was a child, when he first frightened away the birds with his singing, he has dreamed of being a jester. Not just an amusing frolicker, but a true jester, someone who practices the high art of dressing wisdom in the garb of humor. Bumbelwy the Mirthful, he calls himself."

"Bumbelwy the Painful suits him better."

"I know, I know. As I've said before, *Bread yearns to rise beyond its size.*"

The townspeople, meanwhile, seemed every bit as dismal as Bumbelwy himself. Many held their heads in their hands; all wore scowls. One young girl shook loose of a woman's arms and ran into a nearby house, her black hair streaming behind her. While the woman stayed in her seat, she looked as if she envied the girl.

I turned back to Cairpré, scowling myself. "Why does anyone listen to him?"

"One of his, ah, humorous recitals, as he calls them, can ruin your next three meals. But like every other resident of Caer Neithan, he gets to perform in the village circle each year on the date of his birth." Cairpré shook his head. "And the rest of us have to listen. Even those like me who don't live here but are unlucky enough to be here on the wrong day."

He waved at the village circle, his voice no longer a whisper. "To think of all the truly memorable performances this same spot has seen! *Night Hammer. The Vessel of Illusion. Geraint's Vow.*"

Swiveling, he gestured toward one of the smaller, older-looking houses. "Pwyll, whose despairing smile itself inspired volumes of poems, wrote her first poem there." He pointed to a low house with a wooden porch. "Laon the Lame was born there. And let's not forget Banja. Jussiva the Jubilant. Ziffian. They all called this town home. As have so many other fabled bards."

Again I peered at Bumbelwy, whose long arms flailed as he droned on. "The only place he will ever be a jester is in his dreams."

Cairpré nodded grimly. "All of us have our private dreams. But few of us cling to dreams so far removed from our true capabilities! In days long past, Bumbelwy might have been saved by one of the Treasures of Fincayra, the magical horn known as the Caller of Dreams. Think of it, Merlin. The Caller, when blown by someone immensely wise, could bring a person's most cherished dream to life. Even a dream as far-fetched as Bumbelwy's. That is why it was often called, in story and song, the Horn of Good Tidings."

Lines deeper than the scars on my own face appeared on Cairpré's brow. I knew that he was remembering how Rhita Gawr had perverted the magic of the Caller of Dreams to bring only evil tidings to life. In the case of this very village, he had brought about the most terrifying dream of any poet, bard, or musician: He had silenced completely the voices of all who dwelled here, rendering useless the very instruments of their souls. That was why the Town of Bards had been as quiet as a graveyard when I last came here. Cairpré's tormented expression told me that, while the curse itself had departed with the collapse of the Shrouded Castle, its memory lived on.

The bells on Bumbelwy's hat started jangling again, louder than before. If I had not been holding my staff, I would have covered my ears. Nudging Cairpré, I asked, "Why don't you try the Caller of Dreams on him yourself?"

"I couldn't."

"Why not?"

"First of all, my boy, I'm not about to try to take anything—certainly not one of the Treasures—from the Grand Elusa's cave where they now reside. I'll leave that to someone much braver. Or stupider. But that isn't the main reason. The fact is, I am not wise enough to use the Caller."

I blinked in surprise. "Not wise enough? Why, the poet Cairpré is known throughout the land as—"

"As a rhymer, a quoter, an idealistic fool," he finished. "*Have no illusions, I brim with confusions.* But at least I am wise enough to know one important thing: how little I really do know."

"That's ridiculous. I've seen your library. All those books! You can't tell me you don't know anything."

"I didn't say I don't know anything, my boy. I said I don't know *enough*. There's a difference. And to think that I could command the legendary Caller of Dreams—well, that would be a terrible act of hubris."

"Hubris?"

"From the Greek word *hýbris*, meaning arrogance. Excessive pride in oneself. It's a flaw that has felled many a great person." His voice dropped again to a whisper. "Including, I am told, your own grandfather."

I stiffened. "You mean . . . Tuatha?"

"Yes. Tuatha. The most powerful wizard Fincayra has ever known. The only mortal ever allowed to visit the Otherworld to consult with Dagda—and return alive. Even he was susceptible to hubris. And it killed him."

The Flowering Harp felt suddenly heavier, the sling digging into my shoulder. "How did he die?"

Cairpré leaned closer. "I don't know the details. No one does. All I know is he overestimated his own power, and underestimated Rhita Gawr's most fearsome servant, a one-eyed ogre named Balor."

He shook himself. "But let us speak of more pleasant things! My boy, tell me about the Harp. You've made quick work of the Dark Hills if you're already down here in the plains."

I shifted uncomfortably, rubbing my hand over the knotted top of my staff. As I felt the deep grooves, the scent of hemlock spiced the air, reminding me of the woman whose fragrances had filled my childhood. The time had come to tell Cairpré what I wanted to do—and what I had left undone.

Taking a deep breath, I declared, "I haven't finished my work in the hills."

He caught his breath. "You haven't? Did you meet trouble? Warrior goblins on the loose?"

I shook my head. "The only trouble is of my own making."

The bottomless pools of his eyes examined me. "What are you saying?"

"That I've discovered something more important than my task." I faced the poet squarely. "I want to find my mother. To bring her to Fincayra."

Anger flashed across his face. "You would place us all in danger because of that?"

My throat tightened. "Cairpré, please. I will finish the task. I promise! But I need to see her again. And soon. Is that so much to ask?"

"Yes! You are putting all the creatures of this land at risk."

I tried to swallow. "Elen gave up everything for me, Cairpré! She loved her life here. Loved it to the depths of her soul. And she left it all just to protect me. During our time in Gwynedd, I was—well, her only companion. Her only friend. Even though I never did much to deserve it."

I paused, thinking about her sad songs, her healing hands, her wondrously blue eyes. "We had our problems, believe me. But we were much closer than either of us knew. Then one day I left her there, all alone. Just left her. She must be miserable, in that cold stone room. She might even be sick, or in trouble. So while I want to bring her here for me, it's also for her."

Cairpré's expression softened slightly. He laid a hand on my shoulder. "Listen, Merlin. I understand. How many times I myself have longed to see Elen again! But even if we put aside the Dark Hills, to bring someone here from the world beyond the mists—well, to do that is impossibly dangerous."

"Are you certain? The sea has spared me twice."

"It's not the sea, my boy, though that voyage is dangerous enough. Fincayra has its own ways, its own rhythms, that mortals can only guess. Even Dagda himself, it is said, dares not predict who may be allowed to pass through the curtains of mist."

"I don't believe it."

His gaze darkened. "There would be dangers to anyone brought here from outside, and dangers to the rest of Fincayra as well." He closed his eyes in thought. "What you may not understand is that anyone who arrives here—even the tiniest little butterfly—could change the balance of life on Fincayra and cause untold destruction."

"You're sounding like Domnu," I scoffed. "Saying I'm going to be the ruin of all Fincayra."

He swung his head toward the village gates, no longer aglow with golden light. Beyond them, the Dark Hills rolled like waves on a stormy sea. "You could be just that. Especially if you don't finish what you've begun."

"Won't you help me?"

"Even if I knew a way, I wouldn't help you. You're only a boy. And a more foolish one than I had thought."

I pounded my staff on the ground. "I have the power to make the Harp work, don't I? You yourself told the Great Council that I have the heart of a wizard. Well, perhaps I also have the power to bring my mother here."

His hand squeezed my shoulder so hard I winced. "Don't say such things, even in jest. It takes far more than heart to be a true wizard.

You need the spirit, the intuition, the experience. You need the knowledge—enormous knowledge about the patterns of the cosmos and all the arts of magic. And, even more, you need the wisdom, the sort of wisdom that tells you when to use those arts, and when to refrain. For a true wizard wields his power judiciously, the way an expert bowman wields his arrows."

"I'm not speaking about arrows. I'm speaking about my mother, Elen." I drew myself up straight. "If you won't help me, then I will find another way."

Cairpré's brow creased again. "A true wizard needs one thing more."

"What is that?" I asked impatiently.

"Humility. Listen well, my boy! Forget this madness. Take the Harp and return to your work in the hills. You have no idea of the risks you are taking."

"I would take many more to bring her back to me."

He looked skyward. "Help me, O Dagda!" Returning his gaze to me, he asked, "How can I make you understand? There is a proverb, as old as this island itself, saying that only the wisest shell from the Shore of Speaking Shells can guide someone through the mists. It sounds simple enough. And yet no wizard in history—not even Tuatha—has ever dared to try. Does that give you some sense of the danger?"

I grinned. "No. But it does give me an idea."

"Merlin, no! You mustn't. On top of all the other dangers, there is yet another. To you. Attempting such an act of deep wizardry will tell Rhita Gawr exactly where you are—and more, I'm afraid. When he returns, bent on conquering this world and the others, he will pursue you. Mark my words."

I tugged on the sling of the Harp. "I don't fear him."

Cairpré's brambly brows lifted. "Then you had better start. For with hubris like that, you will offer him the sweetest revenge of all. Making you one of his servants, just as he did your father."

My stomach clenched as if I'd been struck. "You're saying I'm no better than Stangmar?"

"I'm saying you are just as vulnerable. If Rhita Gawr doesn't kill you outright, he will try to enslave you."

Just then, a man's shadow fell upon us. I whirled around to face Bumbelwy. Apparently he had finished his recital and approached us, and we had been too absorbed in conversation to notice that he had been listening. He bowed awkwardly, causing his hat to fall to the ground with a noisy rattle. He retrieved the hat. Then, shoulders slumped, he faced Cairpré. "I did miserably, didn't I?"

Cairpré, still glaring at me, waved him away. "Some other time. I'm talking with the boy right now."

Turning his frowning chins toward me, Bumbelwy said glumly, "You tell me, then. Did I do miserably or not?"

Thinking that if I answered him, he would leave, I frowned back at him. "Yes, yes. You were miserable."

But he did not leave. He merely bobbed his head sullenly, clanking the bells. "So I botched the delivery. Too true, too true, too true."

"Merlin," growled Cairpré. "Heed my warnings! I only want to help you."

My cheeks burned. "Help me? Is that why you tried to dissuade me last time from going to the Shrouded Castle? Or why you didn't tell me that Stangmar was really my father?"

The poet grimaced. "I didn't tell you about your father because I feared that such a terrible truth might forever wound you. Make you doubt, or even hate, yourself. Perhaps I was wrong in that, as I was wrong in thinking you couldn't destroy the castle. But I am not wrong in this! Go back to the Dark Hills."

I glanced at the village gates. Shrouded by shadows, they stood as dark as gravestones. "First I am going to the Shore of Speaking Shells."

Before Cairpré could respond, Bumbelwy cleared his throat, making his multiple chins quiver. Then he swirled his cloak about himself with dramatic flair. "I am coming with you."

"What?" I exclaimed. "I don't want you to come."

"Too true, too true, too true. Yet I will come all the same."

Cairpré's dark eyes gleamed. "You will regret your choice even sooner than I expected."

VI

THROUGH
THE MISTS

Like the sour taste that stays in your mouth long after biting into a piece of rotten fruit, Bumbelwy, his bells jangling, stayed by my side. Only with fruit, you can wash your mouth and get rid of the taste. With Bumbelwy, nothing I said or did would make him leave. Although I walked as briskly as I could, not even pausing to strum the Harp, I could not escape his presence.

He followed me out of Caer Neithan's gates, as Cairpré stood watching in silence. He followed me over the rises and dips of the plains, trekking until long after dark, camping with me beneath an old willow, and then continuing through the sweltering sun of the next day. He followed me all the way to the grand, pounding waterway that I knew to be the River Unceasing.

All the while, he mumbled about the heat, the stones in his boots, and the arduous life of a jester. As we approached the river, he asked me several times whether I would like to hear his famous riddle about his bells, promising it would lift my spirits. Whenever I told him that I had no desire to hear his riddle—or, for that matter, his bells—he simply sulked a bit and then asked me all over again.

"Oh, but this is a royal, ranting *romp* of a riddle," he protested.

"A riddler's regular riddle. No, that's backward. Curses, I botched the delivery again! It's a regular riddler's riddle. There, that's right. It's funny. It's wise." He paused, looking even more somber than usual. "It's the only riddle I know."

I shook my head, striding toward the River Unceasing. As we neared its steep, stony banks, thundering rapids boiled beneath us. The spray rose high into the air, lifting rainbow bridges that shimmered in the sunlight. The splashing and roaring grew so loud that, for the first time since the Town of the Bards, I could not hear Bumbelwy's bells. Or his pleas to tell his riddle.

I turned to him. Above the pounding of the river, I shouted, "I have far to go, all the way to the southernmost shore. Crossing the river will be dangerous. You should go back now."

Glumly, he called back, "You don't want me then?"

"No!"

He made a six-layered frown. "Of course you don't want me. Nobody wants me." He peered at me for a moment. "But I want you, you lucky lad."

I stared at him. "Lucky? That's one thing I'm certainly not! My life is nothing but a string of disappointments, one loss after another."

"I can tell," he declared. "That's why you need a jester." Frowning gravely, he added, "To make you laugh." He cleared his throat. "By the way, did I ever tell you my riddle about the bells?"

With a snarl, I swung at his head with my staff. He ducked, stooping lower than usual. The staff skimmed the back of his cloak.

"You're no jester," I shouted. "You're a curse! A miserable curse."

"Too true, too true, too true." Bumbelwy heaved a moaning sigh.

"I'm a failure as a jester. An absolute failure. A jester needs to be only two things, wise and funny. And I am neither." A fretful tear rolled down his cheek. "Can you imagine how that feels? How it makes me ache from my thumbs down to my toes? My fate is to be a jester who makes everyone sad. Including myself."

"Why me?" I protested. "Couldn't you pick somebody else to follow?"

"Certainly," he called above the raging rapids. "But you seem so . . . unhappy. More so than anyone I've ever met. You will be my true test as a jester! If I can learn how to make you laugh, then I can make anyone laugh."

I groaned. "You will never make anyone laugh. That's certain!"

He thrust his chins at me and started to swirl his cloak about himself with a flourish. At the same time, though, he tripped on a stone and pitched sideways, losing his hat and almost skidding over the bank. Grabbing his hat, he jammed it back on his head—upside down. With a snarl, he righted it, but not before he tripped again and plopped down on the muddy ground. Grumbling, he regained his feet, trying to wipe the clumps of mud off his bottom.

"Well then," he declared with a jangle of bells, "at least I can give you the pleasure of my company."

I rolled my eyes, then glanced over my shoulder at the River Unceasing. Perhaps, if I leaped into the rushing water, it might carry me far downstream. Away from this endless torment in the form of a man. Still, as tempted as I was, I knew better. The river at this stretch was flowing far too fast, and jagged rocks protruded like daggers. I would surely damage the Harp, and probably myself as well. Where was Rhia when I needed her? She would know how to speak to the spirit of the river and calm the waves. I cringed, thinking of how we had parted. Yet it was more Rhia's fault than mine. She had been so sure of herself. It had delighted her, no doubt, to see me humbled.

I pulled the Harp higher on my shoulder. At least, once I crossed the river, I wouldn't be surrounded by these parched plains, stretching on and on like the ashen sky above, that reminded me constantly of my unfinished task. South of here, I recalled, the river widened considerably. There I could cross. Then I would continue on to the Shore of the Speaking Shells. With or without Bumbelwy.

To my dismay, it turned out to be with him. The gloomy jester, sleeves flapping and bells clanging, shadowed me past a series of roaring falls, through soggy marshland, and over stretches of smooth stones in the river's floodplain. Finally, reaching the shallows beneath a group of huge, egg-shaped boulders, we stumbled across the River Unceasing. Frigid water slapped against my shins, as the soft bottom sucked at my boots with every step. I felt, somehow, as if the river itself were trying to hold me back.

Emerging from the water, we continued to trek along the western shore. For several hours we plodded along avenues of jagged-edged reeds. To the right, towering trees of Druma Wood stretched skyward, covering the land with a blanket of green as far as the distant Misted Hills. Bright-winged birds flitted among the branches—birds that I knew Rhia could identify. All the while, I did my best to ignore the drooping figure and the jangling bells that followed me.

At last I spied a row of undulating dunes, with a rolling wall of mist behind. My heart leaped. Even with the limits of my second sight, I was struck by the strong colors ahead. Golden sand. Green leafy vines. Pink and purple shells. Yellow flowers.

My boots sank into the loose sand as I climbed the first dune. Reaching the crest, I finally saw the shore itself, rippling with waves.

The tide was low. Beneath the thick curtain of mist, clams and mussels covered the sand. I could hear them squirting and squelching, joined by the chatter and splash of water birds with long, scooped beaks. Tiny mussels by the thousands clung to the rockier places. Huge red sea stars, wide-mouthed whelks, and glistening jellyfish lay everywhere. Crabs skittered, dodging the feet of the birds.

Filling my lungs with the air of the sea, I smelled again the aroma of kelp. And salt. And mystery.

I bent down to grasp a handful of sand. It felt warm and fine as it poured through my fingers. Just as it had before, on the day I first landed on this very spot. Fincayra had welcomed me on that day, giving me refuge from the storms I faced at sea as well as those I carried beneath my brow.

I plucked a few grains of sand and watched them tumble down the slope of my fingertip, bouncing into my palm. They glittered brightly as they rolled, almost as if they were alive. Like my own skin. Like Fincayra itself. Somehow, I realized, I was beginning to feel attached to this island. As unhappy as I had often been here, I felt a surprising pull to its striking terrains, its haunting stories, and—despite the way they had often treated me—its varied inhabitants. And to something else, harder to define.

This island was, as my mother used to say, an *in between place*, a place where immortal and mortal creatures could live together. Not always harmoniously, of course. But with all the richness and power and mystery of both worlds at once. Part Heaven, part Earth. Part this world, part Otherworld.

I stood there, drinking in the sounds and smells of Fincayra's shore. Perhaps, one day, I might feel truly comfortable here. In some ways I already did, at least more than I had ever felt in that miserable village in Gwynedd. If only one particular person were here, Fincayra might even feel like home. Yet right now that person was far away. Beyond the mist, beyond the black rock coastline of Gwynedd.

Swinging the Harp around, I cradled it in my arm. I had not plucked its strings for some time now, since before I had left the arid plains. What, I wondered, could I produce in a place so rich, so teeming with life, as this?

I plucked a single string, the highest one. It tinkled, like an icicle shattering. As the note vibrated in the air, out of the seaward side of the dune popped a single red flower, shaped like an enormous bell. Seeing it sway in the briney breeze, I yearned to touch it, to smell it.

But there was no time. Not now. Dropping the Harp and my staff on the sand, I checked to make sure that Bumbelwy would not disturb them. He was already seated on the beach, frowning as he washed his swollen feet in the waves. His three-cornered hat, its bells silent at least for now, lay beside him. Though he wasn't far away, he seemed fully occupied.

I scanned the beach in both directions. With every slap forward and wash backward of the waves, shells of all sizes and colors rolled across the sand. The sheer breadth and beauty of this beach awed me, just as it had on the day I first landed. On that very day, a shell from this beach had whispered some words to me, words I could barely comprehend. Would I find another one today? And would I understand what it said?

Somewhere out there was the right shell. The trouble was, I had no idea what it might look like. All I knew were Cairpré's words. *There is a proverb, as old as this island itself, saying that only the wisest shell from the Shore of Speaking Shells can guide someone through the mists.*

Beginning with a spotted conch near the base of my staff, I started hunting for shells. Flat ones, round ones, curling ones, chambered ones, all found their way into my hands. Yet none seemed right. I wasn't even certain how to look. I could almost hear Rhia saying something as nonsensical as *Trust in the berries.* Ridiculous, of course. Yet I knew I had to trust in something. I only wished I knew what.

My intellect, perhaps. Yes. That was it. Now, what would the wisest shell look like? It would be striking. Impressive. An emperor of the shore. As large in size as it surely was in wisdom.

Bumbelwy cried out as a large wave splashed over him. As the wave withdrew, grinding against the sand, it revealed the edge of a spiral-shaped shell, bright pink, that was larger than any of the others around. It lay just behind him, although the fellow didn't seem to have noticed it. Could it be the one I was seeking? Just as I started to move closer, Bumbelwy shook himself, grumbling about the cold water, then leaned backward. As his elbow landed on the shell, I heard a loud crunch. He screeched and rolled to the side, clutching his wounded elbow. Shaking my head, I knew that my search had only begun.

Only the wisest shell . . .

I followed the sandy shore, looking for any shells that might seem right. Despite the wide array of shapes, colors, and textures, none were imposing enough. The few that came close I placed against my ear. But I heard nothing except the endless sighing of the sea.

In time I came to a rocky peninsula that jutted seaward, vanishing into the curling mist. As I stood there, wondering whether to search among the wet rocks, an orange crab ran across the toe of my boot.

The crab paused, raising its little eyes as if it were examining me. Then it skittered onto the peninsula and disappeared.

For some reason I felt drawn to this little creature that, like me, wandered this shore alone. Without thinking, I followed it onto the peninsula. Mist enveloped me. I moved carefully across the rocks, trying not to slip. Although the crab seemed to have vanished, I soon spotted another spiral shell. It lay on a flat slab coated with green algae. Even larger than the one Bumbelwy had destroyed, this shell was almost as big as my own head. It glowed with a deep blue luster, despite the unusual shadow that seemed to quiver on its surface. Certain that the shadow was only a trick of the rolling mist, I approached.

With each step I took toward it, the shell seemed more lovely. Gleaming white lines framed its graceful curves. I felt strangely drawn to it, captivated by its radiant hues.

Only the wisest shell . . .

At that moment, a powerful wave surged out of the mist, crashing over the peninsula. Struck by the spray, I felt the sting of salt on my scarred cheeks. The wave receded, pulling the spiral shell off the rock. Before I could grab it, the shell splashed into the water and disappeared in a swirl of mist.

Cursing, I turned back to the flat rock. Although the shell had vanished, the strange shadow still quivered on the algae. I almost reached down to take a closer look, then hesitated. I was not sure why. Just then the orange crab emerged from beneath a nearby rock. It skittered sideways over the peninsula, passing under a ledge before emerging from the other side. As it skirted the rim of a tide pool, it plunged into a tangle of driftwood.

Having lost any interest in following the crab, I turned away. My gaze fell on another tide pool, clear and still. From the bottom, something glistened among the fronds of kelp. Bending lower, I saw only a rather plain shell, brown with a large blue spot, nestled among some purple sea urchins. Still, it aroused my curiosity. Careful to avoid the sea urchins' sharp spines, I reached into the cold water and pulled out the shell.

Unremarkable as it appeared, the shell fit comfortably in the palm of my hand. Almost as if it belonged there. I hefted it, gauging its weight. It felt much heavier than I would have guessed for something so compact.

I brought it to my ear. Nothing. Yet there was something remarkable about this shell. My voice uncertain, I asked, "Are you the wisest shell?"

To my astonishment, I heard a spitting, crackling voice. "You are a fool, boy."

"What?" I shook my head. "Did you call me a fool?"

"A stupid fool," spat the shell.

My cheeks grew hot, but I held my temper. "And who are you?"

"Not the wisest shell, by any means." The shell seemed to smack its lips. "But I am no fool."

I felt tempted to hurl it into the waves. Yet my determination to bring back my mother remained stronger than my anger. "Then tell me where I can find the wisest shell."

The brown shell laughed, dripping water in my ear. "Try someplace where wood and water meet, foolish boy."

Puzzled, I turned the shell over in my hand. "The nearest trees are on the other side of the dunes. There isn't any wood by the water."

"Are you sure?"

"Absolutely sure."

"Spoken like a fool."

Reluctantly, I scanned the peninsula. At length, I noticed the scraps of driftwood where the crab had disappeared. Rotting seaweed draped over the wood like tattered rags. I wagged my head in disbelief. "You don't mean that sorry little pile over there."

"Spoken like a fool," repeated the shell.

Not at all sure I was doing the right thing, I dropped the brown shell into the pool and stepped over to the driftwood. Peeling off the seaweed, I searched for any sign of a shell. Nothing.

I was ready to quit when I noticed a tiny shape in a crack in the wood. It was a sand-colored shell, shaped like a little cone. It could have fit easily on my thumbnail. As I lifted the shell toward me, a black, wormlike creature pushed itself partially out of the opening at the base, then quickly shrunk back inside. Hesitant to bring such a thing too close to my ear, I held it some distance away. Although I could not be sure, I thought I heard a faint, watery whisper.

Cautiously, I brought the object closer. The watery voice came again, like a wave crashing in the tiny shell's innermost chambers. "You, *splashhh*, have chosen well, Merlin."

I caught my breath. "Did you say my name?"

"That I did, *splishhh*, though you know not mine. It is, *splashhh*, Washamballa, sage among the shells."

"Washamballa," I repeated, cradling the moist little cone against my earlobe. Something about its voice made my hopes rise. "Do you also know why I have come?"

"That, *splashhh*, I do."

My heart pounded. "Will you—will you help, then? Will you bring her back to Fincayra?"

The shell said nothing for several seconds. At last its small, gurgling voice spoke again. "I should not help you, Merlin. The risks, *splishhh*, are so great, greater than you know."

"But—"

"I should not," continued the shell. "Yet I feel something in you . . . something I cannot resist. While you have so much more to learn, *sploshhh*, this may well be part of it."

As Washamballa paused, I listened to its watery breathing. I dared not say anything.

"We might succeed, *splashhh*, or we might fail. I do not know, for even success may be a failure in disguise. Do you still, *splashhh*, wish to try?"

"Yes," I declared.

"Then hold me tight, *splashhh*, against your heart, and concentrate on the one you long for."

Clasping the shell in both hands, I pressed it against my chest. I thought about my mother. Her table of herbs, pungent and spicy. Her blue eyes, so full of feeling. Her kindness, her quiet demeanor. Her stories about Apollo, Athena, and the place called Olympus. Her faith—in her God, and in me. Her love, silent and strong.

Mist curled about me. Waves licked my boots. Yet nothing more happened.

"Try harder, *splishhh*. You must try harder."

I felt Elen's sadness. That she could never return to Fincayra. That she could never see her son grow into manhood—and that he, in all those years in Gwynedd, had refused to call her Mother. A simple word, a powerful bond. I winced, remembering how much pain I had caused her.

Slowly, her presence grew stronger. I could feel her embrace, how safe I once felt in her arms. How, for brief moments at least, I could forget all the torments that haunted us. I could smell the shavings of cedar bark by her pillow. I could hear her voice calling me across the oceans of water, the oceans of longing.

Then came the wind. A fierce, howling wind that threw me down on the rocks and soaked me with spray. For several minutes it raged, battering me ceaselessly. Suddenly, I heard a resounding *crack*, as if something beyond the mist had broken. The billowing clouds before me began to shift, gathering themselves into strange shapes. First I saw a snake, coiling to strike. Before it did, though, its body melted into the misty form of a flower. The flower slowly swelled, changing into a huge, unblinking eye.

Then, in the middle of the eye, a dark shape appeared. Only a shadow at first, it grew swiftly more solid. Before long, it looked almost like a person groping in the mist. Stumbling to shore.

It was my mother.

VII

HEADLONG
AND HAPPILY

She collapsed, sprawling on the dark, wet rocks. Her eyes were closed, and her creamy skin looked pale and lifeless. Long, unbraided hair, as golden as a summer moon, clung in ragged clumps to her deep blue robe. Yet she was breathing. She was alive.

Giving the little shell a quick squeeze of thanks, I replaced it among the scraps of driftwood. Then I ran to my mother's side. Hesitantly, I reached toward her. Just as my finger touched her strong, high cheek, she opened her eyes. For a few seconds she gazed up at me, looking confused. Then Elen of the Sapphire Eyes blinked, raised herself up on one elbow, and spoke in the voice I had thought I would never hear again.

"Emrys! It is you."

Though gratitude choked my voice, I replied, "It is me . . . Mother."

At hearing me say that word, a touch of pink flushed her cheeks. Slowly, she extended a hand. Though her skin felt as wet and chilled as my own, her touch sent waves of warmth through me. She sat up, and we embraced.

After a few seconds, she pushed back. Running her fingers gently over my burned cheeks and eyes, she seemed to be looking under my skin, into my very soul. I could tell that she was trying to feel every-thing I had felt in the months since we parted.

Suddenly, as she touched my neck, she caught her breath. "The Galator! Oh, Emrys. It's gone!"

I lowered my sightless eyes. "I lost it."

How could I tell her that I had lost it on the way to finding my own father? And that, in finally meeting him, I had lost even more?

I raised my head. "But I have you again. We're together, here on Fincayra."

She nodded, her eyes brimming with tears.

"And I have a new name, as well."

"A new name?"

"Merlin."

"Merlin," she repeated. "Like the high-flying hawk."

A pang of sorrow shot through me, as I recalled my friend Trou-ble, the little hawk who had given his life to save my own. I dearly hoped that he was still soaring, somewhere up there in the Other-world. Even now, I missed the familiar feeling of him strutting across my shoulder.

And, the truth was, I missed my other friends as well. Friends I had known for a time—and then lost. Cairpré. Honn. T'eilean and Garlatha. Aylah, the wind sister. Even Shim, who had shambled off to the mountains weeks ago. And, yes, Rhia.

I squeezed my mother's hand. "I won't lose you again."

She listened to my vow, her expression both sorrowful and loving. "Nor I you."

I turned toward the dunes. Bumbelwy sat by the water's edge, pol-ishing his bells on his sleeve. He seemed determined to ignore the sea gulls who kept tugging on his mud-splattered cloak. The Flowering Harp, along with my staff, remained where I had left them on the sand. Not far beyond, the luscious red flower swayed in the breeze off the sea.

"Come." I stood, pulling my mother to her feet. "I have something to show you."

We crossed over the rocky peninsula to the fine-grained sand of the beach. As we moved, arms around each other's waists, I savored the joy of walking with her again. Of being with her again. And when I thought about showing her the Harp, and all that I could make it do, my heart raced.

I was feeling my own power now, just as she had predicted long ago. She had told me that Tuatha himself came into his powers as he entered his teenage years. So it made sense that I should, as well. After all, hadn't I already done something that Tuatha, for all his wizardry, had never attempted? I smiled to myself. Even the shifting mists surrounding this isle could not resist me.

As we neared the Flowering Harp, she gasped in wonder. Given her affection for anything alive and growing, I was not surprised to see that it was not the Harp that had caught her attention. It was the red flower sprouting from the dune. Indeed, the flower seemed even more beautiful now than after it had just emerged. The deep cup of its petals, shaped like a bell, sat gracefully upon its arching stalk. Bright green leaves, perfectly round, ringed the stem like dozens of jewels. Dewdrops glistened from the edge of every petal.

"I must smell that flower," she declared.

"Of course." My grin broadened. "After all, I made it."

She halted, turned to me. "You did? Really?"

"With a stroke of my finger," I said proudly. "Come. Let's look closer."

As I drew nearer to the flower, my own urge to smell it grew stronger and stronger. Not just to sip a little of its fragrance, but to immerse my whole face in its petals. To drink deeply of its glorious nectar. To plunge into it, headlong and happily. I hardly noticed the strange, quivering shadow that moved across the petals. Just another trick of the misty light, as I had seen before. And no shadow, however dark, could possibly obscure the radiant beauty of this flower.

My mother's arm fell from my waist, as my own fell from hers. We continued walking toward the flower, wordlessly, as if we were in a trance. Our feet slapped on the wet sand, leaving a trail of dark prints behind us. All I could think about was breathing the flower's wondrous aroma. Only a step away, the briny breeze blew against our faces. Heedless, both of us bent toward the inviting cup.

I hesitated for an instant, wondering if I ought to let her go first. She would enjoy it so much. Then the shadow quivered again—and my urge to smell the flower grew even stronger, so much stronger that I forgot everything else. I lowered my face. Closer. Closer.

Suddenly a green shape leaped over the crest of the dune. It crashed into me, bowling me over backward. I rolled to a stop, covered with sand, then whirled around to confront my assailant.

"Rhia!" Full of rage, I spit some sand from my mouth. "Are you trying to kill me?"

Bouncing back to her feet, she ignored me completely and turned toward my mother. "Stop!" she cried with all the force of her lungs. "Don't do it!"

But Elen paid no attention. With one hand, she pulled her hair back from her face and bent toward the red flower.

Seeing this, Rhia started to dash up the slope of the dune. A terrible scream arrested her—even as it froze the blood in my veins. A dark mass leaped out of the center of the flower, straight into my mother's face. She staggered backward, clutching her cheeks with both hands.

"No!" I shouted to the sky, the sea, the mist. "No!"

But it was too late. My mother stumbled, rolling down the dune. When she stopped, I saw that her entire face was covered by a writhing shadow. Then, to my horror, the shadow slithered into her mouth and disappeared.

VIII

THE LANGUAGE
OF THE WOUND

I rushed to her side. She lay crumpled near the base of the dune. Wet sand smeared her blue robe and one of her cheeks. The sea breeze rose, sending shreds of mist across the beach.

"Mother!"

"She is your mother?" asked Rhia, joining me. "Your real mother?"

"That I am," Elen answered weakly, as she rolled onto her back. Her blue eyes searched my face. "Are you safe, my son?"

I brushed the sand off her cheek. "Safe?" I cried. "Safe? I am destroyed. Totally destroyed. I didn't bring you here to have you poisoned!"

She coughed savagely, as if she were trying to expel the shadow. Yet her face only grew more pained, more frightened.

I turned to Rhia. "I wish you had saved her instead of me."

She pulled at one of the vines woven into her garb. "I'm sorry I didn't arrive sooner. I've been searching all over for you. Finally I came to Caer Neithan, several hours after you had left. When Cairpré told me what you were doing, I followed you as fast as I could." Sadly, she looked down at Elen. "It must feel horrible. Like swallowing a bad dream."

"I—I am all right," she replied, though her wretched expression told differently. She tried to sit up, then fell back onto the sand.

Bells jangled behind me. A familiar voice moaned, "I feel death in the air."

I spun around. "Go away, will you? You're as bad as that poisonous flower!"

His head drooped even lower than usual. "I share your sorrow. I really do. Perhaps I could lighten your burden with one of Bumbelwy the Mirthful's humorous songs?"

"No!"

"How about a riddle, then? My famous one about the bells?"

"No!"

"All right," he snapped. "In that case I won't tell you it was not the flower that poisoned her." He scowled several times over. "And I certainly won't tell you it was Rhita Gawr."

My stomach tightened, even as my mother gasped. I grabbed his wide sleeve and shook him, making his bells rattle. "What makes you say such a thing?"

"*The death shadow*. I have heard it described, many times. Too many times for even a fool like me to forget. It's one of Rhita Gawr's favorite means of gaining revenge."

Elen shuddered and groaned painfully. "He speaks the truth, my son. If I hadn't lost my wits to the spell, I'd have remembered sooner." Her face contorted, even as the breeze swelled again, as if the ocean itself had heaved a great sigh. "Why me, though? Why me?"

I felt suddenly weak. For I knew in my bones that the death shadow had not been meant for my mother. It had been meant for me. Yet because of me—my own stupidity—it had struck her down instead. I should have listened to Cairpré! I should never have brought her here.

"Rhita Gawr saves this method only for those whose death he truly relishes," intoned Bumbelwy. "For it is slow, painfully slow. And horrible beyond anything words can describe. The person afflicted suffers one whole month—through four phases of the moon—before finally dying. But the final moments of dying, I have heard, hold more agony, more torment, more excruciating pain, than the entire month before."

Once again, Elen groaned, drawing her knees into her chest.

"Enough!" I waved my arms at the dour jester. "Stop saying such things! Do you want to kill her sooner? Better not to talk at all— unless you know the cure."

Bumbelwy turned away, shaking his head. "There is no cure."

I started to open my satchel of herbs. "Maybe something in here—"

"There is no cure," he repeated mournfully.

"Oh, but there *must* be," objected Rhia, kneeling beside my mother and stroking her forehead. "There is a cure for every ailment, no matter how horrible. You just have to know the language of the wound."

For a flickering instant, Elen's face brightened. "She is right. There might be a cure." She studied Rhia for a long moment. Then, her voice weak, she asked, "What is your name, young one? And how do you come to know so much about the art of healing?"

Rhia patted her suit of woven vines. "The trees of the Druma taught me. They are my family."

"And your name?"

"Most people call me Rhia. Except for the wood elves, who still use my full name, Rhiannon."

My mother's face creased in pain—but not, it seemed to me, from her ailing body. It might have been a different kind of pain, felt in another kind of place. Yet she said nothing. She merely turned her face toward the billowing mist beyond the beach.

Rhia moved nearer. "Please tell me your name."

"Elen." She glanced my way. "Though I am also called Mother."

I felt a stab of pain in my heart. She still had no idea that this was all my fault. That I had brought her here against Cairpré's strongest advice. That I had tried, in my ignorance—no, my arrogance—to act like a wizard.

Rhia continued stroking Elen's brow. "You feel hot already. I think it will get worse."

"It will get worse," declared Bumbelwy. "Everything always gets worse. Far worse."

Rhia shot me an urgent look. "We must find the cure before it's too late."

Bumbelwy began pacing across the sand, swishing his sleeves. "It's already too late. With this kind of thing, even too early is too late."

"Maybe there's a cure that nobody has found yet," retorted Rhia. "We must try."

"Try all you want. It won't help. No, it's too late. Far too late."

My mind spun in circles, torn between the urgent hopefulness of Rhia and the gloominess of Bumbelwy. Both could not be true. Yet both seemed plausible. I wanted to believe one, but I feared the other was right. A pair of gulls screeched, swooping overhead to land on a bed of sea stars and mussels. I bit my lip. Even if there were a cure, how could we possibly find it in time? Here on this remote beach, with nothing but sand dunes and rolling waves, there was no one to turn to. No one to help.

I straightened suddenly. There *was* someone to turn to! I jumped up and sprinted across the beach to the mist-shrouded peninsula. Ignoring the waves on the slippery rocks, I stumbled several times. Worse yet, in the swirling vapors, I found no sign whatsoever of the pile of driftwood where I had left the wise old shell. Had a powerful wave washed it away? My heart sank. I might never find it again!

Painstakingly, on hands and knees, I combed the wet rocks, turning over slippery jellyfish and examining tide pools. At last, soaked with spray, I spied a shard of driftwood. And there, with it, rested a little shell. Was it the same one? Quickly, I placed the sand-colored cone against my ear.

"Washamballa, is it you?"

No answer came.

"Washamballa," I pleaded. "Answer me if it's you! Is there any cure for the death shadow? Any cure at all?"

Finally, I heard a long, watery sigh, like the sound of a wave breaking very slowly. "You have learned, *sploshhh*, a most painful lesson."

"Yes, yes! But can you help me now? Tell me if there is any cure. My mother is dying."

"Do you still, *splashhh*, have the Galator?"

I grimaced. "No. I . . . gave it away."

"Can you get it back, *splishhh*, very quickly?"

"No. It's with Domnu."

I could feel the shell's despairing breath in my ear. "Then you are beyond any help. *Splashhh*. For there is a cure. But to find it, *splashhh*, you must travel to the Otherworld."

"The Otherworld? The land of the spirits? But the only way to go there is to die!" I shook my head, spraying drops of water from my black hair. "I would do even that if it would save her, I really would. But even if I took the Long Journey I've heard about, the one that leads to the Otherworld, I could never get back here again with the cure."

"True. The Long Journey takes the dead, *splashhh*, to the Otherworld, but it does not send them back again to the land of the living."

A new thought struck me. "Wait! Tuatha—my grandfather—found some way to travel alive to the Otherworld. To consult with the great Dagda, I believe. Could I possibly follow Tuatha's path?"

"That was the path that finally killed him. *Sploshhh*. Do not forget that. For he was slain by Balor, the ogre who answers only to Rhita Gawr. Even now Balor guards the secret entrance, a place called, *splashhh*, the Otherworld Well. And he has sworn to stop any ally of Dagda who tries to pass that way."

"The Otherworld Well? Is it some sort of stairwell, leading up to the land of the spirits?"

"Whatever it is," sloshed the voice of the shell, "to find it is your, *splashhh*, only hope. For the cure you seek is the Elixir of Dagda, and only Dagda himself can give it to you."

A cold wave washed over my legs. The salt stung the scrapes from my falls on the rocks. Yet I barely noticed.

"*The Elixir of Dagda*," I said slowly. "Well, ogre or no ogre, I must get it. How do I find this stairway to the Otherworld?"

Once again the shell sighed with the breath of despair. "To find it you must come to hear a strange, enchanted music. *Splashhh*. The music, Merlin, of wizardry."

"Wizardry?" I nearly dropped the little cone. "I can't possibly do that."

"Then you are, indeed, lost. For the only way to find Tuatha's path is to master, *splashhh*, the Seven Songs of Wizardry."

"What in the world are they?"

The wind leaned against me, fluttering my tunic, as I waited for the shell's reply. At last I heard again the small voice in my ear. "Even I, the wisest of the shells, do not know. All I can say is that, *splishhh*, the Seven Songs were inscribed by Tuatha himself on a great tree in Druma Wood."

"Not . . . Arbassa?"

"Yes."

"I know that tree! It's Rhia's house." I furrowed my brow, recalling the strange writing that I had found there. "But that writing is impossible! I couldn't read a word of it."

"Then you must try again, Merlin. It is your only chance, *splashhh*, to save your mother. Though it is a very small chance indeed."

I thought of my mother, lying in the shadow of the dune, afflicted with the death shadow, her breath growing shorter and shorter. I had done this to her. Now I must try to undo it, whatever the risks. Even so, I shuddered to recall Cairpré's description of the qualities of a true wizard. Qualities that I surely lacked. Whatever the Seven Songs might be, I had almost no chance of mastering them—certainly not in the brief time before the death shadow completed its terrible work.

"It's too much," I said despondently. "I am no wizard! Even if I somehow succeed at the Seven Songs, how can I possibly find this Otherworld Well, elude Balor, and climb up to the realm of Dagda, all within four phases of the moon?"

"I should never, *sploshhh*, have helped you."

I thought about the faint new moon that I had glimpsed last night. Only the barest sliver, it had been nearly impossible for my second sight to find. That meant I had until the end of this moon, and not a day beyond, to find the Elixir of Dagda. On the day the moon died, my mother would die as well.

As the moon grew full, my time would be half gone. As it waned, my time would be almost ended. And when it disappeared at last, so would my hopes.

"I wish you all the luck, *splashhh*, in Fincayra," said the shell. "You will need it, *splashhh*, and more."

IX

ROSEMARY

Since my mother was already too weak to walk, Rhia and I made a rough-hewn stretcher by weaving some vines from the dune between my staff and the branch of a dead hawthorn tree. As we worked, threading the vines from one side to the other, I explained some of what I had learned from the shell, and asked her to lead us through the forest to Arbassa. Yet even as I said the name of the great tree, I felt a strong sense of foreboding at the thought of returning there. I had no idea why.

Rhia, by contrast, didn't seem concerned or surprised to learn that the writing on Arbassa's walls held the secrets I would need to find the Otherworld Well. Perhaps because she had seen Arbassa give so many answers to so many questions before, she merely nodded, continuing to tie off the vines. At last, we finished the stretcher and helped my mother slide into place. Laying my hand on her brow, I could tell that she had grown hotter. Yet despite her worsening condition, she did not knowingly complain.

The same could not be said about Bumbelwy. We had barely started walking, with him taking the rear of the stretcher, when he began doing his own imitation of a speaking shell. When at last he realized that his audience did not find this at all amusing, he switched to describing the intricacies of his bell-laden hat, as if it were some sort of royal crown. When that, too, failed, he began complaining that carrying such a heavy load might strain his delicate back, hampering his abilities as a jester. I didn't respond, although I was tempted to silence both him and his jangling bells by stuffing his hat into his mouth.

Rhia led the way, with the Flowering Harp slung over her leafy shoulder. I took the front of the stretcher, but the weight of my own guilt seemed the heaviest burden of all. Even crossing the dune, passing beside the bell-shaped flower, felt like a strenuous march.

Before entering Druma Wood, we passed through a verdant meadow. Ribbed with streams, the grasses of the meadow moved in waves like the surface of the sea. Every rivulet splashed and rippled, lining the plants along the banks with sparkling ribbons of water. I thought how full of beauty this spot might have seemed to me under different circumstances, beauty not caused by a magical instrument or a great wizard. Beauty that was simply there.

Finally, with a crackling of twigs and needles underfoot, we entered the ancient forest. The bright meadow disappeared, and all went dark. Powerful resins, sometimes pungent, sometimes sweet, spiced the air. Branches whispered and clacked overhead. Shadows seemed to drift silently behind the trees.

Once again, I felt the eeriness of this forest. It was more than a collection of living beings of varied kinds. It was, in truth, a living being itself. Once it had given me my hemlock staff. But now, I felt certain, it was watching me, regarding me with suspicion.

I stubbed my toe on a root. Though I winced with pain, I held tight to the stretcher. My second sight had grown stronger since I was last here, but the dim light still hampered my vision. Sunlight struck just the topmost layers of these dense groves, while only a few rare beams reached all the way to the forest floor. Yet I was not about to slow down to get my bearings. I didn't have time. Nor did my mother.

Following Rhia, we pushed deeper into the forest, bearing the stretcher of vines. The strange sensation that the trees themselves were watching, following our every move, grew stronger with every step. The clacking branches sounded agitated as we passed beneath them. Other creatures seemed aware of us, as well. Every so often I glimpsed a bushy tail or pair of yellow eyes. Squeals and howls often echoed among the darkened boughs. And once, from somewhere very near, I heard a loud, prolonged scraping sound, like sharp claws ripping at a layer of bark. Or skin.

My arms and shoulders ached, but hearing the swelling groans of my mother hurt more. Bumbelwy, at least, seemed moved enough by her suffering to contain his grumbling, although his bells continued to jangle. And while Rhia moved through the woods with the lightness of a breeze, she often glanced back worriedly at the stretcher.

After hours of marching through the dark glades draped with mosses and ferns, my shoulders throbbed as if they were about to burst. My hands, nearly numb, couldn't hold on any longer. Was there no shorter route? Was it possible that Rhia had lost her way? I cleared my dry throat, ready to call out to her.

Then, up ahead, I glimpsed a new light in the branches. As we pushed through a tangle of ferns, which clung to my ankles and thighs, the light grew stronger. The spaces between the trunks widened. A cool breeze, as fragrant as fresh mint, slapped the sweaty skin of my brow.

We entered a grassy clearing. In the center, rising from a web of burly roots, stood a majestic oak tree. Arbassa. Older than old it looked, and taller than any other tree we had seen. Its massive trunk, as wide as five or six trees fused into one, lifted several times my height before its first branches emerged. From there it soared up, up, until at length it merged with the clouds.

Set in the midst of its lower branches, made from the limbs of the oak itself, sat Rhia's aerial cottage. Branches curled and twisted to form its walls, floor, and roof. Shimmering curtains of green leaves draped every window. I remembered first seeing the cottage at night, when it had been lit from within and glowed like an exploding star.

Rhia lifted her arms like rising branches. "Arbassa."

The great tree quivered, raining dew on all of us. With a pang, I recalled my clumsy attempt to make the beech tree in the Dark Hills bend down to me. On that day, Rhia had called me a fool for trying such a thing. Whether or not she had been right, I knew, as I gently lowered my mother's stretcher onto the grass, that I had been far more of a fool on this day for trying something else.

"Rosemary," said Elen, her voice hoarse from moaning. She pointed at a shrub, decked with leafy spires, that was growing near the edge of the clearing. "Get me some of that. Please."

In a flash, Rhia plucked a sprig and offered it to her. "Here you are. It's so fragrant, it reminds me of pine needles in the sun. What did you call it?"

"Rosemary." My mother rolled it between her palms, filling the air with its striking scent. She brought the crushed leaves to her face and inhaled deeply.

Her face relaxed a bit. She lowered her hands. "The Greeks called it *starlight of the land*. Isn't that lovely?"

Rhia nodded, her curls bouncing on her shoulders. "And it's good for rheumatism, isn't it?"

Elen gazed at her in surprise. "How in the world did you know that?"

"Cwen, my friend, used it to help her hands." A shadow crossed Rhia's face. "At least she used to be my friend."

"She made a pact with the goblins," I explained. "And almost killed us in the bargain. She was a tr—Rhia, what did you call her?"

"A treeling. Half tree, half person. The very last one of her kind." Rhia listened for a moment to the whispering oak leaves above us. "She took care of me ever since I was a baby, after she found me abandoned in the forest."

My mother winced in pain, though her eyes remained fixed on Rhia. "Do you . . . do you miss your real family, child?"

Rhia waved her hand lightly. "Oh, no. Not at all. The trees are my family. Especially Arbassa."

Again the branches quivered, showering us with dew. And yet I couldn't help but notice that, despite Rhia's carefree words, her gray-blue eyes seemed sad. Sadder than I had ever seen them.

Bumbelwy, frowning with his eyebrows, mouth, and chins, bent down next to the stretcher and touched my mother's forehead. "You are hot," he said grimly. "Hotter than before. This is just the occasion for my riddle about my bells. It's one of my funniest—especially since I don't know any others. Shall I tell it?"

"No." I pushed him roughly aside. "Your riddles and songs will only make her feel worse!"

He pouted, all of his chins wobbling above the clasp of his cloak.

"Too true, too true, too true." Then he drew himself up a little straighter. "But someday, mark my words, I will make somebody laugh."

"You think so?"

"Yes. It might even be you."

"Right. And the day you do that, I'll eat my boots." I scowled at him. "Get away, now. You're worse than a curse, a plague, and a typhoon combined."

Elen moaned, shifting her weight on the stretcher. She started to say something to Rhia, her blue eyes wide with anxiety. Then, for some reason, she caught herself. Instead, she took another sniff of rosemary. Turning to me, she asked, "Fetch me some lemon balm, will you? It will help calm this headache. Do you know where any grows?"

"I'm not sure. Rhia might know."

Rhia, her eyes still darkened, nodded.

"And some chamomile, child, if you can find it. It often sprouts near pine trees, alongside a little white mushroom with red hairs on the stem."

"The trees will guide me to it." Rhia glanced up at Arbassa's mighty boughs. "But first we'll bring you inside."

She peeled off her snug shoes, made from some kind of bark, and stepped into a small hollow in the roots. Then she spoke a long, swishing phrase in the language of an oak. The roots closed over her feet, so that she stood like a young sapling at Arbassa's side. As she opened her arms to embrace the huge trunk, a leafy branch lowered and laid itself across her back. All at once the branch lifted, the roots parted, and the trunk creased and cracked open, revealing a small, bark-edged doorway. Rhia entered, beckoning us to follow.

As I bent to pick up the front end of the stretcher, I looked at my mother. Perspiration flecked her cheeks and brow. Such torment in her face! Seeing her this way felt like a spear twisting in my chest. Yet . . . I couldn't shake the feeling that not all of the pain she was feeling this day had been caused by me.

Bumbelwy, grumbling to himself, picked up the rear. Together, we stumbled across the maze of roots toward the doorway. When I was only two paces away, the bark-edged door began to close. Just as it had done before, when I first came to Arbassa! Once again, the tree did not want to let me inside.

Rhia shrieked. She waved her hands, swishing a stern reprimand. The tree shuddered. The belligerent door stopped closing, then slowly opened again. Rhia shot me a glance, her expression grim. Then she turned and began to climb the gnarled, spiraling stairway within the trunk. As I followed, ducking my head to pass through the door, I was struck by the smells, rich and moist like autumn leaves after a rain. And by the sheer enormity of the trunk. Arbassa seemed even larger inside than it had outside. Even so, I had to concentrate hard in the dim light not to bump the stretcher against the walls or tilt it so far that my mother might slip off.

Carefully, we climbed the stairs of living wood. Strange writing, as intricate as a spider's web, flowed across the walls. Its interwoven runes filled the entire stairwell from top to bottom. But it was as incomprehensible as before. My hopes sank further.

Finally we came to the thick curtain of leaves that marked the entry into Rhia's cottage. Pushing through, we stepped onto a wide floor of woven boughs. All around us, wooden furniture sprouted straight out of the interlaced branches. I recognized the low table by the hearth, the pair of sturdy chairs, the honey-colored cabinet whose edges were lined with green leaves.

"Oh," breathed Elen, as she shifted slightly to see better. "It's so beautiful."

I nodded to Bumbelwy and we set down the stretcher as gently as possible. Even as he straightened himself stiffly, his frowns lessened ever so slightly. He looked around, captivated by the interior of the cottage. My own thoughts, however, remained in the stairwell below.

As if reading my mind, Rhia touched my arm. "I have some herbs to fetch for your mother." She removed the Flowering Harp from her shoulder, placing it against the wall near the stretcher. "And you, if you still hope to save her, have much work to do."

X

ARBASSA'S
SECRET

Deep within Arbassa, I toiled. I tried everything possible to find the key to the puzzle. Time after time, I trudged up the spiral stairs and down again, searching for the right place to start. I backed away, scanning the walls for some sort of pattern. I came very close, laying my forehead against the cool wood, examining each individual rune in turn. To no avail.

Hour after hour, I pored over the mysterious writing on the walls. Writing that might somehow guide me to the cure Elen so desperately needed. Yet while the intricately carved script seemed full of hidden meaning, it left me empty of understanding.

Sunset came and went, and the dim light in the stairwell faded away completely. For some time I struggled to use my second sight, even less reliable than usual in the darkness, until finally Rhia brought me an unusual torch. It was a sphere, as big as my fist, made of thin but sturdy beeswax. Within it crawled a dozen or more beetles that glowed with a steady, amber light. It was enough to illuminate at least a small portion of the script.

Grateful though I was for the torch, I accepted it without a word. The same was true for the two bowls, one filled with water and one with large green nuts, that Bumbelwy brought me sometime later.

Despite the fact that he tripped on the stairs, spilling half the water on my neck, I hardly noticed him. I was too absorbed in my work. And also my guilt. For all my concentration on the strange runes, I couldn't keep myself from hearing the recurrent sighs and moans from the woman lying on the floor above me. The woman I had brought to Fincayra.

Outside, I knew, a pale new moon was rising over Druma Wood, painting Arbassa's boughs with the faintest glow of silver. Now I had one month, less one day, to find the cure. As difficult, perhaps impossible, as that task would be, I could not even begin it until I deciphered the script. And the script showed no sign of sharing its secret.

Wearily, I lay my hand against the wooden wall. Suddenly I felt a brief spark of warmth from the runes. It barely pricked the palm of my hand before it vanished. Yet it left me with the feeling, deep in my bones, that this writing had indeed been carved by the great wizard Tuatha. Could he have known that one day, years later, his own grandson would struggle to read these mysterious words? That the words would offer the only hope of finding the stairway to the Otherworld and the Elixir of Dagda? And could Tuatha have guessed that the Elixir would be needed to save the life of Elen—the woman he had once predicted would give birth to a wizard with powers even greater than his own?

Some wizard I had turned out to be! When I wasn't bearing a magical instrument, what had my powers wrought? Nothing but misery. To me and those in my wake. I had not only snuffed out my own two eyes, I had nearly snuffed out my own mother's life.

I shambled down to the bottom of the stairwell. Despondently, I leaned close to the wall. Reaching out my hand, I touched the very first rune with the tip of my finger. It looked something like a squarish sunflower wearing a long, shaggy beard. Slowly, I traced its curves and creases, trying yet again to sense even a glimmer of its meaning.

Nothing.

I dropped my hand. Perhaps it was a matter of confidence. Of belief. *I was born to be a wizard, wasn't I? Tuatha himself said so. I am his grandson. His heir.*

Again I touched the first rune.

Again I sensed nothing.

Speak to me, rune! I command you! Still nothing. I slammed my fist against the wall. *Speak to me, I say! That is my command!*

Another painful moan echoed down the stairwell. My stomach knotted. I drew a slow, unsteady breath. *If not for me, then for her! She will die if I can't find some way to learn your secret.* A tear drifted down my cheek. *Please. For her. For Elen. For . . . Mother.*

A strange tingling pulsed through my finger. I caught a whiff of something, not quite a feeling.

Pushing my finger to the rune, I concentrated harder. I thought of Elen, lying alone on a floor of woven boughs. I thought of her love for me. I thought of my love for her. The wood seemed to grow warmer under my fingertip. *Help her, please. She has given me so much.*

In a flash, I understood. The first rune spoke its meaning directly to my mind, in a deep, resonant voice that I had never before heard, yet somehow had always known. *These words shall be read with love, or not read at all.*

Then came the rest. In a flowing, cascading river of words, a river that washed over me and carried me away. *The Seven Songs of Wizardry, One melody and many, May guide ye to the Otherworld, Though hope ye have not any. . . .*

Excitedly now, rune by rune, I read my way up each step of the stairwell. Often I paused, repeating the words to myself before proceeding. When at last I reached the top, the sun's first rays were filtering down the stairwell and trembling over the runes. During the night, the Seven Songs had been carved on the walls of my mind just as they had once been carved on the walls of Arbassa.

XI

ONE MELODY AND MANY

I climbed the last wooden stair and stepped through the curtain of leaves. My mother still lay on the floor, though no longer on the stretcher. Hearing me enter, she stirred beneath a light, silvery blanket, woven from the threads of moths, and tried with effort to raise her head. Rhia sat cross-legged by her side, her face full of worry. Bumbelwy, leaning against a far wall, looked glumly my way.

"I have read the words," I announced without pride. "Now I must try to follow them."

"Can you tell us a little?" whispered Elen. The pink light of dawn, sifting through the windows, touched the pale skin of her cheeks. "How do they begin?"

Grimly, I knelt by her side. I studied her face, so pained and yet so loving. And I recited:

The Seven Songs of Wizardry,
One melody and many,
May guide ye to the Otherworld,
Though hope ye have not any.

"Though hope ye have not any," repeated Bumbelwy, staring blankly at his hat. "Too true, too true, too true."

As I glared at him, Rhia reached for a small, pine-scented pillow. "What does it mean, *One melody and many?*"

"I'm not sure." I watched her slide the pillow under my mother's head. "But it goes on to say that each of the Seven Songs is part of what it calls *the great and glorious Song of the Stars,* so maybe it has something to do with that."

"It does, my son." Elen observed me for a moment. "What else did the words say?"

"Many things." I sighed. "Most of which I don't understand. About seedlings and circles and the hidden sources of magic. And something about the only difference between good magic and evil being the intention of the one who wields it."

I took her hand. "Then I came to the Seven Songs themselves. They begin with a warning."

> *Divine the truth within each Song*
> *Before ye may proceed.*
> *For truths like trees for ages grow,*
> *Yet each begins a seed.*

I paused, remembering that even the mighty Arbassa, in whose arms we now sat, began as a mere seed. Still, that gave me scant encouragement when I remembered the words that followed:

> *Pursue the Seven Songs in turn;*
> *The parts beget the whole.*
> *But never move until ye find*
> *Each Song's essential soul.*

"*Each Song's essential soul,*" repeated Rhia. "What do you think that could mean?"

I touched the woven boughs of the floor. "I have no idea. No idea at all."

My mother squeezed my hand weakly. "Tell us the Songs themselves."

Still pondering Rhia's question, I recited:

> *The lesson Changing be the first,*
> *A treeling knows it well.*
>
> *The power Binding be the next,*
> *As Lake of Face can tell.*
>
> *The skill Protecting be the third,*
> *Like dwarves who tunnel deep.*
>
> *The art of Naming be the fourth,*
> *A secret Slantos keep.*
>
> *The power Leaping be the fifth,*
> *In Varigal beware.*
>
> *Eliminating be the sixth,*
> *A sleeping dragon's lair.*
>
> *The gift of Seeing be the last,*
> *Forgotten Island's spell.*
>
> *And now ye may attempt to find*
> *The Otherworldly Well.*
>
> *But lo! Do not attempt the Well*
> *Until the Songs are done.*
> *For dangers stalk your every step,*
> *With Balor's eye but one.*

Silence fell over the room. Even Bumbelwy's bells did not stir.

At last, I spoke in a hushed voice. "I don't know how I can possibly do all the things the Songs require and return here before . . . ”

"I die.” Elen lifted her hand to my cheek. "Is there any way I could persuade you not to go, my son?” Her arm fell back to the floor. "At least then we'd be together at the last.”

"No! I'm the one who did this to you. I must try to find the cure. Even if the chances are one in a million.”

Her face, already pale, grew still whiter. "Even if it means your own death, on top of mine?”

Rhia touched my shoulder in sympathy. Suddenly, a whoosh of wings stirred in my memory, and I thought of someone else I had lost, the brave hawk who had died in the fight for the Shrouded Castle. We had named him Trouble, and no name could have been more fitting. Yet his actions rang even louder than his angry screeches in my ear. I wondered whether his spirit still lived in the Otherworld. And whether, if I failed in this quest, I might join him there, along with my mother.

Elen stiffened, clenching her fists, as another spasm of pain coursed through her body. Rhia reached for a bowl of a yellow potion that smelled as rich as beef broth. Carefully, she helped my mother drink a few swallows, spilling a little on the floor. Then, raising the bowl, Rhia made a loud, chattering noise with her tongue.

From on top of the cabinet, a squirrel with huge brown eyes suddenly bounced to the floor and loped to her side. It placed one paw on her thigh, waving its bushy tail. Almost before Rhia had chattered another command, the squirrel took the bowl from her hands. With a high-pitched chatter in reply, it bounded off, carrying the bowl in its teeth.

"That's Ixtma,” she explained to my mother. "I found him once in a glade near here, squealing from a broken leg. I set it for him, and since then he often visits, helping however he can. I asked him to refill the bowl for you, after he chops some more chamomile."

Despite her condition, my mother seemed on the verge of laughing. "You are an amazing girl, you are." Then her face tightened, the shadows of leaves quivering on her golden hair. "I only wish I had more time to know you."

"You will," declared Rhia. "After we return with the cure."

"We!" I looked at her in amazement. "Who said you were coming?"

"I did," she replied calmly. She folded her arms across her chest. "And there is nothing you can do to change my mind."

"No! Rhia, you could die!"

"Nevertheless, I'm coming."

The floors and walls of the cottage creaked, as Arbassa swayed from side to side. I could not be sure whether a sudden wind outside had tossed its branches, but I suspected that the wind had sprung from within.

"Why ever do you want to come?" I demanded.

Rhia looked at me curiously. "You get lost so easily."

"Stop that, will you? What about my mother? Someone needs to—"

"Ixtma will do it. We've already arranged everything."

I bit my lip. Turning to Elen, I asked in exasperation, "Are all girls this stubborn?"

"No. Just the ones with strong instincts." Her eyes moved to Rhia. "You remind me of me, child."

Rhia blushed. "And you remind me of . . . " Her voice trailed off. "I'll tell you when we get back."

Bumbelwy cleared his throat. "I shall stay."

I jumped. "What?"

"I said I'll stay. To keep her company, during the excruciating agony of her death. It's going to be miserable, absolutely miserable, that I know for certain. But perhaps I can lighten her load a bit. I'll dust off my most cheery melodies, my most humorous tales. Just the thing for someone gripped by the horror of death."

"You'll do no such thing!" I struck the wooden floor with my fist. "You're . . . coming with us."

Bumbelwy's dark eyes widened. "You *want* me to come?"

"No. But you're coming anyway."

"Merlin, no!" Rhia waved her leaf-draped arms. "Please don't let him come."

I shook my head gravely. "It's not that I want him with us. I want him *away* from her. What he calls humor could kill her in a week instead of a month."

Elen reached a trembling hand toward me and lightly brushed my scarred cheek. "If you must go, I want you to hear what I have to say."

She locked her sapphire eyes on me, so that I could almost feel her gaze penetrating my skin. "Most important, I want you to know that even if I should die before you return, it was worth it all to me just to see you again."

I turned away.

"And something else, my son. I have learned precious little in my time, but this I know. All of us—including me—have within ourselves both the wickedness of a serpent and the gentleness of a dove."

I pushed the hair off my brow. "I have a serpent, that's certain! But I'll never believe you do. Never."

She sighed heavily, her eyes roaming the interwoven branches that framed the room. "Let me say it in another way. You often enjoyed my tales of the ancient Greeks. Do you remember the one about the girl named Psyche?"

Puzzled, I gave a nod.

Once more her blue eyes seemed to search me. "Well, the Greek word *psyche* has two different meanings. Sometimes it means butterfly. And other times it means soul."

"I don't understand."

"The butterfly is the master of transformation, you see. It can change from a mere worm into the most beautiful creature of all. And the soul, my son, can do the same."

I swallowed. "I'm sorry, Mother."

"Don't be sorry, my son. I love you. I love all of you."

Bending low, I kissed her hot brow. She gave me a faltering smile, then swung her head toward Rhia. "And for you, child, I have this." From the pocket of her deep blue robe, she pulled an amulet of twigs bound together with a red thread. "An amulet of oak, ash, and thorn. Take it. You see how the buds are swelling with new life? They are ready to blossom, as are you. Keep it with you, for courage. And to remind you to trust your instincts. Listen to them. For they are really the voice of Nature, mother of us all."

Rhia's eyes glistened as she took the gift and deftly fixed it to her shirt of woven vines. "I will listen. I promise."

"You already do, I think."

"It's true," I declared. "She has even been known to remind other people to trust in the berries."

Rhia blushed, even as she fingered the amulet of oak, ash, and thorn.

"Of course," muttered Bumbelwy, "you have nothing for me."

I scowled at him. "Why should she?"

"Oh, but I do," said Elen weakly. "I have a wish."

"A wish?" The lanky figure came closer and knelt upon the floor of branches. "For me?"

"I wish that one day you will make someone laugh."

Bumbelwy bowed his head. "Thank you, my lady."

"Merlin," whispered my mother. "Perhaps your Seven Songs are like the seven labors of Hercules. Do you remember them? They were thought to be impossible. Yet he did them all, and survived."

Although I nodded, I felt no better. For Hercules' most difficult labor was to carry the weight of the entire world on his shoulders for a time. And the weight I bore now seemed no less than that.

PART TWO

XII

TUATHA

The bark-edged door creaked open, and I emerged from Arbassa. Before leaving the darkened stairwell, however, I took one last breath of the moist fragrance of the inner walls—and one last glance at the runes carved by Tuatha so long ago. I read again the words of warning that had haunted my thinking more than any others:

> *Pursue the Seven Songs in turn;*
> *The parts beget the whole.*
> *But never move until ye find*
> *Each Song's essential soul.*

What could that final phrase mean? *Each Song's essential soul.* It would be difficult enough just to make sense of the Seven Songs, but to master the soul of each seemed utterly impossible. I had no idea even where to begin.

Rhia stepped through the open door onto the grass. Her curly brown hair glowed from a ray of light piercing Arbassa's branches. She bent low and gently stroked one of the roots of the great tree. When she rose, her gaze met mine.

"Are you sure you want to come?" I asked.

She nodded, giving the root a final pat. "It won't be easy, that's certain. But we have to try."

Listening to Bumbelwy's jangling bells coming down the stairs, I shook my head. "And with him along, it will be even harder."

Rhia cocked her head toward the doorway. "I'd rather hear a broken harp all day than listen to those bells. They remind me of an iron kettle rolling down a hillside."

I thought back to the lilting music of the Flowering Harp, music that had accompanied me for so many weeks. Rather than risk damaging it, I had decided to leave the Harp behind, stowing it safely next to Rhia's hearth. Arbassa would guard it well. Yet I knew that I would miss its melodic strains. And something more.

I studied Rhia's face, as forlorn as my own. "I should never have turned away from my task in the Dark Hills. I placed all of Fincayra at risk. Now I've done the same to my own mother." Grinding the base of my staff into the grass, I sighed. "The truth is, I never deserved the Harp. You saw me strutting around with it, like some sort of wizard. Well, I'm no wizard, Rhia. I'm not powerful enough. Not wise enough."

Her eyebrow lifted slightly. "I think you're already a little wiser."

"Not wise enough to master the souls of the Songs! I don't even know where to begin."

The massive boughs above our heads suddenly stirred. Branches shook and clattered against one another, sending a shower of leaves and twigs to the ground. Although the smaller trees surrounding Arbassa remained perfectly still, the great oak itself was swaying, as if caught in a fierce gale.

A bolt of fear surged through me. I grabbed Rhia's arm. "Come! Before a branch falls on us."

"Nonsense." She wriggled free. "Arbassa would never do that. Just listen."

As I shook the leaves from my hair, I realized that the snapping and swishing branches were indeed making another sound. A sound that repeated itself over and over. *Tttuuuaaathhha. Tttuuuaaathhha.* The swaying slowly diminished. The branches grew quiet. The majestic tree towered above us, just as it had before. Yet one thing had changed. For while I still knew nothing about the souls of the Songs, I now had an idea where I might go to find out.

"Tuatha's grave," I declared. "Our quest begins there."

Rhia bit her lip. "If Arbassa believes it might help, then I believe it, too. But I don't like the idea of going there. Not at all."

Just then Bumbelwy, looking more pained than usual, poked his head out of the doorway in the trunk. He staggered onto the grass, clutching his belly. "What a storm that was! My tender stomach is turned inside out."

The lanky fellow straightened himself, jostling the bells on his hat. "But fear not, no, fear not. Weather like that follows me everywhere, so I am quite used to it."

Rhia and I traded worried glances.

"I am still coming," he continued, rubbing his side. "Even though this new injury will make it more difficult to entertain you on the way. Still, a jester must do his best to try!" He pulled his cloak over his head and started hopping around the roots of Arbassa, his bells jangling in muffled bursts.

I frowned. "Better you try to entertain us than my mother."

Bumbelwy removed the cloak from his head. "Oh, don't worry about her," he said casually. "She still has plenty of time. She has almost a month of unremitting pain before she must die." He glanced thoughtfully at Rhia's aerial cottage. "If you like, I could go back up there and give her a few laughs before we leave."

I raised my staff as if to strike him. "You fool! You have no more ability to make people laugh than a rotting corpse!"

He frowned with all of his chins. "Just you wait. I *will* make someone laugh one day. That I will."

Lowering my staff, I said scornfully, "I can taste my boots already."

The massive trunk of Arbassa creaked, as the doorway slid closed. I gazed at the trunk, following it higher, higher, until it disappeared in a mesh of branches above our heads. For a moment, I peered into the branches, woven like the threads of a living tapestry. Leaves glinted in the sun; moss sprouted like fur under every bough.

"Do you think," I asked Rhia, "that someday Arbassa might open its door to me willingly? Perhaps even gladly?"

At my words, the entire tree shuddered, raining more leaves and broken bits of bark on us.

Rhia's eyes narrowed. "Arbassa is being protective of me, that's all."

I searched her gray-blue eyes. "You don't have to come."

"I know." She pursed her lips in thought. "Are you sure, though, about going to Tuatha's grave?"

Bumbelwy gasped, wringing his hands. "The grave of the great wizard himself? Nobody goes there. Nobody who survives, that is. It is a haunted place, a terrible place. Too true, too true, too true."

"We're going there," I snapped.

"But I can't lead you," protested Rhia. "I don't even know where it lies."

"I do. I have been there once before, maybe even twice, though I need to go there again to be sure." I rubbed the top of my staff, filling the air with the scent of hemlock. "If you can guide us to that big swamp just below the Misted Hills, I can take us from there."

She shook her curls doubtfully. "We will lose precious time by doing this."

Bumbelwy shook his jangling head. "We will lose more than that."

"So be it." I thumped my staff on the grass. "Let's go."

Rhia cast a longing glance at Arbassa's boughs, then turned and strode across the grassy meadow, disappearing into a gap in the trees. I followed behind. Bumbelwy took up the rear, grumbling to himself about haunted graves and vengeful wizards.

For some time we followed a twisting trail marked by the prints of foxes, bears, and wolves, as well as others I could not identify. Then the trail vanished and we struggled to cross a wide swath of fallen trees, downed by some ferocious storm. When, shins bruised and bleeding, we finally found our way back to standing groves of pine and cedar, Rhia led us to higher ground. There the spaces between the needled trees were greater, letting more shafts of light reach the forest floor. That helped my second sight, so at least I could avoid tripping over every root and jabbing against every branch.

Even so, it was not easy to keep up with Rhia. Like me, she was driven by the urgency of our task. And, perhaps, by the tempting possibility of losing Bumbelwy somewhere in the forest. But helped by his long, spindly legs, he managed to stay with us, rattling with every step. Meanwhile, Rhia loped along as gracefully as a deer, sometimes breaking into a quick run up a slope. Watching her reminded me of the Greek story about Atalanta, the girl who could run impossibly fast. Yet even as I grinned at the comparison, I frowned to think about the woman who had first told me the story.

I pushed to keep up. Perspiration stung my sightless eyes. As the sun rode high above us, the land grew wetter. Moss sprouted from the sides of every tree, rivulets bubbled out of the ground, and mud clung to our boots. Dark pools of stagnant water appeared more frequently. It was the smell, not the sight, of this terrain that I recognized. Dank, rotting, and ominous, it dug into my memory like claws into flesh.

"Here," I announced, veering to the east.

Rhia turned to follow me, stepping lightly through the mud, unlike Bumbelwy who skidded and stomped just behind. I led them to a shadowed glade of cedars. The sounds of the forest died away, succumbing to an eerie stillness. Not even the whir of a beetle's wings broke the silence.

At the edge of the glade, I halted. With a backward glance, I told the others to remain where they were. Rhia started to speak, but I raised my hand to quiet her. Slowly, cautiously, I advanced alone.

A sudden wind moved through, tossing the branches of the cedars. Instead of making their usual crackling sound, they vibrated strangely, as if they were singing a low, mournful dirge. A song of loss and longing. A song of death. The glade darkened, until I could barely make out the shape of my boots on the needle-strewn soil. All around me, the wailing of the branches swelled. At last, I entered a small clearing, surrounded by the circle of ancient cedars that I knew marked the grave of Tuatha.

Slowly, very slowly, the clearing brightened. Yet the new light did not come from the sun. It came from the ancient cedars themselves, whose swaying branches had begun to glow with an ominous blue light. As the branches waved in the wind like the beards of old men,

I wondered if those trees might hold the spirits of Tuatha's disciples, doomed to watch over his grave, ever mourning.

Twice before, I now felt sure, I had stood on this spot. Once, not long ago. And once as a small child, when I had been brought here on the back of my father's black horse, Ionn, to witness the funeral of Tuatha. I remembered very little from that event, except the feeling of sorrow that permeated the glade.

My gaze fell to the narrow earthen mound in the center of the clearing. Twelve polished stones, perfectly round, bordered its rim. They gleamed like blue ice. As I drew a bit closer, I was struck by the sheer length of the mound. Either Tuatha had been buried with his hat on, or he had been very tall indeed.

"Both are true, you impudent young colt."

The deep voice sounded in my ears. It was the same voice that I had heard while reading the runes in Arbassa. It was the voice, I knew in my bones, of Tuatha himself. Yet beyond my fear, beyond my dread, I felt a strange sense of longing. Training my mind on the burial mound, I gave words to my thoughts.

"I wish I had known you, great wizard."

The blue stones glowed brighter, until they outshone the circle of ancient cedars. Candles seemed to flame within the stones, candles whose flames arose from the very spirit of Tuatha.

"You mean you wish I had saved you from your own folly."

I shifted uneasily, scraping the ground with the base of my staff. "That, too. Yet I also wish I had known you just to be with you. To learn from you."

"That chance was stolen from us," declared the voice bitterly. *"And do you know why?"*

"Because you were felled by the ogre Balor?"

"*No!*" thundered Tuatha, making the stones light up like torches. "*You have answered how, not why.*"

I swallowed. "I—I don't know why."

"*Think harder, then! Or is your skull no less thick than your father's?*"

My cheeks burned at the insult, yet I tried not to show my outrage. I furrowed my brow, probing my mind for the answer. Suddenly I remembered Cairpré's words of warning at the gates of the Town of the Bards.

"Was it . . . hubris?"

"*Yes!*" thundered Tuatha's spirit. "*It was my most grievous flaw, just as it is yours.*"

I bent my head, knowing too well the truth of his words. "Great wizard, I do not deserve your help. But Elen does. And if I am to have any hope of saving her, I must know something."

The stones flickered ominously. "*How do I know that you will not abandon her, even as you have abandoned the Dark Hills to the designs of Rhita Gawr?*"

I shuddered. "You have my word."

"*The Great Council, too, had your word.*"

"I will not abandon her!" My gaze swept the circle of cedars, who seemed to be shaking their branches disapprovingly. My voice barely a whisper, I added, "She means everything to me."

For a long moment, I heard nothing but the sighing branches. At last the blue stones glowed anew.

"*All right then, fledgling. What is it you wish to know?*"

Cautiously, I stepped closer to the mound. "I need to know what it means to find the soul of a Song."

The stones flamed bright. "*Ah, the soul of a Song. So little, yet so much! You see, young colt, as brief as the Seven Songs you have read may seem, they reveal the secret wellsprings of the seven basic arts of wizardry. Each Song is but a beginning, a starting point, leading to wisdom and power beyond your imagination. Far beyond, I say! And each Song holds so many verses that it would take several centuries to learn but a few.*"

"But what is the soul of a Song?"

"*Patience, you beardless infant!*" The stones seemed to smolder. "*The soul is the Song's essential truth. Its first principle. To find it is as difficult as catching the scent of a wildflower from across a wide lake. You cannot see it, or touch it, yet still you must know it.*"

I shook my head. "That sounds difficult even for a wizard, let alone a boy."

The branches waved more vigorously, as the voice of Tuatha echoed again. "*You may yet become a wizard, young colt—that is, if you survive. But remember this. As little time as you have, you will be tempted to pass over some of the Songs. Resist such folly! Do not try to find the Otherworld Well until you have found the souls of all the Songs. Heed well my words. Finding only five or six is no better than finding none. Without all seven, you shall lose more than your quest. You shall lose your very life.*"

I drew an uncertain breath. "How will I know, great wizard? How will I know when I've found the soul of each Song?"

At that instant, a tower of blue flame shot out of the stones. It sizzled and crackled through the air, striking the top of my staff like a bolt of blue lightning. I shook with the force of the blow, yet somehow I did not drop the staff. My fingers felt only slightly singed.

The deep voice filled my ears again. "*You will know.*"

I stroked the staff. It felt no different than before, yet somehow I knew that it was.

"*Now you must go, young colt. Remember what I have told you.*" The light began to fade from the stones. "*May you live to look upon my grave once again.*"

"Please," I pleaded, "tell me one thing more. Is the prophecy true that only a child of human blood can defeat Rhita Gawr, or his servant Balor?"

The glow did not return. I heard no sound but the mournful sighing of the branches. "Tell me. Please."

At last the stones glimmered. "*The prophecy may be true, and it may be false. Yet even if it is true, the truth often has more than one face. Now . . . be gone! And do not come back until you are wiser than your years.*"

XIII

STRANGE
BEDFELLOWS

As I emerged from the glade, the trees fell eerily silent again. I clung tight to my staff, aware that it, like myself, had been touched by the spirit of Tuatha. And that it, like myself, would never be quite the same.

Rhia and Bumbelwy came toward me as I stepped out of the cedars. Although they walked side by side, the contrast between them could not have been starker. One, who moved with the liveliness of a young fox, wore the greenery of the forest. The other, as stiff and glum as a tree stump, wore a heavy brown cloak and, of course, a hat of drooping bells. Yet both, at least for now, were my companions.

Rhia reached for me, wrapping her forefinger around my own. "What did you learn?"

I squeezed her finger. "A little. Only a little."

"That won't be enough," said Bumbelwy. "Nothing is ever enough."

"Where do we go now?" asked Rhia, glancing at the darkened boughs behind me.

Chewing on my lip, I pondered the first of the Seven Songs. "Well,

I must somehow find the soul of the art of Changing. And to do that, I need to find a treeling. *The lesson Changing be the first, A treeling knows it well.*" I caught my breath. "But didn't you say that Cwen was the last of the treelings?"

She nodded, her face grim. I could tell that she felt even now the sting of Cwen's treachery. "She was the last. The very last. And she's most likely gone, too. Probably bled to death after that goblin sliced off her arm."

I spun the staff's gnarled top in my hand. "But then how can I find the soul of the Song? It has something to do with the treelings."

Rhia ran her hands through her curls. "You do have a taste for challenges, Merlin! Your only hope is to go to Faro Lanna, the treelings' ancestral home. I don't think you will find much there, though."

"How far is it?"

"Far. All the way to the southwestern tip of Fincayra. And we'll have to cross the full length of the Druma, which will slow us down more. The only way to avoid that would be to cut across the Misted Hills to the coast, then head south—but that means passing through the land of the living stones. Not a wise idea!"

Bumbelwy's head jangled in agreement. "Sound advice, young woman. The living stones have an uncanny appetite for travelers." He gulped, wiggling his layered chins. "Especially jesters, I understand."

"They must have strong stomachs," I added sardonically. Facing Rhia, I asked, "That's the region where the Grand Elusa lives, isn't it?"

Bumbelwy shuddered. "Another excellent reason to avoid it! Even the living stones are afraid of that gargantuan spider. Her appetite is worse than theirs. Far worse."

I drew a deep breath of air, scented by the boughs surrounding us. "All the same, Rhia, I want you to take us the shorter way, through the Misted Hills."

Both the girl and the jester started. Even the silent cedars jostled their branches, seeming to gasp.

Rhia leaned toward me. "Are you serious?"

"Completely." I pushed the hair off my brow. "If we can save a day, or even an hour, it could be worth my mother's life."

Bumbelwy, his frowns carved deep into his face, grabbed the sleeve of my tunic. "You mustn't do this. Those hills are deadly."

I pulled free. "If you would rather stay here with Tuatha, go right ahead." As his eyes opened to their widest, I struck my staff on the needle-strewn ground. "Let's go."

We left the shadowed glade, trekking through the marshy terrain. Except for the steady rattle of Bumbelwy's bells, we moved in silence. At least, I thought grimly, the Grand Elusa will hear us coming. But would we hear her? And would she hold back her appetite long enough to remember that she had once welcomed Rhia and me as guests in her crystal cave? My legs felt weak at the thought of her slavering jaws.

As our feet squelched through the muddy soil, the trees thinned and I noticed more landmarks. An odd, chair-shaped boulder splotched with yellow lichen. The twisted skeleton of a dead tree. A patch of flaming orange moss. A strange, triangular pit. In the deepening dusk, more water seeped into the soil, as well as our boots. Soon I heard frogs piping in the distance. Water birds joined the chorus, crying in eerie voices. The dank, rotting smell grew stronger. Before long, we arrived at the edge of a wide stretch of tall grasses, dead trees, and dark pools of quicksand. The swamp.

Waving two mud-splattered sleeves, Bumbelwy protested, "We're not going across that now, are we? It's almost nightfall."

"Either we camp here," I replied, "or find some drier ground in the hills. What do you think, Rhia?"

She pulled a handful of purple berries off a low bush and popped them into her mouth. "Mmm. Still sweet."

"Rhia?"

"Drier ground," she answered at last. "Though the berries here are tasty."

As the cry of a swamp crane echoed hauntingly from the shadows, Bumbelwy shook his head. "A lovely choice. Spend the night in a swamp, and get strangled by deadly snakes, or at the Grand Elusa's doorstep, and get eaten as her breakfast."

"The choice is yours." I started off, leaping over a rotting log. I landed with a splash in a puddle. Seconds later I heard two more splashes—along with bells and a lot of grumbling—behind me.

For a while I followed a strip of caked mud that pointed like a finger into the marsh. Yet that soon faded away, making it necessary to slog straight through the grassy pools. Sometimes I sank into water up to my thighs. Long, blackened fingers of submerged branches clutched at my tunic, while mud oozed into my boots. And every so often, strange shapes stirred in the unknown depths.

The light waned steadily. Tonight there would be no moon, however, for thick clouds had rolled in, obscuring the sky. Just as well, I told myself. Seeing the moon would remind me all the more of my vanishing time, as well as hope.

We pushed on in the near-darkness. After another hour of slogging and splashing, all light vanished. A snake hissed somewhere near my boot. I began to fear that we had somehow veered off course. The murk seemed to stretch on endlessly. My legs felt heavier and heavier. Then, little by little, the terrain began to grow more solid under my feet. At first I hardly noticed the change, but in time I could tell that we were climbing gradually onto rocky ground. The rotten pools disappeared, as did their smell. The cries of frogs and birds faded behind us.

We had crossed the swamp.

Exhausted, we stumbled into a level clearing surrounded by boulders. I declared it our camp for the night. In unison, we flopped down on the mossy ground. To warm my cold hands, I slid them into the opposite sleeves of my tunic. My eyes closed, and I fell asleep.

I awoke when a large drop of rain splashed on my nose. Another drop came, and another. A cloud on the horizon flashed suddenly with light, and thunder rumbled over the ridge. The downpour began. Rain pelted us, driven by the rising wind. The night sky grew even darker, as if the clouds had condensed into great slabs of rock. Waves of water poured down from the sky. Even if I could somehow have changed into a fish, I'd have been no wetter. All I needed now was gills.

Shivering from the cold, I moved closer to one of the boulders, hoping to find at least a little shelter. That was when I realized that the boulder was moving closer to *me*.

"Living stones!" cried Rhia. "We've got to get—"

"Aaaaiieee!" screamed Bumbelwy. "It's eating me!"

I tried to roll away from the boulder. Yet the shoulder of my tunic was caught, holding me fast. I tugged on it, trying to break loose. As water streamed down my face, I pounded my fist against the stone.

My fist hit the wet rock—and stuck there. It wouldn't budge! Then, to my horror, the rock started closing around it. Swallowing my whole hand with lips of stone. I shrieked, but a clap of thunder drowned out my voice. In the blackness, in the torrent, I fought with all my strength to pull free.

Soon the stone had consumed my whole hand. Then my wrist. My forearm. My elbow. Hard as I kicked and squirmed, I could not pull away. Though I could still feel my fingers and hand, the pressure on them was increasing steadily. In no time my bones would disintegrate, crushed in the jaws of a living stone.

A sudden flash of lightning brightened the ridge. In that instant, a huge, hulking figure, broader than the boulders themselves, entered the clearing. Its voice, louder even than the thunder, rose above the storm.

"Huuungry," bellowed the great beast. "I aaam huuungry."

"The Grand Elusa!" shouted Rhia.

Bumbelwy screamed again, the scream of a man about to die.

In a single leap, the Grand Elusa landed at my side, her eight legs splattering mud in all directions. Despite the rain and the darkness, my second sight could not miss her massive jaws opening. As I glimpsed the endless rows of jagged teeth, I struggled all the harder to escape. The jaws closed.

Not on me! With a terrific crunch, the Grand Elusa took an enormous bite out of the living stone itself. The boulder shuddered violently, then released my arm. I tumbled backward onto muddy ground. Before I knew what was happening, someone fell on top of me, as a blast of white light seared the ridge.

XIV

THE CRYSTAL CAVE

Light, sparkling like stars, danced all around me. And around Rhia and Bumbelwy, as well, for we lay in a single heap of arms and legs and torn clothing. I pushed someone's dripping foot out of my face and sat up. Aside from being soaking wet and feeling intensely sore in my hand, I was fine. Wherever I might be.

In a flash, I recognized the rows upon rows of glowing crystals, the shimmering waves of light that vibrated over the walls, and the sheer magnificence of this place. Thousands upon thousands of dazzling facets, each as smooth as ice, glittered on all sides, shining with a light of their own. The crystal cave! On my first visit here, I had known that I had never been anywhere as beautiful. Now I knew it again.

Something cracked behind me. I swung my head around to see the Grand Elusa herself, her body so vast that it nearly filled the entire glowing cavern. She had just taken a bite of what looked like the hind quarters of a wild boar. Her huge eyes, faceted like crystals themselves, observed me as she chewed. After swallowing the last morsel, she licked her arms clean with surprising delicacy.

"Welcooome tooo myyy caaave," she bellowed.

Bumbelwy, his bells jingling as he shivered, clutched my sleeve in terror. "Are—are we n-n-next?"

"Of course not," chided Rhia, her damp curls sparkling like the crystals around us. "She brought us here to get us away from the living stones."

"S-s-so she c-could eat us hers-s-self," stuttered the jester.

"Siiilence." The gargantuan spider scratched the white hump on her back. "I haaave saaatisfied myyy huuunger fooor nooow. Luuucky fooor youuu, liiiving stooones taaake sooome tiiime tooo diiigest. Theee boooar waaas meeerely deeessert."

Using the sleeve of my tunic, I wiped the raindrops off my face. "Thank you. But how did you get us here so fast?"

"Leeeaping." The Grand Elusa edged a bit closer, so that I could see myself reflected dozens of times in the facets of her eyes. "Iiit iiis aaan aaart youuu maaay leeearn ooone daaay."

"Leaping is one of the Seven Songs I have to master! Don't tell me I need to learn how to do what you just did. That alone could take a lifetime."

"Maaany liiifetimes." The great white spider continued to examine me. "Espeeecially fooor ooone whoo caaanot compleeete hiiis taaasks. Wheeere haaave youuu leeeft theee Flooowering Haaarp?"

Perspiration beaded on my brow. "It's safe. In Arbassa. But I can't go back to the Dark Hills now! I have another problem to solve first."

"Aaa prooobblem youuu caaaused."

I lowered my head. "Yes."

"Aaa prooobblem," thundered the creature, "thaaat youuu caaan stiiill sooolve."

Slowly, I raised my head. "Are you saying I might really have some chance to save her?"

One of her enormous legs tapped against the floor of crystals. "Aaa minuscuuule chaaance iiis stiiill aaa chaaance."

Rhia crawled a little nearer to me. "So Elen might survive?"

"Sheee miiight, aaand heeer youuung maaan miiight aaas weeell." As the Grand Elusa cleared her throat, the rumble echoed between the curving, crystalline walls. "Buuut heee wiiill neeed tooo surviiive thiiis queeest, aaand maaany mooore, befooore heee maaay ooone daaay fiiind hiiis ooown crystaaal caaave."

"My own crystal cave?" My heart leaped at the idea. "Is that really possible?"

"Aaanything iiis possiiible."

The immense spider slid her bulk to one side, revealing an array of glittering objects. The Treasures of Fincayra! I recognized the Orb of Fire, its orange sphere aglow like the crystals; the graceful horn I knew to be the Caller of Dreams; and the great sword Deepercut, with one edge that could slice all the way into the soul, and another edge that could heal any wound. Just behind them, I glimpsed the plow that could till its own field, the Treasure that Honn had described to his son. Near it lay the rest of the Wise Tools—except for the one that had been lost.

"Iiit iiis eeeven possiiible thaaat, ooone daaay, youuu maaay beee wiiise enouuugh tooo caaarry ooone ooof theee Treasuuures aaand nooot destroooy mooore thaaan youuu creaaate."

I swallowed hard.

"Youuu maaay teeell meee theee Seeeven Sooongs." Not a request but a command, her words boomed in my ears.

I hesitated for an instant, then sucked in my breath and began:

> *The Seven Songs of Wizardry,*
> *One melody and many,*

May guide ye to the Otherworld,
Though hope ye have not any.

Bumbelwy, who was huddled at the far end of the cavern, shook his head morosely, clanging his bells. The spider turned an enormous eye on him, and he instantly stopped.

In the glow of the crystals, I continued, reciting the warning to master each of the Songs in turn. Rhia's bright eyes sparkled like crystals themselves when I spoke the words that were now embedded in my very being: *Each Song's essential soul.* Then I moved through the Seven Songs themselves. When, at the conclusion, I mentioned the eye of Balor, the Grand Elusa shifted her weight uneasily on the faceted floor.

No one spoke for some time. At last the Grand Elusa's voice rang out.

"Aaare youuu afraaaid?"

"Yes," I whispered. "I'm afraid I can't do it all in four phases of the moon."

"Iiis thaaat aaall?"

"I'm afraid of how hard it will be to find the souls of the Songs."

"Iiis thaaat aaall?"

I ran my hand nervously across the crystalline floor, feeling the sharp edges. "I'm afraid of the seventh one, Seeing, most of all. But . . . I don't know why."

"Youuu shaaall fiiind ouuut whyyy, iiif youuu geeet thaaat faaar."

Using three of her arms, she scratched her hairy back. "Youuu maaay leeearn aaa liiittle maaagic, aaas weeell. Iiit iiis aaa piiity youuu wooon't leeearn anythiiing reeeally uuuseful, thooough. Liiike hooow tooo spiiin aaa weeeb. Ooor hooow tooo cheeew aaa stoooone."

Rhia giggled. Then her face grew taut. "What does it mean, that part about Balor's eye?"

The spider's white hairs bristled. "Theee ooogre haaas ooonly ooone eeeye. Aaand iiit kiiills anyooone whooo loooks intooo iiit, eeeven fooor aaan iiinstant."

Rhia leaned toward me. "That must be how Tuatha died."

"Yeees indeeed," declared the Grand Elusa. "Aaand hooow youuu tooo wiiill diiie, iiif youuu aaare nooot caaareful."

I frowned. "The truth is, I may never get past the first Song. When you found us, we were trekking to Faro Lanna, in the hope of learning something that might help. But with no treelings left, it is hardly a hope at all."

"Iiit iiis theee ooonly hooope youuu haaave."

"Faro Lanna is so far away from here," said Rhia despairingly. "It's a good week's walk, even if we don't run into any more trouble."

"A week!" I groaned. "We don't have that much time to spare."

A sudden explosion of white light filled the crystal cave.

XV

CHANGING

We found ourselves sitting on a grassy field at the edge of a sheer cliff that dropped straight to the sea. As I peered over the edge, I viewed colonies of kittiwakes and silver-winged terns nesting on the cliff wall, screeching and chattering and tending to their young. A cool breeze smacked my face. The smell of salt water seasoned the air. Far below me, the white line of surf melted into bright blue and then into green as dark as jade. Across a wide channel of water, I could barely make out the shape of a small island, dark and mysterious. Behind it billowed the wall of mist that surrounded all of Fincayra.

I turned to Rhia and Bumbelwy, also investigating our new surroundings. To think that we had, only seconds before, been inside the Grand Elusa's crystal cave! Wherever we were now, it was far away from there. Such a wondrous skill, to move people like that. She had even remembered to send along my staff. I made a mental note to pay close attention to the fifth lesson, Leaping, should I ever make it that far.

Rhia bounced to her feet. "Look there," she cried, pointing toward the small island. "Do you see it?"

I stood, leaning against my staff. "That island out there, yes. Looks almost unreal, doesn't it?"

Rhia continued to stare. "That's because it *is* almost unreal. That's the Forgotten Island. I'm sure of it."

A shiver shook my spine. "The seventh Song! That's where I must go to learn about Seeing." I glanced at her briefly before turning back to the island, shrouded by shifting vapors. "Have you seen it before?"

"No."

"Then how can you be so sure it's the Forgotten Island?"

"Arbassa's stories, of course. It's the only piece of land in all of Fincayra that's not connected to the main island. No one—not even Dagda himself, it is said—has set foot there for ages. And except for the mer people who live in this inlet, no one knows how to cross the powerful currents, and even more powerful enchantments, that swirl around it all the time."

I dodged a gull that swooped just in front of my face. Yet I couldn't take my gaze from the island. "Sounds like people aren't supposed to go there." My stomach churned uneasily. "For whatever reason."

She sighed, still watching the island herself. "Some people believe it has something to do with how Fincayrans lost their wings long ago."

"Too true, too true, too true," intoned Bumbelwy as he walked mopily toward us, jangling with every step. "That was the saddest moment in the whole sorry history of our people."

Was it possible that the dour jester knew how the wings were lost? I felt suddenly hopeful. "Do you know how it happened?"

His long face swung toward me. "No one knows that. No one."

I frowned. Aylah, the wind sister, knew. But she hadn't wanted to tell me. I wished I could ask her again. Yet that was impossible, as impossible as catching the wind. More than likely, she had blown all the way to Gwynedd by now.

Rhia turned at last from the island. "Would you like to know where we are standing right now?"

I gave her a nudge. "You still sound like a guide."

"You still need a guide," she answered with a half grin. "We're in Faro Lanna, the strip of land that once was home to the treelings."

Listening to the surging waves below us, I scanned the plateau. Steep, cream-colored cliffs bounded us on three sides. But for a few piles of crumbling stones, possibly all that remained of walls or hearths, nothing but grass covered the plateau. Far to the north, a line of dark green marked the edge of a forest. Beyond that, the horizon lifted in a purplish haze, possibly all that was visible of the Misted Hills.

A dingy brown butterfly fluttered out of the grass and landed on my wrist. Its legs tickled, so I shook my hand. Then it flew off, landing on the knotted top of my staff. Its motionless wings blended into the deeper brown of the wood.

With a sweep of my arm, I indicated the grassy plateau. "I don't see how we're ever going to learn about the treelings' art of Changing. If they ever lived here, they didn't leave much behind."

"That was their way." Rhia picked up a white pebble and tossed it over the cliff. "The treelings were wanderers, always searching for someplace better to live. Someplace to sink roots, like true trees, and call home. Their only settlements were here, by the cliffs, but as you can tell from those rock piles, they weren't much. Nothing more than shelters for the very old and the very young. No libraries or markets or meeting halls. Most treelings spent their days wandering across Fincayra, only coming back here when they were ready to find a mate or to die."

"So what happened to them?"

"They got so caught up in their exploring, I guess, that fewer and fewer of them ever bothered to come home. Eventually, nobody at all returned. The settlements fell apart or blew away, since there was nobody around to take care of them. And the treelings themselves died off, one by one."

I kicked at a tuft of grass. "I can't blame them for wandering. It's in my blood, too. But it sounds as if they never felt at home anywhere."

Rhia studied me thoughtfully, the wind off the water ruffling her leafy garb. "And is feeling at home somewhere in your blood, as you say?"

"I hope so, but I'm not sure. What about you?"

She stiffened. "Arbassa is my home. My family. All the family I've ever had."

"Except for Cwen."

She bit her lip. "Once she belonged to my family. But no more. She gave that up for a sackful of goblin promises."

The butterfly lifted off from my staff. It flew over to Bumbelwy, who was still gazing glumly across the channel at the Forgotten Island. Just before landing, the butterfly apparently changed its mind and returned to the gnarled shaft of hemlock. I watched its dull brown wings, one of which was badly frayed, slowly opening and closing.

Looking again at Rhia, I declared, "We must find her."

"Who?"

"Cwen. She might be able to tell me what those piles of stones cannot."

Rhia made a face as if she had eaten a handful of sour berries. "Then we are lost. There is no way to find her, even if she did survive losing her arm. Besides, if we did find her, we couldn't trust her." Fairly spitting the words, she added, "She's a traitor, through and through."

Below us, an enormous wave crashed against the cliff, sending the kittiwakes and terns screeching from the spray. "Even so, I have to try! Surely somebody saw her after she left. If treelings are all that rare nowadays, the sight of one would be noticed, wouldn't it?"

She shook her head. "You don't understand. Treelings not only weren't satisfied to stay in any one place. They weren't satisfied to stay in any one body, either."

"You don't mean—"

"Yes! They knew how to change form! You know the way most trees change their colors in the autumn, and take on a whole new garb in the spring? The treelings went far beyond that. They were always swapping their treelike shape for a bear, or an eagle, or a frog. That's why they were named in the Song about Changing. They were masters of it."

My hopes, already as fragile as the butterfly perched on my staff, vanished entirely. "So Cwen, if she's still alive, could look like anything."

"Anything at all."

Bumbelwy, sensing my despair, spoke up. "I could sing you a song, if you like. Something light and cheery."

Since I didn't have the strength to protest, he started to sing, swaying his bell-draped hat in time to the rhythm.

> *Life's unending curse:*
> *It could be far worse!*
> *Yet I'm full of glee.*
> *None gladder than me.*

Though death fills the air,
I do not despair.
It could be far worse:
Life's unending curse.

Be merry! You see,
Far worse it could be.
So much worse than now!
Just . . . don't ask me how.

"Stop!" shouted Rhia. "If you really feel that way, why don't you just jump off this cliff and put an end to your misery?"

Bumbelwy frowned triply. "Weren't you listening? That's a joyous song! One of my favorites." He sighed. "Oh dear, I must have botched the delivery. As usual. Here, I'll try it again."

"No!" a voice cried out.

But the voice did not belong to Rhia. Nor to me. It belonged to the butterfly.

With a frantic fluttering, the tiny creature left its perch, rose into the air, and started spinning downward. Just before it hit the grass, a loud *crraackk* split the air. The butterfly vanished.

In its place stood a slim, gnarled figure, part tree and part woman. Her hair, as rough as straw, fell over the barklike skin of her face, framing two dark eyes the shape of teardrops. A brown robe encircled her, covering her body down to her broad, knobby feet that resembled roots. Only one arm protruded from the robe, its hand wearing a silver ring on the smallest of six fingers. The sweet scent of apple blossoms clung to her, in stark contrast to the sour expression on her face.

Rhia stood as stiff as a dead branch. "Cwen."

"Yessss," whispered the treeling, her voice rustling like dry grass.

"It issss Cwen. The ssssame Cwen who took care of you assss a baby, and nursssssed you through many a ssssickness."

"And who tried to give me to the goblins!"

Cwen's lone hand ran through her ragged hair. "That wassssn't my dessssire. They promisssssed they would not harm you."

"You should have known they would lie. No one can trust a warrior goblin." She stared at the twisted figure. "Now no one can trust *you*."

"Don't you ssssee I know that?"

A kittiwake landed on the grass nearby and started tugging at some strands with its beak. Though the bird pulled vigorously, the grass wouldn't budge. "Watch thissss," said Cwen, taking a small step closer. In her most gentle voice, she asked, "If I tried to help you build your nesssst, good bird, would you let me?"

The kittiwake screeched and flapped its wings angrily at her. Only after carrying on for some time did it finally settle down and return to work, still watching Cwen warily with one eye.

Sadly, the treeling turned back to Rhia. "You ssssee? Thissss issss my punisssshment."

"You deserve it, every bit."

"I am misssserable, totally misssserable! I thought thingssss could get no worsssse. Then ssssuddenly you appeared." She aimed a knobby finger at Bumbelwy. "With thissss . . . voiccccce of doom."

The jester raised his head hopefully. "Perhaps you prefer riddles? I know a terrific one about bells."

"No!" shrieked the treeling. "Pleasssse, Rhia. I am ssssso full of remorssssse. Won't you forgive me?"

She crossed her leaf-covered arms. "Never."

I felt a strange pang. The word *never* rang in my ears like a heavy door slammed and barred. To my own surprise, a feeling of sympathy rose inside of me. Certainly Cwen had done something terrible. Something she regretted. But hadn't I also done things I deeply regretted?

I stepped close to Rhia, lowering my voice. "It's hard, I know. Yet maybe you should forgive her."

She stared at me coldly. "How can I?"

"The same way my mother forgave me after what I did to her." At that instant, Elen's parting words came back to me. *The butterfly can change from a mere worm to the most beautiful creature of all. And the soul, my son, can do the same.* I bit my lower lip. "Cwen did something awful, to be sure. But she deserves another chance, Rhia."

"Why?"

"Because, well, she could change. *All of us, all living things, have the potential to change.*"

Suddenly my staff flashed with bright blue light. The wooden shaft sizzled, as if it were burning. A split second later, both the light and the sound disappeared. As I twirled the staff in my hand, I found a marking, as blue as the sky at dusk, engraved upon the shaft. It was in the shape of a butterfly. I knew, in that moment, that Tuatha's spirit still touched my staff. And that, somehow, I had discovered the soul of Changing.

Hesitantly, Rhia stretched her hand toward the treeling. Cwen, her slender eyes glistening, took it in her own. For a moment, they regarded each other in silence.

Finally the treeling turned to me. "Issss there any way I can thank you?"

"Seeing you two like this is thanks enough."

"Are you ssssure there issss nothing I can do?"

"Not unless you know the power of Leaping," I replied. "We must go now to the Lake of the Face, far to the north."

"Ten days' walk," moaned Bumbelwy. "No, more like twelve. No, make it fourteen."

Cwen's teardrop eyes probed me. "I don't know the sssskill of Leaping, but the sssskill of Changing may be usssseful to you."

Rhia caught her breath. "Oh Cwen, if only we could swim like fish..."

"It would ssssave you sssseveral days."

I jumped. "Is it really possible?"

A crooked grin spread over Cwen's face as she wiggled her bony fingers at Bumbelwy. "You, voicccce of doom, will go firsssst."

"No," he pleaded, backing away. "You wouldn't. You couldn't."

"Flippna sssslippna, hahnaway sssswish," intoned Cwen. *"Kelpono bubblim tubblim fissssh."*

All of a sudden, Bumbelwy halted, realizing that he had backed up almost to the edge of the cliff. He looked down at the crashing surf, his eyes wide with fright, his sleeves flapping in the wind. He looked back at Cwen, and his eyes grew wider still.

"P-please," he stammered. "I *hate* f-f-fish! So s-slimy, so v-very wet all over! S-so—"

Crraackk.

An ungainly fish, with enormous eyes and quadruple chins under its downturned mouth, flopped helplessly on the grass before finally plunging over the cliff. Yet I found it hard to laugh, for I knew I would be next.

XVI

LIQUID THRILL

Suddenly I couldn't breathe.

Wind rushed past. I fell down, down, down. I fought to take in some air. No use! The howling wind tore at me. Yet I could not fill my lungs with it, as I had always done before. Then, with a splash, I hit cold water. My gills opened wide. Gills! I breathed again at last. As water moved around me, it also moved through me.

No more arms. No more legs. My body was now a single, stream-lined tail, with flexible fins above and below and on both sides. One of the fins curled around a small stick, which I guessed was all that remained of my staff. What had happened to my satchel, boots, and tunic, I had no idea.

It took me a moment to find my balance, for whenever I tried to move my fins, I flipped over on my side. And it took more than a moment for my second sight to adjust to the dim, scattered under-water light. Except for the layer of water closest to the surface, there was practically no light at all. Only gradations of darkness.

After several minutes of struggling, however, my confidence began to improve. I discovered that swimming required completely differ-ent movements than it had with my human form. Stroking was out of the question. So was kicking, at least in the old way. What I needed to do was sway my entire body from side to side, like a living whip cracking. Every single scale on my skin, from my gills to the tip of my tail, joined in the motion. Soon I found I could whip through the waves. And I could move up or down as well as left or right.

A slender fish, mottled with greens and browns, swam over. I knew at once it was Rhia, for although she had been underwater no longer than I, she moved with the grace of the current itself. We waved our fins in greeting. She made some sort of coughing sound, and I realized that she was laughing at the sight of my miniature staff.

At that moment Bumbelwy, trailing a torn ribbon of kelp from his tail, swam slowly toward us. While he wore no bells, there was no mistaking him. From the front, his sagging chins made him look like an eel wearing a ruffled collar. It was the closest he had ever come to being funny, although he had no idea.

Our first task was learning to keep together. Rhia and I took turns in the lead position, with Bumbelwy always following behind. In time, Rhia and I began to swim with increasing coordination. A sixth sense slowly emerged in us, the same sense that binds an entire school of fish together. After the first full day of swimming, the two of us moved almost as a single, connected being.

A quiet, liquid thrill moved through me as we swam through vast forests of swaying kelp or leaped through the rolling waves. I could taste feelings as well as flavors in the currents; I could sense the joy of a family of dolphins, the lonely struggle of a migrating turtle, the hunger of a newborn sea anemone. Yet I never forgot the seriousness of my quest. Even as I reveled in the experience of being a creature of the water, I knew that all of this was merely a means of saving time—and, perhaps, Elen. Still, I promised myself that if I ever survived this quest and one day actually became a wizard, perhaps even the mentor of a young king or queen, I would remember the virtues of transforming my student into a fish.

One of those virtues was discovering the great amount of food that the sea could provide. Why, the sea was really one enormous, floating feast! Day after day, I ate enough insects, eggs, and worms to feel bloated. Rhia, for her part, proved adept at catching tasty little crayfish. While Bumbelwy drew the line at worms, even he tasted many of the sea's strange delicacies.

At the same time, we tried to stay alert to the danger of becoming someone else's delicacy. Once I swam through a tunnel of bright yellow coral only to find a very large, very hungry fish waiting for me at the other end. As quickly as I darted away, I surely would have been caught but for the even larger creature who suddenly appeared, scaring off my pursuer. Although I just barely glimpsed the creature who had helped me, it seemed to possess the tail of a fish and the upper body of a man.

For six days and five nights we swam steadily northward. Often after dark, the pale light of a swelling half moon danced upon the waves. Yet the moon's beauty escaped me. I saw in its face only the face of someone else, someone I feared losing forever. Less than three weeks remained.

At last came the moment when Rhia veered sharply toward the coast. She led us to a small delta where a freshwater stream emptied into the sea. I could taste, mixing with the salty flavors of the wide waters, the purity of melted snow, the playfulness of otters, and the unwavering patience of a stand of ancient spruce trees. We surged up the stream as far as we could. Then, concentrating my thoughts, I repeated the command that I had learned from Cwen.

All of a sudden I stood knee-deep in a tumbling cascade, clutching my staff in one hand and Rhia's arm in the other. Just downstream, Bumbelwy threw himself on the marshy bank, coughing and sputtering. He had, it seemed, forgotten that people tend not to breathe too well with their heads underwater.

While Bumbelwy recovered, Rhia and I shook some of the water from our clothes and ourselves. Meanwhile, she explained that she believed that this stream flowed down from the Lake of the Face itself. Before long, all three of us were trekking along the stony stream bank, climbing with the rising ground. A tangled forest of alder and birch that clung to the bank made the going difficult. Every time Bumbelwy tried to shake free of the branches that grasped at his cloak, his bells rattled soggily.

At one point I paused, panting hard from the climb. Spying a shaggy-topped mushroom growing among the roots of a birch, I pulled it from the ground. "Strange as it sounds," I said as I took a bite, "I'm going to miss those little white worms."

Rhia wiped her brow and grinned at me. She picked her own mushroom. "Maybe you'll find more worms at the Lake of the Face."

"How did it come to have such a name? Do you know?"

She chewed pensively. "Some say it's from the shape, which is a little like a man's face. Others say it's from the power of the water."

"What power?"

"If you look into it, according to legend, you will face an important truth about your life. Even if it's a truth you would rather not know."

XVII

BINDING

We continued on, following the stony stream bank as it climbed through the alders. Though roots tripped our feet and thorns tore our clothing, our pace hardly slackened. Several hours and scraped shins later, the waterway opened into a snug valley surrounded by steep, wooded hills. The spicy scent of pine trees wafted over us. Amidst the trees, outcroppings of white quartz gleamed in the late afternoon sun.

Yet the valley seemed eerily silent. No birds sang, no squirrels chattered, no bees buzzed. I listened closely, hoping to hear the stirring of something alive. Rhia, reading my thoughts, gave a knowing nod. "Animals and birds stay away from this valley. No one knows why."

"They're smarter than people," observed Bumbelwy, still dripping water from his bells.

I watched Rhia walk down to the shore of the lake in the center of the valley. The lake, its water almost black, was so still that hardly a ripple broke its surface. Its contours resembled, from this angle, the profile of a man whose jaw, strong and defiant, jutted outward—much like my own father's. Remembering him, I stiffened. I wished he had been as strong in reality as in appearance. Strong enough to stand up to Rhita Gawr when he had seen the chance. Strong enough to help his own wife, Elen, when she had needed him.

A shriek jolted me out of my thoughts.

There, by the edge of the lake, stood Rhia, gazing into the dark water. She held her hands in front of her protectively, while her back arched in fear. Yet if something in the lake had frightened her, she made no effort to move or get away. She stared straight into the water, completely transfixed.

I ran down to her. Bumbelwy followed me, alternately tripping over his torn cloak and the mesh of vines that grew along the shore. Just as I reached her, she turned around. Her skin, usually full of color, looked deathly pale. She gasped when she saw me, as if she were suddenly afraid. Then she shuddered and grabbed my arm for support.

I braced myself to support her weight. "Are you all right?"

"No," she answered weakly.

"Did you see something in the lake?"

"Y-yes." She shook herself again, releasing my arm. "And you—you'd better not look."

"Fine," declared Bumbelwy, glancing nervously at the dark water. "Let's go."

"Wait." I stepped to the edge of the lake. As I peered into the still water, I viewed my own reflection, so clear that for an instant I thought that my own twin was in the lake, staring back at me. What, I wondered, could have been so frightening about such a perfect reflection? There were my useless eyes, looking like lumps of coal beneath my brows. And my scarred cheeks, ravaged by flames that I could still almost feel. Stroking my cheeks, I wished that I might someday grow a beard to cover those scars. A beard, curly and white, like the one I imagined that Tuatha himself had worn.

I jumped back. The boy in the lake started sprouting whiskers. First black, then gray, then white as the quartz on the hillside, the whiskers grew long and scraggly. They covered most of the boy's face, growing and growing. Soon they fell all the way to his knees. Was it possible? Was the Lake of the Face telling me that I would one day, like my grandfather before me, wear a beard? That I would one day, like him, be a wizard?

I smiled, feeling increasingly confident about peering into the still, dark water. Whatever Rhia had seen had clearly departed. I leaned closer. The boy in the lake, no longer wearing a beard, slowly turned away from me. He ran toward something. No, someone. A huge, muscular warrior, wearing a red band around his forehead, strode out of the depths. Then, as the warrior came nearer, I realized that he had only one eye. One enormous, wrathful eye. Balor!

To my horror, the ogre dodged the boy with ease, grabbed him by the throat, and lifted him high. My own throat constricted as I watched the boy being strangled by powerful hands. Hard as I tried, I could not turn away from the terrifying scene. The boy struggled wildly, trying not to look in the ogre's deadly eye. Yet the eye's power pulled on him. Finally, he succumbed. With a last jerk of his legs, he hung limp in the ogre's hands.

I fell backward on the ground, gasping for air. My head whirled. My neck throbbed. With each breath, I coughed uncontrollably.

Rhia reached for me, as did Bumbelwy. She squeezed my hand, while he patted my brow sympathetically. Slowly, my coughing subsided. But before any of us could speak, someone called to us across the water.

"So," wheezed a gleeful voice, "are you finding the lake's prophecies difficult to, shall we say, swallow?" A full, breathy laughter followed. "Or are you just feeling, shall we say, choked up?"

Regaining my bearings, I scanned the dark surface of the lake. Near what would be the nose of the profile, I spotted an immense, hairy otter, silver in color except for his face, which was white. He floated leisurely on his back, kicking so effortlessly that he hardly caused a ripple.

I pointed. "There. An otter."

Rhia shook her head in disbelief. "I didn't think anyone lived here."

"I only live where I otter," he answered merrily, squirting a jet of water from between his two front teeth. "Care to join me for a swim?"

"No chance," declared Bumbelwy. He waved his long sleeves like fins, causing his bells to dribble water on his face. "I've had enough swimming for a lifetime."

"Then perhaps I should sing one of my water songs for you?" The otter kicked lazily toward us, patting his belly with both paws. "I have, shall we say, a fluid voice." His breathy laughter came again, echoing over the lake.

Supporting myself with my staff, I stood. "No thanks. The only Song we care about isn't about water." Seized by a sudden inspiration, I asked, "You wouldn't happen to know anything about the magic of Binding, would you?"

Rhia frowned. "Merlin," she cautioned. "You don't know him at all! He could be—"

"An expert in matters of Binding," said the otter relaxedly. "My favorite pastime. Next to floating on my back and watching the clouds, that is."

"You see?" I whispered to her. "He could tell us what we need. And I don't see anyone else around this lake who might be able to help."

"I don't trust him."

"Why not?"

She pressed her tongue against her cheek. "I don't know exactly. It's just a feeling. An instinct."

"Oh, confound your instincts! We're running out of time!" I searched the shoreline for any sign of other creatures who could, perhaps, assist us. There were none. "Why would he lie to us? We have no reason to mistrust him."

"But . . ."

I growled with impatience. "What now?"

She hissed at me like a snake. "It's, well . . . confound it all, Merlin! I can't put it into words."

"Then I'm going with what I think, not what you feel. And I think that any creature who lives in this enchanted lake, all alone, must have some special knowledge. Maybe even special power." I turned back to the otter, who had drifted much closer. "I need to find the soul—the first principle—of the art of Binding. Will you help me, good otter?"

Tilting his head toward the shore, he squirted a jet of water at me. "Why should I?"

"Because I asked you, that's why."

He blew some bubbles in the water. "Oooh, that tickles my ears." More bubbles. "You need to give me a better reason than that."

I jammed my staff into the soil. "Because my mother's life is at stake!"

"Hmmm," he said lazily. "Your mother? I had a mother once, myself. She was a terribly slow swimmer. Oh well, I suppose I could help you. Only with the fundamentals, though."

My heart pounded in my chest. "That's what I need."

"Then pull up some of those vines." He floated closer to the shore. "By your feet."

"Vines?"

"Of course," replied the otter, kicking in a slow circle. "To learn about Binding you need to bind something. Go to it, boy! I haven't got all afternoon. Get your smiling friends to help you."

I turned to Rhia, who was still frowning, and Bumbelwy, who had never stopped. "Will you give me a hand?"

Reluctantly, they agreed. The vines, though supple, were thick and heavy, covered with rows of tiny thorns. Hard to grasp, hard to lift. Pulling them up was difficult work. Untangling them from one another was worse.

At last, we succeeded. Several lengths of vine, each three or four times my height, lay at my feet. Bumbelwy, exhausted, sat down with a loud clang, his back to the water. Rhia stayed by my side, watching the otter warily.

I straightened my back, feeling terribly sore in the place between my shoulder blades. Clearly, all the pulling had strained something. "We've done it. Now what?"

The otter continued swimming in a circle. "Now tie one around your legs. Tight as you possibly can."

"Merlin," Rhia warned. She touched Elen's amulet of oak, ash, and thorn, still attached to her leafy shirt.

Ignoring her, I sat down and wrapped one of the vines around my ankles, calves, and thighs. Despite the thorns, I managed to tie it with a triple knot.

"Good," sighed the otter with a yawn. "Now do the same thing to your arms."

"My arms?"

"Do you want to learn about Binding or not?"

I turned to Rhia. "Help me, will you?"

"I don't want to."

"Please. We're losing precious time."

She shrugged. "All right. But it feels all wrong."

The otter, his fur glistening, clucked with satisfaction as he watched Rhia tie my hands together, then bind them to my chest. "Good. You're almost there."

"I hope so," I replied testily. "These thorns are digging into my skin."

"Just one more vine. You are, shall we say, bound to be pleased."

The otter put one paw in the water and splashed Bumbelwy. "You there, lazy fellow! Wrap one around his whole body. Make sure you cover all the places we've missed so far. Even his head. This is, after all, a delicate enchantment we're talking about. Everything must be exactly right."

Bumbelwy glanced at me. "Should I?"

I gritted my teeth. "Do it."

Somberly, Bumbelwy wrapped me up as tight as a cocoon. When he had finished, only my mouth and part of one ear remained exposed. I lay on my side on the soil, unable to move, ready at last to learn the soul of Binding.

My jaw held closed, I asked, "Whad nah?"

The otter wheezed a little laugh. "Now that you are, shall we say, rapt with attention, I will give you the information you asked for."

"Meg id quig." A vine dug into my hip. I tried to roll to the other side, but couldn't even begin to budge. "Peez."

"The first principle of Binding, as with anything, is . . . " He blew a fountain of water into the air. "Never trust a trickster."

"Whad?"

The otter laughed uncontrollably, clutching his ample belly as he rolled over and over in the shallows. "That's why they call me the Trickster of the Lake." Still laughing, he kicked lazily toward the far shore. "Hope I didn't, shall we say, tie you up too long."

I shrieked with anger. Yet I could do no more. However long it had taken to tie me up with the vines, it seemed to take twice as long to untie me. By the time I stood, pacing the shoreline in frustration, the sun had almost disappeared behind the rim of hills.

"I've wasted the whole day," I moaned, tender from the scrapes on my hands, hip, and forehead. "The whole day! I can't believe I trusted him."

Rhia said nothing, though I knew her thoughts well enough.

I swung around to face her. "You should never have come with me! You should have stayed back at Arbassa, where at least you'd be safe."

Her gray-blue eyes examined me. "I don't want to be safe. I want to be with you."

I squashed a vine under my heel. "Why bother?"

"Because . . . I want to." She glanced sadly at the dark water. "Despite what the lake told me."

"What did it tell you?"

She sighed heavily. "I don't want to talk about it."

Remembering my own vision of Balor's eye, I nodded. "All right. But I still don't know why you want to stay."

Something in the sky caught her attention, and Rhia looked up. Following her gaze, I found two distant shapes, weaving their way across the horizon. Although I could barely see them, I knew at once what they were. A pair of hawks, riding the breeze together. They flew almost as one, bobbing and turning in unison, in the way Rhia and I had moved as fishes.

"Aren't they lovely?" she asked, her eyes following the birds. "If they are like the hawks in the Druma, they not only fly together, they build a nest together, a nest they share for their whole lives."

All at once I understood. What tied the hawks to each other, what tied Rhia to me, had nothing to do with vines. Or ropes. Or chains of any kind.

I turned back to her. "I guess, Rhia, the strongest bonds are invisible. Maybe . . . *the strongest bonds are of the heart.*"

With a flash of blue, my staff ignited. As the flame disappeared, I discovered a new marking engraved on the shaft, not far from the butterfly. It was a pair of hawks, bound together in flight.

XVIII

LIGHT FLYER

The blue light had barely faded from my staff before my thoughts turned to the third Song, that of Protecting. I turned from the lake, its smooth surface gleaming darkly, to the forested valley surrounding us. Crossing the steep, thickly wooded ridge would be only the beginning. For the third Song would require yet another long voyage. *The skill Protecting be the third, Like dwarves who tunnel deep.*

To the land of the dwarves! Their realm, Rhia explained, was visited only rarely—and almost never by choice. For the dwarves, while peaceful to their neighbors, did not welcome any intruders. All that was known about their underground realm was that its entrances lay somewhere near the origins of the River Unceasing, on the high plains north of the Misted Hills. This time we had no choice in how to get to our destination. We would have to walk.

Even pushing ourselves each day until long past sunset, it took the better part of a week to work our way over the hills. Our meals consisted mainly of wild apples, crescent nuts, a sweet vine that Rhia discovered, and the occasional egg or two from an unwary grouse's nest. While we avoided any more encounters with living stones, the trekking proved arduous. Vapors swirled constantly, wrapping us in misty shawls, inhibiting our views from even the higher ground.

During one swamp crossing, Rhia lost one of her shoes in a pit of quicksand. We spent much of that afternoon searching for a rowan tree so that she could weave a replacement from its leathery bark. Two days later, we crossed a high pass, slick with ice and snow, but only after walking the entire night of the full moon.

Finally, bedraggled and exhausted, we came to the high plains of the river's headwaters. Countless star-shaped yellow flowers blanketed the plains, filling the air with a tangy scent. In time we reached the rushing River Unceasing itself. There we encountered a pair of cream-colored unicorns, grazing along its banks. Heading north, we followed the river's serpentine path up a series of wide, alpine meadows that ascended like bright green stairs.

As Rhia reached the edge of one of these meadows, she stopped, pointing at the line of snowy mountains in the distance. "Look, Merlin. Behind those peaks lies the city of the giants, Varigal. I've always wanted to see it, even now that it's only a ruin. Arbassa says it's the most ancient settlement on Fincayra."

"Too bad dwarves, not giants, are our goal." I bent down, pulling up a handful of fluffy-tipped grass. "Giants will have to wait for the fifth Song, the one that involves Varigal somehow. If we make it that far."

As we continued trekking after sunset, a gleaming disk emerged from the layers of clouds. Clipped along one edge, the moon was now waning. I pushed harder, practically running along the grassy bank, knowing full well that more than half of my time had vanished, and I had unraveled only two of the mysterious Songs. How could I possibly complete the remaining five, climb up to the Otherworld, obtain the Elixir, and return to Elen, all in less than two weeks? Not even a real wizard could hope to do so much.

By the glow of the moon, we scrambled over yet another steep rise, grasping at roots and shrubs to keep from tumbling over backward. The River Unceasing, now only a splashing stream, flowed down the slope beside us, its little falls and pools sparkling in the silver light. At last we topped the rise. Before us stretched an enormous, moonlit meadow, split by the shining ribbon of water.

Bumbelwy fell in a jangling heap by the stream. "I can go no further without rest. And also food. A jester needs his strength."

Panting in the night air, I leaned against my staff. "It is your audience who needs strength."

"Too true, too true, too true." He mopped his brow with the edge of his heavy cloak. "On top of everything else, I am baking to death! This cloak has me perspiring even after the sun goes down. And during these hot days we've been enduring, it's sheer torture."

Perplexed, I shook my head. "Then why don't you leave it behind?"

"Because without it I may freeze. Turn to ice! Why, it could snow anytime. This hour, this minute, this second!"

Rhia and I traded amused glances. Then she bent down and sniffed the star-shaped flowers. Grinning, she picked a fistful of stems, rolled them into a compact, yellow mass, then handed the roll to me.

"Taste it," she implored. "The astral flower is a trekker's sustenance. It is said that lost travelers have lived on nothing else for many weeks."

Biting into the roll of flowers, I tasted a sweet yet sharp flavor, almost like burned honey. "Mmmm. You know who would like this? Our old friend Shim."

"Yes," replied Rhia. "Or, as he would say, *certainly, definitely, absolutely.*" She handed a fresh roll to Bumbelwy, sprawled on his back by the stream. "Shim loved honey as much as I do! Even before he grew into a giant, he ate enough honey for one." With a sigh, she added, "I wonder whether we'll ever see him again."

Kneeling, I placed my cupped hands into the shimmering water. As I brought the water to my face, however, the moon's wavering reflection appeared within my hands. I jerked backward, drenching my tunic.

"Did you see something?" Rhia studied me with concern.

"Only a reminder of all the damage I've done."

She considered me for another moment. Then, in a voice so soft I could barely hear it above the splashing stream, she spoke. "You still have the heart of a wizard."

My hand slapped the water, splattering us both. "Then give me the simple heart of a boy! Rhia, whenever I tap into those . . . yearnings, those powers, those arts of wizardry, I do something terrible! Because of me, my mother lies at the edge of death. Because of me, much of the Dark Hills remains a waste, just waiting for Rhita Gawr and his warrior goblins to return. And because of me, my own eyes are blind and useless."

Bumbelwy propped himself up on one elbow, clanging his bells. "Such despair, my boy! Could I offer my assistance? Allow me to tell you the riddle about the—"

"No!" I shouted, waving him away. I turned back to Rhia. "The truth is, Domnu is a thieving old hag. But she had it right. I could be the worst disaster ever to come to Fincayra."

Rhia said nothing, and bent to take a drink from the stream. As she raised her head, she wiped the water from her chin. "No," she declared at last. "I don't think so. It's not anything I can put my finger on. It's more . . . the berries. I mean, the Harp actually did work for you, at least for a while. The speaking shell, too, did your bidding."

"All I did was find the right shell. Then it used its own power to bring my mother here."

"Even if you're right, what about Tuatha? He wouldn't have allowed you to read the Seven Songs unless there was at least some chance you could master them and travel to the Otherworld."

My head drooped. "Tuatha was a great wizard, a real wizard. And he did tell me that someday I might become one, too. Yet even wizards make mistakes! No, the only way I'll travel to the Otherworld is when I die. And by then my mother will have died, as well."

She hooked her finger, still wet from the stream, around my own. "There's still the prophecy, Merlin. That only a child of human blood can defeat Rhita Gawr and those who serve him."

Turning away, I gazed at the wide meadow beyond the stream. Though some of its grasses glimmered in the moonlight, most of the meadow lay shrouded by shadows. Somewhere out there, I knew, lay the realm of the dwarves. And somewhere beyond that lay the secret entrance to the world of the spirits, guarded by the ogre Balor.

I pulled my hand away. "That prophecy, Rhia, is worth no more than the person it refers to. Besides, I only want to save my own mother, not battle the warriors of Rhita Gawr." Reaching for a pebble, I tossed it into the silvery stream. "And I doubt I can even do that."

"Ah, misery," intoned Bumbelwy, his face as shadowed as the meadow. "At last you see the wisdom in what I have been telling you all along."

I bristled. "Nothing you have told me remotely resembles wisdom."

"Don't be offended, please. I'm only pointing out that there is only one thing left for you to do. Give up."

My cheeks burned. Seizing my staff, I stood up. "That, you poor excuse for a jester, is the one thing I shall not do! I may be certain to fail in this quest, but I will not fail out of cowardice. My mother deserves better than that." Casting a glance at the moonlit meadow before us, I spoke to Rhia. "Come if you like. The dwarves' realm cannot be far from here."

She drew a long breath. "Yes, but it would be foolish to try to find it now. We need a few hours' rest. And Merlin, that meadow . . . it's full of danger. I can feel it. On top of that, the dwarves' tunnels are surely hidden, by the land if not by magic. They will be hard enough to find even by day."

"Just give up," urged Bumbelwy, reaching for some more astral flowers.

"Never," I growled. Pivoting on the walking stick, I turned to go.

"Don't, Merlin!" Rhia stretched her arms toward me. "Ignore him. Wait for daylight. You could easily get lost."

If I could have breathed fire, I would have. "You wait for daylight! I can take care of myself."

I strode into the meadow, the tall grasses swishing against my tunic. Moonlight streaked the land like luminous claw marks, yet most of it lay shadowed. Then, several paces ahead, my second sight detected an unusually dark patch. Since no rock or tree stood near enough to cast a shadow, I realized that it might be a tunnel, or at least a pit. Not so foolish as to walk right into such a thing, I angled to the left.

Suddenly the earth beneath my feet gave way. I plunged downward. Before I could even cry out, total blackness swallowed me.

When I awoke, I found myself curled into a tight ball, covered with a heavy blanket that reeked of smoke. Something was carrying me, grunting constantly, though I had no idea what form of beast it was or where it was taking me. Thick ropes bound my arms and legs, while a wad of cloth filled my mouth. But for the muffled grunts beneath me, I heard no sound but the beating of my own heart. Jostled and bounced like a sack of grain, I felt increasingly dazed and bruised. My torture seemed to last for hours.

Finally, the jostling came to an abrupt halt. I was heaved onto a floor of smooth, hard stone. I lay there, facedown, my head spinning. The blanket was ripped away. With great effort, I rolled over.

An assembly of dwarves, each one no taller than my waist, stared at me with eyes redder than flame. Most wore tangled beards, while all bore jeweled daggers on their waists. Standing beneath a row of sizzling torches, with feet firmly planted and burly arms crossed on their chests, they looked as immovable as the rock walls surrounding them. One, whose beard showed streaks of gray, straightened his back stiffly, leading me to guess that he had been one of the grunting dwarves who had carried me here.

"Cut his bonds," commanded a sharp voice.

Immediately, strong hands rolled me over again and sliced through the ropes. Someone pulled the wad of cloth out of my mouth. Working my stiff arms and parched tongue, I managed to sit up.

Spying my staff on the floor beside me, I reached for it. A dwarf lifted his heavy boot and stomped on my wrist. I shouted in pain, my cry echoing within the rock walls.

"Not so fast."

It was the same sharp voice. This time, though, I located its source: a thickset dwarf seated on a throne carved of jade, inlaid with rows of gems, that rested on a ledge above the stone floor. She had unruly red hair, pale skin, and earrings of dangling shells that clinked whenever she moved. Her oversized nose looked nearly as big as Shim's before he became a giant. She wore a black robe embroidered with runes and geometric shapes sewn in glistening gold thread, plus a peaked hat to match. In one hand she held a staff, almost as tall as my own.

As I started to stand, the dwarf raised her free hand. "Do not try to get up! You shall be low, lower than me. And do not reach again for your staff."

She leaned toward me, clinking her white shell earrings. "A staff be dangerous, you know. Even in the hands of an upstart enchanter like you, Merlin."

I caught my breath. "How do you know my name?"

She scratched her prominent nose. "No one knows your true name. Not even you, it be clear."

"You called me Merlin."

"Yes," she said with a snorting laugh that seemed to make the torches flame brighter in the cavern. "And you may call me Urnalda. But neither be a true name."

Furrowing my brow in bewilderment, I tried again. "How did you know to call me Merlin?"

"Ah." The white shells clinked as she nodded. "That be a better question." She raised a stubby finger to touch an earring. "The shells told me. Just as a shell told you a few things, some that you be too headstrong to hear."

I shifted my weight on the hard stone floor.

"Not only that, you be an intruder." Urnalda waved her arms, sending their shadows racing across the walls. "And I do so despise intruders."

At this, several of the dwarves reached for their jeweled daggers. One, whose forehead showed a jagged scar, chortled loudly. The sound hovered in the air of the underground room.

Stroking her staff, Urnalda considered me for a long moment. "Even so, I might yet choose to help you."

"Truly?" I glanced at the dwarves, who groaned in disappointment. Then, recalling my experience with the Trickster of the Lake, I felt suddenly suspicious. "Why might you help me?"

She snorted. "Because one day, if you be successful, you might wear a hat such as mine."

Not comprehending, I examined her peaked hat more closely. Its point slouched to one side. Lower down, dozens of tiny holes pierced its surface, allowing Urnalda's red hairs to poke through. But for the silver embroidery, which might have been more attractive if it showed stars and planets instead of runes, it was quite simply the most ridiculous hat I had ever encountered. Why would I ever want a hat like that?

The dwarf's eyes narrowed, as if she could read my thoughts. In a deeper voice than usual, she declared, "This be the hat of an enchanter."

I winced. "I didn't mean to insult you."

"That be a lie."

"All right, then. I am sorry I insulted you."

"That be true."

"Please. Will you help me?"

Urnalda tapped thoughtfully on her staff before finally uttering a one-word answer. "Yes."

A black-bearded dwarf, standing beside her throne, grumbled angrily. In a flash, she turned on him and raised her hand as if to strike. He froze, petrified. Slowly, she dropped her hand—even as his beard dropped right off his face. He squealed, covering his naked cheeks with his hands. Meanwhile, other dwarves hooted and guffawed, pointing at the fallen beard on the floor.

"Silence!" Urnalda shook herself angrily, jostling the shell earrings, as well as the throne on the ledge. "That will teach you to doubt my decisions."

She turned back to me. "I will help you because you might yet defy all the odds and survive. Mayhaps even live to become an enchanter yourself." Slyly, she squinted at me. "And if I help you now, you might one day help me."

"I will. I promise I will."

The torches sizzled, wavering, making the rock walls themselves appear to vibrate. Urnalda leaned forward, her shadow enlarging on the chiseled surface behind her. "Promises be serious things."

"I know." I gazed at her solemnly. "If you help me find the soul of Protecting, I will not forget."

Urnalda snapped her fingers. "Bring me a light flyer. And a carving stone, with hammer and chisel."

Still wary of some sort of trick, I asked, "What is a light flyer?"

"Be still."

But for the sizzling of torches, silence filled the cavern. For several minutes, no one stirred. Then heavy boots clomped into the underground room, as a pair of dwarves approached the throne. One of them hunched under a huge black stone, as rough as the walls themselves, that must have weighed twice as much as he did. At a nod from Urnalda, he lowered his shoulders and dropped the stone with a thud on the floor.

The second dwarf bore a hammer and chisel in one hand, and some sort of small, glowing object in the other. It seemed to be an upside-down cup made of clear crystal, resting with its rim against his palm. Within the crystal, an unsteady light flickered. At Urnalda's nod, he set the tools by the stone. Then he carefully placed the cup on the floor, taking care to slide his hand away quickly so that something inside it would not escape.

Urnalda gave a snorting laugh, and the torches flamed brighter. "Inside that crystal cage be a light flyer, one of Fincayra's rarest creatures." She grinned crookedly at me, a look I did not like. "Your next Song be Protecting, be it not? To learn what you need to know, you must find the best possible way to protect the light flyer from harm."

Observing the hammer and chisel, I swallowed hard. "You mean carve a cage . . . from that big stone?"

She scratched her nose pensively. "If that be the best way to protect the fragile little creature, then that be what you must do."

"But that could take days. Or weeks!"

"It took dwarves many years to carve the tunnels and halls of our realm."

"I don't have that much time."

"Silence." She pointed her staff at a hole in the ceiling, which glowed with a subdued light of its own. "That tunnel, like the one you fell down, provides us with air as well as light. There be hundreds of them, each one carved as smooth as the floor you be seated on, each one concealed on the surface by enchantment. That be why dwarves stay so well protected. That be why you came here to learn the soul of the Song."

"Are you sure there is no other way?" I protested.

The earrings swayed from side to side. "There be no other way to learn the lesson yourself. Your task be to protect the little creature from harm. Now begin."

With a final clink of her shells, Urnalda left the room, followed by her entourage. I gazed at the sizzling torches on the walls, watching the shadows cast by her throne grow, then shrink, then grow again. That very throne, like the walls themselves, had been hewn from unforgiving stone. The same stone that the dwarves, over centuries, had molded into an entire realm.

And now it was my turn to mold stone.

XIX

PROTECTING

The hammer and chisel gleamed coldly in the wavering light of the torches. Grasping the tools, I regained my feet and approached the massive black stone. It came almost to my waist. I raised the hammer and struck my first blow. My hand, my arm, my whole chest shook. Before the ringing of the hammer died away, I struck a second blow. Then a third.

Time passed as I worked, but without its usual rhythms. For in the subterranean throne room of Urnalda, the only sign of day or night came from the air tunnel in the ceiling above my head. While by night its circular mouth gleamed with the silver light of the moon, by day it glowed bright with the golden light of the sun.

Yet day or night made no difference to me. The torches on the walls sizzled constantly. I hammered incessantly—on the flat top of the chisel, on the black stone directly, and occasionally on my poor swollen thumb. The hammer rang to the rhythm of my own breathing. Chips flew into the air, and sometimes my face. Yet I continued, stopping only long enough to eat some of the thick, smoky porridge provided by the dwarves, or to nap fitfully on the blanket.

Three bearded dwarves guarded me at all times. One stood over my staff on the stone floor, his burly arms folded on his chest. In addition to his dagger, a double-sided axe hung from his belt. The other two, holding tall spears fitted with blades of blood red stone, positioned themselves at either side of the entry tunnel. All wore the same grim expressions, which only deepened whenever Urnalda herself entered the hall.

She sat upon her throne on the ledge, for hours it seemed, watching me work. She seemed lost in thought, despite the constant banging of the hammer in my blistered hands. Or perhaps she was trying to probe my innermost thoughts. I did not know—and did not care. All I knew was that I would not, as Bumbelwy had suggested, give up. When I thought of his proposal, or of my mother's condition, sparks flew from the stone. Yet I felt increasingly aware of the limits of my time. And of my ability as a stone carver.

The glow from the light flyer flickered and wavered, playing on the black stone as I worked. Bit by bit, more pieces of the stone chipped away. In time I had made a shallow groove. If my thumb and aching arms held out, I would widen this into a hollow large enough to invert and cover the light flyer. How much more time that would require I could not tell. Judging from the shifting light in the air tunnel overhead, two days and nights had already passed.

Throughout my labor, I kept hearing in my mind Urnalda's final command: *Your task be to protect the little creature from harm.* Once in a while, as the hammering continued, I wondered whether there was a clue buried in those words. Could there be some other way to keep the light flyer safe? Some way I was missing?

No, I told myself, that couldn't be. Urnalda herself had credited tunnels of stone with keeping the dwarves safe. While even stone will not last forever, it is stronger than anything else. The message was clear. *I must build a cage of stone, just as the dwarves built this underground realm. I have no choice.*

Still, as I hammered and pried, trying to split the stone along its cracks, I wished there were some easier way. Like the way I had wielded the great sword Deepercut, in the battle of the Shrouded Castle! I had used not my hands, but some hidden powers of my mind, to make the sword fly through the air. Somehow in that moment, without knowing how, I had tapped into the magic of Leaping. Just as the Grand Elusa had done, sending us to the abandoned land of the treelings. Could I possibly tap into that same power again? Could I make the hammer and chisel do my work now, thereby sparing my stiff back, sore arms, and blistered thumb?

"Be not a fool, Merlin."

I looked up from the stone to face Urnalda, watching me from her jade throne. "What do you mean?"

"I mean be not a fool! If, indeed, you made Deepercut fly to you, it be less because of you than because of something else. That sword be a Treasure of Fincayra. It be possessed of its own powers." She leaned forward on her jade throne, clinking her earrings. "You did not wield the sword as much as it wielded you."

I dropped the hammer, which clanged on the stone floor. "How can you say that? I did it! I used the sword! With my own power. Just as I—"

Urnalda smirked. "Finish your sentence."

My voice fell to a whisper. "Just as I used the Flowering Harp."

"Exactly." The torches wavered as she examined me, scratching her bulbous nose. "You be a slow learner, but there may yet be hope for you."

"I have a feeling you're talking about more than my skill with stone."

She snorted, straightening her hat. "Of course. I be talking about your skill at Seeing. No wonder that, of all the Seven Songs, you fear that one the most."

I blanched.

Before I could say anything, she declared, "You be a slow learner with stone, too. You would never succeed as a dwarf in the tunnels! Which be why I doubt the prophecy can turn out to be true."

"What prophecy?"

"That you will one day rebuild a great stone circle, as great as *Estonahenj*."

I sputtered like one of the torches. "Me? Rebuild something of that size? That's likely! Just as likely as I will pick up *Estonahenj*, stone by stone, and move it across the ocean to Gwynedd."

Her red eyes gleamed strangely. "Oh, it be prophesied that you will do that, too. Not to Gwynedd, but to a neighboring land called Logres, or Gramarye by some. But that prophecy be even less likely than the other one."

"Enough," I declared. I blew on my blistered palm, then reached again for the hammer. "Now I've got to get back to my real work. Carving a stone cage, as you commanded me to do."

"That be a lie."

My hammer raised, I froze. "A lie? Why?"

Shadows skipped around the room, as her earrings clattered softly. "I commanded you, Merlin, yet that be not my command."

"You gave me this stone."

"That be true."

"You told me to protect the light flyer from harm."

"That be true."

"And that means carving something stronger than that crystal cup over there."

"That be your decision. Not mine."

Slowly, hesitantly, I lowered the hammer. I set it down, along with the chisel, and moved closer to the crystal. The creature within it trembled like a tiny flame.

"May I ask you a question, Urnalda? About the light flyer?"

"Ask."

I watched the wavering light of the crystal. "You said it's one of the rarest creatures in Fincayra. How does it . . . survive? How does it stay safe?"

Urnalda's face, lit by the torches, showed the hint of a crooked grin. "It be safe by roaming in the bright sunlight where it cannot be seen. Or, at night, by dancing in the places where moonbeams meet water."

"In other words . . . by being free."

The shell earrings clinked gently, but she said nothing.

I reached to touch the crystal cup. Spreading my fingers over its glowing surface, I felt the warmth of the creature caught inside. With a sudden flick of my wrist, I turned the cup over.

A shimmering spot of light, no bigger than an apple seed, floated into the air of the cavernous hall. I heard only a faint hum as it rose past my head. The light flyer lifted swiftly to the ceiling, slipped into the mouth of the air tunnel, and was gone.

Urnalda pounded with her fist on the arm of her throne. The two dwarves guarding the entrance instantly lowered their spears, aiming the blades straight at me. Again she pounded. "Tell me why you did that."

I drew a halting breath, "Well, because even a cage of stone will eventually crumble. *The best way to protect something is to set it free.*"

At that instant, blue flame erupted from my staff. The dwarf standing over it yelped and leaped his own height into the air. Even before he fell back to the floor, I could make out the new marking, etched in blue, on my staff. It was a cracked stone.

XX

RIVERS COOL
AND WARM

By the time I found the others at their camp by the headwaters, not far from where I had left them, we had been separated more than three full days. The meadow grasses, painted several shades of green, rippled in the breeze. Seeing me approach, Rhia ran to meet me. Her worried face relaxed as soon as she glimpsed the third marking etched on my staff.

She touched my hand. "I was so worried, Merlin."

My throat tightened. "With good reason, I'm afraid. You told me I might get lost, and I guess I did."

"You found your way back, though."

"Yes," I replied. "But it took me too long. Ten days, no more, remain."

Bumbelwy joined us, almost tripping on his cloak as he hopped over the splashing stream. Although he wore his usual stack of frowns, he seemed genuinely glad to see me. He clasped my hand and shook it vigorously, jangling his bells in my ears. Then, sensing that he was about to try again to tell his famous riddle of the bells, I turned and walked away briskly. Both he and Rhia followed. Before long we had put some distance between ourselves and the realm of the dwarves. Yet far more distance lay ahead.

For the fourth Song, Naming, had something to do with the Slantos, a mysterious people who lived at the extreme northeastern tip of Fincayra. While to get there we would not need to climb any more snowbound passes, we would have to cross the entire breadth of the Rusted Plains. That alone would take several days. Then we would be hard-pressed to find a route past the sheer cliffs of Eagles' Canyon, not to mention the northern reaches of the Dark Hills. And while I knew that danger lurked in all these places, it was the notion of crossing the Dark Hills that left me most unsettled.

To cross the plains, we rose each day at dawn, when the first morning birds and the last evening frogs sang together in chorus. We stopped only occasionally to pick berries or roots—and once, thanks to Rhia's ability to speak the buzzing language of bees, to eat a bit of honeycomb, dripping with sweet syrup. She also seemed to know just where we might find water, leading us to hidden springs and quiet pools. It was as if she could somehow see into the landscape's secret mind as easily as she could see into my own. The moon offered enough light to trek into the night, so trek by moonlight we did, across the sweeping plains. Yet the moon, like our time, was quickly disappearing.

Finally, after three long days, we reached the edge of Eagles' Canyon. We sat on the rocky rim, gazing out over the broad stripes of red, brown, maroon, and pink that lined the cliffs and buttresses. Gleaming white pinnacles protruded from the opposite wall. Far below, a shallow river snaked along the base of the cliffs.

Tired though I was, I couldn't help feeling a rush of strength when I recalled the stirring cry of the canyon eagle that had marked the beginning of the Great Council of Fincayra. If only I could soar like an eagle myself! I could sail over this colorful gorge, as swiftly as the wind. Just as I had done, ages ago it seemed, on Trouble's feathered back.

But an eagle or a hawk I was not. Like Rhia and Bumbelwy, I would have to descend into the canyon by foot and find some route up the other side. With my second sight, I followed the line of cliffs, searching for some way to cross. We were, at least, far enough north that the walls were not completely impassable. Farther to the south, they lifted into a yawning chasm that sliced through the very center of the Dark Hills.

Rhia, the most surefooted of the three of us, led the way. She soon discovered a series of narrow ledges that crisscrossed the cliff walls. By following each ledge until we found a place to drop down to the one just below, we gradually moved lower into the canyon, sometimes sliding on our backs, sometimes climbing over crumbly outcroppings. Finally, soaked with perspiration, we reached the bottom.

The river, though muddy, was much cooler than we were. Bumbelwy, sweltering under his thick cloak, plunged straight in. Rhia and I followed suit, kneeling on the round stones that lined the river bottom, soaking our heads and rinsing our arms, splashing water on each other. Once, though I could not be certain, I thought I heard the distant screech of an eagle from somewhere above us on the cliffs.

At last, feeling refreshed, we began the arduous climb out of the canyon. Before long I needed to use both hands, and thrust my staff into the belt of my tunic. As the slope grew steeper, Bumbelwy's grumbling grew worse. Yet he struggled to keep up, climbing just below Rhia, finding his handholds in the footholds she had just vacated.

As we scaled a particularly steep buttress, my shoulders ached from the strain. I leaned back as far as I dared without losing my grip, hop-

ing to glimpse the top of the canyon wall. But I found only more layered maroon and brown cliffs rising far above us. Glancing below, I
viewed the muddy river, which seemed no more than a thin trickle
on the canyon floor. I shuddered, tightening my grip on the rock.
For as little as I wanted to climb upward, I wanted even less to tumble so far downward.

Rhia, who was slightly to my left on the buttress, suddenly called
out. "Look! A sharr. On the pink rock there."

Careful not to lose my balance, I turned to find a light brown, kit-
tenlike animal, basking in the sunshine. Like a cat, it lay curled in a
little ball, purring quietly. Unlike a cat, it had a pointed snout, lined
with soft whiskers, and two paper-thin wings folded across its back.
The delicate wings fluttered with every purr.

"Isn't it lovely?" asked Rhia, gripping the wall of stone. "Sharrs
are found only in high, rocky places like this. I've seen only one before, from much farther away. They're very shy."

Hearing her voice, the sharr opened its blue eyes. It tensed, watching her intently. Then it seemed to relax. The purring resumed.
Slowly, Rhia shifted her footholds. Then, grasping the crumbling cliff
with one hand, she reached toward the creature.

"Careful," I warned. "You might fall."

"Shhh. You'll frighten it."

The sharr shifted slightly, placing its furry paws on the rock as if it
were preparing to stand. Each of the paws had four little toes. As
Rhia's hand came nearer to its face, the sharr's purring grew louder.

Just then I noticed something strange about the paws. At first I
couldn't identify what it was. For some reason, they seemed a
bit . . . odd.

All of a sudden, I knew. The toes were webbed. Like the feet of a duck. Now, why would a creature of the high, rocky canyons have webbed feet? In a flash, I understood.

"Don't, Rhia! It's a shifting wraith!"

Even as I started to shout, however, the sharr began to transform. Quick as lightning, the wings evaporated, the blue eyes reddened, the fur became scales, and the cat's body changed into a serpent with daggerlike teeth. The air crackled as it threw off a brittle, transparent skin, like a snake that is shedding. All this happened in the blink of an eye. Hearing my shout, Rhia had barely enough time to duck before the serpentine creature, jaws open wide, leaped at her face, claws extended. With a savage scream, the attacker flew just over her head, plunging into the canyon far below.

Although its jaws missed her, the shifting wraith's tail whipped against her cheek. Thrown off balance, she lost her footing. For an instant she clung to the buttress with one hand, swaying precariously. Then the stone beneath her hand crumbled. She fell, right on top of Bumbelwy.

Clinging tight to the rock face, his fingers turning white, the lanky jester howled at the impact. Yet somehow he held on, managing to break Rhia's fall. Still, she was left hanging upside down on his back, struggling to right herself.

"Hold on, Bumbelwy!" I cried, watching them from above.

"I'm doing my best," he groaned. "Though that's never good enough."

Suddenly, the stone supporting his hands broke loose, splitting into shards that clattered down the cliff. The two of them screamed in unison. Arms and legs flailing, they slid down the rock face, striking a narrow ledge that stopped their fall. There they hung, high above the canyon floor.

Like an ungainly spider, I climbed down the cliff, my staff swinging from my belt. Rhia and Bumbelwy were sprawled below me on the ledge, moaning painfully. The jester's bell-draped hat lay beside him, covered with red dust. Rhia tried to sit up, then fell back, her right arm dangling at her side.

Working my way across the narrow ledge, I reached her at last. As I helped her sit up, she gasped when I brushed against her twisted arm. Her eyes, full of pain, searched my face. "You warned me . . . just in time."

"I wish it had been a few seconds sooner." A sudden flurry of wind sprayed us with dust from the cliff wall. After it subsided, I took a pinch of herbs from my satchel and dabbed the scratch on her cheek.

"How did you know it was a wraith?"

"The webbed feet. Remember when we found that alleah bird in the forest? That was when you showed me that shifting wraiths always have something odd about them." I indicated myself. "A lot like people, I suppose."

Rhia tried to lift her arm and winced painfully. "Most people aren't that dangerous."

Moving carefully on the ledge, I came around to her other side to get a better view of the wounded arm. "It looks broken."

"And let's forget about poor old Bumbelwy," the jester whimpered. "I did nothing useful. Nothing at all."

Despite her pain, Rhia almost grinned. "Bumbelwy, you were wonderful. If my arm weren't ready to fall off, I'd give you a hug."

If only for a moment, the dour jester stopped moaning. He blushed ever so slightly. Then, seeing her injured arm, he frowned with his brow, cheeks, and chins. "That looks rather bad. You'll be incapacitated for life. Never able to eat or sleep again."

"I don't think so." Gently, I laid the arm across Rhia's lap, feeling for the break.

She winced. "What can you do? There's nothing—oh, that hurts!—around here to use for a splint. And without two—oh!—arms, it's going to be impossible climbing out of here."

"Impossible," echoed Bumbelwy.

I shook my head, knocking some pebbles from my hair. "Nothing is impossible."

"Bumbelwy's right," protested Rhia. "You can't fix this. Oh! Even that satchel of herbs . . . can't help. Merlin, you should leave me here. Go on . . . without me."

My jaw clenched. "Absolutely not! I've learned more about Binding than that. We are together, you and I, like those two hawks on the wind."

A frail light flickered in her eyes. "But how? I can't climb . . . without my arm."

I stretched my sore shoulders, then drew in a deep breath. "I'm hoping to mend your arm."

"Don't be ridiculous." Bumbelwy crept closer on the ledge. "To do that you'd need a splint. A stretcher. And an army of healers. It's impossible, I say."

Feeling the break, I placed my hands gently on top of it. Although it made no difference to my second sight, I closed my eyes in concentration. With all my power, I imagined light, warm and healing, gathering within my chest. As my heart brimmed with the light, I allowed it to flow down my arms and into my fingers. Like invisible rivers of warmth, the light flowed out of me and into Rhia.

"Ohhh," she sighed. "That feels good. What are you doing?"

"I'm just doing what a wise friend once told me to do. Listening to the language of the wound."

She smiled, leaning back against the rocky ledge.

"Don't be fooled," warned Bumbelwy. "If you feel better now, it's only because you're going to feel ten times worse later on."

"I don't care, you old bother! It feels stronger already." She started to lift her arm.

"Don't," I ordered. "Not yet."

As the warm light continued to pour out of my fingertips, I concentrated on the bones and muscles beneath her skin. Patiently, carefully, I felt each strand of tissue with my mind. Each strand I touched with gentleness, coaxing it to be strong again, to be whole again. One by one, I bathed the sinews, smoothed them, and knitted them back into place. Finally, I removed my hands.

Rhia raised her arm. She wiggled her fingers. Then she flung her arms around my neck, squeezing with all the strength of a bear.

"How did you do that?" she asked as she released me.

"I really don't know." I tapped the knotted top of my staff. "But I think it might be another verse in the Song of Binding."

She released me. "You have truly found the soul of that Song. Your mother, the healer, would be proud."

Her words jolted me. "Come! We have less than a week left. I want to get to the Slantos' village by tomorrow morning."

XXI

THE SHRIEK

By the time we finally pulled ourselves over the rim of the canyon, the sun had just set. Shadows gathered on the sheer buttresses, while the Dark Hills rising before us looked almost black. As I gazed at the hills, the lonely cry of a canyon eagle echoed somewhere nearby, reminding me of the eagle's cry that had begun the Great Council of Fincayra. And of the fact that those hills would have been restored to life by now had I kept my promise with the Flowering Harp.

The three of us trekked in the deepening dusk. The flat rocks under our feet quickly turned into dry, flaky soil, the kind of soil that I had learned to identify with the Dark Hills. But for the occasional rustling of leaves from withered trees, we heard only the crunching of our boots, the rattling of Bumbelwy's bells, and the rhythmic punching of my staff on the ground.

Darkness pressed closer. I knew that whatever brave animals might have returned to these hills since the collapse of the Shrouded Castle must have found secure places to hide after sundown. For that was the time when the warrior goblins and shifting wraiths—and whatever other creatures lived beneath the surface—might be tempted to emerge from their caves in the rock outcroppings and crevasses. I shuddered, remembering that at least one such creature had dared to appear in broad daylight. Rhia, uncannily aware of my feelings as usual, gave my arm a gentle squeeze.

Night fell as we continued to ascend the Dark Hills. Twisted trees stood like skeletons, their branches rattling in the wind. Staying on our northeasterly course was made more difficult because heavy clouds obscured most of the stars and the remaining moon. Even Rhia walked more slowly in the gloom. Although Bumbelwy didn't complain openly, his mutterings grew increasingly fearful. My own weary legs tripped often over stones and dead roots. At this rate, we were more likely to get lost than attacked.

When at last Rhia pointed out a narrow gully running down the slope, all that remained of a once-surging stream, I agreed that it would be wise to rest there until dawn. Minutes later, the three of us lay on the hard soil of the ravine. Rhia found a rounded rock she could use as a pillow, while Bumbelwy curled himself into a ball, declaring, "I could sleep through an erupting volcano." Given the danger, I tried my best to stay awake, but was soon slumbering along with the others.

A high-pitched shriek rang out. I sat up, fully awake, as did Rhia beside me. Both of us held our breath, listening, but heard nothing beyond Bumbelwy's snoring. A feeble glow behind the clouds was all that we could trace of the moon, and its light barely brushed the surrounding hills.

The shriek came again. It hung in the air, a cry of sheer terror. Although Rhia tried to stop me, I grabbed my staff and stumbled out of the gully. She followed me onto the darkened slope. Searching the shadows, I stretched my second sight as far as I could, trying to detect any movement at all. Yet nothing stirred, not even a cricket.

Suddenly I spotted a hulking figure traversing the rocks below us.

Even if I had not glimpsed the pointed helmet, I would have known instantly what it was. A warrior goblin. Over the goblin's muscular shoulder writhed a small, struggling creature whose life was clearly about to end.

Without pausing to think, I dashed down the slope. Hearing my footsteps, the goblin whirled around. He tossed aside the prey on his shoulder and, with amazing speed, drew his broad sword. As he raised it over his head, his fiery eyes narrowed with rage.

Weaponless except for my staff, I planted my feet and hurled myself straight at him. My shoulder crashed into his armored chest, throwing him backward. Together, we rolled and bounced down the rock-strewn slope.

I came to a stop, my head still whirling. But the warrior goblin had recovered faster. He stood over me, snarling, his three-fingered hand still grasping the sword. As the moon above us broke out of the clouds, the blade gleamed darkly. Just as he brought down the sword, I rolled to one side. It slammed into the ground, splintering an old root. The warrior goblin growled wrathfully. He raised the sword again.

I tried to stand, but tripped on a gnarled stick. My staff! In desperation, I lifted it to shield my face, even as the goblin's sword came slicing toward me. I knew the thin shaft would hardly slow the blade at all, yet I could do nothing more.

As the blade struck the wood, a sudden explosion rocked the slope. A tower of blue flame soared high into the sky. The goblin's sword lifted with it, spinning like a branch borne aloft by a gale. The warrior goblin himself roared in anguish. He stumbled backward, collapsing on the hillside. He wheezed once, tried to raise himself, then fell back, as still as stone.

Rhia ran to me. "Merlin! Are you hurt?"

"No." I rubbed the shaft, feeling the slight indentation where the sword had struck it. "Thanks to this staff. And whatever virtue Tuatha gave to it."

Rhia kneeled, her curls frosted with moonlight. "I think it was as much you as the staff."

I shook my head, observing the motionless form of the warrior goblin. "Come now, Rhia. You know better."

"I do," she declared crisply. "And I think you are denying it because you want so much for it to be true."

Stunned, I gazed at her. "You read me, in the same way I came to read those runes on Arbassa's walls."

Her bell-like laughter rang out. "Some things I still can't understand, though. Like why, instead of hiding when you saw the goblin, you charged straight at him."

Before I could reply, a small voice spoke behind us. "You must be magical."

Rhia and I spun around to see a short, round-faced boy, crouching on the ground. He couldn't have been older than five. I knew at once that he was the unfortunate creature whose shriek had awakened us. His eyes, themselves glowing like little moons, seemed full of awe.

I glanced at Rhia. "That's why." Turning back to the boy, I beckoned. "Come here. I won't hurt you."

Slowly, he rose to his feet. Hesitantly, he approached, then stopped himself. "Are you good magical or bad magical?"

Rhia stifled a laugh, wrapping her leafy arms around the boy. "He is very good magical. Except when he is being very bad."

As I growled playfully at her, the boy frowned in confusion. He wriggled away from Rhia and started backing down the shadowy slope.

"Don't listen to her. I am an enemy of warrior goblins, just like you." Leaning on my staff, I stood. "My name is Merlin. This is Rhia, who comes from Druma Wood. Now tell us your name."

The boy studied me, patting his round cheek thoughtfully. "You must be good magical, to slay the goblin with only your staff." He sucked in his breath. "I am Galwy, and I've lived all my life in the same village."

I cocked my head. "The only village near here is—"

"Slantos," finished the little fellow.

My heart raced.

Galwy looked away sheepishly. "I didn't mean to stay outside the gates after dark. Really, I didn't! It's just that the squirrels were playing, and I followed them, and when I realized how late it was . . ." He glared at the twisted form of the fallen warrior goblin. "He wanted to hurt me."

I stepped to the small boy's side. "He won't hurt you now."

Eyes shining, he tilted his head to look up at me. "I think you really are good magical."

XXII

AMBROSIA
BREAD

When we returned to the ravine, we found Bumbelwy still snoring. Although the explosion of flame had not been a volcano, his prediction of sleeping soundly had certainly proved true. Rhia and I carefully tucked Galwy, who was so tired he could barely stand, under a portion of the jester's cloak. Then, feeling our own exhaustion, we joined them on the ground. Clutching my staff, I soon fell asleep.

Before long, the first fingers of morning light tickled my face. I woke to find Bumbelwy already doing his best to impress young Galwy with his skills as a jester. From the solemn expression on the boy's round face, I could tell he hadn't progressed very far.

"That is why," the dour fellow was explaining, "they call me Bumbelwy the Mirthful."

Galwy stared at him, looking as if he were about to cry.

"Let me show you another of my jesterly talents." Bumbelwy gave his head a vigorous shake, clanging his bells, and drew his cloak tightly about him. "I will now tell you the famous riddle of the bells."

Rhia, who was also watching, started to protest. But I held up my hand. "Let's hear this confounded riddle. We've been hearing *about* it for weeks."

She smirked. "I suppose so. Are you ready to eat your boots if any of us laugh?"

"Ready." I licked my lips in mock satisfaction. "Then, with any luck, we'll find something more tasty at the Slantos' village."

Bumbelwy cleared his throat, making his drooping chins quiver. "I am now ready," he announced. He paused expectantly, almost as if he could not quite believe that he was finally being allowed to tell his riddle.

"We're waiting," I declared. "But not all day."

The jester's wide mouth opened. Then shut. Opened again. Shut again.

I leaned forward. "Well?"

Bumbelwy's eyebrows arched in consternation. He cleared his throat once more. He stomped his foot on the dry ground, rattling his bells again. But he did not speak.

"Are you going to tell this riddle of yours or not?"

The jester bit his lip, then shook his head glumly. "It's been . . . so long," he grumbled. "So many people, over so many years, have stopped me from telling it. Now that I may, I can't . . . remember it." He heaved a sigh. "Too true, too true, too true."

As Rhia and I rolled our eyes, Galwy smiled broadly. He turned to me. "Could you take me back to the village now? With you, I feel safe."

I tapped Bumbelwy's hunched shoulder. "Perhaps, one day, you'll remember it."

"If that ever happens," he replied, "I'll probably botch the delivery."

Moments later, we were trekking toward the rising sun. As usual,

Rhia and I led the way, although now I bore Galwy on my shoulders. Bumbelwy, more somber than ever, kept to the rear.

To my relief, we soon began a long, rolling descent, leaving behind the parched slopes and shadowed rock outcroppings of the Dark Hills. I could not rid myself of the uneasy feeling that the goblin we had encountered was only one of the first of Rhita Gawr's warriors to emerge from hiding. Nor could I forget how little I had done to make this land habitable for other creatures.

Before long, we entered a wide, grassy plain. Piping birds and humming insects appeared, as clusters of trees with hand-shaped leaves grew more common. A family of foxes, bushy tails all erect, crossed our trail. Sitting in the boughs of a willow tree sat a wide-eyed squirrel who reminded me of Rhia's friend Ixtma—and of the dying woman in his care.

The first sign of the village was the smell.

Grounded in the rich, hearty aroma of roasting grains, the smell strengthened as we crossed the grassy plain. With every step, it intensified, reminding me of how long it had been since I had eaten a crust of freshly baked bread. I could almost taste the grains. Wheat. Corn. Barley.

Other aromas, too, wove through this fragrant fabric. Something tangy, like the bright orange fruits that Rhia and I devoured long ago beneath the boughs of the shomorra tree. Something sharp and fresh, like the crushed mint that Elen often added to her tea. Something sweet, like the honey that bees made from clover blossoms. And more. Much more. The smell contained spicy flavors, robust flavors, and soothing flavors as well. It also contained, more often than not, a hint of something that was not really a flavor at all. More like a feeling. An attitude. Even . . . an idea.

When at last we entered the valley of the Slantos, and their low, brown buildings came into view, the smell grew overpowering. My mouth watering, I remembered tasting the Slantos' bread once before, in the underground den of Cairpré. What had he called it? *Ambrosia bread*. Food for the gods, the Greeks would have surely agreed. I remembered biting into the stiff crust, as hard as wood at first. Then, after some vigorous chewing, the bread had exploded with zesty flavor. A wave of nourishment had coursed through me, making me feel taller and sturdier. For a moment, I had even forgotten about the perpetual soreness between my shoulder blades.

Then I remembered something else. Cairpré, through a mouthful of ambrosia bread, had given me a stern warning. *No one from other parts of Fincayra has ever tasted the Slantos' most special breads, and they guard those precious recipes with their lives.* I gripped my staff as a new wave of fear surged through me. If the Slantos were not even willing to part with their recipes, how in the world was I going to get them to part with something much more valuable—the soul of the Song of Naming?

At the sight of the village gates in the distance, Galwy released a whoop of joy, jumped down from my shoulders, and scampered ahead of us, his arms flapping like the wings of a young bird. Beyond the gates, smoke poured from the hearths of many low buildings. The structures, while varied sizes, were all made from wide, brown bricks lined with yellow mortar. I almost smiled, noting that they looked like giant loaves of buttered bread themselves.

Bumbelwy, who had remained silent all morning, smacked his lips. "Do you think they're in the habit of giving visitors a crust of bread? Or do they turn people away hungry?"

"My guess," answered Rhia, "is that they're not in the habit of having visitors at all. The only people on this side of Eagles' Canyon are in—" Abruptly, she caught herself, glancing at me.

"In prison, in the caverns south of here, you were about to say." I pushed some stray black hairs off my face. "Like Stangmar, the man who was once my father."

Rhia eyed me sympathetically. "He's still your father."

I strode more briskly toward the gates. "Not anymore. I don't have a father."

She swallowed. "I know how you feel. I never even knew my father. Or my mother."

"At least you have Arbassa. And the rest of Druma Wood. As you've said before, that's your real family."

She worked her tongue, but said nothing.

As we arrived at the wooden gates, which were affixed to two tremendous spruce trees, a guard stepped out of the shadows by one of the trunks. Shaking the thinning locks of sand-colored hair that fell over his ears, he scowled at each of us in turn. Though his sword remained in its scabbard, one of his hands grasped the hilt. Even more than the roasting grains that filled the air, I began to smell the likelihood of trouble.

Warily, he examined my staff. "Be that the magical staff that felled the goblin?"

I blinked in surprise. "You know about that already?"

"Half the village knows by now," snorted the guard. "Young master Galwy has been telling everyone he can find."

"You'll let us pass, then?"

The guard shook his locks again. "I didn't say that." He pointed at the staff, eyeing it cautiously. "How do I know you won't use that to harm any villagers?"

"Well, for the same reason I'm not using it to harm you right now."

His face tightened, and he gave his sword an anxious tug. "You'll have to do better than that. You could be an infiltrator, after our secrets. Or an errand boy for the goblins, for all I know."

Rhia, bristling, stepped forward. "Then why would he have slain the goblin last night?"

"As a ruse, leafy girl." He ran a hand through his thinning hair. "Tell me, then. Why would a boy, a girl, and a . . . " He paused, observing Bumbelwy. "And a beggar, of whatever kind, travel all the way to Slantos? Not by chance, I'll wager."

"No," I answered carefully. "Your village is famous, far and near, for its breads. My friends and I would like to learn some of the bread maker's art."

His eyes bored into me. "I suspect that's not all you'd like to learn."

Remembering Cairpré's warning, I swallowed. "I seek nothing that won't be given freely."

The guard lifted his face to the spruce boughs above him, as if somehow seeking their counsel. He drew a long, slow breath. "Well, all right. I shall let you in—not for what you've said, which leaves me quite suspicious, I'll tell you. But for what you did to help master Galwy."

With a final shake of his dangling hair, he moved aside, stepping into the shadows under one of the trees. Although I could feel his eyes watching me warily, I didn't look back again. Nor did the others.

Immediately upon stepping through the gates, I spotted a high, spiraling structure in the middle of the common. Children squealed and jumped, playing around its base, while a steady stream of adults shuttled to and from it. Laden with buckets, baskets, and jugs, they resembled a colony of ants, hauling all the burdens of their society on their backs. Then I noticed a strange rippling on the gold-colored surface of the structure. As if it were moving somehow. As if it were alive.

Except for the few who pointed to my staff, whispering furtively, most of the villagers seemed too preoccupied with their tasks to pay any attention to us. Stepping over a cluster of children playing some sort of game with sticks, I moved cautiously closer to the structure. It seemed to be the source of at least some of the delicious smell that emanated from this village. And its surface was, indeed, moving. A thick, golden liquid flowed slowly from a spout at its highest point, down several spiraling troughs, all the way to a wide pool at its base. Out of this pool, people labored to draw the golden liquid by the bucketful, which they carried briskly into the buildings. At the same time, other people poured flour, milk, and other ingredients into the many vents that ringed the base.

"A fountain." I stared, utterly amazed. "A fountain of bread."

"Dough, you mean." Rhia bent over the churning pool. "They must use the golden stuff—doesn't it remind you of honey, but thicker?—as dough to start some of their breads."

"All of our breads, in fact."

We whirled around to see a plump, fair-haired man with ruddy cheeks, who was filling two large pitchers from the fountain. His ears, like other Fincayrans, were slightly pointed at the top. Yet his voice, like his face, seemed quite unusual, both scornful and mirthful at once. He was, I felt sure, one or the other. Which one I could not tell.

When the pitchers had nearly overflowed, he pulled them out of the pool. Resting them on his sizeable belly, he observed us for a moment. "Visitors, eh? We don't like visitors."

Unsure whether he was being unfriendly, or merely playful, I spoke up. "I would like to learn a little about bread baking. Could you help me?"

"I could," he answered gruffly. Or teasingly. "But I'm too busy now." He started to walk away. "Try some other day."

"I don't have another day!" I ran over to his side, keeping with him as he strode toward one of the buildings. "Won't you please show me a little of your art?"

"No," he declared. "I told you I'm—"

He tripped, tumbling over two scruffy boys, about the same age as Galwy, who were fighting over a loaf of blue-speckled bread. While only one of the pitchers fell to the ground, it smashed into dozens of pieces, all oozing with golden liquid from the fountain.

"Now see what you've done!" With a growl that was clearly serious, not playful, he stooped down to gather the broken pieces. Seeing me start to assist, he waved me away angrily. "Go away, boy! I don't need your help."

Glumly, I turned back to the bread fountain. I trudged toward it, barely noticing the rich aromas it continued to spill into the air. Rhia, having seen what happened, shook her head in dismay. She knew, as did I, that all of our efforts up to this point would be worthless unless we could find what we needed here in Slantos.

As I passed the two squabbling boys, who looked like twin brothers, I could tell that their argument was about to explode into a full-scale fight. Fists clenched, voices snarled. One boy tried to step on the blue-speckled loaf, which lay at the other one's feet. The second boy's nostrils flared. He roared angrily and charged at his enemy.

Slipping my staff through my belt, I stepped between them. Holding one boy by the collar of his tunic, and the other by the shoulder, I tried my best to keep them apart. Both shouted and struggled against me, kicking wildly at my legs. Finally, when my arms were about to give out, I released them and quickly snatched up the loaf of bread.

I raised the loaf, now more dirty brown than blue. "Is this what you're fighting about?"

"It's mine!" cried one.

"No, mine!" shouted the other.

Both of them lunged at the bread, but I held it just out of reach of their grasping hands. Ignoring their angry squeals, I waved it above them. Still warm, it smelled of sweet molasses. "Now," I demanded, "would you like to know how you can both have some?"

One boy cocked his head skeptically. "How?"

I glanced furtively over my shoulder. "I can tell you, but only on the condition that you keep it a secret."

The boys considered the idea, then nodded their heads in unison.

I kneeled down, then whispered something to them. Eyes wide, they listened intently. Finally, when I had finished, I handed them the loaf. They sat down on the spot, and within seconds, both of their mouths were bulging with bread.

"Not bad."

I looked up to find the plump man gazing at me. "Tell me, boy. How did you ever get them to share the loaf?"

Standing up, I pulled my staff from my belt. "Simple, really. I merely suggested that they each take turns having a bite." I grinned slightly. "And I also told them that if they couldn't manage that, I would eat the bread myself."

The man released a deep, guttural sound that could have been either a laugh or a groan. Scrunching up his face, he appeared to regard me with new respect. Or new concern. It was hard to tell. At last he spoke, removing any doubt. "If you'd like to learn a little about bread baking, boy, follow me."

XXIII

NAMING

The man strode to one of the loaf-shaped buildings at the far edge of the common. Before entering, he tossed the fragments of his broken pitcher into a pail outside the door. Then he wiped his plump hand on his tan tunic, already stained by many other wipings. Laying the hand on the wall by the door, he gave the brown bricks a grateful tap.

"Ever seen bricks like this?"

"No. Are they made from a special kind of mud?"

His expression turned grumpy. Or amused. "Actually, they're made from a special kind of flour. The ingredients give it unusual hardness, you see." He tapped the bricks again. "Knowing your ingredients, boy, is the first principle of baking bread."

Something about how he said *knowing your ingredients* made me think he meant something more than merely recognizing different grains and herbs. Tempted though I was to ask him to explain, I held my tongue for fear of pushing too hard.

"This one," he continued, "we call brickloaf. Baked six times for extra strength." He pressed his stubby fingers against the wall. "These bricks will outlive me by a hundred years."

Rhia, who had followed us, gazed at the bricks in wonder. "I've eaten some hard bread before, but not that hard."

The rotund man turned to her. Suddenly he started to laugh, so hard that his belly shook and golden liquid sloshed out of his remaining pitcher. "A good one, forest girl."

She smiled. "You may call me Rhia."

"And me Merlin."

The man nodded. "And me Pluton."

"Pluton," I repeated. "Isn't that a Greek name? From the story of Demeter and the first harvest of corn?"

"Why yes, boy. How do you come to know about the Greeks?"

My throat went dry. "My mother taught me."

"Indeed, as did mine. No child is born in Slantos who doesn't learn the tales of harvesting and baking from many different lands. And it's not unusual to give a child a name from one of those tales." He gave me an ambiguous look. "Of course, that's not my true name."

Rhia and I traded glances. Remembering Urnalda's comment about true names, I felt tempted to ask more. Besides, it troubled me that I could see no connection between the domestic art of bread baking and the magical art of Naming. But I held back. Things had taken a positive turn, and I did not want to alter that. Better to wait for another moment to learn about Naming.

Pluton lifted the door latch. "Come on in, both of you."

As we started to follow him inside, I suddenly remembered Bumbelwy. Scanning the bustling common, I quickly found him, still standing by the bread fountain. He was leaning against its base, peering hungrily at the pool of golden liquid. Children, probably curious about his belled hat, were gathering around him. He seemed unlikely to get into any trouble, and I didn't want to stretch Pluton's hospitality any further than necessary, so I decided just to leave him there.

As we entered the building, a new wave of aromas washed over us. I smelled roasting barley, some nectar as sweet as roses in bloom, and several spices I could not identify. The main room looked like the kitchen of a bustling inn, with pots boiling on the hearth, dried herbs and roots and bark shavings dangling from the ceiling, and bags of grain and flour sitting on the shelves. The room held six or seven people busily stirring, pouring, slicing, mixing, testing, and baking. From their expressions, it was clear that they both enjoyed their work and took it quite seriously.

Sunlight streamed into the room through rows of narrow windows. Yet the main source of light was the hearth itself, a complex of stone ovens and fire pits that covered almost an entire wall. Rather than burning wood, the hearth's fires used some sort of flat, gray cakes as fuel. No doubt they came from another mysterious recipe of the Slantos.

Above the hearth, high enough to be well out of reach, hung a massive sword, its hilt blackened by many years of fires beneath it. The metal scabbard had rusted with age; the leather belt had been eaten away. Something about the old sword made me curious to examine it more closely. Yet with the swirl of activity in the room, I soon forgot about it.

A tall girl, with apple cheeks and black hair that fell to her shoulders, approached Pluton. She looked quite different from anyone else I had seen in the village, partly because of her dark hair, partly because of her slender form. Her eyes, as black as my own, glowed with intelligence. The girl reached for the pitcher of golden liquid, then froze when she noticed Rhia and me standing to the side.

Pluton flicked his hand toward us. "This is Merlin, and Rhia. They're here to learn a bit about baking." Indicating the girl, he added brusquely, or just distractedly, "This is my apprentice, Vivian. Came to me when her parents, whom I'd known from my travels in the south, died in a terrible flood. How long ago was that now?"

"Six years, Breadmaster Pluton." She took the pitcher, her hands embracing it with the care of a mother holding a newborn. Still watching us warily, she asked, "Are you not concerned about them?"

"Concerned? My, yes." He studied her inscrutably. "But no more concerned than I was about you."

She stiffened, but stayed silent.

"Besides," Pluton continued, "I heard a story in the common about a boy who beat off a huge warrior goblin with nothing more than his staff. Saved one of our own children, he did." He cocked his head toward me. "Might that have been you?"

A bit embarrassed, I nodded.

He waved his stout hand at my staff. "And might that have been your weapon?"

Again I nodded.

"Not much of one against a goblin," he said casually. "Unless of course it's touched by magic."

At that, Vivian caught her breath. Her coal-dark eyes fixed on my staff. Instinctively, I turned the shaft around so that the markings from the Songs faced the other way.

Pluton reached out and took a steaming loaf of yellow-crusted bread from the tray of a man walking past. Breaking it into two halves, he filled his lungs with the freshly roasted smell. Then he handed the halves to Rhia and me. "Eat now," he suggested, or commanded. "You'll need your strength."

Without any hesitation, both of us bit into the crusts. As the warm, chewy bread touched our tongues, tasting of corn and butter and dill and many things more, our gazes met. Rhia's eyes sparkled, like the ocean sky at sunrise.

Pluton turned to Vivian. "We'll keep them to the simplest tasks. Stirring, mixing, slicing. No recipes."

He picked up a pair of wooden buckets, dusted with flour, and handed them to Rhia. "You can fill these, one with barley and one with wheat, from those sacks over there. Then carry them to the grinding wheel, in that room beyond the high shelves. You can learn a bit about milling and sifting in there."

He brushed some flour off his tunic. "And you, boy, can do some chopping. Over there at the table preparing heart bread."

Vivian seemed startled. "Really, Breadmaster?"

"That's right," declared Pluton. "He can chop some seeds." Ignoring her look of surprise, he turned to me. "If you do a good job, boy, I'll show you more. Might even let you taste a little heart bread itself, which will fill your belly even as it fills your heart with courage."

Swallowing the remains of my crust, I said, "Thank you, but I need no bread beyond what you just gave me. It's delicious."

His round face glowed. "As I said, it all comes from knowing your ingredients." A secretive smile touched his lips, then vanished. "You'll need a chopping knife for the seeds, and we're quite short on them right now. Ah, good, there's one left at the table. Vivian, why don't you take him over there and show him how it's done? I'll come by to check on his progress shortly."

Hearing this, the girl brightened. Smoothly, she stepped between Rhia and me. In a voice far gentler than before, she whispered to me, "Most people call me Vivian, but my friends call me Nimue." A warm smile graced her apple cheeks. "I'd be glad to help you. Any way I can."

"Ah, thank you, Viv—I mean, Nimue," I mumbled. Was I merely flattered by her attention, or was there something else about this girl that made my heart beat faster?

Rhia, the light gone from her eyes, nudged her aside. "You can start by getting him a knife." She shot me a harsh look of warning.

Her intrusion annoyed me. What did I need to be warned about, anyway? She was treating me like a child again.

"Come," said Nimue, brushing past Rhia. Gently taking my hand, she slowly slid her fingers up the length of my forearm. A new warmth filled me as she led me over to a table covered with vegetables, seeds, roots, and herbs. An elderly woman sat at one end of the table, deftly sorting the ingredients into piles. At the other end stood a young man, thinly bearded, peeling the skin off an enormous nut that looked like a giant acorn.

"Let's start here." Nimue guided me to the middle of the table. She slid over a bowl containing a stack of square, purple vegetables, steaming from having just been cooked. Pulling a battered knife from a block of wood on the table, she deftly sliced open the vegetable and removed a flat seed that glowed with a deep red luster. Then, laying her warm hand over my own, she showed me the sharp, twisting motion that would allow me to chop the seed into tiny pieces.

"There now," she said kindly, allowing her hand to linger on mine. "You are most fortunate, you know. Heart bread is one of Breadmaster Pluton's great specialities. He hardly ever lets an outsider help prepare it, certainly not chop the essential seeds." She flashed her most lovely smile. "He must see something special in you."

With a slight squeeze, she lifted her hand. "I'll come back to check on you in a while." As she started to step away, she pointed to my staff, propped against the side of the table. "That staff of yours is going to fall. Should I put it somewhere safe for you?"

A vague shiver ran through me, though I wasn't sure why. After all, she was only trying to be helpful. "No thank you," I replied. "It's fine where it is."

"Oh, but I wouldn't want it to get damaged. It's so very . . . handsome."

She reached out to touch it. Just then the elderly woman happened to bump her knee against the table. The staff slid sideways along the edge, falling against my hip. I grasped it by the shaft and slid it into the belt of my tunic.

"There," I said to Nimue. "It's safe now."

For the briefest instant, her eyes seemed to flash with anger, though the look of kindness returned so swiftly that I couldn't be sure. In any case, she quickly turned and walked away. After a few paces, she looked back, smiling warmly.

I could not help but smile in return. Then I turned back to the table and took one of the purple vegetables. Still steaming, it sliced open easily. Carefully, I removed the lustrous seed. As I started to chop it, however, the worn blade suddenly split into shards. Rotten luck! I cast aside the useless knife.

I needed to perform my task well, not to bungle it! Pluton, I felt sure, was testing me. Why else would he have given me such unusual responsibility? He had even promised to show me more, if only I did my job well. And if I failed, I couldn't possibly gain his trust. Frantically, I cast about with my second sight, searching for another blade that I could use.

Nothing. Every single knife in the room was being used by someone for carving or slicing. I rose, still carrying my staff in my belt, and looked again. On the shelves. By the hearth. Under the tables.

Nothing.

No blade of any kind.

Then my gaze fell on the tarnished sword hanging above the hearth. It would be clumsy to wield, and grimy to hold. But it was at least a blade.

No, I told myself, the idea was ridiculous. I had never seen anyone use a sword for chopping. I chewed my lip, searching the room again. No knives anywhere. And time was wasting. Pluton would be checking on my progress soon. I turned again to the grimy blade.

Spying a small ladder leaning against the tallest set of shelves, I placed it next to the hearth. Climbing up to its top rung, I reached as high as I could. Yet . . . I couldn't quite reach the hilt of the sword. I looked around for someone taller who might be able to help, but all the people in the room were deeply immersed in their own tasks.

Standing on tiptoes, I tried again. Almost there! I stretched even higher. Almost, almost . . . but no. I simply could not reach it.

I glared at the sword, cursing to myself. Why had it been placed so high, anyway? To be of any help, it needed to be reachable. And I could certainly use its help now. Not just for chopping the seeds for heart bread. Much more was at stake. If I couldn't win over Pluton, I couldn't possibly save Elen.

I concentrated on the old sword, searching for some way to reach it. If only I could make it fly to me, as I had done long ago with Deepercut. But, as Urnalda had taught me, that had been possible only because of Deepercut's own magic.

At that instant, I noticed some very faint scratches on the hilt. They could be nothing but random marks . . . or, perhaps, they could be something more. Runes. Letters. Could this sword, like Deepercut, possess some sort of magic? Yet even as the thought struck me, I knew that the chances were extremely small. Why would a magical sword be hanging, rusted and unused, in a remote village devoted to baking bread?

Still, the runes seemed to beckon to me. Perhaps they described the sword's history. Or, if indeed it were magical, perhaps they gave instructions on how to use it. How to make it fly to me!

Straining to focus my second sight, I tried to make some sense of the scratches. Beneath the layers of dust and soot, I detected a rhythm, a pattern, to the marks. There were straight lines. And curves. And corners. Throwing all my power into the task, I followed the hidden indentations.

The first letter came clear. I could read it! Then . . . the second. And the third. The fourth, the fifth . . . all the way to the end of the word. For that was all the hilt contained. A single, unusual word.

I spoke the word, not out loud, but within the walls of my mind. Pronounced it slowly, carefully, savoring the richness of the name. And, in return, the sword spoke to me. It declared its grand past, and its even grander future. *I am the sword of light, past and present. I am the sword of kings, once and future.*

Suddenly, the sword detached itself from the wall. At the same time, all the grime vanished from the hilt, revealing the brilliant silver forged beneath. Scabbard and belt were reborn, transformed into polished metal and sturdy leather, studded with purple gemstones.

As gracefully as a leaf borne aloft by the wind, the sword floated over the hearth and into my hands.

Only then did I realize that the entire room had fallen silent. No one moved. No one spoke. All eyes were trained on me.

My heart sank, for I felt certain I would now be labeled an infiltrator. Rhia and I would be banished. Or worse.

Pluton, looking either annoyed or astonished, stepped forward. Hands on his wide hips, he regarded me for a while. "Didn't think much of you at first. That's certain."

"I—I'm sorry about your sword."

He ignored me, continuing his thought. "Still, like a good lump of dough, you have risen, boy. Beyond anything I ever expected. You just needed time enough to rise."

"You mean . . . I can use it?"

"You can keep it!" thundered Pluton. "The sword is yours."

I blinked, trying to take all this in. I caught sight of Rhia, watching me with pride. And Nimue, hands on her hips, watching me with . . . something else. Something more like envy.

"But all I did was read its name. It's called—"

"Hush, boy!" Pluton held up his hand. "A true name should never be spoken aloud, unless it's absolutely necessary. You gained power over the sword by recognizing its true name. Now you must guard that name faithfully."

I scanned the room, aglow with light from the hearth, rich with the smells of freshly ground flour and baking bread and a thousand spices. "I think I understand," I said at last. "Here in this village you learn the true names of each and every ingredient before using them. That allows you to master their powers, and release them in your breads. That is why your breads are so full of magic."

Pluton nodded slowly. "Ages ago, that sword came to this place carried by a flock of enchanted swans. It was foretold that it would, one day, fly like a swan itself into the hands of the one person who could read its true name. Because we, of all the peoples of Fincayra, most value the power of true names, the sword was entrusted to us. Until this day. Now it is entrusted to you."

He swiftly affixed the belt around my waist and adjusted the scabbard. "Use this sword wisely and well. And keep it safe. For it was also foretold that one day it would belong to a great, though tragic, king—a king whose power would be so profound that he would pull the sword from a scabbard of stone."

I looked into Pluton's face. "Then he, too, will know its true name. *For a true name holds true power.*"

At that instant, my staff sizzled with a burst of blue light. A new marking appeared, in the shape of a sword. A sword whose name I knew well.

XXIV

NO WINGS,
NO HOPE

Only after Rhia and I had sampled nine different varieties of bread (including ambrosia bread, even better than I had remembered), did we finally extract ourselves from Pluton's kitchen. At last, the master baker stuffed some freshly baked heart bread in my satchel and sent us on our way. No sooner had we stepped out of his door, rejoining the bustle of the common, than we found Bumbelwy, slumped against the base of the great bread fountain.

The lanky jester was holding his swollen belly, moaning painfully. His face, down to the bottommost chin, looked blueish-green. Lumps of golden dough streaked his hooded cloak and clung to his hair, his ears, and even his eyebrows. His three-cornered hat, also clogged with dough, sat soundless on his head.

"Ohhh," he moaned. "Death by overeating! Such a painful end."

Despite myself, I almost laughed. Remembering my pledge about my boots, however, I caught myself.

As he explained to us in halting phrases between moans, Bumbelwy had stood by the bread fountain, watching and smelling the rich, thick liquid flowing out of its spout, until finally he could stand it no longer. He had leaned closer, drinking in the aroma. Then, with both hands, he had scooped some wondrous dough straight out of the pool and into his mouth. Liking the taste, he had taken some more. And some more. What he hadn't realized until too late was that the dough had only begun to rise. So then rise it did—in his stomach. The result was a bellyache too horrible for even him to describe.

Leaning my staff against the fountain, I sat down beside him. Rhia joined us, wrapping her arms around her knees so that she resembled a bundle of green and brown vines. Slantos villagers scurried past, pursuing their tasks with all the speed and purpose of an army.

I sighed, knowing that while we had purpose aplenty, we had no speed. And we still had very far to go.

Rhia reached a leafy arm toward me. "You're worried about the time, aren't you? The moon is waning fast." She hesitated. "No more than five days left, Merlin."

"I know, I know. And for Leaping we must go all the way back to Varigal. We'll have to cross Eagles' Canyon again, and we'll probably find trouble in the Dark Hills again." I ran my finger along the scabbard I now wore on my waist. "More trouble, I'm afraid, than even a magical staff and sword can handle."

Rhia nodded toward Bumbelwy. "And what about him? He can't even sit up, let alone walk anywhere."

I considered the moaning figure, studded with lumps of dough. "This may surprise you, but I just don't feel right about leaving him. He really did his best for you back there on the cliff."

She smiled sadly. "It doesn't surprise me."

"So what should we do?" I stretched my aching shoulders. "If only we could fly."

Rhia swallowed a crust of ambrosia bread. "Like the Fincayrans of old, before they lost their wings."

"I need more than wings," said Bumbelwy, stirring to roll over on his side. "I need a whole new body."

I observed the staff, propped against the base of the fountain. There, etched darkly, were the images of a butterfly, a pair of soaring hawks, a cracked stone, and now a sword. We had come so far, accomplished so much. Yet it all amounted to nothing if I could not discover the souls of the remaining Songs before time ran out.

I recited them to myself, trying to find a hint of hope:

> *The power Leaping be the fifth,*
> *In Varigal beware.*
>
> *Eliminating be the sixth,*
> *A sleeping dragon's lair.*
>
> *The gift of Seeing be the last,*
> *Forgotten Island's spell.*
>
> *And now ye may attempt to find*
> *The Otherworldly Well.*

My heart sank as I considered the vast distances that the Songs required. Even if I did have wings, how could I possibly cover so much ground? Not to mention the challenges that still would remain: finding the Otherworld Well, evading the ogre Balor, and climbing up to the realm of Dagda to get the precious Elixir. All this . . . in five short days.

If only I could compress things somehow! Skip one of the Songs. Go straight to the land of the spirits. Yet even as I considered the notion, I remembered Tuatha's warning to avoid such folly.

I slammed my fist against the ground. "How can we do it all, Rhia?"

She started to reply when a group of four men tottered over to the fountain, staggering under the weight of a huge black cauldron. Oblivious to anyone who might happen to be in their path, they pushed and bumped their way across the common. As they moved between Rhia and myself, they nearly stepped right on poor Bumbelwy. Even as he groaned and rolled aside, they propped the cauldron on the edge of the fountain's pool and began to pour. A creamy brown mixture that smelled of cloves emptied into the pool, gurgling and splattering.

As they departed with the empty cauldron, a small, round-cheeked boy ran up to me. Excitedly, he tugged on my tunic.

"Galwy!" I exclaimed. Then, seeing the worry on his face, I froze. "What's wrong?"

"She took it," he panted. "I saw her took it."

"Took what?"

"The goblin slayer! She took it."

Puzzled, I squeezed his stout little shoulders. "Goblin slayer? What—"

Suddenly I looked at the fountain. My staff was gone!

"Who took it?"

"The girl, the tall one." Galwy pointed at the village gates. "Ran that way."

Nimue! I flew to my feet, shoved my way through the villagers near the fountain, leaped over a sleeping dog, and sprinted through the wooden gates. Standing beneath one of the towering spruces, I scanned what was visible of the grassy plains, although a thick blanket of fog obscured everything beyond the foreground.

No sign at all of Nimue. Or of my staff.

"Leaving already?"

I whirled around to see the guard. He was watching me from the shadows, still grasping the hilt of his sword. "My staff!" I cried. "Did you see a girl just now with my staff?"

Slowly, he nodded. "That one called Vivian, or Nimue."

"Yes! Where did she go?"

The guard tugged on the shreds of hair dangling over his ears, then waved at the rolling fog. "Somewhere out there, beyond the sea mist. Maybe toward the coast, maybe toward the hills. I have no idea. I save my attention for people coming in, not going out."

I kicked at the ground. "Didn't you see she had my staff?"

"That I did. Your staff is hard to miss. But it's not the first time I've seen her convince a fellow to part with something precious, so I didn't think much of it."

My eyes narrowed. "She didn't convince me! She stole it!"

He grinned knowingly. "I've heard that a few times, too."

In disgust, I turned back to the clouded plains. Stretching my second sight to the limit, I tried to find any sign of the thief. Yet all I found was fog and more fog, endlessly shifting. My staff. My precious staff! Filled with the vitality of Druma Wood, touched by the hand of Tuatha, marked by the power of the Songs. Gone! Without the staff's ability to tell me whether I had found the soul of each Song, I had no hope.

Head bowed, I trudged back through the gates and into the common. A man, arms laden with bread, bumped into me and dropped several loaves. But I hardly noticed. I could think of nothing but my staff. As I reached the base of the fountain, I collapsed beside Rhia.

Wrapping her forefinger around my own, she searched my face. "So it's lost."

"Everything is lost."

"Too true, too true, too true," moaned Bumbelwy, rubbing his swollen belly.

Rhia reached for my satchel and opened it. Pulling out Pluton's heart bread, she tore off a chunk and placed it in my hand. A sturdy, robust smell, as rich as roasting venison, filled the air.

"Here. Pluton said it will fill your heart with courage."

"It will take more than courage to save my mother," I muttered, taking a small bite of the bread.

As I chewed, the bits of seeds burst in my mouth, releasing their powerful flavor. And something more. I straightened my back and drew a hearty breath, savoring the new strength that I could feel surging through my limbs. Yet, even as I took another bite, I could not forget the truth. My staff was lost, as was my quest. What could I possibly do—without the staff, without the time, without the wings to fly to the other end of Fincayra?

Tears brimmed in my sightless eyes. "I can't do it, Rhia. I can't possibly do it!"

She slid closer on the ground, brushing aside some hardened lumps of dough. Gently, she touched the amulet of oak, ash, and thorn that Elen had given her. "As long as we still have hope, we still have a chance."

"That's just the point!" I jabbed at the air with my fist, almost hitting the base of the bread fountain. "We have no hope."

At that instant, something warm brushed against my cheek. A light touch, lighter than a caress. Lighter than air. "You still have hope, Emrys Merlin." The familiar voice breathed in my ear. "You still have hope."

"Aylah!" I leaped to my feet, lifting my arms skyward. "It's you."

"There, you see?" said Bumbelwy sadly. "The strain was too much for the poor boy. He's lost his mind. Now he's talking to the air."

"Not the air, the wind!"

Rhia's eyes brightened. "You mean . . . a wind sister?"

"Yes, Rhiannon." A soft, whispering laughter rose out of the air. "I am here to take you, all of you, to Varigal."

"Oh, Aylah!" I cried. "Is it possible, before you take us there, to go somewhere else first?"

"To find your staff, Emrys Merlin?"

"How did you know?"

As a spring bubbles out of the ground, pouring over the soil, the wind sister's words tumbled out of the air. "Nothing can long hide from the wind. Not a stealthy girl, nor the secret cave where she hides her treasures, nor even her desire one day to wield great power through magic."

My blood surged angrily. "Can we still catch her before she reaches her cave?"

A sudden gust of wind swept the village common. Hats, cloaks, and aprons lifted into the air, swirling like autumn leaves. All at once my boots, too, rose off the ground. In an instant, Rhia, Bumbelwy, and I were airborne.

XXV

ALL THE VOICES

As we lifted off from the village common, several people standing near the fountain shrieked in fright—though none shrieked as loud as poor Bumbelwy. For my part, I swung my legs freely in the open air, alive with the thrill of flight. It was a thrill that I had known only once before, nestled into the feathers of Trouble's back. Yet this time the feeling was even more powerful, if also more frightening. For this time I was borne aloft not by another body, but by the very wind itself.

Aylah carried us swiftly higher, supporting us on a blanket of air. As the loaf-shaped buildings of Slantos melted into the fog, the golden pool of the bread fountain faded into tan, then brown, then white. Clouds swallowed us whole, leaving nothing visible beyond ourselves. I could hear the whistling of air all around, yet it wasn't too loud, for we were flying with the wind and not against it.

"Aylah!" I cried. "Can you still find her in the fog?"

"Patience," she replied, her airy voice springing from both above and below. The clouds thickened as we dropped lower and banked to the right.

Rhia turned to me, her face showing her own growing exhilaration. We were riding, it seemed, on a cloud itself, close enough to touch each other and far enough apart to feel completely free. And, in the case of Bumbelwy, completely miserable. His face, still splattered with dough, turned greener with every jostle and sway.

Suddenly, just below us, a figure emerged from a gap in the fog. Nimue!

She strode purposefully across the grassy plain, her long black hair falling over her shoulders. In her hand, she clutched my staff. I could almost hear her clucking to herself in satisfaction. No doubt she was considering what place of honor to give my staff in her cave of treasures. Or how she might find some way to turn its hidden powers to her advantage. A thin smile spread across my own face as we drew nearer, casting a trio of ghostly shadows on the ground.

Sensing something, she whirled around. She shrieked, seeing me and my companions dropping right out of the sky on top of her. Before she could turn and run, I reached down and grasped the gnarled top of the staff with both hands.

"Thief!" she wailed, clinging tightly to her prize.

We tugged against each other, trying to twist the staff free. As Aylah bore me aloft again, Nimue herself rose off the plain, her legs kicking wildly. My back and shoulders ached from the strain, but I held on. Currents of air slapped against her, shoving her body this way and that. Yet she refused to let go. We dropped a bit lower, just as a tangle of brambles came into view. Straight through it flew Nimue, the thorns tearing at her legs and ripping her robe. Still she did not release her grip.

I felt the staff slip lower in my perspiring hands. Her weight made my shoulders scream with pain. My arms were starting to feel numb. All the while, Nimue twisted and writhed, trying her best to break free.

Banking hard to the left, we veered toward a pile of jagged rocks. An instant before she collided, Nimue caught sight of the approaching obstacle. With a terrified shriek, she let go at last.

With a thud, she dropped to the ground, landing on her back next to the pile of rocks. Weakly, I pulled the staff to me, gazing again at its familiar markings. The sign of the paired hawks glistened with my own perspiration. I felt whole again, my staff and my hope both restored.

As the mist thickened, I glanced down at Nimue. As she sat up, her eyes flashed angrily. She kicked her heels on the turf like an infant, waving her clenched fists at the air, cursing and crying for revenge. Smaller she grew, and smaller. An instant later, she disappeared in a shroud of fog, her shouts replaced by the whistling wind.

I twirled the staff in my throbbing hands. "Thank you, Aylah."

"You are welcome, Emrys Merlin. Ahhh yes."

The wind bore us higher, until the fog began to pull apart, shredding into white waves that rose and fell like the rolling sea. Ships of mist, sails billowing, lifted their prows, only to dash upon vaporous shores. The cloud waves rolled over us, soaking us with spray, churning ceaselessly.

I turned to Rhia, her eyes as joyful as Nimue's had been wrathful. "You were so right about her. I don't know how, but she had me, well, confused at first. I wish I had your . . . what did my mother call them?"

"Berries," she said with a laugh. "Also called instincts." She flapped her arms in the mist, stretching them like wings. "Oh, isn't this wonderful? I feel so free! Like I'm the wind myself."

"You are the wind, Rhiannon." Aylah's wispy arms encircled us.

"You have all living things within yourself. That is what instincts are, the voices of those living things inside you."

I watched the shredding clouds, as Aylah's voice whispered in my own ear. "You, too, have instincts, Emrys Merlin. You simply do not hear them very well. You have all the voices, old and young, male and female."

"Female? Me?" I scoffed, tapping my sword, as the air whooshed past. "I'm a boy!"

"Ahhh yes, Emrys Merlin, you are a boy. And a wonderful thing that is to be! One day, perhaps, you will learn that you can also be more. That you can listen as well as speak, sow as well as reap, create as well as construct. And then you may discover that the merest trembling of a butterfly's wings can be just as powerful as a quake that moves mountains."

Hardly had those words been spoken than a sudden current of air jolted us. Rhia and I rolled into each other, while Bumbelwy cried out, flailing his arms and legs. His bell-draped hat flew into the air, and nearly sailed away before Rhia caught it. As she snatched the hat, several chunks of dough flew off, causing it to rattle noisily again.

All at once we burst out of the clouds. As swiftly as hawks, we rose above their fluffy contours. Far below, Fincayra revealed itself now like a tapestry unfurling, full of dazzling colors and intricate patterns. There lay the Dark Hills, swathed in shadows, the flowing ridges broken only by the occasional cluster of trees or jumble of rocks. There ran the red and maroon gorge of Eagles' Canyon, winding away to the south. And there, dappled with sun, stretched the rolling sweep of the Rusted Plains.

I leaned forward, stretching myself prone on the carpet of wind.

Soaring headlong over the lands below, I felt for a moment as if I had become a fish again, gliding through an ocean of air rather than water. Buoyed by invisible currents, sailing weightlessly, I flew through the very substance of my breathing.

To the north, I followed the contorted coastline of a dark peninsula, until it melted into mist. Twisting rivers sparkled below, as hills started swelling beneath us. Dimly, beyond the hills, I glimpsed the grim profile of the Lake of the Face. An icy finger ran down my spine as I recalled the image I had seen in those dark waters, the image of Balor's deadly eye.

Then, above the whooshing wind, I heard a faint rumbling. It came from somewhere in the snowy mountains ahead, whose crested summits gleamed in the late afternoon light. The rumbling grew louder and louder, rolling like avalanches down the slopes. It seemed that thunder itself must be part of this land.

And indeed it was. For we had arrived in the land of the giants. The rumbling swelled as Aylah set us down on a knoll bristling with short, stubby grass. Rising out of a steeply sloping, rocky ridge, the knoll was one of the few patches of green around. The ground beneath us, like the cliffs on all sides, shook from the noise. Or from whatever caused the noise.

As soon as Bumbelwy's feet touched down, he tottered unsteadily over to an enormous pile of leaves, branches, and ferns that had been left on the knoll for some reason. It covered nearly half of the knoll, rising like a miniature mountain of brush. He fell into the pile, crawled higher, then sprawled on his back. Above the rumbling, he called, "If I'm going to die in an earthquake, I might at least be somewhere soft!"

He smoothed some broken branches beneath his head. "Besides,

I have some difficult digesting to do. Not to mention recovering from that ride." He closed his eyes, wriggling deeper into the ferns. "Imagine! Almost killed twice in the same day." He yawned, shaking his bells. "If I weren't such an optimist, I'd say something even worse will happen to me before the day is over."

Seconds later, he was snoring.

"I wish you well, Emrys Merlin." Louder than usual because of the rumbling, the voice spoke in my ear. "I wish I could stay with you longer, but I must fly."

"I wish you didn't have to go."

"I know, Emrys Merlin, I know." Aylah's warm breath caressed my cheek. "Perhaps, on another day, we will meet again."

"And fly again?" Rhia lifted her arms as if they were wings, "Like the wind?"

"Perhaps, Rhiannon. Perhaps."

With a sudden swirl of air, the wind sister departed.

XXVI

LEAPING

A great thud sounded, from somewhere in the steep-walled valley below the knoll. The ground shook again, knocking both Rhia and me over backward. A plump thrush, its purple wings dotted with white, shrieked and flew away from its perch in the bristly grass. Sitting up, I looked over at Bumbelwy, still snoring peacefully in the pile of leaves and brush. What it might take to awaken him, I could not imagine.

Crawling on hands and knees, Rhia and I crept slowly to the edge of the knoll. Peering over, we gazed into the valley below. At that instant, an entire section of cliff above the valley cracked open, dangled precariously, then tumbled down in a cloud of rubble and dust. Another rumble filled the air, and the ground beneath us shook violently again.

Then, as the dust cleared, I recognized the figures laboring below. Even from this distance, the giants looked enormous. And frighteningly powerful. While some of them split boulders apart with hammers the size of pine trees, others hauled the chunks of rock to the center of the valley. Lifting even one such stone would have required fifty men and women, yet the giants moved them around like bales of summer hay.

Not far away, more giants worked, cutting and shaping the gray and white stones. Still others fit them carefully into the towers and bridges of a growing city. So this was Varigal! Destroyed by Stangmar's army of warrior goblins, Fincayra's most ancient city was being completely rebuilt, rock by rock. Already its rough-hewn walls and spires mirrored the cliff walls and snowy spires that surrounded the valley.

As they labored, the giants chanted in low, rumbling tones. Their words echoed from cliff to cliff, pounding and cracking like stones themselves.

> *Hy gododin catann hue*
> *Hud a lledrith mal wyddan*
> *Gaunce ae bellawn wen cabri*
> *Varigal don Fincayra*
> *Dravia, dravia Fincayra.*
>
> *Hud ya vardann tendal fe*
> *Roe samenya, llaren kai*
> *Hosh waundi na mal storro*
> *Varigal don Fincayra*
> *Dravia, dravia Fincayra.*

I remembered, ages ago it seemed, hearing those same voices chanting the Lledra during the Dance of the Giants that had finally brought the Shrouded Castle crashing down. And I remembered hearing Elen sing that same chant to me when I was barely more than a babe in her arms.

> *Talking trees and walking stones,*
> *Giants are the island's bones.*

While this land our dance still knows,
Varigal crowns Fincayra.
Live long, live long Fincayra.

Giants breathe and tempests blow,
Touch the waves and rivers slow.
In the island's realm of snow,
Varigal crowns Fincayra.
Live long, live long Fincayra.

Bumbelwy snorted, rolling over on his bed of branches. A sprig of fern had caught in his hair and seemed to be growing straight out of his ear. With every breath, his bells rattled like a potful of pebbles. Yet the jester slept on, undisturbed.

I turned back to watch a wild-haired female giant, at the near end of the valley, push the base of a stone tower into place with her bare shoulder. From this distance, she looked much like the giant on whose immense frame the eagle had landed at the start of the Great Council. I suspected that, somewhere down there, my old friend Shim was also working. Or, more likely, doing his best to avoid working. Yet as much as I wanted to see him again, there would be no time to try to find him.

"So," spoke a melodic voice behind us, "why do you come to the land of the giants?"

Rhia and I spun around. Seated on a rounded, mossy rock—a rock that had been empty only seconds before—was a tall, pale woman. Her golden hair, stretching almost to her knees, fell about her like rays of light. She wore a simple, light blue robe, yet her very posture made it seem like an elegant dress. Her eyes shone unusually bright, as if intense flames burned inside her.

Winsome though she was, I steeled myself. *I may not have Rhia's instincts, but I won't let what happened with Nimue happen again.* Reaching for my staff in the grass, I pulled it closer to my side.

The bright-eyed woman laughed gently. "I see you don't trust me."

Rhia, while still sitting on the grass, straightened her back and seemed for a moment to study the woman's face. Then she drew in her breath. "I trust you. We came here to learn about Leaping."

I nearly jumped out of my boots. "Rhia! You don't know her!"

"I know I don't. And yet . . . I do. She makes me want to—well, trust in the berries. There's something about her that, I don't know . . . that reminds me of the stars shining at the darkest time of night."

The woman rose slowly, her hair swirling about her waist. "That is because, dear girl, I am the spirit of a star. You know me, in fact, as one of your constellations."

Despite the quaking ground, Rhia rose to her feet. "Gwri," she said softly, so softly that I could barely hear her above the continuing rumble. "You are Gwri of the Golden Hair."

"Yes. I live in your westernmost sky. And I have watched you, Rhia, as well as you, Merlin, even as you have watched me."

Dumbfounded, I too clambered to my feet. It seemed so long ago, that night under the shomorra tree, when Rhia had first shown me Gwri of the Golden Hair. And how to see constellations in a completely new way. To find their shapes not just in the stars themselves, but in the spaces *between* the stars.

Rhia took a small step closer on the grassy knoll. "Why did you come all the way here?"

Gwri laughed again, more heartily than before. This time a circle of golden light glowed in the air around her. "I came here to help the giants of your land rebuild their ancient capital. For, you see, I also came here ages ago when Varigal was first built. I stood by Dagda's side, providing the light he needed to work through the night when he carved the very first giant from the stony side of a mountain."

"You came such a long way."

"Yes, Merlin. I came here by Leaping."

My legs nearly buckled beneath me, though not because of the quaking ground. "Leaping? Will you—can you tell me what I need to know?"

"You already know the soul of this Song," the star declared. "You only need to find it within yourself."

"We have so little time! The moon is barely a quarter full. And my mother . . . " My throat tightened, reducing my voice to a whisper. "She's going to die. All because of me."

Gwri studied me intently. She seemed to be listening to my innermost thoughts, oblivious to the continuing rumble from the valley below. "Just what did you do?"

"I found the speaking shell, whose power brought her here."

Gwri tilted her head, sending a cascade of hair tumbling over her arm. "No, Merlin. Think again."

Puzzled, I rubbed my chin. "But the shell—"

"Think again."

I caught Rhia's eye. "You mean . . . it was me. Not the shell."

The woman nodded. "The shell needed your power to do it. Your power of Leaping, unformed as it is. One day, perhaps, you may master that power. Then you may send people, or things, or dreams. You could travel through the worlds, or even through time, as you choose."

"Time?" A vague memory stirred within me. "When I was very young, I used to dream about living backward in time. Honestly! Just so I could relive my favorite moments over and over again."

A spare smile touched her face. "Perhaps you will come to master that, as well. Then you could grow younger every day, while everyone around you grows older."

As much as the idea intrigued me, I shook my head. "That's only a dream. I'm afraid I'll never master anything. Look what disaster I caused when I brought my mother to Fincayra."

"Tell me," said Gwri, "what have you learned from that?"

Another quake shook the ground. Rocks from the cliff nearest us broke loose, sending up a cloud of dust as they clattered down to the valley below. I grasped my staff for better balance. "Well, I've learned that Leaping, like all magic I suppose, has limits."

"True. Even the great spirit Dagda has limits! For all he knows about the powers of the universe, he cannot bring someone back to life who has died." Gwri looked suddenly pained, as if she were recalling something that had happened long ago. After a long pause, she spoke again. "Have you learned anything else?"

I hesitated, shifting my weight on the grass. "Well . . . that you must think carefully before bringing someone or something to a new place, since what you do could have unintended consequences. Serious ones."

"And why do you suppose that is so?"

Squeezing the knotted top of my staff, I thought hard. The wind whistled across the ridge, chafing my face. "Because, you see, one action is connected to another. Throwing a single pebble in the wrong place could start a rockslide. The truth is, *everything is connected to everything else.*"

Gwri burst into laughter just as my staff erupted in blue flames. A golden circle of light glowed in the air around her, even as the image of a star inside a circle appeared on the shaft. I let my fingers stroke it.

"You have learned well, Merlin. Everything plays a part in the great and glorious song of the stars."

Remembering the phrase from the walls of Arbassa, I nodded. "I only wish I knew enough to use the power of Leaping right now. For I must find my way, and quickly, to a dragon's lair, though I don't have any idea where to look."

Gwri turned to the east, her long hair shimmering. "The dragon you seek is the same one who was lulled into enchanted sleep ages ago by your grandfather, Tuatha. And yet even your grandfather's powers were not great enough to resist Balor, the guardian of the Otherworld Well. If you should survive the dragon and make your way there, do you really expect to fare any better?"

"No. I only hope to try."

For a long moment, she studied me. "The sleeping dragon's lair lies in the Lost Lands, just across the water from here. As it happens, it also lies not very far from the Otherworld Well—though that matters little to you, since you must still voyage all the way to the Forgotten Island before you go there."

With my finger, I traced the new marking on my staff. "Could you, perhaps, send us to the dragon's lair?"

Gwri's eyes shone a bit brighter. "I could, yes. But I prefer to let someone else do it. Someone you know, who can get you there almost as fast as I can."

Rhia and I traded perplexed glances.

The star motioned toward the dour jester, sprawled on the enormous brush pile. "Your sleeping friend over there."

"Bumbelwy? You can't be serious!"

Gwri's laughter rang out. "Not him, though I daresay he may yet show himself capable of some surprising leaps." Again she pointed. "I mean the sleeping friend beneath him."

Before I could ask what she meant, Gwri grew brighter and brighter, until she glowed so intensely that even my second sight could not bear to watch. Like Rhia, I turned away. A few seconds later, the light suddenly diminished. We turned back, only to find that Gwri of the Golden Hair had vanished.

At that instant, the brush pile itself stirred.

XXVII

ANOTHER
CROSSING

The pile of brush lurched suddenly to the side, hurling the sleep-ing Bumbelwy into the air. His bells clanged like a blacksmith's ham-mer. And his shriek, easily heard above the rumbling from the valley below, joined with the surprised shouts of Rhia and me.

Spraying branches, leaves, and fern fronds across the grassy notch, the pile of leaves bent, twisted—and sat up. Two enormous arms stretched to either side, while a pair of hairy feet kicked free from the debris. A head lifted, showing wide pink eyes and a cavernous mouth that opened in a yawn. Just below the eyes, a gargantuan nose bulged like a swollen potato.

"Shim!" cried Rhia and I at once.

Finishing his yawn, the giant looked down on us in surprise. He rubbed his eyes, then looked again. "Is you a dream? Or is you real?"

"We're real," I declared.

Shim scrunched his nose doubtfully. "Really, truly, honestly?"

"Really, truly, honestly." Rhia stepped forward and patted one of his feet, which towered over her. "It's good to see you again, Shim."

With a great smile, the giant reached out with one arm and gen-tly scooped us into the palm of his hand. "I thinks I is still dreaming! But it's you, the truly you." He brought his nose a little closer and took a sniff. "You smells like bread. Goodly bread."

I nodded. "Ambrosia. Like we had that night with Cairpré. Do you remember, good Shim? I wish we'd brought you some! But we're in a hurry, you see. A great hurry."

The immense nose scrunched again. "Is you still full of madness?"

"You could put it that way."

"Ever since that day we firstly meets, you is full of madness!" The giant rocked with a thunderous laugh, swaying on the grassy knoll, shaking loose some rocks that bounced down into the valley. "That day you almost gets us stingded by thousands of bees."

"And you were nothing but a blundering ball of honey."

Rhia, who had managed to rise to her knees in the fleshy palm, joined in. "You were so small I was sure you were a dwarf."

Shim's pink eyes glowed with pride. "I is small no more."

Another tumultuous crash from the valley filled the air, rocking the ridge. Even Shim's mighty arm swayed like a tree in a gale. Rhia and I clung to his thumb for support.

His expression turned serious. "They is workings hard down there. I is supposed to brings the branches, for cookings the supper." He looked suddenly sheepish. "I only wanted to rolls in the branches, then takes a little nap! A briefly little nap."

"We're glad you did," I replied. "We need your help."

A long, painful moan came from the loose branches at the far end of the notch. Before I could say anything, Shim reached over with his free hand and lifted out Bumbelwy by his heavy cloak. Draped with drooping ferns and broken branches, frowning with his whole face down to his layered chins, the gloomy jester looked half alive at best.

Rhia watched the dangling jester with concern. "Did you see him go flying when Shim woke up?"

I gave her a sardonic grin. "Maybe that was the leap that Gwri was talking about."

"Ohhh," groaned Bumbelwy, holding his head. "My head feels like a rock that just bounced down one of these cliffs! I must have rolled off that pile of—" All at once, he realized that he was being carried over the knoll by a giant. He struggled, swatting at the huge thumb that was hooked under his cloak. "Helllp! I'm about to be eaten!"

Shim grunted and shook his head at the bedraggled jester. "You isn't very tasty, that's easily to see. I wouldn't puts you in my mouth for anythings."

I waved at Bumbelwy. "Don't worry. This giant's a friend of ours."

Bumbelwy, swaying before Shim's nose, continued to flail wildly. "Such a tragedy!" he wailed. "All my humor and wisdom, lost forever down a giant's gullet."

Shim dropped him into the palm of his other hand. Bumbelwy landed in a heap beside Rhia and me. He struggled to stand, took a swing at Shim's nose, tripped, and fell flat on his face again.

An enormous grin spread across Shim's face. "At leastly he's funny."

Bumbelwy, who was trying to stand again, froze. "Do you mean that? Funny enough to make you laugh?"

"Not that funny," boomed Shim, his voice so powerful it almost blew us all over the edge of his palm. "Just enough to makes me grin."

The jester finally stood, trying to keep his balance while squaring his shoulders and straightening his cloak. "Good giant. You are more intelligent than I had thought at first." He bowed awkwardly. "I am Bumbelwy the Mirthful, jester to—"

"Nobody." I ignored his glare and spoke to Shim. "As I was saying, we need your help. We need to get to the lair of the sleeping dragon, the one Tuatha battled long ago. It's somewhere across the water."

The giant's grin faded, as the rising wind howled across the cliffs. "You must be kiddingly."

"I fear he's not," said Bumbelwy, his usual glumness returned. "You might as well eat us all now, before the dragon does."

"If it's really a sleeping dragon," asked Rhia, "just how dangerous can it be?"

"Verily," thundered Shim, his whole frame swaying like a great tree in a storm. "For starters, the dragon is still hungrily, even while it sleeps. For enders, it could wakes up anytime." He paused, tilting his huge head in thought. "Nobodies know when Tuatha's sleeping spell will wears off, and the dragon will wakes up. Although the legends say that it will happen on the darkest day in the life of Fincayra."

Bumbelwy sighed. "Sounds like a typical day for me."

"Hush!" I gazed up at Shim. "Will you take us there right away?"

"All rights. But it is madness! Certainly, definitely, absolutely." Scanning the knoll, strewn with brush, he bit his great lip. "But firstly I needs to brings these branches down to Varigal."

"Please, no," I begged. I scanned the afternoon sky, afraid to see the rising sliver of the moon. "Every minute counts now, Shim. I'm almost out of time."

"I supposes I is already late with these pokingly branches."

"Then you'll do it?"

Shim replied by standing and taking a single, enormous stride along the spine of the ridge. Rocked by the jolt, we fell together in a jumble on his palm. Untangling ourselves was made more difficult by the giant's bouncing gait, but we finally succeeded. Except for Bumbelwy, whose cloak had wrapped itself tightly around his head and shoulders. As he struggled to free himself, his bells were mercifully silent under the cloak.

Rhia and I, meanwhile, crawled to the edge of Shim's palm and peered through the gaps in his fingers. Wind rushed past our faces as we watched the landscape transform. So great were Shim's strides that the chanting of the giants, and the rumbling of their labors, soon faded away completely. He stepped over boulder fields as if they were mere clusters of pebbles, crushing rock ledges with his feet. Mountain passes that would have taken us days to scale he climbed in a few minutes. He traversed yawning crevasses with the ease of a rabbit hopping over a stick.

Before long, the terrain began to flatten. Hillsides of trees replaced the snow-draped ridges, while the valleys widened into broad meadows painted with purple and yellow flowers. Shim paused only once, to blow on the boughs of an apple tree, showering us with fruit. Unlike Bumbelwy, who hadn't yet regained his appetite, Rhia and I ate the apples avidly.

Shim sped along, so fast that I had only barely noticed the expanding sweep of blue ahead, when his heavy foot splashed into water. In another moment, he was wading through a channel, surrounded by a flock of screeching gulls. His voice boomed, frightening the birds. "I remembers when you carries me across a ragingly river."

"Right!" I shouted to be heard above the wind and screeching gulls. "The crossing was so rough I had to carry you on my shoulder."

"That would be hardly now! Certainly, definitely, absolutely."

Turning my second sight across the channel, I noticed a line of dark hills, as rugged as a row of jagged teeth, on the horizon. The Lost Lands. Well I remembered the words Cairpré had used to describe that territory. *Uncharted and unexplored*. With a deadly dragon sleeping somewhere in those hills, I didn't wonder why. Instinctively, I reached for the hilt of my sword.

Minutes later, Shim stepped out of the channel, his hairy feet slapping on the shore. He set us down on a wide bank of flat rock. No flowers, nor even grasses, sprouted here. Even the glowing light of approaching sunset brought no softer hues to the land. Only a shiny, black ash coated the rocks, stretching to the hillsides far inland. The air reeked of charcoal, like an abandoned fire pit.

I realized that this entire coastline, and everything that once grew on it, must have been scorched by powerful flames. Even the rocks themselves looked cracked and buckled, seared by repeated blasts of extreme heat. Then, scanning the rugged hills, I found the source: a thin curl of smoke rising from a hollow not far inland.

"That's where we're going," I declared.

Shim bent his worried face so low that his chin almost touched the top of my staff. "Is you certainly? Nobody goes to visit a dragon on purposely."

"I do."

"You is foolishly! You know that?"

"I know that. Too well, believe me."

The giant's moist eyes blinked. "Then good luck. I misses you. And you, too, sweetly Rhia. I hopes to makes another crossing with you one daily."

Bumbelwy's bells jangled as he wagged his head. "With the

dragon's lair just over there, we probably don't have another day."

With that, Shim straightened his back. He gazed down on us for another moment, then turned and strode straight into the channel. The setting sun, streaking the western sky with lavender and pink, outlined his massive shoulders and head. High above, a pale crescent moon lifted into the sky.

XXVIII

ELIMINATING

Rather than try to approach the lair of the dragon at night, I decided to wait until dawn. While the others slept fitfully on the blackened rocks, I sat awake, thinking. For the sixth lesson, the lesson of Eliminating, could mean only one thing.

I must slay the dragon.

My stomach knotted at the very thought. How could one boy, even a boy armed with a magical sword, possibly accomplish such a thing? Dragons, as I knew from my mother's stories, were incredibly powerful, astonishingly quick, and supremely clever. I recalled the night when, her face aglow from the fire in our earthen hut, she had described one dragon who destroyed a dozen giants with a single swipe of his tail, then roasted them for supper with his fiery breath.

How, then, was I to succeed? Unlike the wizard Tuatha, I knew none of the magic that might help. I knew only that, asleep or not, a dragon would be terrifying to approach, and nearly impossible to eliminate.

As the first rays of sunlight touched the charred shoreline, spreading like fire across the waves, I reluctantly stood. My hands felt cold, as did my heart. I pulled one of Shim's apples from the pocket of my tunic and took a bite. Crisp and flavorful though it was, I hardly tasted it. When nothing but the core remained, I tossed it aside.

Rhia sat up. "You didn't sleep at all, did you?"

I merely gazed at the jagged line of hills, now brushed with pink. "No. And I don't have even a hint of a plan to show for it. If you have any sense, stay here. If I survive, I'll come back for you."

She shook her head, so vigorously that some of the leaves en-meshed in her brown curls tumbled to the ground. "I thought we discussed that already. Back at the Lake of the Face."

"But this time the risks are too great. Rhia, you've been warning me ever since the Dark Hills that I could get lost. Well, the truth is there is more than one way to be lost. And that's how I feel right now." I blew a long, slow breath. "Don't you see? Only a wizard, a true wizard, can defeat a dragon! I don't know what it takes to be a wizard, really—strength, or skill, or spirit. Cairpré said it's all that and more. All I know is that whatever it takes, I don't have it."

Rhia's face pinched. "I don't believe it. And neither does your mother."

"For all your instincts, this time you're wrong." I glanced at Bum-belwy, huddled under his thick cloak. "Should I give him the same choice as I gave you?"

The lanky jester suddenly rolled over. "I'm coming, if that's what you mean." He stretched his long arms. "If ever you needed my wit and good humor, it's now, on the day of your certain death."

With an expression as somber as one of Bumbelwy's own, I turned toward the hills. From one of the wedgelike hollows between them rose a dark column of smoke. It twisted skyward, marring the sunrise. I took a step toward it. Then another. And another. At each step, the base of my staff clicked on the rocks like a door snapping shut.

Across the scorched land I marched, with Rhia by my side and Bumbelwy not far behind. Knowing that stealth was essential, we tried to tread as softly as foxes. No one spoke. I rested my staff on my shoulder to keep it from striking the rocks. The jester even clamped his hands over his hat to muffle his bells. As we drew nearer to the smoking hollow, my feeling of foreboding deepened. While the dragon might wait for Fincayra's darkest day to wake, my own darkest day had certainly arrived.

A low, roaring sound reached us across the blackened flats. Deep as the bass strings of a titanic harp. Regular as breathing. It was, I knew, the sound of the dragon snoring. It swelled steadily as we approached.

The air grew hot, uncomfortably hot, as the rocks lifted into the charred hills. Pace by pace, keeping quiet, we drew nearer to the column of smoke. Here the rocks had not just been seared by flames, but also pounded and trampled by enormous weight. Boulders had been crushed. Gulleys had been flattened. All living things had been destroyed. Eliminated.

Hardly daring to breathe, we crossed a pile of crushed stone. Suddenly Bumbelwy slipped and fell. Rocks skittered down the pile, smacking into the rubble at the bottom. That sound, however, was obscured by the clamorous banging of his bells. They rang out, echoing among the hills like a clap of thunder.

I glared at him, whispering, "Take off that cursed hat, you clubfooted fool! You'll wake the dragon before we even get there!"

He scowled. Reluctantly, he pulled off his three-cornered hat and stuffed it under his cloak.

I led the way into the steep-walled hollow, wiping my brow from the heat. Even through my boots, the soles of my feet burned. The sweltering air rippled like water, vibrating with the snoring sound. Everything reeked of charcoal. With every step I took, the walls of rock drew closer together, submerging me in darkness.

Suddenly I halted. There, partly shrouded by shadows, lay the dragon. He was even larger than I had feared, as huge as a hillside himself. Coiled like a great serpent, his green and orange body, covered with armored scales, could have almost filled the Lake of the Face. His head, smoke pouring from the nostrils, lay across his left foreleg. Beneath his nose ran a row of scales, so blackened from smoke that they resembled a huge moustache. Every inhale revealed his rows of sharp-edged teeth; every exhale flexed his powerful shoulder muscles and shook the vast wings folded against his back. Claws, as sharp as the sword on my belt but ten times as long, glistened in the early morning light. Midway down one claw, like an oversized ring, sat a skull large enough to have belonged to Shim.

Beneath his scaled belly, treasures gleamed and sparkled. Crowns and necklaces, swords and shields, trumpets and flutes—all crafted of gold or silver, all studded with jewels. Rubies, amethysts, jades, emeralds, sapphires, and huge pearls lay strewn everywhere. Never in my life had I imagined that such a vast hoard existed. Yet I felt no desire whatsoever to comb through it, for scattered throughout were skulls of all sizes and shapes, some gleaming white, others scorched by fire.

I crept deeper into the hollow, with Rhia and Bumbelwy just be-hind. We cringed as one at the slow, roaring rhythm of the dragon's breathing. His enormous eyes were closed, though not completely, revealing slits of smoldering yellow. I couldn't shake the feeling that this beast was as much awake as asleep.

At that instant, the dragon's jaws opened a crack. A thin tongue of flame shot out, scorching the black rocks and some stray skulls. Bumbelwy jumped backward, dropping his bell-draped hat out of his cloak. It hit the rocks at his feet with a jarring clang.

The dragon suddenly snorted and shifted his gargantuan bulk. His eyelids quivered, opening a sliver more. Bumbelwy gasped in fright. His legs wobbled. Seeing that he looked about to faint, Rhia grabbed his arm.

Then, with gruesome slowness, the dragon raised the claw wear-ing the giant skull. Like someone about to eat a rare delicacy, he brought it to his nostrils, savoring its aroma. His eyelids trembled, but did not open, as he released a searing blast of flames. At last, the roasting completed, the dragon's purple lips grasped the skull and tore it from the claw. A loud crunching echoed in the hollow, the sound of enormous teeth reducing the morsel to splinters. With an immense puff of smoke, the dragon resumed snoring.

The three of us shuddered in unison. Glancing grimly at Rhia, I handed her my staff. At the same time, I lay my right hand on the silver hilt of my sword. Slowly, ever so slowly, I drew it from the scabbard. As it emerged, the blade rang faintly, like a distant chime. The sleeping dragon suddenly growled, releasing a puff of thick smoke from his nostrils. His pointed ears pricked forward, listening to the ringing sound. Meanwhile, his dream seemed to alter. He growled viciously, bared his teeth, and slashed at the air with his claws.

I stood as rigid as a statue. My arm began to ache from holding the heavy sword above my head, but I dared not lower it for fear it would make another sound. After several minutes, the dragon seemed to relax a little. The growling subsided, and the claws fell still.

Cautiously, I crept forward on the rocks, taking one small step at a time. The dragon towered over me, each of his scales as big as my entire body. Perspiration stung my eyes. *If I have only one blow, where to strike?* Those armored scales covered his chest, legs, back, tail, and even his orange ears. Perhaps, if I ran the sword through one of the closed eyes, that might do it.

Closer and closer I edged. The smoky air made me want to cough, but I did all I could to resist. My hand squeezed the hilt.

All at once, the tail lashed out like a monstrous whip. I had no time even to move, let alone to run. As the tail exploded to its full length, one of the barbs at the end coiled tightly around my chest, squeezing the air out of my lungs. In the same instant, the other barb wound around my arm holding the sword, preventing me from moving it at all.

I was totally helpless.

Rhia released a muffled shriek. I felt the dragon tense again, squeezing me all the harder. Yet the yellow slits of his eyes opened no wider. He seemed to be still asleep, or half asleep. And, judging from the curl of his lips, he seemed to be about to enjoy a thoroughly realistic dream about swallowing a boy with a sword.

At the edge of my second sight, I watched Rhia fall to her knees. Bumbelwy knelt awkwardly beside her. His head hung low on his paunchy chins. Then, unaccountably, he started to sing. It was, I soon realized, a funeral dirge, sung in low, moaning tones. As much as I squirmed in the dragon's grip, I squirmed still more at his words:

> *A dragon savors all he eats*
> *But values best the living treats*
> *Who squirm and squeal before they die,*
> *The filling of a dragon's pie.*

> *O dragon, 'tis my friend you eat!*
> *Alas, how sweet the dragon's meat.*

> *The dragon's loves the crunch of bones*
> *And all the dying cries and groans*
> *Of people gone without a trace,*
> *Into deep digestive space.*

> *O dragon, 'tis my friend you eat!*
> *Alas, how sweet the dragon's meat.*

> *My friend, in dragon's mouth interred,*
> *Was even robbed his final word.*
> *For down he went into that hole,*
> *His parting sentence swallowed whole.*

> *O dragon, 'tis my friend you eat!*
> *Alas, how sweet the dragon's meat.*

Even before Bumbelwy had finished, the dragon's jaws opened. I watched, aghast, as the rows of jagged teeth, charred by flames, revealed themselves. With all my strength, I struggled to escape. But the tail only squeezed harder. The jaws, meanwhile, opened wider.

Suddenly, out of the depths behind the open jaws came a gruff, hoarse sound that could be only one thing. A laugh. A deep, belching, hearty laugh. A billowing cloud of smoke came as well, blackening the air. The laugh continued, rolling right down the dragon's serpentine form, shaking first his head, then his neck, then his gigantic belly, then finally his tail. Before long, the entire beast quaked in raucous laughter, swaying on his hoard of treasures.

The tail released me. I dropped to the ground, breathless, dazed, but alive. Quickly, I crawled through the black cloud, dragging my sword. A moment later, Rhia ran to my side and helped me to my feet.

Coughing from the smoke, we stumbled out of the hollow. Behind us, the dragon's coarse laughter began to grow quieter. In a matter of seconds, his roaring snores had returned. I glanced back to see the thin slits of his eyes shining in the shadows. When at last we were well away from the dragon's lair, we collapsed on a bench of black rock. Rhia threw her arms around my neck. So different from the embrace of the dragon!

I squeezed her in return. Then I turned to Bumbelwy. In a hoarse voice I declared, "You did it, you know. You made the dragon laugh."

Bumbelwy's head drooped. "I know. A terrible, terrible thing. I am humiliated. Devastated."

"What do you mean?" I shook him by the shoulders. "You saved me!"

"Terrible," repeated the dour jester. "Just terrible. Once again I botched the delivery! I was singing one of my saddest, most sorrowful hymns. One that should break anyone's heart." He bit his lip. "But what did it do instead? Tickled him. Entertained him. When I try to amuse, I sadden, and when I try to grieve, I amuse! Oh, I'm a failure. A miserable failure."

He sighed morosely. "And to make matters worse, I've lost my hat. My jester's hat! So on top of not sounding like a jester, now I don't even look like one."

Rhia and I traded amused glances. Then, without further delay, I pulled off one of my boots.

Bumbelwy watched me gloomily. "Injure your foot, did you?"

"No. I have a promise to keep."

With that, I sunk my teeth into the leather tongue of the boot. I ripped a section loose and chewed vigorously. No amount of chewing could soften the leather, though it did fill my mouth with the flavors of dirt, grass, and perspiration. With great difficulty, I swallowed.

Bumbelwy suddenly caught his breath. He straightened his back slightly. His downturned chins lifted a notch. He was not smiling, nor even grinning. But, at least for a moment, he was no longer frowning.

As I began to take another bite, he laid his hand on my back. "Hold there. One bite is enough. You may need that boot for another purpose." An odd, muffled sound, almost like a smothered giggle, erupted from his throat. "I really did make him laugh, didn't I?"

"Indeed you did."

The frowns returned. "I doubt I could do it again, though. Just a fluke."

Slipping on my boot, I shook my head. "It was no fluke. You could do it again."

Thrusting out his chest, Bumbelwy stood before me. "Then when you go back into that smoking oven to try to slay that beast, I will go with you."

"As will I," declared Rhia.

I looked at their loyal faces for a moment, then slid my sword back into the scabbard. "You won't have to." I leaned closer on the scorched rock. "You see, I'm not going to slay the dragon."

Both of them stared at me. Raising the staff, Rhia asked, "You have to do it, don't you? How else can you learn the first lesson of Eliminating?"

I reached for the gnarled shaft of hemlock, spinning it slowly in my hand. "I think, perhaps, I already have."

"What?"

Fingering the staff's knotty top, I glanced toward the shadowed lair. "Something happened to me when the dragon laughed."

"Right," agreed Bumbelwy. "You broke free of his tail."

"No, I mean something else. Did you hear how full and hearty that laugh was? It made me feel that, well, as vicious and bloodthirsty as the dragon is, he couldn't be completely evil. Or else . . . he couldn't laugh like that."

Bumbelwy looked at me as if I had lost my mind. "I'll wager that dragon has laughed every time he has destroyed a village."

I nodded. "Perhaps so. But something about his laugh gave me the feeling that, somehow, he isn't so completely different from you and me. That he has some worth. Even if we don't comprehend it."

Rhia almost smiled.

Bumbelwy, though, furrowed his brow. "I don't understand what this has to do with Eliminating."

Lifting my right hand, smudged with charcoal, I touched the lids of my sightless eyes. "You see these eyes? Useless. Scarred forever, like my cheeks. And do you know why? Because I tried to destroy another boy's life! I don't know whether or not he survived, but I doubt it. I tried to eliminate him."

His brow wrinkled still more. "I still don't understand."

"The point is this. Eliminating is sometimes necessary. But it comes only at a price. It may be to your body. Or to your soul. But the price is always there. Because *every living thing is precious somehow.*"

The shaft of my staff sizzled with a blast of blue light. Where bare wood had been before, there was now the image of a dragon's tail.

"The sixth Song is done!" exclaimed Rhia. "Now you have only one left, the Song of Seeing."

Tapping the top of the staff, I examined the dragon's tail, etched not far from the glowing star within a circle. Shifting my gaze to the lifeless stretch of coastline, as blackened and burned as the inside of a fire pit, I viewed the deep blue channel and the distant peaks of Varigal beyond. "There may be only one Song left, but there are only a few days left, too."

Bumbelwy slumped lower. "No more than three, judging from the moon last night."

"And we need to get all the way to the Forgotten Island and back."

"Impossible," declared the jester. He shook his head for emphasis until he remembered that he no longer wore any bells. "Merlin, you have done well, impossibly well, to get this far. But you, like the rest of us, caught a glimpse of that place from the cliffs of the treelings. No one in living memory has ever gone to the Forgotten Island! How can you hope to find your way there and back in only three days?"

I tried to imagine the route we would need to travel—across water, over peaks, through forests, and past whatever barriers of enchantment shielded the Island. The entire breadth of Fincayra, full of untold dangers. Sadly, I turned to Rhia. "For once, I am afraid, Bumbelwy's right. This time, we don't have the wind, or a giant, to help us."

Rhia stomped her foot on the charred rock. "I'm not giving up. We've come too far! You have six of the seven Songs. And I even have the location of the Otherworld Well."

I jumped to my feet. "You have *what?*"

"The location of the stairwell. Where Balor stands guard." She ran a hand through her hair, twisting some curls in her fingers. "Gwri of the Golden Hair gave it to me—sent a vision of it right into my mind—when she told us the Otherworld Well wasn't far from the dragon's lair."

"Why didn't you tell me?"

"She told me not to! She thought you might be tempted to skip the Forgotten Island entirely."

Slowly, I sat down again on the bench of black rock. Putting my nose almost to hers, I spoke softly but firmly. "That is exactly what we're going to do."

"You can't!" she protested. "You'll need to find the soul of Seeing before you stand any chance at all against Balor. Don't you remember the words you found in Arbassa?

> *But lo! Do not attempt the Well*
> *Until the Songs are done.*
> *For dangers stalk your every step,*
> *With Balor's eye but one.*

"You'll die for sure if you try to fight Balor without all seven of the Songs."

My stomach knotted as I recalled Tuatha's own warning to me. *Heed well my words, young colt! Without all seven Songs, you shall lose more than your quest. You shall lose your very life.*

I cleared my throat. "But Rhia, if I don't drop the seventh Song, my mother will surely die! Don't you see? It's our only hope. Our only chance."

Her eyes narrowed. "There's something more, isn't there? I can feel it."

"No. You're wrong."

"I am not. You're afraid of something, aren't you?"

"Those instincts again!" My hands closed into fists. "Yes, I am afraid. Of the lesson on Seeing. It frightens me more than all the others combined. I don't know why, Rhia."

Shaking her head, she leaned back against the charred rock. "Then whatever awaits you on the Forgotten Island is important. You must go there, Merlin. For you as well as for Elen! And there's another reason, too."

"Another?"

"Gwri told me something else. She said that while you are on the Forgotten Island you must find a bough of mistletoe. Wear it, she said, when you enter the Otherworld Well. It will help you make your way safely to the realm of Dagda. Without it, your task will be much harder."

"My task could not be any harder as it is! Please, Rhia. No bough of mistletoe is going to make enough difference to justify using up what little time is left. You must help me. Show me the way to the Otherworld Well."

She scuffed her boot of woven bark on the blackened rock.

"Well . . . if I do, and you somehow survive, will you promise to do something?" Her eyes grew suddenly moist. "Even if I'm not around to hold you to your promise?"

I swallowed. "Of course I will. And why wouldn't you be around?"

"Never mind that." She blinked back her tears. "Promise me that, if you should survive, you will one day go to the Forgotten Island and learn whatever it is you're meant to learn there."

"I promise. And I'm going to take you with me."

She stood abruptly, scanning the bleak ridges. "Then let's go. We have some hard trekking ahead of us."

PART THREE

XXIX

THE FINAL
TREK

Wordlessly, Rhia led us deeper into the wasteland of rubble. Somewhere on these ridges lay the entrance to the spirit world—and the deadly ogre who guarded it. Yet if Balor indeed lived here, he lived without the company of anything that breathed or sprouted or moved. For where the Dark Hills had seemed devoid of life, except for the occasional withered tree, these hills seemed utterly hostile to life. The dragon's fiery blasts had not left a single tree, nor shrub, nor clump of moss anywhere. Only charcoal. I wished that I still carried the Flowering Harp on my shoulder, and that I might use its magic to bring even a few blades of grass to these slopes.

No landscape could have been more different from Rhia's home in the lush glades of Druma Wood. Yet she moved with as much confidence and grace over the piles of scorched rocks as she would have moved through groves of scented ferns. She headed due east, never veering. If staying on course meant scrambling straight up a crumbling rock fall, or leaping over a deep crevasse, then that was where she led us. Hour after hour.

Still, as much as I admired her endurance, I admired some of her other qualities even more. She loved life, and all living things, true to her childhood in the boughs of a great oak tree. She carried with her a quiet, soulful wisdom, reminding me of the tales of the Greek goddess Athena. And, even more, of my own mother.

I felt a surge of gratitude that Rhia had allowed her life to entwine with my own, wrapping us together as tightly as the woodland vines of her garb. And I found myself appreciating as never before the virtues of her garb itself. The tight yet flexible weave around her elbows. The broad green leaves across her shoulders. The playful designs along her collar.

As we trekked over the desolate ridges, her suit of woven vines lifted my spirits, if only a little. Its very greenness somehow gave me hope that even the bleakest lands might be coaxed again to flower, that even the gravest fault might one day be forgiven. For, as Rhia herself knew well, those woven vines held a surprising truth. No wizard's magic, however impressive, could be greater than Nature's own magic. How else could a new sapling spring from lifeless soil? And was it possible that I, like every living thing, might actually share in some of that magic of renewal?

Because the ridges lay in parallel lines, running north and south, we couldn't turn down any of the valleys without changing direction. So we climbed up the steep slopes only to plunge immediately down the other sides. We reached the valley floors only to start climbing again. By the time the sun hung low in the sky at our backs, and long shadows fell from the blackened rocks, my knees and thighs wobbled from the strain. Even my staff hardly helped. It was clear from Bumbelwy's constant stumbling, often on the hem of his own cloak, that he felt no sturdier.

Still worse, we found not even a trickle of water. My own tongue felt like a dry sliver of wood inside my mouth. I might have been more thirsty than the others thanks to my bite of boot leather, but probably not much. The long day of trekking over the rubble had left us all parched.

Yet Rhia never slowed down. Though she said nothing, she seemed more grimly determined than ever. Perhaps it was simply the urgency of our quest. Or perhaps it was something else, something that only she knew. In any case, my own mood was no less grim. The voice of Tuatha still thundered in my ears, kindling my fears just as it had kindled the light in the blue stones surrounding his grave. Immensely wise and powerful though he was, he had still lost his life to Balor's deadly gaze. And why? Because of hubris. Wasn't I guilty of the same flaw, daring to confront Balor with only six of the Songs to my name?

Yes—and no. My hubris had spawned this whole mess to begin with. Yet now my actions were driven more by desperation. And also by fear. For Rhia had been right. I was relieved, truly relieved, to have avoided the Forgotten Island and whatever the Song of Seeing might have entailed. That Song haunted me like a terrible dream, as terrible as the one that had made me claw at my own face on that night in the Rusted Plains. I doubted that I could ever find the soul of Seeing, with my useless eyes and limited second sight. And I suspected that to see like a wizard could require something else entirely, something that I surely lacked.

And that was only the beginning of my fears. What if there were no truth to the prophecy that only a child of human blood could defeat Rhita Gawr or his servant Balor? Tuatha himself had hinted as much. *The prophecy may be true, and it may be false. Yet even if it is true, the truth often has more than one face.* Whatever the prophecy might have meant, I certainly couldn't rely on it. The sad truth was, I couldn't even rely on myself.

A loose rock clattered down the slope from above, barely missing the toe of my boot. I looked up to find Rhia disappearing over the top of an outcropping that jutted from the ridge like a chiseled nose. How odd, I thought. With so much of this ridge yet to climb, why had she chosen to go straight over such an outcropping rather than around it?

The answer struck me as I noticed a glint of moisture on the rocks ahead. Water! But from where? The higher I climbed up the outcropping, the more wet patches I discovered. Even a scraggly tuft of moss, alive and green, had rooted itself in the crack between two stones.

When, at last, I reached the top, I stopped short. For there, not ten paces away, bubbled a small spring, forming a clear pool of water. Rhia was already drinking from it. I ran to her side, plunging my whole face into the pool. With the first swallow, my tongue tingled ever so slightly. With the next, it sprang back to life, feeling the slap and sting of coldness. Like Rhia, I drank and drank, filling myself with liquid. Bumbelwy, too, collapsed beside the spring, his slurps and gasps joining with our own.

At last, when I could hold no more, I turned to Rhia. She was sitting with her knees drawn close to her chest, watching the setting sun paint streaks of red and purple across the western sky. Water dripped from her hair onto her shoulders.

I wiped the trickle from my chin and slid a little closer on the rocks. "Rhia, are you thinking about Balor?"

She nodded.

"I saw him in the Lake of the Face," I said. "He was . . . killing me. Making me look into his eye."

She swung her face my way. Though sunset pink glowed in her hair, her eyes looked somber. "I saw Balor in the Lake of the Face, too." She started to say something more, then caught herself.

My throat tightened. "Are we—are we close?"

"Very."

"Should we push on and get there tonight?"

Bumbelwy, who was arranging some rocks so that he could lie down beside the pool, jumped. "No!"

Rhia gave a sigh. "There's almost no moon left, and we need the sleep. We might as well camp here tonight." She felt the rough contours of the charred rocks, then reached for my hand, wrapping her forefinger around my own. "Merlin, I'm afraid."

"So am I." I followed her gaze to the horizon. Above the jagged hills, the sky now loomed as red as blood. "When I was little," I said quietly, "I sometimes felt so afraid that I couldn't sleep. And whenever that happened, my mother would always do the same thing to help me feel better. She would tell me a story."

Rhia's finger squeezed mine tighter. "Did she really? What a wonderful idea, telling a story just to ease someone's fears." She sighed. "Is that the sort of thing a mother does?"

"Yes," I answered softly. "At least a mother like her."

Her head, streaked with red from the sunset, drooped lower. "I wish that I had known . . . my own mother. And that I had heard some of her stories, stories I could remember right now."

"I'm sorry you didn't have that, Rhia." I tried to swallow, but couldn't. "But there is one thing almost as good as hearing stories from your mother."

"Yes?"

"Hearing stories from your friend."

She nearly smiled. "I would love that."

I glanced at the first star shimmering overhead. Then I cleared my throat and began. "Once, long ago, there lived a wise and powerful goddess by the name of Athena."

XXX

BALOR

Night fell cold and dark. Although after my story Rhia had seemed to drift off to sleep, I continued to lie awake, turning over and over on the rocks. For a while I watched the westernmost sky, recalling Gwri of the Golden Hair, but mostly I stared at the ghostly remnant of the waning crescent moon above our heads. In the morning, at most two days would remain.

Throughout the night, I shivered from the chill air of these treeless hills. And from the thought of that merciless eye, whose merest glance meant death. The vision that I had seen in the Lake of the Face stalked me. When I dozed, which wasn't much, I struggled and flailed.

I awoke as the first rays of light touched the rock-strewn slope. No chirping birds or scurrying beasts greeted this dawn. Only wind, howling in long, lonely gusts across the ridges. Stiffly, I stretched, the place between my shoulders throbbing painfully. I bent to the clear pool, which wore a delicate collar of ice, and took a last drink.

Cold, hungry, and grim, we set off. Rhia strode solemnly over the spiky rocks, her bark shoes blackened by charcoal. Wordlessly, she led us in the direction of the sunrise. Yet none of us paused to savor the rich bands of orange and pink that were spreading across the horizon. Absorbed in our own thoughts, we continued to trek in silence. Several times, the loose rocks gave way beneath my feet, sending me sliding backward. Once I fell over, slicing my knee on a rock.

Late that morning, as we reached the top of another slope, Rhia slowed her pace. She halted, casting me a worried glance. Without a word, she raised her arm, pointing to the next ridge. A great gouge split the crest, looking as if the jaws of a mythic beast had clamped down on it ages ago, ripping away the very rocks. Even as I stared at the gouge, it seemed to stare back.

I chewed my lip, certain that the Otherworld Well stood on that spot. Why hadn't the mighty Dagda simply descended from on high and struck Balor down? Surely, as the greatest warrior of all, he could have easily done so. Perhaps Dagda was fully occupied with battling Rhita Gawr himself. Or perhaps he didn't want mere mortals to enter the Otherworld, whatever their reasons.

I took the lead. Rhia stayed at my heels, so close that I could hear her anxious breathing behind me. As we dropped down into the next scorched valley, I found myself scanning the rubble for any sign at all of something green, something living. But no springs bubbled here, no moss filled the cracks. The rocks lay as bare as my own hopes.

Slowly, we climbed toward the great gouge. When at last we reached its very edge, Rhia grabbed the sleeve of my tunic. For several seconds, she probed me with her gaze. Then, her voice a whisper, she spoke her first words of the day.

"The eye. You mustn't look into the eye."

I clasped the hilt of my sword. "I'll do my best."

"Merlin, I wish we'd had a little more . . . time. For sharing days. And sharing secrets."

I furrowed my brow, unsure of what she meant. But there was no time now to find out. Setting my jaw, I handed her my staff. Then I marched into the gouge.

As I stepped between the dark cliffs that rose sharply to either side, I felt as if I were striding into the open mouth of a monster. Pinnacles, as jagged as the dragon's teeth, jutted from the rims of the cliffs. A frigid wind slapped my face, screaming in my ears. As I moved deeper into the gouge, the air quivered ominously, as if shaken by footsteps that I could neither see nor hear.

Yet I found nothing else. But for the jagged, black rocks, shining in the morning light, the place seemed utterly empty. No Balor. No stairwell. No sign of anything living—or dead.

Thinking I might have missed something, I started to turn, when all of a sudden the wind lashed me again. The air before me darkened, then quivered. This time, however, it parted like an invisible curtain. Out of the air itself stepped a huge, muscled warrior, standing at least twice my own size.

Balor! Towering above me, he seemed almost as broad as the cliffs themselves. His deep, wrathful growl echoed within the great gouge, as his heavy boots slammed down on the rocks. Slowly, he lifted his gleaming sword. I caught sight of the horns above his ears, and the dark brow over his one enormous eye, before turning my second sight aside.

I must look at something else. Not his head! The sword. I'll try the sword.

Barely had I focused on his broad, gleaming blade than it clashed against my own. My arm reeled from the powerful blow. To my surprise, the ogre grunted at the impact, as if the magic of my own sword had caught him off guard. Again he growled, then swung his weapon with even more force.

I leaped to the side just as his blade crashed against the rocks where I had stood only a split second before. Sparks flew into the air, singeing my tunic. As if the blurred edges of my second sight weren't enough of a disadvantage, I could not look directly at him for fear of glimpsing his eye. As the ogre raised his arm to strike again, I thrust at him. But he spun away in time. Pivoting with uncanny speed, he charged straight at me, his sword slashing the air.

Caught by surprise, I backed away. Suddenly my heel struck a rock. I hopped backward, trying desperately to keep my balance, but tumbled over in a heap. Balor released a vengeful snarl as he marched toward me, lifting his sword high. It was all I could do to avoid looking into his face, his eye.

At that instant, Rhia sprinted out of the shadows and threw herself at the ogre. She lunged at his leg, holding tight to his thigh. He tried to kick free, but she continued to cling to him. This distracted him just long enough for me to roll to the side and leap to my feet.

Before I could renew the attack, however, Balor roared angrily at Rhia. He seized her by the arm, ripping her loose. Then, roaring again, he whipped her around and hurled her headlong at the cliff wall. Face first, she slammed into the rocks. She staggered backward, then slumped motionless on the ground.

My heart split in two at the sight. Just then Bumbelwy emerged from hiding and ran to her side, waving his arms wildly. Seething with rage, I charged straight at the ogre, swinging my sword while still averting my gaze. Yet Balor sidestepped me with ease. His fist smashed into my shoulder, sending me sprawling. The sword flew out of my hand and clattered on the rocks. I crawled madly after it.

A huge boot kicked me in the chest. I flew through the air and landed with a thud on my back. My ribs screamed with pain. The pinnacles of the cliffs seemed to wobble and whirl above me.

Before I could try to sit up, Balor's immense hand closed around my throat. He squeezed until I gagged. Then, with a sharp jerk, he lifted me into the air. My head swam. I flailed my arms and legs, swaying helplessly. But he only squeezed tighter, throttling me. I pounded on his arm, trying desperately to breathe.

Slowly, he lowered me, until our faces almost touched. His grip tightened. His snarl tore at my ears. Then, pulled by a spell I no longer had the strength to resist, I looked into his dark eye. Like a pit of quicksand, it drew me in.

With all my remaining power, I fought to break free. But I couldn't resist the eye. It pulled me deeper, deeper, sucking out my strength. Darkness shrouded my vision. I felt myself go limp. *I should just give in. Just let go.* I stopped trying to fight, stopped trying to breathe.

Suddenly, I heard Balor roar in agony. He released my throat. I fell onto the rocks, coughing and gasping. Air filled my lungs again. The darkness clung to me for another moment, then faded away.

Weakly, I raised myself up on one elbow, just in time to see Balor collapse on the rocks. He fell with the force of a toppled tree. From his back protruded a sword. My sword. And standing behind him was Rhia, half her face bloody. Her neck bent strangely, as if she couldn't straighten it. Then her own legs gave out and she crumpled next to the fallen ogre.

"Rhia!" I called hoarsely, crawling to her side.

Bumbelwy appeared, looking grimmer than grim. He lifted me by the arm so that I could stand. As I stumbled over to Rhia, I heard him moan, "I told her she'd kill herself if she moved, but she wouldn't listen."

I knelt by her side. Gently lifting her head with my hands, I tried to straighten her neck. Above one ear I found a deep gash. It bled profusely, staining her suit of woven vines, as well as the rocks. Carefully, I sprinkled some of the herbs from my satchel on the wound.

"Rhia. I'll help you."

Her blue-gray eyes opened halfway. "Merlin," she whispered. "This time . . . there's nothing . . . you can do."

"No." I shook my head vigorously. "You're going to be all right."

With difficulty, she swallowed. "It's my time . . . to die. I'm sure. When I looked . . . in the Lake of the Face . . . I saw you fighting Balor . . . and losing. But I . . . also saw . . . one of us dying. It wasn't . . . you. It was . . . me."

Holding her, I tried to pour strength into her head and neck. I tore off the bottom of my sleeve and pressed it against her skin, willing the gash to heal as I had willed her bone to knit itself together in Eagles' Canyon. Yet I knew that these injuries were far more severe than a broken arm. Even the torn vines of her garb seemed to be fading a little with each passing second, their vibrant green showing hints of shadows.

"It doesn't have to be that way, Rhia."

"Oh yes . . . it does. I never told you . . . but I was told . . . a long time ago . . . that my life would be lost . . . to spare yours. That staying with you . . . would mean my own death. I wasn't sure whether to believe it . . . until now."

"What nonsense!" I concentrated harder on the wounds, but the blood continued to flow, soaking the cloth and seeping through my fingers. "What fool ever told you such a thing?"

"No fool. Arb . . . assa. That's why . . . you were never welcome . . . inside the door."

I winced. "You can't die now! Not because of some foolish prophecy!" I bent lower. "Listen to me, Rhia. These prophecies are worthless. Worthless! A prophecy said that only a child of human blood could kill Balor, right? Well, you saw what happened. Balor had me in his death grip. I was helpless—I, the child of human blood! It was you, not me, who killed him."

"That's because . . . I too . . . have human blood."

"What? You're a Fincayran! You're—"

"Merlin." Rhia's eyelids quivered, as the wind wailed beneath the cliffs. "I am . . . your sister."

I felt as if Balor's boot had once again slammed into my ribs. "My what?"

"Your sister." She drew a difficult breath. "Elen is . . . my mother, too. That's another reason . . . I had to come."

I pounded the black rocks with my fist. "It can't be true."

"It is true," declared Bumbelwy. He bent his lanky frame to kneel beside me. "When Elen of the Sapphire Eyes gave birth to you in a wrecked ship somewhere on our shores, she also gave birth, a few minutes later, to a daughter. She named the boy Emrys, and the girl Rhiannon. The bards of Fincayra all know that story."

His glum sigh melted into the wind. "And also the story of how that daughter was lost as an infant. Her parents were traveling through Druma Wood when they were attacked by a band of warrior goblins, the soldiers of Rhita Gawr. A fierce battle ensued. The goblins finally scattered. But in the turmoil one of Elen's twins, the girl, was lost. Hundreds of people searched for weeks, without success, until at long last even Elen stopped looking. Heartbroken, all she could do was pray to Dagda that her daughter might someday be found."

Rhia nodded weakly. "And she was. By . . . a treeling. Cwen. It was she . . . who brought me . . . to Arbassa."

"My sister!" Tears welled in my sightless eyes. "You are my sister."

"Yes . . . Merlin."

If the towering cliffs had caved in and crushed me just then, I would have felt no greater pain. I had found my only sibling. And yet, as had happened so many times before, I was about to lose what I had only just found.

Tuatha, I remembered now, had warned me that the prophecy about a child of human blood could have an unexpected meaning. *It may be true, and it may be false. Yet even if it is true, the truth often has more than one face.* How could I possibly have known that it would be the face of Rhia?

"Why," I asked in a quavering voice, "didn't you tell me before?"

"I didn't want . . . you to change . . . your course to try . . . to protect me. What you do . . . with your life . . . is important."

"Your life is just as important!"

I threw away the bloody rag and tore a new piece off my sleeve. Even as I tried to mop the gash, I recalled a night long ago in Cairpré's room full of books. So this was why he had hesitated so strangely in telling me the story of my birth! I had suspected then, and knew now, that he was on the verge of telling me something more. That a sister had been born on that same night.

I cradled Rhia's head in my lap, feeling her warm breath on my arm. Her eyelids had nearly closed. The shadows on her garb deepened. As a tear slid down my cheek, I said, "If only I could have seen."

Her eyelids fluttered. "Seen? Are you talking about . . . your eyes?"

"No, no." I watched the blood dripping from her brown curls. "This isn't about my eyes. It's about something else, something my heart has known all along. That you are, well, more than someone I just happened to meet that day in Druma Wood. My heart knew that from the very start."

She made a slight movement with her lips that could have been a grin. "Even when I . . . hung you up . . . in that tree?"

"Even then! Rhia, my heart could see it, but my head just didn't understand. I should have paid more attention to my heart, I'm telling you! *The heart can see things invisible to the eye.*"

A blue flash erupted from the rocks where Rhia had left my staff. Without even looking, I knew that it bore a new marking, in the shape of an eye. For I had discovered, somehow, the soul of Seeing. Yet my gain paled in comparison to my loss.

In that same instant, the air began to shimmer near the out-stretched arm of the fallen ogre. The invisible curtain parted, re-vealing a low circle of polished white stones. A well. Not a stairwell leading up, but a deep well leading down.

I could see it! And I also understood, for the first time, that the pathway to the Otherworld—to Heaven and also to Hell—meant going down, not up. Down into the very deepest places, not up to somewhere in the universe far removed from myself.

The bitter wind swept over us, howling. Rhia spoke so faintly that I could hardly hear her. "You will be . . . a wizard, Merlin. A . . . good . . . one."

I lifted her head to my chest. "Don't die, Rhia. Don't die."

She shuddered. Her eyes closed at last.

I held her tight, sobbing quietly.

Then, as if the dawn were breaking within my very arms, I sensed the presence of something that I had not noticed before. Something within Rhia's body, yet apart from it as well. Passing through my fingers like a breeze of light. Her spirit. Leaving her body on its way to the realm beyond. In a flash, an idea seized me.

I called to her spirit. *Please, Rhia. Don't leave me. Not yet.* I pulled her head close to my heart. *Come with me. Stay with me. Just for a while.*

I glanced toward the circle of white stones, the entry to the Otherworld. The pathway to Dagda. Even if it were too late for him to save Elen, maybe—just maybe—he could still save Rhia. And, if not, at least we might be together for a little while longer.

Come with me. Please.

I inhaled deeply, drawing far more than air. And with that breath, a powerful new feeling flooded into me. It was vibrant. It was robust. It was Rhia.

I turned to Bumbelwy, whose drooping cheeks showed the streaks of his own tears. "Help me up, will you?"

Solemnly, he eyed me. "She is dead."

"Dead." I felt the new life force within me. "But not gone, my good jester."

With difficulty, Bumbelwy helped me to my feet. In my arms I bore the empty body of Rhia, her head dangling. "Now bring me my sword. And my staff."

Shaking his head, the dour jester pulled the sword out of Balor. He used his boots to wipe the blade clean. Then he gathered up my staff from the rocks. Returning to me, he slid my sword into its scabbard and the staff into my blood-soaked belt.

He studied me somberly. "Where are you going with her?"

"To the Otherworld."

His eyebrows lifted. "Then I will wait here for you. Even though you won't ever return."

I started toward the ring of white stones, then stopped and faced him again. "Bumbelwy, in case I don't return, I want you to know something."

He gave me a many-layered frown. "What is that?"

"You are a terrible jester. But a loyal friend."

With that I turned toward the Well. I strode across the rocks, my arms as heavy as my heart.

XXXI

INTO
THE MIST

A gust of warm air struck my face as I looked into the Otherworld Well. A spiraling stairway, made from the same polished white stones as the entrance, dropped down from the center of the circle. I couldn't tell how far down the stairs went, though I suspected it was far indeed.

Holding Rhia's limp body in my arms, I stepped carefully onto the first step. With a deep breath, perhaps my last, of Fincayran air, I started down the spiral. Downward I plunged, taking care not to stumble. As much as my ribs, throat, and shoulders ached from my battle with Balor, my heart ached still more to be bearing the body of my friend. My sister.

After descending more than a hundred steps, I noticed two surprising things. First, the Well never grew any darker. Unlike it would in a drinking well or tunnel hollowed out of the ground, the light did not diminish at deeper levels. In fact, it seemed to grow stronger somehow. Soon the white stones of the stairs glowed with the luster of pearls.

Second, the spiraling pathway did not need any walls. Only mist, curling and shifting, surrounded the stairs. The deeper I went, the more intricate and tangled the fingers of mist became. Sometimes they would twirl around my legs, or the curls of Rhia's hair. Other times they would condense and twist themselves into strange shapes I could not identify.

The mist of this Well reminded me of the mist surrounding Fincayra's shores. Not so much a boundary, or a barrier, as a living substance possessing its own mysterious rhythms and patterns. Elen had often spoken about *in between* places like Mount Olympus, Y Wyddfa, or Fincayra. Places not quite our world and not quite the Otherworld, but truly *in between*. In the same way that this mist was not really air and not really water, but something of both.

And I thought of the day when, on the dirt floor of our hut in Gwynedd, she had described Fincayra to me for the first time. *A place of many wonders*, she had called it. *Neither wholly of Earth nor wholly of Heaven, but a bridge connecting both.*

As I dropped deeper into the mists, drawing nearer to the Otherworld with every step, I wondered what kind of world it might be. If Fincayra were indeed the bridge, where then did the bridge lead? Spirits lived there, I knew that much. Powerful ones, like Dagda and Rhita Gawr. But what of the simpler, quieter spirits, like my brave friend Trouble? Did they share the same terrain, or did they live elsewhere?

Turning endlessly on itself, the spiral stairway led me downward. It struck me that there might be no difference between day and night in this world. Without the sunrise or sunset, or the moon sailing overhead, it would be difficult to tell time. There might not even *be* any time, or what I would call time. I vaguely remembered Elen saying something about two kinds of time: historical time, which runs in a line, where mortal beings march out their lives, and sacred time, which flows in a circle. Could the Otherworld be a place of sacred time? And if so, did that mean that time there turned in on itself, turning in circles like this spiraling stairway?

I stopped, tapping my boot on one of the steps. If there was a different kind of time in this world, I could return to the surface—if I ever did return—too late to save Elen! I might easily spend my two remaining days, and months besides, without even knowing it. I arched my back, lifting Rhia higher on my arms. Her weight, like the weight of my quest, felt heavier than ever.

All I could do was try to find Dagda as soon as possible. Let nothing delay me or throw me off course. I started again down the stairs.

As I followed the Well deeper, something about the mist began to change. Instead of hovering close to the stairs, as it had near the entrance, the mist pulled farther away, opening into pockets of ever-changing shapes. Before long the pockets expanded into chambers, and the chambers widened into hollows. With each step downward the misty vistas broadened, until I found myself in the middle of an immensely varied, constantly shifting landscape.

A landscape of mist.

In wispy traces and billowing hills, wide expanses and sharp pinnacles, the mist swirled about me. At some points I encountered canyons, cutting into the cloudlike terrain, running farther and deeper than I could guess. At other points I glimpsed mountains, towering in the distance, moving higher or lower or both ways at once. I found misty valleys, slopes, cliffs, and caverns. Scattered throughout, though I couldn't be sure, moved shapes, or half shapes, crawling or striding or floating. And through it all, the mist curled and billowed, always changing, always the same.

In time I discovered that the stairs themselves had changed. No longer stiff and solid like stone, they rippled and flowed with everything around me. Although they remained firm enough to stand on, they were made from the same elusive fiber as the landscape.

An uneasy feeling swelled in me. That what surrounded me was not really mist at all. That it was not even something physical, made from air or water, but something . . . else. Made from light, or ideas, or feelings. This mist revealed more than it obscured. It would take many lifetimes to comprehend even a little of its true nature.

So this was what the Otherworld was like! Layers upon layers of shifting, wandering worlds. I could plunge endlessly deeper on the stairs, move endlessly outward among the billows, or travel endlessly inward in the mist itself. Timeless. Limitless. Endless.

Then, out of the flowing landscape, a shape appeared.

XXXII

A GOLDEN BOUGH

Small and gray, the shape rose aloft from a burgeoning hill. As I watched, it spread two misty wings. It sailed toward me, floating on a current, then suddenly changed direction, climbing so steeply that I almost lost sight of it. Abruptly, it veered and plunged straight downward, until it spun into a series of loops and turns that seemed to have no other purpose than the sheer joy of flight.

Trouble!

My heart leaped to watch the hawk fly again. Although my arms were wrapped around Rhia, I could still feel the leather satchel against my hip. Within it, along with my mother's herbs, rested a banded brown feather from one of Trouble's wings. Nothing more had remained of him after his battle with Rhita Gawr. Nothing, that is, save his spirit.

Out of the billowing mists he came soaring to me. I heard his screech, as full of spunk and vigor as ever. I watched his final flying swoop as he approached. Then, with a rush of warm air, I felt his talons grab hold of my left shoulder. He folded his wings upon his back, prancing up and down my shoulder. Though his misty feathers had changed from brown to silver gray, streaked with white, a touch of yellow still rimmed his eyes. He cocked his head toward me and gave a satisfied chirp.

"Yes, Trouble! I'm happy to see you, too." Then my moment of gladness vanished as I hefted the limp, bloodstained body in my arms. "If only Rhia could, as well."

The hawk fluttered down to the leaf-draped girl's knee. He studied her for a moment, then piped a low, somber whistle. With a shake of his head, he leaped back up to my shoulder.

"I carry her spirit within me, Trouble. I'm hoping that Dagda might still be able to save her." I swallowed. "And also my mother."

Suddenly, Trouble gave a loud shriek. His talons squeezed my shoulder, even as the mist before me billowed strangely.

"Ahhh," said a slow, almost lazy voice from somewhere in the mist. "How nice, how terribly nice, of you to come."

Trouble whistled anxiously.

"Who are you?" I called into the clouds. "Show yourself."

"I intend to do just that, young man, in a moment's time." The mist before me swirled like soup in a gently stirred bowl. "And I also have a gift for you, a terribly precious gift. Ahhh, yes."

Something about the voice's slow, relaxed tones made me feel a bit more at ease. Yet a vague sensation, from someplace within me, made me feel more cautious than ever. Better, I decided, to err on the side of caution.

I adjusted Rhia's weight in my arms. "I haven't time for manners right now. If you have something to give me, then show yourself."

"Ahhh, young man. So impatient, so terribly impatient." The mist churned. "But you needn't worry. I shall heed your request, in just a moment's time. You see, I'd like to be your friend."

At that, Trouble gave a shrill whistle. With a powerful flap of his wings, he lifted off from his perch. He whistled again, circled me once, and flew off, disappearing in a cloud of mist.

"You have no need to fear me," murmured the voice. "Even though your hawk friend certainly seems to."

"Trouble doesn't fear anything."

"Ahhh, then I must be mistaken. Why do you think he flew away?"

I swallowed, peering into the flowing mist. "I don't know. He must have had a good reason." I turned back to the spot from which the voice seemed to come. "If you'd like to be my friend, then show me who you are. Quickly. I need to keep going."

The mist bubbled slowly. "Ahhh, so you have an important meeting, have you?"

"Very."

"Well then, that is what you must do. Ahhh, yes." The voice sounded so relaxed as to be sleepy. "I'm sure you know how to get wherever you're going."

Instead of answering, I searched the billowing mist for Trouble. Where had he gone? We had only just met again! And I'd hoped that he might be able to lead me to Dagda.

"Because if you don't," continued the soothing voice, "my gift may be useful to you. Terribly useful. Ahhh, I offer you the gift of serving as your guide."

That feeling of caution, from whatever source, rose in me again. Yet . . . perhaps this person, when he finally revealed himself, could really show me the way through the swirling clouds. It could save precious time.

I shifted my weight on the misty step. "Before I can accept your offer, I need to know who you are."

"In a moment's time, young man. In a moment's time." The voice yawned, then spoke as gently as the wisps of mist that brushed against my cheek. "Young people are in such a hurry, such a great hurry."

Despite my doubts, something about the voice made me feel increasingly relaxed. Almost . . . comfortable. Or maybe I was just feeling tired. My back ached. I wished I could set Rhia down somewhere. Just for a moment.

"Ahhh, you bear a heavy burden, young man." Another agonizingly slow yawn. "Would you allow me to lighten your load just a little?"

Against my will, I too yawned. "I'm fine, thank you. But if you'd like to guide me to Dagda, I will let you." I caught myself. "First, though, show me who you are."

"To Dagda, is it? Ahhh, the great and glorious Dagda. Warrior of warriors. He lives far, terribly far, from here. Still, I would be pleased to guide you."

I straightened my stiff back. "Can we go now? I'm running out of time."

"Ahhh, in a moment's time." Curling arms of mist swayed before my face. "It's a pity, though, you can't take a little rest. You look as if you could use one."

Still holding Rhia, I crouched down, resting her on my thighs. "I wish I could. But I must get going."

"Whatever you say. Ahhh, yes." The voice gave the longest, sleepiest yawn yet. "We shall leave directly. In a moment's time."

I shook my head, which felt strangely clouded. "Good. Now . . . you were going to do something first. What was it? Oh, yes. Show yourself. Before I follow you."

"Why, of course, young man. I am almost ready." The voice heaved a slow, relaxed sigh. "It will be pleasing, terribly pleasing, to help you."

The feeling of caution nudged me again, but I ignored it. I moved the arm that had supported Rhia's thighs, resting my hand on a damp step. I wondered how it might feel to sit down, if only briefly. Surely a little rest couldn't hurt.

"That's right, young man," purred the voice in its most soothing tone. "Just let yourself relax."

Relax, I thought dreamily. *Just let myself relax.*

"Ahhh, yes." The voice sighed sleepily. "You are a wise young man. So much wiser than your father."

I nodded, feeling half dazed. *My father. Wiser than . . .*

The feeling of caution surged through me. How did he know my father?

I yawned again. Why worry about my father now? He wasn't anywhere near the Otherworld. My head felt foggy, as if the mist surrounding me had somehow flowed into my ears. What was I in such a hurry about, anyway? A little rest would help me remember. Crouching on the stairs, I lowered my head against my chest.

Once again, so weakly that I could barely detect it, the feeling of caution pricked me. *Wake up, Merlin! He's not your friend. Wake up.* I tried to ignore it, but couldn't quite do so. *Trust in your instincts, Merlin.*

I stirred, raising my head slightly. There was something familiar about that feeling, that voice inside me. As if I had heard it somewhere before.

Trust in your instincts, Merlin. Trust in the berries.

With a sudden jolt, I awoke. It was Rhia's voice! Rhia's wisdom! Her spirit was sensing what I was not. I shook the fog from my head.

Taking my hand from the step, I wrapped it tightly around Rhia's legs. With a grunt, I slowly stood up again.

"Ahhh, young man." An edge of concern had crept into the sleepy voice. "I thought you might rest a little while."

Clutching Rhia firmly in my arms, the leaves drying but still soft against my hands, I drew a deep breath. "I am not going to rest. I am not going to let you lull me into enchanted sleep. For I know who you are."

"Ahhh, you do?"

"Yes I do, Rhita Gawr!"

The mist started to froth like a boiling pot. It bubbled and whirled before me. Out of the swirling vapors stepped a man, as tall and broad as Balor, wearing a flowing white tunic and a thin necklace of gleaming red stones. His hair, as black as my own, lay perfectly combed on his head. Even his eyebrows looked exquisitely groomed. It was his eyes, though, that caught my attention. They seemed utterly hollow, as vacant as the void. As much as the memory of Balor's deadly eye made me shudder, these eyes frightened me more.

Rhita Gawr lifted one hand to his lips and licked the tips of his fingers. "I could have taken any number of forms." His voice, harsh and snapping, held none of the lazy tones I had heard before. "The wild boar is one of my favorites, complete with the scarred foreleg. We all carry scars, you know."

He stroked one eyebrow with his wet fingers. "But you have seen the wild boar before, haven't you? Once on the shore of that rock pile you call Gwynedd. And once again, in a dream."

"How . . . " Perspiration formed on my brow as I recalled the dream, and the feeling of daggerlike tusks growing into my very eyes. "How do you know about that?"

"Oh, come now. Surely a would-be sorcerer has learned at least a little about Leaping." He licked his fingertips, as his lips curled in a smirk. "Sending dreams to people is one of my few amusements, a brief distraction from my many labors." The smirk expanded. "Though there is something I enjoy even more. Sending the death shadow."

I tensed, squeezing Rhia's lifeless form. "What gave you the right to strike down my mother?"

Rhita Gawr's vacant eyes fixed on me. "What gave you the right to bring her to Fincayra?"

"I didn't mean . . . "

"A little touch of hubris." He ran his hand over his scalp, patting the hairs into place. "That was your father's fatal flaw, and your grandfather's as well. Did you really expect to be any different?"

I straightened up. "I am different."

"Hubris again! I thought you would have learned by now." The white tunic fluttered as he took a step toward me. "Hubris will bring your death, that is certain. It has already brought your mother's."

I reeled, staggering on the misty step. "That's why you delayed me all this time!"

"But of course." He licked his fingertips with care, one at a time. "And now that you know you have failed to prevent her death—the death that you yourself brought on—I shall relieve you of any further misery. I shall kill you, here and now."

I backed up one step, trying not to stumble.

Rhita Gawr laughed, while he stroked his other eyebrow. "Your hero, Dagda, isn't here to save you this time, as he did on Gwynedd. Nor is that fool bird, whose rashness prevented me from finishing you off at the Shrouded Castle. This time, I have you."

He took another step through the mist toward me. His enormous hands flexed, as if they were preparing to crush my skull. "Just so you know the extent of your folly, your hubris, let me explain something to you. If only you hadn't tried to avoid your lessons, you might know that if only you had worn a mantle of mistletoe, that cursed golden bough, you could have traveled straight to Dagda's lair. I could not have waylaid you as I have."

I blanched, remembering Rhia's plea to take a bough of mistletoe with me to the Otherworld. And I had dismissed her advice out of hand!

Once again Rhita Gawr smirked. Arms of mist, sprouting out of his head, clawed at me. "I do so love arrogance. One of humanity's most endearing qualities."

His hollow eyes narrowed. "So much for your lessons. Now you shall die."

At that instant, a winged shape shot out of the clouds. A screech echoed across the shifting landscape of mist, even as Trouble soared straight at me. Behind him he trailed a loose, flowing bough of gold. Mistletoe. Rhita Gawr roared with rage and leaped at me.

Only a fraction of a second before he could seize me, the golden bough fell over my shoulders like a cape. I felt his powerful hands closing on my throat. Suddenly, I became vapor, dissolving into the mist. The last thing I felt was a pair of talons grasping my shoulder. And the last thing I heard was the wrathful cry of Rhita Gawr.

"You have escaped me once again, you runt of a wizard! You will not be so fortunate next time."

XXXIII

WONDROUS THINGS

Skin, bone, and muscles dissolved. Instead, I consisted of air, water, and light. Plus something more. For now I belonged to the mist.

Rolling like a cloud of vapor, I stretched my limitless arms before me. As the golden bough of mistletoe propelled me along the hidden pathways to Dagda's home, I swirled and swayed, melting into the air even as I moved beyond it. Through the spiraling tunnels and twisting corridors of mist I flew. And while I couldn't see them, I could sense that Trouble and Rhia, in whatever form, traveled with me.

Too many times to count, I glimpsed other landscapes and creatures within the vapors. Boundless variety seemed to inhabit each and every particle of mist. Worlds within worlds, levels within levels, lives within lives! The Otherworld, in all its vastness and complexity, beckoned.

Yet I had no time now to explore. Elen's life, and Rhia's as well, hung in the balance. I might have lost my chance to help one or both of them, thanks to my own supreme folly. Even so, as Rhia herself had declared when my staff vanished in Slantos, *as long as you still have hope, you still have a chance*. And hope remained with me, though it seemed no more substantial than the shifting clouds.

My thoughts, rolling like the very mist, turned to Dagda. I felt a deep pang of fear at the prospect of facing the greatest of all the spirits. While I expected that he would judge me harshly for my many mistakes, would he also refuse to help? Perhaps saving my mother's life would disturb some delicate cosmic balance that only he understood. Perhaps he would simply not have time to see me. Perhaps he would not be in his realm at all when I arrived, and instead be somewhere far away, in this misty world or another, battling the forces of Rhita Gawr.

I wondered what so powerful a spirit would look like. Surely, like Rhita Gawr, he could assume any form he chose. When he had appeared on the day I washed ashore on the coast of Gwynedd, he had come as a stag. Immense, powerful, with a great rack of antlers. What had struck me the most, though, were his eyes. Those brown, unblinking pools had seemed as deep and mysterious as the ocean itself.

Whatever form he might take, I knew it would be as strong and imposing as Dagda himself. A stag in human form, perhaps. What had Rhita Gawr called him? *The great and glorious Dagda. Warrior of warriors.*

Like a cloud flowing into a hollow in the hills, my forward motion slowed, little by little, until finally it stopped. Then, imperceptibly at first, the mist around me started to dissipate. Slowly, very slowly, it thinned and shredded, pulling apart like a wispy veil. Gradually, I could discern the outline of a tall, towering form behind the veil. Dark and brooding, it hovered before me.

All at once, the remaining mist melted away. The towering form, I realized, was actually an enormous, dew-coated tree. As tall and mighty as Arbassa it stood, with one prominent difference.

This tree stood upside down. Its massive roots reached upward, disappearing into the tangled threads of mist. They curled majestically around the clouds, as if they embraced the entire world above. From these soaring roots hung countless boughs of golden mistletoe, swaying gracefully. Down below, at the base of the trunk, burly branches stretched across a wide plain of steaming mist. And the entire tree, covered with thousands upon thousands of dewdrops, sparkled like the surface of a dancing stream.

So captivated was I by the sight of the tree that it took me a moment to realize that I, too, stood on the misty plain. My body had returned! Rhia slumped in my arms, while Trouble made soft, gurgling sounds in my ear. A bough of mistletoe, just like the ones dangling above me, draped over my shoulders. My sword hung at my side, while the staff still rode under my belt.

I looked into Trouble's yellow-rimmed eyes. "Thanks, my friend. You saved me once again."

The hawk released a high, almost embarrassed whistle and fluttered his gray wings.

"Welcome to the Tree of Soul."

I spun to face the source of the weak, unsteady voice. It came from a frail, old man, whose right arm dangled uselessly at his side. Although he sat on the floor of mist, leaning against the branches, he was so small and slight that I had not noticed him at all before. His silver hair glistened like the dew-covered bark around him.

"Thank you. Very much." I spoke stiffly, not wanting to be fooled again. Still, with time so scarce, I had no choice but to be direct. "I am looking for Dagda."

Trouble's talons pinched my shoulder. He squawked at me reproachfully.

The old man smiled gently, soft lines crinkling his face. Laying his withered arm across his lap, he studied me intently.

Suddenly I noticed his eyes. Deep, brown pools, full of compassion, wisdom, and sadness. I had seen them before. On the great stag.

"Dagda." I bit my lip, gazing at the frail, little man. "I am sorry I didn't recognize you."

The elder's smile faded. "You did, in time. Just as you may, in time, come to know the true source of my power. Or do you already?"

I hesitated, unsure how to respond. "I know nothing, I'm afraid, about your power's true source. But I believe that you use it to help living things take their own course, whatever that may be. That's why you helped me on the day I washed ashore."

"Very good, Merlin, very good." His brown eyes sparkled with satisfaction—and a touch of annoyance. "Even if you did try to avoid one of the Songs."

I shifted uncomfortably.

He examined me, as if he could see into my deepest heart of hearts. "You carry a great load, in addition to the friend in your arms. Here. Lay her down beside me."

"Can you—can you help her?"

"We shall see." His brow, already webbed with wrinkles, creased some more. "Tell me of the Songs, Merlin. Where does the soul of each lie?"

"And my mother? If she has any time left, it isn't much."

"She, too, must wait."

Stooping on the vaporous ground, I gently laid the body of my sister beside Dagda. Curls of mist flowed over her shoulders and across her chest, covering her like a wispy blanket. He glanced at her, looking profoundly sad, then returned his gaze to me.

"First. Show me your staff."

Trouble clucked with admiration as I drew the staff out of my belt. I held the knotted top toward Dagda, twirling the shaft slowly. All of the markings, as deep blue as the dusk, gleamed before us. The butterfly, symbol of transformation. The pair of hawks, bound together in flight. The cracked stone, reminding me of the folly of trying to cage the light flyer. The sword, whose name I knew well. The star inside a circle, calling back the luminous laughter of Gwri of the Golden Hair. The dragon's tail, which somehow reminded my tongue of the taste of soiled leather. And, last of all, the eye, so different from Balor's, yet in its own way just as terrifying.

Dagda nodded. "You carry a sword now, I see."

I patted the silver hilt.

"Guard it well, for the destiny of that sword is to serve you until the time comes for you to place it into a scabbard of stone. Then it shall pass to a boy, no older than you are now. A boy born to be king, whose reign shall thrive in the heart long after it has withered on the land."

"I will guard it well."

"Tell me now, my son. What melodies have you heard within the Seven Songs? Start with the first one, Changing."

I cleared my throat. "I learned from a butterfly—and from a traitor, a treeling, who redeemed herself—that all of us, all living things, have the potential to change."

The old man studied me intently. "It is no accident that this was your first Song, Merlin. I believe you have been hearing its strains for some time."

"Yes." I looked into the dewy boughs for a moment. "I see now why the Greek words for butterfly and soul are the same."

"Good. Now tell me about Binding."

I glanced at Rhia's face, pale and still. "The strongest bonds are of the heart. I learned it from watching a pair of hawks soaring together."

Trouble pranced proudly across my shoulder, preening his wings.

"And from a trickster, perhaps?"

I sighed. "That, too."

A shred of mist passed over Dagda's left hand. With a deft twirl of his fingers, he wove the mist into a complex knot. Then, with a pensive nod, he let it drift away.

His gaze returned to me. "Next you found your way into the underground realm of my old friend Urnalda. She is wiser than she appears, I can assure you! No doubt she enjoyed the chance to be your teacher."

I shook my head. "I'm not sure how much. I was a rather slow learner. Eventually, though, with the help of a light flyer, I finally found the soul of that Song."

"Which is?"

I pointed to the image of the cracked stone. "The best way to protect something is to set it free."

Dagda leaned back, gazing upward into the burly roots of the Tree of Soul. As he raised an eyebrow, a curl of mist spiraled up the trunk. "The next lesson, I believe, came as a surprise for you."

"Naming. It took awhile—and a broken bread knife—to teach me that a true name holds true power." I paused, thinking. "Is my true name Merlin?"

The elder shook his silvery head.

"Then would you, perhaps, know my true name?"

"I know it."

"Would you tell me?"

Dagda considered my request for a while. "No. Not yet. But I will do this. If we should meet again at a happier time, when you have won over the most powerful enemy of all, then I will tell you your true name."

I blanched. "The most powerful enemy of all? You must mean Rhita Gawr."

"Perhaps." He pointed to the star within a circle. "Now Leaping."

"That's an amazing skill. The Grand Elusa used it to send us all the way to the land of the treelings. Gwri of the Golden Hair used it, too—to give Rhia a vision of the Otherworld Well." My voice lowered. "And Rhita Gawr used it to send the death shadow to my mother."

The silver eyebrows lifted. "To your mother?"

My boots shifted uneasily on the misty ground. "Well, no. To me. But it felled my mother instead."

"So what is the soul of the art of Leaping?"

My attention turned to the flowing mist that surrounded us. Gracefully, it wound its way around Dagda and myself, touching both of us as it touched the upside-down tree, embracing the great roots that themselves embraced the world above. "Everything," I declared, "is connected to everything else."

"Good, my son, good. Now what of Eliminating?"

"That one I learned from a sleeping dragon. And from . . . a jester." I grinned slightly. "They showed me that every living thing is precious somehow."

Dagda leaned toward me. "Even a dragon?"

"Even a dragon."

He stroked his chin thoughtfully. "You will meet that dragon again, I believe. When it awakens."

I caught my breath. Before I could ask anything, however, he spoke again.

"Seeing. Tell me, now, about Seeing."

My tongue worked against my cheek before any words came. At last, in a voice not much louder than a whisper, I said, "The heart can see things invisible to the eye."

"Hmmm. What else?"

I thought for a moment. "Well, now that I know a little about seeing with the heart, I can, perhaps, see better into myself."

Dagda's deep brown eyes regarded me. "And when you look into that place, my son, what do you see?"

I cleared my throat, started to speak, then stopped myself. Searching for the right words, I paused before starting again. "It's . . . well, it's like going down into the Otherworld Well. The deeper I go, the more I discover." Turning away, I said under my breath, "And what I discover can be truly frightening."

The old man watched me with compassion. "What else do you see?"

I heaved a sigh. "How little I really do know."

Dagda reached toward me, taking my hand in his own. "Then, Merlin, you have learned something invaluable." He drew me nearer on the floor of mist. Shreds of vapor curled about us both. "Truly invaluable! Until now, you have been searching for the souls of the

Songs. But knowing how little you really know—having humility—that, my son, is the soul of wizardry itself."

Puzzled, I cocked my head.

"In time, I believe, you will fully understand. For humility is nothing more than genuine respect for the wondrous, surprising ways of the world."

Slowly, I nodded. "That sounds like something Rhia would say." Looking again at her lifeless form, I asked anxiously, "Can you still save her?"

Dagda gave no answer.

"Can you?"

For an extended moment, he watched me in silence. "I know not, my son."

My throat constricted as if Balor still held me in his grasp. "I've been such a fool! I've caused so much harm."

Dagda pointed a finger at a rolling ribbon of mist, which instantly straightened. At the same time, he glanced at another wispy line, which suddenly changed into a tight little ball. Then, turning back to me, he smiled sadly. "So you have come to see both the dark and the light within yourself. The dragon as well as the star. The serpent as well as the dove."

I swallowed. "When you first greeted me, you said I might come to know the true source of your power. Well, I'm not sure, but I think your power is quieter, subtler than other kinds. It is guided by your head and your hand, but it springs from your heart. Really, your power is about the seventh Song. Seeing not with the eyes, but with the heart."

His eyebrows lifted ever so slightly.

"There was a time," I continued, my voice a mere whisper, "when

I would have given anything to see again with my own eyes. I still want to see that way again. Very much. But now I know there are other ways to see."

Lightly, Dagda squeezed my hand. "You see well, Merlin."

He released his grip, then observed me for a long moment. "And I will tell you this. As much pain as you have known and are yet to know, wondrous things await you, young man. Truly wondrous things."

XXXIV

ELIXIR

Dagda's deep eyes turned to the trunk of the tree, sparkling with diamonds of dew. He followed the column higher and higher, to the gnarled roots that melted into the mist far above. His gaze lingered there momentarily, as if he could see through the mist into the lands beyond. At last he spoke. "Now for your friend, bound to you by love as well as by blood."

He reached for Rhia, lying on the vaporous ground, with his uninjured arm. She seemed so still, so silent, the color drained from her skin as well as her garb of leaves. My stomach churned in anguish, for I suspected that her body had grown too cold for even the greatest of the spirits to revive. Hadn't Gwri told me that Dagda, for all his power, could not bring back to life someone who had died?

Ever so gently, he lifted her limp hand, closing his eyes as he did so. He seemed to be listening for something far away. Then, without opening his eyes, he gave me a command. "You may release her, Merlin."

I hesitated, suddenly fearing that this would surely mean her death. Once her spirit had left me, once it had flown, I could never hope to see her live again. As much as I yearned to hear her laugh again, still more I feared that by letting her go I would lose her forever.

"Merlin," repeated Dagda. "It is time."

At last, I released her. Deep within, I could feel her spirit stirring subtly. Then it began to flow out of me, at first like a trickle of water, gathering strength, until finally it felt like a river bursting through a dam. My sightless eyes brimmed with tears, for I knew that whether or not Rhia survived in mortal form, she and I would never be so utterly close again.

Slowly, very slowly, I exhaled. Shreds of mist knitted themselves in the air between us, creating a shimmering bridge linking my chest and hers. The bridge hovered, glowing, for barely an instant, before fading away completely.

Just then I noticed the gash on the side of her head. It started closing, healing from within. As the skin pulled together, the bloodstains, now more brown than red, evaporated from her curly hair, her neck, and her suit of woven vines. Color began to flow into her cheeks. Her garb softened, as the green vitality returned to every leaf and stem.

Rhia's forefinger trembled. Her neck straightened. Then, at last, her gray-blue eyes opened, along with Dagda's. Gazing up into the roots draped with mistletoe, she drew a halting breath of her own. Turning her face toward Dagda, she smiled, even as she burst into speech. "You live with a tree, just like I do!"

Her bell-like laughter rang out. I joined her, while Dagda erupted with a full, resonant laugh of his own. As he shook with mirth, the great tree, too, began to sway on the misty plain. Droplets of dew fell from above, spinning and shining in the air. Even Trouble, perched on my shoulder, piped a joyous whistle. It seemed to me that the universe itself had joined in our laughter.

Her eyes alight, Rhia sat up and swung her head toward me. "Merlin, you did it. You saved me."

"No. Dagda saved you."

"Not without your help, young man." The elder pushed a few silver hairs off his brow. "By holding so lovingly her spirit as well as her body, you kept her from truly dying, long enough that I could still revive her."

His gaze moved to Rhia. "And you helped, too."

"I did?"

The old man nodded slowly. "Your spirit is a radiant one, Rhiannon. Exceptionally radiant. You possess a force of life that is as powerful as the one I placed in one of the Treasures of Fincayra, the Orb of Fire."

Rhia's cheeks flushed.

I recalled the glittering orange sphere that I had rescued from the ruins of the Shrouded Castle. "It has something to do with healing, doesn't it?"

"Healing, yes. But of the soul, not the body. For the Orb of Fire, in the hands of someone wise, can rekindle hope and joy, even the will to live."

Dagda turned to me. "You, Merlin, know more than anyone how bright the spirit of your sister shines."

I realized that I could still feel, deep within me, a touch of Rhia's spirit. A bit of my sister had remained with me. And, I knew, always would.

"Yes," declared the frail, silver-haired man. "Your training as a wizard has only begun. Yet embracing the wisdom, as well as the spirit, of your sister has been part of it. An important part."

"My eighth Song, you could say."

"Yes."

I looked at Rhia. "Aylah tried to tell me, but I didn't understand. Now, though, I think I have a glimmer."

She touched her amulet. "Or you could say . . . an instinct."

Trouble made a clucking sound that resembled a laugh.

Passing my hand through the mist rising from beneath us, I searched the face of Dagda. "I have an instinct that Fincayra is my true home. And yet . . . I have another instinct that it's not. Which one is right?"

The old man gave a sad smile. "Ah, you are learning! Just as true love often melds both joy and grief, true instinct often mixes contrary feelings. In this case, though, I can help you. Humans are not meant to live long on Fincayra. As much as you have come to feel at home there, you must one day return to Earth. You may stay a while longer, for you still have work left to do, but ultimately you must leave."

I bit my lip. "Can't you just allow me to stay?"

Compassion in his eyes, Dagda shook his head. "I could, but I will not. The worlds must remain apart, for each has its own fabric, its own spirit, that must be honored." He sighed gravely. "That is why I am forced to wrestle with Rhita Gawr on so many fronts. He would pull apart the fabrics of Otherworld, Earth, and Fincayra—in order to weave them into his own twisted design. He wants only to rule them all, as his kingdom."

"Is that why the Fincayrans lost their wings?" asked Rhia, glancing at the swirling clouds. "They forgot how to honor the fabric?"

"Your instincts are indeed strong, Rhiannon. You are on the right track, but the rest you must discover for yourself."

"Dagda, may I ask you something?" I hesitated, searching for the right words. "There's a prophecy. It says that only a child of human blood can defeat Rhita Gawr or his servants. Is that true? And if it is, is the human child one of us?"

The elder ran his hand over a sprig of mistletoe hanging nearby. "Though I cannot tell you all you wish to know, I can say this. The prophecy carries much weight. Yet while it was your sister who vanquished Balor, the only person who can stop Rhita Gawr in Fincayra is you."

I tried to swallow, but my throat had tightened again. Suddenly I remembered the death shadow, plunging down the throat of Elen. When I spoke, it was in a whisper. "If I must die fighting Rhita Gawr, you must tell me this. Is there any way—any way at all—that our mother can still live?"

Rhia turned anxiously from me to Dagda. Trouble paced across my shoulder, fluttering his wings.

The old man drew a long breath. "You still have time, though not much. Only a few hours remain before the moon's fourth quarter expires. And when it does, so will your mother."

"The Elixir," I pleaded. "Can you give it to us?"

Dagda reached down to a burly branch. Carefully, he touched one of the dewdrops with the end of his finger. As it came free, it covered his fingertip with a thin, glistening cup. Using his other fingers, he removed the cup. It sat upright in the palm of his hand, like a tiny, crystalline vial.

He winced slightly. At the same instant, the little vial filled with a single drop of red fluid. Dagda's own blood. When the vial brimmed full, its mouth sealed tight.

"There now." He spoke thickly, as if he had been weakened by his act. Quivering slightly, he handed the vial to me. "Take it."

Even as I opened my leather pouch and placed the Elixir inside, I felt Trouble's talons digging into my shoulder. The hawk nuzzled his soft feathers against my neck.

Dagda knew my question before I could ask. "No, Merlin, he cannot join you. Your friend Trouble gave his mortal life at the Shrouded Castle to spare yours. He belongs here now."

The hawk whistled faintly. As the mist billowed around us, the gaze from his yellow-rimmed eyes met my own. We looked at each other for the last time.

"I'll miss you, Trouble."

The bird nuzzled my neck again, then slowly moved away.

Dagda's expression, too, showed pain. "It may not lighten your heart now, Merlin, but I believe that one day, in another land, you will feel the grip of a different bird's talons on your shoulder."

"I don't want a different bird."

"I understand." The elder stretched his one able hand toward me, brushing my cheek. "You must take separate paths now, I am afraid. Though no one knows all the turns those paths may take."

"Not even you?"

"Not even me." Dagda lifted the mantle of mistletoe from my shoulder. "Go now, my children, and be brave."

Trouble's final screech sounded in my ear, even as the swirling mist swept over me like a wave, swallowing everything.

XXXV

A WIZARD'S STAFF

The flash faded into darkness. The only light came from the sprinkling of stars overhead. I found myself still kneeling, with Rhia still sitting by my side. Yet jagged rocks and steep cliffs replaced the steaming mist; a circle of polished stones replaced the Tree of Soul. Not far away, the corpse of a huge warrior lay still and silent.

I took Rhia's hand. "We're back at the Well."

"Too true, too true, too true." The hunched figure of Bumbelwy approached in the near-darkness. "I never thought you'd return. And I see you've brought back the body of—"

"Rhia," she interrupted. "Alive and well."

Bumbelwy froze midstep. Even in the dim light, I could see his eyes grow wider. Then, for a brief instant, his mouth and multiple chins turned upward ever so slightly. It lasted only a fraction of a second. Yet I felt certain that he had actually smiled.

I turned my gaze toward the sky, searching for any sign at all of the moon. Yet I could find nothing. Nothing at all. I bit my lip. If only I hadn't wasted those precious minutes with Rhita Gawr.

Rhia suddenly pointed to a faint glimmer of light that had just emerged from behind a cloud. "Oh, Merlin! That's all that's left of the moon. It will be gone before dawn!"

I leaped to my feet. "So will our mother, unless we can get to her first."

"But how?" Rhia stood, facing the southern sky. "Arbassa is so far away."

As if in answer, the entire ridge shook with a sudden tremor. Then came another, still stronger. Another. Another. Rocks tumbled down from the cliffs on both sides of us. I pulled my walking stick out of my belt and leaned on it for balance. Then my second sight perceived a new shape rising on the horizon. Like a swiftly growing hill, it blocked out the stars behind. Yet I knew at once that this was no hill.

"Shim!" I shouted. "We're over here!"

A moment later, the giant's immense form towered above the three of us. As his feet crushed against the loose rocks, he lowered a great hand. Quickly, Rhia and I climbed into his palm, followed reluctantly by Bumbelwy.

Beneath his bulbous nose, Shim grinned crookedly. "I is gladly to sees you."

"Seize us," moaned Bumbelwy, his hands wringing his cape. "He's come to seize us."

"And we're glad to see you!" I replied, ignoring the jester.

"How did you know we needed you?" asked Rhia. "And where to find us?"

Shim lifted his hand as he straightened himself. Though I tried to keep on my feet, I tumbled into the fleshy palm, barely missing the huddled form of Bumbelwy. Rhia, for her part, sat down beside us with the grace of a landing swan.

"I is asleepily, dreamings of . . . " The giant paused, pursing his enormous lips. "I can't remembers! Anyways, the dream changes into a bird. A hawk, like the one who once rides on your shoulder, except he is all whitely gray instead of brown."

I cringed. I could feel the old pain between my shoulder blades, and another one besides.

"Then this hawk screeches at me, so loudly I wakes up." Shim scrunched his nose. "With the powerfully feeling that I needs to find you! And, most strangestly, a picture in my mind of where to go."

Rhia smiled. "Your dream was sent by Dagda."

The giant's bushy eyebrows lifted.

"You are a loyal friend, Shim! Now take us to Arbassa." I glanced at the trace of the remaining moon. It seemed even fainter than just a moment before.

A bracing wind swept over us, blowing against my tunic as if it were a sail, as Shim turned and started lumbering back across the hills of the Lost Lands. In three or four strides he scaled slopes that had taken us hours to climb, his hairy feet crunching on the rubble. No sooner had he reached a valley floor than he had nearly gained the next ridge. In minutes, a hint of smoke scented the air and I knew we had reached the hollow of the sleeping dragon.

As Shim veered south to cross the channel, sea fog swirled around us. His pink eyes gleamed. "Didn't I tells you I hopes to make another crossing with you one daily?" His laughter rolled across the waves that slapped against his legs. "Certainly, definitely, absolutely!"

Yet none of us joined in his mirth. Bumbelwy hugged his belly, muttering about the demise of a great jester. Rhia and I, meanwhile, studied the night sky, trying to keep track of the swiftly fading moon.

By the sounds and smells that moved through the darkness, as well as the shifts in Shim's strides, I could sense some of the changes in terrain. After emerging from the channel, he marched over the rising coastal plane and swiftly mounted the hills. Soon his steps shortened as the grade steepened. We moved higher into the snowy ridges near the city of Varigal. At one point I thought I heard deep voices chanting in the distance, though the sound quickly died away.

The alpine air grew misty and damp as we descended into a maze of hills and swamps. Somewhere near, I knew, lay the crystal cave of the Grand Elusa. Was the great spider there herself, curled up among the Treasures of Fincayra? Or was she out prowling for wraiths and goblins to satisfy her limitless appetite?

The crashing and snapping of limbs below announced our entry into Druma Wood. Rich, resiny smells tickled my nostrils. Immense shadows, some nearly as tall as the giant who bore us, pushed skyward. I couldn't help but recall Shim's ardent wish that he had confided in me so long ago. *To be big, as big as the highlyest tree.*

His wish had been granted, to be sure. Sitting in the great palm, I stared all the harder at the dying moon, glimmering high above us. And I felt increasingly sure that my own deepest wish would not be granted.

Just when I began to wonder whether I could still detect the moon at all, or whether I was only imagining its pale glow, a new shadow loomed before us. Taller and fuller than the rest, it stood with all the grandeur of Dagda's Tree of Soul. Here, at last, rose Arbassa. In its immense branches, glowing like a star, sat the aerial cottage that held Elen of the Sapphire Eyes.

Shim bent low, placing his hand on the oak tree's burly roots. I grabbed my staff and leaped to the ground, followed closely by Rhia and a stumbling Bumbelwy. With a shout of thanks, I turned to Arbassa, hoping that this time the tree would not resist allowing me to enter.

At that instant the enormous trunk made a low, grinding sound. The bark creased, cracked, and opened. I plunged through the doorway. Taking the stairs two at a time, I bounded upward, not even bothering to glance at the runes carved on the walls. As I burst through the curtain of leaves at the top of the stairwell, Ixtma, the large-eyed squirrel, shrieked. He whirled around, dropping a bowl of water on the floor. Then, seeing Rhia come in just behind me, he scampered over to her, chattering noisily.

Elen, her eyes closed, lay on the floor just where we had left her. The same pine-scented pillow supported her head, while the same shimmering blanket covered her chest. Yet, as I set down my staff and knelt by her side, I could tell that much had changed. Her once-creamy cheeks looked whiter than dried bones; her brow showed the furrows of prolonged suffering. She seemed much thinner, as wispy as the vanishing moon. I lay my head upon her chest, hoping to hear the beating of her heart, but heard nothing. I touched her cracked lips, hoping to feel the slightest breath of air, but felt nothing.

Rhia crouched beside me, her face nearly as pale as our mother's. She watched, motionless, as I reached into my satchel and removed the vial containing the Elixir. Touched by the light from the hearth, it flashed with brilliant red, the color of Dagda's own blood. The whole room flooded with scarlet hues.

Barely able to breathe myself, I dropped the Elixir into my mother's mouth. *Please, Dagda, I beg of you. Don't let it be too late. Don't let her die.*

I barely noticed when Ixtma whimpered, wrapping his bushy tail around Rhia's leg. Or when Bumbelwy entered the room, shaking his head morosely. Or when the first faint rays of dawn touched the leaves draping the eastern windows. Yet I noticed with every particle of my being when my mother opened her eyes.

Seeing Rhia and me, she cried out in surprise. Rosy hues flared in her cheeks. Drawing a tentative breath, she weakly lifted a hand toward each of us. We clasped her hands in our own, squeezing the living flesh. Tears brimmed in my eyes, while Rhia sobbed quietly.

"My children."

Rhia smiled through her tears. "We're here now . . . Mother."

Elen's brow creased slightly. "Forgive me, child, for not telling you before you left. I thought that, if I died, your pain would be too great."

"You didn't have to tell me." Rhia touched the amulet of oak, ash, and thorn upon her chest. "I already knew."

I nudged her and grinned. "Whatever this girl knows about instincts, she learned from me."

We laughed, mother and daughter and son, as if all our years of separation had never occurred. For even if someday hence we might be forced to part again, right now a single, unalterable truth filled our hearts. On this dawning day, in the boughs of this great tree, we sat together. Reunited at last.

Only after much more laughter and much more talk did we pause to eat a hearty breakfast of Ixtma's honey-soaked nuts and rosemary tea with plenty of mint. And only after my fifth helping did I catch sight of the glittering object resting by the hearth. The Flowering Harp, its magical strings aglow, leaned against the wall of living wood. Suddenly I caught my breath. Behind the Harp, several more objects lay stacked. Staring at them with amazement, I licked the honey from my fingers, pushed myself up from the floor, and stepped closer.

I couldn't believe it, yet I knew it was true. All of the Treasures of Fincayra were here! Right here in Rhia's cottage.

There, gleaming darkly, sat the Caller of Dreams, the graceful horn that Cairpré had once told me could stir any dream into life. Beside it rested the double-edged sword Deepercut. When I reached to touch its hilt, the powerful blade hanging on my belt rang softly, reminding me that my sword, too, had been wrought to fulfill a remarkable destiny. Next to the twining branches of the wall rested the fabled plow that could till its own field. Beside it stood the hoe that nurtures its own seeds, the saw that cuts only as much wood as is needed, and the rest of the Wise Tools, except of course the one that had been lost. I wondered, for an instant, what sort of tool it was—and where it might be now. Then my attention turned to the last of the objects, the Orb of Fire. The orange sphere glowed like a radiant torch. Or, as Dagda had said, like a radiant spirit.

"The Treasures," I said aloud, unable to turn away from them.

Rhia, who had silently joined me, took my arm. "Ixtma told me the Grand Elusa brought them here, not long before we arrived." Hearing the squirrel chatter angrily, she grinned. "He reminds me that she only brought them to the clearing outside Arbassa. Since she was far too big to carry them inside herself, she asked—well, commanded—Ixtma and his family to do the rest."

Perplexed, I ran my finger over the Harp's oaken sound box. "Dagda must have sent the Grand Elusa a message, as he did Shim.

But why? The Treasures were safe enough where they were, in her crystal cave. She had agreed to guard them for all time."

"Not for all time. Only until she could find someone wise enough to choose the right guardians to take care of them. The Treasures, before Stangmar, belonged to all Fincayrans. The Grand Elusa believes it should be that way again. And I agree."

More confused than ever, I shook my head. "But who is wise enough to choose the guardians? Surely the Grand Elusa herself could do that better than anyone else."

Rhia observed me thoughtfully. "That's not what she thinks."

"You don't mean . . . "

"Yes, Merlin. She wants you to do it. As she told Ixtma, *The isle of Fincayra holds a wizard once more.*"

I swallowed, glancing again at the objects stacked by the wall. Each of them, regardless of shape or size or materials, possessed a magic that could enrich all the inhabitants of Fincayra.

Rhia grinned at me. "So what are you going to do?"

"I really don't know."

"You must have some ideas."

Bending down to the floor, I retrieved my staff. A wizard's staff. "Well . . . I think the Caller of Dreams should go to Cairpré, wisest of the bards." I indicated Bumbelwy, still stuffing himself with nuts and honey. "And I think a certain humorless jester deserves the honor of delivering it to him."

Her grin broadened into a smile.

Warming to my task, I grasped the handle of the plow that tills its own field. "I'm not sure just yet about most of the Wise Tools. But this plow is different. I know a man named Honn who will use it well. And share it gladly."

Then I bent to retrieve the glowing Orb of Fire. I hefted it, feeling its pulsing warmth. Without a word, I handed it to Rhia, whose leafy garb danced with the orange light.

Surprise filled her face. "For me?"

"For you."

She started to protest, but I spoke first. "Remember what Dagda told us? The Orb of Fire can rekindle hope, joy, and even the will to live. It belongs in the care of someone whose spirit shines as bright as it does."

Her eyes glistened as she studied the sphere. "You've given me something even more precious than this."

For a long moment, we held each other's gaze. At last, she pointed to the Flowering Harp. "Now what about that?"

I grinned. "I think it ought to go to two people with a garden. A garden that flourished even in the middle of the Rusted Plains, when everything around it lay dying."

"T'eilean and Garlatha?"

I nodded. "And this time, when I carry the Harp to their home, I'll expect nothing more than to be welcomed as their friend." Again I touched the oaken sound box. "First, though, I will take the Harp myself for a while. I have some unfinished work to do in the Dark Hills."

As she lifted her gaze to Arbassa's arching boughs, Rhia's face glowed. "Well, as it happens, so do I."

"Really?" I raised an eyebrow. "What work do you have there?"

"Guiding. I have a brother, you see, who gets lost easily."

THE FIRES OF
MERLIN

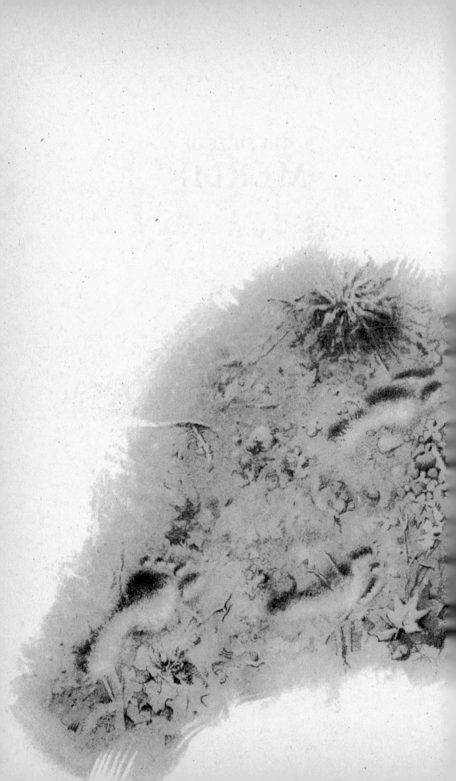

T. A. BARRON

THE FIRES OF
MERLIN

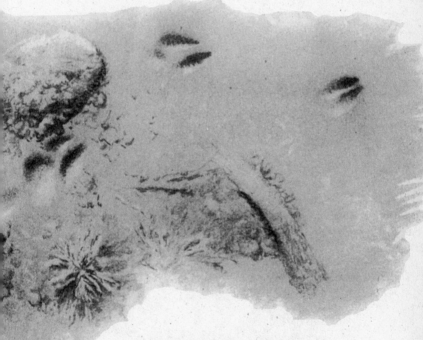

BOOK THREE OF
THE LOST YEARS OF MERLIN

PHILOMEL BOOKS ◆ NEW YORK

This book is dedicated to
Madeleine L'Engle
who has kindled the fires of inspiration in so many

with special appreciation to
Larkin
age two, whose own fires burn so bright

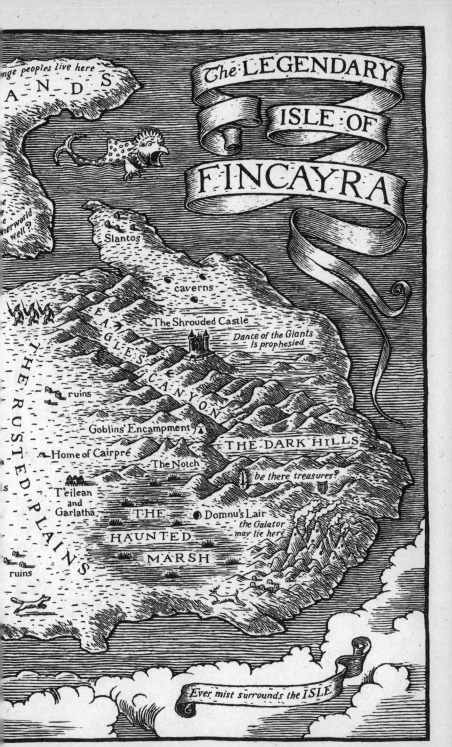

The LEGENDARY
ISLE · OF
FINCAYRA

ge peoples live here

A N D S

nerworld
well?

Slantos

caverns

The Shrouded Castle

Dance of the Giants
Is prophesied

E A G L E S

ruins

C A N Y O N

Goblins' Encampment

THE · DARK · HILLS

Home of Cairpré

The Notch

be there treasures?

T'eilean
and
Garlatha

THE

Domnu's Lair
the Galator
may lie here

HAUNTED

MARSH

ruins

Ever mist surrounds the ISLE

A · Detail · of · Southeastern · FINCAYRA

TO THE DARK HILLS

be there Kreelixes?

Domnu's Lair
the Galator may lie here

THE

HAUNTED

MARSH

The Wheel of Wye

hidden caves

This way to

THE

RUSTED

PLAINS

The Legendary
Carpet Caerlochlann
found here

The Region of

THE SMOKING CLIFFS

Ancient home of the Mellwyn-bri-Meath clan

IAN SCHOENHERR

MCMXCVIII

CONTENTS

PART THREE

AUTHOR'S NOTE

Once again, this wizard is full of surprises.

As those who have read the first two volumes of *The Lost Years of Merlin* epic already know, Merlin first surprised me long ago. In his typically mysterious way, he pointed out that despite all the books, poems, and songs that have been written about him over the centuries, virtually nothing had been told about his youth. For there to be such an enormous gap in the lore about a character so rich, complex, and intriguing was strange indeed. So when Merlin invited me to serve as his scribe while he revealed at last the story of his lost years, I could not refuse.

Even so, I hesitated. I wondered whether it was really possible to add a new strand or two to the already wondrously woven tapestry of myth surrounding Merlin. And, even if it were possible, would the newly created threads feel integral to the rest of the weaving? Would their color, weight, and texture, while original, still feel part of the whole? Would they, in short, feel true?

Somehow, I needed to hear Merlin's voice. Not the voice of the worldly enchanter, all-seeing and all-knowing, whom the world has come to celebrate. Far from it. Down inside of that legendary wizard, buried beneath centuries of struggles, triumphs, and tragedies, was another voice: the voice of a boy. Uncertain, insecure, and utterly human. Possessed with unusual gifts—and with a passion as great as his destiny.

In time, that voice at last came clear. Although it rang with vulnerability, it also carried deeper undertones, full of the mythic and spiritual richness of ancient Celtic lore. The voice sprang partly from those Celtic tales, partly from the mysterious hooting of the owl in the cottonwood tree outside my window—and partly from somewhere else. And it told me that, during those years of his youth, Merlin did not merely disappear from the world of story and song. Indeed, during those years, Merlin *himself* disappeared—from the world as we know it.

Who was Merlin, really? Where did he come from? What were his greatest passions, his highest hopes, his deepest fears? The answers to such questions lay hidden behind the shroud of his lost years.

To find the answers, Merlin must voyage to Fincayra, a mythic place known to the Celts as an island beneath the waves, a bridge between the Earth of human beings and the Otherworld of spiritual beings. Merlin's mother, Elen, calls Fincayra an *in between place*. She observes that the swirling mist surrounding the island is neither quite water nor quite air. Rather, it is something akin to both and yet something else entirely. In the same sense, Fincayra is both mortal and immortal, dark and light, fragile and everlasting.

On the first page of Book One of *The Lost Years of Merlin*, a young boy washes ashore on an unknown coast. Almost drowned, he has no memory of his past—not his parents, not his home, not even his own name. Certainly he has no idea that he will one day become Merlin: the greatest wizard of all time, the mentor of King Arthur, the captivating figure who strides across fifteen hundred years of legend.

That book begins Merlin's search for his true identity, and for the secret to his mysterious, often frightening, powers. To gain a little, he must lose a lot—more, even, than he comprehends. Yet somehow, in the end, he manages to unravel the riddle of the Dance of the Giants. As his journey continues in Book Two, he searches for the elixir that could save his mother's life, following the winding path of the Seven Songs of Wizardry. Along the way, he must surmount his share of obstacles, though one remains far more difficult than all the others. For he must somehow begin to see in an entirely new way, a way befitting a wizard: not with his eyes, but with his heart.

All this Merlin had revealed to us when the time came to begin Book Three—the final installment, I had thought, of the story. Then came the wizard's latest surprise. He told me in no uncertain terms that the tale of his lost years could not possibly be told in just three volumes. When I reminded him that in the beginning he had promised me this would be a trilogy, itself at least a five-year project, he merely waved away my concerns. After all, he said with his unfathomable grin, what is a little extra time to someone who has already lived fifteen centuries? Let alone someone who has learned the art of living backward in time?

I could not object. This is, after all, Merlin's story. And like Merlin himself, the other characters in the tale—Elen, Rhia, Cairpré, Shim, Trouble, Domnu, Stangmar, Bumbelwy, Hallia, Dagda, Rhita Gawr, and others yet to come—have taken on lives of their own. Thus, a projected trilogy has become a five-book epic.

In this volume, Merlin must confront fire in many different forms. He feels the fires of an ancient dragon, of a mountain of lava, and for the first time in his life, of certain passions of his own. He may find that fire, like himself, holds an array of opposites. It can consume and destroy, but it can also warm and revive.

In addition, Merlin must explore the nature of power. Like fire, power can be used wisely or abused terribly. Like fire, it can heal or devour. The young wizard may even need to lose his own magical power in order to discover where it truly resides. For the essence of magic, like the music of the instrument he has made with his own hands, may lie somewhere else than it appears.

The more I learn about this wizard, the less I really know. Even so, I continue to be struck by the remarkable metaphor of Merlin himself. Like the boy who washed ashore with no memory, no past, and no name, without any clue about his wondrous future, each of us begins anew at some point in life—or, indeed, at several points over the course of a lifetime.

And yet, much like that half-drowned boy, each of us harbors hidden gifts, hidden talents, hidden possibilities. Perhaps we also harbor a bit of magic, as well. Perhaps we might even discover a wizard somewhere inside of ourselves.

As in the prior volumes, I am grateful for the advice and support of several people, most especially my wife, Currie, and my editor, Patricia Lee Gauch. In addition, I would like to thank Jennifer Herron, for her bright spirit; Kathy Montgomery, for her contagious good humor; and Kylene Beers, for her unwavering faith. Without them, Merlin's surprises would surely have overwhelmed me by now.

T. A. B.

Splendour of fire . . .

Swiftness of wind . . .

I arise today
Through the strength of heaven:
*   Light of sun,*
*   Radiance of moon,*
*   Splendour of fire,*
*   Speed of lightning,*
*   Swiftness of wind,*
*   Depth of sea,*
*   Stability of earth,*
*   Firmness of rock.*

—From a seventh-century hymn
by Saint Patrick called
THE CRY OF THE DEER

PROLOGUE

The mists of memory gather, the more with each passing year. Yet one day remains as clear in my mind as this morning's sunrise, although it happened those many centuries ago.

It was a day darkened by mists of its own, and by smoke thick and wrathful. While the fate of all Fincayra hung in the balance, no mortal creature suspected. For the mists of that day obscured everything but the fear, and the pain, and only the slightest hint of hope.

As still as a mountain for years beyond count, the massive gray boulder quite suddenly stirred.

It was not the fast-flowing water of the River Unceasing, slapping against the base of the boulder, that caused the change. Nor was it the sleek otter whose favorite pastime had long been sliding down the cleft between the boulder and the river's muddy bank. Nor the family of speckled lizards who had lived for generations in the patch of moss on the boulder's north side.

No, the stirring of the boulder on that day came from an entirely different source. One that, unlike the lizards, had never been seen at the spot, although it had in fact been present long before the first lizard ever arrived. For the source of the stirring came from deep within the boulder itself.

As mist gathered within the banks of the river, resting on the water like a thick white cloak, a faint scraping sound filled the air. A moment later, the boulder wobbled ever so slightly. With shreds of mist curling about its base, it suddenly pitched to one side. Hissing with alarm, three lizards leaped off and scurried away.

If the lizards had hoped to find a new home in the moss atop one of the other boulders, they were destined to be disappointed. For more scraping sounds joined with the constant splashing of the current. One by one, each of the nine boulders lining the river began to wobble, then rock vigorously, as if shaken by a tremor that only they could feel. One of them, partly submerged by the rushing river, started rolling toward a grove of hemlocks on the bank.

Near the top of the first boulder to come to life, a tiny crack appeared. Another crack split off, and then another. All at once, a jagged chip broke away, leaving a hole that glowed with a strange orange light. Slowly, tentatively, something started pushing its way out of the hole. It glistened darkly, even as it scraped against the surface.

It was a claw.

◆　◆　◆

Far to the north, in the desolate ridges of the Lost Lands, a trail of smoke rose skyward, curling like a venomous snake. Nothing else moved on these slopes, not even an insect or a blade of grass trembling in the wind. These lands had been scorched by fire—so powerful that it had obliterated trees, evaporated rivers, and demolished even rocks, leaving behind nothing but charred ridges coated with ash. For these lands had long been the lair of a dragon.

Ages before, at the height of his wrath, the dragon had inciner-ated whole forests and swallowed entire villages. Valdearg—whose name, in Fincayra's oldest tongue, meant *Wings of Fire*—was the last and most feared of a long line of emperor dragons. Much of Fincayra had been blackened by his fiery breath, and all its inhab-itants lived in terror of his shadow. Finally, the powerful wizard Tuatha had managed to drive the dragon back to his lair. After a prolonged battle, Valdearg had at last succumbed to the wizard's enchantment of sleep. He had remained in his flame-seared hol-low, slumbering fitfully, ever since.

While many Fincayrans grumbled that Tuatha should have killed the dragon when he had the chance, others argued that the wizard must have spared him for a reason—though what that reason could possibly be no one knew. At least, in slumber, Wings of Fire could cause no more harm. Time passed, so much time that many peo-ple began to doubt that he would ever wake again. Some even ques-tioned the old stories of his rampages. Others went further, wondering whether he had ever really existed, although very few indeed were willing to travel all the way to the Lost Lands to find out. Of those who did set out on the dangerous trek, very few ever returned.

Very little of what Tuatha had said at the conclusion of the Bat-tle of Bright Flames had been understandable, for he spoke in rid-dles. And many of his words had been long forgotten. Still, a few bards kept alive what remained in the form of a poem called *The Dragon's Eye*. Although the poem had many versions, each as ob-scure as the others, all agreed that on some dark day in the future, Valdearg would awaken once more.

Even now, these lands reeked of charcoal. Near the hollow, the air shimmered with the unremitting heat of the dragon's breath. The low, roaring sound of his snoring echoed across the blackened ridges, while the dark column of smoke continued to pour from his nostrils, lifting slowly skyward.

✦ ✦ ✦

The claw pushed higher, tapping the edge of the rock-like shell as cautiously as someone about to step on a frozen pond would tap the ice. Finally, the dagger-sharp tip of the claw dug into the surface, shooting cracks in all directions. A muffled sound, part screech and part grunt, came from deep inside. Then, all at once, the claw ripped away a large section of shell.

The enormous egg rocked again, rolling farther down the riverbank. As it splashed in the surging water, several more pieces of the shell dropped away. Although the morning sun had started to burn through the mist, its light did not diminish the orange glow radiating from the gaping hole.

More cracks snaked around the sides. The claw, curved like a huge hook, slashed at the edges of the hole, spraying fragments of shell in the river and on the muddy bank. With another grunt, the creature inside shoved the claw completely out of the hole, revealing a twisted, gangly arm covered with iridescent purple scales. Next came a hunched, bony shoulder, dripping with lavender-colored ooze. Hanging limp from the shoulder was a crumpled fold of leathery skin that might have been a wing.

Then, for whatever reason, the arm and shoulder fell still. For a long moment the egg neither rocked nor emitted any sound.

Suddenly the entire top half of the egg flew off, landing with a splash in the shallows. Rays of orange light shot into the shredding mist. Awkwardly, hesitantly, the scaly shoulder lifted, supporting a thin, purple neck flecked with scarlet spots. Hanging heavily from the neck, a head—twice as big as that of a full-grown horse—slowly lifted into the air. Above the massive jaw, studded with row upon row of gleaming teeth, a pair of immense nostrils twitched, sniffing the air for the first time.

From the creature's two triangular eyes, the orange light poured like glowing lava. The eyes, blinking every few seconds, gazed through the mist at the other eggs that had also begun to crack open. Raising one of her claws, the creature tried to scratch the bright yellow bump that protruded from the middle of her forehead. But her aim was off and instead she poked the soft, crinkled skin of her nose.

With a loud whimper, she shook her head vigorously, flapping her blue, banner-like ears against her head. After the shaking ceased, however, her right ear refused to lie flat again. Unlike the left one, which hung almost down to her shoulder, it stretched out to the side like a misplaced horn. Only the gentle droop at the tip hinted that it was, in fact, an ear.

◆　◆　◆

Deep within the smoking cavern, the gargantuan form shifted uneasily. Valdearg's head, nearly as broad as a hill, jerked suddenly, crushing a pile of skulls long ago blackened by flames. His breath came faster and faster, roaring like a thousand waterfalls. Although his enormous eyes remained closed, his claws slashed ruthlessly at some invisible foe.

The dragon's tail lashed out, smashing against the charred wall of stone. He growled, less at the rocks that tumbled onto the green and orange scales of his back than at the torments of his dream—a dream that pushed him to the very edge of awakening. One of his vast wings batted the air. As the wing's edge scraped the floor of the hollow, dozens of jeweled swords and harnesses, gilded harps and trumpets, and polished gems and pearls flew in every direction. Clouds of smoke darkened the day.

• • ◦•

The creature in the egg, her nose still throbbing, flashed her eyes angrily. Feeling an ancient urge, she drew a deep breath of air, puffing out her purple chest. With a sudden snort, she exhaled, flaring her nostrils. But no flames came, nor even a thin trail of smoke. For although she was, indeed, a baby dragon, she could not yet breathe fire.

Crestfallen, the baby dragon whimpered again. She lifted one leg to climb the rest of the way out of the shell, then halted abruptly. Hearing something, she cocked her head to one side. With one ear dangling like a thin blue flag and the other soaring skyward, she listened intently, not daring to move.

Suddenly the hatchling drew back in fright, teetering in the remains of the egg. For she had only just noticed the dark shadow forming in the mist on the far bank of the river. Sensing danger, she huddled deeper in the shell. Yet she could not keep her one unruly ear from poking over the rim.

After a long moment, she raised her head ever so slightly. Her heart thumped within her chest. She watched the shadow draw slowly nearer, wading through the churning water. As it approached, it started to harden into a strange, two-legged figure— carrying a curved blade that gleamed ominously. Then, with a start, she realized that the blade was lifting to strike.

PART ONE

I

THE LAST STRING

J ust one more."

Even as I spoke the words, I could scarcely believe them. I slid my hand across the scaly, gray-brown bark of the rowan tree whose massive roots encircled me, feeling the gentle slopes and curves of the living wood. In one hollow, as deep as a large bowl, sat some of the tools I had been using over the past several months: a stone hammer, a wedge of iron, three filing rods of different textures, and a carving knife no bigger than my little finger. I reached past them, past the knobbed root that served as a hanging rack for my larger saws, to the thin shelf of bark that had so recently held all eight strings.

Eight strings. Each one cured, stretched, and finally serenaded under the full autumn moon, according to ancient tradition. Thankfully, my mentor, Cairpré, had devoted weeks before that night to helping me learn all the intricate verses and melodies. Even so, the moon had nearly set before I finally sang every one of them correctly—and in the right order. Now seven of the strings gleamed on the little instrument propped on the root before me.

Grasping the last remaining string, the smallest of the lot, I brought it closer. As I twirled it slowly, its ends twisted and swayed—alive, almost. Like the tongue of someone on the very verge of speaking.

Late afternoon light played on the string, making it shine as golden as the autumn leaves speckling the grass at the base of the rowan tree. It felt surprisingly heavy, given its short length, yet as flexible as the breeze itself. Gently, I draped it on a cluster of dark red berries hanging from one of the rowan's lower boughs. Turning back to the instrument, I inserted the last two knobs, carved from the same branch of hawthorn as the others, whose month-long kiln drying had ended only yesterday. Rubbing against the oaken soundboard, the knobs squeaked ever so slightly.

At last, I retrieved the string. After tying the seven loops of a wizard's knot on each of the two knobs, I began twisting, one to the right and the other to the left. Gradually, the string tightened, straightening out like a windblown banner. Before it had grown too tight, I stopped. Now all that remained was to insert the bridge—and play.

Leaning back against the trunk of the rowan, I gazed at my handiwork. It was a psaltery, shaped something like a tiny harp but with a bowed soundboard behind all the strings. I lifted it off the root, studying it admiringly. Though it was barely as big as my open hand, it seemed to me as grand as a newborn star.

My own instrument. Made with my own hands.

I ran my finger along the strip of ash inlaid at the top of the frame. This would be much more than a source of music, I knew. Unless, of course, I had bungled any of the steps in making it. Or, much worse, unless . . .

I drew a slow, unsteady breath. Unless I lacked the one thing Cairpré couldn't teach me, the one thing he couldn't even describe—what he could only call *the essential core of a wizard.* For, as he had so often reminded me, the making of a wizard's first instrument was a sacred tradition, marking a gifted youth's coming of age. If the process succeeded, when the time finally came to play the instrument, it would release its own music. And, simultaneously, an entirely new level of the youth's own magic.

And if the process did not succeed . . .

I set down the psaltery. The strings jangled softly as the soundboard again touched the burly roots of the tree. Among these very roots, Fincayra's most famous wielders of magic—including my legendary grandfather, Tuatha—had cobbled their own first instruments. Hence the tree's name, written into many a ballad and tale: the Cobblers' Rowan.

Placing my hand over a rounded knob of bark, I listened for the pulse of life within the great tree. The slow, swelling rhythm of roots plunging deeper and branches reaching higher, of thousands of leaves melting from green to gold, of the tree itself breathing. Inhaling life, and death, and the mysterious bonds connecting both. The Cobblers' Rowan had continued to stand through many storms, many centuries—and many wizards. Did it know even now, I wondered, whether my psaltery would really work?

Lifting my gaze, I surveyed the hills of Druma Wood, each one as round as the back of a running deer. Autumn hues shone scarlet, orange, yellow, and brown. Brightly plumed birds lifted out of the branches, chattering and cooing, while spirals of mist rose from hidden swamps. I could hear, weaving with the breeze, the continuous tumble of a waterfall. This forest, wilder than anyplace I had ever known, was truly the heart of Fincayra. It was the first place I had wandered after washing ashore on the island—and the first place I had ever felt my own roots sinking deeply.

I smiled, seeing my staff leaning against the rowan's trunk. That,

too, had been a gift of this forest, as its spicy scent of hemlock reminded me constantly. Whatever elements of real magic that I
possessed—outside of a few simple skills such as my second sight,
which had come to me after I lost the use of my eyes, and my sword
with some magic of its own—resided within the gnarled wood of
that staff.

As did so much more. For my staff had, somehow, been touched
by the power of Tuatha himself. He had reached out of the ages,
out of the grave, to place his own magic within its shaft. Even with
the blurred edges of my vision, I could make out the symbols
carved upon it, symbols of the powers that I yearned to master fully:
Leaping, between places and possibly even times; Changing, from
one form into another; Binding, not just a broken bone but a broken spirit as well; and all the rest.

Perhaps, just perhaps . . . the psaltery would take on similar powers. Was it possible? Powers that I could wield on behalf of all Fincayra's peoples, with wisdom and grace not seen since the days of
my grandfather.

I took a deep breath. Carefully, I lifted the little instrument in
my hands, then slid the oaken bridge under the strings. A snap of
my wrist—and it stood in place. I exhaled, knowing that the moment, my moment, was very near.

THE ROOT CHORD

Done," I announced. "It's ready to play."

"Done, you say?" Cairpré's shaggy gray head poked around from behind the trunk of the great rowan. He looked frustrated, as if he couldn't find the one remaining word he needed to complete an epic poem about tree roots. As his dark eyes focused on my little instrument, his expression clouded still more. "*Hmmm.* A fair piece of work, Merlin."

His tangled eyebrows drew together. "But it's not done until it's played. As I've said someplace or other, *For the truth shall be found, Not in sight but in sound.*"

From behind him, on the brow of the knoll, came a hearty laugh. "Never mind that your poem referred to a meadowlark instead of a harp."

Cairpré and I swung our heads toward my mother as she stepped lightly over the grass. Her dark blue robe fluttered in the breeze that smelled so strongly of autumn, while her hair draped her shoulders like a mantle of sunlight. It was her eyes, though, that drew my attention. Eyes more blue than sapphires.

Watching her approach, the poet straightened his smudged white tunic. "Elen," he grumbled. "I should have guessed you'd return just in time to correct me."

Her eyes seemed to smile. "Somebody has to now and then."

"Impossible." Cairpré did his best to look gruff, but could not hide his own fleeting smile. "Besides, it's not a harp the boy has made. It's a psaltery, though a small one, after the Greek *psaltérion*. Did no one ever teach you about the Greeks, young lady?"

"Yes." My mother stifled another laugh. "You did."

"Then you have no excuse whatsoever."

"Here," she said to me, pouring some plump, purple berries into the hollow in the root holding my tools. "Rivertang berries, from the rill across the way. I brought a handful for you." With a side-long glance at Cairpré, she flicked a single berry at him. "And one for you, for agreeing to give me a tutorial on Grecian music."

The poet grunted. "If I have time."

I listened, curious, to their bantering. Whatever the reason, their conversations often took such turns lately. And this puzzled me, since their words themselves didn't seem to be what mattered. No, their bantering was really about something else, something I couldn't quite put my finger on.

Watching them, I popped a few berries into my mouth, tasting the zesty flavor. Here they were, talking as if Cairpré thought he knew everything, more perhaps than the great spirit Dagda himself. Yet my mother realized, I felt sure, that he had never lost sight of how little he really did know. As much as he had taught me during the past year about the mysteries of magic, he never began one of our tutoring sessions without reminding me of his own limitations. He had even confessed that, while he knew that I must follow a series of intricate steps in making my first instrument, he wasn't at all certain of their meaning. Throughout the process—from choosing the proper instrument to shaping the wood to firing the kiln—he had behaved as much like my fellow student as my mentor.

Suddenly something nipped the back of my neck. I cried out, brushing away whatever insect had taken me for a meal. But the culprit had already fled.

My mother's blue eyes gazed down at me. "What's wrong?"

Still rubbing the back of my neck, I rose and stepped free of the burly roots. In the process, I almost tripped over my scabbard and sword that lay in the grass. "I don't know. Something bit me, I think."

She cocked her head questioningly. "It's too late for biting flies. The first frost came weeks ago."

"That reminds me," said Cairpré with a wink at her, "of an ancient Abyssinian poem about flies."

Even as she started to laugh, I felt another sharp nip on my neck. Whirling around, I glimpsed a small, red berry bouncing down the grass of the knoll. My eyes narrowed. "I've found the biting fly."

"Really?" asked my mother. "Where?"

I spun to face the old rowan. Raising my arm, I pointed to the boughs arching above us. There, virtually invisible among the curtains of green and brown leaves, crouched a figure wearing a suit of woven vines.

"Rhia," I growled. "Why can't you just say hello like other people?"

The leafy figure stirred, stretching her arms. "Because this way is much more fun, of course." Seeing my grimace, she added, "Brothers can be so humorless at times." Then, with the agility of a snake gliding across a branch, she slid down the twisted trunk and bounded over to us.

Elen watched her with amusement. "You are every bit a tree girl, you are."

Rhia beamed. Spying the berries in the hollow, she scooped up most of what remained. "*Mmmm,* rivertang. A bit tart, though." Then, turning to me, she indicated the tiny instrument in my hand. "So when are you going to play that for us?"

"When I'm ready. You're lucky I let you climb down that tree on your own power."

Surprised, she shook her brown curls. "You honestly expect me to believe that you could have lifted me out of the tree by magic?"

Tempted though I was to say yes, I knew it wasn't true. Not yet, at least. Besides, I could feel the deep pools of Cairpré's eyes boring into me.

"No," I admitted. "But the time will come, believe me."

"Oh, sure. And the time will come that the dragon Valdearg will finally wake up and swallow us all in a single bite. Of course, that could be a thousand years from now."

"Or it could be today."

"Please, you two." Cairpré tugged on the sleeve of my tunic. "Stop your battle of wits."

Rhia shrugged. "I never battle with someone who is unarmed." Smirking, she added, "Unless they boast about magic they can't really use."

This was too much. I extended my empty hand toward my staff resting against the trunk of the rowan. I concentrated my thoughts on its gnarled top, its carved shaft, its fragrant wood that carried so much power. Out through my fingers I sent the command. *Come to me. Leap to me.*

The staff quivered slightly, rubbing against the bark. Then, suddenly, it stood erect on the grass. An instant later it flew through the air, right into my waiting hand.

"Not bad." Rhia bent her leaf-draped body in a slight bow. "You've been practicing."

"Yes," agreed my mother. "You've learned a lot about controlling your power."

Cairpré wagged his shaggy mane. "And much less, I'm afraid, about controlling your pride."

I glanced at him bashfully as I slid the staff into my belt. But before I could speak, Rhia chimed in. "Come now, Merlin. Play something for us on that little whatever-it-is."

My mother nodded. "Yes, do."

Cairpré allowed himself a grin. "Perhaps you could sing with him, Elen."

"Sing? No, not now."

"Why not?" He regarded me thoughtfully, his face both anxious and hopeful. "If he can, indeed, make the psaltery play, it will be true cause for celebration." For some reason, his expression seemed to darken. "No one knows that better than I."

"Please," urged Rhia. "If there's any celebrating to do, there's no better way to do it than with one of your songs."

My mother's cheeks flushed. Turning toward the rippling leaves of the rowan, she pondered for a moment. "Well . . . all right." She opened her hands to the three of us. "I shall sing. Yes, a joyful song." Her eyes darted to the poet. "For the many joys of the past year."

Cairpré brightened. "And of the years to come," he added in a whisper.

Again my mother blushed. Just why didn't concern me, for I,

too, shared her joy. Here I stood, with family, with friends, increasingly at home on this island—all of which would have seemed utterly impossible just over one year ago. I was now fourteen years old, living in this forest, a place as peaceful as the autumn leaves I could see drifting downward. I wanted nothing more than to stay in this very place, with these very people. And, one day, to master the skills of a wizard. Of a true mage—like my grandfather.

My fingers squeezed the psaltery's frame. If only it would not fail me!

I drew a deep breath of the crisp air buffeting the hilltop. "I am ready."

My mother, hearing the tautness in my voice, brushed her finger against my cheek—the same cheek that, long ago, had been scarred by a fire of my own making. "Are you all right, my son?"

I did my best to force a grin. "I'm just imagining how my strumming is going to compare to your singing, that's all."

Although I could tell she didn't believe me, her face relaxed slightly. After a moment, she asked, "Can you play in the Ionian mode? If you will just strike the root chord, and play for a while, I can fit my song to your melody."

"I can try."

"Good!" Rhia leaped up to catch hold of the rowan's lowest branch. She swung to and fro, releasing a bell-like laugh as golden leaves rained down on us. "I love to hear a harp, even a tiny one like yours. It reminds me of the sound of rain dancing on the summer grass."

"Well, the summer has passed," I declared. "Yet if anything can bring it back, it will be Mother's voice, not my playing." I turned to Cairpré. "Is it time, then? For the incantation?"

Even as the poet cleared his throat, his expression darkened again—this time more deeply, as if a strange, contorted shadow had fallen across his thoughts. "First there is something I must tell you." He hesitated, selecting his words. "Since time beyond memory, any Fincayran boy or girl with the promise of deep magic has left home for an apprenticeship similar to yours. With a real wizard or enchantress, preferably, but if none could be found, with a scholar or bard."

"Like you." What was he leading up to? All this I knew.

"Yes, my boy. Like me."

"But why are you telling me this?"

His brow grew as wrinkled as his tunic. "Because there's one more thing you should know. Before you play your psaltery. You see, that apprenticeship—the time of mastering the fundamentals of enchantment, before even starting to make a musical instrument—normally takes . . . a long time. Longer than the eight or nine months it has taken you."

My mother cocked her head at him. "How long does it usually take?"

"Well," he fumbled. "It, ah, varies. Different, you see, from one person to the next."

"How long?" she repeated.

He observed her glumly. Then, under his breath, he answered. "Between five and ten years."

Like Elen and Rhia, I started—nearly dropping the psaltery.

"Even Tuatha, with all his gifts, needed four full years to complete his own apprenticeship. To do it all in less than one year is, well, remarkable. Or you could say . . . unheard of." He sighed. "I've been meaning to tell you this, really, but I wanted to find the proper time and setting. *The opportune time, As rare as good rhyme.*"

Elen shook her head. "You have another reason."

Sadly, he nodded. "You know me too well."

He looked at me imploringly, as he ran his hand over a root of the Cobblers' Rowan. "You see, Merlin, I haven't wanted to tell you because I haven't been sure whether your speed, your swiftness in mastering whatever lessons I gave you, was due to your own gifts—or to my deficiencies as your tutor. Did I forget any steps? Misread any instructions? It's been nagging at me now for some time. I've checked all the ancient texts—oh yes, many times—just to make sure that you've done everything right. And I truly believe that you have, or I would not have let you go this far."

He straightened. "Even so, you ought to be warned. Because if the psaltery doesn't work, it may be my fault instead of yours. That's right. And, as you know, Merlin, a youth gets just one chance at making a magical instrument. Only one. If it should fail to summon high magic, you will never have another."

I swallowed. "If my training really moved that fast, it's possible that the reason is something else altogether. Something unrelated to how good you might be as a mentor—or I might be as a student."

His eyebrows lifted.

"Maybe I had some help. From someplace neither of us suspected. Just where, I'm not sure." Pensively, I ran my thumb over the handle of my staff. Suddenly it struck me. "My staff, for example. Yes, yes, that's it! Tuatha's magic, you know." I rolled the tapered shaft under my belt. "It's been with me from the start, and it's here with me now. Surely, in playing my instrument, it will help again."

"No, my boy." Cairpré held my gaze. "That staff may have helped you in the past, it's true—but it's no use to you now. The texts are as clear as autumn air on this. Only the psaltery itself, and whatever skills you may have brought to its making, will determine whether you pass this test."

My hand, holding the tiny frame, began to perspire. "What will the psaltery do if I fail?"

"Nothing. It will make no music. And bring no magic."

"And if I succeed?"

"Your instrument," he said while stroking his chin, "should start to play on its own. Music both strange and powerful. At least that's what has happened in the past. So just as you have felt magic flowing between you and your staff, you should feel it with the psaltery. But this should be a different level of magic, like nothing you have ever known before."

I worked my tongue to moisten it. "The trouble is . . . the psaltery hasn't been touched by Tuatha. Only by me."

Gently, the poet squeezed my shoulder. "When a musician—no wizard, just a wandering bard—plays the harp skillfully, is the music in the strings, or in the hands that pluck them?"

Confused, I shook my head. "What does that matter? We are talking about magic here."

"I don't pretend to know the answer, my boy. But I could show you tome after tome of treatises, some by mages of enormous wisdom, pondering that very question."

"Then someday, if I'm ever a mage myself, I'll give you my answer. Right now, all I want to do is pluck my own strings."

My mother looked from me to Cairpré and back to me again. "Are you sure it's the time? Are you really ready? My song can certainly wait."

"Yes," agreed Rhia, twisting one of the vines that circled her waist. "I'm not so much in the mood for music now."

I studied her. "You don't think I can do it, do you?"

"No," she replied calmly. "I'm just not sure."

I winced. "Well, the truth is . . . I'm not sure myself. But I do know this. If I wait any longer, I may lose the courage to try." I faced Cairpré. "Now?"

The poet nodded. "Good luck, my boy. And remember: The texts say that if high magic does come, so, too, may come other things—surprising things."

"And song," added my mother gently. "I will sing for you, Merlin, whatever happens. Whether or not there is any music in those strings."

I lifted the psaltery, even as I lifted my gaze to the boughs of the ancient rowan. Hesitantly, I placed the instrument's narrow end against the middle of my chest. As I cupped my hand around the outer rim, I could feel my heart thumping through the wood. The breeze slackened; the rustling rowan leaves quieted. Even the gray-backed beetle on the toe of my boot ceased crawling.

My voice a whisper, I spoke the ancient incantation:

> *May the instrument I hold*
> *Usher forth*
> > *A magic bold.*
>
> *May the music that I bring*
> *Blossom like*
> > *The soul of spring.*
>
> *May the melody I play*
> *Deepen through*
> > *The passing day.*
>
> *May the power that I wield*
> *Plant anew*
> > *The wounded field.*

Expectantly, I turned to Cairpré. He stood motionless but for his roving eyes. Behind him, the lush hills of Druma Wood seemed frozen—as fixed in place as one of the carvings on my staff. No light swept across the branches. No birds fluttered or whistled.

"Please," I said aloud, to the psaltery, to the rowan, to the very air. "That's the only thing I want. To rise as high as I possibly can. To take whatever gifts, whatever powers, you can give me, and use them not for myself, but for others. With wisdom. And, I hope, with love. *To plant anew the wounded field.*"

Feeling nothing, my heart began to sink. I waited, hoping. Still nothing. Reluctantly, I started to lower the psaltery.

Then, ever so slightly, I felt something stir. It was not the leaves above me. Nor the grasses at my feet. Nor even the breeze.

It was the smallest string.

As I watched, my heart drumming against the wooden rim, the remotest tip of one end of the string began to twirl. Slowly, slowly, it lifted, like the head of a worm edging out of an apple. Higher it rose, pulling more of the string with it. The other end also awoke, curling about its knob. Soon the other strings started to move as well, their ends coiling and their lengths tightening.

Tuning itself! The psaltery was tuning itself.

In time the strings fell still. I looked up to see Cairpré's growing smile. At his nod, I prepared to pluck the root chord. Wrapping my left hand more firmly around the rim, I curled the fingers of my right. Delicately, I placed them on the strings.

Instantly, a wave of warmth flowed into my fingertips, up my arm, and through my whole body. A new strength, part magical and part musical, surged through me. The hairs on the back of my hands lifted and swayed in unison, dancing to a rhythm I could not yet hear.

A wind arose, growing stronger by the second, waving the branches of the Cobblers' Rowan. From the forested hills surrounding us, leaves started drifting upward—first by the dozens, then by the hundreds, then by the thousands. Oak and elm, hawthorn and beech, shimmering with the brilliance of rubies, emeralds, and diamonds. Spinning slowly, they floated toward us, like a vast flock of butterflies returning home.

Then came other shapes, swirling around the rowan, dancing along with the leaves. Splinters of light. Fragments of rainbow. Tufts of shadow. Out of the air itself, shreds of mist wove themselves into more shapes—wispy spirals, serpents, knots, and stars. Still more shapes appeared, from where I could not fathom, made not from light or shadow or even clouds, but from something else, something in between.

All these things encircled the tree, drawn by the music, the magic, to come. What, I wondered, would the power of the psaltery bring next? I smiled, knowing that the time to play my instrument had finally arrived.

I plucked the strings.

III

THE DARKEST DAY

At the instant my fingers plucked the chord, I felt a sudden blast of heat—strong enough to scorch my hand. I shouted, jerking back my arm, even as the psaltery's strings burst apart with a shattering twang. The instrument flew out of my grasp, erupting into flames.

All of us watched, dumbfounded, as the psaltery hung suspended in the air above us, fire licking its rim and soundboard. The oaken bridge, like the strings themselves, writhed and twisted as if in agony. At the same time, the shapes swirling around the rowan vanished in a flash—except for the multitude of leaves, which rained down on our heads.

Then, in the very center of the flaming psaltery, a shadowy image started to form. With the others, I gasped. For soon the image hardened into a haggard, scowling face. It was a face of wrath, a face of vengeance.

It was a face that I knew well.

There were the thick jowls, the unruly hair, and the piercing eyes I could not forget. The bulbous nose. The earrings made of dangling shells.

"Urnalda." The name itself seemed to crackle with fire as I spoke it aloud.

"Who?" asked my mother, gaping at the flaming visage.

"Tell us," insisted Cairpré. "Who is it?"

My voice as dry as the fallen leaves at our feet, I repeated the name. "Urnalda. Enchantress—and ruler—of the dwarves." I fingered the gnarled top of my staff, remembering how she had helped me once long ago. I remembered the pain of it. And how she had extracted from me a promise, a promise that I suspected would cause me greater pain by far. "She is an ally, maybe even a friend—but one to be feared."

At that, the blazing rim of my psaltery exploded in sparks, writhing even more. Shards of wood broke loose and sailed into the air, sizzling and sputtering. One ignited a cluster of dry berries on the overhanging branch, which burst into flames before shriveling into a fist of charcoal. Another flaming shard spun toward Rhia, barely missing her leaf-draped shoulder.

Urnalda, her face ringed with fire, scowled down on us. "Merlin," she rasped at last. "It be time."

"Time?" I tried to swallow, but couldn't. "Time for what?"

Tongues of flame shot toward me. "Time for you to honor your promise! Your debt be great to my people, greater than you know. For we helped you even though it be against our laws." She shook her wide head, clinking her earrings of fan-shaped shells. "Now it be our time of need. Evil strikes the land of Urnalda, the land of the dwarves! You must come now." Her voice lowered to a rumble. "And you must come alone."

My mother clasped my arm. "He can't. He won't."

"Silence, woman!" The psaltery twisted so violently that it snapped in two, releasing a fountain of sparks. Yet both halves remained in the air, hovering just above our heads. "The boy knows that I would not call on him unless it be his time. He be the only one who can save my people."

I shook free of my mother's grasp. "The only one? Why?"

Urnalda's scowl deepened. "That I will tell you when you be here at my side. But hurry! Time be short, very short." The enchantress paused, weighing her words. "This much, though, I will tell you. My people be attacked, this very day, as never before."

"By who?"

"By one long forgotten—until now." More flames leaped from the rim. The burning wood cracked and sizzled, almost burying her words. "The dragon Valdearg sleeps no more! His fire be kindled, as well as his wrath. Truly I speak, oh yes! Fincayra's darkest day be upon us."

Even as I shuddered, the flames suddenly vanished. The charred remains of my instrument twirled in the air for another instant, then fell to the grass and leaves in twisted trails of smoke. All of us stepped backward to avoid the shower of coals.

I turned to Cairpré. His face had hardened, like a craggy cliff, yet it showed the shadowed lines of his fear. His wild brows lifted as he repeated Urnalda's final words. *"Fincayra's darkest day be upon us."*

"My son," whispered Elen hoarsely. "You mustn't heed her demand. Stay here, with us, in Druma Wood, where it's safe."

Cairpré's eyes narrowed. "If Valdearg has truly awakened, then none of us is safe." Grimly, he added, "And our troubles are worse than even Urnalda knows."

I stamped my boot on a glowing coal. "What do you mean by that?"

"The poem *The Dragon's Eye*. Haven't I shown you my transcription? Took me more than a decade to tie together the pieces and fill in the gaps—most of them, at least. Rags and ratholes! I planned to show you, but not so soon. Not like this!"

My gaze fell to the remains of my psaltery, nothing more than broken bits of charcoal and blackened strings amidst the leaves strewn over the grass. Near one of the rowan's roots, I spied a fragment of the oaken bridge. It was still connected to part of a string— the smallest one of all.

Bending low, I picked up the string. So stiff, so lifeless. Not at all like the willowy ribbon I had held only moments before. No doubt if I tried to bend it now, it would shatter in my hands.

I raised my head. "Cairpré?"

"Yes, my boy?"

"Tell me about that poem."

He let out a long, whistling breath. "It's full of holes and ambiguities, I'm afraid. But it's all we have. I'm not even sure I can remember more than the last few lines. And you will need to know more, much more, if you are, in fact, going to confront the dragon."

At the edge of my vision, I saw my mother stiffen. "Go on," I insisted.

Doing his best not to look at her, Cairpré cleared his throat. Then, with a jab of his hand, he pointed to the distant, mist-laden hills. "Far, far to the north, beyond even the realm of the dwarves, lie the most remote lands of this island—the Lost Lands. Now they are scorched and reeking of death, but once they blossomed as richly as this very wood. Fruited vines, verdant meadows, ancient trees . . . until Valdearg, last emperor of the dragons, descended. Because the people of the Lost Lands had rashly killed his mate—

and, by most accounts, their only offspring—he set upon those people with the wrath of a thousand tempests. He tortured, plundered, and destroyed, leaving no trace of anything alive. He became, for all time, Wings of Fire."

Cairpré paused, looking up into the branches of the towering rowan. "Finally, Valdearg carried his rage southward, to the rest of Fincayra. It was then that your grandfather, Tuatha, engaged him in battle—driving him back into the wastelands. Although the Battle of Bright Flames lit up the skies for three years and a day, Tuatha finally prevailed, lulling the dragon into enchanted sleep."

I peered at the fragment of the psaltery in my hand. "Sleep that has now ended."

"Yes, which is why I spoke of *The Dragon's Eye*. That poem, you see, tells the story of their battle. And describes how Tuatha relied on a weapon of magic, great magic, to triumph in the end."

"What was it?" asked Rhia.

He hesitated.

"Tell us," she insisted.

The poet spoke softly, yet his words thundered in my ears. "The Galator."

Instinctively, my hand moved to my chest, where the jeweled pendant, possessing powers as mysterious as its strange green radiance, had rested so long ago. Rhia's eyes, I could tell, caught my movement. And I knew that she, too, was recalling the Galator—and its loss to the hag Domnu, that thief of the marshlands.

"The poem," continued Cairpré, "ends with a prophecy." Grimly, he studied my face. "A prophecy whose meaning is far from clear."

He seated himself on a bulging root, his gaze focused on something far distant. After a long moment, he began to recite:

When Valdearg's eye opens,
Too many shall close:
The darkest of days brings
The deepest of woes.
Together with terror
That swells into pain,
Disaster shall follow
His waking again.

By anger unending
And power unmatched,
The dragon avenges
His dreams yet unhatched.
For when he awakens
To find those dreams lost,
Revenge shall he covet
Regardless the cost.

Lo! Nothing can stop him
Except for one foe
Descended from enemies
Fought long ago.
In terrible battle
They fight to the last,
Reliving the furor
And rage of the past.

Yet neither opponent
Shall truly prevail.
The enemies' efforts
All finally fail.
Though striving to vanquish,
They perish instead:
The dragon's eye closes,
His enemy dead.

Then air becomes water
And water is fire;
Both enemies fall to
A power still higher.
Thus only when elements
Suddenly merge
Shall end the dragon,
Shall end the scourge.

But for the rustling of rowan leaves, there was no sound on the knoll. No one stirred, no one spoke. We stood as still as the charred scraps of my musical instrument. And as silent. Finally, Rhia stepped toward me and wrapped her forefinger around my own.

"Merlin," she whispered, "I don't understand what all that means, but I don't like its sound. Its feeling. Are you sure you want to go? Maybe Urnalda will find some way to stop the dragon without you."

I scowled, pulling my hand free. "Of course I don't want to go! But she did help me once, when I truly needed it. And I did promise to help her in return."

"Not to fight a dragon!" exclaimed my mother, her voice frantic.

I faced the woman who had, only moments before, been jubilant enough to sing. "You heard Urnalda. She said I'm the only one who can save her people. Why I'm not sure, but it must have something to do with the prophecy. No one can defeat the dragon except for one person—the one *Descended from enemies Fought long ago*. That means me, don't you see?"

"Why?" she implored. "Why must it be you?"

"Because I am the one descended from Tuatha, the only wizard—out of all those who must have battled him down through the ages—who finally bested him. Who defeated him, at least for a time." I tapped the top of my staff. "And I am the only one, it seems, who might have a chance to do the rest."

Her sapphire eyes dimmed as she turned to Cairpré. "Why didn't Tuatha kill the dragon when he had the chance?"

Slowly, the poet ran both of his hands through his hair. "I don't know. Just as I don't know what the prophecy meant by the dragon's lost dreams. Or by air becoming water and water merging with fire."

With an effort, he tore his gaze from Elen and turned to me. "Yet some of it seems plain. Too plain. It does, I fear, point to you as Valdearg's foe—and as the only one who can stop him from reducing most of Fincayra to ashes. For once he begins, he won't be satisfied just to wipe out the dwarves' realm, or even this forest. He will thirst to destroy everything he can. And so, Merlin, it may well be your part to confront the dragon, just as your grandfather did in the Battle of Bright Flames. But this time the outcome will be different. This time . . . both of you will die."

He swallowed. "Every bard I know understands the importance of this poem. That is why I spent so many years transcribing it, trying to piece it all together. While much remains debatable, no one—no one at all—disagrees on the outcome of the battle. *The dragon's eye closes, His enemy dead.* Whoever vanquishes the dragon will die as well."

Even as she tucked a loose vine back into her sleeve, Rhia examined him closely. "But there's more, isn't there? Something important that the other bards don't agree with you about?"

His cheeks flushed. "You have your mother's way of seeing right through my skin." He indicated the sphere, glowing softly with orange light, hanging from her woven belt. "Perhaps that is why Merlin gave you the Orb of Fire."

Thoughtfully, Rhia stroked the Orb. "The truth is I'm still not sure why he gave it to me." She glanced at me. "Even though I'm grateful. But that doesn't matter now. Tell us the rest."

The wind strengthened, rattling the branches above us as a warrior rattles sword and shield. The leaves rustled at our feet, while more leaves, twigs, and flakes of bark twirled downward. I felt a touch of winter chill in the air, even as my fingers still smarted from the heat of my burning psaltery.

Cairpré brushed a twig off his ear. "I'm not at all sure about this, but I think the key to the prophecy may be that obscure reference near the end: *A power still higher.* Whatever it means, it must be something stronger than the dragon. And stronger than . . ."

"Me. Someone whose magical instrument never played a single note."

"I know, my boy." He studied me anxiously. "Yet, even so, this power may be something you could still master. And if you could, perhaps you could use it somehow to overcome the dragon."

"What is it?" I demanded. "What could be more powerful than a dragon?"

"Rags and ratholes, boy! I wish I knew."

Rhia slapped her thigh. "Maybe it's the Galator! After all, we know it helped before."

I waved the idea away. "Even if you're right, there's no time now to try to get it back. It's all the way on the other side of the island. And Urnalda needs help right now! It's going to take several days, as it is, just to reach her borders. If only my Leaping were strong enough to send me there right away . . . But it's not." I rolled the blackened string between my fingers. "And probably never will be now."

Somberly, I shook my head. "No, let's hope that this higher power means something else besides the Galator. And that I can somehow find it."

Her voice weak, my mother protested once more. "But you don't even have a plan."

"Nothing unusual for him," observed Rhia. "He'll try to make one up as he goes along."

"Then I shall make a plan of my own," Elen replied grimly. "To pray. And to try not to grieve before I must."

Cairpré heaved a sigh. "Are you sure you want to do this, Merlin? No one would blame you if you chose to stay right here with us."

My gaze fell to the brittle string and shard of wood in my hand. All that remained of my psaltery. My failed attempt at higher magic. How could I, with only my staff and sword to help me, even hope to challenge a powerful foe? Let alone Valdearg himself? I lifted the lid of my satchel of healing herbs and precious objects, started to slip the charred remains inside—then caught myself. Why should I keep such a thing? It was useless to me, or anyone else. I let it fall from my grasp onto the ground.

At the same time, my fingertip, already inside the satchel, brushed against something soft. A feather. I smiled sadly, remembering the feisty young hawk who had given me so much, including my own name. Who had never shied away from a battle, even the one that finished his life.

At last my head lifted. "I must go."

IV

A DISTANT CHIME

Cairpré's hand brushed a pair of leaves from my shoulder. "Before you go, my boy, you should take this with you."

He bent to pick up the blackened string from my psaltery that I had discarded. Carefully, he retrieved it from the leaves and grass by my feet. Resting there in his open palm, it looked like the twisted, blackened corpse of a snake—killed in its very infancy.

I pushed his hand away. "Why would I want that?"

"Because you made it, Merlin. Crafted it with your own hands."

"It's worthless," I sneered. "It will only remind me that I failed the test."

His tangled brows climbed higher. "Perhaps. And perhaps not."

"But you saw what happened."

"I did indeed. *With my very own sight: Find the light, find the light!*" He brushed back some graying hair. "And I saw you never had a chance to play. You were interrupted by Urnalda before you—or the strings—could make any music. We don't know what might have happened if you had been allowed to finish."

I glanced at the gnarled roots of the great rowan tree, where I had worked for so many months to make the psaltery. And at the tools, of so many shapes and purposes, that I had finally learned to wield. "But now we'll never find out. You said yourself, I'll never get another chance."

Slowly, he nodded. "To make a magical instrument, yes. But it's just possible, though very unlikely, that your chance to play this one may not yet be over."

"He could be right, you know," said Rhia, stepping through the fallen leaves. "There's always a possibility."

I scowled at her. "You can't make music out of a burned ember!"

"How do you know?" replied Cairpré. "You may have powers you don't yet comprehend."

"Powers I'll never get to use—dragon or no dragon!" Angrily, I snatched the psaltery string from his hand. "Look at this, will you? You know as well as I do that unless a young wizard can make music flow from his instrument, his growth—his chance to become, well, *whatever* he might have become—is ended."

The poet's soulful eyes regarded me for a long moment. "Yes, my boy, that's true. Yet there is much about all this that we—most certainly I—don't understand."

"Remember all the leaves?" asked Rhia. "Even before you started to play, you were attracting things from all over. Not just the leaves, but magical things, too. Even Urnalda! Maybe the psaltery was already starting to show its power."

"That's right," added Cairpré. "And who can tell? Perhaps that power drawing all the leaves, all the magic, was also drawing something else. Something that hasn't yet arrived, that's on its way to you even now."

Skeptically, I studied the contorted string and what was left of the bridge. "I don't believe there is anything left in this. I just don't. But . . . I suppose there's no harm in keeping it for a while."

As I slipped the remains into my satchel, I cast a glance toward my mother, standing in silence by the rowan's trunk. "What I really need is something strong—very strong. To help me against Valdearg."

Cairpré touched my arm. "I understand, my boy. Believe me, I do."

Suddenly, Rhia pointed skyward. "What's that?"

The poet looked up—then hunched, as if struck by an invisible club. Like the rest of us, he gazed at a pair of dark, jagged wings emerging from a cloud. And the blood red mouth baring enormous teeth. Or fangs. As the shape circled high above us, we shrank toward the trunk of the old rowan.

"Not the dragon," prayed my mother, stepping over a massive root. Then, seeing the shape bank sharply to one side, she shook her head. "No, no, look! It's not big enough. It's more like a gigantic bat. What in Dagda's name is it?"

Cairpré made a choking noise. "It can't be! The last of them died ages ago." He rubbed his hand against the rowan's ragged bark. "Stay close to the tree, all of you! Don't move, lest it see us."

"What is it?" I grabbed his arm. "And why do I feel such fear, down inside? For more than our lives."

"Because, Merlin, that thing has come not for our lives, though it could easily take them. It has come . . . for your powers."

Before he could say anything more, a high, piercing shriek echoed across the wooded hills. It jabbed at me, slicing at my chest like a sword of sound. Then, as a wintry gust slapped the rowan, branches flailed, moaning and creaking, while more leaves and berries scattered across the knoll. In that instant, the winged beast wheeled sharply in the air. Downward it plunged, straight at us.

Rhia gasped. "It's seen us!"

"What is it?" I demanded.

Cairpré squinted to see through the waving branches. "A kreelix! Feeds on the powers—the magic—of others."

He tried to place himself in front of Elen, wedging her into a crevasse in the trunk. But she pushed him away. "Forget about me!" she cried. "Protect *him*."

Cairpré's eyes stayed fixed on the bat-like creature. "Those fangs . . ."

Aghast, I stared at the dark shape descending, drawing closer by the second. Already I could see the three gleaming fangs. And the hooked claws jutting from the leading edges of the wings. I could almost feel them tearing at my flesh, my ribs, my thundering heart.

At least I could draw the beast away from the others! I glanced down at my sword, half buried by leaves at the base of the tree, then suddenly remembered a more powerful weapon. My staff! I tore it free from my belt.

Cairpré seized my arm. "No, Merlin."

I wrenched free. Clutching the staff, I leaped clear of the knot of roots.

The shriek of the kreelix cut through the air, drowning the poet's own shout. At the same instant, its enormous, hook-winged shadow fell across the rowan. The beast skimmed the very top of the tree, shearing off dozens of smaller branches as it passed. Debris showered me.

I brandished my weapon, calling on all the powers embedded in its wood. *Now. I need your help now!*

The kreelix careened, ripping at the air with its wings. Then it plunged toward me, the thick brown fur that covered its head and body flattened from the force of the wind. Its mouth opened even wider, thrusting its fangs outward. I realized that the creature lacked any eyes—that, like me, its ability to see came from some other source.

As the three fangs arched toward me, I stepped back, catching my heel on one of the rowan's roots. Though I struggled to keep my balance, I tumbled over backward. The staff flew from my hand, rolling down the hillside.

I started to push myself to my feet—when my hand struck the leather belt of my scabbard. The sword! I grasped the hilt. As I pulled the blade free, it rang faintly, like a faraway chime.

Scrambling to my feet, I had barely enough time to raise the sword before the kreelix struck. It flew straight at me, its wings and voice screaming as one. Now I could see the veined folds of its ears, the dagger-like edges of its claws, the scarlet tips of its fangs. Its shadow raced over the trees below the knoll, then up the grassy slope.

Planting my boots, I reared back. *Do not fail me, sword!* I braced myself. *You are all that stands between us and death.* I swung.

All at once, a blaze of scarlet light exploded inside my head. At the same time, a powerful force slammed into me. Even as it threw me backward, it seemed to reach deep into my chest. To rip the strength from my body, and the sword from my hands. I spun through the air, unable to breathe. With a thud I landed, then rolled to a stop.

I found myself on my back. On grass. And leaves. Yes, it felt like leaves. But where was this place? A short, labored breath. Air at last! I tried to rise, but could not. The clouds spun above me. And something else, something darker than a shadow.

"Merlin, watch out!"

Though I couldn't tell whether the cry came from within me or without, I forced myself to obey it. Weakly, I rolled to the side. A split second later, something slashed into the ground, barely missing my head. It rang softly, like a distant chime. Like . . . something else, something I could not quite remember.

Straining, I sat up. Blurred, unconnected shapes swam before me. A branch . . . a claw . . . or a blade? The broad trunk of a tree—no, it looked more like . . . I wasn't sure. Hard as I tried, I could not focus. Could not remember. Why was I so dizzy? Where was this place, anyway?

With great effort, I concentrated on the blood red shape that was growing steadily larger before me. It had two, no three, gleaming points in its center. It was round, or almost round. It was hollow, and very deep. It was . . .

A mouth! All of a sudden, my memory flooded back. The kreelix was almost upon me! It stood on the knoll, its back to the rowan tree, its wings spread wide. Its fangs glistened, as did the sword it held in a clawed fist. My own sword!

I made an effort to stand, but fell back to the ground, exhausted. The mouth drew nearer. I tried to wriggle away. My body felt heavier than stone.

There was no strength left in my limbs. Nor in my mind. The cavernous mouth started to blur at the edges. Everything looked red. Blood red.

I heard a crack, like splitting wood. The piercing shriek came again. Then silence—along with total darkness.

V

NEGATUS MYSTERIUM

I awoke to find myself, once again, on the leaves. Something brittle and tasteless clung to my tongue. I spat it out. A twig! Someone—my mother—lifted her head from my chest, where she seemed to have been listening. Tears stained her cheeks, but her sapphire eyes shone with relief.

Lightly, she stroked my brow. "You have awakened, at last." She looked up into the rustling boughs of the rowan tree and closed her eyes in thanks.

At that instant, I glimpsed just behind her a pair of huge, bony wings. The kreelix! I rolled to the side, smacking into her full force. She cried out, tumbling down the slope like an apple dropped from a branch. With a single leap, I landed on my feet. Wobbly though I was, I positioned myself between her and the dreaded beast.

Then I caught myself: The kreelix hung as limp as a discarded scarf, suspended by the branches of the rowan tree. Thick, gnarled boughs wrapped around each of its wings, while several more pinned the furred body against the trunk. Its claws, once so threatening, dangled lifelessly, while its head drooped forward, obscuring the fangs. A deep gash, stained with purple blood, cut across its neck.

"Don't worry." Cairpré's hand closed on my shoulder. "It's quite dead."

My mother puffed up behind us. "So am I, almost."

I whirled around. "I'm so sorry! I thought . . ."

"I know what you thought." She forced a grin, even as she rubbed a tender spot on her shoulder. "And I am glad to know beyond doubt, my son, that your strength has returned."

I turned again to the kreelix, draped against the tree. "How . . . ?" I began. "But . . . it was—how?"

"I do so love someone who can ask a clear question." Rhia emerged from behind the trunk, grinning sassily at me. In her hand she held my sword, gleaming in the scattered sunlight of the knoll. She lifted the scabbard from the ground, thrust in the blade, and handed them to me. "I thought you'd prefer your sword without all that blood. Such a ghastly purple color. Reminds me of a rotten fish."

Seeing the confusion on my face, she glanced at Cairpré and Elen. "I suppose we ought to fill him in. Otherwise he'll be peppering us with unfinished questions all day long."

"Tell me!" I roared. "What in the world happened? To me—and that flying maggot over there."

Cairpré's head wagged. "I tried to warn you. It all happened too fast. A kreelix lives on magic, you see. Eats it. Sucks it right out of its prey, as a bee takes nectar from a flower. Since I, like everyone else, thought the last kreelix died centuries ago, I never bothered to tell you about them before. *Foolish error, Greatest terror.* A better tutor would have taught you that the only way to battle one— as the wizards of old learned the hard way, I'm afraid—is slyly. Indirectly. The worst thing you can do is to confront it head-on, exposing all your magic."

"As I did." Buckling the sword, I shook my head. "I had no idea what hit me. There was this flash of scarlet light . . . Then all my strength, all my life it seemed, was ripped away. Even my second sight felt crippled."

The eyes beneath the bushy brows gazed at me solemnly. "It could have been worse. Far worse."

I tried to swallow, but my throat felt rougher than the rowan's bark. "I could have died, you mean. So why didn't I? Right then?"

His hand reached over and tapped my wrist. At first I noticed nothing. Suddenly I spied the puncture, smooth and round, in the sleeve of my tunic. A thin ring of charcoal surrounded it. Something seemed to have melted—not ripped—right through the cloth.

"The fang," he declared, "struck here. A finger's width to the side and you would have died. Without question. Because even the tiniest contact with the fang of a kreelix will destroy the power, as well as the life, of any magical creature. No matter how strong, or large."

Pensively, he ran a hand through his mane. "That was why the ancient wizards and enchantresses tried so hard to avoid face-to-face battles. Especially with weapons that held their own magic, which simply gave the kreelixes more to dine upon."

"Like my sword here."

"Yes, or like the great sword Deepercut you rescued some time ago. One of the island's oldest legends tells how Deepercut was hidden, buried somewhere, for more than a hundred years—just so no kreelixes could find it." He chewed his lip. "Now you see, my boy, why I didn't want you to wield your staff. For it carries, I suspect, more magic than a dozen Deepercuts."

I glanced toward the magical staff lying among the leaves. "How then did they fight the kreelixes? If they couldn't do it face-to-face?"

"That I don't know. But I can promise you this: I intend to find out." His eyes narrowed. "In case there are any more left."

I blanched. "So how did you stop this one?"

He glanced gratefully at the Cobblers' Rowan. "Thanks to your friend over there. And your talented sister."

All at once, I understood. "Rhia! So you did it! Using tree speech! You spoke to the tree, and it snatched the kreelix from behind."

She gave a nonchalant shrug. "Barely in time, too. Next time you try to get yourself killed, at least give us a little warning."

Despite myself, I grinned. "I'll do my best." Then, as I glanced at the giant, bat-like form hanging limply from the branches, the grin disappeared. "Even a tree as powerful as this one couldn't have held any creature that could fight back with magic. So why didn't the kreelix? Surely, if it lived on others' magic, it must have had some of its own."

"Magic?" Cairpré rubbed his chin thoughtfully. "Not as we normally think of it. But it did possess something. What the ancients called *negatus mysterium,* that strange ability to negate, or swallow up, the magic of others. That was the scarlet flash—*negatus mysterium* being released. If directed at you, it can numb some of your magic, at least temporarily. But it won't kill you. That part is left to the fangs."

He scooped up a handful of leaves, then let them drift back to the ground. "Yet the kreelix's own powers ended there. Leaping, Changing, Binding—all the skills you've been trying to develop— the beast itself couldn't command. So it had no power to strike back once caught by the tree."

I indicated the corpse. "Or to keep you from using my sword to finish it off."

"No," answered Rhia, her face clouded. "Before any of us could try to get the sword, it used the blade on itself."

Cairpré nodded. "Perhaps it feared us so much that it chose to slit its throat before we could. Or perhaps," he added darkly, "it feared we might learn something important if it had lived."

"Like what?"

"Like who has kept it alive, and in hiding, all these years."

I shot him a questioning look. The poet's face, already grave, grew more somber still. He fingered the air, as if turning the pages of a book that only he could see. "In ancient times," he half whispered, "there were people who feared anything magical—from the merest light flyer to the most powerful wizard. They saw all magic as evil. And, too often, wizards and enchantresses would abuse their powers, justifying such fears. These people formed a society—Clan Righteous, they called themselves—that met secretly, plotting to destroy magic wherever they found it. They wore an emblem, concealed most of the time, of a fist crushing a lightning bolt."

He drove his own fist into his palm. "Eventually, they started to breed the kreelixes, beasts as unnatural as their appetites. And to train them, as well—to attack enchanted creatures without warning, to wipe out any magical powers completely. Even if the kreelixes themselves died in the process, their victims would usually also die."

Soulfully, he gazed at me. "Their favorite targets, I'm afraid, were young enchanters like you. The ones whose powers were only just ripening. A kreelix would be assigned to watch each of them, to stay hidden until the very moment those powers began to emerge. It might have been the youth's first Changing, first triumph in battle—or first musical instrument. At that moment, the beast would sweep down from the sky, hoping to prevent the young wizard or enchantress from ever growing up."

Seeing Elen's morose expression, he grimaced. "This, truly, is Fincayra's darkest day."

I cringed, as if the shadow of the kreelix had passed over me again. I knew now that whoever had sent it had done so for one particular purpose. To destroy me. To keep me from using whatever powers I possessed. Or—was such a thing possible?—to keep me from ever facing Valdearg.

VI

Two Halves of Time

Unable to sleep, I rolled from one side to the other on the bed of pine needles. I tried crooking an arm beneath my head, bunching the tunic under my knees, or staring at the thick web of branches above me. I tried thinking about the evening mist, filtering through stands of trees at sunset; or the starlit sea, sparkling with thousands of eyes upon the waters.

Nothing helped.

Again I rolled over. Eh! A spiky pinecone jabbed the back of my neck. I brushed it aside, nestled my shoulder deeper into the needles, and tried once again to relax. To rest, at least a little. To move beyond the doubts, the wonderings—so vague I couldn't even put them into words—that poked at me like a pinecone of the mind.

I drew a deep breath. The fragrance of pine, sweet and tangy, flowed over me like an invisible blanket. Yet this blanket lacked enough warmth to ward off the chill night air. I shivered, knowing that before long the first snow would fall in this forest.

Another deep breath. Normally the smell of pine calmed me right away. Perhaps it reminded me of the quieter days of my childhood, long before the pieces of my life began to shift like river pebbles under my feet.

In those days I often climbed up to my mother's table of healing herbs. Sometimes I simply watched her sifting and straining, while the wondrous aromas filled my lungs. Other times, though, I mixed my own combinations, meshing whatever colors and textures pleased me. All the while—the smells! Thyme. Beech root. Sea kelp. Peppermint (so strong that one whiff popped open my eyes and tingled my scalp). Lavender. Mustard seed, straight from the meadow. Dill—which always made me sneeze. And, of course, pine. I loved to crush the needles, so that my fingers would smell like a pine bough for hours.

So why, tonight, did they do so little for me? They only pierced my shoulders, my back, and my legs like so many little daggers. Curling myself into a ball, I tried again to relax.

Something nudged the middle of my back. Rhia's foot, no doubt. Maybe she, too, was having trouble sleeping.

The nudge came again. "Rhia," I grumbled, not bothering to roll over. "Isn't it enough you insisted on following me—" I paused, correcting myself before she could. "Guiding me, I mean, when it made things that much worse for our mother? You don't have to come over here and kick me, as well."

Again—this time harder. "All right, all right," I admitted. "I know you promised her you'd turn back at Urnalda's lands. And, yes, I did agree to the idea! But I agreed because you could save me half a day or more. Not because you'd keep me up all night!"

When I felt another nudge, I flipped over and angrily grabbed—

A hedgehog. Hardly bigger than my fist, it curled itself even tighter, burying its face in a mass of bristles. Embarrassed, I grinned. Poor little creature! It was clearly frightened. Probably cold, too.

I hefted the prickly ball. Though I couldn't see its face, I recognized the darker markings of a male. No more than a few months old, most likely. The little fellow could have been lost, separated from his family. Or simply cold enough that he had abandoned any caution for the warmth of my back.

Holding his belly in my palm, I started gently stroking along his spine. While I had learned much in the last year about the language of trees (having moved well beyond the simple swishing of beeches, I could now carry on a rudimentary chat with an elm or even an oak), I still knew practically nothing about the speech of animals. Even so, I managed to produce a piping *yik-a-lik, yik-a-lik,* which I had once heard a mother hedgehog sing to her brood.

Very slowly, while I continued stroking, the ball began to uncurl. First came the leathery pads of the rear feet, each no bigger than my thumbnail. Then came the front feet. Then the belly, swelling like a dark bubble in a peat bog. At last an eye emerged, then the other, blacker than the shadows of night surrounding us. Finally came the nose, sniffing the skin of my thumb. As I stroked more vigorously, he released a tiny, throaty sigh.

Rhia would enjoy this little creature. Even if it meant waking her—and admitting my own folly. I could already hear her bell-like laugh when I told her that I had mistaken him for her foot.

Sitting upright on the bed of needles, I turned my second sight toward the cluster of fern where she had fallen asleep. Suddenly my heart froze. She was gone!

Setting down the hedgehog, I ignored his plaintive whimpers as I clambered to my feet. My second sight stretched to its fullest, peering through the shadowy branches and dark trunks of the grove. Where had she gone? Having trekked with her so often, I was accustomed to her daytime roamings, whether to forage for food, follow a deer's tracks, or plunge into the cool water of a tarn. But she had never before left camp at night. Had something sparked her curiosity? Or . . . brought her harm?

I cupped my hands around my mouth. "Rhia!"

No reply.

"Rhia!"

Nothing. The forest seemed unusually quiet. No branches clacked or groaned; no wings fluttered. Only the continuing whimpers of the hedgehog broke the silence.

Then, from somewhere beyond the ferns, came a familiar voice. "Do you need to be so loud? You'll wake every living thing in the forest."

"Rhia!" I grabbed my staff, sword, and leather satchel. "Where in Dagda's name are you?"

"Out here, of course. Where else did you expect me to watch the stars?"

Buckling the belt of my sword, I hurried through the mass of ferns. As often as I ducked to avoid the pine boughs, a jagged limb would clutch at my tunic. All of a sudden, the trees parted. A chill breeze splashed my face. I stood at the edge of a small, rock-strewn meadow.

To my left, a spring bubbled out of the ground, forming a pool enclosed by reeds. Beside it rested a flat slab of moss-rimmed stone. There, her arms wrapped around her shins and her face turned skyward, sat Rhia.

As I approached, whatever frustration I harbored melted away. She seemed so at peace, so at home. How could I blame her? I leaned my staff against the stone, sat down beside her—and gazed.

Stars, an immense swath of them, arched above us. Like singers in a grand, celestial chorus, they marched across the sky, linked through outstretched arms of light. It reminded me of the phrase, carved into the wall of the great tree that was Rhia's home—as well as my own memory: *The great and glorious Song of the Stars.*

Rhia continued scanning the sky, her curls sparkling with starlight. "So you couldn't sleep? Neither could I."

"You found a better way to spend the night than I did, though. I was just tossing around on pine needles."

"Look there," she cried, pointing to a plummeting star. Brightly it burned for an instant, then swiftly vanished. "I've often wondered," she said wistfully, "whether a star like that one falls somewhere in our world, or in someone else's."

"Or into a river beyond," I offered. "A great, round river that carries the light of all the stars, flowing endlessly into itself."

"Yes," she whispered. "And maybe that river is also the seam binding the two halves of time. You remember that story? One half always beginning, the other half always ending."

Propping my elbows on the stone, I leaned farther back. "How could I forget? You told it to me on the same night you showed me how to find constellations not just in the stars themselves, but in the spaces between them."

"And you told me about that horse—what was his name?"

"Pegasus."

"Pegasus! A winged steed, prancing from star to star. With you hugging his back." She laughed, a bell pealing in the forest. "How I'd love to fly like that myself!"

I grinned. "It reminds me of the thrill—the freedom—of my first time on horseback."

"Really?" For the first time since my arrival, she turned from the glittering vista. "When did you ever ride horseback?"

"Long ago. So long ago! It was a great black stallion, belonging to our . . . father." I didn't say the rest: before Rhita Gawr corrupted him, filling him with the wicked spirit's lust to control Fincayra. Those words still left such a hateful taste in my mouth. "I don't remember much about that horse, except that I loved to ride him—with someone holding me, of course. I was so small . . . but I loved the sound of his hooves beneath me, pounding, pounding. And the warm breath from his nostrils! Every time I visited him at the castle stable, I brought him an apple, just so I could feel his warm breath on my hand."

Softly, she touched my shoulder. "You really loved that horse."

I sighed. "It's all so blurry now. Maybe I was just too young. I can't even remember his name."

"Maybe it will come back to you in a dream. That happens sometimes. Dreams can bring back the past."

My teeth clenched, as I thought about the only dream that brought back the past for me. Over and over and over again. How I hated that dream! It struck at unpredictable times—but always carried me to the same place. Beyond the swirling mists surrounding Fincayra, across the sea, to a ragged village in the land called Gwynedd. There, a powerful boy—Dinatius by name—attacked me. In my rage I called upon my hidden powers and caused a fire, a fire that exploded out of the very air. The blaze! It scorched my face, searing the skin of my cheeks and brow. I lost my own eyes in those flames—while Dinatius, I fear, lost his life.

The dream always ended in the same way: Dinatius, shrieking in mortal agony, his arms crushed beneath the blazing branch of a tree. I always woke up the same way, as well. Sobbing, clutching at my sightless eyes. Feeling the pain of those flames. And what made the dream worse was that it was true.

Even as I shuddered, Rhia twirled one of her fingers around my own. "I'm sorry, Merlin. I didn't mean to upset you. Were you thinking about . . . the dragon?"

"No, no. Just dragons of my own."

She released my finger and ran her hand across the stone's rough surface. "The worst kind."

I swallowed. "The very worst."

"Sometimes those dragons are different from what they seem."

"What do you mean?"

She faced me squarely. "The Galator. You know it could help you defeat Valdearg. Why, it could be your only chance! So why aren't you going after it first? Before you have to face him?"

My cheeks grew hot. "Because there's no time! Why, you heard—"

"Is that all?" she interrupted. "Your only reason?"

"Of course it is!"

"Really?"

"Of course!" I pounded the stone with my fist. "You don't think I'm doing this because I'm scared of . . ."

"Yes?" she asked gently.

"Of Domnu." I stared at her, amazed. How could she have known? Just the thought of that treacherous old hag made me shudder. "Cairpré was right. You really do know how to see under someone else's skin."

"Maybe," she replied. "Sometimes it's easier to see someone else's dragons than your own, that's all. As to this one, I don't know whether you should go right to Urnalda's lands, or not. Time is short, as you said. But I do know that you're scared of Domnu. Very scared. And you need to know it's affecting your thinking. And, more than likely, your sleeping."

I couldn't help but grin. "You're a lot of trouble, you know. But every once in a while . . . you're almost worth it."

"Thanks," she said, returning the grin.

My brow furrowed. "I think, though, I still should go straight to Urnalda. There's my promise to her—and she needs the help now. Remember her words? *My people be attacked, this very day, as never before.*"

"If you do manage to help her somehow, she doesn't seem the kind of person who's going to give you any thanks."

"Oh, she would—in her own way. She's crusty, all right. And easily angered. But you can trust her, at least. Not like Domnu! All Urnalda really wants is to keep her people safe." I reflected for a moment. "Even if I could regain the Galator, I couldn't possibly do it in time to help her. On top of that, I never did find out how it works. So even if I found some way to get it back from Domnu, how much better off would I be?"

I glanced at the sea of stars above us. "There's also this: Maybe Urnalda knows something about the dragon that could help. In the same way the Galator helped win the last battle. She is, after all, an enchantress."

My gaze met Rhia's. "And, finally, there's one more thing." I took a long, slow breath. "I'm scared of Domnu. Just as much as I am of that dragon."

Sparks danced on her head as she nodded sympathetically. "Her name—what does it mean?"

"Dark Fate. That's all anyone needs to know about her! She calls on magic so ancient that even the most powerful spirits— Rhita Gawr, or Dagda himself—just leave her alone. And as much as I'd like to see her humbled, that's exactly what I'm going to do."

Just then my staff slid off the stone. I reached down among the grasses to fetch it—when something pricked the back of my hand. I jumped, startling Rhia so much that both of us nearly tumbled off.

At that instant, I started to laugh. I lowered my hand into the grass. And I picked up the little hedgehog, stroking his bristly back.

VII

STONE CIRCLE

Through most of the following day, we trekked north through Druma Wood. Thanks to Rhia's knowledge of the hidden pathways made by fox paws and deer hooves, we covered much ground. And quickly. Only twice did our speed slacken: in crossing a thick stretch of thorny brambles, as high as our hips in places, that ripped our clothing and raked our shins; and in climbing a buttress of rock whose shadowed face already wore a slick layer of ice.

Most of the time, though, Rhia's relentless pace left me breathless. She charged up hills, leaped across rivulets, and ran effortlessly through glades of oak, beech, and hemlock. Half deer herself she seemed, as I struggled to keep up with her. Whenever she spotted some tangy mushrooms or sweet berries, I felt doubly grateful—since they staved off our hunger and also gave us a chance to pause.

Yet I never complained about our pace. Urnalda's urgent plea still rang in my ears. Time leaned on me, as heavily as a toppled tree. If only I could get there faster! And if only I had a better idea what to do once I arrived.

Early that afternoon, we entered a grove of cedars that skirted the base of a hillside. Suddenly, the wind grew stronger. Branches waved wildly, slapping and scraping. Trunks twisted and moaned.

Rhia halted, listening intently to the cacophony around us, looking grimmer by the minute.

At length, she turned to me. "The trees—I've never heard them so agitated before."

"What are they saying?"

"Turn back! Over and over they keep saying *the boy of the wizard's staff will . . .*" She paused, working her tongue. *"Will die. As surely as a sapling smothered in flames."*

I cringed, touching the still-tender scars on my face. "But I can't turn back. If I don't face Valdearg, then you and everyone else—including every tree in this forest—will have to face him. The Druma will be a graveyard." The spicy scent of cedar pricked my nostrils. "If I must die, though, I only wish . . ."

I paused, listening to the clacking and creaking of the trees. "That I could be certain I will slay him, too."

Rhia's gray-blue eyes narrowed, but she said nothing.

"The question," I said gravely, "is how. I'm not ready to battle a dragon. Let alone slay one! Never will be, probably. Not after what happened . . . back there at the rowan. No, I'm still just *the boy of the wizard's staff.* Not a true wizard."

A branch snapped just above us, splintering as it struck the ground at our feet. Rhia, biting her lip, turned to go. Buried in my thoughts, I followed.

In time, the sound of our boots squelching through muddy soil replaced the wailing of the branches. Puddles filled every path. Trees grew sparser, except for the whitened skeletons of those whose roots had long ago drowned. Water birds whistled in the rising mist, while the first traces of a rotting smell fouled the air.

I turned to Rhia as we walked. "Is this the great swamp at the Druma's northern edge? Or a different one?"

She planted her boot of woven bark against a mound of peat, testing its firmness before plodding across. "It's part of the great swamp. But more than that I can't say. We're much farther east than the stretch I usually cross, since I took the most direct route. I thought it would save some time." Her voice dropped. "I hope I was right."

The mud sucked at my boots. "So do I."

The swamp, I knew, was not the only treacherous land ahead. When we reached the other side, we would find the fog-laden gullies of the living stones. Too often I had heard tales of travelers whose legs, arms, or heads had been suddenly removed from their bodies, crushed in jaws of rock. Nor could I shake the memory of the time when the lips of a living stone had nearly swallowed my own hand.

We began sloshing through a flooded stretch, stepping over decaying trunks and branches. By the time we reached a thick stretch of bog grasses, the sun had vanished behind a sheath of clouds. I looked over my shoulder at the western horizon. Rhia glanced in the same direction, then at me.

"Clouds are gathering, Merlin. There won't be any stars to guide us tonight. If we haven't reached the other side before nightfall, we'll need to rely on your second sight to find our way."

I took a deep breath, though the air reeked of things rotting. "That's not what worries me. It's what lives in this swamp. And what stirs after dark."

Silently, we trekked on, slogging through water up to our knees. In the waning light, strange sounds began to bubble up from the bog. From one side came a thin, unsteady hum; from behind us, a sudden splash—though we whirled around to see nothing. Then a *thwack*, and a screech of pain, as if someone's skull had been split. Soon the darkening mists echoed with distant wailing.

Without warning—something slithered past my shin. I jumped, leaving behind my boot in the process. Whatever it was quickly vanished, but we lost several minutes extracting my boot from the muck.

Sunset came and went without any change in the gloom. As dusk deepened around us, the wild sounds swelled. Suddenly Rhia stumbled, falling into a reeking pool. When she climbed out, I saw a huge leech, as long as my forearm, clinging to the dripping leaves on her back. It squirmed toward her neck. With a swipe of my staff, I knocked it away. The creature hissed shrilly before landing with a splash.

The light faded steadily. I began probing with my staff to help us avoid pits of quicksand—and whatever else lurked in the depths. We slogged on, trying always to head northward. But how could we keep our bearings without sun, moon, or stars? Each stumble, each twist in the route, took its toll. Merely staying together proved more difficult by the minute.

In the deepening darkness, strange shapes, twisting and writhing, rose out of the marsh. At first I tried to convince myself they were nothing but gasses bubbling up from below. Or shadows—a trick of the waning light. But their ghoulish forms didn't move like gasses. Or shadows. They moved . . . like things alive.

The shapes began sighing, almost weeping. Then came sudden cries of anguish—cries that jabbed like icicles in my ears. As fast as we tramped, the shapes pressed closer. A hand, or what seemed to be a hand, grasped at my tunic. I dodged it, nearly tripping in the process.

Just then, in the near blackness, I detected a vague, sloping contour ahead. But for the high mound in its center, it looked as rounded as the back of a great turtle. An island! Though the writhing shapes hampered my vision, the island seemed devoid of life.

"Rhia," I called. "An island!"

She halted. "Are you sure?"

"Looks that way."

She leaped to the side to avoid one of the shapes. "Let's go, then! Before these things—get away, you!—drown us in the muck."

Taking her by the elbow, I rushed forward. The shapes writhed more frantically, swirling about us, but we eluded them. Finally, we reached the edge of the island. While the wailing cries continued, we trudged ashore, leaving the eerie shapes behind.

Total darkness embraced us as we climbed higher. Despite the squelching of slick vines underfoot, the land seemed fairly dry. And solid. With my second sight, I surveyed the area. Only the massive mound, brooding and mysterious, broke the island's smooth surface.

"Nothing lives here," I noted. "Not even a lizard. Why, do you think?"

Rhia stretched her back wearily. "I don't know. I'm just glad those *things* aren't here."

I approached the mound. It was, I realized, a great boulder, about as high as a young oak tree. I froze. "There are no living stones around here, are there?"

"No. They keep to the higher ground, in the hills beyond. Here, in the swamp, we have other creatures to worry about."

Cautiously, I drew nearer to the boulder. I tapped it with my staff. A flake of moss broke off, spinning lazily to the ground. I placed my hand upon the surface, leaning into it until I felt certain of its solidity. Its stoneness.

"Well, all right," I declared. "But it still seems odd—a huge boulder, sitting all by itself in the middle of a swamp like this. As if someone placed it here for some sort of reason."

Rhia squeezed my arm. "If it's all by itself, then at least you can be sure it's not a living stone. They always travel in groups, five or six together." She yawned. "Merlin, I'm about to drop. How about a little rest? Until dawn?"

"I suppose so." I yawned myself. "We're not going back out there until the light returns anyway. Go ahead and rest. I'll take the first watch."

"You'll stay alert?" She waved at the swamp, whose chorus of harrowing sounds continued. "We don't want any visitors."

"Don't worry."

In unison, we collapsed at the base of the boulder. Tired though I was, I propped myself stiffly against the rock, determined to stay awake. A sharp knob pushed into the tender spot between my shoulder blades, but I didn't move. Better to have the security of something solid behind me. No more swamp creatures would surprise us this night.

Rhia, stretched out by my feet, gave my ankle a squeeze. "Thanks for taking the first watch. I'm not used to having someone look after me on a trek."

I grunted wearily. "That's because nobody can keep up with you on a trek." Then I added, "It's our mother, I'm afraid, who needs looking after. She must be so lonely right now."

"Mother?" Rhia rolled to her side. "She's upset, worried sick about us probably—but not lonely. She has Cairpré. He'll stick to her like resin to pine."

"Do you really think so?" My fingers slid down the shaft of my staff. "He always has so much to do. I thought he would get her settled somewhere, then go on his way."

Rhia's laughter joined the noises bubbling out of the swamp. "Haven't you noticed what's been happening to them? Really! You must be as thick as this boulder to have missed it."

"No," I snapped. "I haven't missed anything. You're not telling me they . . . well, have some *interest* in each other, are you?"

"No. They're well beyond that already."

"You think they're falling in love?"

"That's right."

"Come now, Rhia! You're dreaming even before you've fallen asleep. That sort of thing doesn't happen to . . . well . . ."

"Yes?"

"To mothers! At least not to *our* mother."

She giggled. "Sometimes, dear brother, you amaze me. I do believe you've been so wrapped up in your training the past few months that you've missed the whole thing. Besides, falling in love could happen to anyone. Even you."

"Oh, sure," I scoffed. "Next you'll try to convince me that we'll find a tasty meal in a pool of quicksand."

A despairing sigh was her only response. "I'm too tired to convince you of anything right now. In the morning, if you like, I'll enlighten you."

Tempted as I was to reply, I held my tongue. Right now we needed to rest. I adjusted my back against the boulder. Enlighten me, indeed. How could she be so sure of herself?

Even as I grumbled silently about Rhia, I stretched my second sight all the way across the island. Nothing stirred; nothing approached. The night progressed, full of the ongoing cacophony of the swamp. Yet no creatures joined us on this shore. I began to wonder whether the boulder itself might somehow deter visitors, though I could not understand why. Still, in an eerie way, it seemed more than it appeared.

Perhaps it was some quality of the rank air of the marsh, or the result of my own exhaustion. Or perhaps it was some silent magic of the living stone itself. Whatever the cause, it was only when I felt Rhia's hand pulling wildly on my foot that I realized that I had been swallowed by a mouth of stone.

And by then it was too late.

VIII

CIRCLE STONE

First, *silence.*

No wind whispering, no swamp voices echoing, no gasses bubbling. No shrieking, chattering, or hissing. No thumping of my living heart. No whooshing of my very breath.

No sound. No sound at all.

What sound can I remember? Quickly! I must not forget. The stream we crossed this morning? Yes! I heard it long before I saw it. Spraying sound as well as vapor, it pounded down the banks. Ice, touched by the first finger of dawn, crackled and burst. Water spilled and splashed, thrummed and gurgled, singing like a chorus of curlews.

Yet . . . this silence, so complete, so enormous, slowly overwhelms the singing. With each passing moment, the sound of the stream grows more distant. I begin to hear instead the quiet, in all its richness. Soft enough to roll in, deep enough to swim in. No more clanging, no more dissonance. Only silence. Who could desire more than to hear the heartbeat of the void?

I could! I must struggle to remember. I must. Yet all the sounds I would remember feel so separate, so strangely far away.

Second, darkness.

Light is gone. Or never existed? Oh, but it did! I can still call it back, still see its glow. Luminous. Eternal. First light on the clouds, radiant footsteps ascending the sky. A gleam on the horizon, a flame on the candle, a tremble on the star. And another kind of light, bright in the eyes: Rhia laughing, Mother knowing, Cairpré probing.

Still, darkness pulls on me, coaxes me to sleep, to let go. Why fight for the wavering flame? So easily it fails, returns to the dark. So gracefully the night ever follows the day. Darkness is all; all is darkness.

Light! Where are you? I am so lost . . . so frightened . . .

Third, stillness.

As long as I can move, I am alive. As long as I can feel—the wind against my cheeks, the earth under my toes, the petal between my fingers. Yet all I feel now is hardness. Everywhere. Closing in, crushing me. Move, fingers! Move, tongue! They do not respond. They do not exist. Gone are my bones. My blood. My flesh. Squeezed into nothingness.

I cannot move, cannot feel, cannot even breathe. Whatever is left of me is pressed and condensed. I long to snap like a whip, to spin like a leaf. Yet, even more, I long to rest. To be still.

Now I hear only silence. I see only darkness. I feel only stillness. I begin to accept, to understand, to become. I am solid and strong; I have the patience of a star. I am ageless, unyielding.

For now I am stone.

Almost. Something remains of that former self, that former me. I cannot touch it—cannot name it—yet it stays with me still. Down, deep down, in the center of my core. Too small to see; too large to hold. Snarling. Flaming. Twisting. It prods me to remember. To escape if I can! I have a longing. A life. A self. Yes, I can still hear my own voice, even as another, ancient voice swells around me, urging me to let go of all the rest.

Be stone, young man. Be stone and be one with the world.

No! I am too much alive, even now, encircled in rock. I want to change, to move, to do all the things stones cannot.

You know so little, young man! A stone comprehends the true meaning of change. I have dwelled deep within the molten belly of a star, sprung forth aflame, circled the worlds in a comet's tail, cooled and hardened over eons of time. I have been smashed by glaciers, seized by lava, swept across undersea plains—only to rise again to the surface upon a flowing river of land. I have been torn apart, cast aside, uplifted and combined with stones of utterly different origins. Lightning has struck my face, quakes have ripped my feet. Yet still I survive, for I am stone.

And I answer: I want to know you. Nay, more than that, I want to be you! But . . . I cannot forget who I was. Who I am. There are things I must do, living stone!

What is this strange magic that surrounds you, young man? That makes you resist me? You should have succumbed to my strength long ago.

I know not. I only know that my own self clings to me still, even as clusters of moss cling to you.

Come. Join me. Be stone!

I yearn even now to join you. To feel your depth; to know your strength. And yet . . . I cannot.

Ah, the stories I could tell you, young man! If only you would release yourself completely, allow yourself to harden. Then I could share with you all that I know. For a stone, while separate, is never far from the mountains and plains and seas of its birth. A stone's power springs not from itself alone, but from all that surrounds, all that connects.

I want to learn from you, living stone. Truly, I do. Yet I want still more to live the life I was born to live. Though it may be futile, and fleeting—it is nonetheless mine. You must set me free!

You are a strange one, young man. Although I have very nearly destroyed you, I cannot seem to consume you. There is something in you I cannot reach, cannot crush. That leaves, I am saddened to say, but one possibility.

What is that?

It is not the best for you, nor the best for me. Yet it is, alas, my only choice.

IX

SMOKE

With a thud, I landed on my back on the ground at the base of the living stone. Although Rhia's sudden shriek would normally have chilled my blood, I was glad to hear it. I was glad to hear anything at all.

"Merlin!" She threw her arms around me and squeezed.

"Not so hard, will you?" I wriggled free, patting my sore chest. It ached, as did my arms, legs, and back. Even my ears. In fact, I felt as if one gigantic bruise covered my whole body. Then, seeing Rhia's tear-stained face, so relieved, so thankful, I beckoned her to embrace me again.

She gladly accepted the invitation—more gently this time. "How?" she blurted. "How did you do it? I've never heard of a living stone releasing anyone it's caught."

Despite my sore cheeks, I grinned. "Most people don't taste as bad as I do."

She released me, her laughter echoing across the swamp. Then, for a long moment, she observed me. "There must be something in you that even a living stone couldn't crush."

"My thick head, perhaps."

"More likely, your magic."

Although my ribs throbbed, I drew a deep breath. "As little as there is, I suppose you could say it's my core. Essential—and undigestable."

With her leafy forearm, she brushed some chips of stone off my shoulder. "Well now, look at you! Your tunic is ripped, and there's so much dust in your hair that it's more gray than black." She smiled. "But you're alive."

"How long was I in there?"

"Two or three hours, I'd guess. The sun came up just before you returned."

Warily, I gazed up at the enormous boulder that had ejected me. I stepped slowly toward it, my heart pounding. Rhia tried to hold me back, but I waved her away. Placing a tentative hand on a flat, mossy spot, I whispered, "Thank you, great stone. One day, when I am stronger, I should like to hear more of your stories."

Though I could not be sure, I felt the rock beneath my fingers shiver ever so slightly. Removing my hand, I bent to retrieve my staff, still lying on the ground. The shadow of the living stone did not diminish the wood's lustrous sheen. I grasped the gnarled top—which, as always, fit my hand perfectly. For a few seconds, the scent of hemlock pushed aside the reeking smells of the swamp.

Rhia gasped. "Your sword! It's gone."

I started. Indeed, my sword, scabbard, and belt had vanished. They must have remained inside the living stone!

Whirling around, I pleaded, "My sword, great stone! I need it! For Valdearg."

The stone did not stir.

"Please . . . oh, please, hear me! That sword is part of me now. And it has magic of its own. Yes! I've been entrusted to bear it—

until the day, far in the future, when I shall give it to a boy. A boy born to be king. A boy of great power. So great that he will pull that very sword from a scabbard of stone."

The boulder remained motionless.

"It's true! The sword will be held—not by you, not by a living stone, but by a stone that will guard it, awaiting that very moment."

No response.

My nostrils flared. "Give it back."

Still, no response.

"Give it back!" I demanded. Grasping the shaft of my staff, I raised it to strike the living stone. Then, noticing my thumb on top of the carved image of a sword—symbol of the power of Naming— I halted. The name! The sword's name! Which, like all true names, held a magic of its own. Perhaps, just perhaps . . . I leaned toward the stone.

Abruptly, I caught myself. I had not used any magic since—since plucking my psaltery. If I called on my powers again, would another kreelix attack? And succeed where the other one had not? I cringed, remembering the gaping red mouth, the jagged wings, the ruinous fangs. Yet . . . if I let the elemental fear of another attack rule my actions, then what was I? A coward. Or worse. Whether or not another kreelix appeared, it would have already robbed me of my powers.

I gritted my teeth and bent closer to the stone. Mist, rank with decay, blew off the marsh, shrouding us completely. The swamp's eerie gasping, hooting, and wailing pressed closer. I could hardly hear my own thoughts for the noise.

Concentrating, I cupped my hands over my mouth. So that no one, not even Rhia, might hear the sword's true name, I spoke it softly. Then, with my full voice, I added: "Come to me, from the depths of stone. Wherever you are, I summon you."

Glancing nervously over my shoulder, I saw nothing but the curling trails of mist. Suddenly I heard a rumbling, growing louder by the second. It swelled steadily, like an approaching wind, until it obscured even the sounds of the swamp.

The living stone suddenly wrenched. Chips of rock broke loose, along with flakes of yellowish moss. Small cracks appeared all over its weathered surface. The whole stone rocked from side to side, as if struck by a violent tremor. An instant later, the surface split open, pursed, then spat out my sword and scabbard. They thudded on the ground.

I lunged for the prize, even as the living stone rolled to cover it. Rhia shouted, leaping aside. Together we ran across the island. As we reached the shore, vines squelched and popped under our boots. The mist grew thinner, shredding rapidly, revealing again the swamp.

Before plunging into the mire once more, I quickly strapped on the sword's leather belt. Then I gazed back at the living stone, rocking sullenly on the ground, and called to it. "Do not be angry, great stone! This sword would be difficult for you to digest. No less than its master! Someday, perhaps, you and I shall meet again."

With a deep rumble, the boulder started rolling toward us. Not wanting to wait to learn more about its mood, Rhia and I splashed into the putrid waters of the swamp. Yet as the ooze seeped into my boots, splattered my legs, and assaulted my nose, I felt somehow grateful even as I felt repulsed. Grateful to smell and hear again. And grateful to move freely—my legs pushing through bog grasses, my arms swinging by my side.

For most of that morning, we slogged northward through the marsh. Except for the pool of quicksand that tried to tear my staff from my hand, we had no great difficulties. Still, our hearts leaped when we reached drier ground at last. Eagerly, we shook the mud off our boots. An old apple tree, springing from the side of a low hill, offered us the remains of its autumn harvest. Withered and small as they were, the apples burst with flavor. We ate all we could hold. Nearby, Rhia found a clear, cold stream where we washed away the lingering odor of the swamp.

Continuing north, we trekked rapidly toward the realm of the dwarves. The land rose gradually in a series of grassy plains, lifting like stairs to the high plateau where the River Unceasing bubbled out of the ground. There, I knew well, we would enter the dwarves' terrain. Valdearg's terrain. If only I could find Urnalda before the wrathful dragon found me! Maybe I really could help her somehow. And maybe . . . she could also help me.

In midafternoon, we paused to feast on some shaggy gray mushrooms sprouting among the roots of a leaning elm. And to take advantage, for a moment at least, of the chance to sit down. Wiping the perspiration off my brow, I stretched my legs and surveyed the grassy plains surrounding us. While the River Unceasing flowed well to the east, my second sight could still make out the twisting corridor of mist that marked its channel.

I knew well the river's path: After gathering in these plains, it grew steadily wider and stronger, surging straight through the heart of Fincayra. Along most of that way, steep banks and pounding rapids made crossings difficult. In fact, between the headwaters and the Shore of the Speaking Shells far to the south, I had found only one reliable place to cross—a shallow stretch marked by nine rounded boulders. We couldn't be far from that spot now. For some inexplicable reason, I felt a gnawing urge to go there again.

After tossing another mushroom to Rhia (which she popped right into her mouth), I pointed toward the mist. "What about crossing the river over there? At the place with the boulders."

Still chewing, she shook her head. "I've had enough of boulders for one day! Besides, the shortest route is to keep going due north, up the plateaus, until we meet the headwaters. Crossing there won't be difficult, especially at this time of year when the waters are low."

Though I knew she was right, I continued to stare at the snaking mist. "I don't know why, but I feel drawn to that crossing."

"Whatever for?" She eyed me skeptically. "That would cost us half a day. As it is, the light will only last another couple of hours." She sprang to her feet. "Let's go."

"You're right. Haste is everything." With a final glance at the misty corridor, I followed her through the tall grasses.

A large flock of geese passed overhead, so close we could hear the rhythmic creaking of their wings. Like all the other birds we had seen that day, they were traveling in the opposite direction from us. After them came what looked at first like a spinning knot of dust—until we heard the buzzing and realized it was, in truth, an immense swarm of bees. Following close behind came a wide-winged heron, a pair of tattered gulls, a sandpiper, several swallows, and an elderly raven, flapping arduously. Then, hidden by the grass, a family of foxes nearly charged straight into us. Seeing their wide eyes glowing with terror, Rhia shot me a worried glance. Though we continued to ascend the terraced meadows, her pace slackened a little.

As late afternoon light brushed the grasses with gold, we reached the lip of another plateau. Both of us halted, struck by the same sight. The sky ahead of us loomed unusually dark. A heavy veil draped over the horizon . . . yet it seemed thinner, flatter than any thundercloud. Could it be a shadow caused by the lowering sun? At that moment, a gust of wind fluttered my tunic. I caught the first whiff of a scent that smote me like a broadsword.

Smoke.

I released a groan. The sky ahead had been darkened not by clouds, nor by shadows, but by Valdearg.

Rhia turned to me. Her face, usually so bright, looked utterly grim. "Until now, Merlin, I've been able to push aside my doubts. Because I thought it was right to help you. But now . . . I'm not so sure. Look there! The land burns, like Valdearg's angry heart. It seems so—well, *foolhardy* to walk right into his mouth like this."

"Have faith," I countered bravely. But my croaking voice betrayed how little faith I had myself. I shook my head. "Foolhardy it is, I admit. What else can I do, though? The longer I wait to confront Valdearg, the more he's sure to destroy. My only hope is to reach Urnalda soon. Perhaps she knows something useful. She might even know what the prophecy meant by *a power still higher.*"

Rhia set her clenched fists upon her hips. "All I remember about that prophecy is that, even if you do somehow slay this dragon, you're going to die with him! So either he kills you and survives, or kills you and dies himself. Either way, I lose a brother."

With my staff, I jabbed at a mound of grass. "Don't you think I know that already? Look. Here we are, at the very edge of the dwarves' realm, and what weapons can I really count on? My staff, my sword—and whatever magical powers, still unformed and untrained, that I carry inside me. Put together, they don't amount to a single scale on Valdearg's tail."

I scanned the smoky horizon. "And that's not the worst of it."

She cocked her head. "Meaning?"

"Meaning I just can't rid myself of the idea that Valdearg isn't all I need to worry about."

Incredulous, she stared at me. "Wings of Fire himself isn't enough? What are you talking about—the kreelix? Or whoever might have secretly raised it?"

"No. Though they might also be part of this, for all I know."

"Who, then?"

My voice lowered. "Someone who longs to take Fincayra in his hand. To squeeze it like a gemstone. To make it his own."

For an instant, Rhia's face went as white as birch bark. "Not . . . Rhita Gawr? What makes you think he's involved?"

"I, well . . . I'm not really sure. It's vague. But I wonder why the dragon woke up now, after sleeping for so many years. And who might know enough about magic—or *negatus mysterium*—to have caused such a thing. I don't know whether it's Rhita Gawr or someone else . . . or if I'm just imagining things. Yet I can't help wondering."

She scowled at me. "You're hopeless, really! Listen, Merlin. Rhita Gawr has not set foot on this island since the Dance of the Giants routed him and his forces over a year ago! You'd be better off worrying about the enemies you know—rather than creating any more for yourself."

I twisted my staff into the turf. "All right, all right. You speak wisely, I'm sure. It's just that . . . well, forget it. Here, what do you say we stop talking about enemies—of all kinds—for just a moment. Let's dine on some of these astral flowers."

"Before Valdearg dines on you?"

Ignoring her comment, I picked a fistful of the yellow, star-shaped flowers speckling the grass. As she looked on glumly, I rolled them into a compact mass that produced a sharp, tangy aroma. "I remember when you first showed me how to eat these. You called them *a trekker's sustenance.*"

"Now I'll call them my brother's last meal."

Tearing the mass in half, I handed one part to her. "None of us will eat many more meals unless Valdearg is stopped."

She nodded, her curls ignited by the golden light. "True." She took a bite of the astral flowers, chewed thoughtfully, and swallowed. "That's why I'm coming with you."

"You are not!"

"You will need help." Her eyes bored into me. "I don't care if Urnalda wants you to come alone! I've saved your skin before."

I fingered my staff. "That you have. This time, though, we're talking about Wings of Fire. He could wipe out every single life we know." Wrapping my forefinger around hers, I added gently, "Including our mother's. She is the one who needs you most, Rhia. She is the one you must protect. Not me."

Her head bowed.

"Remember, you promised her that you would come back. That you would take me no farther than the dwarves' borderlands."

Rhia lifted her head slowly. "At least . . . let me give you something." She reached for the Orb of Fire at her side.

"Not the Orb. That's yours to keep."

"But I don't know how to use it!"

I squeezed her finger. "You will, someday."

Releasing me, she deftly unwove a bit of vine from her sleeve. Then, without a word, she tied the bracelet of vibrant green around my wrist.

"There," she said at last. "This will remind you of all the life around you, and the life within yourself." She studied me sternly, though I could see the clouds in her eyes. "What it won't do is help you stay out of trouble."

Now it was my turn to bow my head. "Nothing can do that, I'm afraid."

Numb as I was, I could still feel her leafy arms wrap around me. Then I strode off without her, my future as dark as the veil of smoke on the horizon.

PART TWO

X

Hunter and Hunted

Within the hour, shafts of glowing crimson streaked the sky, like the strings of a celestial psaltery. I soon reached a winding stream, flowing red in the waning light: the headwaters of the River Unceasing. Crossing the narrow channel, a mere trickle of water compared to the torrent it would become in the spring snowmelt, proved easy. Just as Rhia had predicted.

As my boots ground against the rounded stones in the channel, I wondered if her other, more fearful predictions would also prove true. And whether I would ever see her again. Like the nameless horse from my childhood we had talked about under the stars, Rhia was more than a companion, more than a friend. She was part of me.

Stepping onto the northern bank, I surveyed the lands of the dwarves. Somewhere out there, in those rolling, rocky plains, lay the hidden entrances to their underground realm. While Urnalda would, I knew, be grateful for my help, I doubted that she guessed how much I would also need hers. It still puzzled me why she had declared that I, and I alone, could help her people. Perhaps she, too, knew the prophecy of *The Dragon's Eye*:

Lo! Nothing can stop him
Except for one foe
Descended from enemies
Fought long ago.

I shuddered, for while I did indeed carry Tuatha's blood in my veins, I did not possess either his wisdom or his weaponry. And I shuddered again to think of the unmatched power of Valdearg. *Disaster shall follow His waking again.* Slaying the dragon, in itself, would be difficult enough. Evading the prophecy, and somehow surviving the battle, would be—I felt sure—impossible.

Squeezing the shaft of my staff, I debated how best to find Urnalda. Or, more likely, to help her find me. If I made myself too visible, Valdearg might well spot me first. If, on the other hand, I hid too well, I might waste valuable time. Keep to the open, I decided at last. And stay ever alert.

Soon the stench of smoke grew stronger. My eyes began to water. I entered a stretch of plain that looked more like an abandoned fire pit than a field. The base of my staff no longer swished through tall grasses, but rather crunched against brittle stems and parched soil. Scorched brambles clawed at the smoky air. Boulders, scattered over the plain, resembled lumps of charcoal. And always the smell!

With my second sight, I frequently scanned the darkening sky for any sign of the dragon. As large as he would be, giving me the chance to spot him at a distance, I expected he would also be fast. Terrifyingly fast. And even while watching for him, I also watched the shadowy terrain at my feet, for I preferred not to tumble into one of the dwarves' cleverly disguised tunnels. Every indentation, no matter how slight; every unusual shadow, no matter how small—all these I checked carefully.

Just then a gruff voice barked a command. It came from just behind a mass of brambly gorse to my left. Cautiously, I crept closer.

Crouching behind the charred thorns, I spotted a pair of dwarves, their leather leggings and red beards catching the last rays of light. Although they stood not much taller than my waist, their stout chests and burly arms gave warning of their surprising strength. Heavily armed, each of them bore a double-sided axe, a long dagger, and a quiver of arrows. They had just drawn their bows, in fact, and were hurriedly nocking their arrows.

I turned to see a pair of deer, a doe and a stag, cowering at the back of a steep gully rimmed by blackened boulders. No doubt the dwarves had driven them into this trap, hoping to fell one or both of them before they could escape. The doe, tensing her powerful thighs, tried to leap up the side of the gully, but slid back down with a clatter of rocks and a cloud of ash. The stag, meanwhile, lowered his massive rack and prepared to charge straight at the hunters. The points of his antlers gleamed dangerously, yet I knew they would prove worthless against speeding arrows.

The peril of the deer made my stomach clench. Myself, I never ate venison—ever since the day long ago when Dagda himself, disguised as a stag, had rescued me from certain death. Yet I had never deigned to interfere with anyone else's enjoyment of deer meat. Still . . . I had never before stumbled upon one of the graceful creatures' execution.

At the instant the arrows nocked into the bowstrings, the doe suddenly turned in my direction. Whether she saw me or not through the brambles, I could not tell. Yet the sight of her wide, intelligent, brown eyes—stricken with terror—hit home.

"Stop!" I shouted, leaping into the air.

Startled, the dwarves jumped. Both of their arrows went wide, skidding off the rock-flaked walls of the gully. At the same instant, the doe and the stag bolted across the turf before the dwarves could reach for their quivers again. In a single, magnificent leap, their forelegs tucked tight against their chests, the deer sailed over their attackers' heads and bounded out of range.

"What fool are you?" demanded one of the dwarves, pointing his reloaded bow straight at my chest.

"I come in peace." Emerging from the tangle of gorse, I lifted my staff into the smoky air. "I am Merlin, called to join you by Urnalda herself."

"Pshaw!" The dwarf scowled at me. "Did she also command you to ruin our hunt?"

I hesitated. "No. But I couldn't do otherwise."

"Couldn't *what?*" The other dwarf stomped angrily, threw his bow to the ground, and pulled out his axe. "You miserable, long-legged oaf! Methinks we should bring back man meat instead of deer."

"A fine idea," snapped the first. "These days meat of any kind is hard to come by. You won't taste nearly as good as venison—the first we've found in many days, mind you—but you'll do. Did Urnalda never tell you that your race is forbidden to enter these lands?"

"Go ahead," urged his companion. "Shoot him now. Before he tries one of his man tricks on us."

"Wait," I protested, my mind racing to find some way to escape.

"You say these lands are forbidden, yet I have been here before." Although my knees were wobbling, I stood my tallest on the charred soil. "And I have come back to help your people, even as you helped me."

"Pshaw!" He drew back his bow. The arrow point glinted darkly. "Now I know you're a liar as well as a thief. Our laws tell us to kill human trespassers, not help them! Not even Urnalda, whose memory is as short as her plump little legs, would forget that."

"Be that so?" demanded a sharp voice from the shadows.

Like myself, both dwarves whirled to face a squat figure standing beside one of the boulders. Urnalda. She wore a hooded cloak over her black robe that glittered with an embroidery of runes. Her ragged red hair, surging out of the hood, held many jeweled clasps, ornaments, and pins. She wore earrings of conch shells, each almost as large as her bulbous nose. One of her thickset hands curled around her staff, while the other hand pointed at the dwarf holding the bow. Her eyes, as bright as the flames that had consumed my own psaltery, burned with rage.

"Urnal-nalda," fumbled the first dwarf, lowering his bow. "I didn't mean to insult you."

"No?" The enchantress eyed him for a long moment. "An insult be an insult even if the person it maligns be out of hearing."

"B-b-but you are mis-mistaken."

"Be I?" Urnalda stepped fully out of the shadows. "Far worse than your insult to me, huntsman, be your threat to our friend here." She nodded toward me, swaying her shell earrings. "You be about to skewer him before I arrived."

My own chest relaxed, even as the dwarf panted in fright. Nervously, he pawed his beard. "But he—"

"Silence! He may be a man, but he still be a friend. Oh, yes! A valued friend. And more than that, he be our only hope." She glared at him. "You seem to be forgetful of my command to keep him safe after he came to our realm. Be that so?"

"Y-yes, Urnalda. I forgot."

A flash of light burst from Urnalda's hand. At the same instant the dwarf yelped in surprise. He stood in his same leggings, though they fell like loose sacks around his boots. I thought his pants had fallen—then realized the truth.

"My legs!" he wailed. "You shortened them!" He tried standing on his toes, though he still only reached his companion's elbow. "They're only half as long as they were."

"Yes," agreed the enchantress. "So now your memory be no longer than your legs."

He dropped to his knees, now only a little higher than the tops of his boots. "Please, Urnalda. Please give me back my old legs."

"Not until you give Urnalda back her faith in your loyalty." Her eyes flicked toward the other dwarf, who stood shivering. "I would do the same to you, but I be short of huntsmen just now."

Slowly, Urnalda turned to me. Her face, though still wrathful, seemed a touch softer. "I be sorry your return be so unpleasant."

I bowed respectfully. Then, with a grateful sigh, I leaned against my staff. "I am glad you arrived when you did. Very glad."

The conch shells swayed as Urnalda bowed her head slightly. "Your timing be just as good as my own, Merlin. You see, this be the night that Valdearg will come back here."

Stiffening, I glanced at the sky, darkened both by twilight and the hovering streaks of smoke. Gradually, my puzzlement overcame my fear, and I asked, "You know he will come back tonight?"

"That be true."

"How can you be sure?"

Her cheeks pinched. "Because, my young friend, I made a pact with him. Oh yes! A dragon be a most intelligent beast, aware of what he really wants. And in this case, I be sorry to say, what the dragon really wants . . . be you."

XI

THE PACT

Before I could begin to move, Urnalda waved her hand. A flash of scarlet seared my mind. I flew backward from the impact, landing with a thud on the charred turf. For an instant I felt my heart had been ripped away, and my lungs crushed completely. The pain in my chest! The shadowy sky, tinged with scarlet, careened above me.

Haltingly, I took a breath of smoky air. My throat stung. I forced myself to sit up. There—the swirling face of the enchantress, smirking confidently. So dizzy . . . Not far away, my unsheathed sword lay on the ground. Much farther away, my staff. I could barely keep the images distinct; everything blurred together. Hadn't I felt this way before? Recently? I vaguely recalled . . . but when? I couldn't quite remember.

My sword, I told myself. *If I can just get it back, I can protect myself.*

Stretching out a trembling hand, I tried my hardest to halt the spinning, to concentrate my thoughts. *Come to me, sword. Leap to me.*

Nothing happened.

Although I could hear Urnalda sniggering in the background, I did not let my thoughts veer from the sword. *Leap to me, I say. Leap!*

Still nothing.

Once again I tried. Gathering all of my power, I poured every drop of it into the sword. *Leap!*

Still nothing.

"Sorry to say, Merlin, you be a little lighter now." Grinning broadly, the enchantress stepped over to the sword and snatched it. "I be taking something that once be yours."

"My sword." I tried to rise, but fell back weakly. "Give it back to me!"

Urnalda's eyes flamed. "No, it not be your sword I mean." Bending toward me, she spoke in a chilling whisper. "I be taking not your sword, but your powers."

Suddenly I remembered when I had felt this way before. With the kreelix! My stomach twisted in knots; my mind whirled. Gasping for breath, I forced myself to stand. Though I felt as wobbly as a newborn colt, I faced her.

"Urnalda. You can't! I am your friend, aren't I? You said so yourself! How can you do this?"

"Easily," she answered. "A bit of *negatus mysterium* be all it takes."

My legs buckled, and I fell back to the sooty ground. "Why, though? I could help you! I'm the only one who can defeat Valdearg. That's the prophecy of *The Dragon's Eye.*"

"Bah!" scoffed the enchantress. "Such prophecies be worthless. What matters be my pact with Valdearg himself." Her stubby fingers played with one of her earrings as she studied me darkly. "You see, the dragon awoke from his spell of sleep because someone destroyed the most precious part of his waking life, the one thing he treasured over everything else."

I shook my spinning head. "What was that?"

"I think you be pretending, Merlin. I think you already know."

"I don't! Believe me."

"All right, then. I shall humor you. Valdearg awoke because someone—someone most clever—found the secret hiding place of his eggs. His only offspring! Then that bloodthirsty someone killed his young ones. Every last one of them. That be a most dangerous thing to do."

Angrily, she slashed at the air with my sword. "Since the dragon eggs be hidden near the land of the dwarves, Valdearg blamed this deed on my people. The innocent, upright people of Urnalda! So he flies down here, burns my lands, pounds the ground with his tail to make my tunnels collapse, roasts alive dozens of my huntsmen." Her slashing grew more violent. "Ruin! Devastation! Until finally—yes, finally—I convinced him that the killer be not a dwarf after all."

I started to speak, but her torrent of words overwhelmed me.

"Urnalda, so clever, so wise, examined what be left of the eggs most carefully. And I found proof that the killer be not a dwarf, but a man. A poison-hearted man! It be no easy task to convince Valdearg himself to look close enough to see the proof, since even flying high above the remains fills him with rage. Uncontrollable rage." She jabbed at the air with a vengeance. "Even so, I persisted—and finally succeeded. When Valdearg realized the killer be a man, he decided that only his old foe Tuatha—or a descendant if Tuatha no longer be alive—would be capable of doing such a terrible thing."

My cheeks burned. "Where did he get such an idea?"

"That be simple." Her taut lips scowled at me. "It be true."

"But it's not!" I started to stand, but she slashed at me with the blade until I sat down again.

"So I, Urnalda, made a pact with Wings of Fire. Indeed I did! We agreed that if I could deliver you to him, he would leave my people in peace. Forever. But dragons be not patient. He refused to wait very long."

She stabbed at the ashen earth. "We agreed to meet tonight. If I did not yet have you as my prisoner, he promised me just one more week—seven days, no more. If, on the night of the seventh day, I could not produce you—then he vowed to annihilate every last one of my people. And anyone else in his path until he found you."

"But I never killed his young! How could I? For months, I haven't done anything but work on my instrument."

"Bah! You could be slipping away quite easily, with no one ever knowing."

"It's not true."

She looked at me skeptically, her eyes glowing like a dragon's flame. "In many ways, it be a bold and visionary act. Rid this land of dragons! Destroy their despicable race altogether!" She twisted the sword into the ground beside me. "Yet you should be knowing that it bring harm to the dwarves. The people of Urnalda."

"I didn't do it, I tell you!"

Raising the weapon, she swung it over my head, barely missing me. "It be in your blood to kill! Do you deny it? You relish the feeling of power, of strength. You know my words be true, Merlin! Look what Tuatha's only son—your father, Stangmar—did to the dwarves and the rest of Fincayra! He poisoned our lands. He murdered our children. How can you tell me that you, his own son, be any different?"

"But I am!" I pushed myself into a crouch. My second sight, no longer spinning, focused on Urnalda's flashing eyes. "I am the one who finally defeated him! Haven't you heard that? Ask Dagda himself if you doubt me."

The enchantress grunted. "That means nothing. Only that you be still more ruthless than your father." She pricked the edge of my sword with her fingernail. "Answer me truly. Do you deny that you would be glad to see Fincayra rid of dragons forever?"

"N-no," I admitted. "I can't deny that. But—"

"Then how can I believe you be not the killer?" She thrust the sword at my neck, holding the tip just a finger's width away. Her lips curled in a snarling grin. "Now, however, you must understand. Whether or not you really did it be unimportant. Yes, irrelevant."

"Irrelevant?" I slammed my fist on the charred soil, sending up a cloud of ash. "It's my life you're talking about."

"And the life of my people, which be much more important." She nodded, clinking the conch shells dangling from her ears. "What counts be that the dragon *believes* that you be the man who killed his young. Whether or not you really be him—that be meaningless. All he needs be a few bites of man flesh to ease his appetite for revenge." She leaned closer, pressing her bulbous nose against mine. "You be the man."

In desperation, I started crawling toward my staff. Urnalda, though, moved too quickly. Waving her hand in the direction of the staff, she caused it to rise off the ground and twirl in the smoky air. The two dwarves looking on gasped in amazement.

"Now," she snapped, "do you doubt that I stripped you of your powers? Do you think to use your wizard's staff against me?" Before I could answer, she spat out a strange incantation. With a sizzling flash of scarlet light, my staff completely disappeared.

My chest ached with emptiness. *My powers. Gone! My staff, my precious staff. Gone!*

Urnalda examined me severely. "Undeserving as you be, I still be merciful. Oh yes! I be leaving you with your second sight so that you will give the dragon the satisfaction of believing you can defend yourself—at least for a minute or two. That way, after he slays you, he be more likely to keep his bargain. For the same reason, I give this back to you."

She hurled my sword high into the air, at the same time barking a command. It fell back toward me, before suddenly swerving in midair and sliding straight into the scabbard at my waist. "Be warned, though," she growled. "If you be thinking about trying that blade against me, I be using it to cut your legs as short as my huntsman's over there."

The recently shortened dwarf, clasping his baggy leggings, released a whimper.

Urnalda drew in her breath. "Now be the time. Up, I command you!" She pointed with her staff toward a rocky, pyramid-shaped rise across the plateau. "March to that hill. The dragon be arriving there soon."

Weakly, I struggled to my feet. My mind reeled, even as my body ached. I had feared—even expected—that I would lose my life in the end to Valdearg. But not like this. No, not at all like this.

And although some of my strength had returned, I felt more than ever that emptiness in the middle of my chest. As if my very center had been torn away. My future as a mage was already clouded—bad enough. But now whatever powers I possessed, those gifts of magic I barely even understood, had vanished. And with them, something more. Something very close to my soul.

XII

TO CIRCLE A STORY

Just then one of the huntsmen cried out. All of us turned to see a large doe bounding across the darkened plateau. With grace and speed, she sprinted over the rolling plain like a flying shadow. I could not tell whether it was the same wide-eyed doe from the gully. I could only hope that her legs would soon carry her far away from this land of ruthless hunters—and traitorous allies.

"*Mmmm,* venison." Urnalda clacked her tongue. "Quick! Before it be gone."

Before she had finished her sentence, the arrows were already nocked. Both dwarves, brawny arms bulging, drew back their bows. This time, I felt sure, at least one of their arrows would find its mark. And this time I could do nothing to prevent it.

An instant before they let fly, the doe leaped high into the smoke-streaked air. For a heartbeat she hung there, floating, the perfect target.

"Shoot!" commanded Urnalda. "I said—"

An immense bulk suddenly plowed into her from behind. With a terrified screech, she flew into the pair of dwarves, sending their arrows skittering across the ground. The huntsmen, just as surprised as Urnalda, collapsed under her weight. Apparently stunned, she lay on top of them, moaning. The recently shortened dwarf tried to free himself and stand, but tripped over his loose leggings. He landed directly on Urnalda's face, crushing one of her shell earrings.

Simultaneously, a huge rack of antlers scooped me up and lifted me into the air. I toppled backward, falling across an enormous neck, bristling with fur. The stag! All at once we were bounding across the plain. It took all my strength just to hold on, my legs entwined with the antler points and my arms wrapped around the powerful neck. Coarse fur scratched my cheeks as the great body bounced beneath me. Soon the cries of the dwarves faded away and all I could hear was the pounding, pounding of hooves.

I have no idea how long I rode this way, though it seemed half the night. The muscles of the stag's neck felt as hard as stone. Pound, pound, pound. At least once I fell off, thudding into the ground. In a flash, the antlers scooped me up again and the brutal ride continued.

Finally, dazed and bruised, I tumbled off again. This time, no rack of antlers retrieved me. Rolling onto my back, I felt the coolness of wet grass against my neck. My battered body gave way, at last, to exhaustion. Vaguely, I thought I heard voices, almost human but different somehow. Finally, my head pounding as incessantly as the hooves, I fell into heavy slumber.

When I awoke, it was to the sound of a stream. Water bounced and splattered somewhere nearby. Finding myself facedown in a bed of grass, I turned over stiffly. My neck and back ached, especially between my shoulders. Bright light! The sun rode high above, warming my face. The air, while still mildly smoky, seemed lighter and clearer than last night.

Last night! Had all that really happened? Despite the painful stiffness of my back, I sat up. Suddenly, I caught my breath. There, seated on a toppled tree trunk beside the bubbling stream, sat a young woman about my own age.

For a long moment she and I sat in silence. She seemed to be looking past me, at the stream, perhaps out of shyness. Even so, I could tell that her immense brown eyes were watching me cautiously.

Handsome did not describe her—just as, I well knew, it did not describe me—yet there was a strong, striking air about her nonetheless. Her chin, unusually long and narrow, rested upon her hand. She seemed relaxed, yet poised to move in a fraction of a second. Her braided hair glinted with the tans and auburns of marsh grasses. The braid itself swept across her shoulder and over the back of her yellow robe that seemed to have been woven from willow shoots. She wore no shoes.

"Well, well," declared a deep, resonant voice. "Our traveler has awakened."

I spun around to see a tall, broad-chested young man approaching us through the grass. Wearing a simple, tan-colored tunic, he stepped with long, loping strides. His chin, like the girl's, jutted strongly. He possessed the same rich brown eyes, though not quite so large as hers. And he, too, had bare feet.

At once, I knew that these two were brother and sister. At the same time, I felt the gnawing sense that they were somehow more, and less, than they appeared. Yet I couldn't quite identify how.

Pushing myself to my feet, I nodded to both of them. "Good day to you."

The young man nodded in return. "May green meadows find

you." He held out his hand, although the motion seemed slightly awkward for him. We clasped, his sturdy fingers curling around my own. "I am Eremon, son of Ller." He cocked his head toward the trunk. "That is my sister, Eo-Lahallia. Though she prefers to be called just Hallia."

She said nothing, but continued to watch me warily.

He released his grip. "We are, you could say, people of these parts. And who are you?"

"I am called Merlin."

Eremon brightened. "Like the hawk?"

Sadly, I smiled. "Yes. I had a friend once—a dear friend. A merlin. We . . . did much together."

Eremon's wide eyes gleamed with understanding. He seemed to know, somehow, what I had left unsaid.

"Unlike you," I went on, "I am not from this region. You could, as you did before, call me a traveler."

"Well, young hawk, I am glad your travels brought you here. As is my sister."

He glanced toward her hopefully. She did not speak—although she shifted uneasily on the trunk. And while she continued to avoid my own gaze, she shot a direct look at Eremon: a look of mistrust.

Turning back to me, he indicated the patch of matted grass where I had been sleeping. "Your travels have drained you, it seems. You might have slept a full week if your fitful dreams hadn't wakened you."

A full week. All that remained—and now, less! Valdearg would return one week from last night. To devour me. And if not me, everyone and everything in his path.

Seeing me suddenly tense, Eremon placed his hand upon my

shoulder. "I have not known you long, young hawk. Yet I see you are troubled." His gaze flowed over me like a wave washing over a rocky shore. "I have the feeling, somehow, that your troubles are also ours."

Hallia sprang to her feet. "My brother!" She paused, hesitant, before saying any more. At last, in a voice quieter but no less resonant than Eremon's, she asked, "Shouldn't you . . . wait? You are, perhaps, too quick to trust."

"Perhaps," he replied. "Yet the feeling persists."

Still without looking straight at me, Hallia waved in my direction. "He only just awoke, after all. You haven't even . . . circled a story with him."

Puzzled, I watched Eremon close his brown eyes thoughtfully, then reopen them. "You are right, my sister." He turned to me. "My people, the Mellwyn-bri-Meath, have many traditions, many rhythms, some of which have come down to us all the way from Distant Time."

With the agility of a sparrow turning in flight, he moved to the stream's edge and knelt by a strip of soft mud. "One of our oldest traditions," he continued, "is to circle a story, as a way of introducing ourselves. So in meeting someone from a different clan, or even a different people, we often invoke it."

"What does it mean, to circle a story?"

Eremon reached into the stream and pulled out a slender, gray stone. He shook the water from it, then drew a large circle in the mud. "Each of us, starting with you as the newcomer, tells part, but only part, of a tale." Using the stone, he divided the circle into three equal portions. "When we have finished, the parts combine, giving us a full circle."

"And a full story." I stepped to the stream bank and knelt beside him. "A wonderful tradition. But must we do it now? I am, well, much better at listening to stories than telling them. And right now my thoughts are . . . elsewhere. My time is short. Too short! Indeed, I really should go." Under my breath, I added, "Though I'm not quite sure where."

Hallia nodded, as if my reaction had confirmed her suspicions. "Now . . . see there?" she said to her brother, her voice still hesitant, but urgent all the same. "He does not like stories."

"Oh, but I do!" I pushed some hair off my brow. "I have always loved stories. It's miraculous, really, where they can take you."

"Yes," agreed Eremon. "And where they can keep you." He studied me. "Come, young hawk. Join our circle."

Something behind the rich brown of his eyes told me that staying a moment longer, in this particular place with these particular people, could be important. And that my part of the story would be heard with interest—and judged with care.

"All right, then," I replied. "How do I begin?"

"However you like."

I bit my lip, trying to think of the best way to start. An animal—yes, that felt right. One who lived as I did now: alone. I filled my lungs with air. "The story begins," I declared, "with a creature of the forest. A wolf."

Hallia started at my choice. Even her brother, whose wide eyes continued to scan me, flinched. I knew, beyond doubt, that I had chosen poorly. Yet I could not be sure why.

"This wolf," I went on, "called himself Hevydd. And he was lost. Not on the ground, but in his own heart. He wandered through the high hills, exploring and sleeping and hunting wherever he liked. He sat for hours upon his favorite stone, howling to the pearls of the night sky. Yet . . . his forest felt more like a prison, with every tree another bar on his cage. For Hevydd was alone—in ways he could not fathom. He hungered for answers, but he didn't even understand the questions. He longed for companions, but didn't know . . ." My dry throat made me cough. "Didn't know where to look."

Eremon frowned—whether from sympathy or dismay, I could not tell. Yet I knew, as did he, that my portion of the story had finished. Deftly wielding the stone, he began to draw in the upper third of the circle. A symbol, I realized, of my part of the story. But instead of the head or body of a wolf, as I myself would have drawn, he drew a paw print. The wolf's track.

Looking not at me, nor at Hallia, but at the circle, Eremon began to speak. "Hevydd did not realize," he intoned, "that the forest was no cage of bars—but an endless maze of overlapping trails. Where one trail ended, another one began. Deer loped this way; badgers ran that. A spider dropped from one branch; a squirrel climbed another. Along the floor slithered a newborn snake; across the sky soared a pair of eagles. Each of these trails connected to each other, so that when the wolf padded along the ridge by himself, he was really traveling alongside all the others. Even when he veered from his path to stalk his next meal, the trails of hunter and hunted became one."

His voice fell until I could hardly hear it above the splattering stream. "So Hevydd did not notice when the last oak perished, causing the squirrels to move away. Nor did he mourn when plague struck the rabbits' warren, killing every single one of them. Nor did he mark the day when the yellow-backed butterflies stopped flitting through the groves, along with the jays and ravens who dined upon them."

He stopped, drawing a dozen different tracks in his portion of the circle—the prints of all the animals he had named, and more. As he was finishing, Hallia stepped closer, still avoiding me with her round eyes. For a moment she peered thoughtfully at the drawing in the mud, while playing with her auburn braid.

"The forest," she began, "grew quieter . . . by the day. So very quiet. Fewer birds chattered in the branches; fewer beasts strolled through the underbrush. From his stone on the ridge, though, Hevydd howled more often. He howled from greater hunger, since food was more scarce. And he howled, as well, from greater loneliness."

Bending gracefully, she took the slender stone from Eremon's hand. She started to speak again, then paused for a while before the words finally came. "The day arrived . . . that a new creature entered the forest." With deep, harsh strokes, she filled the remaining portion of the circle with another track: the booted foot of a man. "This creature came . . . with arrows and blades. Stealthily, craftily, he approached Hevydd's howling stone. No birds remained to rise skyward in warning. No animals scattered from his path. And no one was left to mourn when the man killed Hevydd . . . and cut out his heart."

XIII

TO RUN LIKE A DEER

Hallia, her portion of the story finished, gazed solemnly at the splattering stream. Though I had been struck by the brutality of her words, I had been struck even more by the anguish in her voice.

Eremon rose slowly to face her. "Would it be fair to say, my sister, that Hevydd might have lived if he had understood more?"

"Perhaps," she replied, pausing even longer than usual before she continued. "Yet it would also be fair to ask: Did the fault belong to him, or to the man who slew him?"

"Both," I declared, standing once more. "That's usually the way of it. With fault, I mean. I've seen how often my own faults combine with someone else's to make things worse."

While Hallia backed away, to the very edge of the stream, Eremon remained still, watching me quizzically. "And how, young hawk, do you know so much about your faults?"

Without hesitation, I answered: "I have a sister."

His whole face wrinkled in a smile—which vanished as soon as Hallia glanced at him sharply. "Tell us, now. What brought you here? And why do I feel so much of the lone wolf in you?"

Feeling the sudden urge to lean against my staff, I instinctively scanned the grass. All at once, I remembered. My staff was gone. Destroyed. Along with my powers.

The boy of the wizard's staff, the trees of the Druma had called me. I cringed at the memory. "I had something . . . unusual. Something precious. And now it's lost."

Eremon's thick eyebrows drew together. "What is this thing?"

I hesitated.

"Tell us, young hawk."

Gravely, I spoke the word. "Magic. Whether or not I might ever have become a true wizard, I still had some gifts. Gifts of magic." I paused, reading the doubt in both of their faces. "You must believe me. I came to the realm of the dwarves at Urnalda's request, to help her battle Valdearg—Wings of Fire. Then she turned on me. Stole my powers." I touched my chest. "I feel, well, this emptiness now. My magic, my essence, was just ripped away. If only you could feel it . . . you would know I speak truly."

Eremon's ears, slightly pointed at the top like those of all Fincayran men and women, quivered for an instant. "I can feel it," he said softly.

Turning to his sister, he asked by his expression whether or not she agreed. Yet Hallia's face showed only mistrust. Slowly, she shook her head, her long braid glinting in the sun.

My jaw tightened. "If you believe nothing else, at least heed this. In just six and a half days, all of Fincayra will know Valdearg's rage. Unless, that is, I can find some way to stop him."

Eremon's eyes widened.

"And I have no idea even where to begin!" My hand squeezed the air as it would have my staff. "Should I just submit to the dragon now? Let him devour me? It might satisfy him. Urnalda said it would. But it might not! He could just continue on his rampage, destroying whatever he likes. I've got to prevent that."

"You ask a lot of yourself," observed Eremon.

I sighed again. "One of my faults." My attention fell to the circle in the mud at our feet. "It's hopeless, really. Like the wolf in our story." In frustration, I struck my fist against my palm. "Those two deer should have just left me to die!"

Hallia started. "What did you say?"

I winced. "If you doubt the rest, then you'll never believe this part."

For the first time, she looked straight at me. "Tell us . . . about the deer."

"Well, it's enough to say that two brave deer—for whatever reason—risked their lives to save me last night. It was they who brought me here. No, it's true! I wish I could thank them—even though things would be simpler if they hadn't bothered. I haven't any idea where they are now."

Hallia's deep eyes probed me. It seemed to me that a new doubt, different than before, shone in them. Then, suddenly aware that I was returning her gaze, she turned shyly away.

Her brother bent toward her. "Say what you will about his words. I, for one, judge them true."

She took him by the arm. "Part of what he says may be true . . . but only part. Remember, he is a—" She caught herself. "A creature not to be trusted."

Her brother shook loose. "A creature not so different from ourselves." He pushed a hand through his nut brown hair and faced me. "That Wings of Fire has reawakened is no secret. Nor that he has done much recently to punish the dwarves. Because the dwarves have very few friends in other parts of Fincayra, most of us who live on their borders have just assumed they brought this trouble on themselves. But no—if your tale is true, Valdearg's anger must spring from another cause altogether."

Grimly, I nodded. "It does." A cold wind arose, ruffling the grasses. "His eggs—his only young—were murdered."

Hallia tossed her braid over her shoulder. "I feel . . . no sorrow for him. He has wasted so many lands, so many lives. Still, I can't help but feel sympathy for his hatchlings, murdered like that. Without even a chance to escape."

I frowned. "I feel no sympathy for them. They would have only grown up to be like . . ." My words trailed off as I realized what I was about to say. *Like their father.* How different was that from what Urnalda had said about me?

Eremon's voice resonated clearly. "For my part, I feel sympathy for them all. They did not seek to be born as dragons, but merely to be born." He paused, watching me. "Do you know who killed them?"

"A man."

His ears trembled once more. "And who was that man?"

I swallowed. "Valdearg believes it was me. Since I am descended from his greatest foe—Tuatha. But it was not. I swear it was not."

His brow knitted as he studied me for a long moment. At last he announced, "I believe you, young hawk." He drew a deep breath. "And I will help you."

"Eremon!" cried his sister, all her hesitancy gone. "You can't!"

"If his words are true, all of Fincayra should rise to help."

"But you don't know!"

"I know enough." He stroked his prominent chin. "Yet I wish

I knew one thing more: where those dragon eggs have lain hidden these many years. If only we could find whatever is left of them, we might find a sign. Something that could tell us who is the true killer."

"I've thought of that, as well," I replied. "But the remains of the eggs could be anywhere! We have no time to search. Besides, what we need to find most is not the killer—but some way to stop Valdearg."

At that, the wisp of an idea rose within me. A desperate, outlandish idea. And, with it, an overwhelming sense of dread. "Eremon! I know what I must do in whatever time remains. It's a foolish hope, yet I can think of no other." I faced him squarely. "And it's far too dangerous to ask anyone else to join me."

Hallia's somber face lightened. Eremon, for his part, regarded me gravely.

"One of the few things I know about my grandfather's battle with Valdearg, ages ago, is that he triumphed only with the help of an object of great power. A pendant—full of magic—known as the Galator."

Both pairs of brown eyes stared at me.

"For a time I myself wore it around my neck. Yet I learned very little of its secrets." My shoulders started to droop as I realized that, without my own powers, the Galator's magic might be useless to me. And yet . . . there was, at least, a chance. I tried to stand taller. "I must get it back somehow! If I can, it just might defeat the dragon once again."

"Where is it now?" queried Eremon.

I bit my lip. "With the hag Domnu—also called Dark Fate. She lives at the farthest reaches of the Haunted Marsh."

Hallia inhaled sharply through her nose. "Then you had best . . . devise another plan. You cannot possibly walk all the way there and back in just six and a half days."

I winced at her words. "You're right. It would be difficult enough even if I could run like a deer."

Eremon threw back his head. "But you can."

Before I could ask what he meant, he turned and started running across the grass, his feet moving effortlessly. He loped faster and faster, until his legs became a blur of motion. He leaned forward, his broad back nearly horizontal, his arms almost touching the ground. The muscles of his neck tightened as his chin thrust forward. Then, to my astonishment, his arms transformed into legs, pounding over the turf. His tunic melted away, replaced by fur, while his feet and hands became hooves. From his head sprouted a great rack of antlers, five points on each side.

He swung around, flexing his powerful haunches as he bounded back over the field. In an instant he stood before us again, every bit a stag.

XIV

EREMON'S GIFT

Astonished, I gazed into the deep brown eyes of the stag. "So it was you who saved me."

Eremon's antlered head dipped. "It was," he declared, his voice even richer than before. "My sister and I only wished to come to your aid, as you had come to ours."

Her brow creased in worry, Hallia reached up and, with her slender hand, stroked the thick fur of the stag's neck. Quietly, she said, "Once should be enough, my brother. The favor is exchanged. Do you really need to do more?" She glanced at me, and her expression hardened. "And for the sake of a man? Need I remind you that men stole our parents' lives? That they cut out our mother's and father's shoulders for a meal . . . and left the rest of their bodies to rot?"

Their eyes met. At length, Eremon spoke with a new softness. "Eo-Lahallia, your pain, like all you feel, is great. Yet I fear that instead of stepping through your pain, as you and I have stepped through many a marsh, you have let it cling to you, like the bloodthirsty tick that rides our backs for months on end."

Hallia blinked back her tears. "This tick will not fall away." She swallowed. "And . . . there is more. Last night, after we regained our two-legged forms, a dream came to me. A terrible dream! I entered . . . a dark and dangerous place. There was a river, I think, flowing fast. And right before me, the body of a stag. Blood everywhere! He quivered, at the edge of death. The very sight made me weep! Just as I came close enough to look into his eyes, I awoke."

Eremon kicked anxiously at the grass with his hoof. "Who was this stag?"

"I . . . can't be sure." She wrapped her arms tightly around his neck. "But I don't want you to die!"

As I listened, my heart filled with anguish. I remembered too well Rhia's parting embrace at the headwaters, and my longing to be with her again. "Heed her warning," I urged. "As much as I yearn for your help, Eremon, that would be too high a price. No, whatever I must do, I must do it alone."

Relief flickered in Hallia's eyes.

Eremon observed me. "Was it hard for you to part with your sister?"

His guess took me aback, though I managed a nod.

He tilted his rack so that one of the points lightly brushed Hallia's cheek. "Can a race whose brothers and sisters care so much for each other be entirely evil?"

She said nothing.

The stag lifted his mighty head and addressed me. "My own race, the deer people, have lived too long in fear and rage at yours. I do not know whether helping you will also help to bind us to the race of men and women. Yet I do know this: It is right to help another creature, no matter the shape of his track. And so I shall."

Hallia sucked in her breath. "Is . . . your path firmly set?"

"It is."

"Then," she declared with a shake of her whole torso, "I will join you."

She raised a hand as Eremon started to protest. "Is your choice to be respected, but not mine?" Sensing his anguish, she stroked his ear softly. "If I must weep, I would rather do so by your side than someplace far away from you."

Gently, the stag's moist nose touched hers. "You will do no weeping." After a pause, he added, "Nor, I hope, will I."

With that, Hallia stepped back from her brother. She glanced down at her hands, stretching her fingers in the sunlight. At length, she turned toward the open field, the meadowsweet poignant under the midday sun. In a flash she was running, then loping, then bounding through the green spears with the grace of a deer. She turned and pranced over to us, her hooves springing lightly off the turf.

Eremon flicked his ears, then faced me squarely. "Now for you."

I stepped back in surprise, slipping off the edge of the muddy bank. With a flop, I landed in the stream. Dripping wet, with a trail of mud rolling down my cheek, I clambered back to the grass.

Hallia's eyes averted me, but I could not miss her snickering. "He may be a wizard, but he could use some more practice walking on two legs before he tries four."

"He will learn quickly," predicted Eremon.

"B-but wait," I stammered, wringing out my sleeves. "I have no magic! And even when I did, the art of Changing was still new to me. I could no sooner change into a deer than into a puff of wind."

"There is a way. Although the magic will be mine, not yours, you still can share in it." He lowered his great rack. "Here. Take your sword."

"No!" cried Hallia, kicking her forelegs. "You can't do that."

"Would you rather carry him on our backs the whole way? I barely managed to bring him from the dwarves' land to this place. The lair of Domnu is much farther."

Speaking again to me, he commanded, "Cut off one of my points. A clean swipe will do it."

Gripping the hilt, I pulled the sword free of the scabbard. It rang distantly, like a shrouded bell. Aiming at the point farthest from Eremon's head, I brought down the blade with all my strength.

There was a sudden flash, and the point snapped off, dropping to the ground. A fresh, spicy smell, like a forest glade, enriched the air. I breathed deeply, remembering the hemlock grove that gave me my staff long ago. Eremon raised a rear hoof and stomped heavily on the point. Over and over again. When, at last, he stopped, a small pile of silver powder remained.

I sheathed my sword and kneeled to look more closely. The tiny crystals glistened in the light.

Eremon's foreleg nudged my shoulder. "By rubbing the powder into your hands and feet, young hawk, you will gain, for a time, the power of my people. You may change from a man to a deer and back again, simply by willing it." His voice took on an edge of warning. "Remember, though, that to survive as a deer you must not only look like one, but think like one, too."

Wondering at his words, I swallowed.

"And," he continued, "there is a risk you must understand. The power could last three months—or three days. There is no way to predict."

"And if it wears off while I am in deer form?"

"Then you will remain a deer forever. This gift can never be given to you again, so I cannot help you change back."

For a moment I gazed into his immense eyes. "I accept the gift.

And the risk, as well." Pulling off my boots, I spread the powder on my palms, and rubbed it thoroughly over both my feet and hands.

The stag's rack poked my thigh. "Don't miss a single joint of a single toe."

Finally, having finished, I stood. "When—if—I change into a deer, what will happen to my satchel? And my sword?"

"The magic will conceal them while you are a deer, and restore them when you are a man."

"Then I am ready."

Hallia huffed through her nose. "Not quite! You had better . . . put your boots back on. Otherwise, when you return to man form, you will have bare feet. And, before long, countless blisters."

As much as her tone irked me, I didn't reply.

Eremon gave a low, throaty laugh. "Now run, young hawk! Enjoy your own motion. Be as fluid as the stream over there, and as light as the breeze."

Through the grass I plodded, my wet boots clomping heavily on the ground. Water sloshed under my toes. I did not need to see Hallia to feel her critical gaze.

Faster I raced, and faster. As *fluid as the stream*. I leaned forward, dangling my arms. *As light as the breeze*. My knees bent backward. My strides felt surer, stronger. My chin stretched outward. Both hands—no, something else—met the turf. My back lengthened, as did my neck. All at once, I was bounding across the field.

I was a deer.

My sleek shadow flew across the grass. Atop my head rode a small rack with two points on one side and three on the other. *This is not so difficult*, I told myself. Glancing back over my shoulder, I saw the handsome stag and doe beside the tumbling stream. Deciding to lope back to them, I whipped around sharply. My left rear hoof struck the inside of my right foreleg. Caught off balance, I twisted and fell.

Barely had I righted myself, knees wobbling, before Eremon and Hallia were at my side. The stag nudged me with concern. My flank less bruised than my pride, I trotted a few steps to show him that I hadn't injured myself. As for Hallia—well, I really didn't care what she thought.

"Come," boomed Eremon, curling his long lips. "We must leave for the river crossing. With any luck, we can be well into the plains before dark."

He loped back toward the shining stream, ears cocked forward, and cleared the channel with a single leap. Hallia followed, the picture of grace. I bounded behind, far less smoothly. Although I tried to clear the stream as easily as the others, my hind legs splashed into the cold water, soaking my underside. I scuttled up the bank, doing my best to catch up.

Eremon led us due south for a while, reversing the route over the stairway of meadows that Rhia and I had crossed just the day before. In time, the rhythm of running through the tall grasses and late-blooming lupines began to seep into my muscles and bones. So gradually that I didn't notice it happening, I started to move less woodenly, less even like a body than like the air itself.

Bounding through the grasses, tinted rust by the onset of autumn, I realized that my sight was good. Very good. No longer relying on my second sight, which in daytime had never measured up to true eyesight, I relished the details, the edges, the textures. Sometimes I even slowed my running just to look more closely.

Dewdrops clinging to a spiderweb, tufts of grass bending as grace-fully as a rainbow, airborne seeds drifting on the wind. Whether my eyes were still coal black, or brown like my companions', I could not tell. Yet that mattered not at all, for they were, at last, open windows to the world.

As good as my eyesight had become, my sense of smell had grown even better. Intimate aromas came to me from all around. I smelled, with relief, the diminishing traces of smoke as we moved farther from the dwarves' lands. And I drank in, unrestrainedly, the subtle aromas of this bright autumn day. A coursing rivulet. An old beehive in the trunk of a birch tree. A fox's den hidden among roots of gorse.

Yet the newest of all my senses, it seemed, was my hearing. Sounds that I had never known existed washed over me in a con-stant stream. I heard not only the continual pounding of my own hooves, and the distinctive weight and timing of the hooves of the two deer ahead of me—but also our echoing reverberations through the soil. Even as I ran, I caught whispers of a dragonfly's wings humming and a field mouse's legs scurrying.

As the sun drew closer to the western hills, I realized that my ability to hear went even beyond having sensitive ears. Somehow, in a mysterious way, I was listening not just to sounds, but to the land itself. I could hear, not with my ears but with my bones, the tensing and flexing of the earth under my hooves, the changing flow of the wind, the secret connections among all the creatures who shared these meadows—whether they crawled, slithered, flew, or ran. Not only did I hear them; I celebrated them, for we were bound together as securely as a blade of grass is bound to the soil.

XV

THE MEANING
IN THE TRACKS

The sun had nearly reached the horizon when Eremon turned his great rack toward the corridor of mist that I knew marked the banks of the River Unceasing. As I followed, the rush and splatter of rapids grew louder. Arms of mist encircled me. Slowing my gait, I realized that the stag had brought us to the crossing that I knew well. The same strange longing that I had felt before with Rhia, to see the great boulders at the river's edge, welled up in me again.

Though I could hear the crashing waters plainly, I could not yet see the river through the knotting mist. Eremon and Hallia, their tan coats shining with sweat, trotted to a patch of dark green reeds. Affectionately, Hallia nudged her brother's shoulder with her own. Then, lowering their heads, they began browsing on the shoots.

When I approached, the stag lifted his rack and greeted me with an approving nod. "You are learning to run, young hawk."

"I am learning to listen."

Hallia, seeming to ignore us, ripped out a tuft of reeds. Her jaws crunched noisily.

I, too, began nibbling at the reeds. Though they tasted almost bitter, I could feel new strength in my limbs almost instantly. Even the velvet covering of my antlers seemed to tingle. I took another, larger bite.

While munching, I nodded approvingly. "What is, *crunchunchunch*, this reed?"

"Eelgrass," Eremon replied between bites. "From the days when my clan of deer people lived by the sea. Feel the texture on your tongue? It's like the dried skin of an eel."

He tore out some more shafts and chewed pensively for a while. "Although we no longer live by the shore, we have kept the reed's name—and many uses. It is woven into our baskets, our curtains, and our clothing. Chafed, pounded, and mixed with hazelnut oil, it starts our fires on winter evenings. It greets our young as a blanket at birth, and sends them on the Long Journey as a funeral shawl at death." His black nose nuzzled another tuft. "Its best use of all, though, is simply as food."

Suddenly Hallia bellowed in pain. She leaped into the air, shaking her head wildly. Even as she landed, Eremon was at her side, stroking her neck with his nose. She continued to cast her head about, whimpering.

"What is it, my sister?"

"I must have bitten—ohhh, it aches! A stone or something. Broke . . . a tooth, I think." Quivering, she opened her mouth. Blood covered one of her rear teeth; a trickle ran down her lip. "Ohhh . . . it hurts. Throbs." She stamped her hoof. "Why now?"

Eremon glanced worriedly at me. "I don't know how to treat such a wound."

Hallia, still casting her head, kicked at the reeds. "I will go . . . ehhh! to Miach the Learned. He will—"

"Too far," interrupted the stag. "Miach's village is more than a full day from here."

A shudder coursed through her. "Then maybe it will—oh! heal on its own . . . in time."

"No, no," declared Eremon. "You must find help."

"But where? Do I just go . . . wandering?" She closed her eyes tightly. As she reopened them, tears gathered on her lashes. "I had wanted . . . to stay with you."

"Wait," I declared. "I may not have any magic of my own, but I do know a little about healing."

"No!" shrieked Hallia. "I won't be healed by . . . him."

Eremon fixed his gaze on hers. "Let him try."

"But he might . . ." She shivered. "He's . . . a man." Cautiously, she curled her tongue to caress the broken tooth. "Oh, Eremon!" Bobbing her head, she said nothing for a long moment. At last, she asked weakly, "You really . . . trust him?"

"I do."

"All right, then," she whispered. "Let him . . . try."

My hoof stomped hard. "Hands. I need hands. How do I change?"

"Just start walking," Eremon answered. "And will yourself to change back."

Though my heart ached at losing my newfound senses, even for a moment, I turned back toward the lands we had bounded across. I strode into the curtains of mist, trying to recall just where I had seen a mass of curled yellow leaves—the plant my mother called *hurt man's blanket*. Many times I had seen her use it to deaden pain, though never in a tooth. I could only try . . . and hope.

After a few steps, my hooves started to flatten, my back to arch upward, and my neck to shorten. My motions suddenly felt clipped, disjointed. And my breath—less deep. Soon my boots, still wet from their plunge in the stream, clomped on the grasses.

As the mist thinned somewhat, I started searching for the yellow cluster I had remembered. For several minutes, I looked—without success. Was my vision now too poor to spot it? Had the roving mist swallowed it completely? Finally—there it was. I hurried over and picked one of the curling, hair-covered leaves. Stiffly, I ran back to the others.

"Here," I panted, holding the leaf in my palm. "I need to wrap this around your tooth."

Hallia whimpered, her whole body quaking.

"It will help," I coaxed. "At least . . . it's supposed to."

She gave a fearful moan. Then, as Eremon gently nudged her neck, she opened her mouth and lifted her tongue, exposing the bloody tooth. Delicately, very delicately, I ran my fingertip along its surface. Suddenly my finger pricked a tiny pebble wedged into a crack. With a tug, I wrenched it free. Though Hallia bellowed again, she continued to hold her mouth open long enough for me to wrap the leaf over her tooth and gum. Just as I finished, she jerked her head away.

"That should do it," I said, sounding less sure than I would have liked.

Slowly, Hallia's lips pinched. She shuddered, tilting her head from one side to the other. I felt certain that she was about to spit out the leaf.

But she did not spit. Instead, her brown eyes flitted toward me. "This tastes terrible. Like rotting oak bark, or worse." She paused, hesitating. "Still . . . it does feel a little . . . better."

Eremon's great head bobbed. "We are grateful, young hawk."

Suddenly feeling as shy as the doe, I turned aside. "Not as grateful as I am, to have been a deer—for a while, at least."

"You shall walk with hooves again soon. And often, if the magic lasts." He glanced at his sister, whose tongue was playing lightly over the crumpled leaf. "For now, though, we are glad you have fingers."

Hallia took a step nearer. "And . . ." she began, taking a slow breath, "knowledge. Real knowledge. I thought men and women had forsaken the language of the land—of the plants, the seasons, the stones—for the language of written words."

"Not all men and women," I replied. Tapping the hilt of my sword, I half grinned. "Believe me, I've learned a few things from stones." My thoughts turned to Cairpré, forever finding treasures between the covers of books. "The written word has its own virtues, though."

She eyed me skeptically.

"It's true," I explained. "Reading a passage in a book is like— well, like following tracks. No, no—that's not it. More like finding the *meaning* in the tracks. Where they are going, why they are sprinting or limping, how they are different from the day before."

Hallia said nothing more, though she swiveled her ears as if she were intrigued. At that instant, the wind shifted. A gap opened in the mist around us, allowing a few gleaming shafts of light to burst through. The rays poured over the shoots of eelgrass, making them seem to glow from within.

She sighed. "How beautiful."

I nodded.

"Don't you love," she said quietly, "the way the mist moves? Like a shadow made of water."

I ceased nodding. "Myself, I was watching the sunlight, not the mist. How it paints the reeds, and whatever else it touches."

"Hmmm." Her ears twitched. "So you saw light, while I saw motion?"

"So it seems. Two different sides of the same moment."

Eremon released a throaty sound, almost a chuckle. Shredding mist wove through his antlers. All of a sudden, the wind again shifted. The stag stiffened, his nostrils quivering.

Hallia chewed nervously on the leaf. "That smell . . . what is it?"

For quite some time, he did not answer, did not move. At last, he lowered his rack. "It is the smell," he declared, "of death."

XVI

DREAMS YET UNHATCHED

Stepping cautiously, we approached the bank of the rushing river. Rapids slapped and pounded. Strands of mist, tinted red from the setting sun, wound around our legs, curling like vaporous ropes. The soil grew soft and slippery under my feet—and the others' hooves.

At the lip of the bank, I paused to watch Eremon and Hallia descend. Despite the unstable ground, they moved as gracefully as a pair of dewdrops rolling down the petal of a flower. Unlike them, I stood upright and vertical—a young man, half human, half Fincayran. Two legs felt so narrow, so unsteady. Even as I curled my fingers, feeling their delicacy, I missed my own hooves. And, still more, I missed my own magic. Thanks to Eremon's gift I had, at least briefly, forgotten the emptiness in my chest.

Change back! Yes. Now. I turned to run along the edge of the bank—when I saw Eremon suddenly halt, his antlered head erect. Hallia, too, froze, the fur on her back bristling.

Like them, I stood motionless. For through the shredding mist, I could now see the edges of the opposite bank. And the scene of slaughter that scarred it.

The boulders that I remembered no longer marked this place.

Only broken shells, their reeking innards clotted with blood. In a flash, I comprehended that they had never been boulders at all. They had been eggs.

Dragon eggs.

Strewn across the muddy shore, the broken remains of the eggs lay in ghastly heaps. I spotted a section of throat, hacked brutally. And a ragged wing, streaked with scarlet and green. Except for the few strips of flesh that fluttered in the spray, everything seemed frozen in the moment of death.

No wolves had dragged away these carcasses. No vultures had carried off the meaty fragments, still glistening with newborn scales. At once, I knew why. For over the whole scene hung something as potent as the fetid odor of rotting flesh—the possibility that Valdearg himself might appear at any moment.

I clambered down the bank to join the others. Mud tugged at my boots, while a growing dread tugged at my heart. As we stepped into the shallows, frigid water slapped against our legs. Yet nothing chilled so much as the devastation before us. At least, I told myself, they were only dragons. Destroyed before they could do the same to anyone else. Even so . . . Eremon's words still nagged at me.

The stag bounded up the opposite bank, then veered sharply to the left. Forehoof raised, he bent over something, studying it intently.

As fast as I could, I scrambled up behind him. Below his hoof, I spied a slight indentation in the soil stained dark orange from blood. All at once, I realized that it was a footprint. The footprint of a man. Here, I felt certain, was the proof that Urnalda had used to turn the dragon's wrath away from the dwarves—and toward me.

Cautiously, Hallia approached. She lowered her head to sniff the print, her nose almost touching it. She glanced at me, the old mistrust back in her eyes. Working her tongue, she spat out the leaf that I had given her. Then, her voice barely audible above the river, she spoke. "This man, whoever he is, has brought much pain."

"And Valdearg will bring even more," added Eremon grimly. "Unless we are successful. Yet our time dwindles. Already the sun is setting on this day."

Sadly, I shook my head. "This print looks so much like my own."

Hallia snorted. "All men's footprints look alike. Heavy and clumsy."

Eremon struck the mud with his hoof. "Not so, my sister. See here? The edge of the heel is blunted, but with a sharp edge. Not in the normal, rounded way caused by walking on turf, or even hard floors."

Hallia turned toward one of my own footprints. After a long pause, she admitted, "There is, I suppose, a difference." Hesitantly, she glanced at me once again. "I'm sorry. I just . . ."

"It's all right," I replied. "Say no more." Facing Eremon, I asked, "So what does the shape of that heel tell you?"

"That it was cut, over time, by something jagged. Perhaps this person lives in some sort of cave, lined with rough stones. Or in a maze of tunnels under the ground."

"Urnalda lives in a realm of tunnels," I mused. "Yet she doesn't wear a man's boots. Besides, why would she ever attack Valdearg's young, knowing it might bring his wrath down on her people?" Slowly, I exhaled. "It doesn't make sense."

Hallia's ears twisted. "There is another possibility. This person, this man, could have left the print on purpose, trying to trick us somehow."

"Possibly," acknowledged the stag. "Men can sometimes be . . ."

"Deceitful," she finished.

His antlers tilted to one side. "Are you saying a deer is never deceitful? Would you never try to trick an enemy?"

The doe straightened her neck. "Only to defend myself." She glanced at the nearest of the heaps, swathed in mist. "Or, one day, my young."

I strode over to the demolished egg. Kicking aside a piece of shell, I froze. Before me lay a severed arm, its claws extended like fingers. Though the arm's shape was not much different from my own, it was at least twice the size. Its underside bore a crest of iridescent purple scales; its wrist seemed as delicate as the neck of a swan. The claws seemed to be reaching, groping for something just beyond their grasp.

Something about this lifeless arm made me want to touch it. With my own hands, my own fingers.

I kneeled and stroked its length. The arm felt soft, despite the rows of scales. Almost like the chubby leg of a newborn baby. Not long ago, it had been alive. And young. And innocent.

At last, I understood the full horror of this tragedy. No life, no creature, no future, deserved to be wasted like this. Murdered like this. No wonder Valdearg's rage knew no bounds.

To myself, I recited the lines from Tuatha's prophecy:

> *By anger unending*
> *And power unmatched,*
> *The dragon avenges*
> *His dreams yet unhatched.*
> *For when he awakens*

To find those dreams lost,
Revenge shall he covet
Regardless the cost.

Suddenly, Eremon jerked his head, his rack spraying drops of water. His body and Hallia's stiffened as one. They were sensing something, feeling something, that eluded me completely.

Then I heard a sound, deep and rasping, like a distant volcano erupting. It came from somewhere far beyond the river, yet it grew steadily louder. A wind stirred; the air felt almost imperceptibly warmer. I picked up the faint scent of smoke. All at once an enormous shadow darkened the reddening mist.

"The dragon!" cried Eremon. "Run!"

The two deer scattered, bounding into the mist, while I stumbled over to the slick bank. The sound of flying thunder rent the air as the shadow passed over again. Terrified, I thought of changing back into a deer myself—when suddenly I slipped in the mud, losing my balance. In a whirl, I rolled down to the river's edge. Frigid water coursed over my legs as well as my sword. Breathless, I regained my feet and dashed across the shallows.

On a steep section of the far bank, I spied an overhang. A thick curtain of grasses, soaked from spray, dangled over the edge. Yet behind the grasses loomed a dark place where the river had washed away the soil. A cavern!

Even as the sound above me swelled into a roar, I threw myself into the cavern, rolling over and over on the mud until I bumped into the arching wall of the bank. For a moment I lay in the darkness, panting. Feeling the chill of the river, I sat up and pulled my knees to my chest. As I gazed through the dripping curtain of grasses I felt a touch of satisfaction. I had eluded Valdearg. Only temporarily, of course. Yet even delaying the inevitable by a handful of days seemed cause enough for pride.

Listening to the rushing torrent outside, I felt grateful for the safety of this cavern. It was cramped, and smelled . . . rancid somehow. Yet who could ask for a better hiding place? Then, without warning, something brushed against my leg.

XVII

POWERLESS

I drew back in fright. Grasping the hilt of my sword, I struggled to wrench it from the scabbard. But the scabbard's mouth
had been so caked with mud that the blade refused to come free.
Hunched beneath the low ceiling, I pulled and pulled without
success.

Hurl myself from the cavern! Now, while I still could. Before
whatever had stirred did so again. Yet . . . I hesitated. Beyond the
grassy curtain Valdearg himself might well be waiting for me. Again
I tugged at my sword. Again it failed to move.

Suddenly a sound like I had never heard before echoed in the
darkness. Part moan, part snarl, part whimper, it grew louder until
at last it abruptly died away. I pressed myself against the earthen
wall. Mud oozed down my neck, but I did not stir. I barely
breathed—yet the rancid smell assaulted me, stronger than ever. I
could only hope that this creature, whatever it was, might just ignore me and leave.

Then, very gradually, a faint orange glow began to illuminate the
cavern. At first I could not tell where it originated, for its flickering caused strange, ungainly shadows to grow and wither on the
walls: giants stalking, snakes writhing, trees crashing to the ground.

Finally, though, I located the source: a triangle of orange light, not far above the floor at the cavern's far end. The light flickered, quavering like a candle in a breeze.

Though fear gripped me, I did the only thing I could think to do. With both hands, I scooped a chunk of mud off the floor, pressed it into a ball, and hurled it straight at the glowing triangle. A splat—and instantly, the light went out. At the same time, the whining, moaning sound returned, this time swelling so loud that I had to cover my ears. I wriggled closer to the rear wall.

All at once, the entire wall shifted behind me. Mud poured over my head. For an instant I thought the riverbank was about to collapse on top of me. Yet the earthen wall did not collapse. Instead, it did the one thing I least expected.

It breathed. Shaking with effort, the whole surface drew a slow, halting breath. Foul-smelling wind rushed over me, swirling around the enclosure. Heedless of Valdearg, I rolled to the curtain of drenched grasses, hoping to escape in time.

Just as I was about to roll out of the cavern, back into the churning waters outside, the long breath choked off. As abruptly as it had started, it ceased. It was, I felt sure, one of the last breaths—if not the very last—of something at the edge of death. Or dead at last. Pausing at the entrance, I studied the path of a single shaft of light, as crimson as the setting sun, that slit the cavern from the place where my shoulder had pushed apart the grasses. It landed on the spot where I had seen the glowing triangle.

My heart froze. For there, tilted on its side in the black mud, lay an enormous head—twice the size of the head of a full-grown horse. It belonged to a dragon.

Its eye, whose eerie light had filled the cavern only a moment before, was now shut. Long lashes rimmed the eyelid. I could see, clinging to the lashes, a few fragments of broken shell. A dull yellow bump protruded from the forehead, while lavender scales ran down the full length of the wrinkly nose. Dozens of teeth, as sharp as daggers, glistened within the half-open jaws. Curiously, only the left ear flopped limply on the mud. The right ear, silvery blue in color, stretched stiffly into the air, like a misplaced horn.

A sudden rush of pity filled me. What vision of terror, I wondered, had driven this young hatchling from its egg and into hiding in this hollow? My skin tingled as I recalled the movement of the great body against my back, movement that was probably its final stirring of life. An inexplicable instinct made me guess that this dragon had been female. If so, she would never have the chance to lay any eggs of her own.

Reaching up, I pulled out several handfuls of the grass that hung over the entrance. More crimson light filtered into the cavern. Probing with my second sight, I spied a pair of sharp claws, flecked with purple, protruding from the mud. Not far from the place where I had momentarily rested, a tail with two hooked barbs lay coiled. Turning back to the head, I smiled sadly at the irrepressible ear. Nothing, not even death, could make it lie down.

I wondered about the dragon's wounds. Had she starved to death? Bled from some fatal gashes I could not see? Or, like any abandoned child, simply suffered from sorrow and fear—until she finally died?

At that moment, another deep moan, weaker than before, rose within the cavern. Still alive! The dragon's immense bulk shuddered, shaking the earthen floor. Clumps of mud dropped from above, splattering my head and shoulders. Her eye opened barely a sliver, fluttered, then closed once again, but not before I caught its look of anguish.

Biting my lip, I hesitated. Then . . . slowly, very slowly, I crawled closer. Gingerly, I lay my open hand over the eye, stroking its delicate lashes. It did not open again. Ever so gently, I moved my hand down the lavender scales of the nose, stopping at the immense nostrils. My whole hand barely covered them. A faint flutter of air warmed my fingers—reminding me of that horse from my childhood, whose name I could no longer recall, but whose misty breath I had never forgotten. But the breath of this creature, I could tell, was rapidly fading.

Yet what if a tiny spark of life still remained? Maybe I could . . . But no! I had no more magic. My jaw clenched, as I cursed Urnalda's treachery. Had she not stolen my gifts, I might have been able to call upon the sky above and the soil below—sources of the power of Binding, which could knit together the threads of the cosmos, and heal even the deepest wound.

Limply, my hand slid from the dragon's nose. I could not call upon that power—or any others. Nor could I do anything for this wretched beast. Helpless! I sighed, feeling more than ever that aching emptiness within my chest.

Something tugged against my hand. One of the dragon's scales had caught on the vine bracelet that Rhia gave to me as we parted. Even in the dying light, the bracelet shone with lustrous green. What had she said as she tied it on my wrist? *This will remind you of all the life around you, and the life within yourself.* I closed my eyes, hearing her voice again. *The life within yourself.*

Yet . . . what use was that to anyone else?

Almost out of habit, I reached into my leather satchel and pulled out a handful of herbs. Rubbing my palms together, I crushed them as best I could. Instantly, scents of rowan bark, beech root, and silver balm enriched the rancid air of the cavern. Then, with effort, I pulled off one of my boots. Using it as a makeshift bowl, I dropped in the herbs, gathering them at the heel. I squeezed some water from my soaked tunic into the boot, mixed the soup thoroughly with my finger, and leaned closer to the dragon. Since her head lay tilted in the mud, I was able to pour a few green, glistening drops into her partly open mouth.

As the drops struck her tongue, I waited for a swallow. But none came.

Once again, I poured some of the potion out of my boot. And I waited, hoping for some sign—any sign—of life. Yet she did not swallow. Or stir. Or moan.

"Swallow!" I commanded, my voice echoing dully in the dank walls. I poured another few drops, which slid off her tongue and fell to the floor.

Long after the last rays of twilight disappeared, and through the unforgiving night, I continued to try. My back ached, my bootless foot throbbed with cold, and my head swam from lack of sleep. Yet I refused to stop, hardly daring to hope that the eyelid might again flutter, that its orange glow might again illuminate the cavern. Or that the dragon might actually swallow something. But my hopes came to nothing.

When my herbal potion finally ran out, I tried rubbing the dragon's neck in slow circles, as my mother had once done for me— long ago, when I had thrashed from fever. It didn't help. Apart from the rare, halting breaths, which grew more frail by the hour, she showed no life at all.

When the first tentative rays of dawn drifted into the cavern, I knew that all my efforts had failed. I studied the motionless form, appreciating the subtle beauty of the scales, the savage curl of the claws. The hatchling lay utterly still, utterly silent.

Glumly, I turned away. The feeling of this hollow now revolted me. Like the devastation across the river, it stank of untimely death. Heedless of whatever danger lay outside, I rolled through the curtain of wet grasses.

XVIII

VEIL OF MIST

Rolling down the slick bank, I slid across the mud, finally stopping at the edge of the river. The surging water pounded in my ears. Cold spray drenched my face. Once again thick bands of mist twined themselves around me.

Cautiously, I scanned the opposite bank for any sign of Valdearg. Or of my companions. I found nothing but the remains of the eggs—broken shells, clotted innards, and hacked pieces of rotting flesh. The twirling columns of mist, and the river itself, were all that moved.

Full of regret, I glanced back at the cavern that held the last of the hatchlings. The last of Valdearg's offspring. Had whoever slaughtered these creatures intended to rouse the sleeping dragon of the Lost Lands, as well as his anger? And had the killer also intended that a man—whether myself or someone else—would be blamed? There was no way to tell. Perhaps simply murdering Valdearg's offspring was enough to serve the killer's purposes.

But what could those purposes be? To eliminate the hatchlings? Or to awaken Wings of Fire and send him on a deadly rampage? Yet that made no sense. Unless . . . perhaps the killer was an enemy of the dwarves, someone who hoped that Valdearg would show them the brunt of his wrath. Or an enemy of my father's race, the men and women of Fincayra. And there were many such enemies, I knew too well. Such a scar on this island, Stangmar's time on the throne! A scar that refused to heal.

I kneeled by the water's edge. Cupping my hands, I dipped them into the chill torrent, then washed my mud-splattered face. Finally, I dug the mud out of my scabbard. After several thick clumps worked loose, the sword at last came free.

I ran my finger over the silver hilt, shining in the spray. Maybe the killer was not just an enemy of dwarves, nor even of men and women, but of all life on Fincayra. Someone who might actually benefit from Valdearg's terror. Someone like . . . Rhita Gawr.

Wiping my face on my sleeve, I frowned. No, no, that couldn't be it. As Rhia herself had chided me, there was no point in creating new enemies. I had enough trouble right now. And yet . . . who else, besides Rhita Gawr, might be cunning enough to find the dragon eggs and ruthless enough to destroy them at birth?

Something soared over my head, darkening the mist. Valdearg! He had returned!

At that instant, a high, piercing shriek sliced through the moist air. It was not, I knew at once, the sound of a dragon. For this sound had assaulted me once before. I could not mistake it.

It was the cry of a kreelix.

I turned skyward just as the bat-like wings appeared out of the mist. The kreelix dove straight at me, its deadly fangs exposed. My hand reached for the hilt of my sword—then froze.

What good was my blade? I could not forget the last time I had faced those fangs, under the Cobblers' Rowan. The shock. The sheer pain. Though I had none of my own magic left, I still had the fear.

Plunging downward, the kreelix opened its blood red mouth. Three deadly fangs arched toward me. Another shriek tore through the swirling mist. The claws raised to slice me to shreds.

Suddenly a dark form bolted out of the fog across the river. Eremon! Clearing the waterway in a great bound, the stag leaped right into the path of the kreelix. With a colossal thud, they met in midair. I jumped out of the way as they came crashing down into the bank. Mud sprayed in all directions.

The two of them tumbled into the river. Eremon gained his legs first and lowered his rack to charge. But the kreelix, shrieking vengefully, lashed out with its claws, ripping the stag's flank. Even so, Eremon plowed straight into the beast, impaling one of its wings. Blood, both red and purple, swirled in the churning waters.

I drew my sword—just as a flash of scarlet light erupted. Above the distant ringing of my blade, I heard Eremon's sharp cry as the kreelix struck again. The great stag faltered, slumping in the middle of the river. I leaped into the spray, swinging my sword as I ran through the waves.

The kreelix whirled around. Like an enormous bat, fangs bared, it swiped at me with its uninjured wing. I dodged—but a bony edge gouged my cheek. As I jabbed my blade at its chest, a river stone slipped under my foot, sending me careening backward. The sword flew out of my hand. Icy water rushed over me.

Before I could right myself, something heavy fell on top of me, pushing me deeper underwater. My ribs collapsed. I gagged, swallowing water, struggling to escape from the mass of fur that crushed my face and chest. My lungs screamed, my mind darkened.

All at once, a strong hand grabbed my arm and pulled me free. Air filled my lungs at last, though I coughed uncontrollably, spewing water like a fountain. Finally, the spasms quieted enough that

I could make out Hallia, in her human form, dragging me from the river. She dropped me, sputtering, at the water's edge, then left immediately.

After a moment, I raised myself on my elbow. Just downriver lay the half-submerged body of the kreelix, the broken shard of an antler lodged in its back. Then a realization colder than the frigid waves washed over me. On the other side of the kreelix lay another body, sprawled on the muddy bank. The body of Eremon.

I rose and stumbled to his side. Hallia, sitting in the mud, was cradling the stag's head upon her lap. Her long face creased in sorrow, she seemed oblivious to the blood seeping into her robe from the puncture in his neck. Wordlessly, she stroked his forehead and his shattered antler, all the while looking into his deep brown eyes.

"My brother," she said softly. "You mustn't die, oh no. You mustn't leave me."

Eremon's chest shuddered as he tried to draw a breath. "I may be dying, my Eo-Lahallia. But leave you? That . . . I will never do."

Her own immense eyes peered into his. "We have so much yet to do, you and I! We still haven't run through the Collwyn Hills in the flower of spring."

His face tightened, and his hoof nudged her thigh. "You know how much I long to run by your side as a deer. And to stand by your side as a man. Yet now . . . I lack even the strength to change back into man form."

"Oh, Eremon! This is worse, far worse, than my dream."

"Here," I offered, starting to rise. "I could make you a poultice that might help."

Eremon's hoof knocked into me. His gaze, stern but kind, seemed to swallow me whole. "No, young hawk. It's too late for such things. Or even for your powers, if you still had them."

I bit my lip. "Whatever powers I once had are just a torment now."

"The kreelix . . ." he began, before taking a halting breath. "It was a kreelix, wasn't it? A magic eater? I thought they had all been destroyed. Long ago."

"So did my tutor, Cairpré."

Eremon blinked. "The bard Cairpré is your tutor? You are blessed indeed."

My brow knitted. "The only blessing I seek is to do something to help you. Now, Eremon."

Ignoring my comment, he asked, "But where . . . did the kreelix come from? Why did it attack you?"

"I don't know. Cairpré thinks someone is raising them, training them to kill."

With difficulty, he swallowed. "The kreelix—it thought you still possessed magic. Or else it wouldn't have attacked you."

I shook my head. "The only magic I possess is what you gave me. It must have sensed that."

Eremon winced. He turned toward his sister. "Forgive me."

Blinking back her tears, she answered bitterly, "I will try."

A wave of spray lifted off the water and settled on the stag with the softness of a candle's glow, caressing his bloodstained body. Another wave of spray came, then another. Almost as if the river itself were grieving, no less than Hallia and myself. Then I noticed that the air around us had begun to quiver, to shimmer, like the veil of mist that separated this world from the Otherworld. In that moment, I sensed somehow that another presence, more elusive than the mist itself, had joined us.

Hallia cocked her head, first in doubt, then in surprise, as she felt something change in her brother's body. His glistening muscles relaxed. His face, newly becalmed, tilted slightly, as if he were listening to someone's whispered words. When at last he spoke, grief still tinged his voice. Yet the old resonance had returned, along with a touch of something else, something I could not quite name.

"My sister, the spirits have come—to take me, to guide me on the Long Journey. Yet before I go, you must know that I, too, have had a dream. A dream . . . about a time when you shall overflow with joy, as the river in spring overflows with water."

Hallia's head fell lower, almost touching his own. "I cannot imagine such a time without you."

His breathing slowed, and he spoke with more effort. "That time . . . will come to you, Eo-Lahallia. And in the days before then, in your moments of fear and in your moments of repose . . . I myself will come to you."

Shutting her eyes, she turned away.

Eremon's hoof quivered, brushing my hand. "Be . . . brave, young hawk. Find the Galator. You have more power . . . than you know."

"Please," I begged. "Don't die."

The deep brown eyes closed, then fluttered briefly. "May green meadows . . . find you."

He exhaled one last time, then lay still.

XIX

THE WHIRLWIND

Swathed in mist, Eremon's blood running down our arms, Hallia and I strained to carry the stag's heavy body over to a protected bend in the riverbank. There a patch of vibrant green grass sprouted, and there we dug his grave in the moist, rich soil. Hallia wove a funeral shawl from shoots of eelgrass, which she carefully draped over his neck. After filling in the grave, I set out to ensure that it would remain undisturbed. Weary though I was, I carried more than a dozen stones to the spot. Hefty ones. Yet as much as my back ached, my heart ached even more.

As I worked, Hallia stood in silence by the grave, an occasional tear drifting down her chin. Although she said nothing, she sometimes clutched her yellow robe or stamped the turf, testimony to the violent storms raging within her. My stone gathering completed, I stood nearby, hardly daring to look at her, let alone comfort her.

At last, without lifting her eyes from her brother's grave, she spoke. "He called you *young hawk.*"

Silently, I nodded.

"It is a name with a meaning for my people."

I said nothing.

Still without looking at me, she continued, her voice sounding far, far away. "There is a story, as old as the first track of the first hoof, about a young hawk. He befriended a fawn. Brought him food when he hurt his leg, led him home when he was lost."

I shook my head. "Your brother had faith in me. More than I do myself."

Her round eyes flitted my way. "In me, too." She sighed heavily. "Soon you will be going, I suppose."

"That's right."

She threw her braid over her shoulder. "Well, if you think I'm coming with you, you are mistaken."

"I never asked—"

"Good. Because if you did, my answer would be no." She kicked at one of the river rocks. "No, I say."

I studied her for a long moment. "I didn't ask you, Hallia."

"No, but *he* did." She glared at the stones. "He asked me. Not with his words, but with his eyes."

"You should not come. You've suffered enough."

Her head bowed. "That I have."

Spying my sword on the bank, I crouched by the river, washing the mud from its blade. Somberly, I replaced it in the scabbard. Then, my feet feeling heavier than the stones I had laid upon Eremon's grave, I stepped slowly over to Hallia. She did not move, merely watching me with her gaze so full of intelligence and grief. A pace away, I stopped.

I felt the urge to take her hand, but held myself back. "I am sorry. Truly sorry."

She did not respond.

For several minutes we stood there, stiff and silent. But for the swirling mist, weaving about our legs, and the churning waters of the River Unceasing, nothing moved, nothing changed. I felt again the profound stillness that I had sensed inside the living stone. And, somewhere deep within, the quiet magic of a deer.

Out of nowhere, a sharp gust of wind struck us. Hallia's robe flapped against her legs. Spray flew off the river, drenching us; mist shredded into nothingness. The wind accelerated—howling, driving us both backward. Hallia cried out as her braid lifted straight up from her head. Hard as I tried to keep my balance, the wind sent me careening on the slick mud. I fell toward the river, about to hit the water, when—

I never hit.

Suddenly I was airborne, carried aloft by the fierce, whirling winds. My tunic flapped and billowed, sometimes covering my face. Hallia's foot struck me as she tumbled through the air nearby, but when I called to her the wind forced the words back into my throat. Spinning wildly, we rose higher into the air.

At one point, through the spiraling mist, my second sight glimpsed the patch of vibrant grass where we had buried Eremon. Just upstream, the remains of Valdearg's eggs lay scattered. Then thick clouds swallowed up everything, even as the wind had swallowed us. The whirling currents screamed in my ears.

Jostled and spun relentlessly, thrown upside down and sideways, I lost any bearings that I might have possessed. My body felt stretched, pummeled, turned inside out. Assaulted—from every side at once. Eyes watering, I could barely breathe amidst the battering winds. Was Hallia doing any better? Wherever this whirling storm was carrying us, I only hoped that we might arrive there alive. Before long, I fell unconscious.

When I awoke, I found myself sprawled facedown on a floor of smooth flagstones. Still whirling, my head pulsed with a roaring sound, as endless as ocean waves. I clung to the stones—they seemed so solid!—for a few more seconds before willing myself to turn over. At last I summoned the strength to roll onto my back. Weakly, my head still spinning, I pushed myself into a sitting position.

Hallia, I realized, lay beside me. Her face looked pale; she breathed fitfully. Her tan-colored hair, no longer tied in a braid, spread across the stones. I reached an unsteady hand toward her, when suddenly I caught myself.

That roaring sound . . . not my head, not the ocean, but voices. Hundreds and hundreds of voices. All around us, all shouting.

The two of us lay in the middle of a great circle of seats, filled with clamoring people. An amphitheater! Although I had never seen one before, I remembered well my mother's descriptions of the Roman amphitheaters during my childhood in Gwynedd. They were, she had explained, colossal arenas for sports—and, sometimes, for sacrifice.

Dizzily, I shook the fog from my second sight, trying to take it all in. The flagstone floor stretched wider than any courtyard I had ever seen, all the way to the rows upon rows of people encircling us. Many waved fists at us, making me feel that their shouts were more likely taunts than cheers.

All of a sudden, a huge pair of doors flung open at the far end of the amphitheater. Out of the darkness galloped an immense black stallion, pulling a wheeled chariot. Seated in the chariot, a muscled warrior raised his burly arms to the crowd. As they bellowed encouragement, he cracked his whip over the horse's streaming mane, driving the chariot directly toward us.

He's going to trample us! The realization shot through me like a bolt of lightning.

Struggling to my feet, I reached under Hallia's arms. Desperately, I tried to lift her onto my back. All the while, above the roaring crowd, I heard the pounding of the stallion's hooves on the stones. Closer drew the chariot, and closer.

At last, shaking with the weight, I managed to lift Hallia off the floor. Glancing behind, I saw the crazed eyes of the horse and the triumphant smile of the warrior bearing swiftly down on us. My heart slammed against my ribs. I took one halting step, then another. The crowd thundered angrily.

My legs buckled beneath me. I collapsed to my knees. Hallia toppled, hitting the floor with a loud moan. I swung my head around, an instant before the chariot crushed us beneath its wheels. Instinctively, I threw myself in front of her.

Just then, the chariot melted into the air. So did the amphitheater, the crowd, the roaring cries. All that remained were the stones, the black stallion, and the warrior himself. Eerie blue lights flickered around the edges of the room, if this really was a room, yet I could see no more. No walls, no ceiling. Only darkness, tinged by the dancing blue lights on the horizon.

With one hand hooked on his gleaming breastplate and the other grasping the whip, the warrior strode over. Grinning down at us, he cackled with evident satisfaction. Then, miraculously, he too began to change. His bearded face grew wider and smoother, as all the hairs vanished. Two triangular ears sprouted, along with a shriveled wart in the center of the high forehead. Across the hairless scalp, wrinkles ran like furrows in a field. Two ancient eyes, blacker even than my own, peered at me. Only the warrior's grin remained, though it was studded with bent, misshapen teeth.

"Domnu," I rasped, my throat suddenly dry.

"Such a pleasure to see you again, my pet." She patted her sack-like robe and began circling us, her bare feet slapping against the stones. "And you gave me such a splendid chance to drive that chariot! The humans, all told, are not much for ideas. But those Romans had a good one there."

She paused, scratching the wart on her forehead. "Or was it the Gaels? The Picts? No matter—humans, of whatever sort. An unusually good idea they had. Even if they lacked the imagination to make it more exciting."

The black stallion stamped his hoof and whinnied loudly. Domnu stopped circling and glanced at the powerful steed. The tips of her teeth showed as her grin widened. Her voice grew more quiet, and even more menacing.

"Are you disagreeing, my colt? Was the excitement too much for you?" She stepped closer and slowly ran her hand down the stallion's nose. While quivering slightly, he continued to hold his head high. "Perhaps you would rather go back to being a chess piece?"

At once, I remembered the chess piece of a black horse that I had seen when I first visited Domnu's lair. He had shown spirit then, as he did now. And he reminded me vaguely of that horse . . . that stallion. What was his name? I chewed my lip, recalling those days, long ago, when I felt my father's strong arms wrapped around me, and the still stronger back supporting us, as we rode around the castle grounds. Whatever else I had forgotten, I could never forget the stallion's prancing gait, his dignified air. And the way he ate apples out of my hand.

As Domnu continued to speak to the stallion, Hallia shifted beside me and opened her eyes. Seeing the hairless hag, she stiffened.

Although a bit of the color had returned to her cheeks, I knew that she was probably still very weak.

"Are you able to stand?" I whispered.

"I . . . don't know." She observed me worriedly. "That wind . . . where are we? Who is that . . . hag? What have I missed?"

"A lot." I gave her a wry smile. "You wouldn't believe me if I told you."

Hallia frowned. Taking my arm, she raised herself to her knees. Her eyes darted to Domnu once more. "She makes me . . . shiver. Who *is* she?"

"Domnu. I think we're in her lair."

"Well, now," interrupted Domnu. "Our second guest is awake." She glanced sharply at the stallion, then slid over to us. Bending toward Hallia, she ran a hand across her wrinkled scalp. "A deer woman, is it?" She clacked her tongue knowingly. "I can always tell by the chin. Bristling bones, I know that shape! So adorably tapered."

Though Hallia stiffened with fright, she did her best to hold her voice steady. "I am, indeed, a deer woman . . . of the Mellwyn-bri-Meath clan." She looked away. "And I beg—no, demand—that you set us free. Imm . . . immediately."

"Demand? Did you say demand?" Once more, the hag started walking in a circle, examining us like a hungry wolf. "Best to make no more demands, my pet. Poor manners, truly poor. I will decide what to do with you in time, just as I will decide how to teach a certain horse a lesson."

At that, the stallion stamped again on the stone floor. He snorted proudly.

Domnu stopped circling. Her dark eyes narrowed. From the

edges of the room, the blue light swelled strangely, crackling like the flames of a heatless fire.

"I understand, my colt." Her voice sounded soothing—and altogether menacing. "You simply need a change. A different perspective on life."

She raised an index finger. Briefly she inspected it, watching the blue light shimmer across her skin. Then she licked it slowly and deliberately. Finally, she held the wet finger before her lips and blew ever so gently.

The stallion reared back, whinnying loudly. He kicked his immense hooves in the air. Suddenly he shrank down into a small, sharp-nosed beast, as thin as a serpent, with dusty brown fur and tiny black eyes. A weasel. The little creature gave us a baleful look, then scurried across the floor, disappearing in the blue flames.

Hallia gasped and clutched my wrist.

Domnu flashed her misshapen teeth. "Poor little colt. This will give him a chance to rest." Her eyes darted back to us. "Of course, I made certain he has no teeth. That way he won't be tempted to use them, shall we say, inappropriately."

"You wretch!" I exclaimed. "That was a terrible thing to do! The horse was only being—"

"Disrespectful." Domnu's face shimmered in the rising blue light. "And I trust that you will not do the same." Thoughtfully, she scratched the prominent wart. "Especially since I plan to feed you a sumptuous meal."

She clapped her wrinkled hands together. Instantly, a full-blown feast appeared on an oaken table in the middle of the floor. Before us lay steaming breads, milk pudding, baked apples, buttered green vegetables, river trout, flasks of water and wine, and an enormous pie that smelled like roasted chestnuts.

My mouth watered. My stomach churned. I could almost taste that pie. Yet one glance at Hallia told me that she felt as mistrustful as I did. We shook our heads in unison. Clambering to my feet, I helped her stand, although she teetered unsteadily. While Hallia looked in the direction of the departed weasel, my own gaze met Domnu's. "We do not want your food."

"Really?" She stroked her scalp. "Perhaps you would prefer venison?"

I scowled. "I would prefer hag."

The blue light at the edges of the room flared, but Domnu watched us impassively. "Surprising, my pets, that you aren't hungry. After all, you have been here for quite some time."

"Some time?" I glared at her. "How long have we been here?"

Domnu started circling again, her feet slapping on the stones. "Oh, how adorable your kind can be when it gets willful! Like little sparrows who are angry that they cannot yet fly! But yes, my pet, it was quite some time ago that my little whirlwind came to fetch you. I was beginning to worry that you might not wake up at all, at least not while I was still in the mood for charioteering."

She scratched a mass of wrinkles by one ear. "I even laid a wager—against myself, there being no one else around just now—that you would never wake up. Though I lost that bet, I also won, if you take my meaning. An admirable outcome." She cackled softly. "I do so love to win."

"How long?" I demanded.

Still circling, Domnu yawned, revealing all her twisted teeth. "Well, now, I should say that it has been at least two days."

"Two days!" I exclaimed. "So I have only three days left!"

"Left, my pet? Do you have some sort of appointment?"

I stepped in front of her, halting her pacing. "I do. An appointment with—" I caught myself, not sure that I should reveal any more. "With someone important."

"Is that so?" asked the hag, with a chilling stare. "Too bad. So too bad. I had thought you might be on the way to meet Valdearg."

I winced. "Yes. That's true. And that is why I was seeking you, Domnu." I straightened my back. "For I have come at last to collect . . . the Galator."

A strange half-grin spread over her face. "How interesting. I was seeking you for the very same reason."

"What do you mean?"

Blue light danced across her brow. "You see, my pet, the Galator has been stolen."

XX

IONN

My knees nearly buckled. "Stolen?"

Blue flames swelled around the room. Wispy shadows, as thin as dead trees, danced across the flagstone floor. "Yes, my pet. The Galator has been stolen. Bones! Breaded bones! Taken from me, its rightful owner."

"No." I placed my fists on my hips. "I am its rightful owner. Not you."

Domnu waved a hand carelessly. "Well, technically, I suppose, you have a claim to it."

"A claim!"

"You might even say that you own it. Still, what is more important, I *possess* it. Or, at least, used to possess it. Whoever stole it will have to return it to me." She squeezed her hand tightly. I heard the distinct sound of bones cracking and splintering, as if she were crushing someone's skull. "And," she added in a low growl, "I will make certain it does not happen again."

Hallia, her doe eyes fixed on Domnu's feet, asked tentatively, "Who . . . would have stolen it?"

Domnu opened her right hand, palm up, and blinked. A silver chalice, brimming with red wine, appeared. Intertwining snakes decorated its rim. She took a slow sip, finishing with a smack of her lips. "The question, my pet, is not who would have done it, but who *could* have done it. My home, while humble, is reasonably well fortified."

My gaze roved over the table arrayed with the feast. Then I looked to the horizon, where the chariot drawn by the stallion had first appeared. Only the ring of blue fire now marked the place. I could hardly believe that I had been convinced I was about to be trampled. Yet it had felt utterly real. No doubt being crushed under those wheels would have felt equally real. "I can't imagine anyone stealing into your lair. Your magic is too powerful."

The hag stopped in the middle of another sip. She glowered at the chalice, which began to melt into a puddle of molten silver, bubbling and steaming, in her palm. Then, with a blink, the remains disappeared. She turned her eyes, which seemed darker than night itself, toward me.

"Just the point, my pet. Whoever stole the Galator was not troubled at all by magic. No, he or she had access to a weapon I have not encountered in many, many ages. A weapon that erases magic itself."

I caught my breath. "You mean . . . *negatus mysterium?*"

Shimmering in the blue light, she nodded. "Because I was confident—too confident—that no more of it remained in Fincayra, I was unprepared. Never again! The person who wielded it simply waited until I left the lair, which I do once every few decades, then pulled loose a few threads of my magical weavings—and walked right in. The *negatus mysterium* erased any signs."

Her bent teeth showed themselves in a sinister grin. "There was one flaw, however." She leaned closer, her voice a hushed whisper. "You may recall that the Galator will only serve its owner if it has been freely given. Which, in this case, it certainly was not."

Running my hand along the leather cord of my satchel, I pondered her words. "So whoever has the Galator cannot use it."

"Precisely, my pet. That mistake is also revealing. It tells me that the thief is someone who knows a good deal about magic, but who is also greedy, arrogant, and impulsive."

I reached inside my satchel and felt the one remaining string from my psaltery. It felt so stiff, so brittle. "I know who the thief is."

Domnu peered at me skeptically. "You do?"

"Yes." Feeling the emptiness within my chest, I nodded. "The same person who stole my powers."

"Explain yourself, my pet."

I traded glances with Hallia. "Before I do, I need your commitment. No treachery this time."

She flashed a mouthful of broken teeth, lit by the flickering flames. "What's wrong, my pet? Don't you trust me?"

"No! And I never will." I watched her warily. "But I might agree to collaborate with you—for a while."

Domnu growled softly. "An alliance, then?"

"An alliance."

"What are the terms?"

My fists clenched. "If together we can regain the Galator, then I can use it to battle Valdearg three days from now. If I should survive, the Galator is yours. I forfeit any claim to it."

Her dark eyes widened. "And if you should not survive?"

"Then it's yours, as well. You may have to argue with Valdearg about it, but I won't be around anymore to trouble you."

"*Hmmm.* Tempting." She studied me severely. "One more term should be added, however. If you can, with my help, regain the Galator, you must show me something."

Puzzled, I cocked my head. "What could I possibly show you?"

The hag hesitated, patting her hairless head for several seconds. "Oh, nothing serious, really. Just a trifle."

"What?"

She bent so close that our noses nearly touched. "I want you to show me how the pendant—especially that green jewel in its center—works."

I stepped backward, almost bumping into Hallia. "You—you don't know? With all your powers?"

Domnu hissed. "Would I ask you if I did? I only know what any wandering bard could tell you. That its powers are truly vast. And utterly mysterious."

Remembering Cairpré's description, I quoted, *"Vast beyond knowing."*

"Quite so. No doubt I could divine all its secrets in a little time. Say, a millennium or two. But someone who knows you made me think you might be able to help me do it faster. Bones! Boiling bones! What was his name? That little fellow who is always playing games with Rhita Gawr."

"Dagda." My face reddened. Little fellow! "His battles with Rhita Gawr are no game."

The hag cackled quietly. "Such naïveté! Charming, my pet, charming." Taking no heed of my contempt, she continued. "One day, perhaps, you will learn that everything is a game. A serious game, perhaps, such as charioteering. Or a meaningless game, full of frivolity—such as life."

I planted my boots, grinding my heels on the stone floor. "You'll never convince me of that."

She waved at the air, her hand awash in blue light. "It doesn't matter. I doubt you will live long enough to learn any better. Even so, I will take the risk that Dagda's remark was true. He told me that, one day, the half-human named Merlin would truly master the power of the Galator."

Surprised, I caught my breath. "Well, I accept your term, though I doubt that prediction will come true. How can it? In all the time I wore the pendant, feeling its weight on my chest, I learned only this: Whatever its magic really is, it has something to do with . . . an emotion."

Suddenly unsettled, Domnu tugged on the folds of her neck. "What emotion?"

"Love."

She made a face like someone who had swallowed curdled milk. "Bones! Are you sure?"

I nodded.

"Well . . . as I said, the risk is mine. I'll just need to find some other way to unlock its power. So there we are, my pet. Allies—for the time being."

"Wait." I glanced toward the flickering lights. "I, too, have an additional term."

The hag eyed me with suspicion. "What is it?"

"Before we go any further, you must return that stallion to his original form."

Hallia started. Her brown eyes gazed at me in astonishment— and, though I couldn't be sure, a touch of gratitude.

"The horse?" asked Domnu. "Why should I?"

I sucked in my breath, remembering the feeling of running upon my own hooves, my own four sturdy legs. "Because you need my help."

The hag grunted. "I suppose I do. All right. Though I doubt that fool beast has learned his lesson yet."

She flicked a finger toward the edge of the room. Suddenly a loud neigh sounded, followed by galloping hooves. The black stallion ran over, keeping his distance from Domnu. Cautiously, he approached Hallia, nuzzling her outstretched hand. Then, his tail swishing, he sidestepped over to me. Gently, I laid my hand on his gleaming coat, feeling its silken surface. He whinnied softly in response.

"He knows you," observed Hallia.

I stroked his black mane, inhaling the horse's familiar smell. Slowly, the edges of my mouth curled upward. "As I know him. His name is . . . Ionn. Ionn y Morwyn. He was my father's horse, and my own first friend."

Domnu shrugged. "How touching. Very well, then. I might consider throwing the horse into the bargain. A sturdy beast, but he's been nothing but trouble to me from the day I, well, rescued him from that drafty old stable."

Ionn gave a loud snort, but she didn't pay any attention. "What I really need is something more docile and obedient—a goblin, perhaps—for my chessboard. So I suppose if you agree to our little alliance, the stallion is yours."

Feeling Ionn's warm breath on my neck, I nodded. "Except that he isn't mine. Or anyone else's, for that matter. This horse belongs to himself. And only to himself."

Ionn nuzzled my shoulder. I continued to stroke his mane, recalling the times I had clung to it as a child. Then, on an impulse, I took an apple from the bowl on the table. The stallion nudged it with his nose, breathing warm air once again on my hand. Wrapping his lips around the fruit, he took his first bite, crunching loudly. Hallia watched, a spare smile on her face.

"So be it, my pet. I will set the horse free."

I watched Ionn take another bite, then turned back to the hag. "Then we are allies."

Domnu reached for one of the still-steaming loaves of bread on the table. Tearing off a chunk, she gave half to me and half to Hallia, who took it reluctantly. "Here. If we are going to be allies, even temporarily, you will need your strength." She pulled off another chunk and popped it into her mouth. *"Mmmm.* Not bad, if I do fffay fffo myfffelf."

Ionn finished the last of the apple, rubbing his soft nose against my wrist as he chewed. At the same time, I took a bite of the bread. Instantly, my mouth filled with its rich, roasted flavor. Before I had even swallowed, Ionn butted my shoulder with his nose. Grinning, I reached over to the bowl and gave him another apple. As he ate, so did I. In time, Hallia too began to nibble.

Together, she and I moved toward the oaken table. With a clap of Domnu's hands, three wooden chairs appeared. Hallia and I fell to the food, eating and drinking ravenously, until we could hold no more. Domnu, for her part, ate the entire pie in just a few seconds, dribbling chestnut sauce on herself. Then, seeing my look of disappointment, she waved her hand. A new pie, speckled with blueberries, suddenly filled the dish. Somehow both Hallia and I found room for hefty slices.

At last, Domnu pushed back her chair. "Now tell me about this person who stole your powers. And why you believe it's the same vermin who took the Galator."

With the back of my hand, I wiped some of the buttery sauce

from the trout off my chin. "I speak of Urnalda, enchantress of the dwarves."

Domnu scoffed. "That old sorceress of the tunnels? She has the arrogance and the greed, to be sure. But she lacks the patience, the cunning, and most of all the understanding of magic. I doubt she could wield *negatus mysterium,* dangerous stuff that it is, without destroying her own magic in the process."

"She used it against me!" I stood, my hands pressed to my ribs. "All my magic, all my power, is gone now." I swallowed. "She even took my staff."

The hag's ancient eyes examined me. "Not true. I perceive magic in you, even now."

Sadly, I traded looks with Hallia. "You must be sensing the magic that was given to me by . . . a friend. Yet that magic allows me to do only one thing."

"Which is, my pet?"

Hallia shot me a warning glance.

"To know . . . a kind of glory." I drew a slow breath. "Though even that won't last much longer."

Domnu's scalp furrowed more deeply. Behind her, the blue flames writhed and twisted, throwing shadows over her burly hands. "Neither will you, I expect. You are quite determined to confront this dragon of yours, I can see that clearly. Well, now, tell me. Do you recall that prediction about you I made when we last met?"

I shuddered, still hearing the sting of her words. "You said that I would bring ruin, utter ruin, to Fincayra."

"That's right, my pet. Don't take it too hard. Besides, I now think my prediction was a bit too harsh."

"Really?"

"Yes." Shadows fluttered like ghouls across the tabletop. "Not because the notion itself was flawed, mind you. But because I now sincerely doubt that you will live long enough to cause much more trouble."

I could only grimace.

"In any case," she went on, "we must consider how to use your remaining time most productively." The flames surrounding us sputtered and crackled. "No, no, I think you would only be wasting what little time is left by seeking out Urnalda."

"But why? I'm sure she's the one."

The hag shook her head, causing ripples of blue light to flow like waves across her scalp. "There is, I suppose, a chance you are right. I sincerely doubt it, though. Still, you have given me an idea. Bones! I should have thought of it sooner. There is a place—an oracle of sorts. It can answer any question, any question at all, posed by a mortal creature. That rules me out, I am afraid. But it ought to work for you."

Uncertainly, I brushed the stray hairs off my forehead. "Where is this place? Is it difficult to get there? My time—it's so short."

"Not difficult at all, my pet. And no whirlwind this time! I could send you there by Leaping." A low cackle filled her throat. "Or, if you like, I could use a chariot. More time-consuming, but ever so much more exciting." Seeing my expression, she frowned. "All right. Leaping, then."

"I'm still not sure. If Urnalda does have the Galator, it could take all the time I have left to win it back."

Domnu reached for the flask of wine, opened her mouth as wide as a crevasse, and poured all the liquid down her throat. "Ah, my pet, don't you understand? If Urnalda does not have it, then you will have used up all your time for nothing. If, however, she does have it, the oracle will tell you that straightaway. This way, you can be certain who really is the thief." She crushed the flask in her fist, spraying shards of glass on the stones. "And that is something—breaded bones, that is something—I would dearly like to know."

Slowly, I gave a nod. "All right, then. Tell me about this oracle. What sort of person is there?"

"Not a person. Not exactly. The oracle lies far to the south, near the sea, in a place surrounded by cliffs—steep, smoking cliffs."

At this, Hallia stiffened. She started to say something, but the hag cut her off.

"It's so simple, my pet! All you need to do is ask it your question." She glanced toward the flickering lights. "That is, after you have surmounted a minor obstacle."

I cringed. "What sort of obstacle?"

Blue light exploded in the room, swallowing everything.

PART THREE

XXI

THE BIRTH OF
THE MIST

Salt. On my lips. In the air.

Suddenly I realized that my legs and back felt wet. Thoroughly wet. I shifted, when something rough scraped the side of my neck. Startled, I sat up—as a bright purple sea star fell from my shoulder, landing beside me with a splash.

Tide pool! I was sitting in a tide pool. A strand of kelp clung to my arm; a sea cucumber, slimy and bloated, draped over my hip. And there, smirking at me, sat Hallia. She leaned against a gnarled piece of driftwood, her back to the waves stroking the shore of black, crystalline sand. Trying to stifle a laugh, she quickly turned aside.

"In the name of Dagda!" I cursed, lifting myself out of the shallow pool. As I stood, water coursed off my tunic and splattered my boots. "Of all the places to land . . ."

Hallia's eyes flitted toward me—then veered away. "You'll dry out," she said quietly, pausing for a long moment to watch the undulating wall of mist beyond the waves. "This place holds more heat than you know."

Unsure what she meant, I rubbed the sore spot on my neck. Though the sting of the sea star was fading, its smell was not. And rubbing made it worse. Much like garlic but stronger, the smell wafted over me, pushing aside even the ocean's briny breath. Hoping to wash it off, I bent down to the tide pool and splashed some water on my skin.

"Just wait a bit," said Hallia, still looking at the mist. "A purple brittlepoint's odor won't last very long. You're lucky it wasn't a yellow one. Their smell can take days to die down. And this beach is full of them."

Annoyed, I peered at her. "How do you know so much about sea stars? And this place?"

She turned her eyes, softer than the mist itself, toward me. "Because this is the place of my childhood. Before my clan, the Mellwyn-bri-Meath, left for the woods of the west."

"Your . . . childhood?" I stepped, boots sloshing, closer to her. "Are you sure? This island has so many beaches."

"Not with sand like this." She ran her fingers through the dark crystals. Then her gaze lifted to something behind me. "Nor with cliffs like those."

I spun around to see a line of sheer cliffs, as black as the sand at our feet. Ominous they stood, like a stand of dead trees. Despite the strong light from the sun, still well above the horizon, the cliffs wore only shadows upon shadows. From several points among their crags, thin trails of smoke climbed skyward.

I shivered, from more than the wet tunic on my back. "The smoking cliffs. The ones Domnu talked about."

"Where lies the oracle—among other things."

Using her big toe, Hallia poked a cockleshell, turning it over on the sand. A long, gray leg instantly emerged from the shell and started to push sideways. In a few seconds, the cockle flipped itself back over—with a squirt of seawater for good measure. Watching this, she smiled wistfully. "It was a good place to live. Full of . . . companions. Even now."

"Companions?" I glanced again at the forbidding cliffs, then at the dark stretch of shore. "Beyond the shells and sea stars, there's no one here but us."

"Oh, no?" She hesitated for a long moment. Finally she shook her head, catching the sunlight in her unbraided hair. "My people are here."

"But I thought you said they left."

"They did—except for those whose tracks had already melted into the sand."

I drew a deep breath of salty air, more confused than ever. "I don't understand."

She waved at the cliffs. "Use your deer eyes, Merlin. Not your man eyes."

Turning, I allowed my second sight to spread over the cliffs. To probe their shadows. To feel their edges. The slapping of the waves behind me slowly faded, transforming into a different sound— somehow nearer, somehow farther away. Thrumming. Drumming. Like an ever-beating heart, an ever-pounding hoof.

In time, I began to discern a faint tracery of lines woven across the vertical slopes. The lines ran in all directions, bending with every surge and scoop of the cliffs. Could they be ancient trails? Worn by countless hooves over countless years?

And . . . hollows. Caves. Darker than the shadows. Full of mystery, as well as something more.

I nodded, understanding at last. "Your ancestors are still here."

With the grace of a doe, Hallia rose to her feet. "That they are, buried in the caves, and a part of me with them." She sighed. "In my heart, I still cling to this shore, just as much as those blue mussels cling to the rocks over there. In my dreams, I find myself floating through this mist—like the silver jellyfish, so delicate, that swims through the shallows, forever breathing the water that becomes its very body."

Her words encircled me, enveloping me like the mist itself. "Why then did you leave?"

"Because of the cliffs. The old lava mountain they surround began to rumble, and then to smoke." Her eyes darted like fretful gulls across the shoreline. "Though it never spewed fire, as it did in Distant Time, the mountain released . . . other things. Evil things."

Under my eye, the tender skin started to throb. The mention of the fire mountain, most likely—reminding me of those flames of my own making, flames that had scarred my face forever. I reached up to stroke my skin, when my hand froze. This scar under my eye hadn't come from those flames. No! It had come from an older wound, years before.

How could I have forgotten? On that long-ago day, on a deserted beach much like this one, a wild boar had attacked—and I was its prey. I could still hear its snarl, still see its slashing tusks, still feel its hot breath. And, with every throbbing pulse, I could still remember my shock at discovering that it was really not a boar at all, but the wicked warlord of the spirit world: Rhita Gawr.

Hallia nudged my shoulder with her own, just as I had seen her do once, as a doe, to Eremon. "You are troubled, I can tell."

Despite the moist air, my throat felt parched. "Those evil things . . . from the mountain. What were they?"

She frowned, then stooped to pick up a moon snail on the sand. Pensively, she ran her finger over the round, spiraling shell, the color of cream. "Something tells me you already know. Spirits—angry ones. Seeking death, not life, for anyone who lived here."

As I nodded, her frown deepened. "They came out of the cliffs, the caves, the sea itself, it seemed. No one knew why. We only knew that sickness and pain followed in their tracks." She winced, remembering something. "And that they had come only once before."

"When was that?"

Gently, she placed the shell on the rim of a barnacle-crusted rock. Before straightening, she paused to touch the flower of a pink sea anemone, limply waiting for the higher tide to return. At last, she stood again and faced me, her eyes now less frightened than sad. "Eremon could have told you. He knew all the ancient stories."

I wrapped my arms around my ribs, hoping to warm myself. "I miss him."

"So do I," she whispered. "So do I."

I watched as her tongue moistened her lips. "How is that tooth healing?"

"It still hurts a little," she said sadly. "But not so much as other places."

"You don't have to tell that story if you don't want to. I just had the feeling . . ."

"I'll try."

Turning her long chin toward the waves, and the billowing mist beyond, she started speaking in a slow, solemn cadence. "In the time before time, all spoken words could be seen and touched and held. Every story, once told, became a single, glowing thread—a thread that wove itself into a limitless, living tapestry. It stretched from these very cliffs all the way down to the sea, across this shore, and under the waves, where it lay beyond reach, beyond knowing. The tapestry—alive with colors and shapes, shadowy places and bright—was called by many names, but to the deer people it was known as the Carpet Caerlochlann."

She watched a crab, decorated with a ragged frond of kelp, strut across the driftwood by her foot. "The Carpet grew more luminous, more richly textured, with each passing season. Until . . . it grew so lovely that it caught the interest of one who wanted it for himself. Not to savor its stories—to feel its layers upon layers of woven yearnings, passions, grievings, and delights—but to own it. Possess it. Control it."

"Rhita Gawr," I said, touching my aching scar.

"Yes. Rhita Gawr. He sent his spirit warriors to haunt the cliffs, chasing away the deer people, poisoning any who dared to remain. Then he took the Carpet Caerlochlann as his own. It is said that on that day, when the sun began to rise, it was so stricken with sorrow that it could not bear to return. So from that moment on, all of Fincayra was cast into darkness."

Waves rolled onto the shore, one after another, nearly slapping our feet. A pair of cormorants soared out of the mist, flapping noisily before splashing down in the shallows. One of them plunged the full length of its neck into the water and came up with a writhing green fish in its beak. Hit by the golden sun, the fish flashed like a living emerald.

"There is sunlight now," I said softly.

"There is, yes. Because the great spirit Dagda confronted Rhita Gawr and won back the tapestry of tales. No one knows just how he succeeded, though it is said that he had to give up something terribly valuable—some of his own precious powers—to do it."

A new kind of cold gripped me, reaching deeper than the skin beneath my sopping tunic. "And what, after paying so dearly, did Dagda do with the tapestry?"

Hallia's round eyes turned to me. "He gave it away."

"He what?"

"Gave it away." She looked toward the slumbering sea, hidden by the vaporous curtain. "First, using the trail of a falling star as his needle, he pulled loose all the threads of story. These he wove together with threads of his own, made partly of air and partly of water. When finally he finished, the new weaving held all the magic of spoken words, and more. It was not quite air, not quite water—but something of both. Something in between. Something called . . ."

"Mist," I finished.

She nodded. "Then Dagda gave the magical mist to the peoples of this island. He wrapped it all the way around the coastline. So that every beach, every cove, every inlet would touch its mysterious vapors. And so that every breath taken upon these shores would mingle with its magic."

Shyly, she shrugged her shoulders. "So that is how, in the tales of my people, Fincayra's eternal mist was born."

For a long moment, neither of us spoke. A gull screeched overhead, while clams squirted by the tide pools. Beyond that, we heard only the waves slapping the shore, sucking the black sand as they pulled back to the sea. Then the lowering sun dropped behind a cloud, and I shivered.

Hallia scrutinized me. "You're cold."

Another shiver. "And wet. What I really need is a fire. Just a small one. Say, if we gather up some of this driftwood—"

"No." She shook her head, tousling her auburn hair. "It will attract *them*."

My eyes widened. "Spirits?"

She glanced at the cliffs, which loomed even darker than before. "They might have departed. It's been many years. All the same . . . it frightens me."

"A small fire, that's all." I flapped my arms. "Just so I can dry out."

"Well . . . if you must."

Without another word, we began picking up shards of driftwood. Higher on the shore, above the clusters of mussels, I found an old tangle of seaweed that had dried into a mass of brittle stems. Pulling it apart with my fingers, shivering all the while, I made a rough-hewn nest. Then, striking two sharp rocks above the kindling, I tried to make a spark. My first several landed not on the nest, but on the wet sand. Finally one struck a stem. Gently, I breathed on it, coaxing it to burn. In time, a thin trail of smoke drifted skyward.

Before long, Hallia and I were warming ourselves before the crackling flames. "As much as I miss having hooves," I observed, "hands can be useful."

She gave a somber nod. "Eremon liked to say that hooves can make speed, while hands can make music."

Remembering my own disastrous attempt to make music—so long ago, it seemed—I grimaced. "Some hands, anyway."

"You have tried?"

I broke some driftwood over my knee and laid the pieces on the fire. "I've tried."

Hallia watched me, as if she hoped I might say more. When I didn't, she scooped some sand in her palm. "Music, real music, is a kind of magic. As elusive as the mist."

Slowly, I drew out of my satchel the charred remains of my psaltery. Holding the remains of the oaken bridge, I twirled the string, blackened and stiff. I tried to imagine it as part of a whole instrument again, cupped in my hand, with all the gleaming strings intact. But the vision exploded into flames, crumbling into charcoal. Gone: whatever magic this string once possessed. Just like whatever magic my own fingers once possessed.

"Cairpré once asked me," I mused aloud, "whether the music lies in the strings . . ."

"Or in the hands that pluck them?" Hallia grinned at me. "My own mother, who taught me how to play the willow harp, asked me the same question."

"And did you answer it?"

"No."

"Did she?"

"No." She pulled a barnacle off a shard of driftwood, then tossed the wood into the flames. "But she did say, while we sat on a rock on this very beach, that an instrument, by itself, makes no music. Only sound."

She furrowed her brow. "I can't remember her words exactly, but she said something else, too. That musical instruments need to tap into something more—something higher. That's it. She called it *a power still higher.*"

I jumped at the phrase.

She eyed me. "What's wrong?"

"That's what I'm going to need if I'm ever going to stop

Valdearg. *A power still higher.* It could mean the Galator. Or it could mean something else." Using the last of the shards, I shoved the burning coals together. "Whatever it is, I don't think I have it."

Hallia studied me, half her face aglow from the flames. "Maybe not, but you do have something."

I looked at her skeptically.

"You have whatever it took to make Domnu give that stallion back his natural form. And, just as important, to set him free." She turned toward the pulsing waves. "That was a noble thing to do. Almost . . . a stag-like thing."

I lifted the flap of my satchel and replaced the psaltery string. "Maybe I have done at least one thing right, then. I only hope that hag keeps her word and sets Ionn free."

Hallia shook her long strands of hair. "I don't trust her any more than you, believe me! She does need your help, though, if she's going to get back that pendant. That's why she told you about the Wheel."

"Wheel?"

"The oracle. The one in the smoking cliffs." Her face tightened. "It's called . . . the Wheel of Wye."

I squeezed her arm. "You know about it?"

"Not much. Just that it's hidden somewhere up there." She paused. "And that it's a place of fear—and has been long before the spirits came to the mountain."

"Do you know what Domnu meant by *a minor obstacle?*"

"No. And I don't want to find out." She drew a halting breath. "There is, though, a village near the cliffs where you might learn more. It's a brutal place. Filled with m—" She caught herself. "With that *kind* of men. Who don't even notice their own tracks, who would kill a deer just for sport. Not like . . . well, another man I know."

For an instant, the fire glowed bright on her cheeks—and, it seemed, on mine. Suddenly she scowled. "That village . . . I've never been there. And never want to! But for you, it's different. It was the place—in my childhood, at least—where most oracle seekers started their climbs into the cliffs. Someone there might know something useful."

Sensing she was preparing to say good-bye, I felt saddened—even as I felt grateful for her suggestion. "Going there, I suppose, could save time."

"Though it's a rough place, and could end up costing you time." She sighed. "The biggest risk to your time, though, is simply finding it, tucked away in its hidden valley. Unless you know the right trails, you might search for days among the folds of cliffs, and the maze of hillocks on their western edge."

She paused, her lower lip trembling. "Which is why . . . I'm going to take you there myself."

My heart leaped.

"The trip will still take time, though. Even more since we can't use our deer forms. Too much risk of hunters from the village."

I looked her full in the face. "Thank you, Hallia."

"It's only what . . . my brother would have done."

"Let's go, then," I declared. "While there's still daylight. Just let me put out this fire."

With my boot, I crunched on the remaining coals. Yet as soon as I lifted my foot, they sprang back into flames. Puzzled, I glanced at my boot. Once again I tried to stamp out the fire; once again it revived. I kicked the largest of the burning embers into a nearby tide pool. It sputtered and sizzled, but continued to flame. Steam rose, mingling with the mist.

"We must leave," she said urgently. "I only hope we'll be leaving alone."

XXII

A CHILL WIND

Hallia guided me over the slippery, mussel-laden rocks to a sharp cleft at the base of the nearest cliff. There we found a thin, winding trail, covered with dust as black as the cliffs themselves. Wordlessly, we followed it inland for some distance, before turning left on another trail, then right on another. Soon we had made so many turns that I would have lost my bearings completely but for the constant presence of the cliffs towering above us.

All the while, as we wormed our way through the sheer buttresses and piles of black rock, we stayed alert for any signs of the mountain spirits. In time, the sounds and smells of the sea began to fade. The trail we were following gradually widened a bit. To our left appeared a string of stubbly fields, while to our right the dark cliffs loomed, separated from us by a row of steep, rocky hillocks. The sun, partly shrouded by a line of clouds, hung low to the west, casting golden rays on the grasses streaked with the auburns and reds of autumn.

By a field where four or five sheep grazed, heedless of us, Hallia stopped. Cautiously, she surveyed the lengthening shadows. "I don't know which worries me more," she said, her eyes darting from side to side. "The absence of spirits—or the presence of men."

"I'm worried about something else," I said grimly. "Time! There's just three days left before I must face Valdearg—with or without the Galator. Even if this oracle can help me find it, I still have to get it back somehow. And learn how to use it."

She gave her flowing hair a shake and began combing its tangles with her fingers. "And one thing more, Merlin."

My eyebrows lifted.

"You still have to get back to the dwarves' territory—no little bound from here. While you can, if you choose, run like a deer, you'll still need to allow at least two days for the journey. Which leaves you only one day to find the Galator."

Pondering her words, I scraped the ground with my boot—the same boot I had used to try to save the baby dragon. I had failed in that attempt. Would I also fail in this one?

A rock suddenly clattered down from the cliffs above. Hallia started. Her hand tugged anxiously at her hair. "The spirits . . ."

I held her gaze. "You don't have to come any farther, you know. You've already done more than I would have asked."

"I know." Her back straightened. "Even so, I shall stay with you a little longer. To the village. But there I must leave you." She glanced at the shadowed cliffs. "And wish you whatever luck is left in this land."

So very much, I wanted to tell her thanks. And something more, something beyond words. Yet my throat had closed as tight as a fist.

As her hands went back to combing her tangled hair, she turned and started slowly down the trail. I stared past her toward the rocky hillocks and the smoking crags behind. The sun's rays, piercing the gathering clouds, had deepened from gold to orange, yet the cliffs seemed darker than ever. Darker than my second sight could fathom.

In silence, we walked. The trail swung straight into the hillocks, which pressed so close to our sides that at times the mountain itself disappeared from view. While Hallia's bare feet made only the slightest shuffle on the pebbles and dust, my boots crunched with every step. Although the trail continued to grow wider, broadening into a rough road, the shadowy rock piles seemed to press all the closer.

As she maneuvered deftly around a yellow-spotted snake, Hallia gave me a worried look. "The Wheel of Wye, as an oracle, must have strong magic of its own. But it may not be stronger than Rhita Gawr's spirits. That might even be why he sent them here—to destroy it, or make it serve his purposes."

I kept striding. Shadows deepened all around us. Under my breath, I replied, "I only hope that he himself is not among them."

She inhaled sharply. "You really think he might be?"

"I don't know. It's just that . . . well, I can't shake the feeling he's somehow more involved than we know. Not just with the spirits' return, but with other things, as well. The kreelixes, for example. Why did they come back just now? And the outbreak of *negatus mysterium*—strong enough to steal the Galator from right under Domnu's warty brow. Maybe even, though I can't explain why, the murder of all those baby dragons."

She studied me doubtfully. "That's like saying the crying of a fawn is connected to the stirring of oak leaves in the wind."

"Exactly," I declared. "For connected they are! I don't understand why or how. Just that, somehow, they are."

Her face pensive, she continued along the rock-strewn road. "You sound almost like . . . someone else."

A moment later, we rounded a bend—and suddenly halted. Before us, lit by the reddening rays, rose three columns of smoke. Not from the cliffs, but from chimneys. The village.

Hallia tensed, one foot twisting anxiously on the pebbles. "I'm . . . frightened."

I took her arm. "You don't have to go any farther."

She shook free. "I know. But I'll decide when I'm turning back. Not you."

Together, we continued walking. The high-walled hillocks on both sides receded, opening into a compact valley. There, scored by shadows, sat a ramshackle settlement, made of the very slabs that dotted its stony field. The huts, seven or eight in all, looked like nothing more than square piles of rock. The roof of one had fallen in, but no one seemed to care enough to repair it. But for the smoke streaming from the chimneys, the sheep gnawing at the few tussocks of grass, and the pair of huddled figures leaning against the wall of the largest building, the whole village could have been mistaken for the rock outcroppings around it. Rising sharply from the far end of the valley, the mountain surged into smoking crags, dark and foreboding.

Hallia rolled her head, sniffing the air. "You see what I was saying about this place? Just look at it! Whatever people live here haven't joined with the land. Never have. See there? Not a single garden, or flower box, or even a bench to sit upon. Most of those huts don't have any windows."

I nodded. "The kind of place where people come to escape from trouble. Or maybe cause it."

A few raindrops splattered us. I glanced at the thick bank of clouds now obscuring the horizon. Arms of clouds, writhing like dark serpents, stretched toward the cliffs. The wind blew cold and hard out of the west, promising more rain shortly. There would be no sunset tonight—and probably no stars for some time.

Grimly, I pondered the cliffs. "I can't hope to climb up there in a storm. Whether or not I can learn something useful, I'll need to wait out the worst of it in the village. As soon as it starts to clear, and some stars emerge, I'll leave. Until then, I'll just say I'm a traveler passing through."

"Two travelers," declared Hallia. She blew a long breath. "Though I'd rather find shelter in the rocks, believe me. No matter how hard it rains."

"Are you sure?"

She lifted her chin a bit higher. "No, but I'm coming anyway."

The chill wind shoved us along the road, which skirted the edge of the village before continuing up the narrow valley. More clouds rolled in, obscuring all but the nearest huts. More quickly than I expected, the rain swelled into a shower, then a downpour. Thunder echoed off the crags, pounding like celestial hooves. By the time we reached the larger building, sheets of rain slapped against the stone roof. The two huddled figures we had seen from a distance had already gone inside, leaving the roughly planked door ajar.

After shaking the water from my hair and wringing out the sleeves of my tunic, I peered inside. Not much to see. Just a peat fire sputtering in the hearth, a few spare tables and chairs, and a bent, white-haired fellow emerging from another room. This was, apparently, some sort of tavern. The old fellow, who wore a waiter's apron, was carrying a clay bowl in his hands. From the room he was leaving, someone bellowed at him—so loudly that he nearly dropped the bowl. Meekly, he nodded, plunging the tips of his sagging moustache into its steaming contents.

"My broth!" roared a man from a table by the fire. "Bring my dog-damned broth!"

Hurriedly, the old waiter brought over the bowl. The man tore it away, planted his feet on the wall beside the fire, then drained the broth in three swallows. He tossed the bowl to the floor, where it shattered into pieces. Even as the old fellow stooped to clean up the mess, the man shouted at him again.

"Fetch some more peat for the fire, will you? I'm wet and cold, can't you see? What sort of rat's hole inn is this that you freeze your guests like corpses?"

The old fellow, his white hair all askew, holding the chips of pottery in his apron, headed toward the adjacent room. He stumbled past the other man who had come in from the rain, now seated in a dimly lit corner, tearing roughly at some dried meat. Although the hood of his black cloak obscured his face entirely, his manner conveyed the same surliness as the man by the fire.

With a frown at Hallia, I pulled open the door. Its squeal was drowned out by the cacophony of the rain on the roof, but the heads of both men immediately turned our way. Even though the hooded man's face remained in shadow, I could almost feel the harshness of his gaze. Hallia, close behind me, hesitated in the doorway.

"By the corpse's death," grumbled the man by the hearth. "Close the dog-damned door!" His eyes, like his coarse beard, glowed red in the firelight. "You'll give me a dog-damned fever, you will."

She looked for an instant as if she were on the edge of bolting, but stepped inside and shut the door. I nodded toward a rough-hewn table at the opposite end of the room. While it sat not far from the other man, whose black hood still dripped from the rain, he seemed likely to be a better neighbor than the ranter by the hearth. As we moved toward the table, the white-haired waiter returned, bending even lower than before under the weight of a few clumps of peat. He barely glanced at us as we passed.

Suddenly the hooded man leaped to his feet. A rusted dagger glinted in his hand. Before I could draw my own blade, he kicked over the table, knocking me backward into Hallia. We fell in a heap on the floor.

The man, bundled in his heavy cloak, scurried past us. Even as we regained our feet, the creaky door slammed shut. I ran after him, pulled open the door, and scanned the rain-soaked road, the stone huts, the dreary field. No sign of him anywhere.

Pushing the wet locks off my brow, I turned back to Hallia. "He's disappeared."

"Why would he do that?" she asked, shaken. "We didn't threaten him."

"Ye came too awfully close, me dear." It was the white-haired man, having rid himself of the load of peat. Still, he hunched so low that his wrinkled brow came no higher than the middle of Hallia's chest. "Ye disturbed his privacy, ye see."

She scowled. "Such a friendly village."

The old man gave a tense, wheezing laugh. "So friendly, me dear, it don't even have a proper name. Or any longtime residents, but for master Lugaid, who owns this public house, an' me, old Bachod. An' a few lame sheep." He glowered at the bearded man by the fire. "It's a mean-hearted place, me dear, I can assure ye that. Jest a place worth avoidin', if ye can."

With a heave, I righted the table. "Do you mind if we sit here a little while? Just to dry off."

Bachod's white hairs, toppling over his ears, wagged from side to side—along with his greasy moustache. "As long as ye pay before ye eat anythin', master Lugaid shouldn't object." He pulled out a rag and began wiping the table. "Jest mind who ye sit near, if ye wish to stay healthful."

"We will." I brushed some moldy cheese off a chair, then sat down next to Hallia. "By the way," I asked, as nonchalantly as I could, "where does that old road out there lead? Surely not up into the cliffs."

The old man continued wiping. "Ah, that little pathway is older than meself, older than the rocks perhaps. It jest curves about this valley like a coilin' snake, not leadin' anywhere." His raspy voice lowered a notch. "Some say it was the ghosts who made it."

"Ghosts?"

"From up the mountain. Ye haven't heard of 'em, me lad? Well then, ye needs to know, that's certain, since ye're journeyin' hereabouts." He ceased wiping and glanced around fearfully, as if the chairs and tables themselves might be listening. Finally he rasped, "They're angry. An' so very vengeful. Yer life is safe, perhaps, in this little valley. But anywhere on the mountain . . . well, ye'd rather be pierced by a thousan' spears before lettin' 'em take ye."

Nervously, he tugged on his moustache. Then he turned to Hallia. His voice lowered ominously. "Death—that'd be a kindness, though, compared to what they'd be doin' to yer heart, to yer innards, an' worse yet, to yer everlastin' soul, if they found ye was . . . a deer person."

Her eyes swelled to their widest. In a flash, she bolted for the door, threw it open, and vanished into the rain.

I glared at Bachod. "You old fool!"

He shrunk away from me. "Jest wanted to be helpful, I did."

Tempted as I was to give him a fright of his own, I turned and sprinted after Hallia. Just as I reached the doorway, I caught a glimpse of her dashing behind the hut with the fallen roof. Beyond, darker than even the sky itself, I could see the ragged edge of the cliffs rising above the valley.

"Hallia!" I cried, charging after her. Mud sprayed from my boots, as rivers ran down my neck and arms. Thunder slammed against the mountainside.

Sliding to a halt by the collapsed hut, I peered into the torrent. Nothing. Nothing but rain.

At that instant I heard a whisper just behind me. "M-e-e-erlin."

I whirled around. There, under an overhanging slab of rock, all that remained of the crumbled roof, cowered Hallia. Ducking under the slab, I joined her in the hollow. I placed my arms around her sopping shoulders, holding her shivering body close to mine.

Several minutes passed. The downpour did not relent. At last, though, her shivers subsided. She began to breathe more normally. I felt her relax, leaning her head against my shoulder. Rain splattered all around, as a chill wind sliced through our clothing. Yet somehow I did not feel cold.

All at once, Hallia stiffened. Before I could move, the blade of a dagger pressed between my shoulder blades.

XXIII

DAGGERPOINT

S teady now," growled the voice behind me. The dagger pressed tight against my back.

I felt Hallia standing by my side, as alert as if she were facing a pack of wolves. Water streamed off the overhanging slab that sheltered us, splattering my left arm. Trying to remain calm, I sucked in my breath. "We have no wish to harm you, good sir. Let us go in peace."

"Fancy words! You must have been mentored by a bard."

Despite the knife, I started. Something about the phrasing, if not the voice, sounded vaguely familiar. Yet I couldn't quite place it.

"Tell me the truth," the man in the shadows demanded. "Have you also learned to play the psaltery?"

Heedless of any danger, I whirled around. "Cairpré!" I threw my arms around him.

"Well met," declared the poet, tossing back his black hood.

Hallia gasped. "You know this . . . ruffian?"

The gray mane bobbed as Cairpré nodded. "Well enough to know that I don't like to use a dagger for anything more dangerous than slicing bread." He slipped the blade in its sheath. "I do hope I didn't give you a fright."

"Oh, no," snarled Hallia, her eyes darting over the shadowy hollow. To my chagrin, she edged away from me. "I had simply forgotten, for a moment, about the treacherous ways of men."

Cairpré's eyes, deeper than pools, regarded her thoughtfully. "You are a deer woman, I see. Of the clan Mellwyn-bri-Meath, if I am not mistaken."

She bristled, but said nothing.

"I am Cairpré, a humble bard." He bowed his head slightly. "I am pleased to meet you. And my heart is pained, for I can see that my own race has brought suffering to yours."

Her doe-like eyes narrowed. "More than you could imagine."

"I am sorry." Cairpré regarded her for another moment, then turned to me. "My disguise was necessary. As was that little scene in the tavern, when I feared you might come close enough to recognize me. Bachod, the old waiter, is—"

"A fool," I declared.

"Perhaps." He wiped a raindrop from the tip of his nose, as sharp as an eagle's beak. "Yet he knows more than he lets on, good fellow. Though his learning comes not from books, he is really, I think, a bard at heart. *Though speech be unlearn'd, The wisdom be earn'd.*"

He glanced again at the black cliffs. "He has already helped me more than he knows, by sharing a few old stories about this land. But to avoid raising any suspicions, I've kept my own identity secret. So Bachod thinks I'm just a wandering bard. He has no idea who I really am, or what brings me here."

The cold wind strengthened, and with it, the downpour. Thunder reverberated again and again among the craggy cliffs. As Hallia and I both drew deeper into the hollow, trying to avoid the drenching gusts, I tried to catch her eye. Yet she avoided my gaze.

Shielding his brow from the rain, Cairpré peered out of the over-hang at the massive clouds that had converged above the valley. "The storm is worsening, I fear. We may be caught here for some time."

Still disbelieving we were together again, I shook my head. "What *does* bring you here, old friend? Are you, too, searching for the Galator?"

The poet's expression darkened. He moved to avoid a new trickle of water from the slab above us. "No, my boy. Not the Galator."

"What, then?"

"I seek the person responsible for the return of the kreelix."

Hallia tensed, as did I. "The kreelix? What have you learned?"

"Precious little, I'm afraid." Gathering his cloak, he sat down on the wet stones, motioning for us to join him. I did so, while Hallia remained standing apart. "Suffice it to say that shortly after you and Rhia departed, I set out myself—to learn whatever I could. Kreelixes have been gone for ages! Their return threatens the life—not just of you, my boy, though that's weighed heavily on my mind—but of all creatures of magic. Indeed, of this whole island."

His bushy brows drew together. "Rags and rat holes, it was hard to leave Elen! Yet I knew that my path could be dangerous, almost as dangerous as your own. Even so, she wanted badly, very badly, to come with me. If she hadn't already promised to wait for Rhia in the forest, I could never have stopped her."

Sadly, I grinned. "Rhia's promise to come back was the only thing that kept her from staying with me, as well."

"No doubt. You two, as brother and sister, couldn't be closer. *So thoroughly bound, As roots to the ground.*"

In the shadows, Hallia shifted her weight. And, though I couldn't be certain, she seemed to edge a tiny bit closer.

Cairpré's fist clenched. "Devourers of magic! I've spent many hours wondering who or what could have brought even one of them back." A sizzling blast of lightning struck the mountain, followed by a crash of thunder. "And I've concluded that there could be only one source so wicked, so cruel, to have done it."

Before he could say the name, I did. "Rhita Gawr."

Grimly, he observed me. "Yes, Merlin. The nemesis of anyone— and any land—he can't control." His head, gray hairs dripping, swung toward Hallia. "That's why he brought his terrible spells to this place. And why he tormented your clan into leaving your ancestral home."

"But . . . why?" she whispered from the shadows. "This was our land. Our home."

The poet waited for another roll of thunder to pass. "Because he needed no interference for a long time—long enough to breed and train the kreelixes. And your people knew too many of this mountain's secrets. You might have gotten in his way. For to bring back those beasts, he needed to tap the mountain's volcanic power. To unleash the *negatus mysterium* within its lava. That's always been the case. Clan Righteous, the people who bred kreelixes long ago, often made lava mountains their hideaways for the same reason."

Lightning struck the cliffs, etching our faces. I remembered, with a shudder, the emblem of Clan Righteous that Cairpré had described once before: a fist crushing a lightning bolt. "So do you think," I asked hesitantly, "that Rhita Gawr has returned?"

"I cannot say. He may still be too enmeshed in his battles with Dagda, relying instead on mortal allies. Or," he added gravely, "he may be nearer than we know." The deep pools beneath his brows surveyed me. "Now, my boy. You said you're seeking the Galator?"

I gazed out of the overhang into the darkening night, the wailing wind, the endless rain. "To use its power, if I can, to stop Valdearg."

Slowly, he nodded. "As your grandfather did, long ago. Yet—why here? Is it hidden among the cliffs?"

"No. But an oracle is—the Wheel of Wye."

"The Wheel! Rags and rat holes, my boy! If the Wheel of Wye exists, and I'm not sure it does, it could be every bit as dangerous as the dragon himself. Why would you ever risk such a thing?"

"I have no choice."

"You always have a choice. Even when it seems otherwise." He laid his hand on my shoulder. "Tell me where you have been since we parted."

As rain slashed against the stone above our heads, I took a deep breath and began my tale. I told of my trek with Rhia, and my narrow escape from the living stone. My confrontation with Urnalda—and her treachery. The poet's hand squeezed my shoulder tightly as I described the shock of how she destroyed my powers. And my staff. I went on, telling of my escape, of Eremon's wondrous gift, and of our discovery of the mutilated eggs, the ghastly remains of Valdearg's offspring.

Then, to the surprise of both Cairpré and Hallia, I described how I had found the last surviving hatchling—and tried to save its life. All through that long night. And how, with no magic left in my hands, I had failed.

Hallia, as gracefully as a falling leaf, sat down beside me. "You really did that? You never spoke of it."

"I didn't do anything worth telling about."

"You tried." Her eyes glistened in the waning light. "To save a life you didn't need to save. Not the sort of thing most . . . men would do."

"Perhaps not," observed Cairpré. "But it was the sort of thing a wizard might do."

I bit my lip. Then, as much to change the subject as to finish my tale, I continued. Briefly, I sketched the attack by the second kreelix—and Eremon's sacrifice. I described (though it made me feel nauseated) the terrible whirlwind. And, at last, our encounter with Domnu. As I felt Hallia's warm breath upon my neck, I explained the disappearance of the glowing pendant, and the hope, however faint, that the oracle might help me find it again in time.

After I concluded, the shaggy-haired bard watched me solemnly for a moment. The last hint of twilight ran along the ridges of his wet brow as he spoke again. "Rags and rat holes, my boy. You do seem to attract your share of difficulties."

Hallia managed a spare smile. "That he does."

I struck my own thigh. "I should start for the cliffs right now! Storm or no storm! Whatever hours I spend huddled here are wasted."

Hallia started to speak, but a sudden clap of thunder cut her off. Finally, she asked, "You would risk climbing a sheer rock wall, slick with rain, in the dead of night? With spirits of evil near at hand? You are more foolhardy than brave."

I started to rise. "But I must . . ."

"She is right, Merlin." Again the poet's hand squeezed my shoulder, coaxing me back down. "Here. In the time we have together, at least let me tell you what I know about the Wheel of Wye."

Reluctantly, I nodded.

Gazing at the gloom beyond the dripping edge of the overhang, Cairpré ran a hand through his wet hair. "If indeed the Wheel exists, and you can manage to find it, the legends say that you will face a choice. A difficult choice."

"The obstacle," said Hallia. "The one Domnu predicted."

Impatiently, I shifted on the stones, wiping some drops of water off my chin. "What choice?"

"You will find that the Wheel itself has not one voice, but several. One, and only one, of those is the voice of complete truth. All the others are to some degree false. If somehow you choose the correct voice, you will be allowed to ask any question and learn the answer. If, however, you choose the wrong one—you will die."

With a groan, I shook my head. "Is that all?"

"No." Cairpré paused, listening to the wind whistling on the crags. "The legends say that the Wheel of Wye will answer only one question of any mortal. So, if you get that far, you will be faced with a choice every bit as difficult as the first: the choice of your one question. Choose well, my boy. For after the Wheel has answered, it will reveal no more to you forever."

Hallia bent close to my ear. "What will you ask, if you are given the chance?"

For a moment, I pondered in the darkness. "The question I want to ask—long to ask. The question that haunts me more than those spirits up there: Is there any way I could regain my powers? Even if I'm never able to follow the pathway of Tuatha. Even if I'm still destined to die in the jaws of that dragon. Those powers were . . . me." My head drooped. "And yet I can't ask that question. For the fate of Fincayra, it seems, hinges on my asking something else: Where is the Galator?"

I blew a heavy breath. "So the truth is . . . I really don't know what to ask."

I could feel, more than see, Cairpré's gaze. "Seek your answer within, my boy. For the choice is different for each different person. Take, for example, your sister, who longs to fly like a canyon eagle. No doubt she would ask how the Fincayrans, in ancient times, lost their wings—and how they could find them again."

Working my stiff shoulders, I nodded. "And what about you?"

"I wouldn't ask where the kreelixes are hiding, for I think I can learn that on my own. Thanks to old Bachod, who still has more to show me about this place—if this storm ever ends, that is. I'm closer than ever now. *Around the bend, My trail shall end.* No, the question that torments me the most, the one I would ask the oracle, is how to *fight* them."

His frown deepened. "I couldn't find anything about that in the texts. All I know is that the weaponry of magic, applied directly, is futile. The ancient mages who battled them must have found something else—something as ordinary, yet as powerful, as air itself. The trouble is, though, nothing but magic seems strong enough to defeat a whole mass of them. And a mass, I fear, is what we will have to face before this is over."

I listened to the thunder echoing over the mountainside. "If only I understood that phrase, the one at the end of the prophecy."

"Not the one that predicts that, if you do fight Valdearg, both of you will—"

"No, not that. *A power still higher.*"

He nodded, stroking his chin. "It could mean the Galator. Or *negatus mysterium,* I suppose. Or . . . something else altogether."

Gently, I spoke to Hallia. "Before I go, tell me. What would you ask the Wheel?"

Her voice so soft I could hardly hear it above the storm, she answered. "Whether, in this world or another, I might ever find . . . the joy in Eremon's dream. How could that ever be? Without his hooves running beside my own?"

The mention of his name suddenly gave me an idea. "It would be much easier for me to climb the cliffs," I said slowly, "with four legs rather than two."

She stiffened. "That's true." A rainy gust swept over us. "And it would be easier still if you had someone with you—someone who knew the trails."

"No, Hallia."

"And why not?" Despite the bravery of her words, her voice quavered. "You would rather go without me?"

"I would rather know you're safe."

"Merlin. I am coming."

"But you—"

"Are the only hope you have! Hear me. This mountain has many trails, many caves. But only one is right."

Knowing she spoke the truth, I could only nod. Slowly, all of us rose to our feet. We stood there, as silent as stones.

Then Cairpré clasped our hands. In a hoarse whisper, he said, "May Dagda be at your side. And at Fincayra's, as well."

XXIV

THE CLIMB

Anyone who could have seen through the sheets of rain that night might have glimpsed two figures dashing from the ruins of the tumbled hut—at first on two legs, then on four. At the start I felt only my own wetness, and the weight of my sopping tunic and drenched boots. Then, seconds later, the weight began to fall away. I felt warmer and drier than I had all day long. The floppy tunic dissolved, replaced by coarse, thick fur. The boots disappeared, changed into sturdy hooves. My back lengthened, as did my neck. The pounding rain joined with a new and deeper pounding.

Racing across the soaked field, I spotted a pair of sheep ahead. I did not go around them, as I would have only a moment before. Instead, I leaped from the turf and sailed over them, as easily as a drifting cloud.

For I could, once again, run like a deer.

Hallia and I bounded up the road toward the end of the valley, splashing through puddles and leaping across gullies that flowed like rivers. Oh, the new strength in my shoulders and hips! The new suppleness of my body! As I ran, the driving rain seemed less to wash off me than to part and fall around me. My nose tingled with aromas of seawater, gulls' nests, and cliff lichen. Best of all, I could truly hear again—not with my ears, but with my very bones.

In time the road narrowed until it was nothing more than a winding gully. Rocks huddled at the sides like crouching figures; water coursed over our hooves. Hallia, more surefooted than I, took the lead. Her ears swiveled constantly, ever alert. Together, we began to pick our way up the increasingly steep slope.

The wind howled constantly, as rain slashed against my nose, my eyes. Bounding over some rocks and around others, we climbed steadily higher, the torrent raging around us. Now that I was no longer running, water rushed over me, flowing down my ears and back and rear-angled knees. I felt as if I'd stepped into a waterfall. My tail, compact as it was, moved constantly, shifting my weight just enough to help me balance on the slippery rocks.

Despite the darkness, I could see better than I had expected. My eyes discerned the jutting edges of outcroppings, the faint shadows of what might have been caves. Even so, I felt grateful for the frequent flashes of lightning as we made our way slowly upward. Often the wind gusted unexpectedly, nearly knocking me over. Several times the rocks under my hooves suddenly wrenched free, sliding down the slope. Only the quick instincts and sturdy legs of my stag's body saved me from falling.

All the while, I couldn't rid myself of the feeling that we were not alone on this stormy slope. Someone, I felt certain, was watching. From those caves, perhaps.

Hallia, climbing just above me, leaped from a long, narrow slab to a flat ledge. Without warning, the slab broke loose. Grinding against the rocky slope, it slid straight at my hind legs. I had no time to do anything but leap. The slab grazed me slightly, but I landed on a sturdier spot, my hooves beside Hallia's own.

Her black nose nudged my shoulder. "You're more a deer by the minute."

I felt as if I'd sprouted a new point on my antlers. "I've been watching you, that's all."

Another round of thunder rolled down the cliffs.

She stiffened, her ears erect. "They're here. Close by. Can you feel them?" Before I could even nod, she bounded away, hooves clattering on the rocks.

Higher we pushed, over steeper and steeper terrain. The wind blew colder, chafing our hides, as the rain took on the sharp edges of sleet. Soon ice appeared, under ledges and along cracks, making the footing more treacherous than ever. Slowly, we struggled upward—one hoof at a time, one rock at a time.

Hallia turned to the right, following a barely visible trail. I felt it more than saw it, my hooves fitting into subtle grooves worn by many hooves before. Meanwhile, the temperature dropped still more. Even as we worked our way upward, sweating with effort, the chill air made us shiver.

We reached a tall pile of rocks, leaning like a dying tree, just as the first hailstones smacked against the slope. As well as our backs. In seconds, the hail—bigger than acorns—started pouring down. Striking like hundreds of hammers, the pellets inundated us. I yelped as one struck the tip of my nose. Hallia pressed close to me as we shrank next to the jumble of rocks.

All at once, the entire pile gave way. Rocks smashed down the slope, nearly taking us with them. Pummeled by hail, we bolted higher. The wind screamed—as did something else, something more like high, shrieking laughter.

A cave loomed ahead, dark against the whitening slope. Instinctively, we dashed toward it—when several pairs of eyes appeared, glowing like torches. More laughter! We veered away, straight into the wind, our hooves sliding on the icy rocks. Thunder pounded, drowning only briefly the raucous laughter from the cave.

Hail! Battering us, biting our hides. My shoulders ached from cold; my ears heard only that hideous sound.

Just ahead of me, Hallia suddenly swerved at the edge of a deep crevasse. Like an unhealed gash it cut across the slope, blocking our ascent. Standing on its lip, she glanced back at me, eyes wide with fright. I knew instantly that she hadn't expected to find the crevasse—and didn't know where to cross it.

Side by side, we tried to work our way along the edge. But the crevasse grew only wider. Only in the instant of lightning strikes could we even see its opposite side. Then . . . yes! It melted away at the base of a sheer outcropping. Muscles straining, we climbed upward. Unstable rocks broke loose under our hooves. Clouds of white came with every frosted breath. Finally, we reached the top—only to find ourselves staring down into the same crevasse as before.

Laboriously, we backtracked, trying to keep our balance on the wind-whipped face. Tiny icicles began forming on my eyelashes, blurring my vision. My lungs stung as the temperature dropped further. Snow started mingling with the hail, coating the treacherous rocks.

At the base of the outcropping, Hallia leaped over a crusted slab. As she landed, her hooves skidded in the snow. Helplessly, she tumbled down the slope, rolling over the rocks. Just at the edge of the crevasse, she managed to plant her hooves and arrest her fall. In the flash of lightning that followed, I saw her leap away, a trail of blood running down her thigh.

A moment later, I reached her side. "Are you hurt?"

"N-n-not badly," she answered, as a brutal shiver coursed through her body. "But I'm lost, Merlin! This crevasse . . . I don't remember it! And we must find a way to cross it soon—or head back down."

"We can't do that!"

"Then we'll die," she cried over the wailing wind. "There's no way to—"

Another clap of thunder cut her off. Then more laughter rang out, piercing us like hunters' arrows. The skin under my eye began to throb—whether from the battering of hailstones or the presence of Rhita Gawr, I could not tell.

The hail slackened, but more snow, thick and wet, fell on us. Rocks, and the gaps between them, were fast disappearing under the blanket of white. In a few moments, the entire slope, and any hope of finding the oracle's cave, would be utterly buried.

Suddenly, a brilliant flash lit the mountainside—revealing a shape, bold and broad, standing beside the crevasse. Both Hallia and I caught our breath. Though it was difficult to see through the swirling snow, it looked almost like a figure we knew well. Almost like . . . a stag! Yet I couldn't be sure. Were those antlers atop its head, or horns, or something else entirely? Before the lightning vanished, the figure turned and charged off, skirting the edge of the crevasse.

"Eremon!" cried Hallia, leaping after him.

"Wait," I called. "It could be just a trick!"

But the doe paid no heed. She bounded off, cutting through the swelling drifts. I ran behind, following her tracks, only hoping we weren't chasing death itself.

Along the edge we raced. Sometimes we veered so close that I could hear rocks, kicked loose by our hooves, skittering down into the depths. The crevasse, even in lightning, showed only shadows—and no place narrow enough to cross. And as the snow deepened, so did my fears. If the wicked spirits meant to trap us, to strand us without any hope of finding our way, this was just the way to do it.

Abruptly, Hallia stopped. My hooves skidded, and I nearly slammed into her from behind. We stood, panting, on a slab jutting into the crevasse. Nothing but darkness loomed before us. The figure—whatever it was—had disappeared.

"Where," I huffed, "did it go?"

"Eremon. I'm sure it was him. He jumped from this spot. Then . . . vanished."

I shook the snow off my rack and leaned into the dark abyss. "It's a trick, I tell you. We can't jump into that."

Her round eyes met mine. "There's a ledge over there, I'm sure. That's why he jumped when he did! Come—it's our only chance."

"No!" I stamped my hoof. "It's madness!"

Ignoring me, she crouched, shuddered once—and sprang. Her legs exploded, her long neck stretched forward. Snow spewed my face as she faded into the darkness. I heard a thud—then nothing.

"Hallia!"

"Your turn," came her cry at last, her voice nearly smothered by the storm. "Come, Merlin!"

I crouched, my heart slamming against my ribs. I tried not to look down, but couldn't help myself. The shadows within the crevasse seemed to reach for me, to snatch at me. "I—I can't. It's too far."

"You can! You are a deer."

A shiver ran up my flank. "But I can't see the other side . . ."

Another gust of snow slapped me, almost throwing me off the edge. Under my hooves, the slab teetered, ready to fall at any instant. Without thinking, I pushed off with all my strength. I flew through the air, suspended by nothing but whirling snow, and landed with a thump on a ledge beside Hallia.

Her shoulder rubbed against my own. "You flew! Really flew! Like the young hawk of your name."

As lightning again seared the sky, I raised my eyes toward the cliffs. For the first time since the storm began, I could see their outlines, thrusting upward like enormous icicles. "Do you really think that was Eremon? Or, perhaps, Dagda himself in the form of a stag?"

Her ears cocked, one forward, one behind. "Let's hope it was Eremon. Because if Dagda is here, then so is Rhita Gawr." She blew a frosted breath. "Besides, I felt him near. More near than I know how to say."

My head beside hers, I whispered, "Then it must have been him."

More lightning. I turned back to the cliffs, gleaming from the flash. They were completely robed in white, but for the dark spots of caves. "The storm," I observed, "might be letting up."

"You may be right." She peered through the thinning veil of snow at the slopes above. "Come! I think I know where we are now."

She bounded off, following a slight indentation in the snow. Picking our way through the drifts, kicking away clumps of ice with our hooves, we moved higher into the crags. From somewhere overhead, I heard the faint cry of kittiwakes. At the next blaze of lightning, I thought I glimpsed one of the birds swooping out of the clouds just above us.

At that instant, the wind shifted. As it flowed over us, it carried a new smell. Smoke—sulphurous smoke. And also a new sound. An eerie, warbling sound. Half sighing, half wailing. A shudder ran through my long body. More spirits!

Hallia froze, as rigid as the rocks. Her ears pricked, then rotated slightly. "That sound—it's so different from that horrid laughing."

"It could still be . . . them."

"Or it could be the oracle."

All at once, she darted higher on the slope. Fast. So fast that I could barely keep up with her. Chips of ice broke under our hooves, while snow sprayed in our wakes. Relentlessly, we pushed up the cliffs. All the while, the haunting sound drifted toward us, now louder, now softer.

A wave of fog, smelling of sulphur, swept down the mountain. Like a phantom avalanche, it rolled over us, burying us completely. Although I kept climbing, I could no longer see Hallia. She had faded away—just like, I realized, the eerie wailing. I started to call for her, when suddenly I bumped into her flank.

She turned sharply. "We must have passed it."

Quickly, she led us back down the slope, pausing only to sniff the air or swivel her ears one way or another. Gradually the sound grew louder, closer. All at once, she halted. The fog before us parted, revealing a feeble glow among the whitened rocks.

A cave! Unlike the others we had seen, this one seemed to be lit from within. Or was that just an illusion? What unnerved me even more, though, was the continuous wailing that poured out of its bowels. For a long moment we stood there, listening. There could be no doubt, I knew with a shiver. The sound came not from wind, nor from sliding rocks—but from voices. Pained, tormented voices.

XXV

One Voice
Out of Many

Together, we planted our hooves upon the ice-crusted rocks at the lip of the cave. From deep within, voices sighed and called, wailed and pleaded. Though I could not make out any words, the voices' tone of anguish and longing could not be mistaken. Hallia and I traded anxious looks. Was this, in fact, the passage to the Wheel of Wye? Or some sort of trap laid by the mountain spirits? And was there any way to find out—except by entering?

I could see in Hallia's eyes that she had reached the same conclusion as I. In unison, we strode forward into the cave. Heeding our silent command, our bodies melted into different forms. Where two deer had stood only an instant before, an unshod young woman and a booted young man stood now. My own sigh joined with those of the voices, for I suddenly felt too vertical, too stiff, too much like wood and not enough like wind.

Wordlessly, we moved deeper into the cave, ducking under a row of icicles that hung like bars across the entrance. The cave did not descend, but rather plunged straight into the face of the cliffs. The air felt thick and humid, as if we were walking inside a cloud. A smoky, sulphurous cloud. At the same time, it felt warmer than I would have expected, reminding us that the lava that had formed these crags so long ago still coursed beneath the surface.

As we continued, plunging deeper into the mountain, the wavering light grew stronger, filtering toward us from somewhere ahead. What, I wondered, was its source? No doubt we'd learn before long. Thousands upon thousands of black crystals coated the floor, walls, and ceiling. Even through my boots, they poked and jabbed at my feet. I marveled at Hallia's ability to walk over them with such ease. She strode as gracefully as a doe crossing a bed of moss, her toes curling gently over the facets.

With every step we took, the black crystals glowed more brightly. Their facets glinted like so many eyes—staring at us and winking at one another as we moved past. Even without my own magic, I could sense that these crystals possessed some strange magic of their own.

Always, I have loved caves. Crystal caves especially. Their quiet depths, their mysterious shadows, their gleaming facets. As we moved deeper, the black crystals created ever more intricate patterns. Circles, waves, spirals—as well as more random designs. While most were black, a few gleamed yellow, pink, and purple. Above our heads draped a row of stalactites, lavender in color. And so ancient in years! They hung like the whiskers of Distant Time itself.

I paused, looking closer—and jumped. There, clinging to the base of one of the stalactites, was a dark, bony creature. Though I knew in an instant it was just a bat, it resembled too much another kind of creature, one I never wanted to meet again.

As the light within the cavern grew stronger, so did the voices. And their torment swelled at the same time. Whether moaning, pleading, or cajoling, they shared a common edge of agony. Yet . . . I couldn't make out any of their words. Only their emotions. If, indeed, they were the many voices of the Wheel of Wye, my stomach churned at the prospect of choosing one—and only one—out of all of them.

The silver light flickered on Hallia's face. "Can you understand them?"

I shook my head. "Not at all. Only . . . the pain." A brittle crystal snapped under my heel. "How will I know which one to choose?"

She slowed, touching a curved arm of crystals protruding from the wall. "Do you remember what Eremon said to you just before he . . . left us?"

"Yes," I answered grimly. *"Find the Galator."*

"No, no. After that. He said, *You have more power than you know.*"

Despondently, I dragged my boot across a bulge of glinting crystals. "He meant his own gift to me—the deer's power."

She scowled at me. "He meant more than that, Merlin. You do have—well, a certain kind of magic. And power. Yes, even now."

I looked at her skeptically. "What kind?"

For several seconds, she considered me. "I'm not sure what to call it. But whatever its name, it was enough to inspire his gift. Enough to make you want to try to help that newborn dragon, even if you couldn't possibly save her. And it just might be enough to help you know what to do at the oracle."

Slowly, I exhaled. "I want to believe you. I really do."

Pace by pace, we marched farther into the cave. Gradually, the passage bent to the left, then grew wider, as well as taller. As we rounded the bend, the ceiling abruptly vaulted high above our heads. Glittering walls of stone arched to meet it. The light in this immense chamber shone intensely bright, reflecting on the crystals. Still, I couldn't find the source.

All at once I understood. The crystals themselves! They were sparkling, glowing with a silvery light of their own.

Directly opposite us, covering almost the entire wall, hung a great, glistening wheel. Slowly, very slowly, it spun, its continual groaning joining the chorus of voices that now clamored in our ears. While the voices themselves were still incomprehensible, they clearly came from somewhere near. Just where, I couldn't tell. Like frogs calling from a hidden pond at night, the voices swam around us, swelling and fading, without ever revealing their source.

We stood there, amazed, watching the wheel turning endlessly on its axis. It appeared to be fashioned from some sort of wood, though its color looked darker than any wood I had ever seen. Each of its five broad spokes, as well as the rim, showed numberless facets, as if whatever hand had fashioned them had carved the surrounding crystals as well.

Five spokes inside a circle . . . just like the star inside a circle that had been carved into my staff. My lost staff! How clearly I remembered that night, long ago, when Gwri of the Golden Hair had descended from the starry sky to meet me on a windswept ridge. The symbol, she said, would remind me that all things, somehow, are connected. That all words, all songs, are part of what she called *the great and glorious Song of the Stars.*

I shook my head. That shape now reminded me of all that I had lost. My staff. My powers. My essence.

At that instant, I noticed three or four dark patches on the floor of the chamber. No crystals glowed, no light radiated, at those spots. Curious, I moved closer to the nearest one. Suddenly, my blood turned to ice. A mass of bones! Splintered and charred by some potent force. From their size and shape I could tell that they were all that remained of a man or a woman—someone who had, no doubt, chosen to listen to the wrong voice.

As I stooped to pick up a fragment of the skull, Hallia seized my arm. "The spokes!" she cried above the reverberating voices. "They're changing."

I gasped, dropping the skull. The facets in the middle of each of the five spokes were, indeed, changing. Gradually, they started to stretch, to lengthen and broaden, drawing themselves together in strange clusters. Some pushed outward into bulbous lumps, while others curled inward to form slashes or pits. The midsections of the spokes started to bulge, as the clusters coalesced and rearranged themselves, burgeoning into larger shapes. Shapes with patterns. Shapes with . . .

Faces. Hallia and I traded glances. For in the middle of each spoke, a face, as distorted as knotty wood, had appeared. While the wheel continued spinning, the faces grew more defined. One by one, they opened their dull yellow eyes, stretched their lips, and turned their gazes on us. As their mouths opened for the first time, each assumed one of the disembodied voices in the chamber. At the same time, the voices adopted the language of Fincayra.

"Free me!" moaned a wide, squarish face that had just risen to the top of the wheel. "Free me and truth shall be yours." As the wheel slowly turned, the face contorted, growing even wider than before. It released a deep, prolonged groan. "Free me! Have you no mercy at all? Freeeee meeeee."

"Ignore that—such a shame, such a shame—voice," snapped a second writhing face on a lower spoke. "He will lead you—what a pity, what a pity—astray. The true voice—such a disgrace—is not his, but mine!"

"Free me, please. Free me!"

"Oh, do be—what a crime—silent."

The sharp nose of a third face jabbed at us. From the pinched mouth came a wrathful hiss. "Don't lissssssten to thosssssse voicesssss! Lisssssssten to me, sssssso you may sssssurvive."

Hallia started to whisper something to me, when a fourth voice cut her off. "Woe to you, who seeks to live; Woe to me, who yearns to give." From a lopsided face with deep-set eyes, the anguished voice wailed: "Choose the right, and it is I; Choose the wrong, and you shall die."

"Sssssuch nonsssssssenssssse!"

"Free me, I beg of you—"

"Stop, plee-ee-ease," squealed a fifth voice, sounding like a dog with a broken leg. "I am the only-y-y voice of truth! You must beli-ee-eve me-ee-ee."

Full of uncertainty, I took a step closer to the revolving wheel. My gaze roamed around the crystalline chamber, from the turning faces, to the worried eyes of Hallia, to the piles of bones at my feet. Then, drawing a slow breath, I addressed all five faces at once. "I have come here," I declared, "to find the truth."

"Plee-ee-ease choose me-ee-ee."

"Choose me! Free me!"

"Sssssilence! You musssssst choose me or you will die."

"One of five shall give you life; All the rest give only strife."

"You must—such a dilemma, such a dilemma—choose me!"

As the voices clamored, the silver light from the crystals grew steadily brighter. Raising my voice above the cacophony, I addressed the wheel again. "Tell me, each of you, why I should choose you."

For a few seconds, the faces on the spokes fell silent. Only the groaning of the turning wheel echoed in the chamber. Yet the light from the crystals continued to brighten, until the walls were almost too dazzling to bear. I sensed that I must make my choice soon, or the crystals' swelling power would somehow explode—like a bolt of lightning—reducing me to another pile of bones. I waved to Hallia to retreat into the passage where she might be safer, yet she stood firmly in place, squinting from the light.

"Free me!" cried one voice, shattering the lull. "Free me and I shall love you always! For I, and I alone, am the truth of the heart."

"Sssselect me," promised another. "I can give you ssssso many thingsssss more! All the wealth you ssssseek, all the power you dessssserve. For I am the sssstrongest truth of all, yesssss! The truth of the hand."

"Choose me—what joy, what joy!" The voice burst into laughter, then suddenly started wailing wretchedly. "I am—such sorrow, such sorrow—the truth of the mind. All that I know, whether merry or grim, soothing or painful, can be yours, all yours."

"Plee-ee-ease," begged the next voice. "I can shower you with wonder, with mystery-y-y! For I shall always be-ee-ee the truth of the unknown."

The last voice, merely a whisper, offered only this: "Truth of the spirit am I; Wisdom and peace I supply."

By now the light had grown so bright that I could no longer even look at the spinning faces, let alone the crystalline walls. The crystals themselves had begun to buzz, as if they could barely contain their swelling power. In seconds, the entire chamber had started vibrating. I knew my time was almost gone.

Concentrating, I forced myself to think. The voices spoke for different kinds of truth—each one important, each one precious. Like the separate parts of the story circle that Hallia, Eremon, and I had created together on the day we met . . .

Truth of the heart, the mind, the hand, the spirit, the unknown. How could I possibly pick only one? What was the truth of the spirit without the truth of the heart? And the heart without the mind?

My thoughts raced, even as the voices, the walls, the wheel all roared at me. The floor shook beneath my feet. What had Cairpré told me? *One and only one, is the complete voice of the truth.*

But which one?

Heart . . . Hand . . . Unknown . . . Mind . . . Spirit . . . which to choose? The walls bent and swayed. I could barely keep my balance. The crystals burned like stars.

Stars! That phrase again flowed through my memory: *the great and glorious Song of the Stars.* All words, Gwri had said, played some part in the song. All words, all voices . . . Could that be the answer? Perhaps the voice of truth was *not* one of the voices I was hearing after all! Perhaps it was another voice entirely—the only voice that could be called *the complete voice of truth.*

"All the voices!" I cried. I raised my hands to the revolving wheel, shouting at the top of my lungs. "All the voices are true!"

Instantaneously, the walls and floor stopped shaking. The light from the crystals dimmed; the buzzing ceased. The Wheel of Wye, however, started spinning faster than ever before. Soon it became a blur, then a shadow. At the same time, the clamoring voices became less distinct. The faster they spun, the more they melted together. When, at last, the wheel was nearly invisible, the voices had merged into a single, resonant tone. Then the oracle spoke—in one unified voice.

"Aaask whaaat youuu wiiill."

Hallia stepped to my side. "You did it, Merlin! But remember, now. You have only one question."

I pushed some straggly hairs off my brow. "I know, I know."

But which one to ask? I had come here, originally, to find the Galator. And yet, with all my heart, I wanted to find my own powers again. They might give me at least a chance against Valdearg. Perhaps I wouldn't even need the magical pendant after all.

I chewed my lip. Tuatha, so long ago, had carried both his own powers and the Galator when he faced the dragon. The problem was—which one did he need most? Or, perhaps . . . which one did Fincayra need most?

"Aaask nooow."

Working my tongue inside my mouth, I turned back to the spinning Wheel of Wye. This choice tormented me even more than the first. How could I be victorious without the pendant? Yet how could I be myself without my powers?

"Aaask nooow."

"Great wheel," I began, my throat suddenly dry. "I seek the powers of . . . the Galator. Where can I find them?"

"Thooose pooowers aaare veeery neeear." The wheel spun all the faster. *"Youuu caaan fiiind theeem iiin—"*

Something as fast as lightning shot out of the passageway behind us and struck the axis of the wheel. Scarlet light exploded in the cavern, or perhaps just in my head. As the axis splintered, an ear-splitting crack rocked the chamber, fading into a distant rumble that seemed to emanate from far beneath us. The voices halted, as did the wheel itself. The five faces on the spokes froze in lifeless stares. Dumbfounded, Hallia and I gazed at the black shape that had lodged like an arrow in the middle of the axis.

A kreelix.

XXVI

THE END OF ALL MAGIC

"Are ye lookin' for somethin', me dears?"

We whirled around to see an old man, standing behind us in the entry to the chamber. Bachod! The glowing crystals around him shone no less than his eyes. For this Bachod looked altogether different from the haggard waiter of the tavern. He stood perfectly straight, his arms folded upon his chest, watching us in the way an owl observes its prey before swooping down to crush its skull. Yet I couldn't mistake his crackling voice, limp moustache, and white hair that brushed the shoulders of his robe.

Crouching by his side, ready to spring at an instant's notice, rested another kreelix. Even with its wings folded on its back, its massive body filled much of the passageway. As it opened its blood red mouth, baring its three deadly fangs, Hallia and I shrank back. I nearly tripped over one of the piles of bones.

Bachod smirked. "I'm so sorry yer little conversation with the turnin' wheel never finished, me dears. Me furred companion, ye see, jest couldn't stop itself in time. Ye needn't worry, though. It won't be botherin' ye anymore."

"You stopped it!" I cried. "Ended its magic! Just when it was going to tell me where to find—" I caught myself before saying more.

Bachod shook his head, swaying his white locks. "Mayhaps I can help ye, me lad. Save ye some time an' trouble." He reached into the folds of his robe. With a flourish, he pulled forth a pendant on a leather cord. Its jeweled center flashed with a stunning green radiance.

"The Galator!" I started toward him, when the kreelix's vicious snarl stopped me. "How—how did you get it?"

"I stole it," answered Bachod with pride. "With some help from a cunnin' friend of mine."

My cheeks burned. "You mean Rhita Gawr!"

His dark eyes glinted with satisfaction. "He taught me about *negatus mysterium,* ye see. An' how to breed an' train the kreelixes to do our work."

"And what work is that?" demanded Hallia, her voice shaking with rage.

"The work of destroyin' magic!" Bachod tossed the glowing pendant into the air. It twirled, sparkling, then fell back into his hand. Gripping it tightly, he sneered, "Magic's the plague of this island. Always has been! Whether from wizards, or pendants, or oracles like this turnin' wheel. It's all evil, an' dangerous, an' worst of all, against nature."

He turned to the kreelix crouching beside him. "That's why these beasts are so useful. For destroyin' the plague." With a glance at me, he chortled. "Or them who spread it—like young wizards."

I almost grabbed a bone from the floor and threw it at him. "So you were the one who tried to kill me."

"Twice, yes—our beasts tracked ye down. Ye may have escaped those times, but never again." He tugged on his sagging moustache. "Me friend, the one ye mentioned, seems to be feelin' a bit angry with ye."

My boot ground into the crystals of the floor. "As I am with him."

"That's yer concern, not mine. Me own concern is magic. Nothin' less than the end of all magic, me dears, can bring lastin' peace to this island. An' that's the work of us who understands."

"Us who understands," I repeated scornfully.

With his free hand, Bachod drew a curved sword from his belt. The blade glinted in the light of the crystals. Seeing it, my heart thundered. For at the base of the blade, burned in black, was an emblem of a fist crushing a lightning bolt.

"Clan Righteous?"

"Yes, me lad! There's only three of us—two bein' up on the cliffs right now, tendin' to the kreelixes—but ye can expect more precious soon." He smiled grimly. "Precious soon. Fer when the word gets out that we're freein' the land from magic, most of Fincayra will rise up to join us."

"You're wrong," I declared. "About Fincayra—and about magic, too. Magic is a tool. No different from a sword, or a hammer, or a cooking pot, except that its powers are greater. And like any other tool, it can be misused. But whether it's ultimately good or evil—well, that depends on the person who wields it."

Hallia nodded. "And don't think wizards are the only ones with magic. No! It lives in quiet places, too—from the hollow log of a tiny light flyer to the meadow grazed by deer people." Her eyes seemed to sizzle. "You have no right to destroy all that . . . and so much more."

Bachod grimaced. "I've every right. Every right, ye see! An' when Rhita Gawr an' I are finished, Fincayra will have no magic left."

"No!" I glared at him. "It will have no *defenders* left. Don't you see? You've been duped, old man! Rhita Gawr is just using you. That's right. To help him wipe out all those who might have any power to stand against him."

He waved his hand contemptuously. "Magic has twisted yer mind."

"It's true," I protested. "Listen! Rhita Gawr could just walk in and declare this world his own if there were no wizards, no Galators, no . . ." I caught myself. "No dragons." I glanced at Bachod's boots, knowing that his heels would show slashes from the sharp stones of this floor, just as Eremon had predicted.

"It was you, wasn't it, who killed the young dragons?"

Bachod smirked. "Of course, me dears. I hadn't planned on wakin' up their father jest yet—but it's jest as well. Havin' him burn a few towns will remind people about the plague."

He studied his sword, flashing in the light of the crystals. "Valdearg's time will be comin' soon enough. Jest as yers will! An' yer friend the bard, a few minutes from now, when I meet him fer a little, ah, stroll up the cliffs." His smirk broadened. "He thinks he's been learnin' about the kreelixes from me, ye see. That he has, me dears, but jest a little bit. All the while I've been learnin' more from him. Much more. He's told me plenty already about the hidin' places of magic."

With that, he grabbed the cord of the Galator, allowing the pendant to swing freely. Sparks of radiant green reflected on the walls of the chamber, dancing with the silvery glow of the crystals. Bachod's grin broadened. "But first, me dears, ye get to watch me destroy this wicked thing." He clucked in anticipation. "I've been so waitful fer the right moment, an' I do believe it's now. With ye both as me audience."

"No!" I cried. "You can't!"

"The Galator is as old as Fincayra itself," pleaded Hallia.

Bachod had already begun uttering a command to the kreelix. The beast's pointed ears stiffened and its shoulders tensed. The dagger-like claws raked against the floor of the cavern. It turned to the Galator, luminous and mysterious, and exposed its fangs.

"Now ye shall see true power," promised the white-haired man, swinging the pendant. "The power of *negatus mysterium*." He chortled softly. "Watch, me dears, as this green glow dies ferever."

Just as he started to utter the final command to the kreelix, I leaped at him. The kreelix screeched, sending a blaze of scarlet light rebounding off the walls of my mind, as well as the cavern. Simultaneously, Bachod toppled over backward. The Galator flew through the air, landing somewhere near the motionless wheel. Even as I fell to the floor, Hallia, springing like a deer, was at my side. Before we could press the attack, however, the kreelix swatted us with an enormous, bat-like wing.

We hurtled into the crystal-covered wall. Sharp facets tore our legs and gouged our backs before we rolled to a halt. Barely had we regained our feet, when a sudden tremor jolted the chamber, knocking us down again.

Several crystals on the ceiling flickered, then exploded, showering the wheel with flaming embers. At the same time, a second tremor rocked the chamber. A great chunk of black rock broke loose from the ceiling, smashing into the crystalline floor only an arm's length from my head. The wheel itself shuddered and creaked as the axis fell away completely. The whole structure tilted forward, tottering precariously on its rim.

Bachod struggled to his feet, then kicked the kreelix in the side.

It snarled, but didn't lash out. "Ye foolish beast! Yer power struck the crystals instead! An' who knows what that could—"

The Wheel of Wye crashed to the floor. Spokes and rim shattered, sailing in all directions. More crystals exploded overhead. Jagged cracks snaked across the walls of the chamber. Then—vents of steam burst open, hissing and snapping. Hotter grew the air, and hotter still.

A sly grin on his face, Bachod mounted the back of the kreelix. "So ye want the Galator, me dears? Well, it's yers ferever more! See how long its magic keeps ye safe now."

The kreelix spread its wings, flapped, and shot into the passageway. At the same instant, another section of the ceiling broke loose. With a burst of sparks, it landed on the remains of the wheel. Flames leaped, blazing with a fury that I had not seen since the fire that had cost me my eyes. I turned to Hallia, even as the wall behind us cracked and buckled, spraying us with chips of stone. Then, to my horror, a sizzling, orange liquid—brighter than the flames around us—started bubbling out of the cracks. Lava.

"Go!" I commanded. "You can still escape in time to warn Cairpré. Run like a deer!"

She glanced up at the crumbling walls. "What about you?"

"The Galator! I've got to find it before—" The wall arching over us shifted, groaning like a dying beast. A spurt of lava erupted from a crack. "Before it's lost for all time."

Hallia seized my arm. *"You'll* be lost for all time if you don't flee now!"

I pulled free. "I, too, can run like a deer. Remember? Please, Hallia. I'll be right behind you."

Her brown eyes, glowing with a light as rich—and unfathomable—as the Galator's, studied me. "All right, but be quick! Even a deer can't run through lava."

"Then, if I have to, I'll fly. Yes—like a young hawk."

She grinned fleetingly, even as she leaped to her feet. Dodging a patch of flaming, sputtering crystals, she dashed for the door. She melted into a tan-colored streak that bounded, hooves pounding, down the passage.

Hastily, I sprang to the spot where the Galator had fallen. A spark struck the back of my neck, burning my skin. I brushed it away—just as a plume of fire erupted by my boot, scorching my leg. Blood from the crystals' scrapings dripped down my forearm. Yet none of this mattered. Only the Galator mattered.

Plunging into the wreckage, I leaped over a smoldering crystal. Wildly, I turned over every piece of fallen stone I could find, searching for the pendant. Then I realized that a broken fragment from the wheel's rim now covered the place where it had fallen. Planting my boots, I tried my hardest to lift the fragment.

It wouldn't budge. Again I braced; again I lifted. The piece shifted only slightly before slipping out of my grasp. A new segment of the ceiling toppled, crashing on the very spot where Hallia and I had sat just a moment before. Crystals sprayed across the floor. More rumbling shook the collapsing walls. The heat was so stifling I could barely breathe.

I planted my feet at a different angle, hoping for better leverage. Wrapping my fingers around the heavy fragment, I pulled. And pulled. My legs shook. My back strained. My head felt as if it would burst. At last, the piece lifted ever so slightly. With a final groan, I shoved it aside.

Not there! I raised my arms, cursing. Where else could the Galator be?

At that instant, an enormous crack slashed across the floor under my feet. Sulphurous smoke belched out. As I leaped aside, the ceiling exploded in a new storm of sparks. Then, to my horror, I spotted a gargantuan slab of rock working loose above the entry to the chamber. I hesitated, scanning the floor one last time, then threw myself into the passage.

Rolling over the crystals, I turned for a final glance at the crumbling walls. Suddenly I saw a flash of green at the far end of the chamber. The Galator! I started to plunge back in again, when the enormous slab tore loose. It smashed to the floor, sealing the opening. A curtain of molten lava flowed over it.

I reeled as if the slab had fallen on top of me. *Gone. The Galator was gone.*

My eyes clouding, I started to stumble down the smoke-filled passageway. Another tremor, more violent than the rest, rocked the cliffs. Vents split open, gushing superheated steam. I pitched to the side, slamming into the wall. *A deer. I must run like a deer.* With all my remaining strength, I tried to run, to become a deer before it was too late.

Nothing happened. I ran harder, my lungs screaming. Nothing happened.

The power! It had vanished! By the new depth of emptiness in my chest, I knew that Eremon's gift had at last abandoned me. He had warned me that it would run out unexpectedly. But why now?

A row of flaming crystals from the roof of the passageway split open, raining sparks and jagged chips on my head. Another section of wall erupted as I passed. I stumbled forward. My head rattled no less than the rocks. All of a sudden the floor buckled beneath me, knocking me sprawling.

I lay there, facedown on the crystals. Though they jabbed and singed my skin, I felt too weak to rise. I could not run like a deer. I could not even run like a man. Here I would die, buried in lava along with the Galator.

XXVII

VERY NEAR

Something hard thudded against my back. A piece of rock, no doubt. Or debris from the shattering crystals. I did not roll over.

A thud came again. And with it, a sound, mixing with the crashing and grinding of the collapsing passageway. A sound I had heard, it seemed, ages ago. A sound like . . . a horse whinnying.

I flipped over. The eyes of a stallion, as coal black as my own, greeted me. Ionn!

His great hoof, raised to strike me again, lowered to the crystalline floor. He shook his mane and whinnied. Half dazed, I raised myself to a crouch. Ionn nudged me with his nose, urging me to stand. I threw an arm around his mighty neck, straightened up, and hoisted myself onto his back. In an instant, we were careening down the passage.

Stone walls broke apart, melting into lava as we passed. The whole passage now glowed brilliant orange—the color of the mountain's deepest fires. Arching forward on the stallion's back, I held on as tight as I possibly could, my fingers clawing at his neck. Crystals flared and sizzled. Steam spurted, barely missing us. Yet Ionn never faltered. His hooves pounded against the quaking floor.

Moments later, we burst out of the passage into daylight. The sun—not lava—cast light on me. Ionn started picking his way down the treacherous face of the snowbound cliffs. From behind, I heard a rumble that gathered into a thunderous roar. Turning around, I saw a fountain of molten rock gush out of the glowing passageway.

Above, the cliffs were disintegrating. As lava flowed over them, great boulders exploded into ashes or simply melted away. Snowdrifts burst into steam. Crevasses tore open, splitting the crags. Caves, whether or not inhabited by spirits, collapsed in flames. Dark columns of smoke belched into the sky, while savage tremors rocked the mountain to its very roots.

Ionn continued to work his way downward, staying just ahead of the streaming lava. Icy rocks, kicked loose by his hooves, clattered down the face. Over the quaking slabs and promontories, he followed a trail of his own making. He managed to avoid the wide crevasse we had crossed during the ascent, skirting its edge for some distance until it narrowed and finally faded away. Often he twisted suddenly to stay clear of a glowing lump of lava, sizzling on the rocks, or leaped to the side to find better footing. Yet bit by bit he made progress, pushing farther down the mountain.

At length, the slope grew less precipitous. The ground beneath us didn't tremble so violently. Mosses and grasses appeared between the cracks; a few scraggly pines clung to the mountainside. Although I knew that soon they would be covered by molten rock, the glimpse of green gave me a spurt of hope that we might yet escape.

Into what? Into the valley and fields that I could see below, warmed by the golden hues of the sun? I knew better. My destination lay far beyond, in the land of the dwarves. And the late afternoon light meant that I had barely two days left to get there.

The thought made me cringe. What did time matter now, anyway? I had no Galator—and no powers of my own. Only the prospect of facing a wrathful dragon alone. And yet, to my own surprise, I still felt sure I must try.

Over the continuous rumbling, I heard a shout. I turned, but saw only the narrow, overhanging edge of a crevasse, marked by a pair of twisted pine trees. The shout came again. Then I noticed, just beyond the pines, a pair of hands and a head topped with shaggy gray hair. Cairpré!

"Ionn!" I cried. "Stop here!"

The stallion halted abruptly. Even so, he looked at the oncoming rivers of lava and whinnied excitedly. I slid off his back. As fast as I could, I ran past the pines, then onto the jutting edge. Cairpré hung there, straining to hold on. Locking both of my hands around his wrists, I heaved with all my strength. I could hear the rumbling around us growing louder. At last one leg lifted over the lip of rock, then the other.

His face white with exhaustion, the poet gazed at me weakly. "Can't . . . stand up."

"You must," I urged, hauling him to his feet. He slumped against me, unable to stay upright.

Without warning, a flying lump of lava struck the trunk of one of the pines. Its resiny wood exploded in flames, as the entire top half of the tree split off, collapsing across the overhang. A wall of fire leaped into the air, roaring furiously, cutting us off completely.

As I stared into the scorching flames, another wall of fire ripped across my mind. *The blaze . . . my face, my eyes! I can't cross that. Can't!*

I staggered, nearly stepping off the edge of the overhang.

"Merlin," panted Cairpré. "Leave me . . . Save yourself."

His legs buckled completely. I struggled just to stand. Beyond the blazing tree, I heard the approaching roar of descending lava. And, in my ear, the labored breathing of my friend.

From somewhere I could not fathom, I found the strength to lean his limp body over my back. With a groan, I lifted him and tottered ahead into the flames. Fire slapped my face, singed my hair, licked my tunic. A branch caught my arm, but I shook free. Stumbling, I fell forward.

Onto solid rock. Ionn whinnied, stamping impatiently. Oncoming lava spat at us. I heaved Cairpré over the horse's broad back, then mounted myself.

Ionn bounded off, widening the gap between us and the molten river of rock. The slope became less steep, giving him sounder footing. Still, it was all I could do to keep both myself and the unconscious poet on his back. Downward he pushed—until, at last, the slope merged into the rocky hillocks. Moments later, we came to the edge of the narrow valley. Ionn instinctively avoided Bachod's village, crossing onto the higher ground on the valley's opposite side.

Behind us, the cliffs continued to glow with orange lava. Above, the sky darkened with clouds of smoke and ash. An immense column of steam rose in the distance, perhaps from lava flowing into the sea. Yet the mountain's tremors had all but ceased. The eruption, it appeared, had spent itself. The land grew steadily quieter.

By a small spring, bubbling through a ring of ice, we rested. I doused Cairpré's head in the spring, which at first made him cough but soon encouraged him to drink. Before long, he had revived enough to talk, and to share some of his salted meat, though his face remained quite pale. Nearby, Ionn tugged at some clumps of grass.

The poet eyed me gratefully. "That was a test of flames, my boy. The mountain's as well as your own."

I tore at a slice of meat. "The greater test is still to come." I hesitated, almost afraid to ask the question most on my mind. "Did you see Hallia?"

The poet hesitated before finally responding. "Yes. I . . . saw her."

"Is she all right?"

Somberly, he shook his gray mane. "No, Merlin. She is not."

I swallowed. "What happened?"

"Well, when the eruption first started, I was a good way up the slope, waiting for Bachod." He paused, weakly running his hand across his brow. "We were supposed to meet there. He was late, and I was growing concerned. The lava mountain seemed to be waking up. All of a sudden, he appeared. Riding on the back of one of those infernal creatures! Rags and rat holes, I was a fool to trust him."

He grimaced. "I did my best to escape, but he finally chased me to the edge of that precipice. Clumsy me—I fell over, barely catching myself. *The vision grows dim, Though ever more grim.* He dismounted, drew his sword on me—when suddenly Hallia bounded over the crevasse. Seeing her, Bachod cursed and leaped onto the kreelix again. Off they flew, chasing her up the slope."

My jaw dropped. "Up the slope? But the lava . . ."

"She knew just what she was doing. If she led him down into the more level terrain, she would have had fewer places to hide. Higher on the slope, she could avoid him longer, buying me a little more time."

"Buying your life with her own," I added bitterly. "So either Bachod got her, or the lava did."

"I fear so. Neither of them came back. But Bachod, I presume, survived. He probably just left me for dead and went about trying to save as many of his kreelixes as he could. Their hideaway, I'm sure, was somewhere up in the cliffs."

He twisted a willow shoot with his finger. "I'm sorry, my boy. Dreadfully sorry. I haven't felt this wretched since . . . I parted from Elen."

The pain in his voice seemed to echo somewhere inside me. For several minutes, we sat in silence, hearing only our own thoughts and the swirling waters of the spring. In time, Cairpré offered me a few slices of dried apple. I chewed for a while, then told him about my discovery of the Wheel of Wye's true voice, my choice of a question—and the incomplete answer. His fists clenched as I described the destruction of the oracle, as well as the Galator.

As I concluded, a slight breeze wafted over us, fluttering my charred tunic. "If I'm going to face Valdearg, I must leave soon."

"Are you sure you want to do this, my boy?"

I splashed some cold water on my face. "Yes. I only wish I knew what to do when I get there. If, that is, I can make it past Urnalda. After the way I escaped from her, she'll probably want to punish me herself before turning me over to Valdearg."

The poet broke an apple slice in two. "I've been thinking about your last encounter with her. It doesn't make sense that she, as a creature of magic herself, would use *negatus mysterium* against you."

"She sees me as her people's archenemy! Or, at least, as their only shield against the dragon. And she's arrogant enough to use any weapons she might have against me."

He frowned, but said nothing.

"If only there were some way I could convince Valdearg that he shouldn't be fighting me—but Bachod, who killed his young, and Rhita Gawr, who made it possible."

Cairpré gnawed on the dried fruit. "Dragons are difficult to convince, my boy."

"I know, I know. But doing that could be my only chance of stopping him from devastating everything! I certainly can't defeat him in battle. Not without the Galator."

"It's just possible that the wheel, like most oracles, might have meant more than one thing by what it said."

I leaned closer. "What do you mean?"

The poet's eyes lifted toward the cliffs, glowing now both with trails of lava and the light of the setting sun. "I mean," he answered slowly, "that it said the powers of the Galator were very near. That could have meant the Galator itself was near—as, indeed, it was. Or it could have also meant *its powers* were very near. Nearer than you knew."

"I still don't understand." Rising, I stepped over to Ionn. The stallion raised his head from the tufts of grass and nickered softly. Running my hand along his jaw, I pondered Cairpré's words. "We knew so little about the Galator's powers—except that they were great."

He stroked his chin. "Were they any greater, do you think, than whatever power brought you and Ionn back together after so many years? Than whatever power gave you the strength to carry me through those flames?"

"I don't know. I only know that any powers I can find, I'm going to need." Drawing in my breath, I pulled myself onto the stallion's back. He gave his head a bold shake as he anticipated my command. "Let us ride, my friend. To the land of the dwarves!"

XXVIII

GALLOPING

Down the narrow valley we rode, and into the night. Ionn's massive hooves thundered in my ears, reminding me of the erupting mountain we had fled. As he pounded over the stones, weaving among the hillocks, his black mane no longer glowed with the reflected light of lava. How often, as a child, I had clung to that very mane . . . I wondered whether this ride, out of one set of flames and into another, would be our last.

Air, as cold as the first breath of winter, rushed over me. Tears streamed down my cheeks from my useless eyes. Though I told myself they came from the wind, I knew they also came from the memory of the many faces I might never see again. Cairpré. Rhia. My mother. And another face, full of intelligence and feeling, with brown eyes that shone like pools of liquid light.

As Ionn galloped, I glanced back at the cliff walls, streaked with bands of orange. I shuddered to think that, somewhere up there, lay the lifeless body of a doe. Whether Hallia had been destroyed by the kreelix or by the onslaught of lava I would never know. It gave me no comfort to imagine that now, at least, she had rejoined her brother.

Ahead, the remaining rays of twilight faded, revealing a few quivering scenes—a twisted tree here, a pair of tilting boulders there. Behind, heavy clouds of ash, darker than night itself, rose into the sky. The rumbling cliffs soon vanished, obscured by the hillocks, which themselves started to diminish as the valley widened. In time, stretches of thick, ragged grass replaced the meager tufts that had interspersed the stones. The valley opened into an expanse of rolling grassland that I knew to be the eastern reaches of the Rusted Plains.

My arms embraced Ionn's broad neck, while my legs pinched his heaving chest. Galloping, galloping, we drove across the plains. Night deepened around us. But for the occasional howl of a wolf in the distance, the only sounds were the relentless pounding of the stallion's hooves and the continuous surging of his breath. Once or twice I almost dozed, but awoke with a start just before I tumbled off his back.

As dawn's first light dappled the grasses, Ionn whinnied and veered to the north. Minutes later, I glimpsed the sparkling surface of a braided stream ahead. Ionn slowed to a trot, then pranced to the water's edge. Stiffly, I dismounted. On unsteady legs, I stepped to the stream and thrust in my whole head. Even with the frigid water washing over my ears, I could still hear the pounding of hooves.

We drank deeply. Finally, we lifted our heads in unison. While I stretched my neck and back, Ionn frisked a bit, seeming to shake the weariness from his bones. I beckoned him toward some tall clusters of grass, but he moved there only reluctantly. I could tell that he, like myself, knew that our time was fast disappearing. Only after he saw me pull some shriveled berries from the vines on the bank did he, too, take time to eat. Soon he nudged my shoulder to mount again.

Onward we rode. The plains rose and fell like gentle waves, tinted with the yellows and tans of autumn. Following the arc of the sun overhead, we pushed westward. By the time the ridges of mist-shrouded hills lifted on the horizon, late afternoon light painted the grasses. As the plains stretched before us, I continued to scan the vista, searching for the fog-filled banks of the River Unceasing. There, I knew, lay the outer edge of the dwarves' realm.

Despite the continual thumping of Ionn's back against me, I felt always aware of the emptiness within my chest. What I would give to sense my old powers coursing through my veins again! To grip the shaft of my staff again.

Was there any chance that Urnalda might be convinced to restore my lost powers? I grimaced, knowing the answer. If she hadn't believed me before I humiliated her—escaping from her very grasp—she would surely not believe me now. Her wrath toward me no doubt rivaled the dragon's. Besides, I doubted she could restore my powers in any case. Cairpré's doubts notwithstanding, I could feel in my depths that they had been utterly destroyed, no less than the Galator itself.

The grasslands seemed to stretch on forever. Another day ended, marked by another sunset. Deep into the night we pressed ahead, with no moon to light our way. I could feel Ionn's muscles straining to keep running. My own back and shoulders ached; my head swam with dizziness and exhaustion.

Sometime after midnight, a new rushing sound mixed with the wind. We pitched forward. Suddenly the stallion neighed and turned sharply. Panic flooded me, along with the fear that Ionn had stumbled. Then a cold wave slammed against my right leg, splashing the side of my face.

The River Unceasing! His mighty frame leaning into the current,

Ionn waded deeper into the waterway. Turning, I viewed with my second sight the ragged mounds lining the bank behind us. Though I caught no more than a whiff of the stench of rotting flesh, that was enough to rekindle the memory of the devastated eggs—and the last of the hatchlings. Somewhere nearby, I knew, her immense young body lay rotting. And not far away, the body of Eremon lay under a mound of river rocks. Through the surging water and chilling spray Ionn pushed, though not fast enough for me.

At last, the stallion clambered up the far bank, his hooves slapping against the mud. Spray, luminous in the starlight, glistened on his coat. I stroked his neck. "Let us rest, old friend. You need it, as do I. But not here. Find us a secluded spot down the river, where no dwarves or dragons are likely to disturb us."

Moments later, we came to a patch of fragrant fern. I dismounted and crumpled to the ground. Though I glimpsed some edible mushrooms, I was far too tired to eat them. With my back hunched, my head between my knees, I fell into a fitful sleep. I dreamed of running through an endless field of fire, with no chance to rest, no chance to escape.

The sun was already riding high when Ionn's wet nose nudged my cheek. With a start, I awoke. Whether from perspiring in my dreams or from the misty air, my tunic was soaking wet. Worse, it was nearly noon. Nearly half a day's travel, I remembered well from my first run as a deer, lay before us. After a brief meal of mushrooms for me and fern stalks for Ionn, we set off again.

Through the meadows and stands of cedar we rode, following the staircase of plateaus into the heart of the dwarves' realm. As the sun dropped lower, the air grew smokier and the signs of recent burning more common. Alert for any dwarves, I scanned the charred fields and scorched rocks that had replaced the verdant lands along the river. No trace of them . . . yet.

The setting sun spilled crimson over the ground as a tall, pyramid-shaped hill came into view. The place where Valdearg would land. "There," I pointed out to Ionn. "That's where we go. But tread carefully. The dwarves could be—"

At that instant, a tumult of shouts filled the air. From behind boulders and bushes, from out of trenches and gullies, leaped an army of the stocky warriors. Waving their spears and slashing their swords, they formed a line between us and the hill. Ionn's ears flicked forward. Galloping ever faster, he bore down on them.

As we neared, more dwarves joined the barrier, their beards and helmets glowing red in the sunset. Now their line was at least four deep. Short as they were, they stood as firmly as oak trees planted in our path. Yet the stallion's speed did not slacken.

Out of the middle of the line jumped a paunchy dwarf wearing a conical hat and a black cloak. "Stop!" Urnalda cried, swirling her cloak about her. "This be my command!"

Ionn only galloped harder. I leaned forward, peering straight into the eyes of the enchantress who had stolen my best hope.

Seconds before the great hooves trampled her, Urnalda raised her staff, as if preparing to stop us by magic. But before she could, Ionn abruptly changed direction, swerving to the right. Somehow, I managed to stay on. He plunged toward a thin section of the line and, with a powerful leap, sailed right over the heads of the awestruck dwarves.

Soon the angry shouts faded behind us. The pyramid-shaped hill loomed closer. Then, without warning, a violent rumbling filled the air.

XXIX

BATTLE TO THE LAST

Like a landslide on high, the rumbling rolled out of the sky, overwhelming Ionn and myself, shaking the charred ground beneath us. An outcropping of rock on the summit of the pyramid-shaped hill broke loose, clattering down the slope. Ionn reared back, arresting his gallop, as we both turned toward the source of the sound.

Valdearg, wings outstretched, plunged at us with incredible speed. Caught by the rays of the setting sun, he looked at first like a clot of crimson against the smoky sky, though soon armored scales of green and orange showed along his tail and wings. Then, as he banked to one side, his terrible claws flashed brightly. Closer he came, and closer, until we could see the smoldering yellow of his eyes.

Writhing columns of smoke poured from his flared nostrils. Beneath his nose, the scales had been so blackened that he seemed to wear a thick moustache. Immense slabs of charcoal clung to the rims of his orange ears, flaking off every time the ears twisted. Several of his claws sported black humps, resembling knuckles. More lumps of charcoal, I thought at first—until the truth struck me like a hammer: They were skulls, burned in the fires of his wrath, worn like so many decorative rings.

As if entranced, we did not move as the dragon descended.

Waves of rumbling rolled over us. If the sky itself had ripped apart, I thought, the noise couldn't have been louder. I was wrong. Soaring straight at us, the dragon opened his cavernous mouth. Row upon row of dagger-like teeth glinted in the reddish light. The gargantuan chest rippled and contracted, releasing an explosive roar so loud that I almost toppled from Ionn's back.

The roar broke our trance—fortunate indeed, for along with it came an enormous, twisting tongue of flame. Ionn whinnied and bolted from the spot. The fire blasted the ground just behind us, splitting the very rocks with its heat. While flames singed my back and Ionn's flank, we galloped away.

"Quick," I cried. "Behind the hill!"

The stallion drove for the pyramidal hill, even as another deafening roar struck our ears. Ionn barely had time to dodge behind a boulder, shaped like an immense fist, before more licks of flames flooded over us. As we cowered behind the wall of stone, blazing fingers curled over the top and around the sides, scorching all they touched. Only the boulder's thickness saved us from being reduced to heaps of ash.

The flames had hardly dissipated when I cautiously lifted my head to check the dragon's whereabouts. He had just landed! He drew his wings to his back and slid his titanic form, nearly as huge as the hill itself, across the ground. Strangely, he was turning—not toward us but to the side. In a flash, I understood why.

I slapped Ionn's neck, and he charged for the rim of the hill. At the same instant, the dragon's massive tail uncoiled. Like a hideous whip, its barbed tips waving, the tail sliced through the air. It slammed into the fist-shaped boulder, sending chunks of stone in all directions. Shards rained on us as we rounded the hill's edge just in time.

"Grandson of Tuatha!" The dragon's voice, deeper than thunder, exploded against the slope. "You murdered my children!"

As Ionn continued to run behind the hill, I bent forward. "Wait. I must answer him."

Although he slowed to a trot, the stallion gave a loud neigh, shaking his head vigorously.

"I must, Ionn."

Again, he protested.

Sadly, I stroked his neck. "You're right—it's madness for us both to go back. Here, I'll dismount, so at least you can run to safety."

Before I could lift my leg, Ionn reared back, forcing me to grab his mane more tightly. He whirled around, turned his muzzle toward me, and scanned me with a dark eye. With a loud snort, he trotted back to the edge of the hill.

From astride his back, I peered cautiously around the charred rocks. Drawing a deep breath, I called as loud as I could to Valdearg. "Your rage burns deep, great dragon! But you must hear me. I did not kill your offspring!" I waited for the wave of rumbling to cease. "It was another man—who serves Rhita Gawr. And who brings the kreelix, the magic eater, back to our land. His name is—"

A torrent of flames erupted, cutting me off and driving me back behind the rocks. "You dare to deny your crime?" Valdearg's voice shook the air, as his tail smashed against the ground. "Even your evil grandfather did not try to hide from his deeds! You do not deserve to bear the title of wizard."

The emptiness in my chest almost throbbed. Grimly, I led Ionn back to the hill's edge. "You speak truly. I don't deserve it. But I did not—did not—murder your young."

The dragon's yellow eyes flashed. Smoke billowed from his nostrils. "And I did not come to hear your prattle about kreelixes and Rhita Gawr. Ages ago I fought the last of all the kreelixes—a battle to the death. His death, not mine! Now I shall do the same to you. And you shall die nine deaths, one for each of my slain children."

"I tell you I didn't kill them!"

"Liar! They must be avenged!"

With that another roar rocked the smoky skies, the charred ground, and all between. The mammoth tail lifted and swept toward me. Ionn needed no command to break into a run. The tail slammed full force into the side of the hill, sending up a shower of broken rocks. I turned just in time to see an enormous slab, heavy enough to crush a dozen people, topple over onto the midsection of the tail. It struck the green scales and bounced harmlessly away.

Ionn galloped with all his strength, trying to put as much distance as possible between ourselves and Valdearg. As we neared the far side of the hill, I glanced to the rear just as the massive head came into view. The dragon's eyes, as bright as suns in the waning light, glared at me. More flames shot out. Fire nipped at Ionn's hooves as we rounded the bend.

Using the hill itself as our shield, we avoided one assault after another. Back and forth Ionn ran, his legs churning, his ears attuned to any sound. For although we could not see our attacker behind the hill, we could still hear him maneuvering, roaring, or slapping his huge tail against the rocks. If his vast bulk slid one way, we dashed the other. We paused, breathless, whenever we could no longer hear him, then galloped off again as soon as he stirred.

Deep into the night the pursuit continued. Once Valdearg tried to take flight, hoping to surprise us in the darkness, but even then the noise of his approach gave him away. Yet I knew that, with enough time, he would surely outlast us. Ionn was bound to make a mistake, to stumble or misread the sounds. And one mistake was all that the dragon needed. Or was he merely toying with us, prolonging his moment of vengeance?

As dawn's first rays caressed the slope, dousing the rocks with gold, I could see that Ionn was tiring. Globules of sweat clung to his lips and mane; his shoulder muscles quivered. He ran laboriously, hardly lifting his hooves.

If only I could do something more than cling to the back of this brave stallion! But what? The prophecy had forecast a terrible battle, fought to the last. Yet, what kind of battle was this? It was merely a pursuit—with a certain outcome.

For a long moment, as the sun lifted over the horizon, Valdearg did not move. Then, suddenly, he started sliding over the rocks, crushing them beneath his weight. Immediately, Ionn bounded in the opposite direction. He rounded the corner at a gallop, then halted so fast that I rammed into his uplifted neck and nearly flew over his head. We were face-to-face with Valdearg! The sound we had heard must have come from loose rocks tumbling down the slope.

Ionn reared back, kicking wildly. But at the same moment, the monstrous tail lashed out. The barbs coiled swiftly around my chest, crushing my ribs, then carried me into the air. In an instant, I hung suspended before Valdearg's snout.

A blast of hot air scorched me as he gave a disgusted grunt. His voice as immense as his open jaws, he demanded, "Why do you not fight me, young wizard? Why do you only flee?"

Barely able to breathe, let alone speak, I rasped, "I have . . . no powers."

"You have powers enough to murder hatchlings still in their eggs!" The yellow eyes blazed. "Well, grandson of Tuatha, you shall flee no more."

"You must . . . believe me," I protested. "I didn't . . . do it."

"Shall I begin by biting off one limb at a time?" His purple lips parted as he wrenched a skull off one of his upraised claws. His jaws compressed, crunching the skull completely. "No, I have a better idea. I shall roast you first."

The rumbling gathered, swelling deep within his chest. It grew steadily louder, while flames started licking his nostrils. At the same time, the tail's grip on me tightened. My lungs couldn't breathe. My heart couldn't beat. The jaws opened wide, as an avalanche of fire rushed toward me.

All at once Valdearg's ears pricked and he cocked his head slightly. The flames shot past, searing my boots but nothing more. Valdearg released a sudden cry of surprise—and his tail released its hold. I thudded to the ground. Ionn raced to my side as I gasped for air. Wrapping one arm around the stallion's neck, I struggled to rise—and to see what had distracted the dragon.

Approaching us on the charred terrain, half hobbling and half flying, came a truly strange creature. At first all I could see was an ungainly mass, as ragged as a storm-lashed sapling. Then I glimpsed a flash of iridescent purple, a crumpled fold of leathery skin, a pair of bony shoulders. And, atop the head supported by a thin, gangly neck, a pair of ears—one of which thrust out to the side like a misplaced horn.

The baby dragon! She had survived!

In a flash, her enormous father spun around, nearly swatting Ionn and me with the bony tip of his wing. He lumbered over to the hatchling, stopping just short of her. His belly rumbled with a steady, soft drone, almost like the purr of an oversized cat, as he placed his snout upon the ground.

Cautiously at first, then whimpering excitedly, the baby dragon allowed his warm breath to blow across her scales. For a long moment they looked at each other, the yellow glow of his eyes melting into the orange glow of hers. Finally, he unfurled his massive wing so that she might crawl into it. Folding its edges around her like a blanket, Valdearg drew his baby near. She gave a contented squeak and huddled closer.

Craning his neck, the dragon lifted his colossal head. To the skies rose a sound unlike any sound heard in Fincayra for ages upon ages, since the birth of Wings of Fire himself. It was a mixture of deep rumbling and high, swirling, ringing notes that flew skyward with the grace of arrows. It was a complex melody, a magical tapestry woven with the lore of generations of dragons. It was, more than anything else, a song of celebration.

Ionn and I listened, transfixed, as Valdearg's song continued for an hour or more. The hatchling, curled tightly inside her father's wing, lifted her own snout from time to time. Her ear, as plucky as ever, stretched out to the side. She seemed to be listening to the song as carefully as ourselves, but with native understanding far beyond our own.

In time, the great dragon lowered his head. Moving with the power of a huge wave surging over the sea, his neck swung toward me. As soon as his gaze met my own, the spell of his song disappeared. Fear raced through me. He was coming after me again! I leaped on Ionn's back, grasping his mane, ready to ride once more.

Just then the baby dragon squealed. The shrill cry arrested me, as it did her father. His orange ears swiveled; his lips curled in puzzlement. She squealed again, this time flapping her little wings frantically. He rumbled, then quieted, as she made several sharp, chirping sounds.

At length, Valdearg's yellow eyes turned back to me. "It seems, young wizard, that some of what you told me was true." A dark cloud of smoke rose from his nostrils. "You are not the man who murdered my children."

Ionn tossed his head, nickering with relief. I gave the side of his neck a pat.

"Yet some of what you said was false: that you have no powers. My daughter here says otherwise." He glanced at her with obvious affection. "She says you saved her by your magic."

I shook my head. "Not with my magic. With my herbs, that's all. It's different."

"Not so different as you think." His huge tail lifted and wrapped around itself, forming a knot of orange and green scales that flashed in the sunlight. "For whatever the magic is called, it has given me back my child."

XXX

WHEN ELEMENTS
MERGE

A high-pitched shriek pierced the sky. Like Valdearg, the hatchling, and Ionn, I looked up. And in that instant, my blood froze.

Not one kreelix, but many—at least a dozen—were plunging toward us out of the smoky clouds. Their mouths, gaping, showed their deadly fangs. And on the back of the leader rode the hunched figure of Bachod, his white hair streaming behind him.

Bachod waved his arm to the kreelixes. Angling their bat-like wings, they immediately fanned out in a wide arc. With an ear-shattering series of screeches, they dived downward. Ionn whinnied and snorted, stamping his hooves angrily. My sword rang bravely as I drew it from the scabbard, though I knew well its limits against *negatus mysterium*. In an instant, the kreelixes would be upon us.

Suddenly Valdearg's tail uncoiled and shot upward. The monstrous whip snapped as it struck one of the kreelixes. The beast screeched and fell lifeless from the sky.

Like a raging swarm of hornets, the remaining kreelixes converged on the great dragon. Diving and swooping, they bore down on him, fangs bared, trying to get close enough to strike. Immense though he was, he moved with dazzling speed—spinning, rolling, and flashing his tail. Yet as long as he remained on the ground, the kreelixes would hold the advantage. At first I wondered why he didn't take to the air, where he could be just as mobile as they.

Then I remembered: the baby dragon. He was protecting her! Deep in the folds of his wing she cowered, safe for the moment. But as long as he held her wrapped in one of his wings, he could not fly. And staying on the ground made him far more vulnerable.

Ionn paced, whinnying anxiously, as we looked on. Though I brandished my sword and shouted at Bachod and the kreelixes, they ignored me. Nothing I did drew their attention away from the flailing dragon. Ionn reared back, kicking at the air, then galloped in a circle around Valdearg. Still the attackers paid no heed. Bachod didn't even look our way.

All at once I understood. Since my deer magic had now vanished, they could sense that I possessed no power! Where I might have been at least a mild threat to them before, I was no threat at all to them now. The empty feeling in my chest ached like never before.

The words from the prophecy of *The Dragon's Eye* echoed in my mind. *Lo! Nothing can stop him Except for one foe Descended from enemies Fought long ago.* A new realization gripped me. Perhaps the prophecy never meant me at all! Perhaps the dragon's ancient foe, the enemy who would either kill him or be killed in the process, was a kreelix!

But if that was the case, what could the rest of the prophecy mean? Would all the kreelixes perish, or just some of them? And what about that phrase—*a power still higher*? Something that could make elements suddenly merge: air into water, water into fire . . .

Roaring and spitting flames, Valdearg continued to hold off the attackers. His eyes, themselves practically aflame, seemed everywhere at once. The ground beneath us shook with the slamming of his tail. Dust and smoke climbed skyward. His one free wing batted constantly at the air above the wing enfolding the cowering hatchling. In all his days of terror, I felt sure, never had he been more worthy of the name Wings of Fire.

Now three burned kreelixes lay as smoldering heaps on the ground. The remains of two more, smashed by the tail, had been trampled in the fray. Still, seven kreelixes, including the one bearing Bachod, remained. They swooped and hovered, always seeking a chance to bury their fangs someplace—anyplace—not shielded by scales. The most exposed target, I suddenly realized, was his wing. Curled tightly around his infant, the wing's leathery folds lay unprotected.

Maybe, with the dragon's immense bulk, it would take more than one gash to destroy him. The thought gave me a spurt of hope. Then I bit my lip, remembering Cairpré's warning that even the smallest contact with the kreelix's fang could end the power—as well as the life—of any magical creature, no matter how large.

At Bachod's command, the kreelixes climbed upward, so high they were nothing more than tiny black dots in the shreds of smoke. Barely, I could see them arrange themselves into a new formation—like the head of a spear. An instant later, they screeched in unison and soared straight at their enemy. Viscerally, I knew they were aiming for Valdearg's wing. And only one of them needed to strike home. The baby dragon, sensing the same thing, whimpered and nestled deeper into the folds.

As they shot toward Valdearg, who seemed now less like a wrathful monarch than a protective parent, he released a defiant roar. Bracing for the assault, he swung his massive head toward me. For a fraction of a heartbeat we gazed at each other. Yet even in that brief instant I could not miss the look that I had never before seen in those glowing eyes: the look of fear.

Twisting Ionn's mane in my hands, I strained my mind to think of something, anything, I could do to help. But what? In seconds, the kreelixes would reach their target.

The baby dragon whimpered, shrinking farther into the wing. How, I wondered, had she revived? Was it possible that I had really given her something more potent than the herbs from my satchel?

Without thinking, I reached inside the satchel. My finger pricked something sharp. The string from my psaltery! What had Cairpré once said it might bring? *High magic, like nothing you have ever known before.* I pulled out the string, warped and blackened by Urnalda's fiery summons. Might it somehow call forth magic even now? From hands without any magic of their own?

I glanced at the sky. Wings folded against their backs, the kreelixes sped downward. Now I could see Bachod riding the leader, the point of the spearhead. And surrounding him I could see seven snarling mouths, seven sets of fangs.

In desperation, I plucked the string. It twanged, releasing a puff of soot—then fell silent. I heard no music. I felt no magic.

Then, out of the very air around me, I heard a voice.

It was Rhia, reminding me: *Remember all the life around you, and all the life within yourself.* Then, joining her, came the ancient, grinding voice of the living stone. *What is this strange magic within you, young man? How can you resist me? A stone's power springs from all that surrounds, all that connects.* The hag Domnu cut in. *My pet,* she declared, *I feel magic in you even now.* Finally, the resonant voice of Eremon called to me. *You have power, Merlin. More power than you know.*

All the life within yourself . . .

This strange magic within you . . .

I feel it even now . . .

More power than you know . . .

The kreelixes screeched, only an instant away. I looked up to see Bachod leering, his eyes fixed on Valdearg's bulging wing that shielded his child. The great creature roared for the last time.

The voice of Cairpré joined the others. *Seek your answer within, my boy.* Then came the many voices, blended into one, of the Wheel of Wye: *Thooose pooowers aaare veeery neeear.*

A wrenching thought struck me. Perhaps I never lost my powers after all! Perhaps Urnalda merely tricked me into believing that! And yet . . . even if I still had magic, how could I use it now? The kreelixes would just consume it, destroy it. Cairpré had said that magic, applied directly, was futile. That the best weapon was something indirect. What was his phrase? *Something as ordinary, yet as powerful, as air itself.*

Air itself! Even as Valdearg's tail lashed out to strike as many kreelixes as it could, my mind raced through the many virtues of air. Bearer of breath. Of wind. Of sounds and smells. Of water.

Water! Was there any way . . .

The dragon's tail struck two of the kreelixes, sending them spinning. Yet he had missed Bachod, now only a fraction of an instant away from striking. Valdearg, unable to whip his tail again in time, was helpless.

With all my strength, I willed the air surrounding the kreelixes to chill. To freeze. The psaltery string in my hand suddenly rang out—like a chime within my very chest. The old emptiness vanished, replaced by a surge of power that I knew to be my own.

Concentrating all my thoughts on the air, I tried to draw away its heat. The air around Ionn and me instantly shimmered with new warmth. I perspired, less from the heat than from the strain.

At the very moment of contact, the air above Valdearg transformed into a mass of ice, encasing Bachod and the rest of the kreelixes. They had no time even to shriek, although my head reeled from the scarlet explosion of *negatus mysterium* being released. The enormous block of ice fell squarely on the dragon's back, just below his folded wing.

As the block of ice crashed to the charred terrain, Valdearg bellowed in anger and pain. He released a torrent of flames, so hot that the frozen block erupted in a conflagration of hissing steam and sizzling bodies. Seconds later, all that remained of the incinerated attackers was a pool of water, blood, and fur, licked by tongues of sputtering flames.

Ionn neighed triumphantly. Casting his head about, he frisked and capered. For my part, I dismounted and moved closer to the steaming pool. My mind was filled with the vision of elements having suddenly merged. For air had indeed turned to water; water to fire.

A high-pitched squeal arrested my thoughts. I started, for it sounded almost like a kreelix. In a flash I realized that it was, instead, the baby dragon. She had emerged from the protective wing, her stubborn ear still protruding. Yet my stomach turned to see the expression of grief on her face. And again to see why.

Valdearg, emperor of the dragons, lay still, his head resting heavily on his foreleg. No smoke curled from his nostrils, while his rumbling sounded thinner, frailer, than before. Although his green and orange scales still gleamed in the light, they seemed somehow to have lost their luster. Yet most telling of all was the dimness of his eyes. While they continued to glow, their light seemed as fragile as the flickering flames at the edge of the steaming pool.

Ionn joined me as I stepped nearer. There, at the base of the wing that had shielded the hatchling, I saw a telltale trickle of blood flowing from a small puncture. While a wound of that size might not normally have been even noticed by a dragon, this wound had come from the fang of a kreelix. The hatchling, whimpering softly, stroked the spot with one of her floppy little wings.

"He is dying," declared a familiar voice.

Ionn and I whirled around. There, facing us, stood a large-eyed doe. Her tan-colored fur was streaked with mud, while her legs bore several scratches and scrapes. Her mud-caked ears cocked toward me.

"Hallia," I whispered through the lump in my throat. "I thought . . . I thought you were dead."

"You underestimate me." She gave a slight snort, pretending to be insulted. "Deer know a few tricks of dodging pursuers, you know. Even kreelixes." Her deep brown eyes observed me. "You know a few tricks yourself, Merlin. I only arrived a moment ago, yet that was time enough to see what you accomplished."

I winced. "And did not accomplish." Turning back to Valdearg, I watched him gazing weakly at his offspring, now curled beside his belly. "My powers have returned, but an instant too late."

Solemnly, I approached the dragon. Warm air flooded over me with each of his rasping breaths. His yellow eyes, now half closed, turned in my direction.

"Grandson of Tuatha," the great creature rumbled. "I was wrong. You deserve to be called . . . a wizard."

My tongue, as dry as wood, worked in my mouth.

He tried to lift his head, then slumped back. "Neither the kreel-ixes nor I . . . survived this battle. At least I had the joy . . . of roasting them in the end." His bulk shook with an anguished cough. "My child, though! What of her? Who will teach her . . . to feed herself, to fly, to master her own magic? Who will . . . show her how to find my hollow, our ancestral home? Who will help her to know . . . the high destiny of a dragon?"

Wishing I had my staff to lean against, I shifted uneasily before answering. "I know very little about dragons. And less about their magic. But I do know the way to your hollow, and my heart would be gladdened to guide her there."

I glanced at Hallia, who now stood on the blackened turf not far from the hatchling. Their eyes, one pair circles of radiant brown and the other pair triangles of glowing orange, were fastened upon each other. Perhaps it was their shared magic, or their shared experience of loss, but I felt certain that these two beings were communicating, speaking to each other in some silent language.

"Your child will be cared for," I declared.

The dragon's eyes glowed brighter, then faded rapidly. "Never have I feared anything or anyone," he rasped. "Until today. Yet what I feared during the battle was not an attack of kreelixes, but the death of my little one." Another cough racked his body down to the barbs of his tail. "And now . . . now I find myself fearing something else."

"What?"

"Death. My own death! A dragon craves life, devours it. Swallows it in great, heaping mouthfuls! He is not slain easily—and does not die tranquilly. He resists . . ." He paused, trying to stifle a cough. "To the last." His baleful eyes, now dull yellow, scanned me. "Yet now I can resist no more. And now, young wizard, I am . . . afraid."

Slowly, I stepped closer to the immense face. My hand extended to touch the prominent brow above one eye. Without knowing where the words came from, I said, "Just look for the light, Wings of Fire . . . Walk there. Fly there. Your child will be with you. And so will I."

With that, Valdearg heaved a final breath, releasing a final wisp of smoke. The light in his eyes extinguished. They closed forever.

XXXI

A POWER STILL
HIGHER

An endless moment followed. We stood as silent as the charred lands around us, as still as the dead dragon. Only the hatchling stirred from time to time, nuzzling the lifeless body of her father.

Finally, Hallia stepped closer to the baby dragon. As she walked, her deer form melted away, replaced by that of a sturdy young woman. All the while, her soulful eyes remained fixed on the hatchling. As she drew nearer, the creature's lavender tail uncoiled and thumped anxiously against the ground. Hallia began to sing a slow, soothing melody, full of images of green meadows and sunlit streams. By the time she had reached the baby dragon's side, the tail fell still. With a single, graceful motion, she sat down, singing all the while.

Following suit, Ionn and I joined them. The stallion, his black coat gleaming in the midday sun, tossed his head in greeting. The baby dragon—half again as tall as Ionn, though much scrawnier—hesitated at first, then responded in kind. When she tossed her own head, though, orange-colored droplets sprinkled the rest of us. Hallia and I traded glances, knowing they were tears.

Hallia stopped singing. Cocking her head to one side, she studied the creature with sympathy. "Your loss is even worse than mine, young one. At least I knew my brother well. So well that I can still hear his breathing as well as his thoughts, almost before I hear my own."

Gingerly, I reached out and stroked the baby dragon's uncooperative ear. Although it protruded as stiffly as a branch, stretching longer than my forearm, it felt amazingly soft. Tiny purple hairs covered its entire length. The dragon whimpered quietly, then lowered her snout toward my feet. Without warning, she grasped one of my boots in her jaws and jerked it toward her, knocking me flat on my back.

Hallia grinned. "She recognizes you."

Despite the ache in my back, I could not keep from grinning myself. "Even more, I think, she recognizes my boot. I used it to feed her when we met before."

The baby dragon tugged again, pulling the boot free. It was, I realized, the same boot that I myself had chewed upon long ago when I had visited her father's lair. Before I could reach to take it back, the hatchling tilted back her head and swallowed it whole. I cried out, but too late. The boot was gone.

Ionn released a snort that resembled a hearty laugh. Suddenly he stiffened. His ears pricked forward. He swung his head to the side, stamping the ground with his hoof. Hallia leaped to her feet. Both of us followed Ionn's gaze.

A band of short, squat figures was approaching from around the edge of the pyramidal hill. Shields and breastplates flashed in the sun. In the center of the group strode a figure bearing a staff, wearing a peaked hat over a mass of unruly red hair. Urnalda.

Though my anger boiled just beneath the surface, I held my

tongue. Despite the lack of my boot, I threw back my shoulders and stood as tall as I could.

Urnalda's earrings of shells glinted as she came near. I could not read the look in her eyes, but her clenched jaw seemed both grim and unremorseful. As the band came within a few paces of us, she slowed and raised a stubby hand. The other dwarves, grasping their axes and bows, halted.

The enchantress stepped forward, examining the corpse of the fallen dragon. She flinched slightly upon seeing the baby dragon nestled there, but said nothing. Her gaze fell to the steaming pool, clotted with the blood and hair of Bachod and the kreelixes.

At last, she turned to me. "I see that your powers be restored."

My eyes narrowed. "They never left, as you know. You only tricked me into believing they were gone."

"That be true." The earrings clinked as she nodded. "The only way a magic-robbing spell can work be if the victim completely believes that his powers be destroyed. Then he and everyone else around him be fooled. It all be part of Urnalda's plan."

My hand, still holding the string from my psaltery, closed into a fist. "And was wiping out all but one of Valdearg's offspring also part of your plan?"

"No," she replied coldly, twirling the tip of her staff in the blackened soil. "Yet that be not a bad result."

"What about the kreelixes? Did your plan account for them? Thanks to your help, they slayed this dragon—and would have gone on to slay you and me and every other creature of magic on Fincayra." My voice lowered to a growl. "In your arrogance, Urnalda, you almost opened the door to Rhita Gawr! It was his plan, not yours, that was guiding your actions. You did it unwittingly, I think, but you still served as his tool."

Her face, normally pale, flushed deep red. "Bah! I never be wrong," she declared. Her eyes lowered for just an instant. "It be possible, though, that I be temporarily deceived."

She extended her hand, palm up. A flash of light split the air, causing several of her dwarves to leap aside, tripping over themselves in the process. There, in her hand, rested my staff. She spat out a few words and the staff floated, twirling gracefully, over to me.

Eagerly, I clutched its shaft, embracing it like the outstretched hand of an old friend. My second sight ran over all the familiar markings—the cracked stone, the sword, the star within a circle, and the rest. All the wisdom of the Seven Songs. Now, at last, I felt completely restored.

Urnalda watched me, playing with one of her shell earrings. "That be for doing what you did to help my people."

Knowing that was as close to an apology as I would ever get from her, I hefted the staff. "Consider my promise fulfilled."

She tilted her head toward the huddled form of the baby dragon. "Now there be only one task remaining. Let us, together, destroy the last of those despicable beasts."

"Wait now," I declared. "The old dragon's death could be an opportunity. That's right—to bridge the ancient divide between the dragons and ourselves. Hard as it will be, couldn't we try to treat her as our fellow creature? Maybe even as our friend? It's possible, at least, she might come to do the same for us."

"Fellow creature? Friend?" she scoffed. "Never! I be seeing far too much of dragons' wrath for that! You may be finding your powers, but you be losing your mind." She clapped her hands. "Guards! Raise your weapons."

Instantly, the dwarves flanking her nocked their arrows and lifted their double-sided axes. They stood poised, awaiting her next command.

I jammed my staff into the ground, splintering a slab of charcoal. "Hear my words, all of you! That dragon shall live." Glaring at Urnalda, I took a single step closer. My head leaned toward hers. "If you or any of your people should ever try to harm that dragon, through whatever means, for whatever reason, you shall face my own wrath. The wrath . . . of a wizard. What happened to those kreelixes over there will be nothing compared to what will happen to you."

For a long moment, the enchantress glowered at me. The air between us sizzled, crackling with tiny sparks. Then, without another word, she turned and strode off the way she had come. Hurriedly, her band of squat warriors stowed their weapons and followed, marching as fast as they could to keep pace with her. I watched as they rounded the bend and disappeared behind the hill.

Ionn nudged my arm. I stroked his neck, still staring at the spot where I had last seen the tip of Urnalda's peaked hat. All of a sudden, Hallia cried out. The stallion and I spun around to see her pointing at the steaming pool, bubbling with the remains of the kreelixes.

Out of the vapors, a shape was forming. A face—with no hair, misshapen teeth, and a wart in the middle of the forehead. I braced myself, knowing it was the image of Domnu. As the hag's mouth creased in a grisly smile, blue flames licked the edges of the pool.

"Well, my pets, you survived. I wouldn't have predicted it." The flames swelled, gathering around her eyes. "Even my little pony over there survived."

Ionn's hoof thudded against the ground. He neighed defiantly.

The vaporous form, vibrating with the rising steam, wrinkled her scalp. "Now, what about our bargain?"

I shook my head. "The Galator is lost. Buried under a mountain of lava."

Blue flames leaped from her eyes. "You wouldn't think of betraying me now, would you?"

"No," I replied. "Unlike some people, I don't go back on my word." I indicated the simmering pool beneath her. "But the thief who stole it from your lair won't bother you again."

Domnu scowled, her whole face writhing. "Bones. Boiling bones! Gone before I had any chance to play with it! Well . . . so be it. I really didn't like the color of the cursed thing anyway. Farewell, my pets."

Instantly, the pool erupted in a swirl of blue flames. When, a moment later, they faded into the rising steam, the face of the hag had vanished. I continued watching the pool, leaning against my staff.

Hallia's resonant voice broke the stillness. "Merlin?"

I turned to face her. How it delighted me to see those eyes again! I felt a new surge of gratitude that she had escaped harm. And, to my surprise, something else, deeper than gratitude.

"Do you recall," she asked softly, "that moment in the oracle's cave, when I said you had a certain kind of power?"

"I do. And I also recall you couldn't put any name to it."

She nodded slowly. "Well, now I can. Call it the power of understanding. Of leaping across barriers, finding meaning in tracks. And as strong as a dragon, or a kreelix, or even a Galator may be, that's something even stronger. For all their power, it's really a power still higher."

Twirling the string from my psaltery, I almost smiled.

"Don't forget, though," she added with a nudge. "Even a great wizard needs two boots, not just one."

I wiggled the toes of my bare foot. "Unless, of course, he can run like a deer."

She watched me thoughtfully. "Or fly . . . like a young hawk."

To all friends of Merlin:

I hope you have enjoyed the first three books of *The Lost Years of Merlin* epic! But while our young hero has come a very long way from the half-drowned boy who washed ashore on the first page of Book One, he still has many adventures to come. And many surprises in store before he becomes, at last, the Great Wizard Merlin of Camelot.

You can read about those adventures and surprises in these two books:

The Mirror of Merlin (Book Four): In this tale, Merlin discovers strange wickedness rising from a remote swamp. To save the enchanted isle of Fincayra, which has become his home, Merlin and Hallia— the deer woman he has grown to love—must go to that swamp and find a magical mirror with the power to change the fate of anyone who looks into it. But when Merlin finally looks into the mirror, he sees something more terrifying, and also more wondrous, than he could have ever imagined.

The Wings of Merlin (Book Five): As winter's longest night approaches, Merlin faces the most difficult challenge of his life: to unite all the peoples of Fincayra against an invasion by the evil warlord Rhita Gawr. And on top of that, he must stop Sword Arms from hunting down innocent children—which means he must solve the mystery of the killer's true identity. Only if Merlin can quickly find dramatic new wisdom and power will he save the children and his homeland . . . and finally regain his people's lost wings.

Both of these books can be ordered wherever books are sold. If you'd like to read some selections and reviews (and view a color map of Fincayra), just visit my website: **www.tabarron.com**.

Enjoy the journey,

T. A. Barron

The Mirror of Merlin (0-399-23455-1)
The Wings of Merlin (0-399-23456-X)